TOUCH

DAVID WILLIS

TOUCH

ARCHWAY
PUBLISHING

Archway Publishing books may be ordered through booksellers or by contacting:

Archway Publishing
1663 Liberty Drive
Bloomington, IN 47403
www.archwaypublishing.com
1 (888) 242-5904

Because of the dynamic nature of the Internet, any web addresses or links contained in this book may have changed since publication and may no longer be valid. The views expressed in this work are solely those of the author and do not necessarily reflect the views of the publisher, and the publisher hereby disclaims any responsibility for them.

Any people depicted in stock imagery provided by Getty Images are models, and such images are being used for illustrative purposes only. Certain stock imagery © Getty Images.

ISBN: 978-1-4808-8197-6 (sc)
ISBN: 978-1-4808-8198-3 (hc)
ISBN: 978-1-4808-8199-0 (e)

Library of Congress Control Number: 2019916691

Print information available on the last page.

Archway Publishing rev. date: 10/22/2019

1

GARLAND SUMMERS WAS born in Puerto Rico, on December 13, 1950. It was a special winter's day, and there was something special about this baby boy. Garland was blessed with some very good musical genes, enabling his musical talent to come naturally and without much effort.

James Summers was an enlisted man in the United States Air Force, where he was destined to make his career. Sissy Summers was a tender and loving mother who dedicated her life to her family. Many times, she was the only parent Garland would be with. Being an air force brat hampered Garland from developing friendships in his early years.

James possessed a talent for several string musical instruments, and Sissy had the voice of an angel. Their harmony comforted Garland. Sissy's voice would always soothe her son. Often, she would sing one of her melodies during the early morning feedings. This custom quickly became a highlight for them both, with Garland gazing into his mother's caring eyes as she sang and rocked him to sleep. It was as if he were memorizing the tunes she created for their magical times together.

In the fall of 1952, the Summers family made their journey to the states for the first time as a new family when James was sent to Fort Worth, Texas. This truly was a homecoming, as both James's and Sissy's families also lived in the North Texas area.

The Summerses' first off-base home was a modest two-bedroom house with a very big backyard. Garland, an energetic toddler, was in love with it, including giving his parents the challenge of trying to catch him. There was nothing like a two-year-old and a big yard.

Soon after the move to Texas, Garland and his extended family would experience the warmth and love of a family Christmas. This truly was going to be a musical feast for his ears. The sounds of the season were always pleasant in the Summerses' house. It was as if Sissy's voice was made especially for Christmas hymns and carols. "Noel" and "What Child Is This?" were her favorites. Even though Garland was two years old, he could always embrace the comfort of his mother's voice and lap. There was not a safer place in the world.

Fort Worth was to be a short tour of duty for the family.

As springtime arrived, the Summerses moved to Roswell, a small town in eastern New Mexico. Roswell was famous from the folklore of aliens landing near it. There, for the first time, Garland began to discover a life with other children.

Roswell was the first place that made the family feel at home. Sometimes those out-of-the-ordinary places were the ones that made military families one big happy family.

When summer arrived, the Summerses found themselves welcoming a new family member. Flipper was a black cocker spaniel that soon became Garland's shadow. It wasn't long before the Summerses realized that Flipper was not a full-blooded cocker spaniel, as he soon grew to twice the size of a typical dog of that breed.

Flipper was always adventurous and into everything he could put his mouth into or onto. Once, Flipper dug up a Gila monster to use as a plaything. The Gila monster was young and did not have any experience with predators. Puppies have a tendency of wanting to chew on just about anything that catches their eye.

One day, Flipper ventured into some castor beans that were growing on the back fence. Fortunately, he was distracted by the trash collectors and left the castor beans alone. He managed to escape two poisonous hazards all within the Summerses' backyard.

Garland and Flipper quickly became inseparable. Many times, Garland referred to Flipper as a little brother.

Roswell's cold winters gave Garland a new experience. On one Saturday morning, Garland and Sissy woke up to a winter wonderland. A six-inch snowfall had blanketed the area. After living in the Caribbean and Texas, snow was a new adventure for Garland and Sissy, and it was for Flipper too. Sissy and Garland had fun making snowballs and a snowman. Unfortunately, the snowman met his fate that afternoon at the paws of a black cocker spaniel.

Garland went to bed that night thinking the day had been almost perfect. If only his dad had been there to experience his first snow day. But James had been sent on a temporary assignment for six weeks. These temporary assignments were tests for any military family, and the Summerses were no exception.

During James's first temporary assignment, the musical connection between Sissy and Garland started to form an even stronger bond between them. Sissy loved to see the look in her son's eyes when she sang to him. Music was soothing to Garland, and anyone who saw him had the feeling music would play an important part in his life. This boy was going to be something special.

When James returned from his assignment, it was obvious that someone else had stolen his wife's heart. One night, when he noticed that Sissy had awoken from her sleep, there was a sound coming from their son's bedroom. James arose and followed the sound. As he approached Garland's bedroom, he gently cracked the door open.

In the shadows of a nearby lamp, he saw something that would be implanted in his mind for the rest of his days. Sissy was singing angelically, even more so than before, and Garland seemed to be keeping time with every musical note, as if he knew what words would be sung next. This was something James had only heard about but never actually thought existed.

After ten minutes of pure enjoyment, James returned to his bedroom and fell asleep.

The next morning, James quietly dressed and left the house. He drove to a local pawnshop and purchased an old Gibson guitar. When

James returned home, he opened the door to his son's bedroom to see the two late-night songbirds still fast asleep. He quietly slipped into the room and placed the guitar in the chair Sissy had sat in earlier. This was a present that would change the family forever.

|||||||||

The tires *clickety-clacked* as they hugged the grooves of the surface of the Mississippi River Bridge outside Vicksburg, Garland awoke from a deep sleep. It took a few moments for him to be alert.

Sissy had turned to see the look on her son's face as he tried to come to life, and she said, "Garland, we are almost halfway there."

The Summers family was headed to their new home in Charleston, South Carolina, which would become their longest stay in one place during James's military career. The family arrived in Charleston on a hot mid-July day, and soon they found a small, two-bedroom house close to the base. This house would be temporary until a new house on the base was finished. It would also bring back memories from when the family lived in Fort Worth. The backyard was large, with many trees—just the thing a growing boy loved.

Garland and Flipper would wear each other out nearly every day as they frolicked in this haven. Garland would climb into the trees and play hide-and-seek with Flipper, who went dizzy trying to find his master. It was as much fun for the dog as it was this six-year-old. It became a contest to see which one would tire the other out first.

The news came one day that soon the family would be moving into their new house on the base. This was the first new house Summerses had ever had.

After several days of packing, the family was a day away from moving onto the base, and then something awful happened! After James awoke that morning to start breakfast for his family, he noticed something lying in the backyard. He slowly opened the back door, hoping the sight was not what he thought it was.

As he approached the site, his fears were justified. Flipper lay there motionless. James knelt and tried to get Flipper to respond. There was no response from the cocker spaniel. The closest thing his son had known to a brother was now dead.

This was going to be one of the hardest things he would ever have to deal with concerning his son. He did not want his son to see Flipper like this. He went into the storage shed and retrieved a shovel to perform a task he was not looking forward to. James went into the little grove of trees at the back of the yard, where Flipper and Garland had played for hours. He knew Flipper would be at home here.

As James began to dig into the loam to create the grave, he heard the back door open and his son call for Flipper, which he did every morning.

Garland caught a glimpse of his dad in the trees, digging. As he ran to his father, Garland could sense something was wrong.

James turned to his son, with the shovel in his hands and Flipper at his side.

Garland froze in his tracks, making sure his eyes were not playing tricks on him. He could not believe what he saw.

James dropped the shovel and moved toward his son to comfort him as he approached his dead best friend.

Garland knelt to pet his dog, just as he had done so many times. This was the last time he would do that.

James had his hand on Garland's shoulder as his son ran his hand along Flipper's side.

"Goodbye, my brother," Garland said to his dog. He then added, "Daddy, I want to finish Flipper's grave."

That day, James saw his son act like a man. This made James very proud of his son.

The next day, the family moved to their new home, minus one family member.

|||||||

As the family car turned the bend, Garland sprang up in his seat, straining to see the new house. This would be the Summerses' home for the next six years. They pulled into the driveway and then into the carport. It seemed as if the car was moving in slow motion, as far as Garland was concerned.

Finally, the car stopped, having arrived at its final resting spot, and the doors opened, releasing an enthusiastic six-year-old. Everything in this house was new, and all the new smells imprinted his senses—new paint, new carpet, new flooring. Everything sparkled and gleamed.

This house backed up to a playground with all the latest playground rides. Garland had never had these amenities before. Before his parents reached the backyard, Garland had sprinted to the playground, headed for the swings. He ran faster than he had ever run before. Grabbing the chains in his hands and pushing his feet against the ground, he began to swing back and forth, gaining speed and height with every movement of his body.

This swing was awesome, and he felt he could touch the sky—a feeling he had never known. The swing began to slow down and lose altitude, coming to a stop. When the swing came to its final resting place, Garland hung his head for a few moments, as if to pay tribute. A slow warm tear from each eye ran down his cheeks. He missed Flipper and wished his buddy could have flown into the sky with him. That would have been heavenly for them both.

IIIIIII

The early September morning began with Sissy not wanting to get up. This morning was the beginning of Garland's first year in public school. As Sissy lay there, she struggled to get the energy to get out of bed. Slowly she began to sit up on the side of her bed, reaching for her slippers. This early morning was very quiet, and a sense of the loneliness she would experience that day and in the days to come began to set in. She and Garland had never been apart before.

Sissy slowly walked to her son's room. It was all she could do to put one foot in front of the other. When she reached the doorway, she saw that Garland's bed was empty. Her heart began to race, beating rapidly in her chest, responding to her fear that something had happened to her son. She suddenly heard little footsteps coming from behind her.

As Garland returned to his room from the kitchen, he said, "Momma."

She turned to her son and asked, "Yes, Garland? Where have you been?"

"I have been eating breakfast in the kitchen," replied her son.

Garland then reported that he had been up for almost an hour.

Sissy could see the excitement within her son as he anticipated his first day of school. There was no better relief for her mind than to see that he was going to be okay and was very excited about the first day of school. She started to recover from that first experience of having an empty nest, but it would not be the last time she had that feeling.

Mrs. Taylor, Garland's teacher, resembled his grandmother remarkably. Her voice gave him the comfort he would need to make it through not only that lonely first day of school, but the next nine months as well. Learning was something that Garland would take to rather easily.

The bell rang for the end of that first day of school, and Garland quickly ran out of the classroom to meet his mother and snuggle into the open arms he had always known to hold him in safety. This first day of school had not been nearly as terrorizing as he had thought it might be, his excitement notwithstanding.

During the ride home from school, Sissy sang along to a song playing on the radio. She turned to her son, amazed as always by his knack of musical ability as he kept time with both her singing and the song on the radio. His love of music seemed to grow stronger and stronger.

Little did they both know at the time that it was going to be an ability that would lead him on a special journey for his entire life. Rock and roll was still in its infancy, but, during the next few years, it would capture the world like no music before it.

||||||||

One early summer day, the family took a trip to Myrtle Beach, South Carolina. Myrtle Beach was famous for its waves, sand, and hot music. Many musical acts played there. Garland and Sissy would listen to the local sounds for hours. Both had such a love for this new form of music. There was such a look of contentment on his face whenever he heard the sounds. It was always as if the music would take him far away into another world and time.

During one of the concerts, Sissy and Garland attended that summer, Garland watched every move by the performer. He began to mimic the singer's dance moves during the performance. The singer looked down into the crowd and saw Garland mimicking his moves. He couldn't believe his eyes watching this young boy moving and singing to his beat and time. As he was about to close his first song, he made his way to the edge of the stage and reached down to Garland. Garland reached up to the singer's hand, and the young star lifted Garland up to be on the stage with him. Sissy and the rest of the audience were about to witness a very special treat.

As the singer performed his next song, with Garland, the two brought the crowd to its feet, cheering. This was pure delight for Sissy. She was so proud of her six-year-old son. She suddenly felt a chill go up her spine. This was the same young man that she and Garland had accompanied on the radio that day coming home from Garland's first day of school. The magic of music had once again touched the Summerses.

IIIIIII

Charleston was becoming the kind of home that the Summerses had never known before. Garland had a personality that allowed him to make friends easily. At Garland's tenth-birthday party, a special friendship developed. Sissy had thrown a mixed birthday party that year for her son. One of his presents that year was a record player and several albums. It was no coincidence his mother had invited nine of his new friends to celebrate this occasion: the party had a perfect mix of five boys and five girls.

As the new music began playing, Garland's eyes focused on one little girl with long blonde hair. Brenda had a very special radiance about her, one he had never noticed before. As would often happen at a mixed party, the mingling of boys and girls of that age took a little time getting started.

Sissy was in the next room, just a wall away. She sensed this party was going nowhere, and so she entered the room with the youngsters and began to pair up the guests.

As fate would have it, Brenda and Garland were matched together.

"It's time to get this party rolling," Sissy said. With that, she placed a record on the turntable.

Each of the couples stared at each other, as if waiting for instructions of what to do next. It was a slow song, which required extra closeness in order to dance.

"What are you doing, Mom?" Garland asked.

Sissy began showing Garland and Brenda how to hold each other and the steps each would need to take. They had been put into the spotlight, much to their surprise.

This isn't so bad, Garland thought.

From the smile on her face, Brenda didn't seem to mind, either.

In fact, both Garland and Brenda had smiles from ear to ear.

Garland stopped when the music stopped, and he played the song again.

It wasn't long before the other couples wanted to see what made Brenda's and Garland's faces light up. The dance finally started, and Sissy had implanted a memory in each of those kids' minds. After that first boy-and-girl party, birthday dance parties became the rage of the neighborhood.

Brenda's birthday was on a very hot August day. To keep up the new tradition, Brenda's mother, Valerie Fisher, decided to throw the party of the year for her daughter. Brenda's birthday party was hotter than the weather that summer's day. Valerie rented the base pool for the occasion. Not only were the same ten kids that had attended Garland's birthday party in attendance but also the entire class from the previous school year. By this time, the music of the sixties had started to become very party oriented.

Garland wanted to really impress his first love on her special day. Shortly after 6:00 p.m. on Saturday evening, all the guests began arriving at the pool, except for Garland. He had returned home with Sissy to get Brenda's special birthday gift from his bedroom closet.

Brenda was confused as to why Garland had not yet arrived. She kept watching the parking lot and the walkway up to the pool. There was a special glow on her face when the Summerses' 1960 Chevrolet pulled into the pool parking lot.

As Sissy and Garland walked up the sidewalk, Garland was carrying something in a large case. Once they arrived poolside, everyone could see it was a guitar case. But why was he bringing for a guitar? None of his friends even knew he had one.

"Everyone, gather around!" Garland shouted. "I have something special I want to share with the birthday girl."

Sissy escorted Brenda into a circle the guests had formed.

Brenda stood with Garland in the center of the circle. She had no clue what was about to happen.

Garland began to play a few chords on the guitar. Even though they were very raw, the tune could be recognized. The look on Brenda's face was worth a million dollars in record sales alone. As Garland's eyes began to look into Brenda's eyes, he began to sing a few lines. As the song progressed along, a tear began to run down Brenda's cheek. She began to recognize the song, raw and unrehearsed as it was.

Garland was playing and singing the song Sissy had played at his birthday party—the first song they had ever danced to.

When Garland finished the song, he leaned over to Brenda, kissed her, and whispered into her ear, "This is our song."

Brenda glowed, and the tears made her eyes sparkle like the stars. She knew her first love was going to be special.

||||||||

The year 1963 was the beginning of a new era for the Summers family. It was also the beginning of Garland's teenage years, and the American music scene was going to be changed forever. The family's years in Charleston were about to come to an end. James would be sent to Thailand during the Vietnam War. This would be a yearlong assignment during which Sissy and Garland would be left behind. Each day would present Garland and Sissy the real thought that James might not return to them.

Shortly after the beginning of the new year, Sissy and Garland packed up to leave Charleston. Charleston had given Garland a lifetime of memories he would cherish the rest of his life. The friends and experiences they had known there had changed their lives.

The Summers family began their trip back to Texas. While they rode along, Garland gazed at a picture of Brenda. He looked at the picture as if he were waiting for Brenda to say something to comfort him.

Sissy watched her son sit restlessly until he finally fell asleep, clutching Brenda's picture next to his face, as if to have her cheek touching his. Sissy had already decided that once the family stopped for the evening, she would surprise her son.

When the 1960 Chevy stopped in Jackson, Mississippi, and they checked into a motel, Sissy reached into her purse to find an address and phone book with a phone number inside. Just as her son finished his bath that evening, she picked up the phone and began to dial the number.

The bathroom door opened slowly, and Garland walked into the room. He saw his mother clutching the phone.

"Garland," his mother said, "there is someone who misses you as much as you do them."

He slowly walked toward his mother, lifting his head and hand to take the phone from her.

"Hello," said a voice over the phone.

The look on Garland's face brought a tear to Sissy's eye. This was the same look he'd had on his face at Brenda's birthday party. At first, he was lost for words. He was shocked to hear his first love's voice coming through the phone. The two adolescents talked for more than fifteen minutes.

Maybe, just maybe, the spark that started that day at the party was to be more than a spark.

2

IN THE SIXTIES, life for teenagers changed faster than it had at any other time in history. Garland's teenage years were going to be met with more changes than most of his friends would come to know. Not only was he leaving his first childhood romance behind, he was also moving to new surroundings.

This time, the Summerses were moving during the middle of a school year. The added pressures of changing schools, coping with new surroundings, and meeting new friends were all new for Garland. It wouldn't be long before he would be the man of the house, as James was about to go overseas for a year.

James left on a cold blustery day in the early winter of 1963. This was the first time Garland would have to face the daily reality that his dad might not come back alive. The Summers family would be reminded of that each night on the evening news, with the death count in Southeast Asia. Garland started to become a very strong shoulder for Sissy to lean on. That meant a very large shoulder for a thirteen-year-old, but it was one he knew would make his father proud.

There was also a new music explosion beginning to develop. Music was changing and becoming more commercial than ever in history. One Sunday evening, Garland and Sissy were watching one of their favorite TV shows. There was this act coming on of four young British singers. The minute they started to play a tune, the girls in the audience became hysterical. They were screaming and yelling so loud, the rest of the audience could barely hear the music the quartet played. Both Garland and Sissy looked at each other in total amazement. They had never witnessed anything like what they were watching. There was electricity in what the group did. Even the flopping of their moppy hair drove the girls wild.

The British Invasion had started, and America would never be the same again musically. From that moment, Garland knew he had the same passion for this new style of music as the audience and the millions who witnessed the event on television had. A passion and a talent he knew he had and wanted to share. At that time, no one knew just how much talent.

The next day at school, all the talk was about the show everyone had witnessed on television. All through the halls you could hear voices singing Beatle songs. The girls would gush at the thought of the boys' hair.

As Garland glanced into the mirror in the bathroom that morning, he began to experiment with his own hair, trying to get the same motion he had seen on TV. No matter how hard he shook his head, it was not the same. He knew he must let it get longer for what he wanted to do.

That night, when Sissy cut his hair, he explained the look he wanted his barber to give him. "Mom, do you think I can have a little trim on the sides and nothing off the top?"

Sissy looked at her son and smiled. She knew what was going through his mind. "I think that can be arranged," she replied.

They both looked into the bathroom mirror and smiled.

Sissy knew her son was going to have an impact on the girls too someday.

Shortly after Sissy finished Garland's haircut, she went into her room to read her latest letter from James. She received letters almost daily. After she read each letter, she always took the time to write one to her husband. She always closed each letter with the count of the number of days until her family would be together again. On this day, while she was writing her letter to James, she heard a noise coming from Garland's room, one she had not heard since Charleston.

She sprang up from her bed and went to see what her son was doing. Garland was sitting on his bed, holding that old guitar his father had bought at the pawnshop when they lived in Roswell. He had not played it since Brenda's birthday party. The strings were loose, and it did not have much of a tune. Garland did not know his mother had entered his room until she placed a hand on his shoulder. He jumped and looked at his mother as she looked into his eyes and smiled.

Sissy sat down next to him, taking the guitar from his hands. It had been a while since she had held it too. Soon it was like an old friend in her hands as she began to adjust the strings and tune the guitar for Garland. After she had it tuned, she began to show him how to tune his guitar. It wasn't long before the strings began to create a sound he had known for some time. His mother did have a talent for singing. A talent Garland would surpass.

Sissy could see how much her son enjoyed playing the guitar and knew her own talent with that instrument was limited. There had to be something she could do. She had written James a few weeks before, expressing her desire for Garland to take lessons. Then, in his latest letter to Sissy, James revealed that he had a friend in Texas who was a musician and Sissy should look him up. The next day, she looked in the phone directory to see if he was still in the area.

The look on her face gave away the answer when Garland walked into the room and asked, "What is it, Mom? You have such a happy look on your face reading the phone book."

Sissy reached into a drawer for a pencil and paper to write down the number. She took her son by the hand, and off to the car the two went.

"Where are we going, Mom?"

His mother did not reply but just looked at him with a smile.

If only this car had wings, Sissy thought to herself.

Garland had never seen his mother do anything like this before.

Soon the 1960 Chevrolet reached its destination. The name on the mailbox read "Kevin English."

As they approached the door, a young boy about Garland's age opened it.

"Is this the home of Kevin English?" Sissy asked the boy.

The boy replied, "Yes."

Sissy introduced herself and Garland to the boy.

"Is your dad at home?" Sissy asked.

"Dad, you have company!" the boy shouted.

Kevin approached the door and introduced himself. He had heard Sissy introduce herself and Garland to his son. The name Summers was familiar.

"Are you related to James Summers?" Kevin asked.

Sissy replied that she and Garland were James's wife and son.

"How is James these days?" Kevin said.

"He is doing well and is stationed in Thailand for another nine months." Sissy said.

Kevin introduced his son to Sissy and Garland. "This is Adam, my son."

Sissy wanted to know if Kevin was still a musician.

Kevin led the Summers into a spare room he had set up as a makeshift music room. There were all kinds of pictures of artists on the walls, and against the wall stood several guitars.

Sissy got straight to the point of why she and Garland were there to see Kevin.

"My son has an incredible hunger to learn to play, and I have taught him as much as I can. I want to give him the opportunity to see how good he can be."

Kevin pointed to an old Gibson acoustic guitar almost identical to the one James had bought in Roswell. "Garland, take Old Magic there, and see how it feels in your arms and on your fingers."

Garland began to strum a few notes.

Each note had a style that shocked Kevin. "Who taught you that?" Kevin said.

Garland just smiled and replied, "Taught? I just feel the music, and it feels me."

Adam, seeing how much fun Garland was having, picked up the

other guitar and began to strum along with Garland. Adam handed Garland a guitar pick. He had never used one before. The notes were even purer, and the tempo was so much faster.

"I would like for you to give my son lessons, Kevin," Sissy said.

Adam replied, "My dad would be glad to teach Garland, Mrs. Summers."

Kevin looked at his son and saw that the two boys had something very, very special. For many years, this relationship would treat the world.

Sissy couldn't wait to write her husband to tell him Kevin was still in the area, and not only did he agree to teach Garland, but he also had a son the same age as Garland. She had just finished her letter to James when Adam arrived. The two boys were going to the local Dairy Queen. Adam had a new record he wanted Garland to listen to. This was a new British group that was burning up the record charts.

"Garland, you will not believe your ears with you are about to hear," Adam said.

This was a sound that made the Beatles seem tame. The Rolling Stones had a much harder sound than that of the Beatles. Their sound was the kind guys were into, whereas the Beatles were more for the girls. Garland could not get over the sounds of the electric guitar. When the two boys arrived back at the Summer's house, it didn't take long to fill the house with music from Garland's record player.

Garland arrived one Saturday afternoon for practice at the Englishes' household. This was the first time Kevin saw Garland's Gibson guitar.

"Garland, let me see who you have there with you. Is this the Gibson James bought? "Kevin asked.

The old Gibson had a unique sound. Garland handed it to Kevin. Kevin played a few notes. He wanted to show his students that even though they had talent, they still had much to learn. He handed the guitar back to Garland.

"Now play me as much as you can of the song you just heard," Kevin said.

Little did Kevin know what he was about to see and hear. Garland began to play every note as if they were words recorded verbatim. There was so much joy coming from the fingers of this young musical prodigy. It was as if the guitar and the guitarist each knew what the other was going to do next. This was pure magic to the ears. Garland finished his tune for his teacher and placed the old Gibson back into its case as if he were tucking it into bed. They were going to be inseparable.

||||||||

One afternoon, Sissy was sitting on a couch, enjoying the beautiful sunlight, when the postman delivered the mail. As she reached into the mailbox, she could feel something was different. There were two letters from James that day, and one was addressed to Garland. Sissy took her son's letter to his room and placed it on his bed. The postal run was always during the time Garland was still in school. Later that afternoon, when Garland arrived home, Sissy told her son that he had a letter from his dad.

Garland went to his room, closing the door behind him. He sat down on his bed and began to open the letter. Inside the letter was a money order made out to Garland. James had sent the money for Garland to buy Sissy a gift for Mother's Day. Mother's Day had an extra special treat this year: it was also Sissy's birthday.

James wanted Garland to buy a special ring for Sissy. It was a mother's ring with Garland's birthstone mounted inside two hearts. The letter also included instructions for Garland to have his mother home on that Sunday at two in the afternoon. This really had Garland puzzled.

The next day, Garland was at the Englishes' house. He let Kevin and Adam in on the secret James had planned for Sissy.

"Mr. English, do you think you can take me to the jewelry store?" Garland asked.

"There is nothing I would like better than to help you and James out with this special gift." Kevin replied.

So off to the jewelry store they went.

Once inside the store, there was a special display of rings. Garland approached the showcase and immediately saw the ring James had told him about.

"Sir, can you have a December birthstone mounted inside the two hearts on this ring? "Garland asked the man in the store.

The man assured Garland it would not be a problem.

"What day would you like to have the ring?" the man asked.

"Well, I would like to have it by next Sunday," Garland said.

The man assured him there would be no problem meeting that time frame.

The Saturday before Sissy's birthday arrived. Garland was fast asleep when he suddenly awoke. His first thought was that this was the day the ring would be ready. He had to run over to Kevin and Adam's house.

Sissy had no clue what the three were up to, much less that her husband was in on it as well.

They arrived just before the jewelry store was to close.

Garland quickly sought out the man who had helped him the week before.

"Hello, Garland. Would you like to see your mother's ring?" the man asked.

Garland smiled and replied, "Yes, sir, very much."

The man opened the box and showed Garland his creation. The ring was even more beautiful than the boy had envisioned. Once the man saw the pride in Garland's face, he took the box and had it specially wrapped with a special card.

The mission had been accomplished, and the three left the store.

Garland had to keep the gift out of Sissy's sight until 2:00 p.m. the next day.

He kept wondering, *Why 2:00 p.m.?*

Sunday finally arrived, and Garland ran into Sissy's room. He glanced at the clock next to his mother's bed and saw that it was only 7:00 a.m. As the morning sun gently brushed her forehead, he could see his mother was a very beautiful woman and the years had been kind to her.

Sissy lay there sleeping for another fifteen minutes, with her son at her side, and then her eyes began to open. She gently reached up to her son's hand, and Garland leaned over to kiss his mother.

That morning, it was hard to tell which one loved the other the most.

"Happy Mother's Day and happy birthday," Garland whispered into his mother's ear and gave her a hug.

The day was surely going to be a long one for Garland.

Garland still had no clue why 2:00 p.m. was such a special time. Slowly but surely, though, 2:00 p.m. approached. Garland began to try to get Sissy settled down in the living room.

"Mother, I need to see you in the living room, please," Garland said.

Sissy took a seat in her favorite rocking chair.

Garland was really lost as to what he was to do, and then he realized that he did not have her present. He rushed off into his room and reached under his pillow where he had kept the box in the pillowcase.

As Garland came back into the living room, the phone began to ring.

What a time for the phone to start ringing! Just as I was about to present the gift to Mom, like Dad told me to, he thought.

Garland reached for the phone to see who had caused this interruption. "Hello," he said.

"Hello, son," the voice on the other end of the line said.

"Dad, is that you?" Garland stammered as his eyes met his mother's.

Sissy sprang to her feet to get to the phone. It had been six long months since she'd heard her husband's voice. Sissy's eyes were like a river rushing out of its banks as her joy overflowed.

"Hi, darling," James said. "Your son and I have a special present for you."

Garland could hear his dad's voice. Taking his mother's free hand, he placed the box inside it.

Sissy handed the phone to Garland to talk to James while she opened her present. It was the most gorgeous ring she had ever seen.

The two hearts became one on the ring to create the special gift. That gift was their son. This Mother's Day and birthday would be one the Summerses would never forget. Even though they were separated by thousands of miles, the love this family had was as strong as if that love were physically in the same room.

||||||||

During the summer of 1963, Garland and Adam became almost inseparable. Kevin acquired the second son he and his wife had always wanted, and Garland began to think of Kevin as a fill-in dad while James was away.

When Garland was at the Englishes' one day, he began to talk to Kevin. Garland wanted to know what a person had to do to write a great song.

"A great songwriter comes from within the heart. Sometimes he has to suffer pain to know a good song," Kevin said.

Garland sat there for moment, thinking. Even though he had never really suffered any pain, he understood what Kevin meant. Sometimes personal pain could give strength to someone. Garland was more musically talented than boys many years older. He could feel the music but never had any idea of how to put the music into words.

Adam came into the room where Garland and Kevin had been talking. He had an idea that would impact their lives.

"Dad, do you think we are good enough to perform?" Adam said.

Kevin grinned and nodded his head yes. He dreamed that, one day, the boys would experiment with a band. It was evident that, while Garland had more musical talent, Adam was the visionary of the two boys. He knew they had a chemistry that was waiting to be discovered, and what better way than in a band?

||||||||

Sissy was reading her latest letter from James one early fall day. The new school year was well under way. She glanced at the September calendar, thinking James would be home in less than three months.

That same day, during lunch, Adam joined Garland, as he normally did.

They were eating when a voice asked, "Are you Garland and Adam?"

Both boys looked up at the same time, acknowledging that they were.

"My name is Brandon Baily. Can I join you two for lunch?" the boy said. "Today is my first day at this school. Mr. Harrison, the music teacher, told me you guys were into music and practiced together."

"We play together," Garland replied.

"Do you play?" Adam asked.

"I have been known to, with the right people," Brandon said.

"What does that mean?" Adam asked as he looked at Garland shrugging his shoulders.

"You tell me when you practice, and where, and I will show you," Brandon said.

Adam wrote down his address and drew a map to his house on a napkin for the boy.

Brandon's confidence intrigued the other two boys, and they were anxious for him to prove himself.

"Come by my house on Saturday at 2:00 p.m.," Adam said.

When Saturday arrived, Adam informed Kevin that there would be an extra person at practice.

"Oh, and what does this person do?" Kevin asked.

"I have no idea, Dad. This guy took Garland and me by surprise the other day. We were so shocked by his confidence that we didn't even ask him," Adam said, relating the rest of their conversation with Brandon to his father.

Kevin knew how to deal with this boy's cockiness.

Garland arrived for practice just minutes ahead of Brandon.

Kevin had just sat down in his favorite chair when the doorbell rang. Walking toward the glass insert in the front door, Kevin could see Brandon waiting impatiently. He was determined to teach this young man a lesson. Brandon could not see Kevin standing there and rang the bell a second time. Kevin waited. Brandon began fidgeting, wondering what the deal was. He began to think he had been set up and this was not the right address. Kevin was beginning to enjoy this. Brandon rang the bell again.

"Hey, is someone going to answer this thing or not?" Brandon shouted.

Kevin did not budge.

Adam and Garland came into the room to see why Kevin would not answer the door.

"Dad, what are you doing?" Adam said.

Kevin began to laugh.

Brandon had left the front porch, throwing his fist into the air with disgust. He took several steps onto the sidewalk when Kevin finally opened the door for Brandon and introduced himself. Without Kevin saying a word and only giving the boy an I-showed-you look, Brandon got the message and introduced himself.

"Brandon, the boys tell me you play, but you only practice with the right people. Just what is it that you *do* play?" Kevin asked.

"Mr. English, I am a drummer." Brandon said.

"You play drums? Are you any good? "Kevin said. He knew he had broken Brandon's cockiness with the "Mr. English" reply.

Kevin led Brandon into the room where the boys did their practicing. There were no drums to be seen.

"Brandon, we keep the drum set out in the garage. This room is for musicians," Kevin said.

Brandon looked at both Garland and Adam, wondering what he had gotten himself into.

Adam and Garland took Brandon into the garage to move the drums into the practice room. Kevin had won the first round with Brandon decisively.

Soon the drums were all set up, almost ready to play.

Garland and Adam began to play a song. Brandon was at a loss. Kevin stopped the two boys from playing.

"Brandon, do you not recognize the beat to this song?" Kevin asked.

"It's not that. I don't have drumsticks to play with," Brandon said.

Kevin reached into a nearby drawer and gave Brandon two drumsticks. He instructed the boys to start back with the same song. He wanted to see Brandon's ability to play.

Again, Brandon did not join in. Again, Kevin stopped the two boys from playing.

"Now what is it, Brandon? Do you still do not recognize the beat?" Kevin said.

"Yes, sir, I do," Brandon said.

"Then why are you not playing?" Kevin said. He grinned, knowing what Brandon was about to say.

"I do not have a stool to sit on, sir," Brandon said.

Kevin walked into the next room to get a stool for Brandon. He had won the second round with Brandon.

Once Brandon was seated on the stool, Kevin had the boys to start again. He instructed them to play another song. This tune was much more difficult than the warm-up one. After a few bars, Brandon had not joined in.

Kevin stopped them for the third time. "Brandon, you have drumsticks and a stool now. Do you not recognize the beat to this new song?"

"Yes, sir, I do." Brandon said.

"Then what is the problem this time?" Kevin asked.

"These guys are very, very good! And I was just enjoying the music," Brandon said.

Kevin again instructed Adam and Garland to start playing.

This time, Brandon joined them.

Garland and Adam looked at each other and grinned.

Kevin turned to look out the window. He did not want Brandon to see the impression he had made with his play.

Brandon gained a lot of respect for Garland and Adam as musicians that day, and their respect for him as a drummer was equal. Brandon might have lost rounds one and two with Kevin that day, but he did not lose the fight. He was a very talented drummer. Brandon and Kevin would eventually come to have an almost father-and-son relationship.

IIIIIIII

James was reading his latest letter from Sissy, dated December 1. He was three weeks away from completing his tour. Garland's fourteenth birthday was on December 13. James did not want to miss his son's birthday but was adjusting to the idea that he would be with his family shortly afterward. He was about to put Sissy's letter away when he received a note to see his commanding officer. James went to Colonel Todd's office immediately, wondering what was going on. The first thought entering his mind was that, for some reason, he would have to extend his tour.

James knocked on the door.

"Summers, that you?" the colonel replied.

"Yes, sir, Colonel Todd," James replied.

"Come in. I have something that has been brought to my attention about your tour. Captain George has informed me that you were not able to take your R & R a few months ago," Colonel Todd said.

"No, sir. We had an emergency, and I was not able to get away," James said.

"Your tour is scheduled to end on December 22. I am going to dismiss your tour here on December 5. You will be home earlier than you had expected. Congratulations, Sergeant Summers, on the job you have done here, and have a safe trip back to the states," Todd said.

"Thank you, sir. I intend to do just that," James said.

James could not get back to his quarters quick enough. He was going to give his son the surprise birthday present of his young life.

The morning of December 5 arrived. James was packed and ready to leave Thailand. He was scheduled to leave on a military transport to Hawaii, where he would catch a commercial flight to California, and then fly to Dallas. Sissy and Garland had accepted the fact that James would be home a week after Garland's birthday. When James arrived in Hawaii, he had a layover of several hours. How was he going to pull off the biggest surprise of his family's life? Who could he get to help him? There was only one person he could rely on.

It was early afternoon in Texas when he placed the phone call.

"Hello," a voice said.

"Is Kevin English there, please?" James asked.

"This is Kevin English speaking. Can I help you?"

"Kevin, this is James Summers. I am in Hawaii, on my way back to Texas in time for Garland's birthday. I want to surprise him and Sissy. Can you help me with the surprise?" James asked.

"James, my friend, there is nothing more I would love to do than to help do that for you and your family," Kevin replied.

James informed Kevin of the arrival time and number of his flight into Dallas.

They agreed it would be a surprise and not to tell Garland and Sissy.

James's flight arrived at Love Field at 10:00 a.m. Kevin dropped Adam off at the Summerses' house before he went to the airport. His son had no idea of what Kevin was up to. It had been several years since the two friends had seen one another, but James and Kevin greeted each other as if the years had never kept them apart. For Kevin, the two-hour trip home seemed like minutes as he caught up with his old friend. But, for James, even though he enjoyed seeing Kevin again, the two hours seemed much longer. It had been a year since he had seen his wife and son.

Garland and Adam were in Garland's room, looking at a new album Adam had brought along.

Sissy sat down at the kitchen table to write another letter to James. She wanted so much for James to be home for Garland's birthday, and the disappointment made it hard for her to start the letter. She'd finally captured the thought to begin the letter when she heard a car pull into the driveway. She could not imagine who would be coming for a visit. The doorbell rang.

"Garland, will you see who is at the front door? I am trying to write your father a letter, and I am really struggling," she called out.

Garland went to the door, only to see Kevin standing on the front porch. "Mom, its Kevin. He is probably here to pick up Adam."

Garland unlocked the door for Kevin, returning to his bedroom.

Kevin opened the door for James. James walked into the living room and set down his things. He quietly walked through the living room and stood in the doorway to the kitchen, watching Sissy sitting at the table with her back to him.

"Adam, your dad is here to pick you up," Sissy called.

Adam walked out of Garland's bedroom to see James walking toward Sissy's back and Kevin holding his finger up to his lips for Adam to be quiet. She sat there with her hand propped against her forehead, trying to write. James was now standing next to her chair. James could see his wife was upset and could hear the sniffles her tears were causing.

Peeking over her shoulder, he saw the few lines she had written him. He was more in love with her now than the day he married her. The sniffles were getting louder and more frequent. James leaned over and began to read the letter, whispering into her ear, and then he kissed her cheek and hugged her around the neck.

The love of her life had pulled off the surprise of her life. Sissy sprang to her feet to grab James and kiss him. These were now tears of joy.

"Mom, are you okay?" Garland shouted from his room. He could hear his mother crying. She did not answer her son. "Mother!" Garland shouted again. There still was no answer.

With their arms around each other, James and Sissy walked down the hallway to Garland's bedroom door.

"Mother, are you okay?" Garland cried. He was beginning to worry why his mother had not answered him. It was not like her.

"Baby, I am finally okay now," Sissy replied to Garland.

This time, he sensed a difference in her voice and turned to see James clutching his mother's hand. Garland jumped to his feet and ran to hug James. This was the first time Garland had seen his father have tears—tears of joy.

James was home. The Summers family was whole again.

3

BRANDON'S MOTHER AND father were divorced ten years before, when he was six years old. His father moved away to another state and remarried. He never even attempted to see Brandon. Brandon's mother did her best to provide for and support him and herself, without any financial help from his dad. Brandon was not the easiest boy to raise. He did have a rather colorful personality and occasionally bent the rules. School was never a priority for him. One Friday afternoon in the spring of 1967, Brandon's life was about to change dramatically.

Brandon arrived home that afternoon from the Englishes', where he and Adam had played around with some new chords and beats they heard on the radio. He walked around to the back door of his house to get the hidden door key, but it was not in its normal hiding place. At first, he didn't remember placing it in another hiding spot. As he sat down, trying to remember where the key was, it dawned on him that he had put it under the flowerpot instead of the doormat. Brandon bent down and moved the flowerpot to get the key. He unlocked the door and entered the house. His mother was at work this time of day.

Several hours passed since Brandon had arrived home. His mother still wasn't home. By this time, Brandon was beginning to really worry. What was happening? He walked into his mother's room and saw an envelope on her bed. He walked over to the bed and sat down. Brandon's name was written on the envelope. He slowly opened the envelope and began to read the letter it held.

As he read, his eyes began to tear up, and it felt like his heart was in his throat. He didn't understand why this was happening to him. Eventually, the shock wore off, and he fell asleep, holding the letter in his hand.

IIIIIII

Saturdays were always a practice session for the three boys, and Brandon was never late. He enjoyed the escape the music provided and the camaraderie he had with Adam and Garland. On this Saturday morning, Brandon was more than an hour late. When he finally arrived, he had a lost look about him.

Kevin was in the next room, observing Brandon not playing very well. He walked into the room where the boys were playing and began to observe. Something was definitely wrong with Brandon. Finally, in disgust, Garland and Adam put down their guitars and walked out of the room.

Kevin and Brandon were very close, but, for some reason, Brandon would not open up to Kevin.

"Brandon, is there something you would like to talk to me about?" Kevin asked.

Brandon did not answer Kevin. He had this catatonic look on his face. One Kevin had never seen. He knew something was terribly wrong.

"Mr. English, would you please give me a ride back to my house?" Brandon asked.

Kevin nodded yes.

Kevin and Adam loaded up the car to take Garland and Brandon home. Both Garland and Adam tried to cheer Brandon up. Once the car arrived at the Baily house, Kevin and Brandon went into the house, followed by Garland and Adam. Kevin wanted to talk to Mrs. Baily about what could be troubling Brandon.

"Brandon, I would like to talk to your mother," Kevin said.

Brandon did not acknowledge Kevin.

"Brandon, where is your mother? Is she at work today?"

Adam and Garland had entered the room where Kevin and Brandon were.

Adam noticed something on Brandon's mother's bed. The room had been disturbed. That was not normal for Mrs. Baily. Adam walked into Mrs. Baily's room and picked up the opened envelope with Brandon's name on it. He did not read it.

"Dad, can you come into Brandon's mom bedroom? There is something I think you need to see!" Adam said.

Kevin walked into the room, while Garland remained with Brandon.

Adam handed the note to his dad.

Kevin began to read the letter. Just as had happened to Brandon the day before, Kevin's eyes watered, and his heart felt like it was lodged in his throat.

The letter read:

> Brandon,
>
> Someday, I hope you will find it in your heart to for-give me. I cannot go on living the way we do. I have tried so hard to provide for us both, but it just doesn't work anymore. Your constant troubles in school are more than I can bear now. The rent on the house is paid up for the month. That should give you time to figure out what to do. I know you will find a way to get by without me. There should be enough food to last you to the end of the month as well.
>
> Aim for the stars, my son; you are a talented boy.
>
> God bless you,
>
> Mom

|||||||

Kevin now knew why Brandon was acting the way he was. He knew that Brandon had kept all of this inside him, and that was unbearable for such a young boy. Kevin walked into the room where Brandon was. The boy was asleep. Kevin wondered if this had been the first time Brandon had slept since receiving the news. He knew Brandon needed a family very much now, and a friend even more.

Kevin knelt and woke Brandon. Brandon wiped his eyes and tried to focus. "Brandon, let's go home. We need to get you some rest. This is too much for you to deal with on your own," Kevin said.

Brandon rose to his feet and went home with Kevin and Adam. Kevin assured Brandon he would always have a place to stay.

When Sunday came, Kevin and Brandon went into the music room. Brandon had never heard Kevin play before that day. Kevin began to play, and Brandon joined in. Kevin knew this was what the boy needed to bring him peace.

Kevin called a family meeting that afternoon. This meeting included Brandon. Kevin had accepted a job in Colorado, as a station manager for a radio station in Denver. He was to have complete control of how the station would be run. He knew that Adam and Brandon had concerns about their friendship with Garland as well as their band. Kevin had a plan that he thought would make everyone happy.

James had retired from the military and was taking some time to determine what kind of career he would pursue next. He and Sissy were discussing what their options were when they heard a car pull into their driveway. A look out of the front window revealed the English family, with their newest member, coming up the sidewalk to the front porch. James met them at the front door and invited them inside. Garland had informed his dad about Brandon. Kevin apologized for coming over unannounced. He had something he wanted to discuss with the Summerses, and he did not want it to wait.

"James, I have been offered the station manager's job at a Denver radio station. I know our boys have become best friends, just as you and I have been. I am prepared to offer you a job at the station as a program director. The station is looking for a new direction, and I think you and I can be the ones to take them there," Kevin said.

James did not know what to say to his friend. Kevin was the best friend James had ever had. James was shocked by Kevin's job offer.

"Kevin, I appreciate the offer, but I am not sure I am the one for this job."

Sissy immediately grabbed James by the hand to show her approval. "James, Kevin would not have offered you the job if he didn't think you could do it, and do it very well. He is putting his confidence in you. He has that much faith in you."

James smiled at his beautiful wife. She always knew just what to say to him.

"Kevin, if you want me, you've got me," James said.

The two friends walked toward each other. Kevin stuck his hand out for James to shake it. James took Kevin's hand, only to pull him closer to hug him.

The two families would soon be Colorado bound.

Moving day for the two families arrived. Garland would be changing schools again during the year. This time, however, would be different. He would be going to a new school in another state, but, this time, he would have two friends joining him. Kevin and James rented trailers to pull all their possessions to Colorado. The trip was to take two days. The Summers family would occupy one truck, and the English family, with their newest member, Brandon, would occupy the other truck.

It was almost 6:00 a.m., when the caravan met to organize their trip. James thought it would be a good idea if they communicated using walkie-talkies. All stops would be coordinated, and, if any emergency should occur, they could alert one another. Highway 287 would provide the route for the first day. Sissy was appointed navigator and would assist in any map reading. She would also provide entertainment for the trip by finding radio stations along the way for musical entertainment. This was also a good way to get some idea of what some of the radio stations were doing to succeed in the market at that time. The music scene was changing again in the late sixties. Kevin would be the one to determine the new format the station would play when he took over the reins.

The first stop was in the small town of Vernon, Texas. Garland had been bored with the trip thus far. He did not have the company of another teenager in the truck he occupied. Adam and Brandon were able to entertain each other.

"Adam, I have an idea. When we leave, can you get the walkie-talkie in your truck and turn to channel two? I need someone I can talk to from time to time," Garland said.

Adam and Brandon agreed this would be a great way to entertain them.

The boys would use the walkie-talkies to play road games between the two trucks and sometimes would find themselves joined by an unexpected listener also using the same devices for communication while traveling. Sometimes they would coordinate radio stations the two trucks would tune in to. The next two days would provide more radio listening time than any of the travelers had done in a long time.

Kevin planned to spend the first night in Dumas, Texas. This was the last good-size town they would see until they reached Raton Pass, New Mexico. After a nine-hour drive, the trucks arrived in Dumas for the night. They would check into a hotel, get cleaned up for dinner, and get a good night's rest.

On the second day, something special occurred. The trip between Dumas and Raton Pass would have a stretch of countryside without any towns or radio signals. That morning after breakfast, Garland was searching through one of the bags in the truck he had packed. He knew he packed the battery-operated tape recorder James had brought him from Thailand. He found it—finally! Garland pushed the Play button to listen to what he had last recorded. The machine would not play. He pressed the Power button again. The recorder did not play. He turned the recorder over, only to discover there were no batteries inside.

"Dad, before we leave can I have some money to get some batteries for my tape recorder?" Garland asked.

James agreed and gave him the money for the batteries.

Once he installed the fresh batteries, Garland hit the Play button; this time, it worked. In a little more than hours, they would be leaving

Texas. Garland did not realize it, but it would be a very long time before he would make it back to the state he had loved so much.

After leaving the Texas state line, the terrain immediately changed as well. The flat farmlands of the Texas panhandle were gone. The landscape was beginning to get rocky, with hills in the distance.

Sissy was having a difficult time tuning a signal powerful enough for the radio. Rather than have static on the radio, she turned the power off.

Kevin's truck was leading the caravan. Brandon was taking in all the scenery. This was the first time he had ever been out of Texas. They came upon a large pasture.

"Hey, guys, do you see over there by that tree? What are those animals? There's probably a hundred of them," Brandon said.

Kevin looked to where Brandon was pointing. He chuckled. "Those are antelope, Brandon, and they are wild around here," Kevin said.

Brandon had never seen antelope before. As the truck came around the next bend, there were even more than in the last group. Kevin was not the only one to get a laugh out of Brandon discovering antelope. Adam had the Transmit button pressed on the walkie-talkie, and the Summerses enjoyed the episode as well.

The trucks were at the halfway point. There was nothing the radio could pick up. And the trip was becoming boring now. The antelope began to lose their amusement factor. Garland was lying down in the backseat. He was looking up at the ceiling of the truck. There was no conversation in the truck for some time now. It was as if everyone was ready for a break.

Sissy sat in the front seat, twirling her fingers through her long black hair. Being back in New Mexico made her remember the quiet early mornings when she rocked and sang to Garland. She began to hum a melody. It was a very soothing melody. Each note seemed to be more perfect than the one before it.

Garland, lying in the seat, with one hand, reached down to the floor and hit the Record button on his tape recorder. With his other hand, he touched the Transmit button on the walkie-talkie. Sissy continued to hit higher notes. Garland remembered the touch he would feel from his mother as she sang to him. How she would stroke his little hands and face. And the touch of her soft lips as she kissed him on his cheeks and neck. The feeling he had when she would sing and hum into his little ears. His mother had the touch of an angel and a voice to go along with that touch. He did not want his mother to stop then, and he didn't want her to stop now. It had been fifteen years since he had heard that sound, and it was the most beautiful sound he had ever heard.

James turned to Sissy, to see her looking out the window with such contentment. It was like he could sense what she was feeling at that minute as well. Not only had her voice touched Garland, it had touched James's heart as well. Sissy continued to get lost in her thoughts of the tune and put more feeling into the song.

The Englishes' truck didn't need a radio frequency that day. They were also treated to a song that touched their souls.

Something else happened that day that was a pure accident. While Garland had held the Transmit button down on the walkie-talkie, Sissy had touched several travelers also. She had performed an angelic concert without even knowing it. Garland released the Transmit button on the walkie-talkie. Sissy was beginning to soften her notes as she was about to end her song.

A voice came over the walkie-talkie, wanting to know who the angel was.

James and Sissy were at a loss as to what the talker was referring to.

Just as the voice finished, another listener commented as well, then another.

Sissy looked at James, wondering what these people were talking about.

A special touch was spread that day. This time, it would not take fifteen years to be heard again. Garland had recorded the entire song. He would have his mother's touch now whenever he wanted it.

The caravan made a fuel stop in Raton Pass. It was during this stop that Kevin and his family approached Sissy and James and told them what they had heard as well.

James and Sissy wished they had heard what all the listeners that day heard.

Garland did not tell his mom and dad that he recorded his mother that day. He had special plans for this. One musical history had never seen before or since.

The Colorado border was less than a half-hour drive from Raton Pass. Raton Pass received its name from the steep inclines the interstate would take to get into Colorado from northern New Mexico.

"James, I would like to stop at the Colorado information center in Trinidad. I want to make sure our trailers are okay for any more altitude climbs," Kevin radioed the two trucks pulled into the remote parking lot at the welcoming center.

Outside the parking lot was a beautiful sign reading, "Welcome to Colorful Colorado."

"Kevin, I would like you to take pictures of James, Garland, and me in front of the sign. And, if you would like, I will take one of your family as well," Sissy said.

The two families took turns taking pictures.

"I have a wonderful idea," said Kevin.

He approached a Colorado state trooper just entering the facility. "Officer, would you do me a big favor and take a picture of the seven of us in front of the sign?" Kevin asked.

The officer smiled and agreed.

While the officer was taking the picture, Garland noticed a nearby bulletin board with some of the state's attractions.

After the photo was taken, Garland approached the board. One area really caught his eye. He could not help staring at the Red Rocks picture area.

Kevin saw Garland was in awe of the formation of rocks and joined him. He instantly knew what Garland was feeling inside.

"Garland, do you know that you are looking at what some people refer to as one of the natural wonders of the world?" Kevin said.

"What is it?" Garland asked.

"You are looking at the Red Rocks Amphitheatre. The natural acoustics there are said to be the best in the world. Every recording artist's goal is to perform there," Kevin said.

"It is my goal too now. I will perform there one day," Garland said.

"You know, Garland, I actually believe you will," Kevin said.

The two families returned to their trucks and started the final leg of their trip.

Interstate 25 would take them to Denver after another four and half hours of driving. Adam and Garland took turns announcing to each other the signs along the way for some of Colorado's attractions.

"Walsenburg's exit is for the Great Sand Dunes," said Adam.

Garland thought that it was hard to imagine desert-like sand dunes anywhere near those mountain peaks with snow on them.

"Pueblo's exit is for the Royal Gorge," said Garland.

Adam had read about the raft trips through the gorge on the Arkansas River. The mountains were becoming more majestic and seemed to have a purple hue to them from a distance. *Just like the verse in "America the Beautiful,"* Adam thought.

"Colorado Springs has several exits, all devoted to the city's biggest attraction, Pikes Peak. It's so tall, you can't see the top. The clouds are hiding it," Garland said.

Sissy interrupted the two tour guides. "Everyone, we will be in Denver in an hour or so. We will find a hotel and a place to eat."

After two long days of driving, they finally arrived in Denver.

Kevin and James were to report to the radio station on Monday. The station's parent company had arranged for them to stay at the Aurora Hotel. The families would need time to find houses and unpack.

Sunday was to be a day for rest and soaking in the new Denver scene.

Kevin went out Sunday morning for a local newspaper.

"Brandon, turn the radio on, and let's see if we can find something to listen to," Adam said.

Brandon turned the power on. He searched up and down the radio dial to find the signal of the station Kevin would soon run. He could not find the station.

"Adam, I thought you said the station was near this end of the dial," Brandon said.

"Dad told me it was," said Adam.

Adam began turning the dial from the lower end of the band, beginning at 500 and going through 1700. There was no signal for the station. The boys had given up when Kevin opened the door and entered the room, holding a newspaper.

Noticing the radio was turned on, Kevin asked, "Did you boys find the station?"

Adam and Brandon looked at each other in disgust and answered simultaneously, "No."

"Is this station still on the air?" Adam asked.

Kevin walked over to the nightstand where the radio was. He picked up the radio and noticed the frequency switch was flipped to the AM band. Kevin giggled.

"Boys, you are on the wrong dial. Our station is not an AM station. We are on the FM band, and we are located at the 90.2 frequency," Kevin said.

The boys had never listened to an FM station. From what they knew about FM stations, the music was like the music you always heard on elevators and would not appeal to a teenager in the late sixties.

Kevin tuned in the station, and just as Adam and Brandon had feared, the music playing was elevator music.

There was a knock on the hotel door. Adam walked over to the door to undo the lock. James and Garland walked in. Garland walked over to the bed to sit down with his friends. Adam and Brandon were sitting there with their heads hanging down. He could hear the music playing on the radio and had not given any thought to what was playing.

"Are we interrupting anything?" James asked.

"No. But I guess it's as good of a time to tell you as any. The boys were looking for the station and could not find it. They were tuning the AM dial, and our station is on the FM band," Kevin said.

"FM dial? "James asked. He was as shocked as the boys were. He had always thought the same thing about FM stations as they did.

"Well, we are going to change what people think about FM radio. The AM frequency will be a thing of the past," Kevin said.

Kevin and James arrived at the radio station on Monday, several minutes ahead of schedule. Two men from the corporate office were seated in the conference room, along with the interim station manager. Kevin and James entered the room. Kevin introduced James to the other men.

"Mr. English, we want to hear some of your ideas on how to turn this station around," one man said.

Kevin had not revealed his plan to James. This was to be news to him as well.

"I have researched the Denver area. The population is becoming younger at a very fast rate, and AM signals are limited by the nearby mountains and the weather conditions as well. We will bring a top-forty music and rock-and-roll format to the FM dial. We have so much potential. We have the greatest stage in the world right here in our backyard. The Red Rocks Amphitheatre will be our stage. We are not going to just be Denver's station but Colorado's station. Our format of music will be delivered better than ever before. Our advertisers will have a larger audience," Kevin said.

The two corporate men turned to each other. There was silence in the room. Both men stood up at the same time without saying a word.

Kevin's mouth was very dry. He grabbed a glass of ice water from the table and took a drink.

The men had not said a word. The interim manager also stood up without saying a word about what Kevin had so enthusiastically presented to them. The silence was suddenly broken by very enthusiastic applause from all three men.

Kevin made an impression on them that they had never anticipated. They left the room, knowing they were lucky to have hired such a talented man.

4

THE ALARM WENT off just as scheduled at the Summers home. James reached over and hit the Off button. Sissy slept with her back toward him. She had been awake into the early hours of the morning, unpacking. James, too, had been up late unpacking. He finally gathered up enough energy for his feet to hit the floor. He really wanted to climb back into bed for another few hours of sleep. There was the smell of fresh coffee brewing, and the aroma was pleasant. James stretched and treated his senses. He left the room and walked down the hallway to Garland's bedroom. James stopped to test his eyes. He thought they were deceiving him. Garland's bed was empty, and his bed had been completely made. This was very odd for a sixteen-year-old.

James proceeded down the hall, toward the kitchen.

Garland sat at the table, enjoying a fresh cup of coffee and eating a piece of toast.

"Good morning, Dad. Would you like some coffee?" Garland asked.

James walked over to the cabinet and opened the door to where the cups were.

"Dad would you like some bacon and toast?" Garland said.

James grinned and nodded at his son.

This time, it was James's turn for Garland's comfort on the first day of school, just as it had been Sissy's turn that morning in Charleston, on his very first day of school.

The scene at the English home was just the opposite. The pressure of a new career and moving his family had kept Kevin up most of the night. He also felt responsible for his best friend's moving his family. He felt the weight of the entire world. Adam and Brandon were still asleep. This was the first time for them to change schools. Both boys were awake into the wee hours of the morning. They wondered if they would fit in at school.

Someone needed to make the first move to get the morning started. But who would it be? Marsha English came to the rescue. Proving true the old proverb that behind every successful man is a good woman, she was that woman for three men that morning. She took control and saved that first day from disaster. Kevin, Adam, and Brandon all arrived at William C. Hinckley High School in time to join James and Garland. Hinckley was one of Aurora, Colorado's best resources, and the school would be entrenched in their memories forever.

Kevin met James at the station after getting the boys enrolled in school. In two weeks, the station would be turned over for his control. He was very confident the new rock-and-roll format would be a winner.

"James, I want to show you something I think the boys would love," Kevin said. He led James into what was an old studio. "What do you think, James?"

James looked at the studio, wondering what Kevin had on his mind. "About what, Kevin?"

"The boys could use this as a studio to rehearse. It's perfect, and we will not be using it," Kevin said.

Kevin was always a step ahead of others when planning was involved.

James could see the excitement in Kevin's face and hear it in his voice as he explained the plans for the room.

"I have a feeling about our boys, James, just as I do about this station. They will be connected in a very special way. I want you to pick the boys up after school and bring them here," Kevin said.

James returned to the station with all three boys. This was the first time the boys visited a radio station. When they entered, they could hear the music being played in the control room on the speakers in the hallways. FM stations at the time did not require dialogue from the DJs. The music was occasionally interrupted with the time or weather. James led them to the end of the hallway and into the empty studio.

Kevin was waiting to see if they had an idea of what they were looking at.

"Do any of you know where you are standing?" Kevin asked.

The boys looked at each other, waiting for someone to take the initiative to answer Kevin.

"Is this a recording studio?" Brandon ventured.

"You are close, Brandon. This room is a sound room for on-air broadcasts. This is the old one, and it is not used any longer. This room will be your new practice studio," Kevin told them.

The boys had not played together in almost a month.

The first day of school and work had been a success.

IIIIIII

As good as the first day of school had been, the second day was not quite as good. In fact, it was almost a disaster.

James had arrived at the station that day to start preparing a playlist for the station. He was working on the current hits of the day to be played, as well as some golden oldies to be mixed in from time to time. Once the word was out about the new format change, record companies were sending new releases daily. He knew he would have to hire DJs as well. This would be very hard to do on such short notice.

James was working on a list of prospects when the phone rang. The call was from Hinckley High School.

"Mr. Summers, this is Principal Roberts at Hinckley. I need for either you or Mr. English to come down to the school at once."

James hung the phone up and informed Kevin he was headed to Hinckley.

James arrived at Hinckley and proceeded to Principal Roberts's office.

Mr. Roberts met James at the door of his office.

"Principal Roberts, I am James Summers," James said.

"Mr. Summers, we had an incident today at lunch with Garland, Adam, and Brandon." Mr. Roberts said. He informed James of what happened and showed him where the boys were waiting.

James entered the conference room where the boys were. All three boys sat with their heads hung. Garland and Adam were both sporting bruises on their faces and torn clothes. Brandon, on the other hand, did not have a hair out of place. James immediately wondered why Brandon was even in the room. From his unscathed appearance, it was apparent he had not been involved.

"What in the world happened to you today?" James asked.

Garland could see the anger in James's face and hear his displeasure in each word he had spoken.

"Dad, Adam and I sat down for lunch today at our normal table and chairs. We were waiting for Brandon to join us. There was this boy who began to mimic our voices. He was making fun of our Texas accents in front of other kids in the lunchroom." Garland said.

"Soon others began to join in the ridicule," Adam added.

"We decided to leave, go outside, and let things die down. But the trouble did not end there. It followed us out into the school courtyard," Garland said. "When we tried to ignore that smart-ass, he stepped in front of Adam and shoved him, daring us. He was not alone. He had three friends who joined in with the insults and the shoving."

"We were outnumbered four to two," Adam said. "They demanded money, or they would kick our asses. They would take turns, one holding us while the other would punch and kick us, and then they would switch," Garland said.

James was shocked to hear what the boys had dealt with.

"Things were not looking good," Garland said.

Garland began to wipe the blood running from the corner of his mouth.

James looked at Brandon, still wondering why Brandon was in the room.

"Brandon, why are you here? You weren't involved. You shouldn't be here," James said.

"Dad, it was Brandon and his new friend, Harley, who came out to help us," said Garland. "You should have seen how Brandon took on those thugs. I had no idea he could handle himself like that."

"He was amazing, and so was Harley," Adam said.

"Mr. Summers, I could not let my two best friends be treated like that. I had to do something. They needed help," Brandon said.

"Let's go home, boys," James said.

The boys walked out of Principal Roberts's conference room.

James could not help looking at Brandon in awe. He could not get over Brandon not having a hair out of place after a scuffle like the one that had occurred that day.

James was taking the boys to the station when Brandon pointed to a boy walking home.

"Look, there's Harley Krause!" Brandon shouted.

"Harley? Was he the boy who helped you guys out?" James asked.

In unison all three boys replied yes.

James pulled the car over to the sidewalk to offer the boy a ride. At first, Harley was not receptive to someone pulling up on him like that. He then looked inside the car and saw Brandon. Harley accepted the ride and climbed inside. James thanked him for what he had done that day and asked him if he would like to ride with them to the station.

Kevin was about to leave the station for the day when James and the boys arrived. The boys took Harley inside to show him the studio, while James filled Kevin in on what happened at school.

Harley had no idea the others were in a band.

"You guys play music in here?" Harley asked.

"Well, we haven't yet, but soon we will," Garland said.

"I would love to sit in with you guys sometime," Harley said.

"Do you play also, Harley?" Kevin asked.

"Yes, sir. I have a bass guitar," Harley said.

"As soon as we get the room ready, we would love to hear you play," Kevin said.

That day, Harley found the niche in life he had always wanted.

|||||||

James had received several résumés for disc jockeys. The latest one had caught his eye. He'd heard some of Chad Royal's work while in Thailand. Chad ran a show on the Armed Forces Radio Network. Chad was unemployed now and could start immediately if needed. James called the phone number listed on the résumé to contact Chad.

"Hello," said a sultry young female voice.

"This is James Summers, and I am trying to contact Chad Royal about an employment opportunity. Is he available?" James asked.

"One moment; he has just entered the house," she said.

"Hello, this is Chad, and to whom am I speaking?" Chad said.

James introduced himself to Chad and informed him why he was contacting him.

Chad agreed to meet James the next morning at the radio station. James hung up the phone, thinking that Chad could be the DJ he could build a team around, with Chad as the featured show each day.

Chad informed his sixteen-year-old daughter, who had answered the phone, that they would be traveling to Aurora the next morning for an interview.

The next morning, James drove to the radio station. Shortly after his arrival, a red Ford Mustang pulled into the parking lot. Three passengers emerged from the car.

Could this be Chad? James wondered. Who are the two passengers with him?

James met them at the front door, introducing himself.

The man reached for James's hand and gave him a very firm handshake.

"My name is Chad Royal. This is my daughter, Suzanna, and my son, Beau," Chad said.

James escorted Chad to his office for the interview.

Suzanna and Beau were waiting in the lobby when Kevin, Adam, and Garland arrived.

Garland was the first to enter the building. His eyes were treated to a wonderful sight. Sitting there was this very gorgeous girl. Her long black hair and brown eyes were like none he had ever seen. Garland immediately approached Suzanna. He tried to speak, but the words were stuck in his throat.

Suzanna smiled at Garland, sensing she had made an impression on this young boy.

Garland again tried to speak, but no words came.

By this time, Adam had arrived at Garland's side to come to his rescue.

"This is Garland Summers," Adam said.

This was the first time in his life that Garland had been left speechless.

Suzanna was all smiles now. She was trying to hide the fact that Garland had made an impression on her as well.

Finally, the words came from Garland's mouth. "Is this your boyfriend?" he asked Suzanna.

She looked at the boy sitting next to her. Like Garland, Suzanna had not yet said a word.

She was about to speak when the boy next to her interrupted. "I am her brother, Beau. This is my twin sister, Suzanna. Our dad is here to interview for the DJ position."

Garland did not want the interview to end. Then, as if a magical spell had been cast upon him, Garland's throat began to release all the words it had been keeping captive.

"I will put in a good word for your dad," Garland said. He definitely wanted to get to know Suzanna.

Two hours had passed by the time James and Chad walked out of James's office.

Beau and Suzanna stood up as Chad approached them.

Adam and Garland were looking out the window when they heard the two men approach Suzanna and Beau.

James shook Chad's hand and welcomed him aboard to the team.

"One thing I forgot to ask, Chad. Do you know anything about the music business? These two boys, along with two others, will start playing together this afternoon," James said.

"Well, Beau has taken some piano lessons and is into electronic keyboards," Chad said.

"Beau, would you like to come sit in as well today? Keyboards are playing a big part in today's sounds," James said.

Without hesitating, Beau told James that he would.

"Suzanna, you can come along too if you would like," Garland said, grinning.

She looked at Garland, shaking her head at the pass he had just made. She could tell he was not experienced with girls, but it did not matter to her.

There were now five members in the new band.

5

THE SUMMER OF 1967 came, and the station's new format was in place. One day, as Kevin opened the mail, he came across a new release of what was to become a masterpiece in the music business. Garland, Adam, Brandon, Harley, and Beau had just arrived for a practice session in the old studio. The packaging was different from any album that had ever been produced. Kevin took the demo down to where the boys were.

"Hey, guys, I have something I want us all to listen to in this room," Kevin said.

He walked over to the turntable and turned the power on.

Everyone had taken a seat and was giving Kevin their undivided attention.

"I want to see if anyone can guess who these guys are," Kevin said.

He began to play the album. The music started. The acoustics in the studio were perfect for the occasion. Each song went right into another; there weren't any pauses between songs. This was something new.

Each of the boys looked at each other, searching for the answer Kevin sought. There were so many different new electronic sounds. New instruments never before used in contemporary rock-and-roll music were on display. The boys were totally blown away by the sounds they heard. The last song had finished, and you could hear a pin drop in the room. The sound captured their minds and took them into another dimension.

"Well, does anyone care to answer the question I posed to you before we started listening to the album?" Kevin asked.

No one had an answer.

Kevin began to ask each of the boys which artists performed the masterpiece they had just heard.

"Guys, you have just heard *Sgt. Pepper's Lonely Hearts Club Band*," Kevin said.

He then took out the album cover and passed it around for the answer. They had just listened to what would become an icon. Never was an album a best seller without having a single released. None of the boys had guessed the Beatles!

After hearing *Sgt. Pepper's,* Garland was getting bored with playing an acoustic guitar. He longed for an electric sound.

James was sitting in his office, going over some new playlists of records being released that summer.

"Dad, I think it's time for us to go to the next level," Garland said.

"I am glad you want to do that, son. What is it you have in mind by going to the next level?" James said.

"I want to start playing the electric guitar; I have these sounds in my head that I cannot produce with the old Gibson," Garland said.

James had a feeling his son had been held back long enough. Kevin always told him that all the great guitar players started out with an acoustic guitar before becoming electric players. James knew his son was great with the acoustic and was ready now.

"I think you are ready, Garland, and I will see what I can do," James said.

Garland left James's office and went back into the studio. He had to hear more of *Sgt. Pepper's*; he would always enter another dimension after hearing that music. Although he wanted to play electric, Garland knew the old Gibson would always be his heart and soul.

That evening, the Summers family was enjoying dinner together as a family.

"Sissy, your son has decided to become electric today. I think it's time," James said.

Sissy had always loved the way her son had played the acoustic guitar. She was sad to see him give it up. She had that empty-nest feeling again.

Garland could see the emptiness in his mother's eyes and face.

To Sissy, it was almost like her son losing his virginity. The acoustic was so pure. She was not so sure the electric would give him that same satisfaction.

"Mother, I cannot play the sounds I hear in my head with the old Gibson. I need to expand. My heart and passion will always be the old Gibson," Garland said. "I can never give up my roots, and the old Gibson is my roots. When I play her, it's like I am in your arms, and I will never give that up."

Sissy approached her son and kissed his forehead. Her little boy was growing up so fast.

The next morning, James and Kevin were going over the latest record charts. The sounds of the times were becoming more sophisticated than those of the early sixties. The record business had become very competitive, and a record's airtime was more important than ever. More airtime led to more record sales. Touring was becoming a big source for artists' income, and what better way to advertise a show than hit records? Hit records could translate into sold-out shows.

During that morning meeting, Kevin noticed that James had been looking at the various electric guitars some of the artists were sporting in some of the music-business publications.

"Kevin, what do you think about electric guitars? Garland wants to diversify his talents with one," James said.

"I think Garland can play any instrument he puts his mind to play, and the boys could do many new sounds and arrangements with two, as well as Harley's bass," Kevin said.

Kevin showed James a magazine photo of a very colorful Fender guitar. These were guitars with psychedelic designs. Some, to keep up with the times, had peace signs, a protest symbol to the war in Vietnam. The late sixties had seen a change in the attitude toward the war in Vietnam. There were protests and peace movements to the war by thousands of artists and their audiences. James knew Kevin knew the recording business very well. He had his eyes on one of the psychedelic Fenders and placed an order to be shipped.

During the next practice session, a delivery truck pulled into the station's parking lot, just as it had many times before. The driver carried his first packages into James's office. James was discussing with Chad a résumé from another disc jockey and paid no attention to the driver. The driver returned to his truck for a second package. He walked over to the table in James's office, next to his desk, and set down the package.

"Mr. Summers, I need your signature for this package, please," the driver said.

James turned to the driver and signed the delivery receipt, never thinking for a minute about what he had signed for. He was impressed with the résumé of this new disc jockey and wanted Chad's input.

Chad finished his meeting with James and left the office to begin his radio show.

James began to go through the packages the delivery man had dropped off. He remembered he'd had to sign for a special package, but which one was it? He did not notice the larger package on the table by his desk. James left his office to get a cup of coffee. When he returned to his desk, he was about to sit down, but then he noticed a large package on the table. Was this the one he had signed for? He then read the receipt from the sender. There was a look of pride lighting up his face as he left his office, carrying the package to the studio where the boys were.

The boys had just finished a tune when James walked in, carrying the package.

"Mr. Summers, is that for me?" Brandon said, jokingly.

James turned to Garland. "Son, I think this was left for you."

Garland walked over to James to accept the package from his dad. He noticed it was not as light as he'd anticipated, and he began to shake the box, wondering what was inside.

"Will you hurry up and open the box?" Brandon said.

Garland began to open the box. All eyes in the room focused on his actions. He removed the bands holding the box together to find a Styrofoam container inside the box. There were more bands holding the Styrofoam together.

What in the world would require so many bands? he wondered.

Finally, the inner container was now open. The look on Garland's face was priceless.

James's face burst with pride.

Garland took the new Fender out of its container. The green, yellow, and pink psychedelic design was the most beautiful thing he had ever seen. He removed the strap from the old Gibson and attached it to the new Fender. Inside the box was also a wire for an amplifier. He plugged the guitar into Adam's amp and began to tune this gorgeous instrument.

The boys found their new lead guitar player that day.

IIIIIIII

The summer of 1967 would bring America the Monterey Pop Festival, a musical event that launched the careers of some of rock and roll's most-popular and best-remembered artists. There had never been an event anything like it before. The Monterey Pop Festival would draw more than two hundred thousand people in the course of three days. Just as *Sgt. Pepper's* changed the recorded-music scene of the day, Monterey would change concerts. These large concerts showcased many artists and were held outdoors in open areas to accommodate the massive crowds they drew. With the increased use of electronic aids, the sound of rock and roll began to become more diverse. The music was much harder than that of the early sixties. Drugs, free love, and protests songs were the themes of many of the most-popular songs.

The hours of practicing were beginning to catch Kevin's attention. There was such chemistry between Garland and Adam. It was as if each boy knew exactly what the other was thinking. The sounds they created were advanced for boys of their age. Kevin had never seen the passion for music that all five of these boys had when they practiced. There was never a time that Kevin had to force them to jam together. They always did it on their own; many times, Kevin or James would have to end the sessions. And yet, even with all the passion the boys had for music, there still was something missing.

The music was blending very well, and they had no trouble learning any new song. The boys always practiced playing musically, but there weren't any vocals. The music had an empty feeling without vocals. If the vocals were as good as the music was, these boys could write their own ticket, and the sky would be the limit. There had to be a way to get the music and the words together.

Kevin had an idea that he was sure would work. Garland usually would cue the others as to what tune they would do. Kevin went into the room next door. There was a reel-to-reel tape recorder dedicated to the studio. The recorder had the capability of laying down tracks of music to be added to other tracks. Different sounds could then be separated. The boys began to play a Rolling Stones tune they all loved. Just as the music began, Kevin turned on the recorder. He wanted to capture the music tracks on tape, undetected by the boys. Kevin captured almost the entire practice session.

After the session, the boys left the room and went home.

Kevin returned to the studio and turned the recorder on for a playback of the session. What he heard amazed him: the music was far better than when he heard it the first time in its live format. Kevin played some of the songs over and over.

Chad was about to finish his show that day and went to see Kevin about an idea. He saw Kevin in the studio.

Kevin saw Chad and motioned for him to come in.

Chad entered the room.

"Have a seat, Chad. I want you to see what your son has been up to," Kevin said.

"What has he done now?" Chad asked.

"Done? I want you to hear something very, very special," Kevin said.

Kevin turned the recorder's Play switch on. Chad had not heard much of the boys' practice sessions. Kevin watched Chad's face as he listened to the recording. He could see the surprise on Chad's face. When the music stopped, Chad sat there speechless—something not typical of a disc jockey.

"I cannot believe what I have just heard," Chad said. "They are this good after such a short time?!"

"We have some very talented sons, Chad," Kevin said.

"The music was awesome, but why weren't there any vocals? Do you know how great this would be with the right lead vocals and harmonies?" Chad said.

"Well, I have an idea that I will spring on them tomorrow when they practice," Kevin said.

Chad was eating breakfast and reading the morning paper. One story caught his eye: the Red Rocks Amphitheatre announced a contest for musical talent. This was a prestigious annual contest. This year, there would be a first in the contest's history. The winner would be the opening act during the 1968 concert season. He wanted Kevin to see this. If the boys could find the words to go with the music, they had a very good shot at doing well in the contest—perhaps even winning.

"Good morning, Daddy. Can I borrow the car today?" Suzanna asked.

Chad had not even noticed her standing in the doorway.

"I can take you to work and drop Beau off for practice," Suzanna added.

Chad had never been able to say no to Suzanna regarding anything. She had him wrapped around her little finger.

"You will have to be back in time to pick us up," Chad said.

"That will not be a problem. I will be there in plenty of time before you are ready to leave for the day. I'll be ready when you and Beau are ready," Suzanna said.

James and Kevin were in their Monday morning meeting when Beau and Chad arrived.

Beau immediately went into the studio.

Chad knocked on Kevin's office door.

"Come on in," Kevin said.

Chad entered the room and approached the conference table where James and Kevin sat.

"The boys should enter the Red Rocks contest," Chad said.

Kevin and James looked at each other. They had no idea what Chad was referring to.

Chad put the contest article on the table for James and Kevin to see.

They all agreed that the boys could do well, but the lack of vocals was a problem.

Kevin insisted that James and Chad follow him to the studio to meet with the boys.

"Boys, have you decided on who wants to take a shot at the lead vocals?" Kevin asked.

The boys looked at each other, but no one came forward to meet the challenge.

Kevin took out the ad for the Red Rocks contest and passed it around for the five boys to read.

"You guys have a great chance of doing something in the contest. Even if you do not win, the opportunity for exposure would be very valuable," Kevin said.

The boys were excited.

Kevin continued, "I want you guys to hear something. I want you to hear how great the five of you sound, and I want to see if you hear what is missing."

Kevin approached the switch on the control panel and turned on the power to the recorder. The music from the last rehearsal began to flood the room. This was the first time the boys ever heard themselves on tape. James had never experienced the sound on tape before and was equally as taken as the boys were. After the tape finished playing, they all agreed the contest was something they wanted to try.

Still, no one wanted to be the lead singer.

The boys were about to start the day's practice session when the door to the studio opened. It was Suzanna, returning from the errands she had attended to.

Garland immediately began to light up. The effect she'd had on him at their initial meeting had not changed. It seemed to him that the butterflies had become very big butterflies.

The other boys were ready to start the session, but Garland would not turn his attention to the work at hand.

"Garland, I hear you are quite bashful," Suzanna said.

Garland began to blush. He did not want Suzanna to see the effect she had on him.

"Where did you ever get that idea? That is the craziest thing I have ever heard," Garland said.

Garland led Suzanna to the spare stool in the studio, insisting that she have a seat.

Kevin sensed that something was about to happen. He left the room and went directly into the next room, where the recorder was. He did not want to miss capturing what he felt was about to happen.

Each of the recorders four tracks could separate different sounds, including vocals.

Garland picked up his guitar and began to play a few chords of the Stones song the boys had played the day before.

Adam, Brandon, Harley, and Beau did not want to miss this.

Garland suddenly began to sing to Suzanna. The words began to flow like a river out of its banks.

Suzanna didn't mind at all. She had never had a boy sing to her before.

The boys did not know Garland possessed such a great voice. They were in awe. Who would have ever thought Garland was this smooth of a vocalist?

James knew it all along. It brought back the memories of that early morning in Roswell when Garland was a little boy and Sissy sang to him. Garland's voice came to him honestly. James could see Sissy's touch in their son. She had passed along her vocal talent to him.

Kevin had just found that missing piece to the music. He hadn't known how big a piece it was until that moment, and all it had taken for him to discover it was a girl.

Kevin quickly rewound the tape of Garland's serenade to Suzanna.

The track recorded was the voice track. The purity was amazing. Kevin then transferred the voice track onto a track of Garland and Adam's guitar tracks. Once the voice track was combined with the music track, he piped the music back into the studio room.

Everyone sat there in complete shock.

Is this really us? the boys thought as they listened intently.

Suzanna was touched that day in a way she had never been before by any boy. She could not keep her eyes off Garland as she listened to every note and word of the song.

Chad had a feeling that the little girl who had him wrapped around her little finger had just given her heart to someone else. There wasn't a boy he could be prouder of for her to fall for than Garland.

When the recording stopped, Suzanna ran out of the room. She did not want anyone to see how much the song had touched her heart.

The contest rules required a demo recording. Kevin made a duplicate copy to send in for the boys' entry. He did not want to risk the chance that the only tape of the session might be lost or damaged.

"Boys, we are ready for the entry to be sent. We only need one more item: a name for the group," Kevin said. "Does anyone have a suggestion? What catchy name can we use to help set us apart?"

"Since our band will be centered on Garland, I think Summers should be part of the name," Brandon said.

Kevin looked at Brandon and nodded his approval.

Beau, the summertime nut of the band, added, "Since the first day of summer occurs with the summer solstice, I like Summer's Solstice for a name. That will pick up on Garland's name."

"Summer's Solstice; that is a great idea," Adam said, giving the name his vote.

Harley agreed.

Garland was deeply touched that the guys considered him the leader of the band and honored that they wanted to use his name in the group's name.

The vote was cast, and it was unanimous. Summer's Solstice was born that day.

Kevin now had all the requirements for the contest. He packaged the demo tape and headed for the post office.

The next few weeks seemed like years as the boys awaited to see if they would have the chance to compete in the contest.

6

SEPTEMBER ARRIVED, BRINGING the new school year. There wasn't any news concerning the contest. Garland and Adam arrived at school that morning, as did Suzanna and Beau. This was the first time Garland had seen Suzanna since that day in the studio. Beau sensed Garland and Suzanna wanted to be alone and suggested he and Adam proceed to the courtyard.

"How have you been, Suzanna? You have been on my mind since that day at the station," Garland said.

Suzanna blushed and replied, "I am okay."

"Are you excited about the new school year at Hinckley? "Garland asked.

"This is our first year here since Dad took the job at the station. I hope I will blend in," she said.

Garland wanted to comfort her. "Which period do you have lunch?" said he asked.

Suzanna unfolded her schedule to find which lunchtime she was assigned.

Garland turned to his schedule as well. He began to compare the two schedules. "We both have lunch during fourth period," Garland said.

Without Suzanna noticing, Garland compared the two schedules to see if they had any other classes together. Garland had this huge smile on his face as he returned her schedule.

The school bell rang and the new school year began.

|||||||

Suzanna had always been a very popular girl and prided herself on the grades she received. She was in the honor society and planned to attend college after high school. Suzanna's first-period class was geometry. Math not being one of her favorite subjects, she was very happy it was her first class. She would be fresh and alert.

Garland, too, had one of his least favorite subjects first period. Algebra 2 was his first-period class, and was relieved to have it finished with the first class.

The first two periods came and went.

Suzanna walked to her third-period history class that first day of school and took a seat. She took out her schedule and wished it was fourth-period lunch. She missed the comfort she felt with Garland. She was looking at the schedule when a voice interrupted her thoughts of Garland. She slowly looked to where the voice came from.

The boy sitting in the row next to her was all smiles.

"I wanted to surprise you. It was all I could do not to say anything when I looked at your schedule," Garland said.

Just as he did that day in the studio, Garland had touched her again with a surprise of the heart. Suzanna reached across the aisle to hold Garland's hand. She really wanted him very much. She smiled and squeezed his hand at the thought of being with him for two back-to-back class periods.

The bell rang, ending the third period. Garland and Suzanna walked to the cafeteria, and soon another bell rang to signal the start of fourth period. Finally, there was some time when she and Garland could be together, just talking, during lunch.

The first day of school came to a close. Garland met Suzanna in the parking lot.

Garland, Adam, and Beau loaded up and went to the station for band practice. They arrived before Harley and Brandon. As they entered the station lobby and passed by Kevin's office, they saw him going through the mail for that day. Kevin had in his hand this large brown envelope almost like the ones he would get for new record promotions from the record labels. In fact, he had at first believed it was one of those promotions. By this time, Brandon and Harley had arrived as well. Kevin opened the envelope, expecting to see details about the record he believed to be inside the package.

Instead, there was a follow-up from the Red Rocks contest.

The letter explained the contest details. Kevin read the letter in silence.

The suspense was about to kill the boys.

"What does it say, Dad?" Adam asked.

"Did they like the tape we sent in?" Brandon wanted to know.

Kevin took a deep breath and then proceeded to inform the boys what was coming next.

"Guys, the number of entries was enormous. So many acts entered that there will be a live audition to narrow down to twenty acts for the finals. We will have two weeks to get ready for the audition, and we have a lot of work ahead of us just to make the top twenty," Kevin said.

The boys hung their heads and walked out of Kevin's office, heading to the studio. This was not the good news they had hoped for. But, at the same time, it wasn't a turndown either. They had made it to the audition round.

Kevin sat in his office, planning his next move. The tape he'd entered was a mix. The boys had never performed music and vocals at the same time. They had never performed harmonies. The entry was one song, and that song would have to wow the judges; otherwise, the boys wouldn't make it to the next round. He needed someone to coach the boys on vocals and harmonies, but who? Who would be able to get those special inner feelings from these boys?

Kevin entered the studio and explained the dilemma they faced.

"Guys, we need someone who knows harmonies. Who can we get with that kind of talent? I have worn my brain out thinking about it," Kevin said. "Does anyone have any ideas?"

There was a long silence.

Garland had an idea. "Kevin, I need to run home. I have something that might help us."

Kevin hoped Garland's idea would be a good one.

James was finishing work for the day when Garland approached him to take him home to retrieve something.

Once Garland and James arrived home, Garland went to his bedroom closet. He searched intently for a canvas bag that he had been keeping for a time like this. At last, he found it and rushed out of his room.

"Mom, will you drive me back to the station?" Garland asked.

At first, Sissy was hesitant, wondering what had come over her son.

"Mom, I really need you to do this," Garland said.

Sissy could see how desperate her son was and agreed to accompany him back to the station.

They arrived back at the station in no time.

Garland took Sissy's hand and led her to the studio where Kevin and the boys waited.

"Kevin, I want you and the guys to hear something. Mother, this involves you as well," Garland said. He reached into the bag to pull out the black tape recorder James had brought from Thailand.

Everyone gathered around to see what Garland had in mind.

"Kevin, I have the answer to what we need right here on this recorder," Garland said.

Garland pressed the Play button, and the treat was about to start. A voice began singing and humming. This was the voice of an angel. Everyone in the room was touched. Kevin stopped the machine.

"This is the voice we heard that day when we were on the road in New Mexico. It was the voice everyone heard on the highway," Kevin said. "This person would be perfect, Garland, but how in the world are we to find the lady singing? She was a passenger on the highway that day, just like we were."

"Kevin, we don't have to look for her," Garland said. He walked over to Sissy and put his arm around her. "The angel we all heard that day was my mom."

Kevin looked at Sissy, who had no idea that Garland had recorded her that day in the car.

"This is a song she would sing to me when I was a baby, and I remember it as much today as I did when I was a baby. She has always been my angel," Garland said.

"Sissy, that was you that day?" Kevin asked.

"Yes, Kevin, I was the guilty one that day. I had no idea my son was recording me," Sissy said. With tears running down her cheeks, she hugged her son.

Kevin smiled at Sissy and Garland, now feeling the problem he had pondered earlier that day could not be in better hands for resolution.

Sissy agreed to help the boys with their vocals and harmonies. It was time to get down to business for the contest.

"Kevin, can you play the tape you sent in for the contest?" Sissy said.

Kevin turned on the recorder.

Sissy liked the song choice the boys had made.

"Will you only play Garland's voice track? I want to hear the range in his voice," she said.

Kevin separated Garland's voice track. There was something about his voice she had never heard before. It was as if his voice had a purpose. Whatever purpose that was, she loved its passion.

"We need to find another voice to complement Garland's voice for two-part harmonies. I want to see which one of the other boys has a voice that will do that," Sissy said. "First, we will have each one of you sing solo, and then a few chorus lines with Garland. "Adam, you can be first. I want to hear your solo."

Adam began his solo. The pitch was not a soothing one.

After a few verses, Sissy interrupted Adam and thanked him.

"Would you like me to do a harmony with Garland?" Adam said.

With just a few bars, Sissy knew Adam was not a candidate for vocals.

"I think the rhythm guitar you bring will be our biggest asset," Sissy said.

Harley was sitting on a stool reading a magazine.

"Harley, let's see what you can do," Kevin said.

Harley stepped up to the microphone and begin to sing the same verses Adam had butchered. Sissy and Kevin looked at each other for an approval. Harley's solo was good, although he did not have the same vocal range as Garland.

Brandon had never shown any interest in expressing himself vocally. He would rather get wrapped up in the beat of the music.

"Beau, it's your turn," Kevin said.

Beau took the microphone in his hand and began to sing. Beau was nowhere as pitchy as Adam, and he was not as smooth as Harley.

Sissy walked to where Kevin was standing. "We can work with Harley, and he will improve. But I am not sure we can use him for any solos. We need another voice."

Kevin motioned for Brandon to join him.

"Brandon, I know you aren't into vocals, but let's see what you can do," Kevin said.

Brandon took the microphone into his hand. He always had a mind of his own and began to sing a different song than that of the other boys. The range and pitch Brandon commanded was amazing. Who would have ever thought this voice would have come from Brandon? Sissy and Kevin could not believe their ears. Brandon's voice would enable them to be versatile.

"Garland, Harley, and Brandon, let me hear you sing a few verses of this song. I want to see how you harmonize together. A three-part harmony would be unique and would set us apart," Sissy said.

Sissy began to lead the boys just like a choir director leads a choir. Brandon and Garland's harmonies were awesome. Harley's wasn't as pleasing, but it was something they could work on. He did have talent.

Sissy gave the boys a few songs to hear how their voices would blend together.

As the boys started their first song, Suzanna walked into the session and took a seat near the control panel. She was wearing a short skirt and boots. Her long black hair draped over her shoulders. Suzanna was becoming a very sultry young woman. Her appearance made Kevin and Sissy do double takes.

The boys stopped singing to be treated to Suzanna's presence.

"Okay, boys, let's try it again," Sissy said.

This time, Garland's voice found the same range that was on the tape Kevin had mixed. Sissy immediately took notice, wondering what had made the difference in him. Garland's eyes never left Suzanna's eyes. She was as lost in the sound of his voice as she had been the day the tape was made. She was beginning to fall for Garland, and no one knew it better than Sissy. As soon as the song was finished, Garland rushed to Suzanna's side. It was evident he was glad to see her, and she was just as glad to see Garland. The session ended that day with Kevin and Sissy pleased with the day's discovery.

||||||||

A week had passed, and there was no word from the contest organizers. The boys' jam sessions were really coming together. Kevin began to show signs of stress, wondering how the boys would react if they didn't make the second round. They were working so hard for this. Kevin placed a phone call to a friend at another station. He wanted to know if a decision had arrived regarding the final twenty. His sources informed him a decision was coming that day, along with the dates for the second round.

Kevin's phone conversation was interrupted by a loud sound coming from the studio. He hung up the phone and went down the hallway. The closer he came to the room, the louder the sound became. He came to the window in the door and peeked inside the room. Kevin did not want to be detected. His eyes and ears both were amazed. There in the studio, practicing so intensely, was Brandon. Kevin had never seen Brandon work this hard at anything. Kevin had discovered Brandon's talent as a drummer years before. However, what he saw today was something even more special: Brandon had begun to blossom into a rare talent.

Kevin was standing by the door with his head hanging down, enjoying the sounds Brandon was performing.

Adam and Garland soon joined Kevin. Both boys were also amazed by the solo their friend was providing.

Another ten minutes had passed when the three of them were interrupted by a tap on Kevin's shoulder.

"Kevin, I have a package for you," a voice said.

Kevin turned to see that it was the delivery driver.

Brandon stopped for a drink of water. He saw a shadow behind the door. Shirtless, with sweatbands on his wrists and head, Brandon approached the window. He saw Kevin, Adam, and Garland standing outside the door, with the silhouette on another person who handed something to Kevin. Brandon took them by surprise as he opened the door.

The package contained the news they all were anxious to receive.

"We are in the second round, guys. Congratulations!" Kevin said.

The boys now had a reason to ramp up their practice: they only had a week until the big day.

The practice sessions were productive and long. Summer's Solstice needed a change of scenery. Kevin wanted to see an audience's reaction to the band. Performing before a live audience would help calm the butterflies he knew they would have at the audition. How could he arrange this? There weren't any shows in the area they could help with. He would have to come up with something, and soon.

Kevin had an idea that just might work. The station was located on the edge of town, next to an abandoned grocery store. He would organize his own show. To promote the show, canned foods would be donated to charity. He would publicize the show at Hinckley and on the station. The parking lot next door could accommodate an audience of one or thousand people. Nothing too large, but something to give the boys some a sense of gratification from performing in front of an audience. This might be the high that would carry them into the next round.

||||||||

The next day at school, the buzz was about the upcoming show. Many of the boys' friends at school knew they had a band, but they never knew how serious the boys were about performing. The boys had permission to place posters in the hallways, and promotions were made daily during the school's morning announcements.

Chad was plugging the show as well on his radio show. Kevin took charge of getting the stage set to perform.

James had a friend donate the use of searchlights and stage lighting.

The speed at which things were coming together was like a dream come true. It was hard for Kevin to believe the response the show was getting.

The boys were now ready for the show.

The day of the show arrived, and excitement stoked the members of Summer's Solstice. The boys arrived at the station several hours before the show was to start.

Kevin and Sissy wanted to have a short meeting with the boys.

"Let's have a great show, guys. We will do the three songs you have been practicing on, "Sissy said.

"Garland, it will be up to you to set the tempo of the show. Make them feel they cannot get enough, and the crowd will be yours; you'll be able to do whatever you want with them," Kevin said.

"Chad will announce you to the crowd," Sissy said.

James arrived to see the boys before they went on.

"How is the crowd?" Kevin asked him.

"There are about two thousand people. I don't think we have room for one more," James said.

The boys left the station and stood behind the stage, out of the crowd's sight.

Chad walked up the steps and onto the stage to where the microphone stood. He took the microphone out of its stand and looked out into the crowd.

"Hello, I am Chad Royal. I want to thank everyone for their contributions tonight. You are here to witness the first public performance of Summer's Solstice." Chad began to walk to the front of the stage. He was getting the crowd worked up. "Aurora, are you ready?"

The crowd began to roar.

Garland walked out onto the stage first. Once on the stage front, he looked to the side, to where Kevin, James, and Sissy were standing. His face lit up when he saw Suzanna. He'd missed her earlier.

Adam and Harley came out next, taking their places on the stage and strapping on their guitars.

Beau and Brandon were the last two out.

Beau went to stand behind his keyboard.

Brandon, with a halfway unbuttoned shirt and drumsticks in his hands, walked to where Garland was standing. The two boys embraced. Brandon then banged the two drumsticks together, teasing the crowd.

Garland, standing behind the microphone, strapped on his Fender.

Brandon ran to his drum set.

"One, two, three, four!" Garland chanted.

The show had started.

Garland's cadence began the moment of a long-overdue reward. Finally, after many long, hard hours of practice, the boys were about to feel what it was like to perform for a live audience. It was a chance to interact with the crowd, and an opportunity for the crowd to respond to and interact with them. The cadence cued Brandon to begin the intro. Then keyboards and bass then followed. Garland glanced at Adam, nodding a count. Adam followed Garland's count. On the fourth nod, the boys came together.

The song began with a three-part harmony from Garland, Harley, and Brandon. The boys had practiced the reps so many times, they could do the song in their sleep. The outdoor sound created a little bit of an echo they were not accustomed to. Playing outside the studio was all new to them. This was what Kevin wanted them to experience. He didn't want the audition to be the first time for echo problems. He wanted to solve any problems before the audition. The applause from the crowd gave the boys a sense of approval.

Garland wanted to hit the audience while they were hot and into the moment. He instantly cued the others for song number two. The second song had much more tempo than the first number. The boys wanted to fire up the audience, and there was no better way than an upbeat, up-tempo version of the Rolling Stones song they knew so well. They knew the crowd was familiar with the song as well; if they performed it well, it would not take long for them to know it.

The response of the crowd grew louder with each note. The louder the crowd's reaction, the harder the boys played.

Garland began to slow down the song. He wanted to showcase the musical talents of his band. He began to direct a short solo for each member. He felt it added a sense of personal satisfaction for each musician, and was he ever right. The crowd ate it up too. The song ended to a standing ovation. Not bad for a new group on its inaugural show: a standing ovation with its second number.

For the final song, the boys played a ballad of the heart. Garland wanted to show how well diversified they could be with their sounds. Again, the crowd responded with a standing ovation. Two standing ovations during their first show. The boys joined each other at the front of the stage to take a bow.

There were already chants of "More! More! More!"

After the final bow, the boys rushed off the stage.

Chad arrived at center stage, awed by the crowd's response.

"How do you feel about Summer's Solstice?" he said.

The crowd cheered.

Chad continued, "Please welcome Harley Krause on bass; my son, Beau Royal, on keyboards; Adam English, on rhythm guitar; Garland Summers, on lead guitar; and last, but not least, Brandon Baily on drums."

Brandon's intro drew the greatest applause from the girls in the crowd.

The boys once again left the stage.

The crowd was not ready for the show to end. It was evident they wouldn't leave until they heard more.

The boys entered the stage again, not knowing what to do.

Garland looked at Kevin for an answer.

Kevin began to motion with his hands as if he were playing a guitar.

The boys stood arm in arm.

"I think we should do an encore. Let's do the chorus from the second song," Garland said softly to the others.

With that, the boys went to their instruments and waited for Garland's signal.

Garland started what he thought would be a short encore. It wound up lasting five full minutes.

Once again, the boys gathered at the center of the stage to take a final bow. Brandon had become shirtless by now, and the girls in the crowd were ecstatic. After the bow, the boys turned for the exit.

Brandon, the free spirit of the group, returned to the crowd. He bent down and gave his drumsticks to two girls in the crowd. And, as if to perform his own personal encore, he threw his sweat-soaked shirt into the crowd.

Kevin shook his head, laughing at what his adopted son had just done. This boy was destined to be the heartthrob of the group, and every group needed one.

|||||||

The following day, Kevin reviewed his mental notes from the show the night before. Which song would stand out over the others? Did they need to change any of the songs' arrangements?

The auditions were divided into two groups of ten. None of the groups were to see any other group's performance. The auditions were to be done simultaneously at two different locations. Each audition was to be judged by five judges in the music business. Scores would be based on musical content and showmanship. In case of a tie, there would be a one-song sing-off. Never in the history of the contest had there been a tie.

The boys still had their work cut out for them, but the biggest hurdle was passed. They had showmanship and were big crowd-pleasers. These were two very big assets for a contest of this magnitude.

7

THE MORNING OF the audition saw all the boys enjoying breakfast together with their families. This was the first time the families were all together at the same time. They wanted the boys to know they were supporting them, and that support to provide strength.

Kevin began the breakfast by telling the boys how proud he was to be associated with them.

"You guys have only been together for a short time, and already I can see how much you care for each other. Don't ever let anyone take that away from you," Kevin said.

"I once was an only child. All my life, making friends has been a struggle for me. Today, I am no longer an only child. I have four brothers," Garland said.

Each of the boys knew exactly what Garland felt.

This bond would be challenged very soon, and their brotherhood was to be tested.

The boys began to load the equipment. Each one took extreme care of the instruments as they were loaded. No one wanted to contend with any sort of equipment problem during the audition.

Garland decided he would take along the old Gibson. He was reaching for his Fender, thinking he would have to make another trip for his old friend. He began to pick the Gibson up as well when a hand reached out for the guitar. As he looked up, the hand grabbed the Gibson's case. Garland had always been very particular about whom he let hold this special friend. At first, he was reluctant to release the case to the hand. As his eyes followed the arm of the hand, a special feeling came over him when he saw the face of the helping hand.

"Can I carry her for you?" Suzanna said.

Garland smiled at Suzanna. "I would really appreciate the help."

Garland helped Suzanna, placing the Gibson in her right hand. He picked up the Fender, making sure to carry it in his left hand. He wanted his right hand to be free.

As they began to walk toward the doorway, Suzanna reached for Garland's hand and held it tightly. The two walked through the parking lot hand in hand.

"Dad, is it okay for Suzanna to ride along with us to the audition?" Garland asked.

Chad saw Suzanna and Garland at the Summerses' car.

"I think you need to let her dad know what you two have in mind," James said.

Chad had overheard Garland asking James.

"Go ahead, sweetheart," Chad said to Suzanna. "We will meet you there."

James and Sissy occupied the front seat, while Garland and Suzanna sat in the rear.

"Son, is there something wrong with the seat?" James asked.

"Wrong? No, Dad. Why do you think anything is wrong with the seat?" Garland answered.

James chuckled and replied, "Well, both of you are sitting on the same side of the car, so I thought there was a problem with the seat."

Suzanna giggled and smiled at how embarrassed Garland had become. She loved it when he blushed.

Meanwhile, in the Englishes' car, Adam asked, "Dad, do we know where we will perform today?"

"For this round, we are assigned to the Denver Center for the Performing Arts," Kevin answered.

The trip was about an hour's drive from Aurora. Adam could hardly wait. He was still riding on the high from their inaugural show.

Brandon shared Adam's enthusiasm.

"Did you see how those girls wanted me? If this is what playing music is all about, I hope the music never gets silent," Brandon said now. The attraction from the girls was as much of a high for Brandon as the music.

The caravan pulled into the parking lot at the performing arts theatre. Kevin suggested they take a tour of the facility. He didn't want the size of the building to overwhelm the boys. Kevin led them inside through the front door of the theatre. The ceilings were so high. The walls were lined with curtains, and the stage was enormous. It was three times the size of the only stage they had ever performed on. The boys walked up to the stage in total awe.

Brandon walked along the stage front until he arrived at the stairs. He ran up the short flight of stairs and proceeded to where the others were standing down in front. He could see his friends were awestruck. Even Brandon knew the shock would not be good for the band.

"Hello, we are Summer's Solstice. Are you ready to get *summerized*?" Brandon bellowed.

Brandon began to imitate Garland, with an awesome display of air guitar, followed by a solo rendition of Beau on the keyboard. Brandon was all over the stage, finally arriving to perform a solo using his chest as his drums. His concert was now complete. Brandon walked up to the stage front and took a bow and then another bow. This brought a loud laugh from his friends. Brandon unbuttoned his shirt, took it off, threw it to Suzanna, and ran off the stage.

The humorous performance notwithstanding, Kevin worried about how he would make the boys feels at home on this stage and in this theater. In the next instant, his worries were no more.

Brandon reached the spot where they all stood, saying. "Suzanna, do you think I can have my shirt back?"

Kevin now knew the boys would be ready.

Each of the acts was to send a representative to the auditorium two hours before the auditions were to start. Kevin did not want the boys to be the last act to perform. He feared the long wait would not be good for his guys.

Chad volunteered to represent the group for the draw. He began the walk to the auditorium, praying their number would be for the first part of the audition. The boys were ready, and, like Kevin, he knew the wait would not be a good thing.

Chad entered the auditorium and joined the other representatives. There was a jar containing ten cards with the numbers one to ten. Each representative would take a card from the jar. Once all ten cards were drawn, the contest organizers would cue the revealing to be made simultaneously. Chad was the last rep to draw from the jar. He slowly reached his hand into the jar, clutching the last card. He slowly began to take his hand from the jar. His wrist had cleared the jar, with only his hand and the grasped card still inside the jar. The card was clearing the mouth of the jar when Chad dropped the card. All the representatives watched to see if the number on Chad's card was visible as it tumbled end over end to the floor. The card came to a rest with the number facing down on the floor. Chad took a deep breath and retrieved the card carefully from the floor, so as not to reveal the number drawn. Then, as cued by the contest organizers, all cards would be turned simultaneously, revealing the order of the competition.

Chad closed his eyes as the cue was given for his card number to be revealed. He prayed his card would reveal a low number. He opened his eyes to see his prayers had not been answered. He closed his eyes again, as if to try to erase the image he first saw. Unfortunately, this did not work.

The drawing was over, and the contest officials instructed the first act to be ready to go onstage in less than an hour and a half.

Chad made his way back to the room where the others waited. As he opened the door, all eyes were glued to him as he met Kevin in the center of the room. Chad handed over the card.

Kevin looked down at the card to see the red number ten. Summer's Solstice would be the last act to perform. This was the last thing Kevin wanted for the boys.

Each boy had his clothes in one suitcase. They took turns dressing. The boys had really done their homework in selecting their wardrobe. The others were dressed, leaving Brandon to be the last to enter.

As he approached the bathroom, Brandon was carrying two bags. "What in the world do you need two bags for?" Beau asked. "I didn't want you boys to be jealous, so I decided I would go last. I hate to show you poor boys up," Brandon said, laughing. "But why do you need two bags?" Beau asked again.

Brandon winked and closed the door.

Brandon looked in the mirror and began to brush his hair. His hair was considerably longer than the other boys' hair. He parted his hair down the middle, making it look even longer than it had before he entered the bathroom. He struggled to get his tight buckskin-colored pants on. His dark hair and skin made the aqua shirt seem to shimmer as he moved in it. He added a belt with a silver buckle.

"What is taking so long in there? If you can join us today, it would be nice. We do have a show today, you know!" Adam yelled.

Brandon ignored the comment from Adam and continued with his outfit.

Inside the other bag were the finishing touches, items reflecting the Native American heritage he was so proud of: knee-high moccasins, complete with the fringes on the tops, and a leather necklace with a turquoise-and-silver hawk. Last, but not least, was a multicolor headband and matching sweatbands around his wrists. He gave one final look in the mirror, turned to open the door, and paused. What had he forgotten? Oh yes! The top three buttons on his shirt were not open. He fixed that, then he opened the door.

All jaws almost dropped to the floor as Brandon walked to the center of the room.

"I came here today to put on a show and for us to get into the next round. I will need my four brothers to kick some ass today. We will be leaving here as the winner of this contest," Brandon said.

Brandon then held out his arm, with the palm of his hand facing downward.

Harley, Beau, Adam, and Garland all joined in, placing theirs hand on top of Brandon's.

"It's Solstice time; time to kick ass," Brandon said, leading the cheer.

Once again, Kevin knew Brandon had come to the rescue. The boys could wait for hours, as long as they had Brandon.

Sissy and Suzanna waited outside in the hall while the boys got dressed.

The signal came from the stage for Summer's Solstice to get ready.

Sissy knocked on the door and said, "It's showtime."

Chad opened the door for the boys to make their way to the stage.

The boys broke their huddle and proceeded out of the room. Harley, Beau, and Adam were the first to exit.

Sissy and Suzanna were leaning against the wall when Brandon entered the doorway.

"Damn," Suzanna said as she saw Brandon.

Brandon stopped in front of Suzanna and Sissy. He winked and then kissed them each on the cheek.

Garland and Kevin were the last to leave the room.

Kevin reached to close the door behind him.

Garland took Suzanna by the arm and walked her to the stage.

Kevin put his arm around Sissy for the walk.

Looking at Sissy, Kevin said, "These boys are going to make you proud today, Sissy. They already have made me proud—win or lose."

The next-to-last act left the stage. There would be ten minutes to get the boys' instruments set up. James and Chad were taking charge of that.

"Sissy, I have a seat for us to watch this. Let's go enjoy the show," Kevin said.

Kevin led Sissy to the VIP seating in the front row. There was nothing more anyone could do now.

James and Chad were almost finished with the instruments.

"Dad, I have an idea," Garland said. "I want to use the Gibson for this song. We are doing the Stones song, and Brandon and I both share lead vocals on this arrangement."

"Are you sure, son? Is this what you and Kevin went over"? James asked.

"Kevin doesn't know about this, Dad," Garland said. "You will have to trust us on this one."

Brandon walked up and put his arm around James, assuring him that it would be okay.

James left the stage to sit next to Kevin and Sissy.

"Guys, we have been waiting for this moment all our lives. Let's make this something special," Garland said.

The boys knew it was their moment, and they were ready. They took their places at their instruments.

The curtains were drawn. The emcee took the stage.

"Our last and final act for today comes from Aurora. I want you to welcome Summer's Solstice," the emcee said.

The emcee left the stage, and the lights went down. The curtains began to open, and the lights began to shine on each of the musicians.

Garland began the introduction with the old Gibson. He began the vocals for the first two verses. The lights gave way to Brandon, who continued the second verse.

Kevin had no idea of this arrangement. He had never heard it.

The tempo began to pick up, and the timing of Brandon's drums was perfect. The combination of the Gibson and the electrical notes from Adam was so different. The melodies were perfect. The harmonics of Brandon, Garland, and Harley were right on the money.

The notes Garland delivered brought a tear to the eyes of one of the judges. The voice was so pure that it gave the audience chills.

James, too, had a chill. He had heard this melody before many times. Even though the words were to a Stones song, the music was the same song they all heard before. James turned to Sissy to see the tears in her eyes.

"Is that the same song you have sung all these years?" James whispered.

Sissy turned to her husband and grinned, nodding her head yes.

The song finished with a harmony of the melody from Garland and Brandon. They had treated the ears and touched the hearts of the standing-room-only crowd.

Summer's Solstice was the only act from that group to receive a standing ovation. At the peak of the ovation, Garland walked to the edge of the stage and jumped down into the crowd. Brandon handed him the microphone. Garland sought out Sissy in the crowd and went to where she was sitting. A spotlight followed his steps to her seat.

"I want to thank my mother, whom I love more than anything in this world, for that song. She is the music in my heart and my soul," Garland said.

Returning the microphone to Brandon, Garland hugged and kissed his mother and once again told her he loved her.

Garland returned to the stage, and Brandon and Adam helped him back onstage.

The boys all came to the center of the stage to take a bow.

The lights were turned on to help the audience find their way to the exits. The lights also revealed that there was not a dry eye in the audience or at the judges' table.

The boys were already winners, with or without the vote of the judges.

The boys and their families gathered backstage to load up the equipment.

Suzanna was touched by the love Garland had for Sissy. She had always heard that a boy who treated his mother well would be a good husband. From what she saw that day, Garland would not be a good husband but a great husband.

Sissy had always been proud of Garland, but never more than she was that day.

"Kevin, you were so right. We do have some great boys," Sissy said.

The judges' decision would be announced in an hour. Everyone remained in the auditorium, waiting for the judges to return with the results. The process was to have taken an hour, but the judges returned in less than half the time.

Five acts from this audition would join five acts from the other audition in two weeks. Those ten acts would be reduced to five for the finals.

"The first act advancing to the next round is Colorado Kool-Aid," judge number one said.

Judge number two announced his choice. "Next, we have Rocky and the Mountaineers."

"That leaves three spots remaining. The next act moving on is Mile High," judge number three said.

The fourth judge came to the microphone. "Next, we have Daily Chores joining the group."

It was coming down to the last spot. Had they done enough to make it through to the next round? Whatever the decision was, the boys knew they could not have done any better. They had given it their all that day and could not have given any more.

Judge number five stepped up to the microphone. "And the final spot goes to the act with the day's highest score. This act received a number one from all five judges. Congratulations to Summer's Solstice."

The boys all jumped to their feet, hugging each other and their parents. It was the boys' turn to shed the tears the audience had shed earlier.

The trip back to Aurora would be a very good one. The first step was behind them, and there were two more weeks until the next round.

The contest officials gave Kevin an envelope detailing the information for round two. This could wait, though. It was time to celebrate this moment.

|||||||

After several days of well-deserved rest, it was now time to plan the second round of the auditions. Everyone assembled in the studio room at the station.

Kevin wanted to go over what they could expect for the next round.

"Guys, I have just learned the group we auditioned with was considered the B group. We were placed in that group because we have not been working at this very long. The A group will be much tougher, and the acts we managed to edge out from our group will be stepping up their game as well," Kevin said.

The audition site was also very much larger. This time, the crowds would play a bigger impact on the acts.

Kevin continued, "We will also have to perform two songs this time around. The first song will be judged by the judges from group A, who have not seen us. The second round will be from group B. We need to make the most of every judge's score."

Kevin left it up to the boys to decide if they wanted to rehearse that day, but he wanted them to know that they would need to step up their game.

Kevin returned to his office, and the boys remained for a meeting of their own.

"Does anyone have any suggestions?" Adam said. "We need to show a diversity of our ranges and talents. You know, the way the Beatles did with *Sgt. Pepper's*."

"Does anyone play other instruments?" Garland asked.

"I can play a harmonica," Beau said.

"Great, Beau. We can try a blues feeling on an arrangement." Adam said.

"Adam, can you play an acoustic guitar?" Garland asked.

"I have played a little on the standard," Adam replied.

"We will meet tomorrow after school," Garland said. "Beau, bring your harmonica. Adam, bring your acoustic guitar. I have an idea."

With that, the meeting was over, and the boys headed home.

IIIIIII

The next afternoon, Beau and Adam were the first to arrive, along with their new instruments. Harley and Brandon made their usual arrival together. Soon an hour had passed, and Garland was still not there. It was not like him to be late.

Kevin had finished his daily paperwork and noticed there were no sounds coming from the studio. Even though it was a studio, there was always a slight sound coming from the room that he could hear in his office when the boys were playing.

Kevin walked down to the studio. He noticed immediately that Garland had not arrived.

"Where is Garland?" Kevin asked.

There was no answer from the boys at first.

He began to look at each boy's face, searching for a clue as to Garland's whereabouts. His eyes stopped at the third face they came to.

"Beau, do you have something you would like to fill us in on?" Kevin asked.

Beau began to look down at the floor, as if to ignore Kevin's question.

"Beau, do you know where Garland is?" Kevin asked pointedly.

Beau looked up and then around at his fellow band members. He did not want to rat out Garland.

Kevin walked over to where Beau was sitting and placed his hands on Beau's shoulders.

"Is Garland in some kind of trouble, Beau?" Kevin asked.

This time, Beau looked at Kevin with a smirk on his face. As he began to answer Kevin, the smirk became even larger. "I know where Garland is, Kevin."

"Well, is he okay? Does he have any plans to join us?" Kevin said.

"I think it is way too late for Garland to be okay, Kevin," Beau said.

This remark brought loud laughter from the other boys.

Beau was beginning to test Kevin's patience.

"Garland came over to our house after school today," Beau said.

"Did he say anything about not showing up for practice?" Kevin asked.

"He didn't say, Kevin. He was not there to see me, though. He was with Suzanna all afternoon long. He said he would be a few minutes late," Beau replied.

This remark brought even louder laugh from the boys. So loud, in fact, that no one, not even Kevin, heard the door open when Garland entered the room.

Garland walked over to see what the laughter was all about.

"Did someone tell a joke?" Garland interrupted.

They all turned to see Garland, with his long uncombed hair.

Kevin walked over to where Garland was standing. When Garland turned his head, Kevin noticed something on the side of his neck.

"Was there a problem with the vacuum cleaner at Beau's house?" Kevin said.

This brought the loudest outburst yet from the boys. They had never seen this kind of humor from Kevin before.

Garland began to blush, just as he did that day in the backseat with Suzanna.

Kevin laughed and patted Garland on the head.

"Now you guys have a good practice," Kevin said and walked out of the studio.

"Thanks, guys, for covering for me. I owe you," Garland said.

The remainder of the session was productive.

Everyone was in attendance the next day, and on time. They had just a little more than a week to come up with another song.

Garland had an idea that would be a departure from the songs they had learned. His idea would have two acoustic guitars, with an intro by a harmonica.

"Adam, do you remember the song we played when we first met?" Garland asked.

Adam responded immediately, not with his voice, but with a few notes he played on the guitar. He continued to play until Garland joined in. The notes were pure with each chord they performed. Everyone else knew the tune they were playing, and with the same instant stroke of the guitar, the song was finished.

"Beau, can you play an intro to that?" Garland asked.

Beau brought the harmonica up to his mouth and slowly picked up the melody of the song.

Garland said, "Brandon, this is your song. With this song, you will have the girls fainting—if you do it right."

The boys spent the rest of the practice session on that one song, and, boy, did they perform it well.

|||||||

Each day, the song was better than the day before. They had no doubt that they were ready with this one. There was nothing more to enhance the arrangement—or so it seemed, until Chad arrived for the close of the session.

Chad finished his radio show and wanted to hear how the boys were doing. The harmonica Beau borrowed was Chad's.

The boys were finishing for the day, but Chad had an idea. The harmonica was truly his specialty when it came to an instrument.

"Beau, try holding your notes for a count longer," Chad said. "Your notes will come across smoother if you hold them a count longer."

Beau began to play the intro with his dad's advice. The boys were amazed at the difference the longer notes made to the sound. This song was now ready to record.

|||||||

Kevin informed the boys that he would pick them up from school that afternoon. He wanted to take them on a special trip. Not only did he surprise them with this field trip, but he also came to Hinckley to get the boys out of school two hours early. The boys were all shocked when the school's office paged them to the office for early dismissal. Kevin borrowed the station's passenger van for the trip. The boys all loaded into the van, having no idea of Kevin's plans.

"Boys, I have a surprise for you. We are going to McNichol's Coliseum. That is where the next round of auditions will be," Kevin said. "I want you to experience what you will see and hear in advance. Again, we are dealing with that awe feeling."

The boys knew he was good at dealing with the awe feeling. They had seen it at work twice. The van arrived at the coliseum's underground parking. Kevin was taking the boys through the same routine the big-time performers went through when doing a concert.

They entered through the special entrance and into the dressing rooms. Once through the dressing-room areas, there was a special hallway up to the stage. This time, there were no stairs. They would take an elevator to the backstage area. The elevator doors opened. The stage was unfinished, and the boys could see the multi levels of the arena. This arena would not have the acoustics of the last auditorium.

"Man, I am going to get a neck strain looking up so high. I guess it's the price I will have to pay for the girls in the upper deck, huh?" Brandon said, winking at his brothers and making them laugh and shake their heads.

Kevin and the boys all knew that this would be a treat for Brandon, not a challenge. That was something Kevin felt the other acts would not have as an advantage.

Brandon let out a loud wolf whistle, as if he were serenading the girls.

"Wow, do you guys hear that? The sound travels all the way to the top," Brandon said.

Kevin laughed. "Yeah, just think how the girls will act when they hear you call them with a microphone."

Brandon smiled from ear to ear and let out a loud, Indian-like yell.

Kevin and the boys spent the next hour exploring the setting of the arena. He wanted an advantage for this next round and seemed to always know just how to find that advantage.

8

KEVIN ORGANIZED A meeting that Friday night before the auditions. With the stakes now higher, he wanted to review the details of their audition. The boys arrived that evening with a definite purpose. Their mood was very serious.

"Tomorrow is a step toward what we have worked very hard for. You guys are ready. I can see it in your eyes and your spirit. Chad will guide you through the schedule," Kevin said.

"The auditions will begin at 7:00 p.m. And we will leave here at 4:00 p.m. Once we arrive, I will check us in. We have been assigned dressing room number seven," Chad said.

"We will get dressed and wait for our time to perform," Kevin said.

Kevin closed the meeting and wished them a good night's rest.

The boys departed the station for their homes.

That is, all but Garland. He called James to inform him the meeting would be a little longer and he would be home as soon as the meeting was finished. Garland was sitting on the bench outside the station's front door, enjoying the bright full moon, when Suzanna pulled into the parking lot.

Suzanna opened the door, to reveal a very low-cut top and short skirt.

Garland met Suzanna halfway to the bench. Suzanna looked very sultry in the moonlight. The two met and embraced.

Garland could feel the heat of her passion in her arms around him, and with that, he kissed her. The two young lovers began to explore their desire for each other. Garland began to kiss her neck and slipped the top down over her shoulders. Suzanna began to squirm until she could no longer resist his intentions. She slipped her top off, and Garland began to kiss all over her exposed neckline, using his fingertips to explore and gently trace her breasts. Suzanna began to kiss Garland very deeply. She could no longer control her desire. She began to slip Garland's shirt over his head, kissing his exposed chest. She began to return the tease of Garland's breast.

Garland was ready for her now. The two went to the car and climbed into the backseat. It was not long before the two inexperienced young lovers would become experienced. Afterward, the two almost fell asleep in each other's arms.

Garland was almost asleep when he realized he was past the hour time frame he'd told his father about. He ran inside to phone home.

Suzanna dressed herself and waited with Garland until it was almost time for James to arrive. She did not want James to know the reason Garland was late that evening.

IIIIIIII

At 4:00 p.m. sharp, the trip to Denver Coliseum began. The mood in the van was solemn. There wasn't a word spoken. The van pulled into the parking garage, and the boys began to unload the equipment. While the boys were unloading the equipment, Kevin went to check-in with the contest officials. He was the first representative to arrive.

"I am here to check in for the Summer's Solstice group," Kevin said.

He began to sign the log for the group and was instructed that the representatives would remain in the room until all the reps had arrived.

The boys finished unloading, and, along with Chad, proceeded to dressing room number seven.

Finally, all representatives were present and signed in.

The head contest official began to inform the group as to the reason for all the reps remaining in the room. "The reason you have been kept here is to determine the order in which your act will appear during the contest. We have decided that the order would be based on the order you checked in."

Kevin had received the lead act to start the competition. He had an hour to get his group ready for the stage.

Kevin entered the dressing room.

"What took you so long to check in?" Adam asked.

"We were the first group to check in today. They would not let any of the reps leave until all the groups were checked in. The judges used the order of the check-in for determining the order of appearance," Kevin said.

"We are the first act?" Adam said.

"Yes. We will do both numbers back to back, and then we will have to wait for the other nine acts to perform," Kevin answered.

This would be a very long wait for the results.

The boys were almost dressed for their performance.

Garland and Adam wore football jerseys. Harley wore a black T-shirt with a pair of white jeans. Beau, with his blonde hair, went more for a beach-boy look. Brandon wore his buckskin pants and moccasins, and did his best to get Kevin to agree to let him perform without a shirt. Brandon now sported several necklaces of different lengths. Going shirtless enabled him to show them off.

Chad, wearing a leather vest, had an idea. "Brandon, why don't you wear my vest for the show? You can wear it open, without a shirt underneath, and still have your necklaces on display."

Brandon was now on top of the world. He was sporting the look he planned.

The boys left room number seven and made their way to the stage.

James and Sissy awaited the group at the backstage door. Earlier, James had taken a peek at the crowd. It was larger than the first round. He was sure the boys wouldn't have any stage fright from the crowd size. He did have a greater concern. James motioned for Kevin to approach him. He wanted to be sure the boys did not hear what he was about to reveal to Kevin.

"Is the crowd very large tonight?" Kevin said.

"It's a very big crowd. But it's not the size of the crowd the boys will be overwhelmed by," James said.

Kevin sensed James had larger concerns.

Kevin walked over to the door to see what James was concerned about. There in the front row was a press section. There were several local newspaper reporters and photographers. The biggest surprise was the TV camera crew for a local news channel. The boys had never been exposed to any press coverage before. How was he to deal with this huge awe factor? This was something he had not anticipated. Kevin began to take several more peeks, trying to come up with something very fast. It was almost showtime.

Brandon saw Kevin peeking through the door and then closing it. He had seen Kevin do this several times, and each time he closed the door, there was this worried look on his face—one that Brandon knew meant he was concern. On Kevin's final peek, Brandon slipped up on Kevin. He looked through the cracked door and at the press without Kevin knowing he was behind him.

"Looks like my fan club has come to see us tonight, Kevin," Brandon said.

Brandon's voice took Kevin by surprise. Brandon patted Kevin on the shoulder. Kevin knew Brandon would come through once again. They closed the door and agreed not to say a word to the others.

"I will take care of my fan club, Kevin, "Brandon said with a grin and winked at Kevin.

||||||||

Kevin led James and Sissy to the VIP section in the first row, next to the press section.

The boys went up the steps to the backstage area. Garland, Adam,

Harley, and Beau took their places on the stage, without noticing Brandon remaining behind.

The crowd was beginning to chant for the show to begin.

Finally, the emcee approached the microphone to open the second round of the auditions. "The first act we have are the boys from Aurora. They were also the winners of group B's first round. Please give a warm welcome to Summer's Solstice."

The spotlights were shining on the group. This cued Brandon to make his entrance. He ran to join the others onstage. Brandon stopped in front of the press area, banging his drumsticks together. He wanted to hide the press from the others.

Beau began his harmonica opening, soon to be joined in by Garland and Adam's acoustic guitars. The song opened without a hint of the media.

Brandon, sensing the shock factor was gone, ran to take his place on the drums joining in the song's intro. He then began the song's vocal on key as the intro led into the song.

The lyrics in the song were familiar to Kevin, but the arrangement was not. The two classical guitars and harmonica gave this song a special feeling, and when Brandon's vocals joined in, the tone was as smooth as silk. The boys always did an up-tempo electrical version, and Beau's keyboards added to Brandon's rhythm and beat.

How could this song have such a different feeling and meaning when delivered in this new form? Kevin wondered.

Brandon's voice was never like this. The range of his voice was awesome. He was hitting notes off the scale.

Soon the song took a different rhythm. Brandon's drum beat came to a halt when he stood up from his drums. Beau began his harmonica solo as Brandon reached for a nearby microphone, removing it from its stand. Soon he would join Harley and Garland at center stage. Beau began to soften his harmonica. The sound became lower as Garland, Harley, and Brandon all joined in for a harmony, accompanied by the lower harmonica sound. Soon there was no music. The audience would be treated to one of the best three-part harmonies any of them had ever witnessed. This was a pure delight. The tune came to an end, and you could hear a pin drop. It was apparent the audience at that moment had been taken away.

There was something magical about a song so well done it made listeners believe they were having an out-of-body experience. This song did, that special night, by these special musicians. It was such an experience that the boys actually did not receive any applause after the number.

What went wrong? they began to wonder.

From the reaction of the crowd, they felt this song was a total failure.

Garland knew the arrangement was special for this song. He knew he would have to gather the boys quickly. Garland and Adam quickly changed into their electrical guitars. The next number was a very fast-tempo rock-and-roll song.

Adam began the song with very hard-sounding strokes. Sometimes it was like there weren't enough frets on his guitar. Kevin watched his son play with more passion than ever before. Garland joined in with as much passion as Adam. The two boys' instrumental opening was a pure delight. They were taking the biggest risk of the day. It was almost unthinkable to do the song "Sgt. Pepper's." This masterpiece was untouchable. The boys knew very well they needed a song that, if mastered, would knock out the rest of the competition. Adam and Garland did just that on this night. They were nailing this song, and they knew it! There was not a better song for a band, which had earlier created a journey of the soul, and then reunited the body and soul together. This song would require harmony during the entire rendition. Garland and Brandon rocked the audience out of their seats.

Summer's Solstice, in just two numbers, took the audience on a journey and a return landing like no one had ever done.

During the final stanza of "Sgt. Pepper's," the flashes from the cameras of the media started to light up the auditorium.

Afterward, one of the members of the media was overheard saying, "The light from the cameras was so intense, I could have read the *Denver Post* that night in that building."

The boys brought the song home to an ovation so loud that it overshadowed the light show of the cameras.

The boys did their customary center-stage bow. As was his tradition, Brandon took off the vest Chad had loaned him and tossed it into crowd, once again leaving with the upper part of his body uncovered. The boys left the stage and rushed into the dressing room. They would have to wait for the next nine acts to perform. This was going to be a long, long night.

IIIIIII

Kevin decided to stay and watch several of the other acts. It would be a long night, and the entertainment would help make the time pass by faster. He was very interested in the five acts from group A. There was a buzz that evening concerning the superior talent among the performers in group A, as compared to those in group B.

There were two men sitting behind Kevin, one of whom had a familiar face. Kevin had seen this face before, but where and when?

Before any of the acts in group A had performed, one of the men suggested that the time had arrived for them to leave, saying, "We have seen what we came here to see."

Kevin wondered about what interest these two men might have in the boys. The man's words lingered with Kevin for the rest of the evening.

The first act from group A, a six-member band, took the stage. These musicians were much older than the boys. The group's sixth member was a saxophone player. Kevin instantly thought about the groups from the late fifties and early sixties, most of which always had a sax player. The group finished their second song. Kevin thought that they were very good; however, both songs sounded similar, and there was no diversity in the two numbers performed. He waited for the crowd's reaction.

The crowd soon let Kevin know they agreed with him. The applause was less than it had been for the boys' performance.

The next two acts were from group B: Colorado Kool-Aid and

Mile High. The performances showed less talent than that of the first act from group A. Three acts had performed now since the boys' performance, with six acts remaining. Kevin knew these three acts fell short of the performance the boys had given.

We need to finish ahead of two remaining acts, Kevin thought, knowing that would place them in the final five for round three.

The emcee announced a fifteen-minute intermission.

Kevin took advantage of the intermission to return the dressing room.

The boys were almost asleep when Kevin entered the room. He could see how tired they were. There was a knock on the dressing-room door. Kevin opened the door to a man with a cart covered by a tablecloth. The man entered the room and removed the cloth. The top shelf contained sandwiches of all sorts. The second shelf was loaded with desserts, and the bottom had beverages.

Not long after the food arrived, the boys found enough energy to eat.

"I have seen three acts perform: one from group A, and two from group B," Kevin told them. "That leaves four more from group A, and two more from group B. Based on what I have seen, I think we must finish ahead of two of the remaining acts in order to make the finals."

Kevin took a sandwich and a drink, left the dressing room, and returned to see the final six acts. As he walked down the hallway, eating his sandwich, he noticed the two men who were sitting behind him earlier. Once again, he wondered why the face of the one man seemed so familiar. He kept thinking about the comment he'd overheard the man make.

After finishing his food and beverage, Kevin took his seat for the second half of the show. While taking some notes, he overheard a lady say that the next act, Purple Majesty, was the winner of group A.

The emcee approached the microphone to start the second half of the show. Purple Majesty already occupied their places on the stage as the emcee walked off the stage. Purple Majesty was also a six-member band. This group had one member dedicated to lead vocals who did not play an instrument.

As the lights began to shine on each band member, the audience could see that Purple Majesty's lead vocalist was a very beautiful girl. The band began to play a sultry rendition of a Motown song. It was evident from the start that this girl had a very strong voice. The harmonies from the backup singers were excellent. The lead singer hit every note and definitely owned both the stage and the audience. Her long blonde hair flowed with every movement of her head, and her dance moves made her seem like a female Elvis Presley. In fact, her hip movements made Elvis's leave something to be desired. She landed a long high note to close the first song. The crowd went wild. Kevin could feel his seat vibrate from the noise level.

Before the crowd died down, she began the group's second song. Purple Majesty, too, wanted to show how well diversified their music was. After their second song, it was very evident there wasn't a tempo of music this girl and group couldn't perform. Their second number also closed to very loud applause. The group came to take their bows at the center of the stage. The band members were deluged with flowers from the audience. Not only were Kevin and the audience impressed, but so was the news-station cameraman. It seemed as if he wouldn't take his camera off the blonde lead singer.

Purple Majesty had lived up to their reputation. If Summer's Solstice wanted to advance to the finals, Purple Majesty would be very hard to beat.

The next two acts were also from group A, and Kevin knew the boys still had two more acts to beat in order to qualify for the final round next week.

Like the first act from group A, the band members of this act were much older. Something about this act just was not impressive. Their tempo seemed boring, and the charisma wasn't there. The vocals were okay, but their song arrangements were boring. Once again, Kevin was pretty much on the money with his assessment of that group, based on the audience reaction.

The next act was the runner-up for group A during the first round of competition. Eight Tracks consisted of five members. This group's dress set them far apart from any of the previous acts. They were very much into the psychedelic movement. They had charisma, they had showmanship, and they had the moves when they performed. They were heavily influenced by the British group the Who. The music was loud, but the vocals did not have the range of Garland or Brandon—or Purple Majesty's lead singer. Nevertheless, Eight Tracks knew how to entertain. Kevin began to think they were in.

There were just three acts remaining. Just as he had done with the previous acts, Kevin used his own assessment, as well as the audience reaction, to get an idea of how well each group did. Eight Tracks received a good level of applause.

At this stage of the competition, Kevin mentally had the boys at no less than third place. This assessment was based on his musical knowledge and the audience response.

The emcee returned to the stage to announce the final intermission of the evening, stating, "After a thirty-minute intermission, we will return for the final three acts."

Kevin returned to the dressing room. He found all the boys asleep, except Garland.

Kevin took a seat next to Garland, asking, "How are you holding up?"

I am a nervous wreck," Garland said.

Kevin continued whispering to Garland, not wanting to wake the others. "I have an idea, Garland. I want you to come with me to watch the final three groups."

The two continued talking about the remaining acts before the judges' decision.

Kevin did not notice the time had slipped away from him.

Meanwhile, back in the auditorium, Rocky and the Mountaineers took the stage. This act had changed considerably since the first round. It was obvious this group wanted to win. Their vocals were much improved from the first round, and the musical arrangements were more detailed.

Kevin looked at the time and realized they would be late. He and Garland made their walk to the auditorium.

Once again, Kevin came upon the same man he had seen earlier in the evening, not once but twice. He still had that same feeling about recognizing the man's face.

Garland turned toward Kevin. "Do you get the feeling you have seen that guy? He looks so familiar to me. But I cannot place where and how I know him."

Kevin looked at Garland, surprised that Garland had the same feeling about this man. Who was this guy?

As they made their final steps toward the auditorium, they could hear that there was something special happening on the stage. The crowd was really into whatever they were witnessing. Kevin opened the door just in time to see the final chorus of the Rocky and the Mountaineers' second song. There was a light show like no other act before them. Each time the lights flashed in a certain way, so as to make the band to appear to be playing in slow motion, the crowd went wild.

Kevin and Garland made their way to their seats without anyone having to move to let them get by. Unbeknownst to Kevin and Garland, the crowd had been on its feet for both of the group's numbers. The ovation for the group was awesome. This made Kevin wish he had been on time for the show. It was clear that he had missed something worth seeing.

Now there were two acts remaining: one from group A, and one from group B.

Daily Chores was the last act from group B to perform. Their show was identical to the show from the first round. The songs were the same from the first show and performed in the same order. Their stage presence did not create any excitement.

Kevin suggested that Garland watch the audience reaction to every act, explaining that the crowd's reaction was a very good indicator for approval or disapproval of the act's performance.

Daily Chores finished their second number, and the crowd had an average response. It was far from the reaction Kevin and Garland had witnessed when they entered the auditorium.

The last act for the night was from group A. Kevin felt that, so far, there were two good acts from the so-called wonder group A. Now to see that group's last performer.

The music for the last act started out slow. There was a very nice keyboard intro into the first number. The vocals were nice; the harmonies were good but not great. It was obvious that the key ingredient to this group was the keyboard player. He was very good.

Back Stage's last number was a first for the competition. Back Stage played an instrumental for their last number. This was different and showcased the talents of the members' abilities on their instruments.

Kevin looked at the judges' area. There was something the judges liked about the last number. What, he had no clue. But he knew they were impressed.

Back Stage ended their second number to very good audience approval.

The second round of the contest came to a close. It was now in the judges' hands to pick the final five for the next round.

Kevin and Garland began their walk back to the dressing room. They were discussing the acts witnessed, and both regretted not seeing Rocky and the Mountaineers. They arrived at the door to the room.

"Congratulations, Garland! You were very good today," a voice shouted down the hall.

Garland and Kevin turned in the direction from where the voice had come. The voice belonged to the man with the face they recognized but could not place. Who was this man, and how did he know Garland?

||||||||

Adam was sitting near the door when Kevin and Garland returned.

"Have the results been announced?" Adam asked.

Both Garland and Kevin laughed at Adam's impatience.

"Maybe the judges will have their decision quickly. The first-round results only took thirty minutes," Garland said.

An hour had passed, and there was no word on the results. The cart's food became only crumbs. The intensity of the wait had increased everyone's appetite.

"I wish the judges would hurry up. I am going to gain twenty pounds. Wouldn't that really make the girls go crazy to see me with a gut as I throw my shirt into the crowd?" Brandon said.

Everyone laughed.

"Just think of the shirts you would save, Brandon! Your fans would throw them back at you," Adam said.

Adam's comeback brought a long and very loud laugh from everyone. The laugh was so loud, in fact, that no one heard the first knock at the door. The second knock definitely interrupted the moment in the room. This knock was delivered with a very hard and determined hand.

Garland opened the door to see one of the ushers.

"The judges are ready to announce the results, and everyone is to assemble at the stage area at once," he said.

The mood in the room changed instantly. Were they ready to face the results? Would they be able to accept the results? The time had finally arrived, and the atmosphere in the room was very tense. It was time to leave the room and learn their fate.

"Hey, Brandon, would you mind putting your shirt back on while it still fits you?" Adam said.

Without saying a word, Brandon once again made it easier for the others to face the music.

The ten judges were all sitting in chairs on the stage.

One judge spoke. "We have come to a final decision. Each judge made a list of the top five. The list ranked the groups in the order of placement by that judge. The lists were then compared to the names on the list and their rankings. Points were given to the groups, based on placement, with the number-one rank receiving five points; second place, four points; third, three points; fourth, two points; and fifth, one point. Each group's total points received were then totaled up. The five groups with the highest number of points will advance to the final five."

The judge paused and then continued, "I will now announce the results in random order. The first group making the final five is Back Stage. Next, we have Eight Tracks."

Kevin noted the first two acts were from group A.

A different judge took the stage to announce the next member. "The third act joining the finals is Rocky and the Mountaineers."

Kevin wished he had seen this act perform. Group B now had a representative.

"Our next group is Purple Majesty," the same judge added.

The announcement of Purple Majesty was well received by the crowd. A rumor among the other groups circulated that Purple Majesty had brought a cheering crowd for this round. It was now clear that this was not a rumor but a fact. Kevin contemplated the effect of this cheering group on the judge's decision.

"We now have one act remaining for next week's final round," the judge said. "Our last group is Summer's Solstice."

The reaction from the crowd was very good. Although their applause was not as loud Purple Majesty's, it was more rewarding. Summer's Solstice received the loudest applause from the other musicians. This was the greatest compliment that could be given. Kevin and the boys were deeply touched by this.

The boys were ready for the final round!

9

THE NEXT WEEK was to be the biggest and the most exciting week of the boys' lives. There was less than a week to prepare for the finals. Kevin received the instructions for the final round. He wanted the boys to be well prepared for the event. This was an event that could change all their lives forever.

Monday morning brought another surprise for the boys. That morning at school, Principal Roberts declared the week as Summer's Solstice Week. Hinckley was behind Summer's Solstice like nothing before. On Friday, there was to be a big send-off for the boys. The boys were beginning to feel special at school—a feeling almost equal to when they performed.

Suzanna was beginning to feel very special when she was with Garland. He was becoming very popular at school, and she was the one he wanted to be with. Being Garland's girlfriend made her popular as well, and she loved the envy of the other girls.

Kevin picked the boys up from school that day. He wanted a meeting to discuss the next round's changes.

Kevin drove to an outdoor stage.

The boys wondered why they were meeting outside.

"Guys, we are at this outdoor arena today for a reason. The next round will be outdoors. I want to go over the final round," Kevin said. "We are to perform three numbers. The first number will be a song the judges will select. Every act will perform the same song. After the first song, one act will be eliminated."

"Can we choose the arrangement for that song?" Garland asked.

Kevin nodded yes to Garland's question and then continued, "The remaining four acts will do an instrumental for their second number. This number will not contain vocals."

Kevin believed this change came about when Back Stage performed their instrumental. He now believed that was the scene he witnessed with the judges.

"After the second round, the judges will eliminate one more act. The final three acts will advance into the finals. The final number will be the group's choice. There has never been a tie. In the case of a tie, there would be a one-song sing-off."

With that, Kevin finished explaining the rules for the final round.

That day, they all knew the winning group would earn a hard victory.

Kevin could see in his boys' eyes that they were ready for this challenge. There were some details Kevin did not inform the boys of that day. He would wait for the proper time to tell them.

"Are you guys ready for the biggest moment of your young lives?" Kevin asked.

Then, almost in perfect harmony, all five boys shouted, "Hell, yes!"

It was time to head back to the station. There were at least two new numbers to learn.

||||||||

Later that evening, Garland began to search for the poster of the Red Rocks Amphitheatre bought their first day in Colorado, at the visitors' welcoming center. He knew the poster was somewhere in his closet. The picture's spirited mystique drew Garland from the moment he saw the awesome rocks of the theater area. This was his most valuable picture. He worked very hard trying to find it. Finally, there in the corner, was this poster sitting on a shoe box. He reached for the poster. Why was this box in this corner? What was inside this box? The shoe box was a box for women's shoes. What was this women's shoe box doing in his closet? Finally, he could no longer resist the temptation of the box's secret. Garland opened the box and began to sift through its contents. There inside the box were some old pictures.

The old memories began to flow through his mind. There were old school pictures, and the snow picture of Roswell with Sissy. Then, there was the picture the police officer took at the "Welcome to Colorado" state sign. He paused for a long look at the next picture he came upon. A tear began to form in his eyes. It was an old picture of Flipper, his first best friend. Garland held the picture, remembering the times they shared; every now and then, the tears would change to a smile and then a laugh as he remembered the good times. There was one last picture remaining in the box, lying facedown. The back of the picture was well soiled from the fingers that had held it. It was obvious something very special was on the other side.

Garland turned the picture over to reveal its secret. The tears for Flipper were a drop compared to the ones he was shedding now. There in his hand was Brenda's picture. The one he clutched that night in the backseat of the car while driving to Texas. There were dried tear marks on her picture. It had been seven years since he had seen that picture. The emotions of the box soon let Garland know the Red Rocks Amphitheatre picture was not the only important picture he owned.

An hour had passed when Sissy walked past his bedroom door. She approached her son's bed. Garland was asleep with his head on a pillow, holding Brenda's picture next to his face as if he were hugging her—just as he'd done seven years before.

IIIIIII

The next day at practice, Kevin revealed the one song each group would be required to perform: "Lucy in the Sky with Diamonds" by the Beatles. This was a song all the boys loved. Beau loved to play the keyboards to this song when he was waiting for the others to arrive. This would turn out to be a big advantage for Summer's Solstice.

For the first time, Beau's talent would step to the forefront. Beau began to play a piano intro for "Lucy." The tempo was slow at first but soon changed into a very rhythmic piano. The way Beau played made it evident that he had great passion for this song.

Garland and Adam were mesmerized by the tune Beau played. What more could they add to this arrangement? It was easy to play a note after what they had witnessed with Beau. Once again, there was a song in which both Adam and Garland could display their love and talent for acoustic guitar.

The arrangement Beau had in mind would require Brandon to perform a lesser beat than he usually provided the group. He didn't know if Brandon would have the same feel for this song that he and the others did.

"Brandon, we will not need your normal drums for this song," Beau said. "Halfway through the song, I want you to stop with the drums and switch to a tambourine for the ending beats this arrangement will require."

"You want me to do what? A tambourine? Do you want me to stand in front of a kettle too, asking for money?" Brandon said sarcastically.

Kevin entered the room just in time. It was clear Brandon did not agree with what he was just asked to do.

"Do you want me to ring a bell too? If I had wanted to be in the goddamn Salvation Army, I wouldn't be wasting my time here!" Brandon shouted.

Kevin tried to reason with Brandon, but it was too late. His feelings had already been hurt by the others. Brandon stormed from the room and left practice.

What had started out as great start for the final round, soon turned into disaster. This was the first time there had been an altercation at any of the boys' practice sessions.

Brandon went home after practice and straight into his room.

Sissy had agreed to take Adam home that day. Kevin needed to finish some reports for the station's ownership group.

"Adam, I need to use your phone to call James," Sissy said.

The boys had informed Sissy about the incident at practice.

Sissy spoke to James, hung up the phone, and walked to Brandon's room. Brandon always opened up to her. She knocked on his bedroom door.

Garland and Adam followed her down the hallway and stood just outside the doorway and out of Brandon's sight.

Sissy walked over to the bed where Brandon was lying.

"Brandon, did I ever tell you the story about the time I played in a talent show?" Sissy asked.

Brandon shook his head no.

Hearing his mother, Garland said softly, "Adam, you are going to love this story."

Sissy continued, "We were to do this certain song. This song would require a special sound that only a tambourine would deliver. Everyone knows that great drummers make the best tambourine players. They are a natural when no one else can even relate to what a tambourine is all about. A drummer can feel the beat of a tambourine and understand what the tambourine is saying."

Brandon sat up, moving to the side of bed and next to Sissy.

"The song we played for that contest required two tambourine players. One was our drummer, and I was the other," Sissy said.

Brandon was aware of Sissy's ability to play several instruments; she was very good on every one she played.

"You were asked to play a tambourine?" Brandon said.

"Oh yes, and I loved every minute of it," Sissy said, adding, "Brandon, you were probably asked to do probably because none of the other boys could play one."

"Do you think I would be any good at the tambourine?" Brandon said.

"I have no doubt you would be great, Brandon. I know you would be much better than I was. Do something special with the tambourine that no one else can do. Make that something special your own," Sissy said.

"Thanks, Sissy. I know if you took pride in the tambourine, then I can too." Brandon said.

Brandon hugged Sissy, thanking her again for helping him.

"Wow, that was some story," Adam said to Garland.

Garland laughed.

"What is so funny about that story? I thought it was great," Adam said.

Garland smiled. "Well, it wasn't the tambourine she was asked to play; it was the piano."

It didn't matter. Brandon would always believe Sissy had played the tambourine, just as he would.

|||||||||

Beau arrived for practice thirty minutes early. He was ready to put yesterday's altercation behind them. The incident had made Beau very upset. He was not able to sleep, worrying about his and Brandon's friendship. How could he patch things up between him and Brandon? He was very sure of the arrangement they were working on for "Lucy in the Sky." He hadn't meant for Brandon to take it as an attack on his drumming ability. There was no doubt in his mind that Brandon was the best drummer in the contest.

Beau was sitting on a stool at his keyboard when he heard this loud commotion coming from down the hallway. The closer the commotion came to the studio, the louder it became. Beau jumped to his feet just as the door to the studio swung open.

Brandon was wearing a western hat and sandals. He approached Beau, playing not one but two tambourines. As Brandon reached the spot where Beau stood, Beau feared something was about to happen. He knew that he would not be any match for Brandon and prayed it would not come to anything physical.

"Beau, you were right about the idea for 'Lucy,'" Brandon said. "The drums fading to a tambourine would be good, but drums fading into two tambourines, would be awesome."

Brandon began to play the idea he had for the song.

"That is incredible, Brandon. Where did you get the idea of two tambourines, and how did you create the sound you were doing?" Beau said.

Brandon had accepted Beau's idea and improved on it as well. Beau sat down at his keyboard, while Brandon continued playing the two tambourines. The sound of the two tambourines and the keyboard blended very well.

Kevin, Garland, and Adam walked through the door. None of them could believe what they saw. This was a sight for sore eyes, and the music wasn't hard on the ears either.

That morning, Kevin a reporter from the *Denver Post* had greeted Kevin on his arrival at the station.

"Kevin English, the *Post* is doing a story about the five finalists for this weekend's finals," the man said.

Kevin began to tell the reporter about the group's brief history.

"These boys have been together how long?" the reporter asked.

"Garland and Adam have been playing for about two years now. Brandon joined shortly afterward. Harley and Beau came aboard after we moved to Colorado," Kevin said.

"This is amazing. I would have thought they were together much longer. They have a chemistry that is unreal," the reporter said.

The story would include interviews from each of the five boys as well, including their own stories and the way they each felt about the group. The story would appear in that Friday's edition.

After the reporter left, the boys began wrapping up their final version of "Lucy in the Sky with Diamonds."

"Beau, I think your idea was very good. You did a very good job," Kevin said.

Beau felt good about coming through for the group. He was now ready for the instrumental.

In their minds, there was only one song for the instrumental. They would perform the Stones song that they had done that night in the parking lot for their first performance in front of an audience of significance. That song was each one of the boys' favorite.

Now there were two songs ready for the competition.

"Guys, I have a surprise for you tomorrow," Kevin said. "So go home and get a good night's rest."

The boys left practice that day in a 180-degree turnaround from the day before.

Kevin waited for the next day to reward the boys with the final details of the contest. He had only hinted of this on the first day's preparation for the final round.

When the boys arrived for practice, he reminded them this round would be outdoors.

"Today, I want to surprise you with the site they have selected for the finals. I think you will like where we are going today," Kevin said.

The van left Aurora and headed west. Their journey would take them to the western side of Denver. After an hour's drive, the van came into the small town of Morrison, Colorado. At first, Morrison did not have a connection with any of the boys. Garland fell asleep during the ride. Brandon shook Garland, trying to awaken him. Garland opened one eye to see what all the commotion was about.

"Garland, we are in Morrison," Brandon said.

Garland turned to his side, trying to avoid Brandon.

Adam stood up from behind Garland's seat to thump him on the back of the ear. "Garland, did you not listen to Brandon? We are in Morrison now!"

Garland sat up in his seat, still in a deep daze from the nap.

"We are in Morrison," Garland repeated.

Finally, the van pulled up into the parking lot. Kevin drove the van up to the entrance of the amphitheater and parked it. As the van rolled to a stop, Garland looked out his window, instantly springing to his feet. It was as if he had awakened from a dream. Wiping his eyes, Garland looked out the window to see the three big red rocks.

"We are performing in the Red Rocks Amphitheatre! Is this real, or am I dreaming?!" Garland said.

Garland rushed out the van door to take in the sights of his dream.

"Guys, this is the surprise. We will do our final numbers on the stage where many of music's superstars have performed," Kevin said.

From the first day he entered Colorado, Garland had dreamed of just seeing a show here. Now he would perform on its hallowed stage. The boys could tell Garland was deeply touched and let him relish the moments of his dream. The boys entered the stadium area. There was an incredible feeling. They, too, now felt the magic Garland had known from just a picture. The sound was so quiet. It was nature's own studio for her artists to perform. Man could have not done it better. After an hour, the theater was to close.

The boys were loading into the van for the trip home. Kevin started the van.

"Wait, Dad, Garland is not in the van!" Adam shouted.

Garland began to make his way to the waiting van. Garland, holding his hands to the back of his head, took one last look to imprint his memory, and entered the van. This would be the inspiration for Garland Summers to give the performance of his young life.

||||||||

Friday was the most special day of the week at Hinckley. It was the day Hinckley rolled out the red carpet as a send-off for Summer's Solstice. Principal Roberts had a surprise for the boys—a secret surprise. Both the faculty and the student body were in on this secret. The boys thought the special event was the send-off they were receiving that Friday afternoon, which was rather like a pep rally, and that was what they wanted the boys believe.

Friday's rehearsal would be the last before the big day. There still was the matter of a third song if they advanced into the final round. It was agreed that "Sgt. Pepper's" would be that last song. What could they do to make this show different from the last show? Garland had an idea that, if pulled off, would put the audience on its feet for the entire number.

Garland's idea was for the boys to switch the instruments they were playing during the song. Garland, Adam, and Harley would switch, playing each other's guitars during the song. Each boy would do a solo on the guitar they did not originally begin with. Harley was the least-talented guitarist of the three. They agreed that Harley would begin with a different guitar, and his solo was to be played on his own bass. They practiced the move that afternoon, and it came off perfectly. The boys loaded up the equipment before leaving that evening.

||||||||

The boys arrived at the station that Saturday morning. This was the day they lived for. This could be the start of something they all wanted very much. During the trip, Garland once again took a nap. Soon the others followed suit. This was the perfect way to unwind and let all the butterflies loose. The boys would report to dressing room number one. It would be theirs for as long as they remained in the contest. The van pulled into a loading area near backstage. This time, the equipment would be unloaded by stagehands provided by the contest. There would be no chances of something physically happening to any performer this day.

The final instructions for the day were posted in each dressing room. For the first round, the performing order was determined alphabetically. Summer's Solstice would perform last for the first round. As usual, all the boys brought one bag, except Brandon. For this occasion, Brandon brought three.

"Why are you bringing three bags, Brandon?" Kevin asked.

"Well, there are three rounds, and I need four shirts," Brandon replied.

"Four shirts?" Kevin asked.

"You don't want me celebrating with all those hot girls afterward without a shirt on, do you? They wouldn't be able to keep their hands off my chest," Brandon said.

Kevin knew that at least one of the boys was ready for the show.

The boys were dressed for the show to begin. That is, all but Brandon, who did his usual primping in the bathroom. Kevin and the other four boys toured the Red Rocks Amphitheatre stage area. They walked down to the stage. Standing by a doorway to the stage, was the same man that had attended the last show. All four boys looked at the man with the same question in their eyes.

"Did you see that guy? How do we know him? Am I the only one who feels like I have seen that face before?" Adam asked.

Everyone agreed they had seen the face before, but, other than Garland and Kevin seeing him at the second round, no one could remember how they knew the face. The man walked away without saying a word.

Back Stage took the stage for the final round's opening act. Their opening song was a new choice for them. They chose to perform an instrumental version of "Lucy in the Sky with Diamonds." Didn't they know each group was required to do an instrumental for their second number? Back Stage was the group with the weakest vocals of the five remaining acts.

Soon after the song started, the members of Back Stage knew performing an instrumental "Lucy in the Sky with Diamonds" was not the right decision. Back Stage's number came to an end and was treated to a mixed reaction from the crowd. This was clearly not what they had hoped for. The boys could see the disappointment in the members of Back Stage as they exited into the hallway. The stagehands began to set up the stage for the second act.

Eight Tracks stepped onto the stage for their opening version of "Lucy in the Sky with Diamonds." This was a song that matched their psychedelic image perfectly. The song began with heavy guitar licks and a perfectly timed vocal. Their drummer seemed to always be a beat behind the lead guitar. It would take him more than half the song to recapture the timeliness of the beat. This was something only other musicians and the judges would pick up on. Eight Tracks also lacked a keyboard player.

Without a keyboard, "Lucy in the Sky with Diamonds" was not "Lucy in the Sky with Diamonds." The song came to an end with heavy guitar licks, just as it had begun. Red Rocks and the psychedelic sound seemed at odds with each. Eight Tracks was greeted to a very good crowd reaction. They were sure their performance was better than that of Back Stage.

There were now two acts down and two more to go, before Summer's Solstice's turn.

Purple Majesty was the next group to perform. The crowd began to get excited with the anticipation. They were dressed as if they were doing an album cover shoot. With darkness beginning to fall, the lights to the stage made Purple Majesty stand out more to the audience. The TV cameras were more apparent with the lights needed for the cameras. The lead singer for Purple Majesty took her place on the stage.

She cued her band to start the song. As she began "Lucy in the Sky with Diamonds," she walked up to a TV camera with a microphone and began to sing into the camera. The camera would follow her across the stage as she made direct eye contact with every one of the judges, winking before she moved on to the next judge. Her hip-hugger jeans showed every curve and crevice of her lower body. Several of the judges did a double take, looking over the tops of their glasses for a better view.

Their arrangement of "Lucy" was by far the most sophisticated and longest of the evening. Purple Majesty's ending of "Lucy" brought the crowd to its feet, just as it had done the last round of the competition. Everyone in attendance knew Purple Majesty once again was the act to beat.

As the stagehands prepared the stage for Rocky and the Mountaineers, Kevin walked back to the room. Brandon had not made his way down to where the rest of the band was waiting. Once again, Kevin came upon that familiar face.

"Are the boys ready to break a leg?" the man asked Kevin.

"Have we met before?" Kevin said.

"No, you and I have never met," the man said, and then he turned and walked away.

Kevin opened the door to find Brandon asleep. "Brandon, it's almost time for us to take the stage!"

Kevin helped Brandon up from his nap, and the two left the room together.

"Rocky and the Mountaineers will be next, and we will follow for the final act of round one," Kevin said.

As they walked down the hallway, Kevin once again tried to remember where he knew that man. His face was very, very familiar.

Purple Majesty exited the stage through the door and down the stairway to where the boys were waiting in the hallway. The blonde lead singer led their way down the stairs. She was looking downward at her feet, making sure not to miss a step and trying not to fall. She was almost on the last step when she heard Brandon and Kevin talking. Brandon's voice took her by surprise. She was not aware of anyone nearby. With this distraction, she took her eyes off the last step and began to do what she had tried very hard to avoid. She completely missed the final step and started to fall. Brandon was now only a few steps away and saw her stumble, falling right into his arms. As Brandon rescued her from the fall, her eyes locked onto his.

"Are you okay?" Brandon asked.

She was deeply embarrassed by her clumsiness and said nothing.

The remaining Purple Majesty members rushed to her side. Brandon had just saved them from withdrawing. Their act relied on the sexy lead singer and her antics on the stage. Those antics would be very difficult on crutches. She gathered up her composure. She then dropped down from the arms that had saved her without so much as a thank-you.

Rocky and the Mountaineers took the stage. Kevin wanted to see how much this group had improved. As "Lucy in the Sky" began, darkness overtook the skies at the perfect time for Rocky and the Mountaineers' light show. Unlike the last round's black-and-white light effect, tonight's performance would have multicolor lights. What an effect these lights created for this song.

The "Lucy in the Sky" lyrics created hallucinogenic images; unfortunately, the musical arrangement did not measure up to the light show. The harmony vocals failed to bail out the lead vocals. Rocky and the Mountaineers' performance on this night was far short of the show during the last round. As "Lucy" came to an end and the lights turned on, the crowd seemed unsure as to how good of a show they had witnessed. The crowd seemed divided in terms of applause. The group walked off the stage, thinking their chances were over for the evening.

The boys gathered at the stage entrance, waiting for their chance to earn a place in the next round. A very loud chant arose from the audience. It was as if the crowd size had suddenly grown larger. The emcee began his introduction for Summer's Solstice but was soon drowned out by the crowd's anticipation. The standing-room-only crowd was now a crowd that couldn't even move. As the emcee left the stage, he motioned for the boys to take the stage, as it was evident they couldn't hear him call them out onto the stage.

As the boys took the stage, they were moved by what they were about to see. The reason for the crowd being so much larger soon became evident. Every wall along the theater, including the rear wall, was occupied. This scene stopped the boys in their tracks. Where had all these fans come from? On the right side of the stage stood a man on stool, making sure he would catch their attention. As he raised his arms, more than five hundred Hinckley students began to show their support for Summer's Solstice. This was the secret surprise the Hinckley students and faculty kept guarded all week. Organizing this was a miracle in itself; with this kind of enthusiasm, there was no way Summer's Solstice would perform badly.

Beau's piano intro calmed the crowd momentarily. The sounds of the piano were so soothing, becoming even more tranquil when Garland and Adam joined in with their acoustics. The tempo began to pick up when Brandon's drums added a measure of rhythm as Harley's and Garland's voices were added. "Picture yourself in a boat on a river ..." took the audience to a faraway place. The chorus was then enriched when Brandon joined in for the awesome three-part harmony.

Midway through the song, the melody changed. Brandon sprang up from his seat to display his talents on not one but two tambourines, adding another level to the trip everyone's mind was traveling.

This was a show the Beatles themselves would have enjoyed that night. There were no light gimmicks, no flirting with the judges—just pure musical talent. This was a band with great talent making a song their own. When the boys finished "Lucy," the crowd approval became deafening.

The boys ran off the stage. The crowd's noise level did not subside; in fact, they wanted an encore. The boys ran to the center of the stage, giving their encore bows. The judges began to take notice of how they owned the crowd. The boys were very appreciative; this was the fuel they needed to advance. Garland, Adam, Beau, and Harley ran off the stage.

Brandon walked slowly to the end of the stage, making sure he had not missed unbuttoning his shirt. Finally, he had his shirt off and tossed it into the air. The shirt began to float down into the crowd. There was a dash to claim the shirt as it landed on a girl's head. Eventually, the shirt was surrendered to its winner, revealing the original landing sight. The shirt found the head of Purple Majesty's lead singer. Brandon winked at the angry girl and then, to make matters worse, blew her a kiss. This night's battle was now on!

The wait for the judges' results began. The boys took a seat in a nearby waiting area. How long a wait it would be was anyone's guess. The boys laughed at Brandon's latest stunt. Although Brandon had not planned the results, the outcome could not have been better. The look on that girl's face was priceless. Finally, word arrived that the judges' decision was about to be announced. Each act was to assemble on the stage for the results.

The emcee approached the microphone to announce which acts were to move into the next round. "For the first time in our history, we have a tie. However, this tie does not involve the leaders. There was a tie for fourth place. Fourth place would have been the last act to advance to the next round."

There was a buzz among the contestants. No one had any idea of the twist to the contest that was about to happen.

The emcee continued, "We have decided, based on consensus among the judges, that neither of these two acts could win the competition. Therefore, Back Stage and Rocky and the Mountaineers will not be advancing to the next round. Since there are two acts being eliminated this round, we will skip the next round and go into the final round. We will begin that round in one hour."

As each of the remaining acts left the stage, they were given an envelope explaining the forum for the next round.

Summer's Solstice returned to their dressing room. They were shocked and excited at the same time.

Kevin opened the envelope to read the next round's instructions, which included the order of the acts' appearance: Purple Majesty would lead off, Eight Tracks would follow, and Summer's Solstice would wrap up the round.

Each act would perform their second-round instrumental and then their choice for the second number. Each group would perform one song and leave the stage. There would be no back-to-back performances. The order of appearance would remain the same for the second song. There would be a twenty-minute intermission in between the round. The judges would meet and then announce the winning decision.

"Are we ready, guys?" Kevin asked. We now have to beat just two acts. You guys have come such a long, long way. I am so proud of you guys. You will not leave here today a loser. Take a look at the lives you have touched at Hinckley. They came here to thank you for the pride you have given them for being their friends."

Garland stood to thank his friends for making this day one they would always remember for the rest of their lives. "You are my brothers, and I love all of you. Are you ready to take home the bacon? It's time to show our skill on the instruments we each love."

The boys left the room, ready to kick ass.

Purple Majesty was about to take the stage with their instrumental. They were to perform an instrumental version of a Stones song. This time, the lead singer was lost without her flirtations to the camera. She tried to disguise her loss to the crowd and went through the motions of being content. This was not her idea of entertainment. As the boys came closer to the stage, they looked at each other in total disbelief. What was the chances of this happening? Were their ears playing tricks on them?

As Purple Majesty wrapped up their instrumental, Kevin, as usual, was waiting to hear the crowd. He knew the boys would be very hard to beat this round. Each member played their instruments very well. Kevin cracked open the door for a peek at the crowd. He first glanced at the stage where Purple Majesty stood. Why was there this look of disappointment? He sensed this band did not have the passion for their instruments. The judges began to enter their scores.

The crowd, however, was not a favorable judge for the song they had just witnessed.

Eight Tracks was the act to be aware of for this round.

Eight Tracks took their turn on the stage. From the start, this group's musical talent was obvious. They were performing both "Sgt. Pepper's" versions as a medley, and, if pulled off, they would be a cinch to become the second-round leaders. Eight Tracks was on target, and it was evident to the audience. Midway through the song, they switched to the reprise version. This was the faster-paced of the two and would provide a chance for the musicians to showcase their respective instruments. They began to own the audience. Then, in the same way that the song had started, the song stopped, with all instruments in time. It was difficult to have timing that precise.

The crowd rose for a standing ovation. Even though the boys had not seen the performance, they, too, were impressed with the sounds of this group. As Eight Tracks went down the stairs from the stage, they were again treated to very loud applause, this time, from an audience who did not have the opportunity to witness their show. Summer's Solstice rewarded Eight Tracks with their own applause.

"You guys were great out there. You really rocked," Garland said.

To Eight Tracks, Garland's compliment was more rewarding than any scores the judges could give them.

The crowd welcomed Summer's Solstice to the stage. The boys began to open the Stones song they all loved and had played so many times. The passion the boys owned for this song began to show through with each note played. The crowd was on its feet, and with their arms stretched into the air, began to wave from side to side. It was as if they had caught this ride of music and never wanted it to end. It wasn't the loud appreciation that Eight Tracks received, but it was a very effective reward. It took a lot of confidence to play the same song a competitor had performed.

Even though it was the same song, there was a world of difference in the way the songs were played. One act played the song with the attitude that they couldn't wait for their performance to end, and the other act did not want theirs to end. The boys finished their instrumental and took a bow to very loud applause.

It was now time for the intermission, with all the stakes at hand on one song.

The boys left the stage, feeling good about their performance. As they walked back to the dressing room, two members of Purple Majesty were standing in the hall. They were arguing about something. As the boys approached, the argument became silent. One of the members was the lead singer. The boys moved to one side of the hallway to pass through to their room. As Brandon passed through, she began to say something, but then, instead, gave a sneering look. Finally, the temptation over took her.

"Hey, Cochise, you'd better bring it this time, or your ass will be done!" she shouted.

The boys stopped in their tracks, about to turn and face this smart-ass, when another voice from down the hall interrupted.

"Hey, blonde bitch, who do you think you are calling Cochise?" the voice said.

No one was prepared for what was about to happen next.

There were two individuals walking toward them. One was a young woman, and the other was an older man. The two Purple Majesty members turned to the two new arrivals and then to where Brandon was standing. At first, it seemed they were seeing double. In fact, if was as if they were seeing triple.

"That is not Cochise, you bitch." the man said.

The boys began to have the same impression as that of Purple Majesty.

"If you want to speak to Cochise, then do it now. He is the son of Cochise," the man said.

In that instant, Kevin and the boys realized why his face was familiar. But the female face seemed just as familiar. Who was this girl?

Brandon approached the two strangers. He was overwhelmed by his feelings. Brandon looked at each of the faces. One face looked like his, only older; the other face was similar as well, only prettier. This face belonged to a very beautiful girl. The man placed one hand on

Brandon's shoulder and the other on the girl's. The man didn't have to tell Brandon who he was or who the girl was.

"Brandon, I am your older sister, Shonda, and he is our father," she said as she smiled, adding, "His name is not really Cochise."

Brandon never knew he had a sister. His dad had left when he was so young.

The boys were shocked but happy for Brandon.

Kevin, meanwhile, thought, *Why now, and what do they want with Brandon?*

"Let's continue this reunion in the dressing room," Kevin said.

They all agreed and went back to the room.

Once in the room, it was obvious this reunion had deeply affected Brandon. Kevin wanted to intervene but knew it was not his place. He sensed this should be a private meeting and instructed the other boys to leave the room.

"Brandon, our mother is very sorry for leaving you. She wanted to be here so much today to see you, but she is sick. She has tuberculosis," Shonda said. "Our father left the family when I had tuberculosis to seek treatment for me."

Brandon's father said, "Brandon, your mother never recovered from the disease she was exposed to. That is why she left. She never wanted you to see what this disease does to someone you love, and she could not bear seeing the pain you would feel."

"Is she still alive?" Brandon asked.

"Yes, but she doesn't have very much time," Shonda said.

Brandon began to break down. "I want to go back with you. For so long, I couldn't understand why she left me. I always thought I had done something wrong."

"It will mean so much to your mother. She wants to ask for your forgiveness," his father said.

"For now, I want you to shut that blonde bitch up, and win," Shonda said.

Shonda's comment made Brandon smile, but only for an instant.

The final round was about to begin.

Purple Majesty took the stage, opening the final round. Soon there would be a winner. Their number began with much more confidence than that of the instrumental round.

The lead singer began the song with an invitation to the audience. "Everybody, clap your hands. Are you ready for a good time?"

With the microphone in her hand, she went to the stage front to reach down, performing finger touches along the awaiting front row. Soon the second row rushed in, trying to get their chance as well. The musical background for her vocals was out of tempo with the lyrics she was singing, but it had no effect on the crowd. She did have a flirtatious means to entertain.

During the guitar solo, she began the movement of those hips that had become famous in the earlier rounds. She was a very good dancer. Purple Majesty was a crowd-pleaser, because of the lead singer's dance movements as much as her vocals. She ended the song with a very long note that she held almost perfectly. The crowd noise on that song was the loudest of the night. The band took their bows at center stage. Once again, the cameraman was locked in on her, and oh how well did she know it! Purple Majesty had just raised the bar for the final round.

Summer's Solstice arrived at the on-deck spot just as Eight Tracks was about to depart. Garland and the rest of Summer's Solstice wished Eight Tracks well. Just as Purple Majesty lacked sportsmanship and class, Eight Tracks had both. Garland and the boys would be rooting them on for a second-place finish.

Eight Tracks took the stage. As the musical introduction began, their lead singer began to thank the crowd, the judges, and the organizers.

"We especially want to wish Summer's Solstice good luck with their number as well," he said.

Eight Tracks began an Elvis song. This song made you want to get up and stomp your feet. Their backup vocals were good. Their harmonies were in a league with those of Summer's Solstice. Eight Tracks was dressed in black leather pants and jackets, completing the Elvis look. This was a classy performance by Eight Tracks. One even Elvis would have enjoyed that night. The more-experienced Eight Tracks nailed their final performance of the evening. Not only was the crowd noise the loudest of the night, it was also the longest. As they exited the stage, the boys were there with hands out, congratulating Eight Tracks. It was their turn next.

The boys took the stage for their final number of the evening. They would need the best performance of their young lives. The plans were to perform "Sgt. Pepper's," with each member changing instruments during the arrangement. This would showcase the talents of each musician. Harley would begin on the lead guitar and, as agreed, would switch out in time to play bass during his solo. Brandon and Beau would remain on the drums and keyboards. Harley started the song. Although he was a little slower than Garland, it was a good start. The boys' harmonies connected well on the chorus lines.

Then, during the first instrument change, things began to happen. Brandon's timing started to lag. The first solo was Garland's on the rhythm guitar. This was where Brandon's vocals should have picked up Garland's while Garland was performing. Brandon's pitch was off key. It was obvious the earlier encounter had affected him.

On the second instrument changeover, Harley began his bass solo. The bass solo relied heavily on the beat. Once again, Brandon was off. This was not to be the performance the boys needed.

Adam turned to get Brandon's attention; he wanted to encourage Brandon. Brandon began to pick up his tempo for the last part of the song. All was well until the final harmony. This was to be a three-part harmony. Something the boys were becoming famous for. The song ended with a two-part harmony. Brandon froze and couldn't deliver his part.

The crowd still loved the boys. They appeared not to notice the errors in the performance. Garland was now wishing the judges might have missed them as well. The boys took their bow at center stage to a loud applause. The boys left the stage. This time, something was missing as well. Brandon did not toss his shirt into the audience. It was apparent he was somewhere far away.

As the boys walked off the stage, Adam and Beau became upset with Brandon. They came at him with resentment.

"Do you realize what you have just done?" Adam said.

"You just lost this for us," Beau added.

Brandon never said a word; he just ran down to the dressing room.

The emcee took the stage and informed the contestants that the judges had reached their decision. All the groups were to be onstage for results. Summer's Solstice would receive the results with one less member in attendance.

"Let's have a round of applause for these very talented musicians," the emcee said.

There was a five-minute standing ovation from the crowd. They had been treated to an awesome night of talent.

"This year's winner will return back here to Red Rocks Amphitheatre to be the opening act for a major group during the summer. I can now tell you this will be the biggest show we have ever booked here," he said.

Adam and Beau were already very upset with Brandon, and the announcement only intensified their anger.

"The winner of this year's Red Rocks contest is Eight Tracks," the emcee said.

With that, Purple Majesty left the stage in disbelief.

Eight Tracks took a stroll across the stage front, reaching out to their fans.

The boys stood there, applauding Eight Tracks. This was Eight Tracks' moment of glory. It was time to leave the stage and let them enjoy it. As the boys were leaving the stage, two members of Eight Tracks caught a glimpse of them leaving. They rushed over to the boys, bringing them out to the stage front, raising Garland's and Adam's arms into the air with their own.

Kevin smiled, witnessing the classiest act he had seen.

Finally, the boys left the stage and headed for their dressing room.

The boys arrived at the dressing room to begin loading up for the trip back to Aurora.

"Before we go into the room, boys, I want you all to know what happened to Brandon today. We all discovered today that the face we had seen before but couldn't place belonged to Brandon's father. It has been many years since he saw his dad. If this wasn't enough shock, he learned of a sister he had never known," Kevin said.

"Dad, I think we were too rough on Brandon after the competition. We blamed him for our loss," Adam said.

"Tell me you didn't," Kevin said. "I only told you half of his shock. His father was here to tell Brandon that his mother is about to die. It was very hard for him. I have never seen him break down until today. He cried like a baby. He didn't have to go out there tonight and perform. That took a lot of guts. He thinks *that* much of all of you."

The boys wanted to apologize to Brandon, hoping he would forgive them. Kevin opened the door for the boys to enter the room.

"Hey, Brandon, they are wondering where your shirt is!" Garland said jokingly.

Once inside the room, they saw that Brandon's things had been removed. His three bags were missing. On the table was a piece of paper. Brandon had written in big letters, "I am sorry. I will always remember you, my brothers."

The boys and Kevin searched the halls for Brandon. As they approached an exit door, there stood a security guard, the one who had let them in earlier that day.

"Have you seen one of our guys?" Kevin asked.

"Are you looking for Brandon? He left with a man and a woman and his baggage," the guard said.

The boys really felt bad; while they were onstage, wanting to get that final applause, they were losing a brother.

They began to walk back to the room when the guard said, "He left these for you, Kevin."

The guard gave Kevin a bag. Inside this bag were Brandon's drumsticks. Summer's Solstice would never perform again.

10

SUMMER'S SOLSTICE CREATED a very special brotherhood in the lives of five boys. The van ride back to Aurora was the quietest ride four teenage boys ever took. Each one hurt deeply from the loss that night. It wasn't the loss from the contest but the loss of a brother that made the pain unbearable. The boys began to reflect on what Brandon's friendship meant to each one of them.

To Garland and Adam, it was that day in the courtyard at school. Brandon protected them, even against the odds he faced by the four thugs. He never thought once about himself; he risked his own safety for that of his two friends.

To Beau, it was the incident caused during his arrangement. Brandon took pride in drumming, but he was a team player; he gave up his own passion for the sake of Beau's dream.

For Harley, it was Brandon's final performance with Summer's Solstice. As bad as he was hurting, he refused to let his friends down, and so he tried to perform.

Brandon was a true friend. He was a giver to those he loved and never expected anything in return.

Even though Kevin always got the credit for easing the boy's stage fears, he knew it was Brandon who really took the fear away, his humor and antics making live performance a fun experience rather than an intimidating one.

When the van arrived at the station, the boys began to unload the instruments. Each boy carried his own instrument to the studio. Only Brandon's drums remained in the van. The boys returned to the van, gathering up Brandon's drums and carrying them into the studio.

Kevin picked up a bag from the floorboard, along with Beau's leather vest, which Brandon had worn that night. He walked into the studio to return Beau's vest.

"Beau, you left your vest in the van," Kevin said as he handed the vest to Beau.

Beau paused a moment and then walked to Brandon's drum set, placing the vest over the back of the chair Brandon used during practice.

The boys walked to the door and turned for one final look.

As Kevin opened the door to turn off the lights, he still held a bag in his hand.

"Dad, what's in the bag?" Adam asked.

Kevin peeked into the bag and closed it without saying a word.

"Let's all go home guys. It's been a long day." Kevin said.

Kevin walked over to the station's award showcase, opening it with his key. He opened the bag and removed its contents. Four sets of anxious eyes watched his every move.

"Those are Brandon's sticks," Harley said.

Holding the drumsticks, Kevin placed them next to an award won by the station several years before. This was to be the station's first award under Kevin's direction, and, as far as he was concerned, there wasn't a more valuable one anywhere. Kevin shut and locked the showcase doors.

IIIIIIII

Now that Summer's Solstice was a thing of the past, there was a tremendous void in Garland's life. You never really know exactly what you have until you no longer have it. For the first time in Garland's life, the desire for music was extinguished. His days of being a fixture at the radio station became fewer and fewer. His studies at Hinckley began to suffer. Garland's thirst for an education was beginning to die as well. Many of his teachers were deeply concerned by his lack of concentration in their classrooms.

Adam, on the other hand, began to use his studies as an escape from the void left in his life. For the first time since their friendship began back in Texas, Adam's grades were much higher than Garland's. The focus of his attention switched to going to college. In those days, a college deferment was a way out of going to Vietnam. The boys had too many friends going to Southeast Asia. Many of them did not return, and some who did return were disabled, whether physically, emotionally, or psychologically, unable to live life as they had known it before their departure.

Without the group, Harley, who had never been a good student, began to miss classes frequently. Many times, he would miss the entire day.

Beau was hooked on his song arrangement of "Lucy in the Sky with Diamonds" from the contest. This was something Beau wanted to do more of, and he began to focus on the music business. Beau began to spend as much of his spare time as he could at the radio station. He had a thirst for learning.

Suzanna observed her friends during this time. As much as she wanted Garland now, she knew the best thing would be for Garland to grieve in his own way. She didn't know the time frame it would take to heal. One spring day, Suzanna made her move. She wanted to be the spark for Garland to be the old Garland again. The one she was falling in love with. As they walked to the school cafeteria that day, Suzanna had a plan. They both walked through the lunch line as usual, arriving at their normal table and seats.

Garland pulled his chair away from the table. He tried to pull the chair back up to the table when the seat was stopped suddenly. As the seat stopped, Suzanna slid down onto Garland's lap, wrapping her arms around his neck. She now had his undivided attention. Suzanna's actions received a lot of attention, just as she'd hoped. Garland looked into her beautiful brown eyes. She returned the look into his eyes, as if to heal his soul. She began to run her hands through his now shoulder-length hair.

Garland took a deep breath and let out a very noticeable sigh. *She is so beautiful,* Garland thought.

Then, without any further hesitation, Suzanna kissed Garland like she never had before. She wanted Garland to feel how much he meant to her. Garland, on several occasions, tried to end Suzanna's kiss. She was not giving in to him on this.

Before long, others at their table began to stare at the action going on. Once again, Garland tried to end this already very long kiss, but he was not successful. Suzanna began to open one of her beautiful brown eyes to peek around them. Now there were two tables watching them. She loved the attention. Their kiss was approaching the five-minute mark.

Finally, a teacher serving as a cafeteria monitor, approached them. "All right, that is enough."

The kiss continued.

The teacher was not amused at being ignored. "I said that is enough of this fornicating."

Suzanna was determined not to let the teacher stop the treatment she was administering to her lover.

This time, the teacher tapped Garland on the shoulder and once again demanded that they stop.

Garland began to get concerned by the tone and actions of the teacher, and he broke the kiss off. Suzanna sprang up from Garland's lap, and the two, hand in hand, ran to the nearest door, leading into the courtyard. As they left the lunchroom, there was a loud round of cheering and applause.

That day, Suzanna gave Garland the healing that he desperately needed.

||||||||

As the spring semester of 1968 was well under way, Harley Krause decided school was not for him. His truancy had now become an obstacle to graduation. To become a high-school graduate, Harley would have to repeat his senior year. This was not an acceptable option to

Harley. Already eighteen, Harley dropped out of school and became eligible for the military draft. He was drafted into the US Army that spring. After six weeks of basic training, Harley was sent to Vietnam.

Garland, Adam, and Kevin met with Harley the night before he was to be sent to Vietnam. They couldn't help thinking that Harley would not be leaving for Vietnam if they had been victorious in the contest. This was now another reminder of their failure that one night.

"Harley, take care of your ass over there," Garland said.

"Garland, they have jeeps in the army now; we don't ride mules nowadays," Harley said jokingly.

They all had a good laugh at Harley's attempt to take away the sorrow each was feeling, not knowing if they would ever be together again.

Later that evening, Garland was sitting on his bed, thinking about why things change. It was just several weeks ago that the world had been his for the taking. Now his world was falling apart, and he couldn't do anything to change it. Two members of Summer's Solstice were out of sight but not out of mind.

Sissy walked by her son's room. "Garland, would you like me to fix you something to eat? You barely touched your supper tonight."

At first, Garland indicated he would like something to eat, but then he said, "Mom, I'm really not hungry."

Sissy found it hard to believe her son wasn't hungry, but she didn't press him. She turned away to walk out of his room.

"Mother, I miss our talks," Garland said. "You always knew just the right thing to say to make things better."

Sissy walked over to his bed and sat beside her son.

"I don't think I will ever play music again. The memories would be too much for me," Garland said.

Sissy knew how much Garland loved music. Her son possessed a passion for music more powerful than she had ever witnessed. There must be a way to reunite Garland with that passion.

Garland began to tell Sissy of the incident at school with Suzanna. "Mother, when I am with her, I sometimes feel like there is hope for me. She makes me feel good about myself. I am afraid I will bring her down."

"My son, I think you underestimate how much Suzanna feels for you. She is in love with you," Sissy said.

Garland paused for a moment and smiled. A tear glistened in one eye as he said, "I know when I am with her, nothing matters. Sometimes, I never want her to be away from me."

Sissy began to sing the song Garland loved. The song made Garland think more and more about Suzanna. This was different. In the past, he always thought of Sissy with that melody.

"Mother, can I borrow the keys to the car?" Garland asked.

"My keys are hanging on the coatrack in the hall. Where are you going this late?" she asked.

"I want to see Suzanna. There's something I want her to know," Garland said.

As Garland left that night, Sissy knew her son was in love.

IIIIIIII

Garland arrived at the Royals' rather late that night. He pressed the doorbell, never looking at the time. It seemed as if no one was going to answer the bell.

Chad was heading for bed when he heard the bell ring. He couldn't believe what he was hearing at this late hour. When someone came knocking this late, it generally meant bad news.

Chad flipped the front porch light on, peeking through the door to see Garland. He then unlocked the front door and invited Garland into his home.

"Garland is there something wrong with James or Sissy?" Chad asked.

"No, sir, they are just fine. Why would you think there was anything wrong with my mom and dad?" Garland said.

"Well, you are here very late; I thought there might be an emergency," Chad said.

By this time, Garland's late-night visit had woken the other Royals.

"I need to see Suzanna. I have to tell her something," Garland said.

"Can it wait until the morning, Garland?" Chad said.

"Garland, is anything wrong?" Suzanna asked as she approached the door.

"I need to tell you something, Suzanna. I don't want to wait until the morning for you to know. Something happened that day in the school cafeteria—you know, during our kiss. I fell in love with you. I never knew what it was until tonight," Garland said.

Suzanna was deeply touched that Garland had come at this hour of the night. It really was special, even more so because Garland could have called on the phone to tell her. She preferred the face-to-face method much more.

"Garland, are you sure you can be in love with someone who has all these curlers in her hair and no makeup on?" Beau said jokingly.

"Well, it's a good thing, Beau, your sister doesn't have any makeup on. Her tears would only make her mascara run," Chad said.

Chad had always been impressed with Garland, even before that night; now he was even more so. Perhaps the days of chivalry were not gone—at least not in Garland's case.

Garland hugged and kissed Suzanna good night.

‖‖‖‖‖

Garland and Suzanna grew closer and closer. Suzanna filled the emptiness within Garland. Everyone was convinced Garland wouldn't perform ever again, that he had turned away from his talent and passion for music.

As Suzanna and Garland's relationship deepened, Adam and Garland's friendship became almost nonexistent. Occasionally, they would pass each other in the halls at school, with no more than a casual hello.

Adam was happy that Garland had a girl in his life; at the same time, he resented her for taking his best friend away from him. Losing a best friend was Adam's void. More and more, Adam came to rely on music to fill his void. He began to play the guitar relentlessly, experimenting with new electronic sound enhancements. Fuzz tones and wah-wah pedals created a new sound. Adam was taking his musical talent to a whole new level, occasionally pausing to wish Garland was alongside him. Adam had no doubt the two would be better than ever before.

Adam began thinking of his other friend, the one who had become almost a brother—to Adam even more so than the other boys. Several months passed without anyone learning of Brandon's whereabouts. Adam thought of how much he wanted to apologize to Brandon. He remembered the last words he'd said to Brandon. Those were not the last words Adam wanted Brandon to remember him saying.

||||||||

One afternoon while Garland and Suzanna were out driving, an announcement came on the radio for the concert at the Red Rocks Amphitheatre. Garland reached to turn the up volume on the car radio. He knew a very big recording star was to appear at the concert. After the act was disclosed, the announcer indicated that there would be a special appearance by Eight Tracks. Sensing how much the radio spot had upset Garland, Suzanna turned off the radio. She did not want Garland to be upset any further. He was beginning to come out of his pain and didn't need a setback. She wanted Garland to make it through the next eight weeks. That was the date of the concert.

High-school graduation was now the focus for Adam, Garland, Beau, and Suzanna. The school year was about to end. The boys had always planned on careers in music. After spending so much time on one passion, it was very difficult to redirect that attention. Even though the boys were very good students, a college education had never entered their minds. Now, though, college would be a way to avoid the war in Vietnam.

Suzanna was afraid of losing Garland if he went away to school. She did not want Garland to leave her behind and began to discourage his idea of going to college; she abandoned her own plan of going to college as well. Adam applied to several universities and was accepted.

He began to narrow down his choices. Life was changing faster than any of them wanted it to. If only they had another shot at their passion.

||||||||

Kevin and James were going over the latest radio-listener ratings for the station. Kevin's secretary informed him there was a phone call.

"Hello, Kevin, this is Rudy Stamps with the group Eight Tracks. I would like to come by your station to meet with you about the upcoming show at Red Rocks," said the voice on the other end of the phone.

Kevin agreed to meet Rudy that afternoon. All morning long, Kevin and James were guessing as to why this young man wanted to see them. He did know Eight Tracks was very gracious to the boys during their performance and even more gracious about their loss.

The time of the appointment arrived. Kevin and James went to the conference room and left instructions for the receptionist to direct Rudy to the meeting room. Two young men arrived right on time and entered the station. The receptionist escorted them to where Kevin and James were waiting. The young men entered the room and joined Kevin and James at the table.

"My name is Rudy Stamps, and this is my brother, Terry. We are doing a promotional ad for the Red Rocks Music Festival," one of the young men said.

Kevin informed the Stamps brothers that he knew all about their performances.

This surprised the brothers. "You saw our performances?" Terry said.

"Yes, and you were almost as good as our sons were that day," Kevin said.

"Your sons?" Rudy asked.

"Yes. Our boys were Summer's Solstice," James explained.

"Your sons are very talented," Terry said. "We heard about what the drummer experienced just before they were to perform. We were very fortunate to win the event. We have talked about that many times. Under any other circumstances, we feel that they would have won easily."

James informed the Stamps brothers that Garland was his son and Adam was Kevin's.

Kevin agreed to promote the show for the boys.

"I'm really glad we met you today, Kevin and James. I only wish we could have met your boys as well. Our other band members are on a promotional tour in Golden today. We are to meet with them at one of the local television stations this evening," Terry said.

Kevin walked the Stamp brothers to the front door, thinking these young men were very classy.

Kevin went back to the conference room to finish up his meeting with James.

"Kevin, I am very glad we have the opportunity to help promote these young men," James said.

Kevin and James walked out of the conference room, noticing a light was on in the old studio room. They exchanged a glance, each one thinking the other was responsible for the light being on. As they approached the studio room's door, the window revealed the person responsible.

Garland returned to the station that afternoon to pick James up from work. This was his first trip back to the station since the night they'd delivered the equipment. Kevin and James stared through the window, watching Garland. There were so many good memories in that room of the boys growing into a band. Garland approached his old Gibson guitar, staring at his old friend. Finally, he embraced and opened the case. Garland took the old Gibson from its case, holding it as if he never wanted to return it to its case. He knew this was a friend that would never leave him.

Kevin couldn't resist the temptation and entered the room. This was the first time he'd seen Garland since the night after the contest. Kevin walked up to Garland as he held the guitar. He did not want to interrupt Garland's reunion. Garland looked at Kevin, with a very lost look on his face. There were no words to describe what he was feeling. Kevin handed Garland a guitar pick from a nearby table.

Garland looked at Kevin's other hand as he took the pick from Kevin. Keven was holding a poster for the Red Rocks Music Festival, with the dates posted in big letters. At that moment, as Kevin thought Garland was about to play something, Garland put the pick in his pocket and put the old Gibson back in its case. Garland left the room without saying a word. It was obvious that the pain within Garland, where the passion for music had once been, was still not healed.

11

GOLDSBORO, NORTH CAROLINA, was the home of Seymour Johnson Air Force Base. This small town was a popular area for retirees. Michael Fisher was one of the many retirees in the Goldsboro area. He liked the small-town atmosphere, and the schools were very good. This was a bonus when raising a teenage daughter. Brenda Fisher was to graduate from high school in the spring.

Brenda and Valerie Fisher were looking through some old childhood pictures. Neither of them could believe how fast the time had gone by. There were the early school pictures from the years when the family lived in Charleston. There were those grade-school pictures, with the missing front teeth and the pigtails. There were all those pictures of classmates that people tended to keep and from time to time, to reminisce about that period of their lives. As Brenda's mother turned to each one, she would quiz her daughter on the person in the picture. Brenda was batting a perfect thousand. She was perfect. As Brenda gave each answer, her mother would turn the card over, revealing the name written on the back of the picture.

Valerie reached for the last picture in the box. There wasn't a name written on the back of this picture. Brenda turned the picture over, revealing its secret. She didn't need a name on this one. Brenda began to cry and quickly left the room.

"Brenda, are you okay, baby?" Valerie asked.

Brenda did not answer her mother.

Valerie picked up the picture, searching for the reason her daughter was so upset. The last picture in the box was of a ten-year-old boy playing a guitar at a pool party. That same picture brought a tear to Valerie's eyes as well. She, too, didn't need a name on this picture.

After regaining control of her emotions, Brenda returned. As she walked into her bedroom, Brenda saw the look in her mother's eyes. Garland's picture also reminded Valerie of the great friendship she'd enjoyed with Sissy. Brenda joined her mother on the side of her bed. She sought comfort from her mother's hug; it was the comfort she'd relied on for her entire life.

Brenda opened the box for another look. As she looked at Garland's picture, she noticed a piece of paper inside the box. It was a love letter Garland had written shortly after the move to Texas. In the letter Garland described his friendship with Adam and playing music. Garland had so much passion for his friend and music. The letter ended with Garland telling Brenda he would wait for her forever. To a thirteen-year-old, forever was almost like the end of time.

As she folded Garland's letter to return it to her treasure box, Brenda noticed there was a phone number.

"Mother, can I call Garland?" she asked.

"I think that is a great idea. I would love to talk to Sissy," Valerie said.

Brenda picked up the phone near her bed and began to dial the number. A very big smile and the glow in her eyes revealed the anticipation Brenda was enjoying as she finished dialing. Her heart began to race as the phone rang on the other end of the line. Valerie felt the same anticipation as she heard the phone ringing.

Brenda's smile suddenly became a frown as she heard a recording informing callers that the number had changed. Brenda hung the phone up.

"Honey, what is wrong?" Valerie asked.

"Their number has been changed," Brenda replied.

Valerie picked up the receiver and began to dial the number. She wanted to be sure that Brenda had dialed correctly. The same recording Brenda heard now played. Valerie thought Brenda might have given up too soon.

Brenda, with her head hanging down, caught a glimpse of her mother writing on the back of Garland's letter. Her mother knew something Brenda didn't: when a phone number was changed, the new number was disclosed at the end of the recording.

Brenda's face once again showed a sign of hope As Valerie began to dial the new number.

Finally, the phone was ringing on the other line. Several rings passed without any answer. Valerie let the phone ring a few more times before she terminated the call. After ten rings, it was apparent the phone would not be answered.

Brenda's roller coaster of emotions once again was on the down side of the hill.

"Baby, at least we know this is a working number now. We may not know if the number is Sissy and Garland's, but we don't know it isn't, either," Valerie said.

Valerie tried dialing the number several times, without any success. Each time, Brenda's face showed less and less hope. It was getting late, and the time had come to stop.

"Maybe we can try calling the Summerses another day," Valerie said.

Valerie left the room and went to finish some chores before heading to bed for the night. Brenda put her treasure chest under the bed and went to sleep as well.

The next day at school was to be a very big one for her. Brenda was meeting with a college representative the next morning to discuss the results of her application for admission. She had applied to Duke University. She wanted to go to law school and become an attorney. Not only was Brenda a very beautiful girl, she was very intelligent as well.

||||||||

Brenda arrived at Goldsboro High School the next morning, with more excitement and a lot of butterflies. Taking a major test was never like this for her. There wasn't any study preparation for this meeting. As she arrived and went to the counselor's office, Brenda took a peek at the picture in her sweater pocket. After looking at Garland's picture the night before, she couldn't help thinking of how much pleasure the picture brought her. She had tucked the picture into her pocket to take it with her on her big day.

She would love to see how much her first love had changed over the years. Was he handsome? Was he tall? Did he have long hair? Did he still have and play the guitar in the picture? All these questions went through her mind. It was those questions that took her mind off the interview she was about to attend.

Brenda knocked on the counselor's partially opened door. The Duke representative was in her office, waiting for Brenda's appointment.

IIIIIII

Valerie Fisher was finishing up her early morning chores. She sat down for a break and noticed the number she'd written down the night before. It was the new telephone number for the Summerses. She held the paper in her left hand as she dialed the number. For several minutes, there was no response from the phone; the call did not seem to connect. Finally, Valerie heard the phone ringing on the other end of the line.

"Hello," a voice answered on the other end.

"I am trying to reach the Summers residence," Valerie said.

"I am James Summers. How can I help you?"

"May I speak with Sissy, please? This is an old friend of hers from Charleston," Valerie said.

"I think she is around here somewhere. Let me get her for you," James said.

Valerie could hear James in the background, telling Sissy she had a call from a friend she knew in Charleston.

"Hello," Sissy said.

"Sissy, this is Valerie Fisher. How are you doing?"

Sissy was very surprised to hear from Valerie. The two women began catching each other up on their lives since those days in Charleston. Sissy was very fond of Brenda. Brenda was once almost like a daughter to Sissy.

Valerie began to fill Sissy in on Brenda's big event that day.

"I know you must be very proud of Brenda. It makes me proud of her just hearing about the news," Sissy said.

"How is Garland doing? Does he still play his guitar?" Valerie asked.

Sissy filled Valerie in on the events of the contest.

"That must be very rough on him to get that close and have it taken away from him just like that," Valerie said.

"It has been. I have never seen him take anything so hard in his life. He will not play his music now. I keep thinking something will happen to bring Garland and his passion together again. But it has not happened," Sissy said.

Sissy began to tell Valerie of the night Garland found Brenda's picture in an old shoe box and how he fell asleep clutching it to his face.

"Sissy, you are not going to believe this, but Brenda found an old picture of Garland with his guitar. It was the picture I took at her tenth-birthday party. Finding his picture moved her like I have never seen her moved before," Valerie said, adding, "Brenda wanted to call Garland last evening. We had a very hard time finding you."

"I have an idea that will help both our kids. I will arrange for Garland to be here at a certain time tonight. I will not tell him who is calling," Sissy said.

Valerie agreed that would help Garland and Brenda very much.

"I will have Brenda call him at 10:00 p.m.," "Valerie said.

Sissy agreed for Garland to be in the house at the arranged time, saying, "10:00 p.m., it is."

Valerie was about to conclude the phone call when she suddenly thought about the time difference: 10:00 p.m. at her house would be

8:00 p.m. in Colorado. The adjusted time was agreed upon, and the two long-lost friends' plan would soon be in effect.

Valerie and Sissy said their goodbyes.

Sissy smiled to herself. It was now her turn to create a phone surprise similar to the one Garland and James had done for her on her birthday back in Texas.

IIIIIIII

Brenda began the Duke interview with very high hopes. Miss Jones, the lady from Duke began to go over Brenda's transcript. Her grades were among the highest being interviewed. Brenda's SAT score was also very high. Both Brenda and Miss Jones began to go over the essay Brenda had written as part of her application for admission.

"Brenda, why do you want to go on to law school?" Miss Jones asked.

"I want to do something with my life that will help people," Brenda replied.

"There are other ways to do that without a law degree," Miss Jones said.

Brenda wasn't prepared for that type of comment. She didn't understand the relevance of the question.

"I think sometimes there are attorneys who are in the profession for the money, not to find the real truth. I want to help anyone who seeks the truth; I do not want to be an attorney for a quick-results paycheck," Brenda said.

"I really believe you will be that type of attorney, Brenda. In fact, if I had a law firm, I would welcome you with open arms," Miss Jones said.

For the first time during her interview, Brenda smiled at Miss Jones.

"You are a very well-qualified candidate for Duke University. I just wish we had one spot left open for you. We didn't receive your information in time for consideration at this time. I am going to see if there is anything we can do to help you get into Duke. You are a definite asset to any university you go to," Miss Jones said.

Brenda left the interview, feeling that her world had come to an end. This was to be a very long day for her at school. School was the last thing on her mind now.

||||||||

Garland arrived home from school that afternoon. He went to his room and began his homework. Today's homework load was more than usual. He was glad the school year was about to be over.

Sissy called him into the kitchen.

"Garland, I need to run an errand this evening," Sissy said. "I am expecting a very important phone call for your father. If I am not here, I want you to take down the information for your dad."

Garland assured Sissy he would fill in for her secretarial duties that evening.

"I am expecting the call to come at around 8:00 p.m.," Sissy said.

Garland returned to his room, carrying a plate with the sandwiches his mother had prepared for that evening.

Sissy really didn't have any place to go; it was her way of ensuring that Garland would take the call when it came.

Meanwhile, Valerie anxiously awaited her daughter's arrival that afternoon. She wanted to share the excitement of her daughter's big day. As Brenda arrived home, her mother instantly knew she was upset. Brenda began to tell her mother about the interview with Miss Jones.

"Brenda, this doesn't mean you will not be getting into Duke; it just means it may not be this year. Let's give Miss Jones a chance to try to help you, though. From what you have told me about the interview, you made a friend," Valerie said.

"Maybe you are right, Mother. I think she will do everything she can to help me," Brenda said.

Valerie couldn't wait any longer.

"I had a very interesting phone conversation this afternoon. I could have talked all day on the phone," she said.

"Mother, you never like to talk on the phone that much," Brenda said with a smile.

Valerie smiled at her daughter, as if she were hiding something.

"Well, it's not every day you get to talk to a friend you have not spoken with for five years," Valerie said.

"You didn't, Mother; tell me you didn't," Brenda said.

"Yes, baby, I did; I talked to Sissy, and she has it all set up. You can talk to Garland at 10:00 p.m., our time this evening," Valerie said.

Brenda could hardly wait. Hearing Garland's voice would take away the void she felt today.

Shortly before 8:00 p.m., in Colorado, Sissy set the stage.

"Garland, I am leaving. If the phone rings, take the message for you father," Sissy shouted to her son in the other room.

Garland acknowledged to his mother that he would take care of the message.

Sissy wanted her son to think she left the house, so she opened and shut the front door, then slipped into her bedroom, undetected.

Brenda sat next to her mother, holding Garland's picture. Valerie dialed the number, then handed the receiver to Brenda. Valerie wanted to give her daughter some privacy and went into the next room. Although she wanted Brenda to have some privacy, she wanted to be there for her if she was needed.

The phone began to ring.

After four rings, Garland answered the phone.

"Hello," he said.

Brenda recognized his voice but couldn't get over how much it had changed. It was so soothing and very sexy.

"Garland, you probably don't remember me," Brenda said very nervously.

Brenda held on to his picture very tightly, almost as if she were trying to get the words she wanted to say to him. From the time she found that picture, she had practiced in her mind what she would say.

"Can you give me a clue? Maybe I can remember who this is," Garland said.

"You were my first love, Garland," Brenda said.

Garland paused as his heart began to flutter.

"My first love was in Charleston," Garland said.

Brenda smiled, with tears in her eyes. Something she couldn't explain came over her. It was if something took control of her.

She then did something totally out of character for her. She began to sing into the phone. As she began to sing, she became emotional over the song she was singing.

Garland was touched. This was his first serenade. As Brenda began the second verse to the song, Garland was sure now who the caller was. Brenda was singing the same song Garland had performed at her tenth-birthday party.

"Brenda, is this really you? You remembered our song?" Garland asked.

With that song, on that night, something changed Garland Summers. Brenda brought the music back into his heart. She was the only person with that special touch.

The two teenagers continued talking for an hour that evening, catching up on each other's lives.

IIIIIII

The next morning, Garland began his day with a special feeling, a feeling he had missed for months. He saw Sissy sitting at the kitchen table, enjoying her morning coffee. Sissy didn't want her son to know she was involved with the prior night's phone call. She really thought she had pulled it off.

"Mother, I am going to school early today," Garland said.

This was very unusual. As he walked through the kitchen to leave the house, Garland stopped where his mother was sitting. It had been a very long time since Garland looked at her this way.

"You are truly one of a kind, Sissy Summers, and I am so lucky to have you as my mother," Garland said as he hugged her and kissed her hand.

This was his way of thanking you for the night before and, at the same time, letting her know she had been busted for her involvement.

Garland went directly to the radio station that morning. He entered the station without anyone detecting his presence. He went to the old studio and retrieved his long-lost friend. This time, when he picked her up, he did not return her to her stand. Garland left the studio, carrying his guitar.

Kevin entered from the rear of the station that morning. He walked up the hall to see the light on in the old studio room. As he turned the switch off, Kevin noticed the old Gibson was missing. The first thought entering his mind was that it had been stolen. Kevin proceeded to the front of the station. He suddenly stopped in his tracks. He was touched by what he saw.

Garland was standing in front of the award showcase with his head bowed. Kevin began to walk to where Garland stood. As he approached Garland, without him noticing, Garland placed his hand on the window where Brandon's drumsticks were on display. It was as if Garland were communicating with Brandon.

"Brandon, it's time for you to come home to your bothers. You belong with us, and we belong with you," Garland said.

Garland did not know Kevin was standing beside him. Garland turned, saw Kevin, and smiled.

"It's time for the music to begin, Kevin," Garland said.

Garland Summers was back, and the music world could thank a teenage girl in Goldsboro, North Carolina, for his return. It would be a very long time before he and the old Gibson would be separated again. Garland took her home that evening and called Brenda. He wanted her to know her place in his heart. The timing was perfect for Brenda as well. She had been accepted to Duke University. Things were looking up for them both.

12

ANOTHER WEEKEND ROLLED around. Weekends were always the week's highlight to teenagers. For some time, Suzanna and Garland had planned a trip to Elitch Gardens for the annual seniors' night bash. Elitch was the very popular amusement park in Denver. Saturday night was the annual senior night at the park. The park was open all night for seniors of the Denver area. The park sometimes hosted concerts on that special night.

Adam English and his date, Toni, approached the park entrance at the same time as Garland and Suzanna. The girls entered the park in adjacent lines, followed by their dates. Garland saw Adam just a few steps ahead of him, But Adam was not aware Garland was in the park. As Adam cleared the turnstile, he turned to see Suzanna. He was about to speak to her, when Garland approached her and took her arm. Not knowing if Garland's feelings for him were healed, Adam shied away from speaking to Suzanna. The two couples went separately into the park.

As the couples proceeded on their separate routes, each route was decorated with posters for that evening's concert. Adam and Toni were into the arcades. He loved the games of skill and the thrill of showing off his winning trophies to Toni. The ringtoss was always a rewarding game for Adam, and tonight was no exception. As Adam won each game, the combined prizes could be exchanged for larger spoils. There was this very large purple gorilla Adam had his sights set on.

"Hey, baby, I am going to win one of those Magilla Gorillas for you," Adam said.

With his last ring, Adam tossed one more winner. There was no way for them to carry the six stuffed dogs he'd already won. It was a no-brainer to trade them for the big purple gorilla. Adam and Toni each carried one of Magilla's arms and began their journey through other areas of the park. Each time they approached Hinckley students, Magilla became the subject of their meetings.

Meanwhile, Garland and Suzanna reached the double-looped roller coaster. This was the most popular ride in the park. The long lines indicated its popularity. As they approached the ride, riders were able to select the car they wanted to occupy for the mile-long ride. Garland looked at Suzanna with an impish little smile.

She knew he was up to something, but what? Without a moment's hesitation, Garland took her hand and led Suzanna to the very first car. The two jumped into the side-by-side front-row car. Garland turned to his date and buckled the seat belt as the safety bar secured them for the journey. Suzanna took Garland's hand and kissed him.

"If we don't make it off this ride alive, I want you to know I love you, Garland," Suzanna said.

Garland smiled at her fear, returning her kiss.

The car began to make its initial assent for the highest climb of the ride. Suzanna began to feel the front car was the safest car for the ride. The car seemed as if it would never reach the top. She began to relax as the car reached its goal of the top.

Then, it happened! That front car took off like a bullet! Before long, the ride's top speed of sixty miles per hour was reached. Climbing over hills and winding around curves, the ride came to the second-highest climb of the journey. This time, the lugging car did not fool Suzanna; she knew there was something more incredible about to happen. Just as the car did on the first hill, it took off like a bullet again. Suzanna's hair was sticking straight out. She opened her eyes for an instant, only to see a pair of back-to-back loops.

Garland was enjoying her fear of the moment. He felt that fear drawing her close to him, and he loved that feeling.

The car began to enter the first loop, which turned the car completely upside down.

Without any hesitation, Garland took Suzanna's hands and then stretched their arms over their heads. He wanted the ultimate ride.

"Baby, it's time to reach for the stars," Garland said.

Suzanna, for a moment, believed him; they would not only reach for the stars, they would catch one as they entered the second nonstop loop.

The ride then began losing speed and soon returned to the terminal.

One of the ride operators helped Suzanna from her seat, and Garland had to pry her hands lose from the safety bar.

As they exited the ride, Garland looked into her eyes. "Let's go ride it again, baby," he said.

Suzanna looked at Garland and almost fainted. Garland laughed.

The two couples, although on different sides of the park, unknowingly were beginning to make their way to the concert area. Garland and Suzanna continued their thrills on the rides. Adam and Toni continued through more arcades. This time, Adam wasn't trying to win. Two at the park was good company, but three, even a stuffed gorilla, was more than a crowd. To make things easier while walking through the crowds, Adam placed Magilla on top of his shoulders.

Garland and Suzanna stopped for a drink and hamburger. As they were eating their meal, Suzanna looked down the row.

"Wow! Do you see that?" she asked.

Garland had no idea what she was referring to.

"Do I see what?" he said.

"Someone has won a purple gorilla. That is the coolest thing I have ever seen," she said.

Garland then noticed the gorilla, thinking he was glad someone other than he was carrying that thing.

Garland and Suzanna began their journey once again. They arrived at a bulletin board containing a map of the park. Across from the map area, a double-sided poster separated two aisles coming together to form one aisle. Garland and Suzanna arrived at one side of the poster to view the concert information. On the other side of the marquee, Adam and Toni arrived. Adam began reading the poster, as did Garland from the other side. The four of them were standing at the end of the marquee, but on different sides.

Then, just as if they'd cued each other, Garland and Adam read aloud the act performing. "Eight Tracks. These are the guys we lost to in the Red Rocks contest," they each said.

Garland and Adam knew this was a show they would have to see. They began to walk to where the aisles merged. Adam began walking backward for a few steps, just as Garland turned from talking to Suzanna. At that moment, Garland turned, bumping into Magilla and pushing Adam into his date. Garland and Adam turned to see what they had run into. Both stopped immediately and, at first, appeared to be about to apologize for running into the other, each thinking it was a stranger. Instead, the boys just nodded to each other, and neither apologized. Not a word was spoken during the incident, and the four proceeded to the concert area.

More time was needed for these feelings to mend.

The two couples made their way to the concert area. As Adam began to walk, he once again placed Magilla upon his shoulders. Giving a huge purple gorilla a piggyback ride was not in his plans for the evening. The couples arrived at the entrance to the arena. There on the marquee, in large red letters, were the words "Eight Tracks."

The boys stopped, reminded of their loss to Eight Tracks.

That sense of abandonment filled Adam.

Didn't Garland know how much he needed his best friend after that day? Why did Garland replace their friendship with Suzanna? Adam couldn't get those thoughts out of his mind. He knew if the two boys were to ever be friends again, he would have to close those thoughts.

Garland, on the other hand, never realized what Adam was experiencing. Garland never recognized that he was the only friend close enough to help Adam heal. He began to realize that Brenda, Suzanna, and Sissy were the ones who got him through the ordeal. Maybe if he were in Adam's shoes, he, too, would feel abandoned.

The arena filled to standing-room-only capacity. Eight Tracks was an unknown group to most of those in attendance that evening. There weren't any chants for the show to begin as there had been during the contest. The lights began to dim as the band entered the stage. Then, just as they had done in the finals of the contest, Eight Tracks began to get the crowd involved.

Rudy Stamps removed the microphone and strutted on the stage front, clapping his hands together and encouraging the audience by shouting, "Are you ready? Are you ready?"

Both Garland and Adam knew the routine Rudy was using to start the show. It was as if the crowd were asleep. Rudy was giving it his best.

Then, as if on cue, even though they sat in different rows and on opposite sides of the stage, Garland and Adam both stood up and began clapping, urging the crowd to join in.

The lights were very dim in the crowd. Rudy wanted to take advantage of this scene. He motioned for the lighting director to spotlight the two boys standing in the crowd, enticing the audience. As the lights found their subjects, Rudy couldn't believe his eyes. He was honored that both Adam and Garland had arrived to his aid.

The two boys were not aware they were both performing for the audience as well. Adam and Garland always seemed to know what the other was thinking—even now, when they hardly saw or spoke to each other. This fact was never more evident than that evening.

Rudy began the vocals to the opening song. His energy was boosted by Garland and Adam. Rudy's younger brother, Terry, added the backup vocals to the song, which was the same one that had won the contest. Eight Tracks was a very good act, and it wasn't long before the crowd knew it too.

Next, Eight Tracks did their version of "Sgt. Pepper's."

Garland immediately noticed the copycat version. Eight Tracks was playing the version of "Sgt. Pepper's" leading into the reprise version, just as Summer's Solstice had performed. The reprise part required a very good drummer.

Adam noticed this as well. His thoughts turned immediately

to how much better Brandon was on this song. *Their drummer is no Brandon,* he thought.

Eight Tracks would go on to perform six more songs that evening.

For their final song of the show, Eight Tracks performed a song they were introducing for the first time. It was written by Rudy and Terry Stamps. Although the song was an original, the arrangement was once again borrowed from Summer's Solstice.

This arrangement was performed with two acoustical guitars. Rudy and Terry were great on the acoustic, but their talent didn't come close to that of Adam and Garland.

Writing their own material was something Garland and Adam wanted to try as well. Seeing Eight Track's attempt that evening fueled Garland's passion for songwriting.

Eight Tracks ended that night's show with a very good encore presentation. That encore that made both Adam and Garland really miss performing. The encore created a higher feeling than either had ever experienced.

Rudy sent the event security guards to the exits the boys were using to leave the event.

As Garland and Suzanna exited, the security guard approached them, escorting them to the backstage area.

"Will you please come with me.? You have been invited to come to the dressing-room areas."

Garland agreed, and he and Suzanna followed the guard.

As Adam and Toni exited the doorway from the other side of the arena, Adam felt someone trying to get his attention by reaching for his arm. His first thought was that someone was trying to steal his Magilla Gorilla. He turned abruptly to confront the would-be thief. To his surprise, it was an event security guard.

"What are you doing, trying to steal my gorilla?" Adam said.

The security guard apologized. He knew how it must have looked to Adam.

"I am here to escort you to the backstage dressing areas," the guard said.

Garland arrived at the area. There, waiting with a cold drink in his hand, was Rudy Stamps. From the other side of the backstage area arrived Adam, Toni, and Magilla. The sight of Adam piggybacking a purple gorilla was truly hilarious.

Rudy greeted both Adam and Garland.

At first, Garland wouldn't acknowledge Adam. He stared at the ground as Rudy began talking. Rudy wasn't aware there had been a problem between the two who had once been best friends.

As Rudy continued talking, Adam began to once again struggle with Magilla, trying to reach a comfortable position. Each time Adam adjusted the gorilla, the others began to laugh. The laughter began to melt Garland as well. This was very funny. This was a side of Adam that Garland had never witnessed.

"Hey, Adam, I think your gorilla would like a banana," Garland said with a smile.

Garland's remarks brought loud laughter from the others.

Adam stood next to Magilla, with his arm leaning on his shoulder, as good pals often do, trying to think of a comeback to Garland's quip. Adam's mind was blank, though; he couldn't think of thing to say. Instead, he walked Magilla over to where Garland stood, took the gorilla's arms, and wrapped them around Garland's neck.

"Magilla, Garland has a banana in his pocket for you," Adam said.

Adam and Garland looked each other in the eyes and hugged each other. Who would have guessed a gorilla wanting a banana would be the medicine to heal their friendship?

"I have thought about the song you guys sang during the final round of the contest. Your dad informed Terry and me about Brandon's misfortunes," Rudy said.

"We were very sorry to hear your group disbanded," Terry added.

Garland was very happy to see Rudy and Terry. He had the utmost respect for the two brothers and their band. "Do you know what group you will be opening for?" Adam asked.

"Yes, the Moody Blues, one of England's best, will be the headliner. We are now just four weeks away from the big night," Rudy said.

Garland wanted to know all about the last number Eight Tracks had just performed.

"I have been wanting to start writing songs as well. I have so many thoughts inside my head. Until tonight, hearing the number you guys wrote, I never knew how much I wanted that," Garland said.

"The more pain a songwriter experiences, the better the songs he can author. The heart is mightier than the pen. Great songs always come from the heart," Rudy said.

This was not the first time Garland had heard that same thinking.

"Hey, guys, I think it's time we get back to the park. I would like something to drink," Suzanna said.

The Stamps brothers invited Adam and Garland to come by and sit in on one of their practice sessions.

The two couples then left the backstage area. This time, they did so as a foursome—or a fivesome if you counted Magilla.

"Do you guys see what I see?" Toni said. "Let's go over to the bumper cars. I have always loved them. It's time to shake things up. Until now, we have just been going through the motions."

The two couples entered the floor. Garland, Suzanna, and Toni rode in separate cars. Adam and Magilla took the last remaining car. As the music began, so did the rush.

Suzanna took the lead as the cars began to make a lap around the floor. She didn't want to be the receiver of a blow; it was the delivering she enjoyed. Just as Adam and Magilla made the first turn, Suzanna swung her car around for a head-on crash. She nailed Adam's car, making him lose control and slam into Garland. The drivers each turned their steering wheels, trying to separate the pileup created by Suzanna.

Once the cars were free, the drivers began to reach full speed again. Toni was the master driver. She would weave in between car after car, avoiding any direct hits. She began taunting the other drivers.

"Catch me if you can. You know you can't hit what you can't catch." Toni shouted.

She became a marked girl. Her taunts not only gathered the attention of her group, but the other drivers as well.

The thrill of now avoiding all ten cars on the floor was becoming more challenging. Toni took her eyes off her route and made a sudden move to avoid a car. She only caught a glimpse of Garland's car from the corner of her eye. She turned to taunt Garland.

Then, as she turned her attention to the floor, Toni's foot slipped off the pedal, and she was instantly rammed by Adam and Suzanna from each side. She was led into a head-on with another car, bringing the car to a stop. *Wham!* A car came from her rear, snapping her head back. Another car hit her car, and then another. Eventually, all ten cars became involved. Now it was the other drivers' time to return the taunts. Toni was a good sport and complimented the victors.

The early hours of that morning flew by. The sun would be up in another hour, and the park would be closed. It had survived another senior night. As the park began to close that morning, the two couples went their separate ways. Garland and Suzanna were stuck in the line exiting the parking lot. Toni and Adam were located two cars behind Garland and Suzanna. The drive back to Aurora was normally a thirty-minute drive, without traffic delays.

This morning wasn't normal. They had not traveled very far when the traffic came to a total halt.

"There must have been a terrible accident," Garland said.

Several cars behind Garland and Suzanna, stuck in traffic, was the car Adam and Toni occupied. Adam and Toni didn't know Garland and Suzanna had left the parking lot ahead of them that morning. They didn't have a clue of how much farther ahead they were. Traffic moved at a snail's pace as the three traffic lanes became one.

A sudden thought went through Adam's mind. Toni could see the concern in his face as their car approached the sight of the accident.

"Adam, is there something wrong? You look as if you just saw a ghost," Toni said.

Adam turned to his date. "What if it was Garland's car in the accident? How would I ever get along without him? He was and still is my best friend."

Toni reached for Adam's hand, holding it very tightly.

"How would he recover, losing two of his close friends in such a short time?" Adam said.

The sight of the wreckage was blocked with emergency vehicles.

As the traffic stopped for the ambulances to leave, Adam could now see that five vehicles were involved, two of which were so mangled, the type of car was barely identifiable.

Garland and Suzanna's car passed the sight. Garland had the same feeling Adam experienced. He could now breathe easier, knowing none of the cars in the accident was Adam's. The traffic for Garland and Suzanna began to move as the one lane returned to three lanes.

Soon Adam and Toni's car passed the wreckage. Adam breathed a deep sigh of relief. His friend was not involved.

The traffic flow soon began to move much faster. The sight of the accident made both Garland and Adam each realize how much the other meant to him. Although they felt sorrow for the ones involved in the terrible accident, it was a celebration deep inside them both that day.

Both cars, for some unexplained reason, drove to the radio station that morning.

Garland and Suzanna arrived first and went straight to the old studio room. Soon afterward, Adam and Toni also arrived. Adam removed the gorilla from the backseat and carried him to the studio. As he approached the room, he saw Garland and Suzanna inside the room. Toni opened the door for Adam, whose arms were filled with the gorilla. He felt his way over to the set of drums and sat the gorilla on a nearby stool behind the microphone stand.

Kevin arrived at the station that morning. As he walked into the lobby and down the hall to his office, Kevin saw five shadows inside the old studio room.

Who are those five people in the room? he wondered.

As he opened the door, much to his surprise, there stood Adam and Garland, each with a beautiful girl on his arm. Kevin had met Toni a few days before and was taken by her from that first meeting. Kevin greeted the kids and began to laugh when he saw what he'd thought was a fifth person.

"Magilla has a special talent for that, Kevin. He is a real charmer," Suzanna said.

"Welcome back, boys. It's good to have you back home together at the same time," Kevin said.

Kevin left the studio and went into his office. There was news coming over the wire services about the accident on the freeway. Wanting more information, Kevin turned on the television. A news reporter was reporting from the scene of the accident. The reporter began to disclose the facts of the accident.

Garland and Adam, with their dates, began to make their way to the lobby. As they walked past Kevin's office, news about the accident played on the television. A highlight news film of Eight Tracks suddenly began to play.

Why are they playing this right now? The same thought went through everyone's mind.

"Three members of the group Eight Tracks were killed this morning in a five-car accident," the reporter said. He later added the names of the casualties. This was a very big shock. Just a few hours earlier, the band had performed for thousands at senior night. Garland and Adam and their dates had been backstage, carrying on with the band members, and now three of them were gone. Rudy and Terry Stamps were not listed as any of the three casualties. This was a very sad day in the Denver area.

"Dad, last night, Rudy Stamps told Garland and me that he and Terry were here at the station doing a promotional visit for the Red Rocks Music Festival," Adam said.

Kevin, still in shock from the news, nodded his head yes. He could not find the words to speak. It is always tragic when a person dies, but when a young person dies a tragic death, the tragedy is very hard to understand.

"Did Rudy leave a number where he can be reached?" Adam asked.

Kevin opened the drawer to his credenza to find the poster information promoting Red Rocks. There wasn't any contact information for Eight Tracks.

"You guys need to get some rest. You have been up all night at the park; you must be exhausted. We can talk about this later." Kevin said.

The boys agreed and left to take the girls home and then go home themselves.

Kevin remained at the station. This accident needed the Denver area's help to heal, and Kevin wanted to do all he could to help.

13

THE DENVER AREA paid its respects to the members of Eight Tracks. The memorial service was the largest anyone in the Denver area could ever remember. This tragedy made the national news. Garland, James, Adam, and Kevin all attended the service. For Garland and Adam, the experience was something new. Death was something not very many high-school students had to deal with.

After the memorial service ended, Garland and Adam wanted to talk with Rudy and Terry. Unfortunately, Rudy and Terry weren't available.

Kevin met with one of the service directors, asking, "Can you please deliver this message to Rudy Stamps? It is very important he gets this message."

The man assured Kevin that he would deliver the message to Rudy.

Several days passed without Kevin receiving any response from Rudy. The Red Rocks Music Festival was nine days away.

Garland and Adam arrived at the station that afternoon. This was a very big night for the Summers and English families: the Hinckley graduation ceremony. After twelve long years of school, the boys were to end one chapter, only to begin another new one.

Adam appeared to be headed off for college, and Garland was contemplating staying at home and enrolling at a local junior college. Attending college was a backup plan for the boys. Their hearts were in music, not academics. Neither of the boys wanted to be in a classroom, and they both felt that college would not benefit their talents.

Kevin was viewing a local television station's coverage of the memorial services held two days earlier. This caught the boys' attention as well. The reporter was interviewing an official from the Red Rocks Music Festival.

The official began to read an official statement concerning that event, stating, "We wish to extend our deepest sympathy to the families of the group Eight Tracks. This tragic incident has deeply moved everyone in the Denver area, as witnessed by those attending the memorial service. We regret that the plans for the Red Rocks Music Festival event will be changed because of this unfortunate accident."

The boys looked at Kevin, confused, while all three awaited further information pertaining to the concert.

The official continued, "The accident has left the winner of the contest without a band. Normally, the second-place band would fulfill the commitment, but Summer's Solstice no longer performs and has ceased to exist. Therefore, the remaining finalist group, Purple Majesty, will be contacted. We regret this decision, and our thoughts and prayers are with the families of Eight Tracks."

"Can they do that?" Adam said.

Kevin did not have an answer for his son.

As Kevin and the boys were about to leave the station to get ready for graduation, Kevin's phone rang. Kevin rushed to his desk to answer the phone.

"Kevin, this is Rudy," said the voice on the other end of the line.

The sudden big smile on Kevin's face let the boys know this was a good phone call.

"Hello, Rudy. I was beginning to think you would not answer my message," Kevin said.

Rudy informed that Kevin he had not received any message. He then said, "I guess you have seen the news on television. With only nine days before the concert, they chose Purple Majesty to do the show."

Kevin informed Rudy he was aware of the news.

"I'm calling because I wanted you to know that we fought the decision of the concert organizers. There was nothing we could do. Terry and I just hate that Purple Majesty will be there," Rudy said.

Kevin agreed and then said, "Rudy, can I call you back tomorrow? We are about to head out; the boys' graduation is this evening."

Rudy did not want to interfere with the boy's big day. He agreed to continue the conversation with Kevin the following day.

This time, Kevin and the boys left the station and made their way home.

llllllll

Garland arrived home for a family dinner before the graduation ceremonies. Sissy was doing everything possible to make Garland's day special. At the dinner table, Garland told his mother and father about the concert's new opening act.

"Somethings in life are not fair," James said. He explained to his son that he understood the dilemma the Red Rocks people faced now. They wanted to award a worthy contestant the right to perform in a big arena for a big show.

"If only there was enough time before the show," Sissy said.

"What do you mean by 'enough time'?" James asked.

"Well, there are three members of Eight Tracks, and three members of Summer's Solstice. The boys and Eight Tracks seemed to hit it off. They have a great chemistry, and they respect each other," Sissy said.

Garland agreed, telling them about the meeting with Rudy and Terry after their show at Elitch on senior night.

"I think the six boys would be awesome. Both groups performed "Lucy," so there is one song you both already know," Sissy said.

Garland's face lit up like a Christmas tree. "I don't know how you do it, Mother, but you always do. There isn't any problem you can't solve."

This solution would only work if the remaining members of Eight Tracks wanted to perform.

||||||||

Garland picked Suzanna up for graduation. This was her and Beau's night as well. Suzanna looked radiant that evening. She glowed, in fact. Garland was speechless at the sight of her. He could not remember a time when she had looked better. They arrived at the school auditorium at the same time as Kevin and Adam.

"Wow, Suzanna, you look very nice tonight," Adam said.

"Suzanna, if I were twenty years younger, Garland would be arriving alone this evening," Kevin said. He winked at Suzanna and patted Garland on the shoulder.

"Where are your dad and brother?" Adam asked.

Suzanna pointed to the red Mustang already in the parking lot. "They should be inside."

Once inside the foyer area of the auditorium, Beau and Chad joined the new arrivals. Garland, Adam, Suzanna, and Beau left to join the graduating class of 1968. Kevin and Chad entered the auditorium, arriving at the seats James and Sissy were saving for the group. The time was approaching for the class of 1968 to graduate.

As the class of 1968 marched in to take their seats in front of the stage, there was a sea of flashes from the cameras of the admirers in the crowd. The graduation more than an hour and a half. There were more than three hundred graduates that year. As their names were announced, each of the students went onstage to receive their diplomas and then returned to their seats.

Since the students were announced alphabetically, Adam was the first of the group to receive his diploma. Adam always insisted he was first because he was ranked highest in the class's grade-point system. Chad had the pleasure of having children who were back-to-back graduates. He was the only parent in the room with that distinction. Garland was the last of the group, alphabetically. Adam and Beau did their best to try to convince Garland that he was actually that far down in the class rankings.

Once all the students received their diplomas, the class stood, and each of them moved the tassel from one side of their caps to the other, signifying that they had graduated. This prompted more than three hundred caps to be tossed into the air simultaneously. School was now officially over for them.

The graduates began to filter out of the auditorium to join their families. This was the time for pictures of the graduates with their family members and other graduates.

James volunteered to be the photographer that evening. He made sure he was well prepared, as he did not want to miss a single shot on this special occasion. James was finishing up the final pictures, about to put away his camera and film, when Sissy reminded him that there were no photos of him and Garland. He was so busy being the photographer that he didn't think of being the subject.

"James, you and Garland stand over there, and I will take your picture. Then, I will take one of Garland and Sissy together. Finally, we will do one of the three of you together," Kevin said.

With that, the photos were now finished, and the memories of a lifetime were preserved.

After the photo session was completed, several of Garland's and Adam's friends came around. This would be the last time some of them would see each other that night. Garland and Adam were talking with Kevin and Beau. From the corner of his eye, Kevin caught a glimpse of two young men dressed in suits. At first glance, they appeared to be just other elated family members in the crowd. As they came closer, it seemed these two young men had sought the boys out of the crowd.

"Congratulations, Garland and Adam. This is your special night!" one of the young men shouted.

Garland and Adam both smiled.

"You guys are the last two people I would have ever expected to see here," Garland said.

The two young men were Rudy and Terry Stamps. Each shook hands with Garland and Adam.

"After I talked to Kevin today, there was no way we wanted to miss this," Rudy said.

"Rudy, you have made our day complete," Garland said.

As Kevin turned to look at the two young men, he, too, felt touched that Rudy and Terry Stamps were there. This was special, especially after what they had been through the last few days.

"We wanted to share your graduation. Terry and I did not graduate from high school. Who knows? Maybe someday we will go back and finish high school," Rudy said.

"We are very glad you came tonight," Kevin said.

Garland and Adam wanted Rudy and Terry to know how sorry they were for their loss. Rudy and Terry thanked them for their concerns.

"I guess you have heard the news about the Red Rocks Music Festival. They will officially announce tomorrow afternoon that Purple Majesty will be the opening act for the Moody Blues," Rudy said.

"We heard that, and it makes me sick to think that bullshit group will get what they did not earn," Garland said.

Garland shocked the others with his statement. They had no idea how he felt about that group.

"Garland, I am glad you think that. I thought I was the only one who felt that way," Terry said.

Garland was waiting for the opportunity to introduce Sissy's idea. He wanted one of the Stamps to indicate that they still wanted to play music.

"A third-place group should not be getting all that attention. I can just see that blonde bitch strutting her stuff on the stage. She always acted like her shit didn't stink," Garland said.

"Has the committee contacted Purple Majesty about being the replacement act?" Kevin asked.

"From my understanding they have been contacted, and will be formally asked to fill in tomorrow at the press conference," Rudy said, confirming what he had indicated earlier.

"Rudy, will you be attending that press conference?" Garland said.

"They have requested that we be there in attendance; that way, they feel that they can express their condolences for the accident and introduce our replacements." Rudy said.

Garland could no longer resist the temptation. He had to put forward Sissy's idea.

Taking Rudy aside, Garland said quietly, "Rudy, I have to say something that has been on my mind. My mother has come up with a perfect solution. I have not mentioned it to anyone, and I won't give you the details until later, but we are going to that press conference with you tomorrow."

IIIIIIII

The next day, Garland and Sissy were to meet Kevin, Adam, and Beau at the press conference. The others did not know of Garland and Sissy's plan. Kevin, Adam, and Beau met Rudy and Terry in a room next to the press conference. Kevin didn't have a clue why Garland wanted the three of them to be in attendance that day. Garland and Sissy arrived shortly afterward.

As they made their way to the meeting with Rudy and Terry, Purple Majesty's lead singer stopped them, saying, "Did you come here to congratulate us?"

Sissy could see the anger in her son's eyes, and she led him to the meeting before he could reply.

Garland and Sissy entered the room. Sissy took a seat, while Garland stood and began to reveal the plan. "Rudy, Terry, I have an idea. I have not discussed this with Adam or Beau. However, I don't believe they will object to what I am about to say."

"What is your idea, Garland?" Rudy asked.

"Rudy, if you guys want to play that show, Adam, Beau, and I would be honored to join you," Garland said.

Garland took Rudy by surprise. He was not prepared for Garland's idea.

"Rudy, the others would want us to play. They were looking forward to this night. This is the right thing to do," Terry said.

Kevin squeezed Sissy's hand, showing his approval. He was as proud of Garland as she was.

"Garland, you have touched me very deeply with your offer, and my brother is right. It is the right thing to do to remember the ones we lost," Rudy said.

Rudy led the others into the press room. Rudy and Terry sat, with the other boys standing behind them. Sissy and Kevin sat at the back of the room. This was to be the boys' doing, and they did not want to miss this. Across the room, Purple Majesty, looked very confident. The lead singer began to blow bubbles with her gum in an attempt to show off. She was enjoying this moment. She still believed they had been robbed with the original results.

As the concert officials approached the microphones, they could not help but notice that the Stamps brothers were not alone.

One official spoke, thanking those in attendance and then stating, "As a result of the unfortunate accident, we are now forced to make changes to the Moody Blues show next week. Eight Tracks was to perform. Now, of course, that is not possible. Our second-place group, Summer's Solstice, disbanded and no longer exists. Therefore, Purple Majesty, will step in as the opening act."

Purple Majesty's lead singer blew even bigger bubbles and then showed that smirk she was known for. Everything was going her way.

The official then opened the floor to questions. He was not prepared for what was about to happen.

Rudy stood. The press, aware of who Rudy was, began to applaud.

The official acknowledged Rudy and gave him the floor.

"My name is Rudy Stamps. Today, I am here with not only my brother, Terry, but my three new brothers as well. We want to play the opening act. But, more important, we *have to* play for those who cannot perform. Terry and I, along with Garland Summers, Adam English, and Beau Royal, the remaining members of Summer's Solstice, need you as much as you need us. We all know of the misfortunes that over-came Summer's Solstice just before they performed, and we all also know they were the best group in the contest. By us joining together, we can heal together. This is the right thing to do."

The officials not prepared for such an act of valor as this. They excused themselves to take into consideration Rudy's new proposal.

"We will return with our decision momentarily," one of the

officials said. "We want to do what is best for the concert's paying customers. They deserve the best, and we want to ensure they receive it."

After fifteen minutes, he returned to reveal the committee's decision.

"Rudy, we appreciate the offer," the official said. "We have to consider the paying customer in this matter. Although they will be coming to see the Moody Blues, we want to provide the best opening act we can as well. I am afraid there is not enough time to do the opening act justice. We therefore stand by our decision to award Purple Majesty the opening act."

The results shocked everyone in the room that day. Disappointment filled almost the entire room.

As the room began to empty, Purple Majesty's lead singer couldn't resist one last taunt. She stood up and did a little victory dance, ending by blowing a kiss to the boys.

"Go for it, Lola!" one of her band members shouted.

The boys felt this was truly one day when the good guys did finish last.

As the boys were leaving the room, Kevin suggested they all get something to eat at the restaurant next door.

"You know, I was really pulling for you guys," one reporter told them. "Both of your groups were very good, and I could hardly wait to hear the combination of the two groups together."

"Thank you, sir. We think we would have been something awesome as well," Rudy said.

"We would like a table for eight," Kevin instructed the hostess at the restaurant.

She led them into a room with an open table. Even though no one was hungry, Kevin knew that a good meal would help relieve some of stress from the press conference. After looking over a menu, everyone agreed they would like the buffet. Their appetites suddenly arrived as well. This restaurant would lose money on this party today. Everyone was stuffed, sitting back and enjoying the relaxation before they departed. Feeling like losers was something these boys were not about to give in to.

Two men entered the restaurant. One of the men was the reporter from the press conference. The two men stopped at the hostess stand. As Kevin directed his attention to the hostess, he felt the men were inquiring about his group. The two men walked into the room, arriving at Kevin's table. Kevin recognized the reporter from the press conference as the one who had written the newspaper article for the *Denver Post* prior to the contest finals.

"Kevin, we are sorry to interrupt your meal. This is my brother, Saul Goldman; we have something your boys might be interested in," the reporter said.

Rudy instantly recognized Saul Goldman.

"Hello, Rudy," Saul said. "I am very sorry to hear about the accident. I know you and Terry were very close to them."

"Thank you, Mr. Goldman," Rudy said. "These are my friends. Garland, Adam, and Beau were in the group Summer's Solstice. Kevin, Adam's father, is the station manager at KARO in Aurora. Sissy is Garland's mother."

"I have seen you perform, Garland," Saul said. "Your group was very good, and I know Rudy's was also good. I agree with my brother that the combination of the remaining members would be something very special."

"Mr. Goldman is the entertainment director at Elitch Gardens," Rudy said.

Saul continued, "I know you guys had your heart on the Red Rocks Music Festival, but I have something I think will benefit you much more. Instead of one show, I want to book you for the entire summer. I am prepared to offer you the Friday and Saturday night shows in our new outdoor arena by the lake. Unlike the Red Rocks Music Festival, you will get paid for these shows."

The boys were speechless. Could this really be happening to them?

"How would you guys like to make music again? "Rudy asked.

Garland stood to shake Saul's hand, saying, "Mr. Goldman, you are going to love the music we will give your audiences."

As they left the restaurant, Lola and Purple Majesty were leaving the press conference.

Garland wanted to make sure Lola would be able to hear the results of the meeting with Saul.

"Mr. Goldman, we thank you for this great opportunity. We will not let you down," Garland said in a loud voice.

Realizing Garland wanted Lola to hear their conversation, Saul said just as loudly, "Elitch Gardens looks forward to having you guys the entire summer. Red Rocks' loss is our gain."

As Saul entered his car, he winked at Lola. There wasn't a bubble or a wiggle this time.

14

ITS DESERT CLIMATE made Tucson, Arizona, an ideal treatment area for people with tuberculosis. The Baily family had been in Tucson for some time. Shonda Baily had just returned home from her mother's funeral when a news story on one of the local Tucson television stations caught her attention. The local channel was airing a story about the accident that had killed three Eight Tracks band members in Denver. She remembered that was the name of the group winning the Red Rocks contest her brother had competed in.

By now, there was plenty of time for Brandon to have returned home after the funeral. Several hours went by, and her brother was still not home. She began to think that she had not only lost her mother that day but her brother as well. All during their mother's illness, Brandon was like a caged cat. It was evident Brandon had never forgiven their mother for leaving him, letting him believe her leaving was entirely his fault.

During the early morning hours of the next day, Brandon returned to the tuberculosis center where his mother had been since leaving him in Texas. He snuck into the rear entrance and arrived at the room his mother had occupied. It was almost twenty-four hours since he'd last slept. As he entered the room, he saw a picture of Brandon and Shonda on the nightstand. This was a picture Brandon never even knew existed. He sat down on the bed and began to stare at the picture.

The stress of the last twenty-four hours began to take its toll on him. It wasn't long before Brandon fell asleep, clutching the picture. One of the care nurses walked past the darkened room, noticing the bed had been disturbed. She approached the bed to find Brandon asleep. The nurse, thinking it was best to let him rest, unfolded a nearby blanket and covered Brandon. Thinking this was Brandon's way of grieving, the nurse left the room.

Several hours later, Shonda's phone rang.

Who is calling me this early in the morning? she thought.

"Hello, is this Shonda Baily?" the voice said.

Shonda answered yes.

"Shonda, your brother is in your mother's old room, asleep. We thought someone should know," the nurse said.

Shonda immediately dressed and went to the treatment center.

As Shonda approached the room, the nurse approached her with some troubling news.

"During the time I spent on the phone with you, Brandon left the center," the nurse said.

"Maybe he's headed home." Shonda said.

Shonda left the center. She wanted to be there when Brandon returned. The day would turn out to be a very long wait. Brandon did not return, and she had no idea of where he would go.

|||||||

Brandon wandered the streets of Tucson for days. Occasionally, he would find a car unlocked. The nights in the desert were often very cold. Although Brandon never damaged any of the cars and never stole any valuables left inside them, he did stay inside them to warm up and catch several hours of sleep. The loose change he found in some of the cars provided his only means to buy food. His daily diet often consisted of nothing more than some slices of bread; if he found additional money, there would be the luxury of a bologna sandwich. Sometimes Brandon would walk by the tuberculosis center and sit out front, never entering the facility.

Then, one day, as Brandon walked the streets, without any idea of where he had arrived, he came upon the cemetery where his mother was buried. He found a nearby visitors' bench and sat down to rest. The lack of food was taking its toll on him. He was very weak and soon fell asleep on the bench. Soon it began to rain. Brandon occasionally rolled from side to side, trying to block the cold raindrops with the back of the bench.

A person in attendance at another funeral reported Brandon to a cemetery security officer. With what little strength he had, Brandon began to resist his removal. As he escaped their grasps, Brandon fell to the ground. As he lay there on the ground, Brandon noticed the earth hadn't settled back to its normal undisturbed state.

As he surrendered to the security guards, Brandon rose on his knees. There was a wreath and a temporary marker on the grave he had fallen upon. The name on the marker read "Baily." He was escorted from the cemetery, and the gates were locked behind him.

This was not a son's proper farewell to his mother.

||||||||

Several weeks passed by. Shonda was beginning to think Brandon had disappeared from the face of the earth. She would visit the surrounding neighborhoods, showing Brandon's picture to people. No one had seen him. Sometimes she would visit the tuberculosis center, searching for a clue. Each time, there were no results. One day, she made a trip to the cemetery. This was the first time she had been there since the day of the funeral.

On her way out of the cemetery, she came upon two security guards.

"Has either one of you seen this guy?" Shonda asked.

One of the men looked at the other.

"Isn't this the guy we had to throw out that day?" he said as he showed the picture to other man.

"Yes, that's the one we found on the Baily grave that day."

"Do you have any idea of how I can find him? He is my brother, and that was our mother's grave," Shonda said.

"Have you tried the homeless center, two streets over?" one of the guards said.

Shonda left, thinking she might finally have found a clue.

IIIIIII

Back in Aurora, things were looking up for Garland and Adam. The music was returning to their lives. Rudy and Terry's musical talent complemented the boys' talent. Kevin was delighted to have the old studio in use again. With school a thing of the past, the boys began to direct all their attention to music.

Well, that is *almost* all their attention.

Garland and Suzanna had become almost inseparable. She often sat in on the practice sessions.

Rudy introduced a song to the others. This was one of his songs. He wanted to perform it at their first show. Kevin walked into the room to witness Rudy's attempt. The music brought back so many good memories. As Rudy began to express his ideas about his song, the boys began to play. Kevin thought the arrangement was very good, but there was something missing.

"Rudy, Rudy, it's the beat that needs to change," Kevin said. Referring to the Eight Tracks drummer, he added, "Sam needs to pick it up. The drumrolls are off from the rest of the song."

For a moment, Kevin thought back to a time when he corrected Brandon.

Sam took Kevin's advice and began to try to change the beat and the drumrolls needed as chorus changes were made. Once again, Sam was off with the beat.

After several takes, it was apparent the other boys would have to make changes to accommodate Sam's talent. Sam was a good drummer, but he wasn't in Brandon's league.

Once, Kevin began to try to help Sam with the arrangement.

"Brandon, I have seen you do much better," Kevin said.

The others were shocked at what Kevin had said.

"Dad, he's not Brandon. This is Sam," Adam said.

Kevin realized Brandon was on his mind. He apologized to Sam, assuring him it was nothing personal.

|||||||

Later, Garland said, "Mother, I think Kevin almost lost it today at practice."

Garland then explained to Sissy what had happened, adding, "I think he was upset with Sam for not being Brandon."

"Garland, I can't tell you how many times I have thought about Brandon. We all miss him and worry about him. You have to remember that Kevin took Brandon in when he did not have anywhere to go. When Brandon left, it was like Kevin lost a son that day," Sissy said.

"You know, sometimes I can feel Brandon. I have not told anyone else. Brandon is in trouble; I can feel it," Garland said.

Sissy began to dismiss Garland's notion, thinking it was just his way of missing Brandon.

"Mother, I know Brandon is trying to get back to us, but he needs help. I have never been so sure about anything before," Garland said.

Sissy then knew her son was serious.

Garland kissed his mother good night. He went into his room and went to bed. This had been an unusual day.

|||||||

During practice the next day, Kevin received a phone call from Saul Goldman. Saul was on his way to meet with the boys. He wanted to go over some of the ideas the park had to promote their shows. When Saul arrived at the station, the boys were brought into the conference room. They all thought highly of Saul and enjoyed being in his company.

"Hey, guys, how are things going? We want to begin the shows in two weeks, and we need to start doing some promotions," Saul said.

"We are working on about ten songs, one of which Rudy has written," Garland said.

Saul was impressed that their show now contained ten songs.

"Most of the shows will be an hour long. Down the road, we want to do a few special shows lasting ninety minutes," Saul said, adding. "Kevin, we also want to involve the station as well. We want your station to be the official station for Elitch Gardens. We will buy advertising time on the station, print some banners, and use our marquee to promote both the boys and the station."

Kevin assured Saul that this sounded like a wonderful arrangement and the station would be delighted to help in any way needed.

"Now we only have one problem we need to address as soon as possible," Saul said.

"What problem, Mr. Goldman?" Rudy said.

"Well, Rudy, we need to come up with a name for your act," Saul said.

With all the practice time they were putting in, a band name had never even occurred to them.

"We will have something for you in a day or two, Mr. Goldman," Garland said. "We want to come up with something that will roll off people's tongues when they say it—something they will easily remember too."

With a smile, Saul informed the boys he would return the next day. He was very pleased with his new stars. He sensed something very special in them, and he wanted to contribute to their success.

After Saul left that afternoon, the boys began to kick around names. They all agreed that the group name wouldn't contain any of their own names. No one member would be any greater than the group, and using one person's name would contradict that idea. They did, however, want the group name to relate to where they were from.

They agreed as to wanting everyone to know that Colorado was their home. Garland, Adam, and Beau wanted something with Aurora in the name. Aurora was a regal sounding name, and it was also part of the name of the famous phenomenon of the northern lights.

Could it be this simple? Maybe we should just use the name Aurora,

Garland thought. But then he thought that perhaps something should be added to the name.

"You know, I can't think of anything that makes the name any more dynamic. The word Aurora is perfect," Terry said.

"Terry, you may be right. Aurora doesn't need another word; it speaks for itself," Rudy agreed.

"Let's put it to a vote. Everyone in favor of becoming Aurora, raise your hand," Terry said.

The vote was unanimous. Elitch Gardens was now home to the band Aurora.

||||||||

Day after day, Shonda went to the homeless center, hoping to find Brandon. Shonda encountered a volunteer whom Brandon had become friends with.

"My name is Shonda, and Brandon is my brother. Can you please tell me how he is doing?"

At first, he ignored Shonda, but then Charlie Redwine could see in Shonda's eyes her concern for Brandon.

"Brandon didn't show up last night. Your brother suffers a great loss. His heart and spirit have been damaged greatly," Charlie said.

Shonda began to tell Charlie about the death of their mother.

"Brandon's pain is for much more than your mother's death," Charlie said. "His heart was once filled with a free spirit. That same spirit has left his heart."

Shonda wasn't sure what Charlie meant by what he told her that day.

Charlie knew Brandon wouldn't be back. He didn't think Shonda was ready to accept the fact that Brandon had left to find his spirit. Shonda returned daily, seeking out Charlie. Charlie always comforted her as much as he could. Eventually, he felt she would accept the fact that Brandon would never return to Tucson.

||||||||

After being there for a while, Brandon had begun to withdraw from the homeless center. He started to hate himself, and he knew that if he didn't resolve this hate, it would destroy him. One night, Brandon found himself once again sleeping inside an unlocked vehicle. Finding a cargo truck with its door unlocked, Brandon climbed inside for a good night's rest.

The next morning, Brandon was awakened by the truck moving. This wasn't in his plans. There were no windows and not much light. In almost total darkness, Brandon did the only thing he could to make the time pass: he went back to sleep, waiting for the truck to stop. It was several hours before the truck made a stop. At last, the truck began to decrease its speed until it finally came to a stop. Once the truck stopped, Brandon felt the motor wasn't running and made his way to the door, fumbling for the latch.

There was the sound of two voices just outside the door. Brandon jumped to the side, hiding behind two large boxes. He didn't want to be detected by the person opening the door. The door suddenly lifted. Brandon's heart felt like it was about to exit his chest. He couldn't get any closer to the walls of the truck in order to stay out of sight.

A moment later, someone climbed into the truck. Brandon prepared to defend himself. As the person climbed inside, Brandon jumped from behind the boxes, taking the person by surprise. He took the person into his arms, and, with a full nelson lock to the head, gained control. His prisoner's boot heels began to scrape down Brandon's shins. Several sharp elbow jabs took Brandon's breath away as the jabs pushed into his diaphragm. The person felt small to Brandon, but there was a tremendous amount of fight inside that little body.

After regaining control of his prisoner, Brandon wanted to see this person who had so much determination.

"I am not going to hurt you. I will let you go if you promise not to yell., Brandon said.

In discomfort from Brandon's head lock, the person nodded in agreement not to create any noise.

Brandon removed his arms from the long hair now tangled around his arms. He began to turn his captive around, revealing the face of the intruder.

"Take whatever you want, but please do not hurt me." the voice said.

"Hey, you put up one helluva fight, for a girl. I am not going to hurt you. I am here for the ride," Brandon said.

"Can we get out of this damn truck? It's hot in here, and you don't smell very good," she said.

Brandon agreed and jumped down to the pavement.

She began to climb down, out of the truck, and into Brandon's arms.

With the sun now shining on her face, Brandon was shocked by the beauty of this little package of dynamite. She had very long, beautiful, black hair, and her eyes were black as coal. They were so dark that Brandon could see himself in them.

"Do you have any idea of where we are?" Brandon asked.

"Yes. We are in White River," she said.

"Where is White River?" Brandon asked.

"White River is located in the Fort Apache Indian Reservation. We are about two hours northeast of Tucson. This is my uncle's truck. We come up here to deliver some supplies to the reservation," she said.

"Do you have any family here?" Brandon said.

"Yes. My grandmother lives here, and we come here a few times a year," she said.

The longer she looked at Brandon, the more she realized Brandon was also Native American.

"You know, I bet if you were cleaned up, you would be an okay-looking guy," she said.

"Oh, you do, do you?" Brandon said with a laugh, adding, "My name is Brandon."

"You look like a Brandon," she said, laughing. "My name is Tobie. We need to find you some clean clothes. I think you are about the same size as my uncle."

Tobie took Brandon by the hand and led him to where her uncle was.

Brandon's spirit returned that day in White River.

|||||||

Saul Goldman's return to the station brought much anticipation for the boys. They were eager to see Saul's reaction regarding their new performing name.

Saul arrived that afternoon to observe one of their practice sessions firsthand. He didn't want his new act not to be aware that he was observing them.

Kevin led Saul into the old control room. Here, someone could watch the activities in the studio room without any detection. This was also the best place to hear the sound. Saul was very proud of his selection. Both Eight Tracks and Summer's Solstice were very good acts by themselves, but, together, they were even better than he had first thought they would be.

After hearing the first song, Saul left the control room and entered the studio.

"Hey, fellas, how is the session going? "Saul asked.

The boys let Saul know that things were further along than they had hoped for.

Adam walked over to a nearby table to retrieve a poster he had made the day before. There, in big bold letters, was the name "Aurora" in yellow and orange. The word *Aurora* looked like it was on fire.

"What do you think of this, Mr. Goldman?" Adam said.

"Wow!" Saul said. "Aurora's fire is very intense. Kind of gives you the impression of *hot*. I like that. Hot music is something we can build on. I like Aurora's Fire."

Fire was a word the boys had never considered, but they agreed that it intensified the name, adding a dimension they had overlooked.

"We will begin printing up posters and banners with the name 'Aurora's Fire,' and they will be displayed throughout the park," Saul said. "The first show will be scheduled the night before the Red Rocks Music Festival."

This left the boys just a few days to plan their first show.

IIIIIII

On the morning of the day of the first show, Garland and Suzanna arrived at the park. Garland wanted to do a final walk-through of all the band's equipment and, at the same time, spend some time with Suzanna. Tonight could be the start of something very big for Garland, and there was nothing more he wanted than to share it with Suzanna.

Suzanna had become very demanding in terms of the amount of time the two of them shared. Unknowingly, Garland became one of her most prized possessions. She didn't want to share *her* time with that of the band. She knew that the more popular they became, the bigger the following they would have. Rock bands were like magnets for young girls. She didn't want to share him with the band, other girls, music—or anything or anyone.

IIIIIII

Showtime was now just a few hours away. The band was backstage in the dressing room, going over the lineup of songs.

Saul came around to wish his guys good luck.

"I also have a surprise for you guys tonight. You may be aware of this surprise during the show, I am not sure; but one thing that is for sure, you will know what that surprise is at the end of the show," he said.

Saul didn't intend to make them any more nervous than they were, but he wanted them to be excited in a positive way.

Adam was watching Garland sitting on a nearby stool. Adam detected his friend's mind was somewhere else at that moment.

"Garland, is something troubling you?" Adam asked.

Garland turned to Adam and said with a smile, "You know, this is the first time we don't have Brandon to get us ready. I was just thinking how much I miss that."

Adam paused for a moment, also thinking of Brandon.

Rudy interrupted their trip down memory lane, saying, "Hey,

guys, it's almost showtime. Let's give them something to remember us by."

The time had flown by. Showtime was now just minutes away.

Saul took to the stage that evening. This was a special night for him and Elitch Gardens, revealing their new headliner show for the summer season.

"Ladies and gentlemen, I am so proud of the act that is about to perform. These young men have survived several tragedies that many of us would have not survived. I am very proud of them and consider them my special friends," Saul said.

The boys looked at each other. Saul's introduction gave them a feeling of urgency. They were going to nail this show.

Saul left the stage as the curtains opened and the light searched for the spot where the first musical note began.

Rudy and Adam began the song's introduction with their electric guitars, and Garland complemented their sound with an electrically enhanced acoustic guitar.

For the moment, the bright lights were hiding the surprise in the audience that night. Saul, watching from the wings, smiled as Garland began the opening vocals. Garland's voice was maturing very well, and his wide vocal range was becoming his trademark.

As the lights started to become lower, Garland could see that the crowd was standing room only and reacted to every command he gave during the song. They fueled his energy, and he fueled theirs. The first song ended in deafening applause from the crowd.

Aurora's Fire was leading into their second number when Saul directed the lights to be dimmed to where the boys could see the crowd in the first row, where Kevin, James, Sissy, Suzanna, and Chad all sat.

Sitting next to the family members was the VIP section for the evening. In this section were the members of the Moody Blues, enjoying the music they were hearing. Each song the boys delivered ended with an emotional, heart-pounding standing ovation. They could not have been welcomed back to the stage by a warmer audience.

After the final note was delivered on the last song, the crowd began to chant, "More, more, more!"

Aurora's Fire obliged their fans with an encore.

There was a buzz in the audience that night about Aurora's Fire. As the stage lights gave way to the lights in the audience, the boys were delighted to see how many of the crowd remained.

The band gathered into the front center-stage area to take a bow. Each member was anxious to see the Moody Blues' reaction to their show. As they gazed into the area where the Moody Blues sat, their hearts dropped when they discovered their seats were empty. The boys left the stage, and Saul returned to the stage, informing the crowd that if they wanted more of the Aurora's Fire, there would be more shows during the summer season.

The boys left the stage, feeling like they were on cloud nine.

"I don't think anything can make me feel any higher than I do right now," Rudy said.

He was wrong! As they entered the dressing-room area for a something to refresh their bodies, there was a large gathering. Who was in this crowd, and why had they assembled in their dressing rooms?

"Guys, I told you about a surprise earlier today. We had a special request by the Moody Blues to attend your show," Saul said.

The boys were speechless when the Moody Blues members began to approach them.

"This is Justin Hayward, Deny Laine, and Graeme Edge," Saul said. "They wanted to meet you guys in person."

The boys couldn't believe it.

"We have heard through several sources that the group opening for us wasn't the best in the contest," Justin said.

"I think everyone in this park who saw you guys do your thing knows, as we do, who the real contest winners were," Denny said.

The boys had their first brush with fame that night. They hoped it would not be their last one.

"Saul, I thought there was nothing to make this night any higher for us. I was very wrong. We are way higher now," Rudy said.

Saul Goldman laughed and smiled at his new stars. These guys were the real thing. Neither Saul nor the boys in the band wanted this night to end.

As they were leaving the park that night, they came across a long line of people waiting to buy tickets. It was strange to see a line this late; it was almost closing time. The boys left that night with their family members and returned home.

15

"KEVIN, THIS IS Saul Goldman. Do you have a minute? I have something you will find very interesting," Saul said over the phone.

"I always have time for good news, Saul," Kevin said.

"Something happened last night after the show, and it has continued into this morning. You aren't going to believe this, but we ran out of printed season passes to the park," Saul said.

"You did what?!" Kevin exclaimed.

"We have sold out of the passes we printed in the spring for what we thought we would sell during the season. When our ticket-sales people asked why the people were buying the passes, they indicated that they wanted to see the boys perform on several occasions during the summer," Saul said.

By the excitement in his voice over the phone, Kevin could tell that Saul felt he'd hit the jackpot.

As the boy s all arrived that morning to do a walk-through of the previous night's show, Kevin informed them of the good news.

"Tonight's show will have an extra incentive," Garland said. This is the night of the Red Rocks Music Festival, and we want to do our best to provide a great show. We want the people in Morrison to be able to hear us here at Elitch."

Kevin laughed. There was nothing he would enjoy more than to drown out the show at Red Rocks.

||||||||

The days Brandon spent at Fort Apache gave him the inner peace he had been searching for since the night of the Red Rocks contest. Brandon was sitting on a rock in the Arizona hills, enjoying the early nightfall. There was a breeze, and the moon would be full and very bright when it rose. As darkness descended, the sky began to fill with fireflies. He loved watching the fireflies and feeling the breeze flowing through his shoulder-length hair. He felt as free as those fireflies. The sounds of the night came, filled with the serenade of crickets.

For a minute, he let himself imagine he was back in Colorado, remembering how much he had wanted this night. Since that night at the contest, Brandon had kept track of time in his mind, and he knew that this was the night of the concert at Red Rocks. The guilt Brandon felt letting his friends down and giving up the only things he had ever loved had hardened his heart.

Tobie slowly walked to where Brandon was sitting. She wanted to surprise him. Brandon was perched on a large rock, sitting with his legs crossed and each foot resting on the opposite knee. Tobie arrived without Brandon detecting her. Standing behind Brandon, Tobie placed her hands over his eyes and whispered into his ears. Her soft words gave him chills.

"Do you feel it, Brandon?" she whispered. She began to hug him from behind. He could feel Tobie's heart beating with each breath she took. "Can you feel it, Brandon?"

Tobie had waited for a night like this since the day she first met Brandon.

He slowly turned around to see the fireflies' reflection in her dark eyes.

"Yes, Tobie, I can feel it," Brandon said.

"Good, baby. I feel it too," Tobie said.

Tobie interrupted Brandon's smile with a kiss. She had wanted that kiss ever since that day in the back of the truck. Brandon began to kiss Tobie with a passion inside him that he never knew existed. This was not a lustful passion; it was something much more special.

Brandon and Tobie made love that night under the Arizona sky. Their music was the sounds of the night in the woods nearby. A sound so pure and perfect, the world's best symphony couldn't have done as well. Tobie healed Brandon's heart that night.

IIIIIIII

The sunrise found the two lovers asleep on the ground in each other's arms. As the sunlight found its way to their faces, Brandon and Tobie began to awaken. The two lovers found warmth from each other's body heat that morning.

"Baby, how do you like my Armstrong Heaters?" Brandon asked.

"Brandon, there are no heaters I would rather have than those Armstrong Heaters of yours," Tobie said with a smile.

"I could lie here with you forever. I never want this moment to end," Brandon said.

As much as they regretted it, Brandon and Tobie began to gather their clothes scattered across the ground and the rock. Tobie began to dress Brandon, and Brandon began to dress Tobie. Each was trying to wear their matching T-shirts, without any success. Brandon had Tobie's shirt, and Tobie had his. They laughed as Brandon tried to fit into her shirt.

Tobie and Brandon sat on the rock, enjoying their last few minutes together. Tobie began to run her fingers through Brandon's long but tangled hair.

"Where are you going?" Brandon asked as Tobie left the rock without saying a word. He couldn't understand why she would just leave without saying a word.

She took a few steps from the rock. Brandon could tell she was looking for something on the ground, but he didn't have a clue as to what she sought.

Tobie began gathering some wild blackberries, putting them into an apron she created with the bottom of her T-shirt. As she was about to return to where Brandon was sitting, Tobie found a large freshly fallen pinecone and added it to her collection. She returned to where

Brandon was perched and began to feed him the berries she had collected, demanding a kiss in return for each berry.

"Baby, we have to do something to your hair," Tobie said.

While Brandon finished off the berries, Tobie gently began combing Brandon's hair. The pinecone made a great comb and left a pine scent as well in his hair.

"Sometimes the best things in life are right under your nose," she said.

IIIIIII

It was daybreak in Aurora. This was the morning after the Red Rocks Music Festival with the Moody Blues. Kevin walked down his driveway for his morning newspaper. As Kevin started to walk back to the house, his next-door neighbor called out to him.

"I bet you must be very proud. I know I would be," the man said.

Kevin had no idea what his neighbor was referring to.

As he walked into the kitchen to pour his morning cup of coffee, the phone began to ring. Who was calling him this early on a Sunday morning?

It was Adam, calling from the Summerses' house. "Dad, have you seen it yet?"

"What do I need to see, Adam?" Kevin said.

"There is a review in the entertainment section. The Moody Blues and our show were both reviewed by the *Denver Post*'s entertainment reporter," Adam said.

Telling Adam he would see him later, Kevin hung up the phone and sat down to read the article.

First, he read the review for the Moody Blues; after all, they were the reason for the show at Red Rocks. The reporter began the review by saying that, although this concert was sold out for months, there were many empty seats. The Blues were great, as they usually were, but the opening act seemed to just be going through the motions. The promoters were pleased with the sellout but were confused as to why there were so many no-shows.

Kevin didn't realize it at the time, but he was reading the article out loud when his wife, Cindy, entered the kitchen. She had overhead the lines about the promoters questioning the empty seats.

"Honey, that's easy to understand. There was a better show last night across town," she said.

Kevin paused from reading the article. "Do you think that is what caused the many empty seats?"

"Well, that is what they are saying on the morning news on channel five," she said.

"Channel five?" he asked.

"Yes, they did a story about the two shows on the morning news," Cindy said.

Kevin stopped reading the review and turned to the next page. There, in headline print, was the review for Aurora's Fire. This was a special day. Not only did the newspaper tell the story of how the boys stole the night, but a local television did as well.

Word was traveling fast that morning in the Denver area. That Sunday evening, one of the national news media services took interest in channel five's story and rebroadcasted the piece nationwide. Brandon and Tobie were in one of the local dining halls on the reservation. They were still on a high from the night before. Tobie had never questioned Brandon about his past. She felt that when, and if, Brandon wanted to share his past, she would love to listen.

Someone walked over to the wall that evening and turned on the television. Sunday was the night for the television show *Bonanza*. This was a very popular show on the reservation and always drew a crowd during the hour it was on the air. The local station's Sunday evening newscast was ending, and, following its usual format, a feel-good human-interest story concluded the newscast. The story began by relating a David and Goliath battle in the music scene of Denver.

The Red Rocks Music Festival was portrayed as the Goliath of the two shows. Brandon couldn't believe what his eyes were seeing and his ears were hearing. The story went on to tell about the empty seats no one had anticipated. Then, the story switched to the David of the two events.

Elitch Garden's new summer sensation consisted of the group that should have been the opening act for the Moody Blues. The story went on to explain how this group came together after a tragic auto accident and the Red Rocks Music Festival committee's abandonment of the group in favor of one they considered better prepared to entertain the audience that night.

Tobie began to notice a look on Brandon's face. This look was all new to her. There was something about this story. Brandon's eyes began to fill with tears. These tears were both of sorrow and happiness. As Brandon faced Tobie, he couldn't hide the fact that his eyes were full of tears. Then, as if instantly knowing exactly what to do, she hugged Brandon, feeling his pain.

Brandon began to regain his composure. It was not like him to display his feelings. He always wondered how his friends were doing back in Colorado. Those were the best days of his life. He missed his friends and his music and longed to have them both in his life. But now, Brandon had something more valuable. He was in love with Tobie.

"Brandon, are you okay, baby?" Tobie said.

Brandon assured Tobie he was okay.

She knew deep down inside that something in that news story meant something to Brandon; but just what it was, she would have to wait to discover.

Brandon walked Tobie home that night to a friend of her uncle's. The walk wasn't the kind of walk Tobie was expecting. Whatever was troubling Brandon remained inside him. Brandon was silent during the walk and only began to speak when the two reached the walk's final destination.

"Tobie, you are very important to me. I want you to know that, no matter what happens," Brandon said.

Brandon's remarks frightened her.

"What are you trying to tell me, Brandon? What did I do wrong?" Tobie said.

"That's just it, Tobie. You haven't done anything wrong. It's just something I have to work out before I can be free," he said.

Brandon kissed Tobie that night. This kiss was far different from any the two had shared; it felt like a goodbye kiss. As Tobie watched Brandon walk away into the night, she knew he wouldn't be back.

|||||||

Tobie began to awaken the next morning. As she sat up and began to gather her senses, she suddenly remembered Brandon. She wanted to assure herself this was all a dream. Tobie rushed over to where Brandon was staying, hoping to find him there. She frantically searched the areas Brandon loved. Each time, Brandon wasn't there, and each location's heartbreaking results began to take their toll on Tobie.

Finally, there was a clue! One of the residents saw Tobie's endless search and approached her.

"If you are looking for Brandon, he isn't here. He left this morning at dawn, headed east." the man said.

"East?" she said.

The man nodded his head yes.

Tobie held her head down and then, suddenly, as if her knees were knocked out from underneath her, fell to the ground in tears.

The man came over to help her to her feet and wiped the tears from her eyes.

She knew Brandon loved her but was searching for something. Even so, Fort Apache wouldn't mean anything to her without Brandon. Tobie gathered her composure and told the man to give her uncle a message.

"Tell him I am headed east, and I will contact him," Tobie said.

Tobie then went after the most important thing in her life, determined to not let him get away.

|||||||

Later that afternoon, Brandon arrived at a service station in a small town; it was the only gas station in town. He took advantage of the service station's restroom to freshen up from the heat of the day. Cold wet paper towels gave him temporary relief. Brandon soaked his long hair with water from the sink's faucet. He approached the service-station attendant.

"Can you tell me how far we are from Interstate 40?" he asked.

The man informed Brandon it was about fifty miles. Brandon thanked him and returned to his journey.

Later, Tobie arrived at the same town's only station. She also used the restroom facilities and freshened up from the afternoon's heat. She didn't want to lose any more time to Brandon's lead. The station attendant entered his office.

"Yes, miss, can I help you?" he asked.

Tobie began to describe Brandon, inquiring if anyone had seen him.

"You missed him. He was here not more than thirty minutes ago. He wanted to know how far it was to Interstate 40," he said.

At least she now had a clue as to where Brandon was headed. She wished she knew the reason why.

||||||||

Brandon caught a ride shortly after leaving the station. The driver of a truck was going as far as Holbrook and would welcome Brandon's company. The man instantly detected Brandon's loneliness.

"Son, where are you trying to get to? I have seen many homeless wanderers, and you are not one. Your shirt is awesome. I have not seen one like it before," the man said.

Brandon thanked the man for his kindness and the ride.

"I am headed east," Brandon said.

"That covers a lot of territory. Where in the east, exactly, are you headed?" he asked.

Brandon had fallen asleep and didn't answer the man's question.

The driver sensed he was tired and decided to let him sleep and awaken him when they reached Holbrook.

Tobie directed her journey to Holbrook as well. A woman and her daughter, who had stopped at the station, heard Tobie inquiries about Brandon. The woman sensed Brandon meant a lot to Tobie and offered her a ride into Holbrook.

Brandon, along with his trucker friend, reached the destination of Holbrook.

Brandon stepped out of the truck and thanked the man for his help.

"I see you are hungry, son. Take my homemade sandwich. You need it much more than I do," the man said.

"Thank you, sir. You have been a big help to me," Brandon said.

He opened the sandwich, taking a bite.

"What kind of sandwich is this?" Brandon asked.

"Is there something wrong with it?" the man said.

"No, sir, it is very good," Brandon said.

"It is a Navajo sandwich my girlfriend made. She and I are Navajo," the man said.

As he finished the sandwich, Brandon told the man of his own Apache heritage.

"Now that you are in Holbrook, you aren't that far from Indian Wells. You can go there to the Navajo Reservation. Look for a man there named Sonny; he is my brother and can help you," the man said.

Brandon thanked him and began to walk into Holbrook. The man entered a gas station after letting Brandon out. After paying for his fuel, he noticed there was a diner across the street from the station. A hot cup of coffee would help him make the trip back home.

IIIIIII

Mrs. Turner, the woman who had offered Tobie a ride, pulled into the same station. The mother and daughter went to freshen up in the restroom, while Tobie stood outside the vehicle, wondering how she would ever be able to find Brandon. The man exited the diner and began to enter his truck parked next to the car where Tobie stood. As he opened the door, he couldn't help noticing the shirt the young girl was wearing. It was a very different shirt, and the chances of seeing that same shirt in less than an hour was odd to him.

"Nice shirt you have there. I can't believe how different your shirt is, and to have seen such a different shirt twice in an hour is rare in itself," he said.

The man's comment didn't register with Tobie at first. She was drained emotionally. As the man began to start his truck, his remarks sank in with Tobie.

"You have seen this shirt before in the last hour?" she asked.

"Yes. I could never forget a shirt like the one the two of you are wearing," he said.

"Can you please tell me where you have seen this same shirt?" Tobie said.

"Sure, I can. I gave a boy a ride and let him out at this gas station an hour ago. He seemed so alone, I sent him to Indian Wells in the Navajo Reservation to look up my brother, Sonny," he said.

Tobie now had her next clue to find Brandon.

The Turners returned to the car in time to hear the man's remarks about Tobie's shirt and Indian Wells. Tobie was still in shock that she was so close to Brandon and yet so far away.

"Tobie, if we are going to make Indian Wells before sunset, we need to get back on the road," Mrs. Turner said.

Tobie slid into the backseat, with the happiest heart in Arizona that day.

||||||||

Brandon, sensing it would soon be dark, climbed up the sloped concrete embankment under the Interstate 40 overpass. This spot, nestled under a steel girder, would be his bed for this night.

Unknowingly, Mrs. Turner drove right past Brandon. Of course, neither she nor Tobie had any knowledge of Brandon's exact whereabouts. Mrs. Turner proceeded to drive into Indian Wells.

Soon after arriving in Indian Wells, Tobie went to seek out Sonny. She knew that if Brandon was there, he would be with Sonny; if he wasn't with him, he would seek him out, just as she did. After searching several buildings, Tobie began to wonder if Sonny existed. There was this small old building with a rusted smokestack in the roof. While the Turners waited in the car, Tobie approached the well-weathered door, lifted her hand, and knocked. As she knocked on the thick wood, she realized that the sound of her knocks did not carry very well; it would definitely be hard for anyone inside to hear her knocking.

The door began to open slowly. A very old man smoking a pipe opened the door. He took a deep draw on his pipe and released some smoke.

"Are you Sonny?" Tobie asked.

"Who in the hell wants to know?" he said in a rusty old voice.

"I was sent here by Sonny's brother. He assured me Sonny would be a great help to me," she said as she was about to cry.

The old man wasn't prepared for this. This young beautiful girl touched his heart. It had been a very long time since anyone had touched it. He took a deep puff off his pipe, as if trying to summon the pipe to answer Tobie.

"I am Sonny Greyeagle," he said, adding, "My brother sent you, huh?"

Tobie was relieved and did something Sonny had never expected. She hugged Sonny with the comforting love a granddaughter gives her grandfather.

Mrs. Turner, seeing Tobie was in good care, turned the car around, and left. She was glad to have played a part in helping such a warm caring young girl.

||||||||

Brandon was exhausted. As loud as the sound of the cars running under the bridge was, it did not interrupt his sleep that night. The night went by very fast for Brandon. He now needed to complete his trip to Indian Wells. Once Brandon reached the highway leading to Indian Wells, he began to try to catch a ride. Soon a man offered the bed of his pickup truck. Indian Wells was now less than an hour away. Brandon climbed in, leaning against the cab of the truck. He would let the cab support his back as he enjoyed the warmth of the sun on his face.

The truck rolled into Indian Wells, stopping at a local market. The driver informed Brandon that they had reached their destination.

Brandon thanked the man for the ride and began his search for Sonny. Fortunately for Brandon, the search for Sonny didn't take long. Brandon noticed the old building with the rusted smokestack. He knocked on the door.

Sonny was bringing Tobie her breakfast when he heard the knock on his door. In less than twenty-four hours, his door had received more visitors than it had during the past six months. He paused, thinking what an annoyance it was.

At first, Sonny was reluctant to answer the door. He soon found out the knocks wouldn't stop, so he had no choice but to open the door. Sonny arrived at the door and began to undo the lock. As he opened the door, he paused. On the other side of the partially open door was a very familiar sight. Sonny stopped instantly and looked at the shirt Tobie was wearing; it was identical to the shirt worn by the person on the other side of the door.

Brandon was confused as to why the door was only partially open.

"What the hell do you want?" Sonny asked through the door.

"I am looking for Sonny," Brandon said.

"I don't know any Sonny," Sonny said.

"I am sorry to bother you, but his brother sent me here to see him. He told me Sonny would help me," Brandon said.

Sonny then opened the door fully. He looked up at the boy with the long hair and the eyes desperately in need of a friend.

"I am Sonny Greyeagle," Sonny said. "But I sure as hell am not the goddamn Red Cross. You are the second person he has sent to find me."

Brandon paused and began to walk away. This man appeared to not want anything to do with him. As Sonny began to close the door, a voice came from the other room.

"Brandon, is that really you, or am I dreaming?" the voice said.

Brandon stopped, thinking his ears were playing tricks on him.

"Tobie, are you in there? What has this old man done to you?" Brandon said.

Without a moment's hesitation, Brandon pushed open the heavy old wooden door as if it were cardboard. Once inside the house, he turned toward a doorway where Tobie stood. Sonny tried to get back on his feet after Brandon's rush toward Tobie knocked him to the floor.

Brandon rushed into Tobie's room. He began to hold and hug her, never wanting to let her go. The two young lovers stood there, soaking up the moment and the sight of each other.

"I have missed you like I have never missed any girl, Tobie. I will never leave you again," Brandon said.

Those were the very words she longed to hear from him. This time, she knew he meant what he said.

Sonny was overwhelmed by what he had just witnessed. Brandon walked over to Sonny and began to apologize for knocking him down. Sonny knew it was Tobie's safety Brandon was concerned with, and he had no hard feelings toward Brandon. He knew if the situation were reversed, he would have reacted the same way.

"Let me get you some breakfast," Sonny said.

The three of them sat down to enjoy the breakfast Sonny had whipped up.

"Brandon, what was it that upset you? Why did you leave me?" Tobie asked.

Brandon explained that it was about the news piece they had seen on TV at Fort Apache.

Tobie remembered the story very well. "What was that all about?"

"You are not going to believe me, but I was in one of the groups in the contest. It was my fault we didn't win that contest. We would have been on our way to the top now if it hadn't been for me. I blew the last song, making us lose," Brandon said.

Tobie walked over to the chair Brandon was sitting in and hugged him. It had to have been terrible to have kept this inside him for so long. No wonder his heart was bitter. He missed his friends and the music.

"I am going to help you two any way I can. You two belong

together. I can see it in your eyes the love you have for each other. Brandon, we are going to get you back to playing music. You will be able to help so many of our people, giving them hope that we can be successful too, "Sonny said.

Brandon told Sonny about the good old days with Summer's Solstice.

"Brandon, you are too young to have any good old days. You might have had some good days, but they definitely weren't old ones," Sonny said jokingly.

"Baby, you are going back to Colorado, and I am going with you. Wherever you go, I will go too," Tobie said.

Brandon promised Tobie that, from that night on, they would never be apart again.

16

ELITCH GARDENS' SUMMER season was in its last weeks. Aurora's Fire was much more than Saul Goldman had hoped for. The park was enjoying a record year for attendance. The last two weekends would see the boys do their ninety-minute shows. The sets for the shows would become more detailed for these special nights. The combination of Elitch Gardens and radio station KARO was almost like a match made in heaven. The station's ratings were beginning to take off.

Kevin began to explore the idea of adding another DJ and dropping one of the syndicated shows from the nighttime station lineup. The extra DJ would also enable the station to shorten the airtime shows of the two DJs currently on the air. Shorter airtimes would allow the DJs to capitalize on their popularity for public appearances.

James's job as program director now entailed greater responsibility.

"James, I have been given approval to add a few more positions here at the station," Kevin said. "I want to shorten our two daily shows from eight hours to six hours and add a third on-air personality."

"Our ratings have almost doubled from the time we took this station over, Kevin. We can increase our audiences and the shorter airtime would allow our DJs to be more creative. We can do a lot with eighteen hours of daily programing," James said.

"The other position I want to add is an assistant for you. You can post the position in the papers and on our bulletin board out front," Kevin said.

James wanted to try the bulletin board first. He felt that an Aurora resident would have more of an interest in the station.

The job posting wasn't creating much interest. James instructed Chad and the other DJ to announce the job opening on their shows. This would reach a broader audience. The price was right for the ad, since it was free.

One Friday morning, a young girl came into the station lobby. She approached the receptionist's desk and informed her why she was there.

"I would like to apply for the station's administrative-assistant job." the girl said.

The receptionist gave her an employment application.

"You can take the application home and return it completed tomorrow. James, the program director, is not in the office at the moment," the receptionist said.

"Thank you very much," the girl said.

As she walked to the front door, she stopped at the trophy case. The drumsticks on display caught her attention. She was staring at them when James entered the building. He could not help but admire this beautiful young girl.

The receptionist informed James that the girl was there to apply for the administrative-assistant job.

"If you would like, you can fill out the application now; or, you can bring it back to me tomorrow morning," James said to the girl.

"I will be here in the morning," she said, promising to return the following day by 10:00 a.m.

||||||||

Kevin was sitting at his desk early the next morning when he received a shocking phone call. The news was bad.

The man on the other end of the line said, "Kevin, we have just received word that Harley was injured last month in Vietnam and is coming back home. Harley is paralyzed from the waist down and is confined to a wheelchair. The army will be discharging him, and he is to receive the Purple Heart."

"Thank you," Kevin said. "I appreciate your calling me. As bad as it seems for Harley, at least he is alive."

Kevin hung up the phone and called Chad to his office. James was arriving for his interview with the young girl that morning. He met Chad in the hall on his was to Kevin's office. Chad informed James about the bad news. Harley's injury was the first tragedy of the war that affected anyone they knew personally. Vietnam was becoming a very unpopular war across the country. Even James, a military retiree, found it difficult to justify. This war wasn't fought to be won, and it was dividing the country.

"James, the young girl from yesterday is here for the interview," the receptionist said.

James met the girl in the doorway and invited her into his office. She sat down in the chair in front of his desk as James began to review her employment application. At first glance of her application, James saw that there wasn't any previous employment history.

"What is your employment experience?" James asked.

"I have been helping with my uncle's business," she said.

"What were your duties with him?" James asked.

"I did anything that needed to be done," she said.

James continued to review her application.

"What is your level of education?" he said.

"I am self-taught and never attended public schools," she said.

James began to carry on a conversation with her. This was his way of determining just how much education she had retained. It wasn't long before James discovered that this self-taught girl was a very bright person. Her personality began to win him over. He wanted Kevin to meet her and offer his impression as well.

Kevin joined the interview. It wasn't long before he concurred with James's impression.

"Your application says you are self-taught," Kevin said. "Your teachers are to be commended. Our school system should be so fortunate to have such talent. Congratulations! You have the job and can start on Monday morning."

She thanked James and Kevin for the opportunity.

KARO radio added their new employee that morning.

IIIIIII

The new set at Elitch Gardens was almost complete. The first ninety-minute show was to be that night. The instruments were being set up for the evening's show. One of the park's new employees was assigned to the concert area. He began to pay special attention to the drums. They were set up all wrong. The sound of the drums was never going to be appreciated in their current setup.

He began to place a wooden stand under the drum set. This would raise the drummer above the other members of the group. Finally, he noticed the stool was too short as well. The stool should be higher than the drum set. This would give the drummer easy access for those really fast drumrolls. He walked around the stage. He didn't want anyone to witness his next act. After determining there was no one around, he climbed onto the stool and began to play. As he continued to play, it was apparent the sound of the drums was greatly improved. They now would be the showcase. Not wanting to draw attention, he left the stage area.

The members of the group began arriving for the show. The traffic on the freeway became an obstacle for an on-time arrival. Saul was there with open arms for the first night of the special season-ending shows. The boys were dressed in mod attire. Striped tight-fitting pants with wide belts and buckles, with vividly colored scarfs draped around their necks gave way to open-necked, pointed-shirt collars. There was a little time before the opening song of the evening.

The new setup for the drums was almost unnoticed until Sam took his seat. The new setup gave Sam a view of the audience. He knew he would love the sight of the crowd and being able to enjoy the pleasure in their faces as the band performed.

Rudy began the intro to a song he wrote. His guitar licks were the cue for the stagehands to open the curtains.

The curtains opened and gave way to spotlights on the band members. This crowd began to feed off Aurora's Fire.

Garland sensed the electricity in the crowd as he began to sing the opening lyrics to Rudy's song. This night's audience was to be a special one: as Garland began the chorus, his voice was drowned out by the singing of the audience. They knew every word of the chorus.

When Garland began to start the second stanza of the song, he was amazed that the crowd singing along did not stop. The fact that the crowd knew this song made the performance very special. It was a very big compliment for an artist's song to be sung by the audience as the band performed. The show ended with a thundering encore from the audience.

There were now only three shows remaining for the season.

||||||||

Kevin and Adam went to Denver's Stapleton Airport the next morning. Harley's plane was to arrive at 9:00 a.m. As the plane rolled off the tarmac and into the gate, Kevin began to wonder if the war might have changed Harley. Handicapped passengers were the first to exit the plane. Harley's wheelchair entered the gate area. The stewardess placed her foot on the pedal behind the wheelchair and set the brake.

Harley's face lit up the minute Kevin and Adam approached him.

"Do you know much I have missed you guy's ugly faces?" Harley said.

"I am sure not as much as we missed your ugly puss," Adam said.

It wasn't long before Kevin and Adam realized Harley was the same old Harley to them.

During the ride back home, Kevin had an idea: Harley was home to stay and would never perform in the music arena again. Harley did have a very soothing voice. He remembered his harmony on many of the songs with Brandon and Garland.

"Do you know what you will be doing now that you are home?" Kevin asked.

"I don't have anything lined up at the moment. I have thought about using a government loan to go back to school," Harley said.

"Well, I have an offer for you Harley—a job I think you would be absolutely perfect for," Kevin said.

"What do you have in mind?" Harley asked.

"We are adding a third show at the station, and I think you would be a perfect fit. I am offering you a job as on-air personality, Harley," Kevin said.

This act really touched Harley. He knew this would be something he would love to do and make his own.

"Kevin, there is no one I had rather work for than you. I am honored that you would think of me for this job. I am yours if you want me," Harley said.

KARO radio now had their new star.

||||||||

For the show on Sunday night, Rudy and Garland would do renditions of some old Elvis Presley songs. Rudy thought it would be a special effect to do a few all-acoustic songs.

"Garland, I want you to meet me at the concert area at 5 p.m., tonight. I have something I want to show you that will blow your mind," Rudy said.

Garland had learned that no one could figure Rudy out. He was a surprise a minute.

The stage crew began to perform their setup for the evening.

Earlier in the day, a courier had delivered a package. The package came with specific instructions that it was to be opened only by Rudy Stamps.

Garland arrived at the time Rudy had requested. He saw the package, and it brought back memories of the day when his Fender arrived at the station.

Rudy and Terry entered the stage and immediately went to where the package was sitting. Rudy picked up the package, and his excitement rivaled that of a kid on Christmas morning.

"This will help our sound become very unique," Rudy said.

"Rudy, we are already unique," Garland said. "The fact that we came together, defying all those people who told us it couldn't be done, makes us unique. Other than our families and Saul, we never had anyone in our corner."

IIIIIII

The rest of the group arrived in time for the grand opening of Rudy's big box. Rudy had been bragging about this new thing and what it would do for them. The drama was beginning to tire them all. If Rudy didn't hurry up and open the damn thing, they would be too exhausted to do the show. Rudy struggled, trying to determine the best way to open the box. He knew what the contents were and didn't want to damage them. Finally, he decided the only way to open the box safely was to just lay it on the floor of the stage and have at it. He took out his pocketknife and began to cut the elastic bands wrapped around the box. One by one, he cut the four bands off the box and began to remove the staples.

Why are there so many staples in the box? the others began to wonder.

Rudy finally removed all the restraints and ripped open the box with one sudden movement. It seemed as if there was a mile of Styrofoam wrapping. At last, Rudy lifted the item from the box. His fellow band members, one by one, began to ogle the box's content. Rudy thought it was the most beautiful thing he had ever seen.

One, two, three, Garland began to count to himself. *Seven, eight, nine, and ten.* Garland was not finished. He then counted eleven and twelve.

"Rudy, this is a twelve-string guitar," Garland said. "There are six strings on two different necks."

Rudy took the guitar and began to tune it.

"Tonight, we will really open some eyes with this, but that will be nothing compared to the ears we will treat," Rudy said.

After watching Rudy glow over his new twelve strings, Sam approached his drum set. Again, the drums were changed from the previous night's show. This time, there was an extra set of tom-tom drums. He knew some new acts were beginning to use multiple drum-set combinations. Using a multiple drum set was for those drummers with extraordinary speed. Although the set was still elevated, the drums were now closer to the stage.

"Who keeps messing with my drum set? Where are the stage-hands? I want these moved back," Sam said.

Garland and Adam both noticed something was upsetting Sam and went over to address his concerns.

"Let me find the stage crew and get them rearranged. Where would you like the drums to be moved, Sam?" Garland said.

Sam pointed to the spot, adding, "They can also remove these extra tom-toms. I don't need the damn things."

Garland went offstage, in search of the stage crew. As he walked down the stairs, Garland couldn't help thinking about why the drums were being changed each night by the stage crew. Eventually, he found one of the stagehands as he was about to leave for the evening.

"Can you guys put the drums back in place?" Garland asked.

"Back in place? Why would we need to put them back in place? We never touch the drums," he said.

"I take it, then, you will not move the drum set?" Garland said.

"All my guys have left for the day. It must be the new guy who moved them. Someone heard the drums being played before you guys showed up last night," he said.

Garland gave up and returned to the stage to give Sam the bad news. The show would have to go on with the current setup. There wasn't enough time to rearrange the stage set.

|||||||

Once again, the audience was standing room only. This was beginning to become habit forming, and the boys loved it!

Saul, as always, did the introduction for to the night's show.

"Ladies and gentlemen, we have a very special show this evening. One that I am sure you will enjoy. The boys will be doing tribute to Elvis this evening. The show is so special, they wouldn't let me know anything about it."

As Saul left the stage, the curtains began to open. The spotlights found the stars on the stage.

The crowd roared when the lights revealed the boys' leather outfits and combed-back hair. The show opened with the Aurora's Fire version of "Jailhouse Rock." This song enabled both Garland and Rudy to showcase their guitar showmanship. Sam's opening drum bit set the tempo for the song, and "Jailhouse Rock" set the tempo for the show.

The boys thought it would be a lot of fun to wrap up the show with "Hound Dog." None of the boys could ever remember performing for an audience that stood, dancing, clapping, and singing along, for the entire show—all ninety minutes. There now was only one more weekend left and just two shows. Next week would be hard for the boys. The summer went by so fast, and then there was the uncertainty as to when they would perform together again.

|||||||

Monday morning arrived at radio station KARO. Today was the first day for two new station employees. Kevin, James, and Chad were in the conference room that morning when Harley arrived. This was the first face-to-face meeting for James and Chad with Harley since his return from Vietnam.

Harley's face is war weathered, James thought. It brought back memories for James, reminding him of his own days in Thailand. *One good thing, though: Harley did not let the war change his personality. He seems to be the same old Harley.*

Kevin said, "Harley, we want to bring you on for the evening show. Todd is on the air now and occupies the time slot from 6:00 a.m. to noon. Chad takes over at noon, and his show ends at 6:00 p.m. We want you're show to fill the time slot from 6:00 p.m. to midnight. From midnight to 6:00 a.m., we will continue running the syndicated national show we've been airing up to now. James and I will work with you in developing your technical usage of the studio equipment. You can view Chad's show jingles to get an idea of what you would like yours to sound like."

"I have a playlist of all the songs you will have access to in our library as well as the weekly chart ratings," James said.

"Harley, I have another new employee starting today. I need to excuse myself and leave you to James and Chad for the rest of the meeting," Kevin said.

Kevin left the meeting, feeling Harley would be a great asset to the station.

Kevin left the conference room just as the station's new assistant was making her way into the lobby. Once again, she stopped at the trophy showcase, wondering why there was a set of drumsticks on display. What kind of award could they possibly represent? As she continued to look at the drumstick display, the glass showed the reflection of Kevin's approach.

"Good morning! I want to welcome you aboard," Kevin said. "Today is a very big day here at the station. We are expanding our on-air personalities as well."

Kevin remembered James saying that Brandon's drumsticks had caught her attention during her first visit to the station.

"Mr. English, can I ask you question?" she said.

"Of course you can. What is your question?" he said.

"Why are these sticks in here with all these awards and trophies? Do the sticks belong to someone famous?" she asked.

"Oh, they are much more than that. These are magical sticks. I have never heard the magic they created, before or afterward. To me, they are the most valuable award we have," Kevin said.

She looked at Kevin, noticing his eyes were teary. He, too, was caught up looking at the drumsticks.

"Let me take you on a tour of the station," Kevin said.

Kevin led her into the live studio areas where the shows were broadcast from. They walked past the studio the boys used. She thought it was strange that this was the only room they did not visit during her tour. The two returned to the conference room to meet James, Chad, and Harley.

Later that morning, Aurora's Fire had a practice session in the studio. This weekend's shows would be the last ones for the Elitch Gardens summer season.

Garland was the first of the boys to arrive that morning. His dad had forgotten to mention that there was a new employee at the station. Garland couldn't resist her beautiful long black hair and coal-black eyes.

"Let me introduce myself. My name is Garland Summers," he said.

"You must be James's son," she said.

As Garland was about to answer her, Adam and Beau walked up behind him.

"I was just returning to the conference room to meet the new DJ," she said.

"We have a new DJ?" Garland said.

"Come along with me, and you can meet him," she said.

The three boys had no problem following her. She could have led them off a cliff that morning.

The boys entered the conference room, walking up to where a man in a wheelchair sat with his back to them. Kevin, James, and Chad began to smile as the boys stopped alongside the wheelchair.

"I want you boys to meet our new DJ," James said with a very large smile.

The wheelchair began to slowly turn around to where the three were standing. When the wheels of the chair stopped, the man turned to the three, his outstretched hand ready to shake theirs.

"My name is—" he began.

Before he could finish his own name, the three boys replied in unison, "Harley."

A handshake would not be enough. The four of them hugged, and the tears began to flow.

Kevin, James and Chad were also touched. This was a very good start for what promised to be a very big week.

Rudy, Terry, and Sam arrived shortly afterward to join the others to practice for their final shows. The six of them went into the old studio to work on the next show.

Rudy walked out to his van. He gathered the case inside and carried it into the studio. The closer Rudy got to the studio, the faster his paces became. He was very excited, and it showed. In the corner was a very special stand to hold his new prized possession.

"I want to introduce the Gibson at our final show," Rudy said.

He began to hold the pearl-white Gibson as if it were a newborn baby, not wanting to hurt it in any way. He strapped the guitar on and plugged her into one of the nearby amplifiers. Rudy decided he would use a thumb pick and began to play one of the group's old songs.

This old song sounded very different. The others couldn't get over the difference the guitar made to one of their old favorites.

The boys practiced for several hours. It was time to call it a day. As they began to leave the studio, Harley was in the hallway. His wheelchair was parked in front of Brandon's drumsticks as the others were about to leave for the day.

Rudy, Terry, and Sam always wondered about the significance of the sticks in the showcase.

Harley turned to the others as they approached the showcase.

"Has anyone heard from Brandon? I feel so bad about what I said to him that last night," Harley said.

"No, Harley, we haven't heard a thing. We all wish we could see him again. We all miss him very much," Adam said.

The Stamps brothers knew of the incident and thought it best not to intrude on the memory of Brandon. They now knew whose sticks were inside the showcase, and why.

All together, the boys began to leave the station.

Harley was on his way to James's office. The girls in the office were leaving for the day as well.

The new assistant was completing her first day at the station. As she left her desk, she met Harley in the hallway. She had seen him looking into the showcase earlier.

"How did your first day go?" Harley asked her.

"I like it very much. I feel right at home here," she said.

"That's good. These people are the closest thing I have to a family in this world," Harley said.

She smiled.

"I never did catch your name," Harley said.

"Well, I never threw it for you to catch," she said with a laugh.

"Aren't you a cute one!" Harley said.

"I will tell you my name, on one condition," she said.

"One condition? All I have to do is ask Kevin what your name is. You know that, don't you? "Harley said.

She laughed and said, "My name is Tobie."

"I like that name, it fits you very well," Harley said, adding, "Tell me, though, what was the condition?"

"I was just curious about the drumsticks in the showcase. They seem out of place. All Kevin would tell me was that they were magical. He wouldn't say to whom they belonged," Tobie said.

"They were used by the best drummer you will ever hear. He had so much charisma. As a person, he would do anything for anyone," Harley said.

Harley began to roll his chair down the hall. "You have a good evening, Tobie. I will see you tomorrow."

Tobie still didn't have the answer she had tried to get, not once but twice. She was determined to find out about those sticks. They were very special, and the owner must have been too. He was missed very much and loved even more than he was missed.

||||||||

On Thursday afternoon, Harley came into the station early. He was almost ready to take over his show. Kevin and James wanted Harley to be familiar with the current top hits. Harley taped some spots of the show and replayed them in the old control room. This way, he could study his voice to gain comfort with feeling what it would be like to be on the air. With each take, Harley became more comfortable with the way his voice came over the airwaves. Each time, there was a sense of less nervousness than the take before.

Kevin was just outside the door, listening to Harley's demo tapes.

"Harley, it would be a great idea to start keeping up with the current events of day. You can review them and add your own little version on how to announce them. Always ask yourself about what you would like to hear. What is it that keeps you interested? Develop your own style and technique," Kevin said.

Harley knew exactly what Kevin was referring to. Harley was about to finish his demo tape when Tobie left her desk to deliver a phone message.

Maybe the third time will be the charm to get the answer about those sticks, she thought.

She entered the studio, exploring its contents. She wasn't aware Harley was in the next room.

Harley left the old control room and headed for the old practice studio. Tobie was still not aware she had been discovered. Harley took Tobie by surprise when he entered the room. Not wanting to scare Tobie, Harley began to wheel over to some of the old guitars.

Tobie smiled when she saw Harley.

In one corner was the control board. Harley noticed the control panel was unplugged from the wall and bent over to plug it in. As the power light turned green, Harley hit the Play button. It was obvious this machine hasn't been used in a long time. Harley was shocked at the sound coming from the tapes. This tape contained some of the old mixes. He began to laugh at the sound of the tape of Sissy and Kevin testing the voices of the boys for vocals.

Tobie listened intently to find the reason of Harley's laughter.

"Is that you singing, Harley?" she asked.

"Yes, unfortunately it is," he said.

"You have a very good voice," Tobie said.

Harley turned up the volume. He wanted to enjoy the voices that were to follow. The next voice appeared on the tape. This voice was so familiar and so beautiful.

As the voice continued, Tobie realized this was a voice she was very familiar with.

"Whose voice is that?" Tobie asked.

"That is the voice of the friend we all lost. His voice was amazing; but, as good as it was, it was only second to his talent as a drummer and entertainer," Harley said.

"Can you replay that piece with his voice?" Tobie asked.

Harley rewound the tape and replayed it. Tobie knew the voice. It was Brandon's. She now had the answer to her question. The drumsticks in the showcase were Brandon's. He really did belong in a band.

IIIIIII

Saturday arrived, and the mood of the boys was sad. Tonight's show could be the last time they performed. Saul made arrangements for a special after-show party. If this was to be their final show ever, he wanted to create something special for them to remember it by. The stage crew was given special instructions detailing the new effects to be used during the group's final number of the evening. The final number would be performed as if in a wild thunderstorm, with fog and lightning effects, including lightning striking the stage on the closing note of the song.

Once again, there was a mysterious movement of the drum set. As usual, it was moved when no one witnessed it. The drum set was given a new raised level, higher than previous shows. For this special show, the boys were paying tribute to the British Invasion of the early sixties. The Beatles, the Rolling Stones, and the Moody Blues were to be the core of the song selections for that evening.

Garland decided to spend time with Suzanna during the hours leading up to the show. James had called Garland earlier in the day, reminding him to pick Sissy up for the show. The hours swept by much faster than he realized. Sissy, realizing the time was running short, drove herself to the gardens.

The much-publicized final show was drawing a record crowd. The attendance at the park was the largest ever. Saul wanted everyone at the park to be able to enjoy the show, even if they didn't have a seat at the show. Several of the theaters inside the park were carrying the show on large screens as well. Sissy, with a later start than she had hoped for, found the parking lots were full. Finally, she arrived at one that wasn't full. The walk to the park was to be a lot farther. With her mind on the show, Sissy began to walk to the park and elected to take a shortcut. She knew this wouldn't be the safest route, but it would enable her to arrive in time to see Garland before the show started. The shortcut paid off, as she arrived early enough to have some time with her son before the show.

The show began with the loudest and largest crowd of the concert season. The crowd began chanting, "Aurora, Aurora, Aurora!" Each time, the chant sent chills up the boys' spines as they prepared for the curtains to open.

This time, the show began without Saul's introduction. Instead, one by one, each member took the stage, introducing themselves to the crowd. Garland and Rudy generated the loudest applause.

The rest of the boys began to strap on their instruments as Sam and Beau played an opening on the drums and keyboard. The crowd had a lot of energy, and it fueled the boys. They felt just as high as the crowd. As the first song came to an end, the crowd stood up and wouldn't sit down for the rest of the show.

Rudy began to sing his own composition. This song was normally the one that ended all their shows.

That night, when the boys came to the chorus of Rudy's song, something happened. Several fans in the first two rows began to turn their cigarette lighters on, as if to pay tribute. The idea quickly spread like wildfire. The sight of all the lights was an awesome tribute for the boys—one that touched them deeply. As the song ended, the boys took a bow to show their appreciation for this special tribute.

This ninety-minute show went by so fast. It was time for the show's closing number. The song was "Lucy in the Sky with Diamonds." The closing refrains were sung in the stormy and foggy atmosphere. Rudy, as always, gave a cue for when it was time to do the ending note to each of the songs they did. Garland, as he sang the refrain over and over, began to wonder when Rudy's cue would come.

Finally, with the crowd standing and swaying from side to side, Rudy's cue came for the others to stop. Just as Rudy cued them to stop, Garland cued them for one more chorus. Doing the lead vocals on a song did have its perks. If this was to be Garland's final song, he wanted it to be something to be remembered.

The applause after the song was deafening.

The boys left the stage, heading straight to the open arms of their families and Saul.

"I wish I had brought my camera," Sissy said.

"I have one in the car out in the first-row parking lot behind the rear entrance," Kevin said.

Sissy, after insisting that Kevin give her the keys, ran to get his camera.

A well-dressed man sitting next to Kevin approached the dressing-room area.

"I want to say that this show was as great as I have heard it would be," the man said. "My name is Joe Moss, and I am with Magic Sounds Inc. We own Magic Sounds Records. We have been watching you guys all summer long, and we want you on our label."

The boys began to hug each other and jump with the excitement. This was something they had always wanted. Garland couldn't wait for Sissy to return for the great news.

||||||||

Sissy exited the back entrance to the park. This part of the park was very secluded and was never recommended for a woman alone. As Sissy was walking down the aisle of cars, her path suddenly became blocked by two men. She stopped and turned around to seek another aisle. She began to walk faster and turned to enter the next aisle; the two men also blocked that entrance. She was so close to the park entrance, but it seemed like miles at the moment. Once again, she turned to take another aisle. She was blocked again. There were now three men.

"If you don't get away from me, I will scream," she said.

The men took no exception to her threat and began to come closer.

"Give us your purse. As loud as the crowd is inside, no one will ever hear you," the tallest of the three men said.

Sissy began to clutch the purse as they grabbed it. She began to struggle but was no match for one man, much less three. Her purse fell to the ground as one man began to tear her clothes. To keep her from screaming, she received a backhanded slap from one of the men, followed by fist. These were sensations she had never felt before. The combination knocked her off her feet. As she fell to the ground, one of the men moved to kick her. She knew she wouldn't leave here alive. For some reason she couldn't figure out, the kick was never landed.

A scuffle suddenly erupted between the three men and another man. The fight didn't last long. The Good Samaritan began to take control of all three of the men. She was about to lose consciousness when a blurred image of a face kneeling down to help her appeared.

"Sissy, are you okay? Let me get you some help. These guys will never harm you again," her savior said.

Before everything went black, Sissy recognized the face and murmured, "Thank you, Brandon."

Brandon flagged down a nearby visitor to the park, shouting, "Please get an ambulance! She's badly injured."

Sissy's concussion caused her to go in and out of consciousness. Each time she regained consciousness, Brandon was there, holding her, not leaving her side.

Finally, the ambulance and the police arrived on the scene. Brandon informed the police about Sissy and the three men lying on the pavement.

"What happened to these guys?" asked the officer.

At first, Brandon did not reply to his question.

"Did you have anything to do with this?" the officer asked.

Brandon looked up at the officer. "I could have killed them for what they did to Sissy."

Once the paramedics arrived, Brandon left Sissy with them and went to the gates to the park. He left word with the security office to contact James in the concert hall. Brandon then went back to work. There was much work to be done taking the stage down for the year.

He would miss setting up the drums; he loved playing them and hoped they appreciated the setups.

IIIIIIII

One of the security guards arrived backstage and told Saul the bad news about Sissy. Garland was standing nearby and could tell the officer had some bad news for Saul. He had never seen Saul this upset before. Saul walked over to where the boys were celebrating. He hated to diminish this special moment.

"James, I have some very bad news for you and Garland. I hate to ruin this moment. Something has happened to Sissy in the parking lot," Saul said.

Garland rushed over to hear what Saul said.

"She was mugged by three men in the parking lot and has been taken to the hospital," Saul said.

"I hope they caught the bastards who did this to my mother," Garland said.

"Better than that, son. All three were beaten very badly by a Good Samaritan. Whoever he was, he saved her life," the officer said.

James and Garland ran to where the car was parked and drove straight to the hospital.

Once Kevin received word about the incident, he, along with Adam and Suzanna, left to go to the hospital. The other band members followed.

In just a few minutes, James and Garland arrived at the hospital emergency room. Sissy was with the emergency-room doctor as they arrived. A nurse came out to talk to them, informing them she had a concussion and was bruised very badly. Hours passed before the doctor came out to talk to them.

"We are going to admit her to a room. We want to observe her for the rest of the night. Your wife will be fine, Mr. Summers. She is lucky to be alive," the doctor said.

As they wheeled Sissy from the emergency room to be placed

in a private room, Garland walked beside her bed, holding her badly swollen hand. This was going to be a very long night.

Kevin and the gang waited in the waiting room down the hall. Garland and James took turns giving them updated status reports. Sissy's condition did not change. Twelve hours passed since she'd first arrived.

The doctor came around that morning to check in on Sissy.

"This is taking longer than I had anticipated it would. I will order a CAT scan of her head to check for any further injuries. I don't think there will be any, but we need to make sure," he said.

Another six hours had elapsed by that time.

Garland and James were sitting in chairs on each side of Sissy's bed. Both were very tired and began to take a well-deserved nap. Just then, Sissy made a sound that woke them both up. They sprang to their feet and rushed to the pillow where her head lay. Sissy began to mumble again, struggling as if she were trying to escape.

Her eyes began to open, trying to focus on the scene in the room. Then, the mumble came again, much clearer than the last one. "Thank you, Brandon," she said.

Garland and James looked at each with the same puzzled look on their faces.

"Did she just say what I think she said?" Garland asked.

"I am not sure what you heard," James said.

After dismissing what they thought Sissy had said, the two fell back to sleep.

IIIIIIII

Twenty-four hours had passed since the incident occurred. The nurse came in to start another drip of glucose. They didn't want any further complications from dehydration.

Once again, Sissy began to open her eyes. Garland and James, sleeping in their chairs, were not aware she was awake.

"How are my two men doing?" Sissy said.

Garland raised his head, as if trying to awaken from a dream.

He was about to put his head back down when he saw Sissy smiling at him.

"Dad, Dad, she is awake!" Garland shouted.

Garland's voice awakened James. Each stood up and ran to hug her.

Sissy slowly began to regain her bearings.

"Where is Brandon?" she asked.

"Baby, Brandon left us several months ago," James said.

Both James and Garland knew it was the injury that made her forget that Brandon had left.

Sissy paused and shook her head, saying, "You don't understand me. I saw him."

"Mother, when did you see Brandon?" Garland asked.

Sissy began to sit up in the bed. She was now totally awake.

"Brandon is the one who stopped those three men. He saved my life," Sissy said as she began to cry.

Both James and Garland were lost for words when they heard her story.

Garland excused himself to inform the ones in the waiting room that Sissy was awake.

|||||||

When Garland arrived in the waiting room, everyone stood and began to hug each other when they heard the great news. Somehow, the news of a recording contract was not as important.

Across from the waiting room were the elevators. An elevator reached the floor where they were sitting, and stopped. The white light came on, and the bell rang, indicating this was the elevator's stop for this floor.

A couple emerged from the open doors. The young woman walked slightly ahead of the young man.

Kevin looked up to see the two walking and said to the young woman, "Tobie, we just got the news that Sissy will be okay," Kevin said.

Kevin was about to start another sentence when he stopped. He suddenly started to cry. At first, Garland and Adam thought it was the news of Sissy regaining consciousness. Then, Kevin dropped everything and ran to Tobie as she approached the waiting room. This took Adam and Garland by surprise. They now knew it was something other than the news of Sissy.

"Brandon, is that really you?" Kevin said, sobbing.

Both Garland and Adam turned instantly, hearing Kevin's question.

"Kevin, I forgot to tell you that I had a boyfriend. This is my boyfriend, Brandon. Somehow, I think you already know him," Tobie said with a very big smile.

Brandon clasped Kevin in a hug that Kevin would remember for the rest of his life.

Garland and Adam rushed to meet their old friend.

Garland began to wonder how Brandon knew they were here. He suddenly knew it was true that a Good Samaritan had saved Sissy's life, just as she and the security guard had told them.

"Brandon, there is someone who would really like to see you now," Garland said.

The two walked down to Sissy's room. Sissy was sitting up in her bed, with the pillows propping her up. James was sitting with his back to the door.

"Mother, you have a visitor. Tobie is here from the station with her boyfriend," Garland said.

James stood up and turned around to greet Tobie and to meet her boyfriend.

Sissy turned to greet Tobie as well. Sissy's tears flowed more heavily than Garland had ever witnessed.

Brandon went over to the bed.

"Hi, baby. How is my best girl doing?" Brandon said.

Sissy hugged Brandon harder than she had ever hugged anyone in her life. She couldn't stop her tears, which flowed from the joy and relief that Brandon was safe and had come home. Even more so, though, she sobbed because Brandon had saved them—just like he always did.

Tobie was very proud of Brandon. Her man had come home to his family.

"Brandon, I want to thank you for saving our dear Sissy's life," James said.

Later that evening when the doctor made his rounds, he noticed how well Sissy had rebounded.

"Looks like your medicine has done wonders," the doctor said.

"Oh, I am much better, Doc, but the medicine that turned me around is sitting right here on the bed," Sissy said as she sat there on the side of the bed, holding Brandon's hand.

17

THE EXCITEMENT STARTED early in the year of 1969. Brandon returned to his friends and adopted family. KARO made the switch of adding a third radio personality. Garland and Suzanna remained inseparable. Gone were the days of Aurora's Fire headlining summer performances at Elitch Gardens.

It was now time to get down to business with Aurora's Fire recording contract. Magic Sounds wanted a single to be released during the first quarter of the year. The single would be the introduction to a twelve-song album.

Things were happening very fast, and the times were very exciting. There was talk of a music festival in upstate New York. This show would be the show of all shows. Woodstock was to be the biggest concert in history. Festival attendees worked on their plans from all over the United States. Some of the biggest rock-and-roll artists of the day agreed to perform. Woodstock would actually be larger than the event organizers planned, lasting several days.

|||||||

Suzanna stopped by the Summerses' home one afternoon. Sissy answered the door. Garland and James were out running some errands. Suzanna said she was in the area and wanted Garland to take her to a movie.

There is something different about Suzanna today, Sissy thought as she invited her inside.

Suzanna seemed disoriented as she made her way into the living room.

"Are you okay, Suzanna?" Sissy inquired.

As Suzanna looked at Sissy, the expression on her face made Sissy think her mind was a million miles away. Suzanna took a seat on the couch, holding her head in her hands. Something was definitely wrong. Once again, Sissy inquired about her well-being.

This time, Suzanna raised her head to answer Sissy, saying, "No, I am not at all well."

"Suzanna, do you wish to tell me what is wrong?" Sissy said.

"I have been offered a modeling job," Suzanna said.

"My dear, that is wonderful. You should be very proud of yourself," Sissy said.

Suzanna sat there, once again in a daze, as if she were searching for the words she wanted to say next.

"No, it's not wonderful. They want me to move to California. That is where the work is. I would have to leave Garland, and I don't want to. But, at the same time, I do not want to pass up this opportunity," Suzanna said.

Suzanna's hair exuded a smoky smell that Sissy was not familiar with.

"Suzanna, is there something I can get for you?" Sissy asked.

Once again, Suzanna had that lost look in her eyes and on her face. She began to answer Sissy, but then, as if pushed over by a feather, she passed out on the couch.

|||||||

James and Garland arrived minutes afterward, to find Suzanna passed out on the Summerses' couch.

"What is wrong with Suzanna? Is she sick, Mother?" Garland asked.

Garland walked over to the couch where Suzanna lay. As he

approached her, Garland noticed the same scent in her hair. Unlike Sissy, Garland knew the scent. He didn't want his parents to know Suzanna had been smoking weed.

"I will get a pillow and blanket from my bed," Garland said.

Garland went to his room and picked up the special pillow his mother had made for him when he was a little boy in Roswell. Returning to the living room, he placed the pillow under Suzanna's head. He unfolded the blanket and gently covered her.

Sissy could see the passion her son had for Suzanna and didn't want him to be hurt.

"Garland, when you get a chance, I want to talk to you in the kitchen," Sissy said.

Sissy went into the kitchen and sat at the table, awaiting her son.

Garland entered the kitchen. He wanted something to drink. He wasn't sure what his mother wanted to talk to him about, but he was sure it was something serious. She had that serious look about her.

"Garland, we need to talk about what is bothering Suzanna. This is something you need to know before it's too late," Sissy said.

"What do you mean by 'too late,' Mother?" Garland asked.

"Suzanna doesn't want you to know that she has been approached to move to California by a modeling agency. She doesn't want to leave you. At the same time, Garland, this is a great opportunity for her. If she stays and doesn't go, she will always hold it against you for being the one who kept her from becoming something special," Sissy said.

Garland was shocked. Suzanna had never mentioned anything about this to him. Modeling would suit Suzanna. She always adored attention; in fact, she thrived on it. He knew his mother was right. If Suzanna didn't leave, she would never forgive him. He had to let her go and, at the same time, let her know just how much she meant to him.

"Do you love her?" Sissy asked.

Without any hesitation, Garland replied that he did.

He knew it was hard for a mother to tell her son something like this. Garland hugged his mother, letting her know how much she meant to him.

The front door suddenly slammed.

"James, is that you? Don't make so much noise. You will awaken Suzanna," Sissy said.

James walked into the kitchen. "I will do what? Is she asleep on the bed in the guest bedroom?"

Garland and Sissy rushed into the living room. Lying on the floor were the blanket and the pillow. Suzanna had left without a word.

Garland ran out the door, carrying the blanket, and drove after Suzanna. He felt he knew exactly where he would be able to find her. The drive would take thirty minutes. He knew Suzanna didn't have that much of a lead on him timewise. He wanted to arrive before nightfall.

As Garland drove into the park, he saw Suzanna's red Mustang parked near the trail leading to a cave they occasionally visited. The dampness of the night was already in the air. Just as he thought, Suzanna sat in the cave with her face buried against her knees. She wasn't aware of Garland's presence.

On the floor of the cave was a partially smoked marijuana cigarette. Garland stepped on the cigarette, putting it out. Suzanna reached to where she had put the cigarette down, with her head still against her knees. She began to run her hand along the cave's floor, searching for the joint. Her hand stopped at the toe of Garland's shoe, then began to roam over his foot, as if to continue the search for the joint. Not satisfied with the results, her hand began to climb his leg, stopping at his knee.

Suzanna took a deep breath before she had the courage to look up to see who was standing next to her in the cave. Her hand began to tremble, and Garland could sense the fear she was now feeling. "Baby" was all Garland had to say. Suzanna raised her head and hugged his leg as she cried. Garland comforted her tears and fear at the same time.

"Baby, let me get something out of the car," he said.

"Okay, but you'd better be right back," she said.

Garland assured her he would be back in a minute.

Garland left the cave to fetch the blanket from the car. He returned to the cave and leaned up against a wall. Suzanna snuggled up next to him as he covered them both with the blanket. After a few deep breaths and sighs, Suzanna fell asleep in his arms.

Sometime during the middle of the night, Garland fell asleep, lying back to back with Suzanna. As the first rays of sunlight entered the cave, signaling the beginning of a new day, Garland felt Suzanna's arm and leg wrapped around his body. Garland savored this moment. This was the first night the two had spent together.

Suzanna's hand explored Garland's body. She began to tease her lover. This was her way of letting Garland know how much she wanted him at that moment. Garland's heart began to race faster with his increasing desires. He felt her hand slip under his shirt, exploring his firm chest and stomach. Her fingertips teased his sensitive navel area, tracing circles around it. Her hand began to gently lift up his shirt, exposing his bare back. Suzanna began to kiss his back and traced his spine with her warm breaths of desire. Her free hand slipped under his body, reaching for his belt and zipper. She began to undo them both sliding down his pants. This was becoming more than he could resist.

Garland leaned back into Suzanna, taking his hand to hold her closer to him. As he drew her in closer, his hand felt her soft, smooth skin. To his surprise, Suzanna was already undressed, lying naked under their blanket. This was the final temptation. Garland quickly turned over to his lover, kissing her. Garland wanted her more now than ever. Suzanna kissed Garland again, pushing him on his back. At first, Garland thought it was her way of backing off. When Garland stopped, flat on his back, Suzanna started kissing him deeper and deeper. She began to squirm, wanting him more. He didn't want this kiss to end. Suzanna stopped her kiss long enough to mount Garland.

"Baby, I am going to make love to you like never before," she said.

The two made love all morning long. The night before was like a piece of coal, but the morning soon became a diamond. This was a night they would never forget.

||||||||

Garland hoped Suzanna would open up to him about her problem. He didn't want her to know Sissy clued him in about their talk. Garland wanted Suzanna to be the one to bring up the conversation of going to California. Neither of the two young lovers wanted the afternoon to end. This was so special, and it was something they both needed.

Suzanna, feeling like she was on cloud nine, began to open up to Garland.

"I have something I need to tell you, Garland. I have worried about this ever since I first received the offer," she said.

Garland knew what was coming next but didn't want to give any indication he already knew, so he simply asked, "What are you trying to tell me?"

Nervous, Suzanna paused for a moment, trying to gather the words she wanted to say. She reached for Garland's hand for security, hoping this would help her with what she was about to tell him.

"You know you mean more to me than anything in this world," she said. "If I go through with this, it will be the toughest thing I have ever done. I have been offered a modeling job with a major advertising agency."

Garland squeezed her hand. "That is what you are worried about telling me?"

"Partly. The job is in California. I will have to move to California. I don't want to leave you," she said.

Garland squeezed her hand with even more authority. He was not ready for this moment, but he knew Sissy was right: he had to let Suzanna pursue her dreams.

"Baby, that's wonderful," Garland said. "I will stand by you with whatever you decide you want to do. This is too good of an opportunity for you to pass up."

Suzanna fell once again into the comforting arms, knowing she would soon miss them.

"Do we have to leave now? Can we stay here longer?" she asked.

Garland began to think there was no reason to leave. They could stay longer.

"Of course, baby, we can stay longer," he said.

Suzanna hugged Garland.

"I want to make love to you again," she said.

Garland smiled and kissed her again.

The two spent the rest of the day together, filling each other's needs. The hours passed by quickly. After several hours of lovemaking, the two fell asleep in each other's arms.

When Suzanna awakened afterward, she wondered what time it was. She remembered it was dark when they were snuggling, but now it was daylight. Her sudden movements woke Garland. He, too, remembered it was dark before they fell asleep.

"Oh no! We have been here all night. People will be worried about us," he said.

They quickly gathered up their clothes and the blanket; arriving home wasn't going to be a pleasant experience.

|||||||

Joe Moss scheduled a meeting with the band the next morning. Everyone was in attendance except Garland. Garland was recuperating from his all-nighter with Suzanna.

"I want to schedule the recording room this Friday," Joe said. "Will you guys be far enough along that we can record some tracks and then give them to the producer and engineers? I have several studio musicians available as well."

Rudy assured Joe there wouldn't be a problem with the song they were working on, adding, "We have been working on a few other songs for the album as well."

"We can lay some tracks for those as well, and save them," Joe said.

As Joe left the station that morning, he couldn't remember a time when he had been more excited about an act.

"James, where is Garland?" Rudy asked.

"I am afraid you guys will have to do without him today. He was with Suzanna for the last two nights," James said.

The boys all laughed, each thinking that if they had been with Suzanna for two nights, they would need a day off too.

IIIIIII

Suzanna was scheduled to leave for California on Saturday. Garland wanted to spend as much time with her as he could. His time away from the band was beginning to negatively affect the practice sessions.

Friday morning arrived at the Magic Sounds Studio. Once again, Garland was late. Kevin had left some papers back at the station. He called Tobie and instructed her to bring them to the recording studio. Joe Moss informed the boys that studio recording time was very expensive, and tardiness would not be tolerated. Kevin assured Joe that, once Suzanna was in California, there wouldn't be any more problems with Garland.

Garland arrived with Suzanna on his arm.

"Hey, Garland, I am glad you could join us today. Joe Moss has eaten our ass out because of you," Rudy said.

Garland turned to his guitar without confronting Rudy. He felt it was best not to respond.

Joe introduced the boys to the producer and the engineer. The producer wanted to hear the ideas Rudy and Garland had for the song.

Rudy began to play the intro to the song, with Garland and the others joining in. Garland would be on the lead vocals for this song. Midway through the song, the producer stopped them.

"Fellas, we need a faster tempo from the drums. The beat is lagging behind," he said.

Once again, Rudy began the intro. Once again, the producer interrupted the song.

"It's still not right, fellas. The beat is all wrong for what we are trying to do," he said.

Sam was becoming frustrated with the producer's attack on his drumming talents.

"We may have to record the drums on a separate track and overlay them into the song," the producer said.

Once again, Rudy started the song. The producer did not interrupt this time. He wanted a replay after the song was finished.

"You guys, take ten; I am going into the control room to hear this take," the producer said.

A few minutes later, Tobie arrived with the paperwork Kevin needed. Brandon had accompanied her for the ride over to the studio. Both Tobie and Brandon saw the frustration in Kevin's face. Something wasn't going very well. The two of them joined Susannah where she sat on a nearby stool.

The producer returned to the studio. "We will have to do another take on the song, guys. It's still not right. Sam, you still need to pick your timing up. Let's get it right this time."

For the fourth time, Rudy began his intro. Sam began to play. This time, the producer stopped Sam even sooner than he had the other times.

"Well, if you think you can do it better, then have at it!" Sam said as he walked away from his drums, leaving the room.

The producer became livid. This type of attitude was all new to him. He really didn't have the time or patience for such disrespect.

Joe was sitting in the control room, listening to the entire incident.

"I Icy, guys, I thought you really wanted this. Maybe we will reschedule for another day," Joe said.

The boys began to pack up their equipment for another day. The studio time was becoming very expensive with each retake.

Kevin thanked Tobie for bringing the paperwork to the studio.

"Kevin, I am sorry the boys' big day was not a good one," Tobie said.

Kevin thanked Tobie for her concern.

Tobie and Brandon stood up from their stools to leave the studio. Well, at least that was what Tobie thought they were doing.

Brandon winked at Kevin and patted him on the shoulder.

"I didn't think you guys were a bunch of quitters," Brandon said. "The guys I know would lick this. Hey, Mr. Producer, let's try this one more time before you call it a day."

"And who the hell do you think you are? Ringo Starr?" the producer said sarcastically.

Brandon had heard enough of the song to know what the beat should be.

"No, but this will be the last take you will need for this song. You don't have anything to lose but a few more minutes, and we are all here now," Brandon said.

The producer dismissed Brandon and began to call the session off.

"I think you'd better listen to what the boy is telling you," Kevin said to the producer.

The producer stopped in his tracks before leaving the studio.

"Okay, one-take wonder," he said. "I will give you one take. That is all you will get."

Smiling and winking at the producer, Brandon said, "I never need more than one take."

Brandon took a seat on the stool behind the drum set. He began to loosen up. This was the first time he had played the drums since working on the crew in Elitch Gardens.

"Hey, Mr. Producer, tell your engineer to get his machine ready," Brandon said.

"Hey, Rudy, are you ready to make your record? Get ready for your introduction. We will be going home soon," Garland said.

Rudy wasn't quite sure how to take this incident, but he followed Garland's advice.

Rudy began his intro once again. Garland began the vocals, and the other instruments fell right into place.

The producer was shocked by the results. The music was awesome, and Garland's vocals worked perfectly with the harmonies. But, most of all, who was this guy who just came in and sat down at the drums, nailing the arrangement for this song?

Garland wrapped up the final notes for the song as Rudy wound down the instrumental.

The producer rushed to the drum set to shake Brandon's hand, saying, "Damn, you are good."

"Well, Mr. Producer, I learned a long time ago that it takes you twice as much time to do something wrong as it does to do it right. So I do it right," Brandon said.

The producer turned to his engineer in the sound room, giving a thumbs-up sign.

"You guys sit tight while I do a replay in the control room," the producer said.

The boys sat down, waiting for the final results. The producer, Joe, and Kevin went into the control room for the playback. The engineer adjusted the sound level and began the playback. Soon the three men were all smiles. The producer had another first that day. There was absolutely nothing he could add that would make this take better. He would record the song as it was. This was a first not only for a group's first time in the recording studio, but for any song he had ever recorded.

IIIIIIII

The Saturday Garland hoped would never arrive eventually did. Suzanna was all packed for her California adventure. Garland stopped off that morning at a local shopping center. He wanted to get Suzanna something very special to remember him by. Shopping for a girl was definitely something he didn't have experience with. He was about to surrender this idea when he came across an item in a local jewelry store's showcase.

This is perfect, he thought.

As Garland entered the store, a clerk greeted him at the main counter. Garland described the item that had caught his attention in the showcase. The clerk excused himself to retrieve the item. Garland took a seat on a stool at the counter, awaiting the clerk's return. As the clerk locked the showcase and began to return to where Garland was sitting, Garland noticed he was carrying two cases.

"This is a very good choice, sir," the man said, opening the case for Garland's approval and taking the item out of its case.

Garland's smile indicated his approval of the item.

"Sir, I told you this was a very good choice, but now I want to show you an excellent choice," the man said as he opened up the larger case, revealing an excellent choice, just as he had promised.

"You are absolutely correct; this is the perfect choice. I can't believe I overlooked it in your showcase. I will take it," Garland said.

The clerk, realizing the importance of this gift, offered to have the item engraved, free of charge.

Garland accepted his offer and requested that the item to be gift wrapped.

Garland left the jewelry store to meet Suzanna. The trip to the cave seemed to take forever. Suzanna's Mustang was parked near the trail to the cave. Garland parked and began the walk to the cave. As he was walking, he began to sing a song along the way. Suzanna loved to hear Garland's voice, and this was very romantic. Garland entered the cave where Suzanna was waiting. She looked absolutely stunning. Her beautiful long black hair was shiny and soft as silk. The white sand dollar necklace complemented her dark tan below her neckline.

Garland approached her with the surprise behind his back. He arrived at the spot where Suzanna was standing, savoring every minute. She was a pure treat for his eyes that day, and he didn't know the next time he would have this treat again. Finally, Garland could no longer resist the temptation of the white-frosted lips, kissing them to determine their flavor. As Garland kissed Suzanna, her hands embraced her lover, exploring the hands holding the box he tried so desperately to hide from her.

Each time, Garland would switch the box from hand to hand, keeping it just out of her reach. The harder Suzanna tried to capture the box, the more tickled he became, until, finally, Garland broke off the kiss, bursting out in loud laughter.

"You win, baby. You have found the hidden treasure," Garland said as he turned over the gift-wrapped box.

Wanting to keep the special gift-wrap paper, Suzanna gently unwrapped her surprise. After removing the paper and folding it, she removed the lid of the box. Several layers of tissue paper protected the box's contents.

Garland seized the box at the moment Suzanna was about to

discover its contents. His desires made sure Suzanna would have to wait for her gift. Not knowing when they would be together again, Garland and Suzanna began an encore performance of lovemaking in their special love cave. There was a sudden loud burst of thunder as a light rain began to fall. A slow rain was very erotic when you were with the person you love. Suzanna's passion for Garland that day was out of this world. Time, as usual, was too fast for the two young lovers. It was getting late; this time, an all-nighter wasn't to be.

Garland retrieved the partially opened box. Suzanna once again began to open the box, removing the tissue paper. She began to cry as she took out the silver anklet. The anklet supported two silver sand dollars joined together. On each sand dollar was engraved a name: "Garland" on one, and "Suzanna" on the other. Garland placed the anklet on her ankle and kissed her. The special moment drained Suzanna. She had fought very hard not to break down. Suzanna regained control of her emotions as she dressed.

Garland walked Suzanna to her car, opening the door for her entry. The moment seemed so final for them both. Sometimes a simple goodbye was the best way. Suzanna started her car and drove off, with Garland standing in the now-steady rainfall. It was hard for him to let go of something so beautiful. Love sometimes means giving the person you love the freedom to go; if it is truly love, he or she will be back.

IIIIIIII

Garland arrived home soon after leaving the love of his life. Sissy was sitting in the kitchen as he entered through the garage.

"Why are you wet?" she asked.

Garland just smiled, saying, "No comment."

Sometimes there were things you didn't need to talk to your mother about. This was one of those times.

"Suzanna is on her way to California," Garland said.

Sissy was impressed with Suzanna's ambition.

"Where will she be staying? California, from what I have been told, is a lot faster paced than Denver," she said.

"She will be living with Chad's sister. She is divorced and has a daughter Suzanna's age. I don't think she would have attempted to do this if it wasn't for that," Garland said.

The stress of the day began to take its toll on him. He kissed Sissy good night and went to his bedroom. Sleep often filled a void better than anything else.

18

JOE MOSS AND the producer met at the Magic Sounds Studio. Both were very impressed with Brandon's talent. They agreed that Sam was a very likable guy, but this was a business decision.

"Kevin, this is Joe Moss with Magic Sounds. My producer and I were going over the tracks we recorded. We are very impressed with Brandon. He is a great talent, and we can do so many arrangements with him in the band."

Kevin agreed with Joe. He knew, better than anyone else, the talents Brandon possessed.

"Do you think he would consider joining the band?" Joe asked.

"Joe, Brandon has been in a healing process," Kevin said. "I promised myself that, as much as I was aware of his talents, I would not pressure Brandon to come back. I wanted him to heal. I knew that, when he was ready, Brandon would let me know. I do believe that what he did in the studio that day is a big step in his healing."

Joe understood what Kevin had told him. He asked Kevin to inform him if Brandon's desire ever changed.

Kevin ended the phone call with Joe Moss and paged Tobie to come to his office.

"Yes, sir, you wished to see me?" Tobie said as she stood in Kevin's office doorway.

"Tobie, that was Joe Moss I was talking to on the phone. He would really like for Brandon to consider playing with the band. I would like to talk to him," Kevin said.

Tobie smiled at the idea of Brandon playing again. She was very impressed by his performance that day in the studio.

"I will talk to him this evening," she said. "I have a secret that might make Brandon decide to come back to the band."

Refusing to give Kevin even a clue as to what it be, she left Kevin's office, smiling to herself.

Tobie indeed had a secret that might bring Brandon back to the band. Now that Elitch Gardens was in its off-season, Brandon's work hours were cut back. His job mostly consisted of repair and maintenance work that the park required. She began to put a plan together in her mind to work things out for the best of one and all.

Tobie arrived home that evening before Brandon. The small apartment they shared was closer to the station than the park. She anxiously awaited his arrival. Brandon arrived to find Tobie very excited. She was in an unusual mood, and he didn't have a clue what had caused it.

"Brandon, I want to talk to you about something," Tobie said. "Kevin wants you to drop by to see him in the morning."

"I think I can do that," Brandon said. "I am off tomorrow. My hours seem to be fewer and fewer these days. What is it he wants to see me about?"

Not wanting to place any pressure on Brandon, Tobie insisted she didn't have a clue as to the reason.

She would only say, "All I can tell you is that I have a secret that will change our lives. That secret that will be revealed tomorrow."

|||||||

Suzanna reached her destination in California. Her aunt and her cousin, Jodi, were very happy to have her there. The photographer who was to create her modeling portfolio had a studio several blocks away. Suzanna began to unload the car, removing the few items she had brought. After unloading the Mustang, Suzanna wanted to call Garland to assure him that she was okay.

"Can I use your phone to call Colorado before it gets too late?" Suzanna asked her aunt.

Jodi showed Suzanna to the room she would occupy during her stay in California. There was a phone on the nightstand beside the bed. Suzanna called Garland.

"Hello," said Sissy's voice on the other end of the line.

"Sissy, it's Suzanna. Is Garland there?" Suzanna asked.

"Suzanna, are you okay? Are you in California?" Sissy asked.

Suzanna assured Sissy everything was okay but she would like to talk to Garland very much.

Sissy placed the phone on the table; Garland was in his room working on something.

"Garland, you have a phone call," she said.

"Tell them I am busy. I am working on something," he said.

Sissy walked over to the bed to see what Garland was working on. He was writing in a notebook.

"Baby, I think you will want to take this call," she said with a big smile.

Garland closed the notebook and went to answer the phone.

Sissy's curiosity got the best of her; she opened the notebook. Inside were the words to a song. She began to read, thinking the words were very beautiful.

"Hello," Garland said as he picked up the phone, then asking, "Baby, is that really you?"

Sissy could hear her son. Not wanting to listen in on his conversation, but also not wanting to get caught snooping in his notebook, she listened for the end of his conversation with Suzanna.

"I miss you, and I love you" were the final words she heard Garland say, indicating the end of the call.

This was Sissy's cue to shut the notebook. She exited the room quickly and softly, smiling to herself. Her son was truly the gem of her life.

||||||||

The next morning, Joe Moss arrived at the radio station to meet with Kevin. Kevin and Joe went into the conference room. The band members were on their way as well. Joe brought along the two tapes the producer had recorded that day in the studio, thinking this would be the best way to address the drumming issue. If everyone heard the same thing he and the producer heard on the playback, their decision might be easier to accept.

"Joe, I have a plan for later on during the meeting," Kevin said. "I do not want anyone else to know. I am not promising anything, but we may have a chance with Brandon."

The boys began arriving and immediately went into the conference room. Garland and Beau were the last ones to arrive.

"Fellas, I have something I want you to hear, and then we have a decision that needs to be made," Joe said.

Joe played a tape of the first take.

The boys looked at each other, thinking they liked what they heard.

"Before you start to congratulate each other, I want you to hear the second tape," Joe said.

Joe then played a tape of the second tape. He immediately detected the difference in the two. From the looks on the boy's faces, they did as well.

"What do you guys think?" Joe asked.

One by one, everyone agreed that the second tape was far better than the first tape.

"We need to use the second tape," Rudy said.

The other boys agreed with Rudy.

The door to the conference room suddenly opened. In came Tobie and Brandon. They were not aware of what had transpired in the room before their arrival.

"I am glad you all agree with me," Joe said. "There is a problem, though. A problem we need to discuss."

"The second tape you heard is of the take when Brandon performed," Kevin said.

The room became very quiet.

Brandon, still having no idea as to why Kevin wanted him there, quickly said, "It's okay to use the demo I played on. I was only glad I could help."

Joe said, "Sam, we think you are a great guy; but this is a business decision. One we all need to agree on."

Brandon quickly interjected, "I didn't come here to create any problems. I don't know why I am even here."

"We are not trying to force you out, Sam," Joe said. "I know you can play other instruments."

Feeling like he was intruding on his friends, Brandon dismissed the idea of replacing Sam as the drummer.

"Brandon, you make us a lot better. Everyone here today is a witness to the difference you make," Adam said.

Sam added, "Brandon, I want to do what is best for all of us. If it means that I step down as the drummer and play another instrument, then I will."

Once again, Brandon refused to be the divider and started to leave the room.

Tobie, standing the closest to the door, stepped in front of Brandon, blocking his exit.

"Kevin, I would like to say something, if I may," Tobie said.

Kevin nodded that it was all right.

Tobie said, "I told you yesterday I had a secret, Kevin. Even Brandon doesn't know about this. Brandon, this will affect you most of all: we are going to have a baby."

Brandon turned to Tobie. "You are pregnant?"

Tobie smiled, with a tear in her eye.

"Yes, baby," she said. "You are going to be a father."

Brandon hugged Tobie, lifting her into the air. This was the happiest day of his life.

"Brandon, we are all very happy for the two of you. You can really use some extra money now, more than ever," Kevin said.

Brandon set Tobie down. Holding hands, the two walked over to Joe Moss.

"Mr. Moss, I would be honored to join Aurora's Fire," Brandon said.

The others then crowded around Brandon and Tobie. This was a happy day for everyone.

|||||||

Suzanna was early for her portfolio shoot.

"Hello, are you here for an appointment?" the receptionist asked.

"Yes, my name is Suzanna Royal, and I am here for my portfolio shoot."

The receptionist escorted Suzanna into the studio.

The photographer smiled as Suzanna entered the studio.

"I am pleased to meet you, Suzanna," he said. "My name is Jean Pierre."

He had a very sexy French accent. Suzanna began to blush. Getting attention from an attractive older man was something new for her, and she liked it very much.

"We will start with some head shots. I want everyone to see your beauty," Jean said.

With each compliment Suzanna received from Jean, her attraction to him grew stronger.

Jean stepped out from behind the camera and began to pose Suzanna for the shots he envisioned.

Suzanna loved the touch of Jean's hands as he positioned her for each pose. This man knew exactly what he was doing: not only was he pushing the right buttons on his camera, he was pushing hers as well.

The glow in Suzanna's eyes let Jean know she was attracted to him.

This was a very handsome, sophisticated man, and he was all hers for the time being.

"Now that we have finished the head shots for your portfolio, I want to do some fashion shots as well," Jean said. "I have some clothes in the other room. Let's start with a blue gown."

Suzanna went into the dressing room. There on the rack was this beautiful blue chiffon gown. She fell in love with it immediately.

Suzanna quickly changed and returned to the studio. As she entered the studio, the look on Jean's face let her know he was pleased. Pleasing Jean Pierre was a turn-on for Suzanna. This, too, was a new feeling for her.

"This time, I want you to pose for me. Show me the feelings you are experiencing at this moment," he said.

Suzanna began to play up to the camera. Each click of the camera's shutter encouraged Suzanna. She was very beautiful, and it was evident she loved the attention.

"Let's wrap up the gown shoot. Select one of the swimsuits on the rack. I want you to choose the one you think complements you the best," Jean said.

He eagerly waited for Suzanna to return from the dressing room.

Suzanna entered the studio, wrapped in a terry-cloth bathrobe. She wanted to surprise Jean Pierre, hoping to turn him on. She began to drop her robe. Underneath was a very small mint-green bikini. Jean Pierre rushed to his camera and began to focus the camera. As he began to snap the pictures, there was something wrong. The camera was not advancing his film. He stood behind the camera and began to laugh out loud. This was a big surprise to Suzanna. He instantly saw the disappointment in her face.

Realizing the sudden laugh might have given Suzanna the wrong impression, Jean Pierre approached Suzanna.

"I laughed because, in the heat of taking your other pictures, I ran out of film," Jean Pierre said, comforting his model.

Suzanna laughed as well. Now she could relax and let the camera know her feelings.

The swimsuit pictures became the highlight of the day's portfolio shoot.

"I will have the proofs ready tomorrow afternoon if you would like to view them," he said.

Suzanna smiled, assuring Jean Pierre she would return the next afternoon.

||||||||

Jean Pierre finished developing Suzanna's portfolio pictures. Never was he prouder of a client than he was of Suzanna. He sensed that, before long, Suzanna would have to turn work down. She was astonishingly beautiful, with a very glamorous, sexy look.

Suzanna entered the studio to view her pictures. Once again, she began to melt seeing Jean Pierre. Having a handsome man paying her this much attention was flattering.

Jean Pierre was devoting his attention to her, and she knew Jean Pierre could have any woman he wanted. Why shouldn't she be the one he wanted? She wanted to give some kind of sign to Jean Pierre that she was attracted to him but didn't quite know the way to display her feelings.

"Can you excuse me, Jean? I need to freshen up in the ladies' room," Suzanna said.

This is my chance to draw him in, she thought as she entered the restroom.

Suzanna looked into the mirror as she applied lip gloss and teased her hair. She was very well endowed and was determined to use this to her advantage. Suzanna unbuttoned the top two buttons of her blouse, hinting at the French bra she wore. She gently sprayed a mist of her perfume om her wrists and, for the final touch, in her cleavage. Suzanna was going for the kill this afternoon. After being in California for only two days, this young girl had grown up very fast. She opened the door and returned to the studio.

Jean Pierre turned as she entered the room. He wasn't prepared for what he was about to see.

"Suzanna, when I was shooting your portfolio, I thought I had witnessed a goddess. I was wrong; I am now seeing a goddess. I have something for this special occasion."

Jean removed two champagne glasses from a cabinet and filled them with very nice imported champagne.

"I want to propose a toast," he said. "To a long-lasting career."

The two interlocked their arms, drinking the champagne.

This is a perfect time for a kiss, she thought.

Jean Pierre looked into her eyes, seeing her desire as he finished his champagne. Suzanna finished her last sip at almost the same instant. She began to move closer to Jean Pierre. She wanted to feel those sexy French lips on hers. She knew that much-anticipated kiss was just a breath away.

"Congratulations, my dear, on your great portfolio," Jean Pierre said as he removed his arm from hers.

Reaching for her hand, Jean kissed it.

Suzanna had totally misread his intentions. Jean Pierre was very professional, but, most of all, he was a gentleman. She now knew the relationship was to be professional and nothing more.

IIIIIII

Suzanna returned to her aunt's home. Jodi was entertaining friends that afternoon before her mother came home. Jodi and her guests were outside on the patio.

"Cuz, is that you? Hey, come on out and meet some of my friends," Jodi said.

Suzanna walked out on the patio, and her entrance drew attention from two of the guys.

"Jodi, this is your cousin? Where have you been hiding her?" one of the boys said.

"Well, she is a hillbilly. She is from Colorado," Jodi said.

Turning to Suzanna, he said, "I'm Brad. I don't know much about Colorado, but if there are hillbillies there like you, I am ready to move there."

After the incident at the studio, ridicule from Jodi was something Suzanna could do without at the moment. She left the patio and went to her room.

Jodi lit up another joint. She didn't know what Suzanna's problem was, and, at the moment, she didn't care.

Brad, sensing Suzanna's feelings might have been hurt, went inside to check on her.

Suzanna was changing into some more-comfortable clothes when Brad stopped at her partially opened door. He enjoyed the view as she finished changing her clothing. Brad, already high from pot, stumbled into her room. Suzanna jumped at his entrance. She wasn't aware she had been followed. She was sitting on her bed as he entered the room.

"I think you'd better leave while you are ahead!" she warned.

"Hey, you want to cool it? I just came here to give you some relief," Brad said.

He reached into his shirt pocket and pulled out a fresh joint, saying, "Let this take the edge off. You look like you need it much more than I do."

Suzanna took the joint and placed it into her mouth as Brad lit the cigarette for her. With each hit, Suzanna began to feel at ease. Suzanna's demeanor quickly changed, and she became very cordial toward Brad as they took turns hitting on the joint. Brad took the final drag off the cigarette.

"Would you like another?" he asked.

Suzanna nodded her approval.

After sharing the second joint, Suzanna took the final draw. She then curled up on a pillow and went to sleep. Brad, higher than Suzanna, passed out on the floor.

Suzanna's aunt arrived home, and the party immediately came to an end.

||||||||

The boys arrived at the Magic Sounds Studio to wrap up the flip side to the single. The boys were divided as to which song was to be the flip side of their first release. The easiest solution would be to do an instrumental or one of the songs performed during their summer engagement at Elitch Gardens.

After several hours of debate, the decision was made to do the instrumental. Doing an instrumental would also allow them to determine which instrument Sam would play from now on. No one wanted Sam out of the group; and yet, at the same time, it was obvious that they were a much better act with Brandon on the drums. Rudy lobbied for a song he had finished to be their flip-side release.

"Rudy, we will do a follow-up release with your song as the featured song. All groups need to have a follow-up song after their first hit," Joe Moss said with a smile.

Joe knew the business, so Rudy agreed. He would hate for his song to overshadow their first record. After all, the bigger this song would become, the more anticipation for his song.

The session ended that day with not only the instrumental song wrapped up, but several other cuts for the album completed as well, one of which would be Rudy's song, which also would be included on the album.

Garland was very excited that their record was completed. It was ready to produce for sale and play on the radio. He wanted Suzanna to share in this big news and rushed home to call her.

"Hello, is Suzanna there?" Garland said.

"Yes, but she isn't in any shape to talk to anyone," Jodi said.

It was a very big letdown for Garland not being able to share his excitement with the person who meant the most to him.

"Is there anything wrong?" Garland asked.

Jodi laughed.

Garland failed to see the humor in his question. He asked, "What is going on? Is there a problem with Suzanna?"

"Well, nothing that will not be cured in several hours. She had to come back down from last night's high," Jodi said.

Garland ended the call, but he still wanted very badly to share the great news with Suzanna.

||||||||

Magic Sounds gave the boys several promotional copies of the hit-side record, to be distributed for special gifts. Garland began to fill out the list of those he would mail or deliver copies to. The local stations would begin playing the song the next day. There were two special packages Garland finished that evening. He autographed the record labels and their jackets, then placed the records in their respective packages. As he finished up the packages, he paused, thinking how special it would be to be there as each person heard the record for their first time. Not wanting to waste another minute, Garland left for the post office. He wanted next-day delivery on the two most-important packages.

The next afternoon, in separate parts of the country, two express-delivery drivers entered the driveways of their respective recipients. The two packages would be approached very differently.

One package was delivered to the home of Suzanna's aunt, in California. The driver approached the front door. There was no one there to accept the package. Researching his instructions, the driver noticed it was okay to leave the package in a secure place, which he did, placing a notice on the front door as to the location of the package.

Jodi was the first to arrive home that afternoon. She read the note on the front door and proceeded to the package's location. Seeing that the package was for Suzanna, when Jodi entered the house, she deposited the package in Suzanna's bedroom.

Suzanna arrived home that evening from her first modeling job. Upon entering her room, she noticed the package. She began to read the return address on the label, and then she put the package where Jodi had left it.

"Suzanna, I have something you would love. Come on out to the patio!" Jodi shouted.

Suzanna went to the patio. There was Jodi, already enjoying a joint.

"I sure could use one now." Suzanna said.

Jodi took a freshly rolled joint from her purse and handed it to Suzanna. Suzanna lit the joint and smiled as she drew her first hit. Jodi and Suzanna shared the final cigarette in Jodi's purse.

This is the life Suzanna, thought.

Suzanna took the last drag from the joint and extinguished it in the kitchen sink. She returned to her room, without giving Garland's gift a thought.

That same afternoon, in Goldsboro, North Carolina, a delivery driver delivered a package. The doorbell was answered promptly by a young Duke University coed.

"I have a package for Brenda Fisher," the driver said.

Brenda acknowledged the driver and gladly signed for the package's delivery. Brenda stepped into the Fishers' living room and began to open the package. She opened the box to find the contents safely packed with protective Styrofoam. Inside she found a note Garland had written especially for her:

> Many years ago, you planted a dream deep inside me.
> Today, that dream sprouted, and I have you to thank.
> I want to thank you for being a friend and also for coming back into my life.
>
> Love,
>
> Garland Summers

Under the note, Brenda found an autographed 45 record. She immediately removed the 45 and placed it on the turntable.

As the record began to play, Valerie Fisher entered the room. It was unlike her daughter to buy records.

"Did you buy this record today?" Valerie asked.

As the music began to play, Brenda didn't immediately answer her mother.

Valerie sensed something was wrong with her daughter and was concerned as to why she was sad.

"Brenda, what has you so upset?" Valerie asked.

Brenda turned to face her mother. Her tears weren't tears of sorrow but happiness.

"Mother, Garland always told me he would be something special one day. I am so, so proud of him. My heart is not saddened by the gift; my heart smiles. He still is my true love," Brenda said.

Ironically, these two packages were sent with the equal affection by Garland, but each was accepted and received in such a different manner.

Garland Summers was on his way to stardom, and Brenda knew it.

19

DURING THE LAST week of May 1969, Aurora's Fire's first record began to receive airtime. Brenda was driving that morning, on her way to class, when a familiar voice began to come through the radio. She instantly recognized the song as the one Garland had sent her. This was the first time Brenda heard the song on the radio. She had played it for many hours on her record player at home.

As her emotions began to overwhelm her, Brenda pulled off the road to enjoy the song. She was very proud of Garland. He was fulfilling his childhood dream. A dream that began one summer afternoon during a pool party. Brenda sat on the roadside until the song was finished. She didn't want anything to interrupt this special moment. As the song finished, the DJ announced that the song had moved into *Billboard*'s top forty for the week ending May 31, 1969.

After driving several miles down the road, Brenda's habit of radio-station hopping took control. It was on the switch to the second station, as if by magic, that she again heard Garland singing on the radio. With a big smile and tears in her eyes, Brenda sat in her car to listen to the song's ending.

As Brenda entered her classroom that morning, several of her friends noticed there was something different about Brenda.

"What did you have for breakfast?" one of her friends asked.

Brenda began to giggle and then replied, "There is no better way to start the day than to have someone very special to you sing to you on your car radio."

This was a very good day!

||||||||

Several hours later, in California, Suzanna was arriving for her latest modeling shoot. She was to shoot a very sexy TV commercial for a popular women's cigarette. If the TV commercial viewed well, there would also be a whole series of print ads using Suzanna as the symbol for the cigarette brand.

One of Jean Pierre's friends was doing the film shoot. The commercial began to run into hours of shooting, with several different wardrobes filmed. The film crew was beginning to tire when the director decided they had captured the desired look for the commercial.

Suzanna went to her dressing room to change into her clothes. There was a knock on her door, and she opened it to find the director, Tony.

"I thought you might like to join me for dinner. You were marvelous today and really put a lot into our shoot," he said.

Suzanna paused to enjoy Tony's handsome face and body.

"I would love to join you. I am actually very hungry," she said.

"You can leave your car here. We can take my Mercedes," he said.

"I know a very special restaurant I think you will like," Tony said. "It also has the best view of the city."

Suzanna smiled at Tony as he drove into the hills above Los Angeles. As the Mercedes made its way into the hills, a song began to play on the radio.

"I can't believe they are playing this song again. I am beginning to believe it's the only song they have on this station," Tony said as he switched stations.

Suzanna didn't have a clue as to what Tony was talking about.

Tony pulled into the restaurant's parking lot and up to the valet's desk. The same song began to play on the new station. This time, Tony didn't change the station. The valet opened the door, and they would soon be inside the restaurant.

"Sir, welcome to the Madrid," The maître d' said.

"We would like a table on the patio," Tony said as he tipped the man twenty dollars.

Tony really knows how to treat a girl and make her feel very special, Suzanna thought. She was not accustomed to this type of treatment.

Tony ordered a bottle of champagne and then ordered food for the two of them. With each flicker of candlelight, Tony saw the beauty in Suzanna.

"You are absolutely gorgeous," he said.

The compliment made Suzanna blush as she took a sip of champagne. This was the first time she was romanced in this manner, and she enjoyed it very much.

"The meal was very good, and the champagne is wonderful," Suzanna said.

She was on her third glass of the imported champagne. The view of the city was very romantic, and the sky was full of stars.

Tony ordered bread pudding with rum sauce for their dessert. The waiter delivered the pudding, along with a special blend of coffee that complemented the sauce fantastically.

"Tony, it's getting late, and I am very tired," Suzanna said.

The champagne had left her feeling very good. Tony walked behind Suzanna's chair and pulled it away from the table. Suzanna stood from her chair, and, as she stepped away from the chair, she lost her balance, falling into Tony's arms. Suzanna's eyes immediately met Tony's eyes. Already in his arms, they were just inches apart. The temptation was too much for both of them. Suzanna shocked herself by kissing Tony. Tony, not wanting to disappoint her, returned the kiss. Tony took Suzanna's hand and led her from the restaurant.

The valet took Tony's ticket and returned with the Mercedes. Tony drove from the valet's desk, stopping at the front parking lot exit. Tony placed the car in park and reached over to where Suzanna was sitting. She knew Tony wanted her, and she wanted him. Tony kissed her deep and long this time. He wanted Suzanna to feel his desire.

"Tony, let's go to your apartment. I don't feel like driving home," Suzanna said.

Tony smiled and assured Suzanna everything would be okay. As they arrived at Tony's apartment's garage, he turned the radio off just as that same song began to play.

Suzanna wasn't aware that Garland was singing this song. She'd had the privilege of only hearing the first few parts. She was so preoccupied with everything going on with her modeling job that she didn't even recognize it as an Aurora's Fire song.

The night was even more spectacular than the dinner. Tony's apartment was the typical playboy pad, designed for partying.

"Suzanna, come into the dining room. I have something you will like," Tony said.

As she entered the dining room, Tony arranged a white chalky substance in rows on a glass plate. Tony gave Suzanna a thin straw. Not wanting to appear to be an inexperienced child, Suzanna waited for Tony to begin so that she could follow his lead.

Tony began to snort the cocaine. As he completed each row, he raised his head and then switched to the other nostril. This was a first, but she didn't let on, not wanting to come across as inexperienced. Suzanna began to snort her first row. Just as Tony had done earlier, she raised her head and switched nostrils for the next row. Her first experience was a burning sensation. And then it started: she became disoriented and light-headed. Still, she did four rows of coke.

Tony then led Suzanna into the bedroom. He began to undress her. It was at this moment that Tony began to realize this was her first time with cocaine. As he began to remover her outer clothing, Suzanna passed out and fell onto the bed. She would be out for hours. Tony's desires wouldn't be fulfilled that evening.

Morning arrived, and Suzanna woke up with a very bad headache. She knew something had made her feel like this but didn't have a clue as to what it was.

Tony entered the bedroom, carrying a cup of fresh coffee. "Good morning. How are you feeling?"

Suzanna whispered, "Please talk softly. The noise is killing my head."

Tony laughed and agreed.

"As soon as you are ready, we can go back to your car. There is no rush," Tony said.

After almost finishing her coffee, Suzanna realized she had been out all night long without notifying anyone.

"I need to leave very soon," she said.

Suzanna dressed, and Tony drove her back to the studio parking lot to get her car.

Suzanna entered her car and left the studio. She began the thirty-minute drive back to her aunt's house. She knew she had been inconsiderate in not letting anyone know that she was all right and was spending the night elsewhere. Suzanna was pulling into the driveway when the song Tony kept referring to began to play on her car radio. This time, she wanted to hear it in its entirety.

Midway through the song, Suzanna began to recognize a familiar voice. She began to dismiss the idea that it was Garland. After all, she was sure he would have told her the good news. As the song finished, the DJ informed his listeners that this song, Aurora's Fire's "Dream Beauty," was the fastest-moving song on the charts, now holding the number-forty spot on the *Billboard* charts.

As Suzanna entered her aunt's house, a very irate cousin and aunt greeted her.

"Do you have any idea what you have put us through?" her aunt said.

Suzanna knew she was wrong and began to apologize, assuring her aunt it wouldn't happen again. After Suzanna and her aunt reached an agreement on the incident, Suzanna informed her that Garland's song was on the radio.

"It really pisses me off that he never called to tell me the news," Suzanna said.

"Did you ever open the package you received two weeks ago?" Jodi asked.

Suzanna looked puzzled by her cousin's question.

"I left it for you in your room, and you put it on the dresser," Jodi said.

All three of them went into Suzanna's bedroom. Suzanna, always in a hurry, had thrown a blouse on top of the package, forgetting its existence.

She began to open the package, finding its contents packed with special care and a note.

"Suzanna, my love, we finally did it. We are now a real recording group. We are on our way, and I want you with me," the note from Garland read.

The carefully packed contents contained a 45 record dedicated to Suzanna.

"I think you have been a little too hard on Garland. You have been so wrapped up in yourself that you didn't take the time to care about anyone else," her aunt said.

Suzanna began to cry. How could she have been so cold toward Garland?

"Can we play the record on your stereo?" she asked her aunt.

The three went into the den and placed the record on the stereo.

Suzanna thought it was the most beautiful thing she had ever had the pleasure of listening to. She played the record for an hour. Each time, she would break down and cry as it ended.

|||||||

Kevin hung up the phone Monday morning, after talking to Joe Moss. The results were in for the previous week's sales and airtime. After climbing from forty to thirty, "Dream Beauty" had leaped another twelve places on the *Billboard* charts. Aurora's Fire now had the eighteenth-most-popular song in the nation. This was after being on the charts for only three weeks. This was great news for everyone.

Kevin called James, who had not yet arrived at the station, to give him the great news. Sissy was standing next to James when Kevin called. Both were just as excited as Kevin.

"I want to give Garland the good news," James said.

As much as she knew Garland would love the news, Sissy insisted, "Garland was up late last night. Wait until he's awake."

"Yeah, he was probably on the phone with Suzanna," James said.

"Well, if he was, it would have been very hard for Garland to hear her. He is writing a song. He was working on the chords for the harmonies," Sissy said.

James didn't have any idea his son wanted to be a songwriter.

Sissy wanted to burst with the excitement but knew it wasn't her place to make the announcement. "I don't want you to let Garland know about this. Let him tell us about it in his own time," Sissy said.

James agreed as he hugged and kissed Sissy goodbye before he left for work.

||||||||

Garland was experimenting with the chorus melody to the song he was working on. Sissy stopped before entering her son's bedroom, listening as Garland began to sing the melody of his song. She wanted to savor this special moment. As he continued singing, Sissy began to recognize the notes. Garland was writing lyrics to the melody the two of them had enjoyed more than eighteen years before—the song she sang to him when he was a baby, the song he had recorded her singing while they drove from Texas to Colorado. Not wanting her son to think she was eavesdropping, Sissy knocked on the door before entering. Garland sat on the side of his bed, with a pencil behind his right ear and a notebook beside him.

As Sissy approached the side of the bed, Garland removed the notebook, providing a seat for his mother. Garland's guilty smile showed he realized his mother knew what he was up to. Garland began to play a melody on the old Gibson as Sissy watched and listened.

After several bars, Garland began to sing, picking up the song's tempo. As Garland sang the first few verses of the song, Sissy began to glow. His voice was so pure and made the lyrics seem very vivid. When Garland came to the chorus of the song, as if she were reading his mind and his heart, Sissy began to sing in harmony, almost word for word.

"How did you know what the chorus would be? I have not decided on what to use," Garland said.

"I think it's a touch of the heart," she said, smiling and with tears in her eyes.

Garland turned to where he had set the notebook. He picked it up and handed it to his mother.

Sissy looked down at the lyrics written on the pad.

"Touch" appeared in capital letters, indicating it was the song's title.

Sissy began to sing the lyrics Garland had written, while Garland accompanied her on his Gibson. Once again, as if each were reading the other's mind, Sissy and Garland sang the same chorus. The harmony was perfect. "Touch" was magical. The words came from the heart and soul, from the love shared between two hearts and two souls.

The two exchanged ideas for the song.

"I wanted to write a song for the new album," Garland said. "I am not sure it will be good enough to add, though."

"Good enough? Garland, how did you come up such beautiful lyrics? This song will touch everyone who hears it," Sissy said.

"Do you really think the others will like it?" Garland asked.

Sissy smiled, "Baby, I don't think they will like it; I *know* they will *love* it."

Garland began to play again for his mother, singing to her.

Garland looked into his mother's eyes as he continued singing, "It is your touch that I have needed so much. It is your touch that comforted my tears. It is your touch that got me through the years. It is your touch that I hold so dear. It is your touch that comforted my tears. It is your touch that I needed so much."

"Garland, you make me feel like the luckiest mother on earth," Sissy said, and then she suggested some more lyrics. "Baby, it's the touch given and not earned. Baby, it's for your touch I will always yearn."

Garland smiled, pausing to take the pencil from behind his right ear again to write in his notebook.

With just one beat of her heart, Sissy added the next verse.

Garland would do whatever it took to record this special song.

||||||||

The next morning, Garland arrived at the old studio recording room at KARO. He wanted to record some tracks on Kevin's machine. This song was to be his masterpiece. The old recorder would enable Garland to record four separate tracks and mix them together. He wanted to create a demo the others would accept.

Garland placed a new tape reel in the recorder and began to play the old Gibson. Immediately after recording, he played back the track, making sure it was exactly the way he wanted it. Garland placed the Gibson in its case and opened the case for the electric Fender. This track was to be electrical, not acoustic.

Garland completed the electrical track and mixed it with the acoustic track. He returned to the studio to replay the mix. The sound was even better than he had envisioned. Overlaying tracks to create one track was a trick Kevin had shown the boys in the early days. Garland would now have three more tracks if he wished to use them.

Sitting in the corner was Beau's keyboard. Garland removed its cover and began to practice the track he envisioned. Keyboards were not his forte, but Garland wasn't the average musician. A key was a key, and if you could play a key on a guitar, then you could master the keyboard as well. Garland played a modest keyboard. The keyboard was a complementary instrument for the song, not a major sound for this arrangement.

Garland completed the keyboard track and returned to the studio for the keyboard playback. The keyboard arrangement wasn't quite the idea he had in mind. Garland returned to his stool for a break.

The studio door opened. Much to Garland's surprise, there was Sissy.

"I came by to have lunch with your father. Would you like to join us?" Sissy said.

"Mother, I am working on the song," Garland said.

"How is it coming along?" she asked.

"Well, I am mixing the keyboard track, but I am not satisfied with it," Garland said, playing the keyboard track for his mother. "I need to do a remix, but, first, I will have to record another keyboard track."

Garland began to practice the track he envisioned. There was something missing with the keyboards, and Garland couldn't quite put his finger on what it was. Sissy sat on a stool, observing her son. Once again, Garland played a chord; once again, he stopped, disgusted.

"I give up. I will finish the keyboards later," Garland said.

Not wanting Garland to give up, Sissy joined him at the keyboard. Garland remembered the story she had told Brandon that day about the tambourine while he and Adam listened in the hall. He knew his mother was very good on a piano but never thought of her as a keyboardist.

"Let me see if I can show you something with that key you want to do," Sissy said.

Sissy took Garland's hand and guided his fingers to a different key. The sound was far different than what Garland had tried. After several adjustments, Sissy encouraged Garland to try his arrangement with the appropriate changes.

"Garland, turn on the recorder. It will enable you to hear the changes," Sissy said.

Garland turned the recorder on and began to play the changed chords. The changes were amazing. Garland began the mixing of the guitar and keyboard tracks. Finally, the music on the tape matched the music in his head. Now only the drums and the vocal tracks still needed to be done.

Once again, the studio door suddenly opened.

"Brandon, what are you doing here today?" Garland inquired when he saw his friend.

"Tobie and I went shopping for the baby today during lunch,"

Brandon said, adding, "What are you and Sissy up to? I see you are using Kevin's mixing recorder."

"Brandon you should hear the song Garland has been working on. He lacks only the percussion and vocal tracks," Sissy said as she turned the mixer on.

"Garland, this is awesome," Brandon said. "I would consider it an honor to do the drums track."

This was something Garland had not thought of.

Brandon took his place on the stool behind the drums, placing the headphones over his ears. Sissy turned the mixed tracks on for Brandon to hear.

"Let me hear the tracks in their entirety," Brandon said.

After hearing the tracks, Brandon began to play. Once again, he instructed Garland and Sissy to replay the mix. This time, Brandon began to play along with the music on the headphones. As usual, Mr. One Take came through. Garland mixed Brandon's drum track into the others. The three sat there admiring their work. The musical tracks were now complete. The vocal tracks were the last to be done.

"Garland, would you like to add your vocals?" Sissy said.

At first, Garland was reluctant to do them. With encouragement from Brandon and Sissy, Garland agreed to do at least one cut. Garland began to play the tracks using the headphones; he then began to add his vocals over the instrumental tracks. Garland's vocals were as awesome as they always were. His vocals gave "Touch" its heart and soul.

The song was good, but there was still something missing. There were no harmonies for the chorus verses. Once again, Brandon had a great idea. This was the first time Brandon had heard the song, but he instantly knew the one thing that would make "Touch" magical.

"I have the final piece Garland. I know the answer for the harmonies," Brandon said.

"You do, huh? And what would that be?" Garland asked.

"I can tell this is a very special song. It is a song of one heart to another. After hearing Sissy sing, I think she would do the perfect harmony with you," Brandon said.

Without any hesitation, Garland agreed. "Brandon, you are so right. Mom, I want you to do the harmonies with me; but, Brandon, I remember how great you are with them as well. We can do a three-part harmony."

Both Brandon and Sissy smiled and agreed with Garland. The three stepped up to the microphones and recorded the backup vocals to "Touch."

Garland overlaid the final track and replayed the finished tape. The song was now complete, and it was awesome.

"I want this to be our secret. I don't want to hurt the feelings of any of the others," Garland said.

The three agreed and called it a day. "Touch" was finished.

"You should be very proud of this, Garland. Your song is very good. You wrote the song, arranged the song, played all the instruments, and did the vocals. That is something never heard of," Brandon said.

"Brandon, you did the drum set for the song. I could have never contributed the set you did," Garland said.

Brandon smiled and said, "This is our secret. You, Sissy, and I are the only ones who know, and I will never tell anyone."

"I hope the guys like it enough to want it on the album," Garland said.

"Garland, it's their loss if they don't. But this is your song, and you do what you want with it. The song is better than the album," Brandon said.

"Mr. Moss wants to follow up 'Dream Baby' with one of Rudy's songs," Garland said.

"Garland, it's hard for Mr. Moss to do otherwise. He doesn't know about your song," Brandon said.

Garland and Brandon again agreed to keep the song a secret. Garland turned the lights out as they left the room. No one had a clue as to what was left behind that day.

20

WITH "DREAM BABY" now in the top ten on the charts, Magic Sounds was ready to release Aurora's Fire's follow-up hit. The album lacked two songs for its release. The first week in July, the song topped out at its height on the charts. "Dream Baby" would reach the number-five spot on the charts and would remain on the charts for another six weeks.

Suzanna and Garland were finding it more difficult to continue a long-distance relationship. With her career starting to boom, Suzanna was never available for Garland. She was always off on some shoot. Not being able to share your first success with the girl of your dreams took a lot of the enjoyment from the high of that success.

||||||||

Brenda was finishing up another semester at Duke. Summer school was a fast way to get extra credit hours. It was her goal to finish school in three years and be admitted to law school. Brenda was well on her way.

One hot summer day while on her way to a final exam of the first summer session, "Dream Baby" was playing on her car radio. She wondered if she would ever see Garland again. She did enjoy the talks they frequently had on the phone, and she couldn't replace the feelings she had after talking to him. Each time, she wanted to climb into her car and drive to Colorado. It was all she could do to fight the temptation.

IIIIIII

Tobie was well into her pregnancy. Shortly after their announcement of the baby, Brandon made an honest woman of Tobie. The two were wed in a traditional Apache wedding ceremony. Brandon was becoming a very good husband, and she knew he would be a very good father as well. With the growing success of Aurora's Fire, Tobie knew the band would soon begin to tour to promote the album. This was going to be a very lonely time for her. Tobie's only wish was to have Brandon home when the baby came.

Joe Moss stopped in at KARO the next morning, to meet with Kevin and the boys.

"Guys, I have some great news," Joe said. "A national television show wants you to perform the follow-up to 'Dream Baby.' This would be great national exposure and publicity for Rudy's song. We have selected the song you guys performed at the final show at Elitch Gardens. We need to strike while you guys are still hot."

Kevin couldn't agree any more with the strategy.

"We need to finish the album as well. If our follow-up song is as successful as 'Dream Baby,' this would give the album two top-ten hits," Kevin said.

Joe added, "Tomorrow morning, radio stations across the nation will debut the new release. This will give us one week to produce the B side of the record."

"When will we do the television show?" Garland asked.

"We will do the television show a week from this Saturday," Joe said.

The boys left the studio that morning, very excited. Their music careers were launched. None of them knew how quickly they would succeed.

Radio stations across the country began playing the new release during their morning drive-time shows. Brenda was on her way to class that morning. This morning was slow. For some reason, she just couldn't get started. The schedule of constant classes was taking its toll. This morning, she wanted a more serene, quiet drive, and she drove in silence. She didn't want the radio to disturb the mental peace she desperately needed this morning. Brenda was sitting at a red stoplight, just blocks away from Duke. A red Camaro convertible pulled alongside her car, with the radio blasting, and now her tranquil moment was gone.

The light changed, and the Camaro pulled away quickly. Brenda pulled into her assigned parking lot. Just as luck would have it, the Camaro was parked behind her space. The driver was sitting in his seat, listening to the radio. Brenda took her mascara brush from her purse and began to liven up her eyes. Applying the finishing touches, she opened the car door as a song began to play on the Camaro's radio. Brenda opened the trunk to retrieve her books for her morning class. She noticed the driver turned up the volume, sensing she was trying to listen in on the song playing. Brenda knew the charts very well, but this song stumped her.

The song had a familiar flavor to it, one she couldn't quite put her finger on. She impatiently awaited the ending of the song.

As the song started to wind down, the DJ announced the artist and the song. "You have just heard the premiere of Aurora's Fire new song, 'From the Start.'"

Brenda paused to relish this special moment. This great news was just what she needed to kick-start the morning. This was much better than caffeine. This morning's class was to be a very long one in her mind. Brenda couldn't wait to call Garland to congratulate him once again.

|||||||

Garland began the morning with the anticipation of the new song's debut.

Sissy tuned the kitchen radio to KARO as she began to prepare breakfast. The Summers family sat down for breakfast as Chad announced the song.

"Today, we are proud to announce the follow-up song by Aurora's Fire," Chad said.

Joe wanted the boys to be surprised with his choice for the follow-up. Garland was in the dark as much as the rest of his family as to which song would be the follow-up. The song began to play.

As the song's vocals began, Sissy instantly knew it wasn't Garland's voice.

"Do you recognize the tune?" she asked.

"Yes, its Rudy's song, 'From the Start,'" Garland said.

Sissy tried to hide her disappointment. She was biased when it came to Garland's vocal talent, just as any proud mother would be.

Garland excused himself from the table. He needed to call Suzanna. It seemed like months since the two had last talked.

Garland dialed Suzanna's number from his bedroom phone.

"Hello," the voice said.

Garland sensed his called had awakened that person.

"Is Suzanna there?" he asked.

"No, she is out," Jodi said.

Garland looked at the clock in his room, noticing that it would be early in California.

"I am sorry to have disturbed you this early in the morning. Do you have any idea when she may be available?" Garland said.

"No, but she cannot be reached for several days," Jodi said.

Garland thanked Jodi and ended the call. This was the second time he wanted to share his great news with Suzanna, only to have it taken away from him.

Once again, Garland was disappointed that he couldn't share the news with Suzanna. He entered the den to relax.

Sissy, sensing her baby was not doing very well, brought Garland some breakfast. As she entered the den with Garland's food, the phone rang. Sissy placed the food on the coffee table to answer the telephone.

"Hello," she said.

Kevin said, "Sissy, are you sitting down? The boys will be doing the national Saturday morning television show in New York and then will embark on a two-week tour. The tour will take them through the Carolinas and down into Florida over the next fourteen days."

"Kevin, this is great news. Just the kind of news Garland needs right now. He is really down about Suzanna," Sissy said.

"Well, tell him also the first royalty checks are in as well. He will have some spending money to take to New York and for the tour," Kevin said.

Sissy told Garland the good news.

His dreams took another step. The good news gave Garland an appetite. He finished his breakfast and left for the studio.

IIIIIIII

Aurora's Fire entered the studio that morning to complete the final two tracks of their album. They decided to record another of Rudy's songs. This would give him a total of eight tracks on the twelve-song album. Three would be remakes of some of the boys' favorite songs.

"We can add a twelfth song, or we can make several of the takes longer to fill the minutes needed to complete album," Joe Moss said.

"Well, if no one objects, I think we can add several more choruses to the songs we have and then fill in the time," Rudy said.

Rudy's suggestion did not sit well with Brandon.

"Mr. Moss, I know I am the new guy here, and my suggestions may not be warranted. But I cannot just stand by and let this happen," Brandon said.

"Brandon, you have a say in what we do here. It doesn't matter how long you have been involved with the group," Joe said.

"I want you to hear something," Brandon said. "I told Garland I would keep his secret, but I can't let this happen. It will be a very huge mistake."

Brandon looked at Garland, walked over to the recorder, and pressed the Play button. The tapes began to roll, playing a song none of the others knew existed.

A silence overcame the room, and the boys were overwhelmed

by what they heard. Once the recording finished playing, Brandon stopped the recorder to take the floor. The others might not want to have this song on the album, but he was determined to go down fighting.

"You have just heard a song in which Garland Summers played every instrument," Brandon said. "He wrote the song and arranged the song. He is by far the most talented guy in this room. I told Garland I wouldn't say anything, but this song is the best song I have ever heard, and it needs to be on the album."

"Brandon, you are right," Adam said. "Rudy has eight songs on our album. I think Garland should have this one. This is much better than doing any extended versions of the songs we have already recorded."

Without any hesitation, Joe made the decision to add "Touch" as the twelfth song. It would be added just as it was recorded. A music producer wouldn't enhance this song.

||||||||

Joe made the arrangements for the boys to fly into New York the Friday before the television show. The boys arrived in New York on Friday afternoon. Joe met with the boys to go over the itinerary for the tour.

"We will leave New York on Saturday, immediately following the television show. We will join the tour and be the opening act with two other groups. We will appear at the University of Florida. I will give you the rest of the tour information once we arrive in Florida for our show tomorrow evening," Joe said.

The boys checked into their hotel rooms. Garland, Brandon, and Adam shared a room; Sam, Rudy, and Beau took the other room.

Brandon and Adam left the room early that evening. This gave Garland several minutes to be alone, and he took advantage of the time to call Suzanna.

"Hello, is Suzanna there?" Garland asked.

Garland could hear there was some sort of party going on in the background.

"Hold on. I will see if she is available," the voice said.

Garland patiently held the line, hoping to finally get a chance to talk to Suzanna.

"Who is this?" the voice said.

"I want to talk to Suzanna. Is she there or not?" Garland said.

Garland could hear the music was now much louder as the receiver was placed down on a table. In the background, Garland could hear what he determined to be two female voices yelling at each other. The voices were then over shadowed by a voice now speaking into the phone.

"Hey, man, Suzanna is not able to come to the phone," the voice said. "You will have to call back some other time."

Without identifying himself, the man to whom the voice belonged hung up the phone, not giving Garland a chance to say another word.

Garland felt like he struck out. Three times he had tried to contact Suzanna without any success. He couldn't imagine the type of life she had resorted to.

For the third time, Garland had called Suzanna; for the third time, Suzanna wasn't aware of his call. She couldn't understand why Garland never called.

Saturday morning arrived, with the boys entering the stage at the ABC studio in New York. Their song would be performed live. "Dream Baby" would be performed during the first thirty minutes of the show, and the new release, "From the Start," would debut during the last thirty minutes.

The show was a big hit across the country with the teenage scene. It was prestigious to perform on the show. This was something only fifty-two acts a year had the privilege of achieving. The show aired at noon eastern time, 11:00 a.m. central time, 10:00 a.m. mountain time, and 9:00 a.m. Pacific time.

The Summers and English households were glued to their sets that morning, as was most of Denver. It wasn't every day that a local band made national news.

The show's host, sitting in the crowd, began his introduction. "Today, we have a group whose debut record reached number five on the charts. They will be a group, I am sure, that will dominate the charts for months and years to come. From Aurora, Colorado, please welcome Aurora's Fire."

The crowd cheered as the opening of "Dream Baby" began to play.

It was 9:00 a.m., in California. Jodi and Suzanna sat down to enjoy breakfast, and, as they normally did on Saturday mornings, turned on the national televised show. Suzanna, with a glass of orange juice at her lips, began to take a drink as the show's host introduced Aurora's Fire. The words coming from the television took her totally by surprise. Suzanna's orange juice ran down her chin and onto her pajama top.

Jodi, watching Suzanna, began to laugh at her cousin's clumsiness.

"Hey, does your chin have a hole in it?" Jodi said, laughing.

Even Jodi's sarcastic remark didn't interrupt Suzanna's fixed gaze on the television.

This was a look unfamiliar to Jodi. Again laughing at her cousin, she said, "You look like you have seen a ghost."

Suzanna's eyes never left the screen during the performance.

Immediately following the song's ending, Suzanna rushed into the living room. Picking up the telephone, she began to dial it.

"Hello, Sissy, I just saw the show," Suzanna said.

"Suzanna, is this really you? Garland has tried many times to contact you," Sissy said.

"Sissy, I didn't know. No one told me he has called," Suzanna said.

"Honey, Garland misses you and wanted to share his special news with you. You know, the phone lines do run both ways. You could have called him," Sissy said.

Suzanna began to cry. She had to make things right again and was determined to make amends with her love.

Suzanna returned to see the interview portion of the show.

"Suzanna, are you okay?" Jodi said. "Oh my God! Is that your brother, Beau?"

Suzanna smiled and nodded yes.

As the host began to interview the band, he introduced each member.

"Oh my God! That is Garland!" Jodi said.

Suzanna, with tears in her eyes, began nodding and shaking.

The boys left the bench they were sitting on, taking their places on the stage for the next number. Once again, the host introduced Aurora's Fire.

"Doing their newest release, 'From the Start,' once again, please welcome Aurora's Fire," he said.

The boys began to play their second number.

This was a special day in Denver. The group that had entertained them all summer long at Elitch grew up that day. They belonged to much more than Denver now.

ǀǀǀǀǀǀǀ

Brenda Fisher watched the show that morning from her dad's hospital room. Watching Garland perform on TV provided temporary relief. Brenda's father was involved in an automobile accident the day before and was in serious condition. He sustained some internal injuries that required many blood transfusions. Some of his fellow military retirees were beginning to organize a blood drive to offset some of his medical costs.

Brenda's mother entered the hospital room to witness the show's end.

"Brenda, we always knew Garland would grow up to be something very special. No one deserves this any more than he does." Valerie said.

Brenda was very, very proud of her first love.

"Tomorrow night, why don't you call and congratulate Garland?" Valerie said. "I know he would love to hear from you."

Brenda smiled at the idea. She really did need a friend during this time.

ǀǀǀǀǀǀǀ

Aurora's Fire left New York that afternoon, headed for the Florida engagement. Playing college campuses were a great way to be noticed by the ever-growing younger population. The plane arrived in Gainesville, Florida, that afternoon. The boys would have three hours before their show at the university.

"Hey, guys, you will be playing in the swamp this evening. The show is a sellout," Joe Moss said.

"Did you say *swamp*?" Brandon asked.

Joe laughed at Brandon's intrigued expression. "Yes, Brandon, it's the football stadium of the University of Florida Gators. It's just a nickname to intimidate the opposing team when they come to play here."

The boys were dressed and ready to be the opening act. Opening the show would enable the boys to have an early getaway. Their next show would take them to Atlanta, Georgia. This was to be a very busy two-week tour. Each show would take place in a different city.

|||||||||

Thinking Garland was in Colorado, Brenda placed a call to congratulate Garland on his national television appearance. Sissy was finishing the dinner dishes as the phone began to ring.

"Hello," she said, answering on the third ring.

"Hi, Mrs. Summers. This is Brenda Fisher. Is Garland there?" Brenda asked.

"Brenda, I am sorry. He will not be home for two weeks. The band is on a two-week tour," Sissy said.

Finally, Brenda's emotions broke lose; she couldn't hold back the tears.

"Is there something wrong?" Sissy asked.

"It's my dad. He is in serious condition at a hospital in Raleigh. He was involved in an automobile accident," Brenda said.

Sissy always had a special talent for comforting those in need. She made Brenda feel as if things would really be all right.

"I will call Garland and let him know you called. I am sure he would love to hear from you, Brenda," Sissy said.

"Thank you, Mrs. Summers. Garland is one of my closest friends," Brenda said.

|||||||

The band, now playing in a different city each night, had fantastic results every time. Each show was sold out.

One night, after a show in Savannah, Georgia, Garland called home.

"How is my favorite girl?" Garland's voice said as Sissy answered the phone.

"Hey, baby, where are you calling from this evening?" Sissy said.

"We are in Savannah, Georgia tonight. Tomorrow night, we will be Columbia, South Carolina," Garland said.

"Today, I received a phone call from Brenda Fisher. Her father is in critical condition in a Raleigh hospital. He was in a terrible automobile accident," Sissy said.

The news silenced Garland; he wasn't prepared for bad news. He wanted the phone call home to be a motivator.

"I will try to call and check in on Brenda," Garland said.

"I think the Fishers would love to hear from you. Brenda does care for you very much," Sissy said.

Garland ended his call that evening, promising to call again before coming home.

Sissy had barely hung the phone up when it rang again.

"Hello, Sissy," the voice said.

"Suzanna, is that you?" Sissy said.

"Yes. Is Garland back home? Has he returned from the show and the concert?" Suzanna asked.

"No. He will not be home for almost two weeks. He is in Georgia tonight," Sissy said.

"I want to surprise him. Where will the tour end? "Suzanna asked.

"I really don't know the specifics, but I believe it will be in the Carolinas. If you contact Joe Moss's office, maybe they will give you the itinerary," Sissy said.

Suzanna thanked Sissy for the idea and agreed that Joe Moss's office would be the best source.

||||||||

The band's time in South Carolina went by very fast. Columbia was the first stop, followed by Greenville, Charleston, and Myrtle Beach. During the Myrtle Beach stop, Garland remembered the summer when he and his mother attended a concert during which the performer gathered him up on the stage. That was his first taste of how special show business was.

Charleston had been his home for almost six years. These were the most formidable years of his childhood. Charleston was also the place where he met Brenda.

This would be the perfect time to call Brenda, he thought.

After ending the sold-out show in the fairgrounds, Garland returned to his hotel room to place the call. The phone only had to ring two times before Brenda answered it. It was almost like she was just waiting for his call.

"Brenda, this is Garland," he said.

Brenda broke down at the sound of his voice. She hadn't wanted Garland to hear her crying.

"Hi, Garland. I am so glad you called me," she said through her tears.

"My mother told me the news about your dad. How is he doing?" Garland asked.

"They have stopped his internal bleeding and want to do surgery as soon as possible," Brenda said.

That evening, Garland and Brenda talked for an hour. He only wished he could have comforted her in person.

||||||||

"From the Start" was now entering the third week after its release. Although it was in the top forty now, the response from the public wasn't as great as what Magic Sounds hoped for. There was now mounting pressure to release the third song. Joe Moss didn't want to lose the momentum they received from "Dream Baby."

Once the tour was over, they would meet back in the studio to determine which song would be the B side to another Rudy Stamps songs.

Joe wanted the release of the third song to coincide with the release of the album. "There's nothing like hitting them while you are hot" was Joe's music-business philosophy.

|||||||

Taking Sissy's advice, Suzanna called the Magic Sounds office to get the Aurora's Fire tour itinerary.

"Can you tell me the remaining dates for Aurora's Fire's current tour?" Suzanna asked.

"After tonight's show, they will have two more shows in North Carolina. The next show will be in Charlotte, and the final show, on Friday night, will be in Raleigh, North Carolina," the receptionist said.

Immediately after hanging up the phone, Suzanna made flight reservations to Raleigh. She wanted Garland to know how important he was to her. You never know what you have until you don't have it any longer. She had experienced that in California, and it was not a good feeling. She wanted to surprise Garland on the road during the last show.

|||||||

The Charlotte show was starting. The crowd for this show was the loudest the boys had yet entertained. Joe wanted the boys to inform the public of their new release during this show. The crowd was like the days at Elitch: eager and excited.

Rudy took to the microphone to thank the crowd. "Tonight, we will open with our newest release. This will be the third release from our new album; both will hit the streets tomorrow."

The third release also featured Rudy's vocal talent. Following Joe's plan, the B side would not be determined until they returned from the tour.

The Charlotte show was also the only stop on the tour to have two acts instead of the usual three. This would give Aurora's Fire more exposure than the other stops. After the show, the boys loaded up and headed for the tour's final stop. One more night, and they would be headed home.

IIIIIII

After playing a much-longer concert set, Joe had made arrangements for the boys to stay in Charlotte for the night and then fly into Raleigh the following day. Friday arrived, and the band departed Charlotte's airport, headed for Raleigh. The band landed in Raleigh after an hour-long flight.

While waiting for his luggage, Garland was reading the headlines in the Raleigh newspaper. There was a story about the pouring out of sentiment for Michael Fisher. The community was behind every effort to ease the cost of his medical expenses. Today was the day of Michael's surgery. The story deeply saddened Garland. There had to be something he could do as well. Garland informed the others that he was headed for the hospital and would meet them at the hotel.

Garland exited the airport and flagged down the first taxi he saw.

"Where to, buddy?" the cabbie said.

"Take me to Raleigh General Hospital, and make it quick," Garland said.

"Anything you say, chief," the cabbie said as he sped out of the airport arrivals' pickup area.

As Garland's cab was leaving the airport, a flight from California was landing—the flight that carried Suzanna.

IIIIIII

Suzanna's plane landed. Without any luggage to collect, she immediately made her way to the front of the airport. Suzanna was approaching the baggage pickup area when a voice shouted her name. She paused for a moment and then thought that the voice must calling for another Suzanna. She didn't know anyone in Raleigh. Once again, the voice shouted her name; this time, it was behind her and much closer than the previous time.

"Hey, Suzanna Royal!" the voice said.

This time, she knew it was intended for her. She turned around to see her brother Beau. He was the one shouting. There *was* someone in Raleigh who knew her that day.

"What are you doing here in Raleigh?" Beau asked.

"I came to see Garland. I wanted to surprise him. I wanted to be here for the last show of your first concert tour," she said.

"Well, you just missed Garland. He is going to the hospital," Beau said.

"Oh my God! Is he okay? Has he been hurt?" she asked.

Beau had never seen his sister like this. "No, sis. Garland is okay. I think he went to see a friend who is in serious condition."

IIIIIII

Garland arrived at the hospital, entering through the main doors. He approached the information desk.

"Where can I find the surgery waiting room?" he asked.

The volunteer directed Garland, who then sought out the elevators. He reached the elevators and pressed the button for the third floor. The volunteer had said that, once off the elevator, the waiting area would be visible.

Garland rushed out of the elevator and entered the surgical waiting room. There, in the corner, was a familiar face. Although it had been many years since he had seen her, Garland recognized Valerie Fisher instantly. As he approached Valerie, her first glance his way told Garland she did not recognize him; after all, he looked a lot different now than he had at thirteen.

"Mrs. Fisher?" Garland inquired.

She looked up with a very worried look on her face. It was obvious she had not rested in several days. One of Valerie's friends took issue with Garland. He didn't want someone to bother her at this moment.

Garland was about to speak when a voice came from behind him, saying, "You will have to excuse my mother's friend. He's only protecting her best interest during this trying time for our family."

Garland turned to answer the voice.

There, more beautiful than he could ever have imagined, was his first love. Garland smiled and took a moment to imprint the view into his memory bank. Garland stared at the beauty and was lost for words.

Once again, the family friend sought to protect the family during this time.

"Is there something you want or are looking for?" said the man asked.

Garland continued to look at Brenda, making her very uncomfortable.

"I am sorry, Brenda," Garland said. "It's just that you are so beautiful, and it has been so many years since I last saw you."

Brenda approached Garland, looking into his eyes. "Oh my God! Oh my God! It's really you."

Brenda grabbed Garland, hugging him like she wanted to erase the lost years. Her actions surprised the others sitting in the waiting room. Brenda's beautiful eyes were full of tears. The tears made her eyes sparkle brighter than any star or any diamond. These were tears of joy.

After the last few days, how could my eyes have any tears left in them? she wondered.

Brenda took Garland's hand and led him to where her mother was sitting. "Mother, you will not believe what I have found today."

Valerie looked at her daughter. This time, Valerie recognized the face. "Garland Summers, is that really you?" She already knew the answer and didn't need a reply from Garland.

Garland smiled at Valerie.

Turning toward Brenda, Garland said, "Brenda, I am sorry to hear the news about your dad. I am here in town for a concert tonight at North Carolina State University and saw the news in the newspaper at the airport."

"I called you after I saw you on television that Saturday morning. Your mother said you were on the road for a two-week concert tour, but she didn't mention anything about you being in Raleigh," Brenda said.

Brenda sat next to Garland, holding his hand, never wanting their fingers to be separated. She had waited a long time for this and wasn't going to miss one minute.

"Is there anyone here from the Fisher family?" Dr. Johnson asked as he entered the waiting room.

Everyone in the room stood up, each of them saying, "Yes."

"The surgery was a success," Dr. Johnson said. "Mr. Fisher lost a lot of blood on account of a ruptured spleen. We had to remove the spleen. He should recover, but it will take time."

Brenda and Valerie thanked the doctor.

"You will be able to see him after he leaves the recovery room," Dr. Johnson said.

Brenda and her mother were spared heartbreak that day.

Garland excused himself from the waiting room, looking for a nurse. He found a nurse, and the two entered a nearby room. After twenty minutes, Garland returned to the waiting room, just in time for the family to move to the recovery waiting room.

Brenda and Garland held hands as they walked down the hall to the other waiting area.

Brenda began to run her hand up Garland's arm, discovering a Band-Aid midway up his left arm. She was about to ask Garland what had caused his injury, when she suddenly noticed it was the kind of Band-Aid the hospital used for blood donors. This explained his absence earlier.

"You really are one of a kind, Garland. Time has not changed you one bit. It has only made you more special than you already were," Brenda said, and then she kissed his hand.

Garland remained that day until the family went to see Michael. He didn't want to intrude on their time.

"Brenda, I have to leave now. I need to get to the hotel in time to get ready for the show," Garland said.

Brenda knew Garland had to leave, but she wasn't looking forward to his departure. She walked Garland to the elevators that afternoon, not knowing when—or even if—she would see him again.

She made her way over to a window that looked out onto the hospital entrance, wanting one more glance at this very special man in her life. As Garland made his way through the front doors, a taxi pulled up. A beautiful girl exited the cab. Brenda watched as the beautiful girl ran up to Garland and began to kiss him like there was no tomorrow.

Suzanna's arrival at the hospital was as big a surprise for Brenda as Garland's had been. In all the excitement of seeing her first love, it had never occurred to Brenda that Garland now belonged to another woman.

||||||||

Garland and Suzanna arrived at the hotel. Garland updated the others on his visit to the hospital that afternoon. Everyone was surprised to see Suzanna. She explained that she had come to surprise Garland for the last show of their first concert tour, as she had told Beau earlier.

"Tonight, I want to play a special song at our show. I want to perform 'Touch' for the first time," Garland said.

Brandon stood up and gave Garland a high five. Garland knew he had Brandon's support for anything he needed.

"Garland, you can do your song, but none of us know the song. We have only heard the song once," Rudy said.

"Garland, you and I will do the song," Brandon said.

Garland smiled at Brandon, giving him a thumbs-up.

"I think I even remember the chorus lines," Brandon said.

The band left the hotel, headed for the closing show of their tour.

Eighteen thousand fans were in attendance that night. Aurora's Fire would open the show, followed by the other two touring bands.

The boys agreed that "Touch" would be the first song after "Dream Baby."

||||||||

The crowd had come to see the final act of the evening. Creedence Clearwater Revival was a special group with a different sound. This night was a night when Creedence would have to share the accolades. Aurora's Fire had come to play, and everyone would soon witness just how good they were becoming. Aurora's Fire's energy was very high that night. After all, they would finally be going home after a hectic two weeks.

With the opening song, Rudy gave the audience just what they had come for. The volume of the applause peaked at the introduction to "Dream Baby," and this fueled the band during the song.

As the crowd began to calm down for the next song, Garland stepped up to make an announcement. The band didn't have a clue to what Garland was about to do. Garland had instructed the ushers to bring in a box for each section; the ushers would move the box from aisle to aisle, as needed.

"Tonight, you will hear the first performance of a song that has been nineteen years in the making," Garland said. "There was a story in the Raleigh newspaper today about the Fisher family and a tragic accident. I want to do something very special for that family. During this next song, ushers will be placing boxes in each section, for donations to help with medical expenses."

The arena lights were turned on, and Garland began his debut of "Touch." As the song began to play, the words touched the audience. Fans made their way to the boxes in droves, donating cash. That evening, the ballad of "Touch" did exactly that. Some fans were overheard saying that they had never found such powerful meaning in a song. It was a masterpiece. The concert ended that night with a special heartfelt meaning, unlike other concerts of that time.

||||||||

As the band boarded their flight back to Colorado the next morning, a news team was heading to Raleigh General Hospital. They had a story the state of North Carolina, and the entire nation, needed to hear. A reporter with a cameraman entered the wing of the hospital that contained Michael Fisher's room.

The Fishers were unaware of the previous evening's events.

At first, the hospital did not cooperate with the news team. The hospital didn't want to create a three-ring circus. The reporter and cameraman entered Michael's room. As the reporter entered the room, she instructed the cameraman to begin filming.

"Fisher family, we are here to present you with a gift. One created last evening at the concert at NC State," the reporter said. "During the concert, Aurora's Fire debuted a new song, 'Touch,' and Garland Summers encouraged people to donate to help with your medical expenses. Boy, did they ever! The donations were only accepted during the song 'Touch.' I want to present you with a donation of twenty thousand dollars from that song."

The moment was too much and overwhelmed everyone in that hospital room that day.

Brenda ran to hug her mother and father. Someday and someway, she would return the favor to her first love.

A group performing its first tour, and as an opening act, couldn't have imagined the lives they touched. This was just the beginning for Garland Summers.

21

AS AURORA'S FIRE drove from the Denver airport, pulling into the city limits of Aurora, there was a sense that something special lay ahead. The van bringing them home turned onto the boulevard that would take them to the radio station. The traffic flow was much slower as the van approached the station.

"Kevin, why are we driving so slowly?" Rudy asked.

"You guys need to see this to believe it," Kevin said.

The boys climbed to the nearest window in the van to witness the streets lined with people. As the van passed by, there was applause from the fans along the sides of the streets. The sight began to overwhelm the boys. This was something that took all of them by surprise. The sides of the building displayed banners emblazoned with "Aurora's Fire" in bold lettering. Standing in the parking lot was a sea of people that parted as the van made its way to the front covered drive.

Slowly the boys began to depart the van, making their way to the front door. There was a stage with several microphones near the door.

Brandon was the last to depart the van. As he began to make his way through the crowd, he suddenly stopped. Standing several feet away was Tobie, glowing in her pregnancy, even though she felt like she was about to explode. She had never looked more beautiful, or sexier, to Brandon than she did that day.

Tobie began to push her way through the crowd, sometimes yelling, "Make way! Pregnant lady coming through."

Brandon pushed his way through until he reached Tobie.

The two weeks Brandon was away had seemed like months to both of them. This was an absence that had definitely made two hearts grow even fonder.

Finally, all of Aurora's Fire reached the stage where Joe Moss welcomed them home, to very loud applause.

Garland thought, *This isn't bad for a group that no one had ever heard of several months ago.*

James and Sissy met Garland and Suzanna, with open arms.

"Welcome home, kids! We have missed you, and we are so proud of both of you," James said.

After a short speech from Joe Moss, the boys began to leave for their homes. Joe informed the boys that they needed to be at the Magic Sounds Studio the next morning. There was an important decision to be made for the new release.

||||||||

Garland and Suzanna left together.

"Baby, I have a surprise for you," Suzanna said.

Garland wanted to be with her very much. It was several months since the two had been together. Suzanna drove her Mustang, keeping their destination a secret. After an hour's drive, Garland didn't have the slightest clue as to where they were headed. Soon the Mustang reached the city limits of Morrison. Garland smiled at Suzanna, thinking she had something planned at the Red Rocks Amphitheatre. His guess soon proved to be wrong as the car passed the exit for the renowned site. Several miles down the road, Suzanna exited the freeway. Driving down a winding, hilly road, the couple reached their destination for the evening.

Suzanna pulled into the Red Rocks Resort. The young couple exited the car and made their way to the front entrance. As they entered the lobby, the sight was the most inspiring Garland had ever experienced in an indoor venue. The lobby's highlights included a huge rock fireplace and a ceiling vaulted with beams of ponderosa pine, creating a welcome-home atmosphere for the resort's guests. Across the lobby, near the desk, were three round, clear elevators making their way to all twelve floors.

After checking into the hotel, Suzanna led Garland into a special dining room. A sign above the door read the "Eagle's Nest." Two large pines stood inside the dining area. The room was filled with the scent of pine, blending with the aroma of the dishes coming from the kitchen.

Suzanna approached the maître d', requesting a table near the window. He led the couple through the pines. They walked until they came upon a small bridge crossing a mountain brook inside the room; this path led to the outer windows. There, next to a window, was a perfect table for two. It was just the way Suzanna had imagined.

After a wonderful meal, the two left to find their room for the evening. They entered the first elevator and pressed the twelfth-floor button. As the elevator began to ascend, Garland and Suzanna turned to enjoy the view of the massive lobby and the Eagle's Nest.

Suzanna turned to Garland and kissed him. She wanted Garland to know how she felt—and wanted everyone around them to know as well.

The elevator reached the twelfth floor, and the two exited. Four rooms away from the elevator was the room the two would occupy for the evening.

Garland opened the door to the Rocky Suite. The room was equipped with a fireplace and a balcony.

As the two entered the bedroom, Suzanna ran back to the door. She opened the door and placed the Do Not Disturb sign on the door, immediately closing it and turning the lock. On this night, Suzanna was determined to make up for all those days she had missed Garland. The two lovers would spend the night leaving no doubt about their feelings for each other. The setting was perfect. Garland was with a beautiful woman, one he had missed for a long time.

The morning sunshine crept through the spaces between the

drapes. Garland's back was to the window. He watched the light shining on Suzanna's beautiful face as she lay there asleep. With his hand propping up his head, Garland gazed at Suzanna, thinking about how lucky he was to have her in his life. Garland walked softly into the next room to order breakfast for the two of them. Afterward, he returned to slip back into the bed. He was addicted to the images of Suzanna with the sun on her beautiful face. He lay there smiling until room service interrupted his thoughts.

When room service knocked on the door, Garland arose from the bed to put on his robe to answer the door. This time, the knock on the door was longer and louder. This knock was intended to awaken the room's inhabitants. The second knock, so much louder than the first, did what it was intended to do. Suzanna stirred as the knocking continued. As she raised her head, Suzanna looked at the pillow next to her. She instantly sat up in the bed. The empty pillow startled her; she had expected to see Garland lying there next to her. She turned to the door, to see Garland pushing the room-service cart over to where she lay in bed.

"Are you ready for some breakfast?" Garland said.

Garland placed a fresh strawberry in his mouth and walked over to the bed. Bending down, his mouth met Suzanna's, feeding her the juicy strawberry. Afterward, he collected a kiss as a reward for his delivery service.

Suzanna put on her robe and joined Garland at the table. The two enjoyed a wonderful breakfast.

After breakfast, Garland went into the bathroom. Suzanna could hear water running as she approached the doorway. As she entered the bathroom, Garland removed her robe, letting it fall to the floor. Garland held Suzanna from behind and began to kiss her shoulder until he reached her neck. Suzanna led Garland to the shower and opened its door. She then turned to Garland and removed his robe, pulling him into the hot shower. She wrapped her arms around his neck and begin to kiss him, very deep and long. She wanted his desire for her to be as hot as the shower's water. She reached for the liquid-soap bottle in the soap tray. Filling her cupped hand with the soap, she began to rub the soap on Garland's body.

The coldness of the soap made Garland flinch. He wasn't expecting the soap to be that cooling. Garland, while kissing Suzanna, took the bottle of soap from her hands and filled his much-larger hands with soap. He was determined to give Suzanna a very hot rubdown. After covering their bodies with the soap, Garland and Suzanna began to kiss for what seemed like several minutes, rubbing their soapy bodies together until they could no longer resist each other. Garland pushed the button for the rain showerhead, rinsing the soap from their bodies.

The pulsating water made them want each other even more. The two made their way over to the shower seat. For the fourth time since arriving at the hotel, Garland made love to Suzanna; this time, in a sensuous shower. Suzanna wanted a fifth time that morning, and there would have been a fifth time if the hot-water supply had lasted.

Realizing that Garland had to be at the Magic Sounds Studio for a meeting with Joe Moss, the two lovers wrapped up their night of passion.

|||||||

That morning, Garland and Suzanna were the last two to arrive at the studio. This wasn't a surprise to anyone in attendance. In fact, there were bets as to how late Garland would be that morning. Beau won the bet!

Joe started the meeting that morning, informing the boys that "From the Start" was dropping in the charts, so it was time to release Rudy's song.

"We will release Rudy's song, 'Forever,' as our next single," Joe said. "We need to determine the B side. If we come to a decision quickly, we can have the record in stores in several days."

Once again, Brandon lobbied for "Touch" to be released as the B side. After all, it was well received at NC State. The song was at KARO's studio, and the group selected the song as the final track on the album. The track was ready to be pressed right onto the flip side of the "Forever" single.

The vote was unanimous to have "Touch" as the B side of "Forever."

|||||||

The first week of August 1969 found radio stations across the nation receiving Aurora's Fire's new record. The press release informed the media that the song title was a single word. During his radio show the Monday after its release, Harley debuted the record.

"This is the new song from our favorite sons here in Colorado. Here is Aurora's Fire's 'Forever,'" Harley said.

As Harley began to play the song, he failed to notice that he had placed "Touch" on the deck. Thirty seconds into the song, Harley realized he had made a mistake. This wasn't "Forever" playing. He had no choice but to let "Touch" finish playing, even though he had debuted it by mistake.

Something very miraculous began to happen that evening. Suddenly, as the song began to finish, the KARO's phone lines began to light up. Many wanted to know the song title and when it would be available for sale. After a deluge of phone calls, Harley had a plan. He would play "Forever," and then play "Touch." He encouraged his audience to call in and vote for which song they enjoyed the most. This time, the phone lines did not just light up, they were overloaded with calls. The vote was unanimous, in favor of "Touch."

|||||||

The next morning, Garland and Sissy were doing some shopping at the nearby shopping mall. One of the stores they entered was playing another Denver station on the radio. As Sissy began to look through some dresses, the DJ introduced "Forever" as the new single from Aurora's Fire. Sissy paused to listen to the song. This was the first time she had the pleasure of hearing the new release. When the song completed its play, she smiled at Garland. She found it hard to believe the way things were beginning to happen for her son.

As Sissy continued her shopping, the DJ took a call from a listener. The listener began to inform the DJ about the song Harley had introduced on KARO.

"Can you play 'Touch'?" the listener said.

"I think you mean 'Forever,'" the DJ said.

"No, I would like to hear 'Touch.' I think it is their new song. Another station played it last night, and the calls coming in were awesome," the listener said.

The DJ was now more lost than ever. He was certain the caller was confused and meant "Forever."

While the other radio station was playing another song on the air, another caller called the station with the same information. The caller informed the DJ that "Touch" was the B side to "Forever." The DJ took the advice of the caller and flipped the record over to find that, indeed, the caller was correct.

Sissy and Garland were in another store, shopping. Sissy went into the dressing room to try on her selections, and Garland remained in the waiting area. This store was playing the same radio station as the previous store.

The DJ came back on after the song finished. He took another call and put the listener on the air live.

"I would like to hear 'Touch,'" the listener said.

This time, the DJ obliged his listener and introduced "Touch."

Sissy made her selections and met Garland outside the dressing area. She wasn't aware of what had just happened. Garland and Sissy made their way to the nearest cashier to pay for her purchase.

As Sissy opened her wallet to pay the clerk, she noticed everyone in the store had stopped what they were doing to listen to the sound coming through the store's speakers. She turned to Garland, wondering if he had witnessed the same thing. A tear ran down Garland's cheek as the song continued to play.

"Garland, are you okay baby?" Sissy asked.

Garland nodded that he was fine and began to hug Sissy.

There were no speakers in the dressing rooms, so Sissy still wasn't aware of what was happening. The shoppers in the store were all standing as if something had stopped time momentarily. Once again, Sissy asked Garland why he had tears in his eyes.

"Mother, the song they just played is my song. Somehow, the DJ is playing 'Touch,' instead of 'Forever,' the A side," Garland said.

As "Touch" was finishing, Sissy began to hear the familiar notes. She understood what was happening that day. "Touch" was more than just a song that was discovered by accident—an accident that was spreading throughout Denver, in just two days.

||||||||

Joe Moss came into KARO the next morning to meet with Kevin.

"Kevin, the other night, one of your air personalities played the wrong side of our newest release. 'Forever' was to be the hit side, not 'Touch,'" Joe said.

Kevin, not knowing quite how to respond to Joe, thought for a moment.

Finally, Kevin asked, "Are you upset about what happened?"

"We have done press releases to all the stations, informing them that 'Forever' was the song," Joe said.

"Joe, Harley made a mistake that evening," Kevin said. "But, in his defense, he played both releases and let his listeners determine which one they wanted to hear. Here at KARO, we will be playing both songs. You know, this could be humongous; it could be a double-sided hit record. The Beatles and the Monkees are the only groups to do that, and only the Beatles had a number one from both sides. I think we would be in an elite company to accomplish that. From what I have been told, other stations have picked up on Harley's discovery and are running with it."

"Kevin, you know, you are absolutely right. I never thought about it like that," Joe said.

Kevin smiled at Joe and wished him a good day. Joe left Kevin's office with a much-different attitude than the one he had arrived with.

IIIIIIII

After a successful tour and two top-forty hits under his belt, Garland's bank account was beginning to grow. With the royalty checks hitting regularly, Garland wanted to do something very special for his family. One day when he was on his way home from KARO, while sitting at a traffic light, a radiant orange Camaro convertible caught his eye. Garland turned at the light and proceeded to enter the dealership.

As luck would have it, there was an empty space next to the car, and Garland took advantage of it. Garland sprang out of the family car just as the salesman approached him. The 1969 Camaro was the most beautiful car Garland had ever seen. The black leather interior and convertible top perfectly complemented the radiant orange.

The salesman greeted Garland and opened the driver-side door. Mounted in the center of the steering wheel was the SS symbol, indicating this was a muscle car as well. At first, the salesman viewed Garland as just another tire kicker. As Garland raised the hood and looked at the awesome engine, he saw another awesome sight. Inside, on the showroom floor, was a brilliant blue Camaro convertible. Without any hesitation, Garland tossed the keys to the salesman and began to make his way to the showroom floor.

As Garland entered the showroom, several salesmen behaved in the same manner as the one who had met Garland on the lot. They viewed him as a young tire kicker. Finally, an older salesman approached Garland.

"Sir, how are you today? I see you have a fantastic eye for awesome cars," the man said.

Soon the other salesmen entered the floor and whispered to the older salesman, telling him not to get excited about this customer.

As Garland opened the door to the blue convertible, the remaining salesmen gathered around. They wanted to see the older salesman get some experience with a tire kicker. Although he was much older than the others, he was new to the car business. They didn't want to miss out on the fun each thought was about to happen.

"Do you mind if I try out the radio? I am really into music," Garland said.

This really brought about a large chuckle from the salesmen.

Everything was going just as if the scene were scripted: young man looking at a sports car and enjoying the radio. Garland began to tune the radio to the FM band. Soon a song began to play, and Garland turned up the volume. The louder the music played, the more the salesmen laughed. As fate would have it that day, the song on the radio was "Touch." As the song finished playing, Harley informed his listeners that "Touch" was now the number-one song not only in Denver but also in the nation.

Garland smiled and raised both hands up into the air, letting out a yell. This was the best news he could have received that day. Garland turned off the radio and stepped out of the car. He handed the keys to the salesman.

"Sir, do you have the keys to the orange convertible as well?" Garland asked the older salesman.

The salesman nodded that he did.

"Well, today is your lucky day. You see, I love orange, and blue is my mother's favorite color. I have been wondering what I could get for her birthday," Garland said.

The other salesmen were all standing with their mouths open.

"I will take them both, and I want them to be delivered," Garland said. "The song you just heard reaching number one nationwide is my song. This is a perfect way to celebrate."

The salesman took Garland's information and led him into the business office. Inside his desk drawer, he removed two sold signs and proceeded to the cars to place the signs inside them. He wanted to return the show for his colleagues, laughing and smiling at each salesman as he walked by. This was a very good day for him as well.

||||||||

Garland drove the family car home and left it in the street, by the curb. He wanted to make sure the new cars would be on display in the driveway. Garland walked into the kitchen, where he found James and Sissy just sitting down for dinner. The family enjoyed a very good dinner that evening. As good as his mother's cooking was, Garland had to force himself to clean his plate. The excitement was more than he could handle.

Garland began to wipe his mouth with his napkin as the doorbell rang. The timing was perfect.

Sissy, sitting closest to the living room, was the first to leave the kitchen. She approached the front door, closely followed by Garland and James. Standing at the front door were two men in suits, one of which was the older salesman from the dealership.

"Ma'am, are you Sissy Summers?" the salesman said.

"Yes, I am Sissy Summers. Why do you ask?" she said.

The man reached into his pocket and handed Sissy the keys to the blue convertible. Afterward, the two men began to hum the first bars of "Happy Birthday."

Sissy turned to James. "Do you know what this is all about?"

James shook his head. He didn't have the slightest clue as to what was happening.

She then turned to Garland, to see the biggest grin she had ever seen on his face.

"Happy Birthday, Mother," Garland said as he approached Sissy to give her a kiss and a hug. "The blue one is for you, and the orange one is mine."

Garland agreed to drive the two men back to the dealership. This would give him the opportunity to visit Suzanna and surprise her with his orange convertible. He wanted everyone close to him to celebrate and share his success with "Touch." It was not every day that you had the number-one song in the nation.

He arrived at Suzanna's apartment. He wanted to see the look in her eyes. Garland pulled up in front of her apartment and began to honk the horn until she opened the door. Garland immediately ran up to the door to take her by the hand.

"Baby, have you heard? 'Touch' is the number-one song in the nation!" Garland screamed.

He lifted Suzanna up into the air, spinning her around and around. Once Garland returned Suzanna to the ground, she immediately bent over and began to throw up.

"Baby, I am sorry. I didn't mean to get you dizzy and make you sick," Garland said.

Garland led her over to the car, and sat Suzanna down in the passenger seat. Suzanna began to get her color back.

"Garland, it wasn't the spinning that made me sick. I am pregnant," she said.

With that announcement, Garland dropped to his knees in shock, as if someone had knocked his feet right out from under him. This was the most eventful day of his nineteen years.

22

"TOUCH" WAS BECOMING the biggest hit of the year. During its third week as the nation's number-one tune, "Touch" broke the plateau of one million sales. "Touch" was showing no sign of relinquishing the number-one spot on the charts. Joe Moss was beginning to put together a short tour to capitalize on the success of "Touch." Not only was "Touch" the number-one single, but the album was at the top of the charts as well. This was the perfect time for a short tour. This time, Aurora's Fire would be the headliner and not the opening act. Being the headliner on a successful tour would also be very lucrative for the boys. Touring was where the money was to be made.

Joe Moss arrived in Kevin's office to wrap up the schedule for the upcoming concert tour. The boys were all in attendance that morning when Joe presented Aurora's Fire with their platinum-record sales plaque for "Touch." The plaque would be displayed in the trophy case in the KARO studio. After presenting the award, Joe opened his brief-case and presented the boys with their royalty checks. The expression on each of their faces quickly showed that these checks reflected the largest amount of money any of the young men had received up to this time.

Joe proceeded to remove another item from his briefcase. He quickly unfolded it reveal a black T-shirt. There would be two differ-ent designs on the front; the back would have the tour dates and their respective venues.

"Several groups have been merchandising souvenirs at their shows," Joe explained. "These T-shirts will help with the tour costs. I am also very close to having us a sponsor as well. These are some of the benefits we will have as the headliner for the tour."

Another two weeks passed, and "Touch" remained the number-one song in the country. It had now held the top spot for five straight weeks. The tour was sold out. This tour would take them to the West Coast, to some of the largest arenas used during that time.

The first stop would take them to Southern California, including an appearance at the Hollywood Bowl and another appearance on a popular late-night television show. If "Touch" remained the number-one song by the time the tour ended, it was almost guaranteed to become a double-platinum record. This would be the first double-platinum hit for Magic Sounds.

The date arrived for the boys to depart on their tour. Garland and Suzanna had agreed to wait until the tour was over to make their special announcement. The time was also getting near for the arrival of Tobie and Brandon's baby. The thought of his being away was very hard on both Tobie and Brandon. Tobie's due date was two days before the tour's last show.

"Baby, I will call you every night to check on you, and I have asked Sissy to check in on you as well," Brandon said.

"Well, you just hurry up and get back for our daughter's birth," Tobie said.

"Daughter? I think you mean our *son's* birth," Brandon said as he kissed Tobie goodbye and entered the bus.

This was going to be a very long two weeks for Brandon now that he had finally found his best friend and the love of his life. He remembered promising Tobie that he would never spending even one night away from her.

||||||||

The first show of the tour, in Los Angeles, showed the boys a crowd far different from the audiences they had entertained in the southeast.

The ways and times of the West Coast were much more liberal than anywhere else in the country during that time. During the opening show, the boys went out for their opening act. The crowd was much less reserved than East Coast audiences. At first, it appeared this was the difference between the two coasts.

As the opening song began, Garland and Rudy looked out into the audience. The audience seemed hazy. Maybe it was the lighting. Both looked at each other, with the same puzzled expression on their faces. Then, the crowd became even fainter. There was also a familiar odor all throughout the stage area. Almost the entire audience was openly smoking pot during the concert. This was something very, very different to them, coming from Colorado.

As the show began to wind down, there was no doubt that most of the audience was stoned, either from smoking their own joints or inhaling the smoke permeating the air.

"At least the crowd was in a good mood," Rudy said.

Garland laughed. If Southern California was this wild, he couldn't wait to see Northern California.

IIIIIII

Brandon called to check on Tobie. He heard the phone ring on the other end of the line. At first, he thought Tobie would never answer the phone. Finally, after many rings, the most welcome voice came over the line. Tobie knew there were only two kinds of calls she could possibly receive at this time of night, one of which she knew she would not be happy to receive, while the other would be the highlight of her day. The voice coming through the phone line soon revealed this would be the better of the two kinds of calls.

"How is my son doing this evening, baby?" Brandon asked.

Tobie began to laugh, and then she answered, "Well, I am not sure how your son is doing, but your daughter is giving me fits this evening. I should have not fed her that spicy food for dinner."

Tobie held the phone to her stomach, wanting to let her baby enjoy its father's voice.

"The TV show is on tonight," Brandon said. "We taped it at 5:00 p.m., and it will air at 11:00 p.m. Tonight, we will perform at Anaheim Stadium. Tonight's crowd will be much larger than the one at the Hollywood Bowl. After tonight's show, we will travel to the Bay Area for a show and some appearances."

They said their goodbyes, and Brandon hung up the phone and went to join the band.

The Anaheim show began with an opening that included some characters from Disneyland. It was obvious that the tone for this show was to be a lot different from the previous night's show. It wasn't everyday a group would be able to serenade Mickey and Minnie Mouse. Brandon, almost a new father, took advantage of the situation and gathered some take-home souvenirs for his soon-to-be-born child. One of these included was a photo of Brandon with both Mickey and Minnie.

"Brandon, I think you will enjoy having a child very much. You seem to still have a lot of child left in you," Adam said.

Brandon laughed. "You have no idea of how much I am looking forward to being a daddy. I want to be the father to my child that I never had as a kid. I know how important that would be to my son."

"Your son? You are confident aren't, you?" Beau said.

The band all had a big laugh and then began their part of the concert. Tonight's crowd was much more like the crowds the group had come to know from previous tours: very interactive with the show—it seemed not being stoned would do that.

The bus left Anaheim for the short trip to San Diego. San Diego would provide a night off before the show. The boys would take advantage of the day off to take in some of Southern California's best venues.

San Diego was a beautiful city, without the chaos of the much-larger Los Angeles area. During their off day, a publicist arranged for the boys to take a tour of the world-famous San Diego Zoo and to enjoy a day of relaxation on one of California's best beaches. This would be a treat for six guys from Colorado.

During the trip to the zoo, Brandon began to watch the many families in attendance. The scene of the families and kids at the zoo was an image he would take home. He anxiously awaited the day when he and Tobie would take their family to the zoo. Several times, the other guys caught Brandon gazing at the families, with the biggest grin on his face. No one could remember seeing Brandon any happier than he was now.

The San Diego show would find a local group opening the show for Aurora's Fire. This group was very talented and featured a female singer. Sand Dollar was a five-member band that featured two-part harmonies with more of a folk sound. Many of their songs used classical guitars. This brought back memories to Garland, Adam, Beau, and Brandon of the days of Summer's Solstice. The Sand Dollar opened the show with a rendition of "Lucy in the Sky with Diamonds." This really painted a vision of the boys' past. Sand Dollar wrapped up the opening of the show. They were a crowd-pleaser.

During the stage setup between the two acts, Garland began to talk to some of the members of the group. He soon discovered these musicians had the same passion for music that he and Adam did in their earlier days.

"You guys are great," Garland said. He then had an idea. "I want you to join us for the remaining tour. Would you like to open one of the shows in Northern California?"

The answer came in unison from the band members.

"I want Joe Moss to hear you perform. I think he will be as impressed as I am," Garland said.

The bus pulled out of San Diego, headed for San Francisco, with the boys accompanied by five new passengers. This would be an all-day bus ride that would give Garland the time he wanted to find out more about their opening act. The much-awaited San Francisco and Oakland shows would be back to back. San Francisco's Haight-Ashbury neighborhood was the scene of the much-publicized love-ins. Frisco was a much more radical city, and the times there were changing faster than anywhere in the country.

When the tour arrived there, it might have been summer as far as the calendar was concerned, but the weather felt like a blustery, cold winter's day. The cable cars and hills with the Golden Gate Bridge as a backdrop were spectacular. The bus pulled into the arena's parking facility for a welcomed rest. There were several radio shows to attend the next morning. The first radio show sponsored a contest for free tickets and wanted the band to make the drawings of winners. These shows would become a very popular item during the rest of the tour. This was a way to put the band in touch with their fans.

|||||||

Sissy went by to check in on Tobie while the boys were in the Bay Area. Tobie was becoming depressed, and her due date arrived. Not having Brandon there scared her. She had always planned for Brandon to be with her for this special day.

"Have you talked to Brandon today?" Sissy asked.

Tobie could not hide the fact that Brandon had not called her. She had no way of contacting Brandon while he was on tour; she always relied on him to call her.

Seeing Tobie's state of mind, Sissy called Tobie's doctor. Sissy had a plan that would help both Tobie and Brandon. After receiving the approval of Tobie's doctor, Sissy called Kevin to discuss her plan. Kevin agreed that Sissy's idea was fantastic. He agreed to meet Sissy and Tobie and at the Summerses' house.

As they were leaving Brandon and Tobie's apartment to meet Kevin, Sissy noticed a scrapbook that Tobie had been working on. There were these pictures of Tobie during her pregnancy, all taken by Brandon. These were very good pictures that captured the special event in a tender way. They were perfect for what Sissy had planned. She grabbed the pictures and dropped them off at the station.

"James, have the video people at Magic Sounds place these pictures onto a slide," Sissy said.

Tobie didn't have a clue as to what Sissy was planning.

As they drove from the station to the Summerses' house, Sissy said, "Tobie, you and I are going to San Francisco. I called your doctor, and he said you will be okay to travel."

Kevin stopped by the Magic Sounds Studio on his way to meet

Sissy and Tobie. He picked up the slide and delivered it to Sissy when he arrived at the house.

"Ladies, are we ready?" Kevin asked.

This was the first time Tobie had traveled by plane. As much as she wanted to see Brandon, there was no way she would have flown that day by herself. Tobie and Sissy boarded the plane and began the ninety-minute flight into Oakland, California. Kevin called to inform Garland that his mother and a guest were on their way to Oakland for the show. He did not tell Garland that Tobie was her traveling companion. Kevin also told Garland to arrange for a screen to show the slide Sissy was bringing as a surprise for Brandon.

IIIIIIII

Aurora's Fire and Sand Dollar made their way to the Oakland arena. It was time to perform the preshow sound checks. Seeing what actually went into the preshow production was a new experience for Sand Dollar. As they arrived at the arena, Joe Moss approached them. He was very curious about the opening act that Garland had told him about. If the group sounded as good as their lead singer looked, Joe knew that they would be a successful act.

Sand Dollar took the stage and began to do a warm-up song. Once again, the song was a rendition of Summer's Solstice's version of "Lucy in the Sky." The two-part harmonies immediately gathered Joe's attention. As Joe and Garland sat watching Sand Dollar, Joe told Garland he thought they could have a hit with their version of "Lucy." He was very impressed. This tour had started to make his marquee act larger; as a bonus, Magic Sounds was gaining another promising recording act.

IIIIIIII

Tobie and Sissy's flight landed in Oakland. Tobie had survived her first flight. From the airport to the arena was an hour cab drive. They had almost two hours until the start of the concert. As the cab driver left the airport, a traffic report informed him that he would need to take a detour because of an earlier accident. He assured his passengers that they would not be late.

The cabbie pulled into the arena parking lot and informed the parking attendants that he needed to let a pregnant lady out at the front door. This not only helped Tobie, but it saved several minutes as well. Tobie and Sissy exited the cab and went to the will-call window.

Garland had left instructions for Sissy's ticket and the slide.

"Please get this slide to the lighting people," Sissy informed the person at the will-call window. "It contains something very special for tonight's show."

Sand Dollar opened the show with "Lucy." Although they were unknown to the audience at the start of the show, after tonight, they wouldn't be forgotten. Each song ended in standing ovations. It was evident that they fed off the audience and the audience fed off them. The rest of the tour was going to love Sand Dollar. Joe Moss was on cloud nine. He couldn't wait to sign the new act. Sand Dollar was brought out onstage to a warm encore. This was their first encore. It would not be their last!

In between acts, the stage crew began to set up something new for Aurora's Fire. A very large paper screen was being installed on the side of the stage, near Brandon's drums. Only Garland knew the reason for the screen's existence.

Sissy and Tobie went to a dressing room that Garland had arranged.

Onstage, the emcee barked, "Hello, Oakland. Tonight, we want to welcome the group with the number-one song in the country, now for the sixth straight week—the Aurora's Fire!"

The band ran out onto the stage, to loud applause and flashing lights. The boys decided to start this show with a fast-tempo song. They wanted this show to really cook and intended for the audience to have a wonderful time. This would be the most special stop on the tour. No one knew just how special it would be. The band went into one song right after another. They didn't stop to pause for one minute. The audience loved every song. They were on their feet the entire show.

Finally, after the seventh number, the band took time out to introduce themselves and for Garland and Rudy to change out their guitars. After a fast-paced start, the show began to slow down into the ballads.

The crowd kept shouting for "Touch." Each time, Garland would turn to Rudy, smiling and shaking his head no. He was saving "Touch" for something very special that night.

After the instrument change, the band began another seven-song set. Once again, there was no interruption in between songs.

That night, something was giving all of them energy like never before. Well, almost all of them. Brandon began to get tired, with the continuous drumming from one number to another.

Garland decided it was time for the show to really become special.

The band still had not performed "Touch." But why? Were they going to skip the biggest song in a decade? Everyone was in shock.

After the last song of the second set, the security guard escorted Tobie and Sissy to an area behind the stage. Tobie stood on the spot where she was directed to stand.

The boys paused for a moment to quench their thirst.

Garland made his way back to Brandon, walked up to his friend, and smiled. He then gave Brandon a hug and a pat on the back.

"Brandon, this is for you, my friend," Garland said.

Brandon was at a loss to understand what Garland was talking about.

Garland returned to his stand and sat on a stool, awaiting Brandon. Garland then began the introduction to "Touch." The crowd went wild! Something began to happen that night with this version of "Touch." Where Garland would normally begin the vocals to "Touch," another musical chorus began. The other band members followed his lead. On the third chorus, something began to happen.

The paper next to Brandon began to perform as a screen. A slide suddenly began to play on the screen. The slide began with a picture of Brandon, followed by one of Tobie. As the slide continued, there were maternity pictures of Tobie, each detailing the months of her pregnancy and the special relationship she shared with Brandon. The crowd grew quiet. Brandon's drumming stopped as he began to watch the love of his life on this screen. The slide was coming to an end when Garland began to sing "Touch."

Garland began "Touch" with different verses this night. This was Tobie's cue. As the crowd and Brandon watched the slide, Tobie walked from behind the screen and onto the stage, next to where Brandon sat. Brandon jumped up from behind his drums and ran to Tobie. With just Garland and his guitar now playing, there was not a dry eye in the house. As Garland began the final words to "Touch," Sissy joined him onstage. "Touch," as big as it was, would never be any larger than it was on this night.

The lights were dimmed, other than those assigned to the stage flooring.

Garland and Sissy joined Brandon and Tobie. Adam and Beau couldn't wait to put their instruments down and meet them as well. As they walked away from the stage and made their way to the dressing room, Tobie made a sudden stop. As she stopped, she grimaced. There was a puddle of water on the floor where she stood.

"Baby, its time," Tobie said to Brandon. "Your daughter is going to be a Californian."

"You mean my *son* will be," Brandon said.

Garland and Adam began to clear a path to the exit for Brandon and Tobie. Immediately exiting the arena, they saw one of the security guard's patrol cars. As luck would have it, the guard was inside the parked car, drinking coffee. The swarming of his car took him by surprise. Soon he realized what was going on and took pleasure in being the driver for this special mission.

The driver knew the quickest route to the hospital, one that would not involve the traffic of the concertgoers.

Brandon sat next to Tobie in the backseat, trying to comfort her during her contractions. Each time, he would wipe her forehead and kiss her hand. He didn't want anything to happen to the love of his life.

As the driver arrived at the hospital, he jumped from the car, running into the emergency room as Brandon began to assist Tobie from the backseat. Several nurses arrived at the car. One pushed a wheelchair that they would use to bring Tobie into the preparation area prior to taking her to the delivery room. She was already well into labor. Brandon went into the predelivery room long enough to change into a hospital gown.

The doctor came in to examine Tobie and immediately ordered the nurses to take her into the delivery room. Brandon went in with her to help deliver their first child. Although Tobie was well dilated, the baby was taking its time. It was at this time that Brandon realized he wasn't having a son.

"Darling, this has to be a girl; this baby is too stubborn to be a boy," Brandon said as he kissed Tobie.

Thirty minutes had elapsed when the baby began to appear. It wasn't long before the baby was out of Tobie's womb and lying on her stomach, waiting for her cord to be cut.

"Would you like to cut your daughter's cord?" the nurse asked Brandon.

Brandon followed the nurse's instructions and cut his daughter's cord.

The nurse removed the baby to take her vital stats.

Brandon bent down and kissed Tobie.

"I love you," Brandon said.

Tobie clutched Brandon's hand. "I love you too, baby. But the next baby we have, it will be your turn to give birth."

The nurse returned with the baby, now wrapped in a pink blanket.

"I have a name bracelet," the nurse said. "Do you have a name picked out?"

Tobie and Brandon had names picked out: one for a boy and one for a girl. Brandon told the nurse the name they had selected, and she wrote it down on the bracelet.

"Brandon, I have something in my purse I want to put on her," Tobie said.

Brandon looked in Tobie's purse, found the items she wanted, and placed them on their daughter.

"You have a room of friends waiting outside," the nurse said.

Brandon took his daughter and left to show her off.

|||||||

The rest of the band sat in the delivery-room waiting area. Garland and Sissy tried to calm the others down. This was the most exciting thing that had ever happened to them. The time seemed to crawl by. They all wanted to know how Tobie and the baby were doing. The doors began to swing open, and the boys jumped to their feet.

Brandon walked into the waiting room, holding a bundle in a pink blanket. As he opened the blanket, in his arms was a little baby with a head full of coal-black hair and eyes as black as onyx. She was wearing a tiny multicolor headband and the tiniest pair of moccasins.

"I want everyone to meet the new girl in my life. This is my daughter, Skye. Her name is Apache," Brandon said.

No one could ever remember seeing Brandon so at peace with his life. This little one was going to be Daddy's girl, and no one knew it more than Brandon.

Garland walked away from the others, with his head down. Sissy sensed something was wrong. It was not like Garland to not want to share in Brandon's excitement. Whatever was troubling him would weigh on her mind during the trip back to Colorado. Garland noticed the change Skye made in Brandon. He wanted that same feeling. He and Suzanna would have to reveal their secret when the tour was over.

23

THE SUMMER TOUR surpassed everyone's expectations. The boys arrived home after selling out all their concert dates, Magic Sounds added another artist, and Brandon and Tobie welcomed home a daughter. The Monday morning after the tour, news arrived at KARO.

After eight weeks of being the number-one song in the nation, "Touch" slipped to number three. Although "Touch" was no longer number one, the album containing the giant hit was still holding its own as the number-one-selling album. Joe Moss called Kevin with the news that the album had reached double-platinum status in sales and was showing no signs of slowing down. Aurora's Fire was the hottest act that summer.

As Brandon, Tobie, and Skye left the station that morning, Garland noticed how happy they were with the addition of Skye. This made Garland want Suzanna very much. He drove to Suzanna's apartment. His new Camaro needed wings that morning. He couldn't wait for the two of them to make their announcement.

Garland arrived at Suzanna's apartment. He used the key Suzanna had given him and let himself into her apartment. He wanted to surprise the love of his life with his return. Garland searched the entire apartment, only to find that it was empty. The emotions of the last two weeks had worn him down. Garland walked into her bedroom and took a seat on her bed. It wasn't long before he fell asleep.

Several hours had passed when Garland awakened. He sat up on the side of Suzanna's bed, trying to gather his senses. Garland was very disappointed that Suzanna still wasn't home. Finally, he gave up and began to make his way out of her apartment. As Garland was about to exit the apartment, Suzanna pulled into the parking lot. She walked up to the front door without noticing that Garland was waiting for her.

"Hey, baby!" Garland said.

Suzanna was shocked to see Garland. It was apparent she wasn't as glad to see Garland as he was to see her. She eventually reached the spot where he stood. Garland bent down to kiss her and followed with a hug. For some reason, Suzanna wasn't receptive.

"Is there something wrong?" Garland asked.

Suzanna could no longer hold the tears back and began to cry as she ran inside her apartment.

Garland followed her into the apartment as she ran into the bathroom, closing the door.

"Suzanna, what is wrong, baby? Please tell me," Garland said through the door.

Twenty minutes passed, with Garland standing outside the bathroom door, and Suzanna not responding to him. Being ignored began to make Garland angry. The silence from Suzanna began to make him worry and wonder if she was okay. Garland took a step backward and kicked the door open. Suzanna was sitting on the floor, with her head on her knees. Garland approached her, and Suzanna raised her head to finally acknowledge him.

"Garland, there isn't going to be a baby," she said.

"What do you mean, there isn't going to be a baby?" Garland asked.

"I am not pregnant," she said.

Garland was at a loss for words. Never in a million years did he expect the news he was hearing at this moment.

Suzanna mumbled something about needing to think of her modeling career. She then insisted that Garland leave. She wanted to be alone. Suzanna's attitude really hurt Garland that day. He did the only thing he could think of, giving in to her wishes and leaving the apartment.

Garland arrived home and went immediately to his bedroom. He wanted to be alone. Today's homecoming wasn't quite the welcome he had imagined. Garland was lying on his bed, with his head in his pillow, when the phone began to ring. After several rings, it was apparent that no one was home to answer the phone.

Maybe Suzanna is calling me, Garland thought.

With that, Garland jumped up to answer the phone. The voice on the line wasn't Suzanna's.

"Garland, how are you?" the voice said.

"You have no idea how good it is to hear your voice," Garland said. He began to explain what had happened that day.

"I am sorry you had to come home to that Garland. I wish there was something I could do to make you feel better," the voice said.

"There is. What are your plans for this week?" he asked.

"Well, as of this moment, I don't have any plans," the voice said.

"Is it all right if I come and see you?" Garland asked.

The voice replied that he was always welcome.

Garland hung the phone up and left a note for his family. He departed the house with only the clothes on his back.

IIIIIII

Soon after Garland left that evening, Suzanna arrived at the Summerses' home. She approached the front door as Sissy and James were arriving from a business meeting.

"Hi, Suzanna. We haven't seen you in a while. How have you been?" Sissy said.

"I am surviving," Suzanna replied. She then said, "I don't see Garland's car. Do you know when he might be home?"

The three of them entered the house and went into the kitchen. There on the table was a folded piece of paper. Sissy opened it to find a note from Garland.

After reading the note, Sissy informed Suzanna that Garland wouldn't be back in Aurora for several days.

"Does he say where he went?" Suzanna asked.

Sensing something was amiss with Suzanna, Sissy promptly answered, "He doesn't say. He only says that he will call me tomorrow."

Sissy didn't want Suzanna to know Garland's destination. What she didn't know wouldn't hurt her. Sissy knew there was something going on.

Without a word, Suzanna left the Summerses' house. She knew Sissy was keeping something from her. As Suzanna left, she squealed the tires, leaving tire marks the entire width of the Summerses' driveway.

||||||||

At the last minute, Garland changed his mind and decided the drive in his convertible would do him good. He wanted the time to think things out. Suzanna was changing, and the change was something he wanted to sort out. He kept thinking about Suzanna's pregnancy. Had she intended for it to be ended? Was it an act of God? All these thoughts raced through his mind.

The drive would take just a bit longer than twenty-four hours. While driving, Garland tuned in a Kansas City radio station. The station carried a national syndicated show with the weekly music countdown. During the show, the host was leading into the number-three spot previously held by "Touch." Another song had replaced "Touch" as the number-three song that week.

Garland was glad he hadn't found the station earlier. He didn't want to hear how far "Touch" had fallen in the countdown. He pulled into a gas station and filled up. The gas stop enabled his legs to get a break as well. With a full tank, Garland fired up the Camaro to continue his trip. The radio host was about to announce the number-one song for the week. He began his introduction by saying that the song he was about to play would make history in the music industry.

The host continued, "After eight weeks as the number-one song in the nation, and then falling to the number-three spot, this week's number-one song has made its way back to the top. This is the first time in the Rock era that a song has achieved that."

With that, he began to play "Touch."

"Touch" was number one again, making it the number-one song for nine weeks. Garland turned up the volume on the car radio, so everyone within earshot could hear.

|||||||

As the hours crept along, Suzanna's demeanor worsened. She began to plot her revenge, furious that Garland had run out on her. Suzanna wanted Garland to pay dearly for not understanding her situation. In her own way, she loved Garland; she just wasn't ready to be a mother. She had her modeling career to think of. Young and attractive, pregnant was the last thing she wanted to be. Garland leaving her at this time only fueled her anger.

|||||||

Garland continued his drive eastward. His journey took him into the hills of western North Carolina. This was the perfect weather and scenery for a drive with the top down. The air was filled with the fragrance of honeysuckle in bloom, and the fresh mountain air took his mind millions of miles away from his troubles. During the drive, he pulled over to enjoy a mother bear and her two cubs enjoying a fruitful berry patch. They were too busy enjoying their feast to even be aware that he was anywhere in the area.

The evening's fading light began to make the mountains seem like they were on fire. The Great Smoky Mountains would leave an image in Garland's mind that would never forget. He paused to think of the beauty the Rockies, which he had taken for granted all this time, vowing inwardly to never make that mistake again.

The next morning, Garland had almost reached his destination. He decided to call home while stopping at a gas station to refuel.

"Mother, can you look up an address for me? I want to surprise them," he said.

Sissy retrieved the address and Garland wrote it down on the back of an empty paper bag from his lunch the day before.

"I will call you tomorrow, after I arrive, to let you know I made it okay," Garland told Sissy.

Garland arrived in the Raleigh area early that afternoon. He was now just an hour away from his final destination. To make things more private, Garland stopped in Raleigh to get a hotel room. He wanted to take this time to freshen up. He took advantage of the hotel gift shop to buy shirt and a pair of shorts; he was still wearing the clothes he had on when he left, and they needed a break. After freshening up and changing into his new outfit, Garland began the last leg of his journey.

Garland arrived at his final destination that evening. He slowly drove passed the house, thinking of a way to make his entrance. After several drive-bys, he finally mustered the courage to stop the car, get out, and make his way up the sidewalk. He approached the door and searched for its bell. However, there was no bell, just an old-fashioned knocker in the center of the door. Garland began to pull the ring of the knocker, pressing it against the plate on the door. The force made a very loud sound, onc he knew would be heard all throughout the house.

While Garland impatiently stood there, waiting for someone to answer the door, the most wonderful aroma treated his nose. This was the aroma of dinner, which embarrassed Garland. He had never intended to arrive just in time for dinner. He began to think of a way to leave without being detected; but, as he soon found out, it was too late to escape. The door opened. There in the doorway stood a very beautiful woman wearing cutoffs and a man's fitted shirt with the shirttails on the outside. The two took a moment to soak up the view of each other.

"Oh my God! Garland, is it really you?!" Brenda cried.

Brenda's excitement was heard in the dining room, where the rest of the family had started their dinner.

"I thought you were kidding about coming to see me. This is the best surprise I have had in a long time," Brenda said.

Garland entered the foyer and stepped into Brenda's open arms. He returned the warmth of her heart and soul with a very intense and heartfelt hug. Neither of them wanted to let go. This was something they both had needed for a very long time.

Brenda took Garland's hand and led him into the dining room to meet the rest of the family.

Valerie Fisher jumped up at the sight of Garland and immediately hugged him.

"My God! This is such a wonderful treat. You truly are a sight for sore eyes," Valerie said with a laugh and smile.

Michael Fisher shook Garland's hand. "I want to thank you, once again, for all your generosity during my accident, Garland."

It was very clear to Garland that the Fishers thought of him as a son.

Brenda interrupted her dad and led Garland to a seat next to hers. She dashed into the kitchen to retrieve another place setting. There was no way Garland was to leave tonight without dining with them. Left-handed Brenda made sure to seat Garland in the chair to her right. As Garland took his seat, the food began to be passed his way. Each time, he was encouraged to take as much as he wanted.

"Garland, you will need to empty the bowls. We don't do left-overs," Valerie said with a laugh.

Garland grinned and obliged the invitation. Although it had been many years, he had not forgotten that Valerie was a fantastic cook.

Brenda turned Garland's wineglass upright and filled it with a zesty blackberry wine. Garland placed his napkin in his lap and began to enjoy the wonderful meal. Brenda smiled as Garland took a peek at her. This made her feel special.

Brenda's face then lit up like a Christmas tree. There was a surprise happening under the table. As the two began to eat, Garland took Brenda's hand. The two would hold hands that way for the entire meal. Sometimes they put their forks down with their free hands to pass a dish to another family member, but they never released their hands from one another.

"Mrs. Fisher, this meal is the best I have ever eaten. Everything is wonderful," Garland said.

"Garland, I am glad you like my cooking. But I have saved the best for last. We are having a family recipe for dessert: my great-grandmother's bread pudding with a hot rum sauce," Valerie said.

"Yes, ma'am! I have a little room," Garland said with a wink.

The bread pudding was to die for. It was so wonderful that Garland asked for seconds. Valerie smiled as Brenda dipped out a second helping, complete with rum sauce. With the completion of dessert, Brenda led Garland into the den.

Michael Fisher joined Garland as the ladies cleared the table and loaded the dishwasher. Garland and Michael enjoyed talking about the good old days in Charleston. Brenda and Valerie soon joined the two men. Brenda sat beside Garland on the leather sofa. Although this was a very long couch, one would have thought it was a sofa made for two.

"Congratulations, Garland on your musical career. You should see the way Brenda's face lights up every time she hears "Touch" on the radio," Valerie said.

Garland turned toward Brenda, smiling when he saw her blushing because of what her mother had said.

Brenda smiled and once again grabbed Garland's hand.

"Brenda has followed every step of your career," Michael said.

Garland returned Brenda's smile. He was very touched that Brenda cared that much for him.

"Brenda has completed her second year of college," Valerie said.

"Speaking of college—" Brenda said, her voice trailing off as she left the room.

She returned to the room, tossing a blue T-shirt into Garland's lap. "You need to wear the Duke shirt, baby, not the North Carolina State shirt."

The whole room burst into laughter.

As Brenda returned to her seat next to Garland, she bent down to kiss him. Garland, much to her surprise, returned the kiss.

The length of the kiss took Brenda's parents by surprise. This was the first time they had ever seen their daughter behave this way.

"Garland, do you have accommodations for this evening?" Michael asked.

"Yes, sir, I have a room at the Marriott in Raleigh," Garland answered.

"Are you driving back to Raleigh tonight?" Valerie asked.

"Yes, ma'am," Garland replied.

"Well, tomorrow night, you will be our guest. We would be glad to have you stay here," Valerie said.

Garland had never anticipated that this would happen.

"I think your mother and I will let you two have some privacy, Brenda," Michael said.

Brenda's parents left the room, leaving the two to catch up on each other's lives.

"How long will you be staying here, Garland?" Brenda asked.

"I am not sure. I need to sort some things out, and I wanted to see you, Brenda. There are some things I need to talk to you about. Afterward, you may not want to see me again," Garland said.

Garland took Brenda's hand and began to tell her about Suzanna. "I thought I had fallen in love with a beautiful girl back in Colorado. The more I thought I knew her, the more I realized I didn't really know her at all. She wasn't the girl I had thought she was."

Brenda held Garland's hand even tighter, realizing how hard this was for him to tell her.

"Just before we left on our West Coast tour, Suzanna told me that she was pregnant. She seemed very happy about it. Something happened while I was away. When I returned home, I went to surprise her at her apartment. She wasn't home when I arrived, so I let myself in with the key she had given me. When she returned, she wasn't glad to see me at all," Garland said.

Brenda could see the pain in his face. Although she had never met or talked to Suzanna, she instantly began to dislike her.

"She became upset with me. She then informed me she was no

longer pregnant and was glad she wasn't." Garland took a deep breath and then added, "I think she had the pregnancy terminated."

Brenda did the only thing she could think of: she hugged him. Garland returned the hug, snuggling like a newborn seeking comfort from his mother's love.

"Brenda, you are the only one who knows about this," Garland said. "There was no one else I felt I could turn to."

The more the two talked, the more obvious it became that each had strong feelings for the other.

The time had flown by, and Garland apologized for the intrusion.

Brenda looked at the grandfather clock in the foyer to see it was after 1:00 a.m. She walked Garland to the door.

"When you come back tomorrow, will you stay with us for a few days?" Brenda asked.

Garland shrugged his shoulders. He didn't have an answer. Once again, Brenda did the only thing she could think of: she grabbed Garland, kissing him long and deep. Once again, Garland was very receptive to her actions. Garland walked out the door, closing it behind him.

With her head hanging down, filled with confusion, Brenda once again reacted to the situation. Garland began to back out of the Fishers' driveway, and Brenda ran down the driveway, reaching his Camaro just in time. Garland stopped and rolled down the passenger window. She reached into the open window to unlock the door, letting herself into his car. She shut the door as Garland turned toward her.

"I am going back to Raleigh with you. I don't want you to be alone tonight," Brenda said.

Brenda's actions were received with mixed emotions by Garland. She was his first love, and he didn't want her family to be worried.

"Your parents will be worried about you," Garland said.

"Baby, as long as they know I am with you, they will not be worried," Brenda said.

Garland accepted her answer and pulled out of the driveway. He began the drive back to Raleigh.

With Brenda along for the ride, the trip back to Raleigh seemed much shorter than the trip from the hotel to the Fisher home. Garland walked Brenda to his hotel room. He unlocked the door, and Brenda turned to him with a big smile. He took her by the hand and led her into the parlor area of the room. Neither could tell who was the more nervous that night.

"Brenda, you can have your Duke shirt, and I will sleep in the NC State shirt," Garland said.

Brenda gave Garland the biggest sly smile he had ever had the privilege of seeing, and then she winked.

Garland began to turn the covers back on the bed, leaving a night-light on one of the nightstands. As he climbed into the bed, Brenda slid under the covers on the opposite side of the bed. The coolness of the crisp sheets made her instantly slide over to Garland's side of the bed, for both comfort and security. Garland wrapped his arms around her. She was an even better fit in his arms than Suzanna was. Brenda found Garland's hand and began to fill the spaces between his fingers with her own. The nervousness they both had experienced earlier left the room.

Garland began to whisper in Brenda's ear. The erotic feeling began to make her writhe. This was something she had waited her entire life for. She remembered that day at Garland's tenth birthday when Sissy taught the two to dance; she had fallen in love with him and never stopped loving him. This was absolutely perfect. Garland sensed Brenda's passion was stirring inside her beautiful body. He lifted her beautiful long blonde hair, so soft in his fingers, and began to trace her neck gently with his fingertips. He began to nibble on her neck as his hand began to trace the curves of her young body.

Brenda was bursting with passion; it was all she could do to control it. Finally, Brenda turned to face Garland and kissed him deeply. It was a long french kiss that took Garland totally by surprise. Brenda was a very good kisser, and he loved kissing her. Kissing was always his weakness. Brenda gently pushed Garland onto his back and got up on her knees in the bed. She began to take her Duke shirt off and then slid her panties onto the floor as well. This was going to be her first time, and she had always wanted Garland to be her first.

Brenda gently began to slide Garland's clothes off, and then she tossed them on the floor next to hers. She began to trace his nice chest, making circles with his chest hair. She began to kiss Garland's chest until she arrived to meet his lips, devouring his hot tongue with her own. She began to feel something for the first time. The moistness in her crotch was beginning to drip down onto Garland's stomach.

"Baby, this is my first time; I hope I don't disappoint you," Brenda whispered.

She slid down onto Garland and began to make love to him. The pain soon was overtaken by pure ecstasy. It wasn't long before Brenda experienced her first orgasm. Just as she was almost finished, another orgasm came, then another—she was out of control. They were coming so frequently, and some were so deep. She bent down to once again kiss Garland when she felt all her wetness become flooded with Garland's orgasm. The heat was much more intense than she had read about. Brenda slowly began to climb off Garland and immediately lay next to her lover. Her first time was heavenly! The two fell asleep in each other's arms, never changing their sleeping positions the entire night.

The morning sunlight found its way through the space between the closed drapes. A fine line of sunlight found its way across the faces of the two lovers. Brenda was the first to awaken that morning. She enjoyed gazing at Garland as he slept. He seemed to be at peace. He needed this peace after the story he had shared with her the night before. She gently ran her fingers through his long hair. Garland began to grin, as if he knew what was going on. Just when she thought he was about to awaken, his eyes seemed to close tighter. Brenda began to snuggle against Garland's warm body.

Garland could no longer resist playing possum. He flipped Brenda over onto her back; it was his turn to return the favor. Garland began to kiss Brenda until she could no longer resist his early morning intentions. Brenda's second time to make love would be more enjoyable than her first time, but it wouldn't be as memorable as the first time. Garland was a wonderful lover. He was patient and gentle. And, boy, was he a great kisser!

Garland left the love nest and began to start the shower. As the shower began to reach the hot-water stage, Garland took a moment to call room service to order breakfast.

"Brenda, it's time to rise and shine. We need to shower before breakfast arrives," Garland said.

Garland led Brenda into the shower and opened its doors. He placed a towel over the top of the door, and the two entered the wonderful pulsating water. Garland removed the top from the shampoo bottle as Brenda stood under the showerhead, enjoying the hot water rushing down her body. Garland led Brenda out from the shower's water and poured the shampoo into her hair. He began to shampoo her long, beautiful hair.

Brenda thought this was a pure treat. It was more than that—it was a dream!

"Baby it's time to wash the soap out of your beautiful hair," Garland said.

With the last rinse of her hair, Brenda turned to Garland and kissed him as the water rushed over their heads and down their bodies. Garland turned the shower's water off. The two took turns drying each other off that morning. The timing was perfect. They exited the steam-filled bathroom just as room service began to knock on the door.

|||||||

That same morning, back in Colorado, Suzanna was becoming very impatient with Garland. She began to call all the members of Aurora's Fire, searching for Garland. Each time, her call ended with no results. With the failure of each call, Suzanna's temper was becoming shorter. She decided to make one final call that morning.

"Sissy, I have been calling everywhere, trying to find Garland. I know you are hiding his whereabouts from me!" Suzanna screamed.

This wasn't the way to get any cooperation from Sissy, as Suzanna soon found out.

"Excuse me! Do you want to run that statement by me again?" Sissy barked back.

Suzanna apologized for her outburst. "I feel lost without Garland. I know I did something terrible."

"If I know Garland, Suzanna, I am sure it's nothing he will not get over," Sissy said.

Suzanna paused and then began to cry. "Well, this is something I know he will never understand. I just hope he will forgive me."

"Suzanna, it can't be that bad. Nothing is unforgivable," Sissy said.

Suzanna wanted to tell Sissy but couldn't find the words. She knew that Sissy would eventually find out.

||||||||

Back in North Carolina, Garland and Brenda made their way back to the Fishers' house. This was something new for Brenda, not just losing her virginity but leaving during the middle of the night. The two lovers entered the front door and made their way into the den, where Brenda's parents were enjoying the morning newspaper and coffee. Brenda and Garland took their familiar seat on the sofa, sitting hand in hand.

Valerie turned to her daughter. Without Brenda saying a word, Valerie knew what the two had been up to. She knew that someday it would happen, and she felt fortunate that her daughter was much older than most girls during that time. Michael, on the other hand, reacted in the same way all fathers do with their daughters.

Garland felt that if looks could kill, he was good as dead, with the look Brenda's dad was giving him.

Brenda did the only thing that she could think of at that moment. She walked over to where her dad was sitting in his lounging chair, picked up his empty coffee cup, and brought it into the kitchen. She refilled his cup, adding just the right ingredients, and returned to his side, placing the cup down on a nearby coaster. She climbed into her dad's lap and hugged him. After a long, loving hug, Brenda leaned back, still sitting in his lap.

"Dad, whatever you think I did last night, you are right. I love Garland. I've loved him ever since I was ten years old. If I had it to do all over again, I would. I have no regrets. I love him very, very, much," Brenda said.

Brenda began to cry. As she turned to where her mother was sitting, she witnessed her mother's tears as well.

Walking over to the chair that Brenda and Michael occupied, Valerie hugged her daughter.

Garland kept his seat on the sofa, not knowing exactly how to react. Although what was happening was awkward, he understood the love in the room.

Brenda left her father's lap and returned to take her seat next to Garland.

"Garland, how do you feel about what happened last night?" Michael asked.

"Sir, we did not plan what happened last night. True love is never planned; it just finds a way," Garland said.

"Garland, I know about the nights you fell asleep with Brenda's picture next to your head. Your mother was very touched by that, and so am I. I know you have always cared for Brenda," Valerie said.

Garland began to blush. At first, he wanted to kill Sissy for telling on him during her talks with Valerie. But then, once he thought about it, her talks made everything feel right. Both of Brenda's parents were very fond of Garland. They knew his feelings for their daughter were honest and real.

Garland began to excuse himself. He was sure he wouldn't be welcomed to stay here during his time in North Carolina. As he was about to exit the room, Valerie Fisher quickly put out her arm to stop him.

"Where do you think you are going?" Valerie said.

Speechless, Garland turned toward Valerie. His brain knew what to say, but his mouth didn't. Finally, his mouth caught up with his brain.

"I am driving back to Raleigh," Garland said. "I don't want to cause any problems between you, Mr. Fisher, and Brenda. Coming between you is the last thing I want to do."

With the same quickness Valerie had used to stop Garland, she moved toward him to give him a wonderful hug.

"Garland, our daughter is not a little girl," Valerie said. "Sometimes it takes a parent a little longer to accept that fact. If you go back to Raleigh and do not accept our original invitation to stay here, we will be very disappointed. Please stay with us as long as you remain in North Carolina."

This made Garland realize how special the Fishers were, and he gladly accepted Valerie's invitation.

The next few days found Garland and Brenda doing almost everything together. Brenda took Garland over to Durham and a tour of the Duke campus. With the summer sessions Brenda had attended, she had sufficient credit hours to become a senior. She would be graduating from college a year early.

On their way back to the Fisher home, the two stopped for a picnic lunch in a Raleigh park. The park was filled with huge oak trees several hundred years old. Brenda loved the stories Garland told about his musical career. She was very proud of his achievement, but, then again, she always knew he was a very, very special person with unmatched talent.

This was evident that afternoon as the two sat on a blanket after enjoying their lunch.

"Do you have a pen in your purse?" Garland asked.

"I should have one; let me find it," Brenda said.

Brenda began to look inside her purse until she found a pen in a side pocket. She handed the pen to Garland.

Garland took the empty deli bag, laid it flat on ground, and pressed it out smooth. He then began to write.

"What are you writing?" Brenda asked.

Garland continued to write, without any hesitance.

Brenda looked over Garland's right shoulder as he wrote down what appeared to be lyrics. The words on the paper began to paint an image in Brenda's mind. As she continued to read these lyrics, her heart began to melt.

As Garland finished the lyrics, he returned to the top of the bag and wrote the last few words. "You Make My Heart Smile" was written that day in the park.

Garland walked Brenda over to the nearby picnic table and sat her down on the tabletop. While Brenda sat on the tabletop, Garland took a seat on the table's bench.

What is he up to? Brenda wondered.

Soon she would have her answer.

There in the park, Garland began to sing to Brenda. As he started the song, Garland gave the bag to Brenda. She immediately began reading the words while Garland sang. Although this song was freshly written, Garland never needed to be reminded of its lyrics. He already knew the song word for word as he continued to serenade her.

Garland's soothing voice began to gather a crowd. It wasn't every day a park visitor would be treated to an act of love such as this. The lyrics made Brenda melt. She began to remember the day in Charleston when Garland serenaded her during her pool party. That song was wonderful, but this song was very special. This song was written for her by the most special man she had ever met.

Garland wound the song up, and Brenda bent down to kiss him. It was at that moment the two realized this special moment was shared by others. A crowd had gathered and began to applaud the two lovers. Many of the park's visitors that afternoon recognized Garland as the star he was swiftly becoming.

This was a day Brenda would have etched in her heart forever.

"I want you to keep this with you forever, Brenda. When you are lonely, I want you take it out and read it. Remember, this is from my heart to yours," Garland said and kissed her again.

The next few days seemed like a few hours. When you were with the person you wanted very much, time went by too fast.

"Mrs. Fisher, if it's all right, I would like to call my mother and tell her I will be coming home tomorrow," Garland said.

"Garland, tell your mother hello for me. She was always a very special friend," Valerie said.

Garland used the phone in the next room and dialed home.

Valerie and Brenda could hear Garland's voice. It began to make them both very sad. The time they all had enjoyed would soon be ending.

Garland ended his call to Sissy and entered the room where Brenda and Valerie were.

"Tonight, I want to return the hospitality you have shown me during my stay here. You choose the restaurant—anywhere you would like—and dinner is on me," Garland said. "We will have a night on the town."

That night, at the restaurant, something happened. Shortly after Garland and the Fishers completed their meal, a young girl approached their table.

"Excuse me. May I please have your autograph?" she asked.

Everyone paused. No one was more surprised than Garland. He was a very humble person, and this really did embarrass him. Garland signed the girl's napkin. This was his first autograph.

The commotion attracted attention from other restaurant patrons that evening as the girl began to share her discovery of Garland. Soon others began to gather around the table; each time, the girls became older. Not wanting to disappoint any of them, Garland obliged them all. Finally, the restaurant manager, realizing Garland's and the Fishers' privacy was being abused, began to escort them to a side door. It was an eventful evening for them all.

The next morning, Garland began to pack the few things he would take back to Colorado with him. The Fishers hated to see Garland leave.

"I want you all to know I consider you family. I love each of you, but I am in love with Brenda," Garland said.

"Honey, let's go inside so Brenda and Garland can say their goodbyes in private," Valerie told her husband.

"Garland, I have always loved you, and I always will. You are the only man I will ever love. You are my first, last, and only love," Brenda said as she began to cry.

Garland held Brenda. He wanted her to feel safe.

"Baby, you have my heart. I will be back soon," Garland said. "I want you to finish school. You are so close. I will call you when I get home. I promise I will be back soon. I want you to come to Aurora. I want to show you off to all my friends and family."

As Garland began to release the hug, he couldn't hide his tears.

"I love you very much, Brenda," Garland said as he climbed into his orange Camaro.

Just like that, he was gone—but never forgotten.

24

GARLAND ARRIVED BACK in Aurora, after taking two days to drive form North Carolina. Sissy was glad to see her son. It seemed like the two never had time for each other these days. Having a famous musician for a son meant she would have to share him with others. Garland began to tell Sissy about the Fishers. This was a trip he had needed in more ways than one.

"The Fishers want you to know how much they miss you, Mom," Garland told Sissy. "They are great people. I had a wonderful time there. They took me in as if I were their own son."

Garland wanted to tell Sissy about Brenda but felt very uncomfortable discussing that with his mother.

Garland kissed Sissy and then went to his room. He picked up the phone and began to dial Brenda's phone number to let her know that he had made it home safely. He didn't want her to worry.

"Hey, baby, I wanted to let you know that I am home and that I already miss you something terrible," Garland said.

Brenda enjoyed hearing from Garland. As the two talked on the phone, it wasn't long before Brenda discovered she was talking to herself. Garland, as tired as he was, fell asleep. She was glad he had made it home before falling asleep.

‖‖‖‖‖

The next morning found Sissy sitting at the kitchen table, enjoying her morning coffee. She loved using the early morning hours to gather her thoughts. Many times, she would reminisce about the early mornings she shared with Garland. That morning, she was enjoying one of those memories when she felt hands upon her shoulders, followed by a hug.

"Good morning, Momma," Garland said as he placed his cheek next to hers.

"Have a seat Garland, and I will fix you cup of coffee. I want to hear more about your trip," Sissy said.

As Sissy prepared his coffee, Garland excused himself to retrieve some things from his car. He returned with a shopping bag, setting it next to his chair as he began to sip his coffee.

"I am glad you had a great time at the Fishers'. I would have loved to have been there with you. I can only imagine how beautiful Brenda has become," Sissy said.

Garland smiled and began to reach into the shopping bag. He removed a smaller paper bag and gave it to Sissy. Sissy reached into the bag and removed two pictures. One was of Brenda, and the other was of Garland and Brenda. She paused, memorizing the smiles of both Brenda and Garland.

"Baby, she is even more beautiful than I imagined," Sissy said. "Although I know she was childhood crush, you two do make a very good couple. I can see in your eyes and smiles in the picture that you two are very happy together."

Garland smiled. "Mother, there is something special about Brenda. She makes me feel like I am alive and that I am very important to her."

"Garland, she will make someone very happy someday. She really is beautiful and, from what I gather, very smart as well. She has it all rolled into one package; one that any man would be very fortunate to share his life with," Sissy said.

"Mother, during my stay in North Carolina, something special occurred. It wasn't planned. Maybe that is what made it so wonderful. Brenda, although she is almost twenty, was still a virgin," Garland said.

Sissy had a feeling she knew where her son was going with this. "But when you left North Carolina, she was no longer a virgin."

Garland turned to his mother and, with teary eyes, shook his head no.

"It was the most wonderful night I have ever known," he told his mother.

Sissy knew Garland's feelings were no longer a childhood crush. Her son was in love.

"Garland, there is something you should know. While you were in North Carolina, Suzanna came by, and she was very upset. A few days later, she called and was even more upset than she was when she was here," Sissy said.

Garland shook his head and then asked, "Did she say why she was upset?"

"She didn't say," Sissy answered.

"I didn't think she would tell you the reason, Mother," Garland said. "She did something I cannot forgive her for."

Sissy sat quietly, waiting for Garland to say more.

"When Skye was born, I saw a happiness in Brandon I had never seen in him before. Suzanna and I didn't want to tell anyone until I was back home from the tour. I wanted both of us to tell you and Dad," Garland said.

Once again, Garland struggled with the idea of telling Sissy about Suzanna.

Sissy sensed her son was deeply troubled about Suzanna.

"Garland, you don't have to tell me anything you are uncomfortable about," Sissy said.

Garland took a deep breath and thought this was as good a time as any.

"Mother, Suzanna discovered she was pregnant before I left on tour. We wanted to tell everyone when I returned, but Suzanna didn't want to be pregnant," Garland said.

Sissy was shocked and had a very good idea of what her son was going to say next.

"Suzanna didn't want a baby to interfere with her career. She thought being pregnant would hurt her modeling career. Mother, Suzanna terminated the pregnancy," Garland said.

Garland's silence revealed the pain he struggled with.

"I just can't believe she did that. Are you absolutely sure that is what happened? That is a very strong accusation, Garland," Sissy said.

"I wished a thousand times I wasn't, Mother, but, yes, I am positive," Garland said.

"I think this will be our secret, Garland," Sissy said. "There is no need for anyone else to know what happened. If anyone else finds out, it will be Suzanna's wish for them to know."

Garland knew Sissy always knew the right thing to do and the right thing to comfort him. He left the kitchen to dress for the day. The torn feelings Garland once had between Suzanna and Brenda were no longer torn. That tear was mended in North Carolina.

Garland returned from his bedroom, dressed for the day. The phone began to ring. Garland and Sissy turned to each other. The first thought entering their minds: was this Suzanna calling? After several rings, Sissy answered the phone. Soon the smile on her face and the tone of her voice made Garland sigh with relief.

"Honey, tell Garland to be at the station within the next hour. Joe Moss has a special announcement to make. He wants the entire group to attend. From the sound of his voice this morning, this is something very, very big," James said.

Sissy relayed the message to Garland and assured James that Garland would arrive at the station on time. Garland grabbed a cold drink from the refrigerator and left for the station.

Garland had just left when Suzanna, feeling her calls were being ignored, pulled into the driveway. She rang the doorbell. Sissy made her way to the front door. She stopped to peep through the window in the front door to see Suzanna on the front porch.

Sissy took a moment to collect herself; she didn't want it to appear that she had any idea of what Suzanna had done. She opened the door and invited Suzanna into the house. Suzanna stopped to hug Sissy. She figured she would get more information from Sissy about Garland by being nice than by being a bitch. Sissy invited Suzanna into the kitchen for something to drink. As Sissy began to prepare a glass of ice-cold lemonade, Suzanna sat down at the kitchen table.

After taking a seat, Suzanna discovered a partially open paper bag on the tabletop. The bag was open enough for her to see that there were two pictures inside it. The top picture was of Brenda and Garland together. Suzanna couldn't see the bottom picture.

Sissy brought the lemonade to the table, handed a glass to Suzanna, and sat down. By the guilty look on Suzanna's face, Sissy could tell that she had discovered the contents of the bag on the table. Sissy decided to play all her cards and opened the bag for Suzanna to see. She didn't want Suzanna to think anything was being kept from her. She placed the pictures in open view.

Suzanna took a drink and peeked at the pictures over the top of the lemonade glass. Her eyes glanced from one picture to the other. Each time Suzanna glanced at the pictures, her teeth began to grind on her glass.

Sissy hadn't realized Suzanna was that thirsty.

"Suzanna, let me get you a refill. You finished that glass in one drink, it seems," Sissy said.

Sissy refilled her glass. "You just missed Garland. Joe Moss had a special announcement and wanted all of Aurora's Fire to be present."

Suzanna didn't respond.

Sissy didn't want Suzanna to have any idea she knew of her incident, so she made small talk. "Do you have any more shoots coming up?"

"I have two very big ones coming up. I have been asked to present the trophies at the upcoming Grammy Awards," Suzanna said.

"That is great news! You will be going back to California for that one, right?" Sissy asked.

"Yes, to Los Angeles." Suzanna said, adding, "Sissy, I am sorry, but I have to go. I didn't come here to talk to you; I came to see Garland."

At first, Suzanna's remarks made Sissy angry. Then, she took control of her anger and thanked Suzanna for coming by.

Suzanna thanked Sissy for the lemonade, and left. She wanted to find Garland.

IIIIIIII

Garland arrived at KARO. This was the first time he had seen or spoken to any of the guys since the tour ended. As Garland pulled into a parking spot at the radio station, a new Oldsmobile Cutlass 442 pulled into a space next to his Camaro. Garland exited his car as the other car's motor shut off. He started his way up the sidewalk as the Oldsmobile's doors began to open.

"Hey, Slick, it's good to see you again!" a female voice said.

Garland stopped, recognizing a familiar voice that he couldn't precisely identify. He was about to turn around to see its source when he heard a cry from a small baby. Garland knew the source now and turned to see Brandon and Tobie, who held Skye in her arms.

"Do you not talk to old married people now, Garland?" Tobie teased.

Brandon hugged Garland, telling him how much he had missed him.

Tobie kissed Garland on the cheek, still holding Skye in her arms.

"Can I hold her?" Garland asked.

This shocked both Tobie and Brandon.

"Please do. We will take any break we can get," Brandon said, laughing.

Garland carried Skye as he, Brandon, and Tobie made their way into the lobby of the radio station and proceeded to the conference room. They were the last to arrive for the meeting. Garland found it good to see everyone again. Brandon, Tobie, and Garland, with Skye in his lap, took the last three seats. The sight of Garland holding a baby touched everyone in the room. He seemed almost as a natural as Brandon.

Joe Moss welcomed everyone to the meeting. First, he announced that Sand Dollar was now under contract and would be releasing their first record within a month. He thanked Garland for bringing Sand Dollar to his attention.

Joe continued, "I want to congratulate you guys with this certified record-sales document. 'Touch' became a triple-platinum record. It is the only record to do that this year, and there are very few singles that have ever attained this achievement."

The boys began to applaud themselves for this once-in-a-lifetime accomplishment.

Joe then said, "The big news today is about the Grammy Awards. The nominations are next month. You have been nominated for four Grammys."

Kevin, James, and the rest of the radio staff gave the boys a standing ovation for their recognition.

"You have been nominated for awards in the four main categories: Best New Artist, Record of the Year, Album of the Year, and, for 'Touch,' Song of the Year, with Garland Summers as the songwriter," Joe said in conclusion.

This was a great day. Winning these awards would be even greater. Everyone in the room started congratulating Garland. It wasn't every day that a song was discovered by mistake and then became a sensation. Almost the entire room was delighted—all but the baby girl in Garland's lap, who had slept through all the commotion. It seemed that Garland hadn't impressed her. Maybe, one day, he would.

||||||||

The news of Garland's nomination garnered great pride back in North Carolina. The Fisher family gathered around the den television set that evening as the nominations were formally announced on the national news. The news was ending just as the phone began to ring.

Valerie answered the phone.

"Hi, Mom," the voice said.

Valerie turned to her family as she answered the phone. She began to smile, and the tone of her voice indicated the caller was someone very special.

Brenda turned the volume down on the television, not wanting to miss a word her mother was saying.

"Garland, we just saw the news about your Grammy nominations," Valerie said. "I can't believe you have accomplished so much in such a short time. I know how proud we are of you, so I can only imagine how proud Sissy and James are of you."

Garland exchanged several more pleasantries with Valerie, thinking of a way to not hurt her feelings by telling her that he hadn't called to talk to *her*.

Brenda began to think Garland would never get to talk to her this evening.

"Garland, I think someone wants to talk to you very much. Let me see if she is around," Valerie said with a laugh.

Brenda immediately grabbed the phone from her mother, not wanting her to monopolize this important call.

"Congratulations, Garland! You deserve these nominations very much," Brenda said.

"Brenda, I am going to send you three plane tickets, so you and your folks can come to Los Angeles for the award ceremony. I want you to be in audience that night. I want to share this moment with you very much," Garland said.

Brenda turned to her family and began to smile. She was like a kid with secret, just dying to let that secret out.

"Mom and Dad, Garland wants us to come to California as his guests for the ceremony. Shall I accept his invitation?" Brenda said. Without waiting for an answer from her parents, she promptly accepted the invitation. "Garland, I can't wait to see you. I have missed you very much in the short time you have been away."

"I will make all the arrangements for your airline tickets and the tickets to the Grammys," Garland said.

Brenda smiled as Garland told her he needed her.

"I need you too, Garland, and I love you very much," Brenda said.

Brenda hung up the phone up and, with a spring in her step, left the room. She had plans to make for the trip.

||||||||

After Garland's phone call to the Fishers, he made his way out into the parking lot. As he approached his car, Suzanna pulled in behind his Camaro, blocking its exit from its parking space. Garland walked over to Suzanna's car as she began to roll her window down. Suzanna also knew of the Grammy nominations; however, she took a different approach.

"Guess who will be onstage as a hostess? I will be one of the models presenting the winners," Suzanna said.

Once again, Suzanna took advantage of the situation to optimize the attention on herself. She didn't want Garland to feel special for his achievement. She made it a point not to congratulate him. She felt the show would be focused on her as much as any of the winners that evening. After all, she was already a winner. Garland would have to wait for his results, and there was the possibility that he wouldn't win. These thoughts filled Suzanna's mind as she drove away.

IIIIIII

The weeks leading up the awards went by fast. There was much to do in a very short time. Two days before the awards ceremony, Garland called the Fishers to make sure everything was still a go. Brenda assured Garland that the family had been ready two days and was counting down the hours.

"Garland, I can't wait to get to California so that I can see you," Brenda said.

Brenda stood up, hung up the phone, and began to walk to her room. She instantly stopped. Her head felt light as she walked to her room. Maybe it was because she had stood up quickly. Whatever the cause, the feeling left as fast as it had come over her.

Brenda's dad began to load up the family car with their luggage. It was almost time to leave for the airport to catch their flight. The flight to Los Angeles would take four hours, and there was a three-hour time difference. Jet lag would take its toll on the Fishers.

Brenda approached her seat on the aircraft. As she began to enter the row with her seat, she retrieved a pillow and blanket from the overhead bin. She wanted to be comfortable during the flight. The excitement from her adrenaline rush was beginning to wear off. She didn't realize how tired she was until she took her seat.

The stewardess, realizing Brenda wasn't feeling very well, offered assistance. "Ma'am, if there is anything we can do to make this flight more comfortable for you, please push the overhead Assistance Needed light. I know a trip like this in your condition can be very uncomfortable."

Brenda's facial expression indicated she didn't have a clue as to what the stewardess was talking about. Soon after the plane took off, Brenda covered up with the blanket and used the pillow as prop for her stomach. She was sure the odd sensation was just butterflies.

As the plane made its descent into Los Angeles International Airport, the butterflies reappeared. There wasn't a passenger on the plane that day any happier to get off the plane. Michael Fisher helped his daughter off the plane. He was puzzled as to why Brenda was the most exhausted of the three. They soon entered the gate into the airport. A tall black man in a black suit stood against a nearby wall, holding a sign. Written in large black lettering was "Fisher family." The sign took the family by surprise.

The family approached the man, informing him that they were the Fishers.

"I am here to help you with you with your luggage and take you to your hotel," the man said.

As they made their way to the baggage pickup area, the man hailed a nearby skycap, requesting his help with the family's luggage.

After collecting the luggage, he instructed the skycap to take the family to the passenger pickup area. He would meet them there. The family and the skycap stood on a nearby curb. Soon a large black limousine pulled up.

"Look, Mother, I think there may be a movie star inside the limo," Brenda said.

Her mother stooped, trying to get a closer look as to who might be inside the limousine. The limousine pulled up just enough for the trunk to be where the skycap stood.

"Can you see who is in the car, Mother? "Brenda asked.

The driver's door began to open, and the tall black man emerged. He hurried around the car and began to open the back doors and the trunk.

"I forgot to introduce myself earlier," he said. "My name is Harry. I will be your chauffeur today."

He escorted the family into the back of the limousine and tipped the skycap, then walking around the car and returning to the driver's seat.

"Harry, we didn't request a limousine," Michael said.

"Sir, are you here to see the Grammys?" Harry asked.

"Well, yes, we are. We have been invited by a special friend. He is nominated for four awards," Michael said.

"Yes, sir, I know. I hope Mr. Summers wins," Harry said.

Harry's comment had the Fishers more confused than ever.

"Harry, who is paying for all of this?" Michael asked.

"Sir, I was told it was your son," Harry said.

Valerie hugged Brenda when they heard Harry's answer. This was like a dream come true, and Garland was the dream maker.

"Today, we will be driving to the Century Plaza Hotel. The hotel is also one of the sites for the Grammys. Part of the show is held in Los Angeles, and part is in New York City," Harry said.

The limousine departed Los Angeles International Airport and began the drive to nearby Beverly Hills. The limousine rolled down the streets, each lined with very tall palm trees. The limo then made its final approach to the hotel.

This isn't any ordinary hotel; this is a city, Brenda thought.

Harry drove into the front area of the hotel. As the limousine stopped, a nearby bell captain opened the door, welcoming the Fishers to the hotel.

The bell captain arranged for a bellhop to deliver the luggage to their room. This was the largest hotel any of them had ever seen. As the site of the Grammys, the hotel was in a festive mood. The excitement was electric, and the guests were enjoying every minute of the special occasion. The Fishers checked into the hotel and followed the bellhop to the elevators. They were being escorted into a private wing of the hotel.

As the elevator reached its floor, Brenda once again felt lightheaded. Perhaps the elevator's ascent was affecting her balance. This time, her dilemma did not go unnoticed by her parents. Valerie remained behind her husband and the bellhop as they went to find the room. Brenda needed her mother at this moment. Valerie helped Brenda to their room. This spell lasted longer than the previous spell. Finally, they entered the room. This wasn't an ordinary room; it was a suite. There was one bedroom for Brenda and one for her parents, each with its own private bath.

The bellhop sorted the luggage as Michael identified each piece, indicating which room the piece was to be delivered to.

Brenda entered her bedroom to find a freshly cut bouquet of flowers on the dresser. Attached was a card. She opened the card, and, as she began to read the words written inside, she could no longer hold the tears back. This was overwhelming for her. No one had ever made her feel this special before. As she sat on her bedside, once again reading the card, the phone began to ring.

Her dad, in the living area, answered it, calling, "Brenda, honey, the phone is for you."

As the voice began to come through the receiver, Brenda's eyes were filled with tears of joy.

"There is a popular song stating how awesome California girls are, with their beauty; today, those California girls wish they were you," the voice said.

Brenda's emotions were changing, and she didn't understand why.

"Are you okay, baby?" Michael asked.

"Yes, I am, Dad. It's Garland. I have never been better in my life," Brenda said.

The Grammys were one day away—a day she would need very much.

"Tomorrow, I will make arrangements for your seating at the ceremony," Garland said. "I have two tables reserved. You will be sitting with some of the family members of our group."

"Will you be joining our table, Garland?" Brenda asked.

"Well, yes, but I hope I have to leave the table at least four times," he said.

"I hope you do too," Brenda said.

"I know it's been a long day, with your flight and the time change. Tell your mom and dad I look forward to seeing them and I hope all of you get some rest," Garland said.

"Yes, for some reason, I am more tired than I thought I would be," Brenda said.

Brenda smiled as she said good night to Garland. She wouldn't need to be rocked to sleep that night.

||||||||

The next morning began with a knock on the door. Room service delivered breakfast. Valerie answered the door.

"Ma'am, I will set the breakfast table in the living area," the hotel employee said.

The aroma of fresh coffee and fried bacon filled the bedrooms with their pleasant smells.

Brenda made her way from her bedroom, stopping to put on the velour hotel bathrobe. For the moment, she felt much better. Perhaps jet lag had made her feel weak and peculiar. She was very hungry this morning, and fruit was always one of her favorite breakfast foods.

After breakfast, the family dressed for the day and left their room. The huge hotel had pulled out all the stops for the Grammys, and the festive atmosphere was very exciting. As they exited the elevator on the main floor, an area was roped off for those attending the ceremonies. The red-carpet arrivals were always the highlight of the ceremony. They walked along the rope until they came upon a section that was not attached, leaving a gap that was perfect for someone to slip through and sneak into the concert hall hosting the evening's main event. The stage was awesome, and there were many camera stands for the live broadcast. Even at this early hour of the day, there was very much activity going into the preparations. Everything had to be perfect.

A stage director approached them.

"If you don't watch out, we will put you to work," he said.

His remark brought about a sudden laugh.

"Will you be attending the awards tonight?" the man asked.

The Fishers, as if in a choir, answered in unison with a definite yes.

"We have a table reserved," Brenda added.

"What is the name of your party?" the man asked.

Michael informed the man of their name. He began to look through a stack of nameplates for the tables. He scanned them once and then began to scan a second time; he wanted to make sure he had not overlooked their name.

"Perhaps it's under another name," the man said.

The Fishers were very disappointed. Maybe the man was right; perhaps the table was under another name.

Not wanting to show their disappointment, the Fishers began to leave. As they began to enter the aisle for the exit, a group of five made their way to the VIP area. The Fishers walked toward the five, with their heads down. The aisle was too narrow to accommodate this many people simultaneously.

"Excuse us, please," Brenda said as the Fishers stopped to let the others through.

A voice suddenly arose from one of the ladies in the group of five. "Oh my God! I cannot believe this."

At first, her outburst shocked the Fishers. They didn't want a confrontation on this special day.

Then, the woman said, "Brenda, is that you?"

Brenda paused, wondering, *Who could possibly recognize me?*

Valerie Fisher turned to the woman and instantly said, "Sissy Summers, you haven't changed one bit."

The two women hugged.

"Garland told us you were coming, and I have waited so long for this moment," Sissy said.

Sissy hugged Brenda. She was the daughter Sissy had always wanted.

Sissy then introduced Kevin and Cindy English to the Fishers.

"I want you to meet someone who is very dear to me," Sissy said. "This is Tobie; she is the wife of our adopted son."

"I wasn't aware you and Mr. Summers had an adopted son," Brenda said.

"Brenda, Brandon is as much of a son to the Summers and English families as Garland and Adam are. You will get to see just how special he is when you get to meet him," Sissy said, adding with a smile, "And you can call us Sissy and James now."

Michael Fisher informed them that there was some kind of mix-up with the table situation.

"Mix-up? "Kevin asked.

"Yes. Garland said we would be joining a table of family members, but when we told the crew our name, there weren't any nameplates for the Fishers," Michael said.

Kevin turned and motioned to the young man setting up the tables that he needed to speak to him.

After several minutes with the young man, Kevin returned with three nameplates in his hand.

"We will all be sitting together at two tables. Tonight, tell them you want the Aurora's Fire guest table," Kevin said with a smiled.

This was a relief to the Fishers: they had a table, and there wasn't anyone they would rather be with on this night.

"I think we will return to our room and rest for the big evening. It was very nice to have met each of you, and I will be honored to be in attendance on this evening with all of you," Michael said.

IIIIIIII

The next hours went by very fast. The time finally arrived to get dressed for the big event. Garland had another surprise up his sleeve that day. Once again, a knock interrupted the moment. Michael answered the door. There in the doorway stood a man with an elegant gown.

"Sir, this gown is for Miss Brenda Fisher. Will you please see that she has it for tonight?" the man said.

Michael gathered the evening gown in its plastic cover. Brenda and her mother stopped in awe at its beauty. It was the most beautiful dress either had ever seen.

"Brenda, I think you will show us all up tonight," her dad said with a proud look.

Brenda relieved him of the dress and returned to her bedroom. Her parents returned to their bedroom. The time to leave was very near now.

Sissy had called their room earlier, and the Fishers agreed to meet the rest of their party at the main entrance. They would enter the building as a group and be seated at their table at once. Although Brenda had talked to Garland several times since arriving in California, she wanted to see him before the big night. She was very proud of her man and wanted to make Garland aware just how much. The usher greeted them and escorted the party to their table. As they approached their table, Brenda was in awe of the stage.

There was a special backdrop of mountains circled by fire. It was truly breathtaking. Theirs was a very large round table, with three empty seats. One of these was next to Brenda. As the time drew closer to the opening of the show, the tables were filled with occupants. A glance around the room indicated there were some very famous people in the audience. It was like a dream to be among them. Occasionally, Brenda found herself pinching herself to be assured this *wasn't* a dream.

Brenda began to worry about Garland. Where was he? It was almost time for the show to start. This was the biggest night of his life, and she didn't want him to miss a minute of it.

"Sissy, I am worried about Garland; he should have been here by now. Is he all right?" Brenda said.

Sissy had also begun to worry not only of Garland's whereabouts but Adam's and Brandon's as well.

"Kevin, do you think they are stuck in traffic?" Brenda asked.

Kevin smiled. It was all he could do to keep the biggest secret of the evening thus far. "Brenda, you need not worry. The boys have a room here at the hotel. Traffic will not be a problem for them tonight."

The room suddenly got quiet. A floor director began to signal the countdown for the start of the show. His countdown would signal the cameras to be directed toward the stage. The countdown neared its mark, the lights of the audience were dimmed, and a fire appeared in the rings surrounding the Rocky Mountains. The television cameras became alive. The fire completed the circle; the crowd cheered. The backlit Rockies illuminated the stage.

As the stage lights illuminated, a sound began from a guitar on the stage, followed by another guitar. It was the introduction that everyone in the audience and on television knew: the biggest-selling song in history. This was the song that touched everyone who heard it; it was perfect.

The lights of the stage became fully illuminated, and Garland Summers took his place at the stage front. As Garland continued to sing "Touch," he did something at that moment totally unexpected. Garland placed his Gibson onto a guitar stand on the stage and jumped down from the stage. A television camera began to trace his steps.

Garland arrived at the table where his family was sitting. As he continued to sing, Garland first approached Sissy, kissing her and never missing a lyric. The camera followed Garland across the table to where Brenda was sitting as the chorus of "Touch" began. Garland kissed Brenda as the chorus began—all captured nationwide on live television. The Grammys had never begun like this before.

As Garland returned to the stage to end "Touch," Kevin had pulled off the huge surprise. It had been all he could do to keep it to himself. He wanted this to be a very special moment for everyone. He was right. This was the first time a new recording artist opened the Grammys, the biggest of all music-awards shows. The audience stood to applaud "Touch." The setting was perfect, both on- and offstage.

As Garland and the band left the stage, Suzanna was standing offstage.

"I hope you don't think that performance will get you any votes. The results are already in," Suzanna said.

The emcee introduced two presenters for the first award of the evening. Suzanna was holding the statuette for the night's first winner.

Garland only wished that the first award was one he was nominated for. He wanted to be a winner very badly.

Aurora's Fire's first nomination wouldn't be for some time into the show.

Suzanna took her place on the stage to present the night's award.

"Sissy, can I ask you something?" Brenda asked.

"Of course, you can. What is it?" Sissy replied.

"That beautiful girl standing on the stage, with the statuette in her hands, that's Suzanna, isn't it?" Brenda said.

Sissy held Brenda's hand. Sissy didn't have to reply; Brenda already had her answer with that hand hold.

"Suzanna is really a very beautiful woman. I had no idea she was this gorgeous," Brenda said as she looked down.

Sissy could tell Brenda was upset, so she said the only thing she could think of. "You are too, Brenda."

Brenda smiled; she knew that Sissy was trying to comfort her and ease her insecurities.

As the night's first winner made his way onto the stage, Suzanna presented the statuette, followed by a kiss. It was now her turn to get Garland's attention. After the opening act and first award, the network scheduled its first commercial break. During the break, two guys arrived at the table, each taking a seat.

Kevin began introducing the two to the Fishers. "This is my son, Adam; he is one of Aurora's Fire."

"You must be Brenda!" Adam said.

Brenda smiled and nodded yes.

The second guy stopped where Tobie was sitting, bending to kiss her. It was a very long kiss. After the kiss, he immediately turned his attention to Sissy, first kissing her hand and then her cheek.

"How is my sweetheart doing tonight?" he asked.

Sissy smiled and hugged him.

"Brenda, I want you meet our Brandon. You will never meet another one like him. He is very special to us all," Sissy said.

"I have heard so much about you, Brandon. Garland talks affectionately about you," Brenda said.

Brandon turned to Brenda. "You have the glow of a diamond, my dear. I can see how you stole Garland's heart. I am glad to meet you, Brenda."

Brandon kissed Brenda's hand. He was about to kiss her cheek, but his kiss was interrupted by a hand.

Brandon turned to see who was stealing his kiss.

Garland laughed and patted Brandon on the shoulder.

Brandon stood and hugged his friend, returning to his seat beside Tobie.

Garland took his seat next to Brenda.

"Garland, you have a look about you I have never seen you have before," Brandon said.

Garland smiled and kissed Brenda. He wanted to enjoy the show, together with his friends and family.

The time was nearing for Aurora's Fire first nomination of the evening.

The presenters approached the microphone to announce the nominees.

"The nominees for Best New Artist are," they began and then named each nominee.

After each nominee was introduced, a short musical clip followed. If the audience's applause after each nomination was any indication, Aurora's Fire would win, hands down.

One presenter began to open the envelope.

"The winner for Best New Artist is Aurora's Fire," he said as the audience got to its feet.

Adam, Garland, and Brandon sprang up from their chairs, as did Sam, Rudy, and Beau, sitting across the room at another table. The six met at the base of the steps to make their way onto the stage. As they approached the microphone, the presenters each shook the hand of every member of Aurora's Fire.

Out from the wings of the stage came Suzanna, with five Grammy trophies. She presented Adam, Sam, Rudy, Beau, and Brandon each with their statuette. Her actions of purposely not delivering Garland's statuette did not go unnoticed by the audience, the presenters, or the Grammy officials. Earlier, the boys had decided that, if they won in the categories of Best New Artist or Album of the Year, Rudy would make the acceptance speech. During his speech, the audience applauded very loudly. Rudy smiled, thinking his speech was well received. From the other side of the stage came the other model to deliver the statuette to Garland. The applause was for Garland's award. Suzanna's snub turned into a gem. The boys all walked off the stage, shortly returning to their seats.

The three musicians returned to their seats, placing the three Grammys in the center of the large table, for their families to cherish.

Once again, Suzanna's actions didn't go unnoticed. During the next presentation, the winner was also a group of six. The model for this award managed to deliver all six trophies. As she walked off the stage, the audience began to applaud.

During a commercial break in between the next awards, Sissy left her seat to hug Adam and Brandon.

"Congratulations! I am very proud of you boys. I know how hard you have worked for this award, and you deserve it very much," Sissy said.

Brenda turned to Garland. Tonight's events were something that, only months before, she would never have dreamed of being a part of.

Kevin looked at the awards schedule, noticing that there were only a few awards before the boys' next nomination would be announced. Their next category was Album of the Year. This award was to be delivered by the previous year's winner. As the presenter made his way to the microphone, the audience gave its approval. He was a very big star with many Grammys on his mantel.

"The nominees for Album of the Year are—" he said, pausing before he announced each artist.

He opened the winner's envelope and, with much excitement, revealed the winner. "Once again, the winner is Aurora's Fire."

As the boys approached the microphone, the presenter stepped aside, applauding their achievement. It was the ultimate compliment to be applauded by such an icon.

This time, Suzanna left the wing of the stage. Another of the models shook her head at Suzanna's inconsideration. She then took it upon herself to deliver all six trophies.

"We would like to thank our families for being there for us. Just a year ago, we did not exist as an act. A tragic accident brought the six of us together. Tonight, I want to remember the three we lost in that accident. I know they are looking down on us tonight," Rudy said.

Rudy's words were heartfelt, and everyone in attendance was familiar with the story of Aurora's Fire.

As Rudy walked off the stage, the presenter joined him, putting his arm around Rudy. This was class.

Once again, the audience stood as the boys left the stage for the second time.

Suzanna made sure she remained out of the boys' sight. Once again, her behavior was noticed by the audience, the presenter, and the Grammy officials.

The boys returned to their tables.

This year was the final year the Grammys were being televised from both Los Angeles and New York. The next award would be presented in New York.

Rudy took advantage of the break to visit Garland's table. He wanted to meet Brenda and say hello to Tobie and Sissy.

"That was very touching, Rudy, paying tribute to your friends who are no longer with us," Kevin said.

Rudy thanked Kevin then added, "You guys have a great looking centerpiece for your table. You must have gotten yours from the same place we got ours."

"I have heard the rest of the centerpiece is on its way. We will make sure they don't forget yours," Adam said as he lined up the six golden trophies now adorning their table.

Rudy laughed and returned to his table.

"Tobie, are you not feeling well this evening? You look like something is wrong," Sissy said.

Tobie smiled at Sissy, with a tear in her eye, holding Brandon's hand very tightly.

Brandon took his free arm and wrapped it around Tobie, trying to comfort her.

"Tonight is the first time I have ever been away from Skye. I will be okay," Tobie said.

"Who is taking care of her while you are away?" Valerie asked.

"Tobie's uncle Charlie is watching her," Brandon said.

"Brandon, you and Tobie should find a pay phone and call in to check up on her. There is plenty of time before the next award we are nominated for will be announced," Garland said.

Tobie smiled, saying Garland's suggestion was a good idea.

Brandon escorted Tobie from the table, and they went to the lobby to find a phone.

The 1970 Grammy Awards ceremony started winding down, with just two remaining awards remaining to be announced. Aurora's Fire was nominated for both awards.

Brandon and Tobie returned to the table. The look on Tobie's face indicated Skye was in good hands. Tobie trusted her uncle; she just needed assurance that everything was okay. The first time a new mother was away from her baby was always the hardest.

The emcee announced, "The next category is the closest competition of the evening. The award is for Record of the Year."

Once again, the nominations were announced, each followed by a short musical clip.

This time, the clips were played with live satellite feeds from each nominee's hometown. Back in Aurora, a large group gathered at KARO for a Grammy-watching party. There were signs from almost everyone in the crowd, including a huge banner held up by Harley and Chad. Seeing the home crowd behind them made the boys feel very special. They wanted this win for the whole town.

The presenter said, "I want all the nominees in this category to know that there is no loser. You are all winners in my book."

As the presenter opened the envelope, she said, "The winner, for the third time this evening, is—"

Thunderous applause and a standing ovation from the audience interrupted the presenter.

"The winner is Aurora's Fire!" she said, shouting into the microphone, her voice still overwhelmed by the crowd's reaction.

There wasn't a person in the room sitting in a chair.

This time, the boys gathered at the steps for a group hug. It seemed to them that this couldn't really be happening. They approached the microphone, arm in arm, and gathered around the stand. They had agreed that Brandon would make the speech if they won in the category of Record of the Year.

Brandon approached the microphone as the audience sat back down.

"Tonight, I wish to thank the academy for this award. I want to thank my fellow band members, some of whom are like brothers to me. Kevin English, who has been like a father to me, and Sissy Summers, who has been like a mother to me, I love you both very much. You have honored us this evening. Next to the day that I married my wife, Tobie, and the night our daughter, Skye, was born, this is the happiest day of my life," Brandon said as he lifted the band's third statuette.

The boys all stood together as the audience showed their approval, not wanting them to leave the stage.

The music cued the emcee to announce the final presenter for the evening's final award.

The boys exited off camera, going down the steps in front and returning to their tables.

The emcee announced the final presenter of the evening. He walked out on to the stage that evening with a biggest ovation up to that point of the evening.

"The final Grammy tonight is for Song of the Year. This is the songwriter's award," he said.

The presenter announced the nominees. Once again, there was a live satellite feed from each nominee's hometown.

"Congratulations to all of the songwriters," the presenter said. "You are the ones who give the music its voice."

He turned over the envelope and began to remove the gold seal from the envelope's flap, removing the results, and unfolding the paper to reveal winner's name.

"The winner is, ..." he said and then paused, adding, "This is the best song I have ever had the pleasure of hearing. The winner is Garland Summers for 'Touch'!"

At that moment, the noise level in the room could have been heard all the way back to Colorado. The large screen immediately switched to Aurora. The crowd was much larger, filling the street in front of KARO. People were honking their car horns, celebrating. They wanted Garland and the boys to hear them all the way from Colorado.

Garland, trying to recover from the shock, rose from his chair as he kissed Brenda. Everyone was standing, including Sissy. Garland then did another first in Grammy history. He took his mother's hand and led her onto the stage. Sissy held her son's hand very tight; she didn't want Garland to leave her on that stage all alone.

Garland and Sissy approached the microphone to a standing and cheering crowd.

Even Suzanna, standing in the wings, applauded, although she and Garland were at odds. There wasn't any way she couldn't applaud Sissy; she was a classy person and was always wonderful to her. They turned to watch the big screen for a moment.

Garland stepped up to the microphone. "Tonight, the academy honors me with this very special award. The woman on this stage tonight is the inspiration for every word in 'Touch.' She created 'Touch' with her love for me, and, tonight, I give this award to her. 'Touch' wouldn't exist if it were not for her. Mother, I am the luckiest son on earth. I thank God for choosing you as my mother."

Garland gave the Grammy to Sissy and kissed her cheek.

Tonight, Sissy felt she was the luckiest mother on earth, not because of the four Grammys, but because she, too, thanked God—for giving her a son like Garland.

As Garland and Sissy returned to their table, guests from the adjoining tables rushed over, telling them how much their relationship touched them.

"The academy is holding a reception for all the nominees and winners. We need to go the main banquet ballroom," Kevin said.

The crowded auditorium began to empty as the VIP guests made their way to the reception. Garland, Adam, and Brandon, carried their three Grammy statuettes. Garland picked up the one remaining statuette and insisted that Sissy carry it—after all, it was no longer his.

Garland took Brenda's hand, squeezing it very tightly as they left the room.

"Garland, I think I need to stop off at the ladies' room before we attend the reception," Brenda said.

Garland escorted Brenda to the nearest ladies' room. Brenda entered the restroom, feeling a little faint. She wanted to freshen up for the party, hoping that would make the sensation pass.

As Brenda looked in the mirror, powdering her face and touching up her mascara, Suzanna appeared, making her way to the sink and mirror next to Brenda.

At first, Suzanna wanted to appear not to have noticed Brenda. Finally, the temptation overcame Suzanna. She tried to sneak a peek at Brenda, trying to remember where she knew Brenda from, but the mirror gave away her intentions. She turned to Brenda and forced a smile her way.

Brenda was brushing her long hair, which she wore in a waterfall. Her hair was one of her biggest attributes, and Suzanna realized it. Suzanna's stares made Brenda feel very uncomfortable.

Suzanna also began to brush her hair, trying to recall just where she had seen that hair before. A waterfall was a difficult hairdo. It was a very special look, and that look was meant for a very special girl. It dawned on Suzanna where she had seen that hair—and that look—before. The smirk on her face indicated Suzanna had her answer. This was the girl in the picture with Garland inside the partially opened paper bag on Sissy's kitchen table. That girl had the same hairdo.

From the moment Suzanna stepped up beside her, Brenda knew who she was, but she tried not to let Suzanna feel that she knew her.

Brenda was about to finish freshening up when she felt faint again. *Why am I experiencing these fainting spells?* she wondered.

Brenda stopped and leaned against the counter, trying to regain her composure.

Suzanna noticed something was not right with Brenda.

"Are you all right? Is there someone I can get for you? "Suzanna asked.

"It has just been a very long day. I will be okay. Thank you for your concern," Brenda said.

Suzanna turned to exit the ladies' room, while Brenda took a few more moments.

As Suzanna exited the restroom, she began to close her purse and accidentally nudged someone on the bench outside the ladies' room.

"Excuse me. I am so sorry; I am not normally this clumsy," Suzanna said as she latched her purse shut.

"It's not a problem. No one got hurt," the man said.

"Garland? What are you doing here on this bench?" Suzanna asked.

Garland was surprised to see that Suzanna was the lady apologizing for her clumsiness.

"I am waiting for someone in the ladies' room," Garland said.

Suzanna giggled with a devilish smile, adding, "Oh, you must be waiting for the girl who is not feeling well."

"What do you mean, 'not feeling well'? Is she all right?" Garland asked.

Once again, Suzanna laughed. As she walked away, she said, "I think she will be just fine as time goes by."

Brenda soon emerged from the powder room.

Garland rushed to her side. "Are you all right, baby?"

Brenda said she was fine. She had missed Garland's incident with Suzanna.

The Grammys' organizers spared no expense for the reception following the awards show.

As she entered the ballroom, Brenda became awestruck.

"Garland pinch me!" Brenda said.

"Pinch you?" Garland said.

"Yes, I want to make sure I am not dreaming. I can't believe I am in the same room with so many of the stars I worshipped as a child. This night is priceless, Garland!" Brenda said.

Brenda's excitement brought smiles to her parents as well as the Summerses.

As they made their way around the room, Garland began to garner the attention of the media members assembled there. Each step found a flashbulb capturing his expressions of the evening. Occasionally, a reporter would ask a few questions. As much as Brenda admired Garland for his talents, she loved him even more—success did not change him.

A voice coming a few feet from where Garland and Brenda stood called his name. A middle-aged man quickly made his way over to the couple. He approached Garland with a handshake, followed by a hug.

"Joe, I want you to meet Brenda Fisher. Brenda, this is Joe Moss; he works for our record label," Garland said.

Joe was about to burst with the news he had just received.

"Garland, we have just completed a very big deal. We will do the American Invasion of Britain. This will be the biggest concert venue to ever hit England from the US, and we are part of it!" Joe said and raised his fist into the air.

This was very big news; it would make Aurora's Fire a world superstar.

The concert news became the topic for the rest of the evening.

Garland, sensing Brenda was tiring, suggested they leave for someplace more private.

"You would walk out on this party to have some private time with me?" Brenda asked.

Garland didn't want Brenda to refuse, so he took her by the hand, leading her to an outdoor courtyard. The two found a bench away from the crowd.

"Garland, it will be very hard for me to leave tomorrow. This experience has been a dream, and you have been a prince through it all," Brenda said.

They both knew she had to go, though.

Garland wanted her to fulfill her dream and finish her last year of college. "You are so close to finishing your degree, baby. We will have plenty of time together after you are done."

An education was very important to Brenda, but not as important as Garland was to her, and she told him so.

Garland wouldn't take no for an answer. He winked at her, and the two went back inside.

"I think it's time to gather the others and call it a night," Garland said.

The biggest night of the boys' lives was coming to an end.

"Tomorrow, I will accompany you to the airport. I want to spend as much time as I can with you," Garland told Brenda.

As the families departed the reception, Brenda and Garland managed to separate themselves. Their parents smiled at the thought of being dumped by their children.

Garland and Brenda walked through the courtyard until they arrived in the hotel's garage. Garland's smile indicated he was up to something. As they continued their walk, Garland stopped at a black limousine. He turned to see if anyone was around. Once determining the coast was clear, he opened the unlocked back door, and the two slipped inside, out of sight. The night would end with the two lovers locked in each other's arms. Neither of them had ever made love in a limousine before.

The two lovers fell into a light slumber, and then awoke and returned to their rooms.

Garland returned for a short nap before running one final errand. There was a special trip he had to make before escorting the Fishers to the airport. Brenda took advantage of the hotel's comfortable bed, sleeping for the next five hours. Garland finished his errand in time to make the trip to the airport. Once again, he took care of the transportation arrangements.

The limousine arrived at the VIP parking area near the hotel's front entrance. As the driver's door began to open, a pleasant face and voice directed their way to the area where the Fishers were waiting.

"Harry, are you here to take us back to the airport?" Michael Fisher asked.

"Yes, sir. I will be your driver once again. I will escort you to the airport, and we will meet Mr. Summers in the lobby," Harry said.

The Fishers entered the limousine and began their trip home.

Harry pulled into the passenger drop-off area. A familiar skycap immediately welcomed the Fishers. Harry informed the skycap which airline and the flight number for the luggage check-in.

"Folks, please follow me through this door. Mr. Summers is awaiting your arrival," Harry said.

The Fishers followed Harry into the lobby. Inside the lobby was the entire Summers family. Garland ran to greet the Fishers.

"I wanted to spend some final minutes with all of you before you returned home," Garland said. "Mother, Dad, Mr. and Mrs. Fisher, please gather around."

Garland paused, waiting for the two families to form a circle. As the circle began to form, Garland stepped into its center. His actions took everyone by surprise. All were wondering what Garland had up his sleeve. Garland placed his hand into his right pocket, searching for its contents. As his hand began to make its way to the top of his pocket, Garland's face beamed with a big smile. He was doing his best not to reveal his surprise.

With his hand still in his pocket, Garland led Brenda into the circle to stand beside him.

"I am having a hard time retrieving my hand from my pocket. Will you help me get it unstuck?" Garland said.

Brenda placed her hand on top of Garland's hand. Slowly Garland began to remove his hand, with Brenda's hand on top of it, from his pocket. As the two hands exited his pocket, Garland's hand was clutching a small box. He slowly opened the box, revealing a one-carat diamond engagement ring.

Brenda stopped moving at the sight of the surprise, covering her lips with her fingertips. She began to tremble with excitement.

"Brenda, I have dreamed of this day ever since my visit to North Carolina. Everything I have achieved will not mean anything if I don't have someone to share it with. Will you be my partner in life and marry me?" Garland asked.

Garland's actions brought tears of joy to Sissy and Valerie, each hoping Brenda's answer would be yes.

"Garland, I have loved you from the day we danced at your birthday party in Charleston. You have made these last few days the happiest of my life. There is nothing I would love more than to be your wife, but I want to finish school first. After I finish my education, if you still want to marry me, we can talk about it then," Brenda said.

Brenda's answer wasn't the answer Garland or the two families anticipated.

Garland closed the box, returning it to his pocket. He wasn't taking Brenda's answer as an actual no. He knew the importance of her education.

A voice over the airport's public-address system announced the boarding of the Fishers' flight. The two families began to say their final goodbyes.

"Garland, don't think my answer is a no. Please understand you are the only one I want to marry. I do love you," Brenda said, with tears in her eyes as she made her way into the plane's tunnel.

As Garland stood there, watching Brenda's every step, Sissy wrapped her arms around her son.

"Garland, make no mistake, Brenda really does love you. Your letting her do this will make her love you even more," Sissy said.

The Summerses watched the plane exit the gate and taxi to the runway. The plane turned onto the runway, gained speed, and took the sky.

A tear ran down Garland's cheek as the plane flew out of sight. He couldn't help remembering the last time Sissy advised him not to interfere with the dreams of the woman he loved.

25

AURORA'S FIRE RETURNED home to the biggest homecoming ever witnessed in Aurora, Colorado. The Denver airport was swamped with press members and fans. As the band members made their way through the airport, a familiar voice welcomed them.

"I want to welcome home my brothers. They have made us all very proud," the voice said.

Garland, Brandon, Adam, and Beau were touched. They had not expected to have such a large crowd welcoming them back home.

Once again, the voice made another announcement. A short clip began to play on several of the airport television sets. The clip was the highlights of the Grammy Awards presentations.

The voice continued, "Today, we are doing a live remote at the homecoming for Aurora's Fire. Tomorrow night, the city of Denver will host a party."

As the boys approached a set of microphones, a wheelchair rolled from behind them. Harley was a welcome sight.

"Harley, we share these awards with you. You have always been a part of our musical family," Garland said.

Harley thanked Garland, hugging him and the other members of the band.

"You're damn right I am part of this. Have you forgotten whose mistake discovered 'Touch'?" Harley said jokingly.

Harley winked at his friends. In his own way, he was a winner too.

|||||||

The Fishers returned to Raleigh and began their final leg back to Goldsboro. The car ride from the airport was very quiet. The trip back to reality would take several days. So much had happened to them—more than they had ever dreamed possible.

Brenda went to her bedroom that evening. She wanted to call Garland to apologize. Maybe she had made a mistake.

She opened the top drawer of her nightstand. A paper bag was folded inside the drawer. She unfolded the bag and began to read the song Garland had written for her that day in the park. Somehow, she needed Garland to understand her feelings. That night, Brenda fell asleep with the song lying beside her on the pillow.

|||||||

Joe Moss called Kevin, informing him of the venue for Denver's celebration party.

"Kevin, the party will be at Red Rocks. That is where the boys began their career," Joe Moss said.

Kevin agreed that the Red Rocks Amphitheatre was perfect for the occasion.

"Afterward, there will be a private party at the country club," Joe said.

"I will be sure to inform the guys," Kevin said.

Kevin hung up with Joe and then began to call the band, informing each of the night's plans.

Beau was the last one Kevin called that morning.

"Hello," a voice said.

Kevin recognized the voice as Suzanna's. He was surprised to find her at Chad's house.

"Suzanna, this is Kevin English. I'm calling to inform Beau that the welcome-home party thrown by the city of Denver will be tonight at the Red Rocks Amphitheatre. Afterward, Magic Sounds is throwing a private party."

Suzanna assured Kevin she would give the message to Beau.

As Suzanna hung up the phone, she paused; an idea entered her mind. Maybe this would be a good time to talk to Garland. She dashed out of the house and drove to her apartment. She had just enough time to prepare for this occasion. It wasn't the public party she was preparing for; it was the private party. If she couldn't dazzle Garland tonight, perhaps she could turn the head of someone who could enhance her career as a model. She was sure Garland wouldn't be able to resist her this evening. Makeup was her specialty.

She searched her closet, looking for that special outfit Garland always loved her in. Laying the dress on the bed, Suzanna took the time to draw a very nice bubble bath. She wanted her skin to be as smooth as silk. This was a special skin treatment she had learned of during one of her modeling shoots. After her bubble bath, Suzanna washed her hair with a special herbal shampoo. This would make her long, dark hair shimmer.

And then, there was the matter of her makeup. As a model for a cosmetics company now, Suzanna was treated to the best makeup materials on the market these days. Everything she treated herself with complemented her features. It was almost like each of these products was made with her in mind. For one final touch, Suzanna began to comb her hair into the waterfall Brenda had worn the night of the Grammys. She was confident that she, too, would look great in the hairdo.

Garland arrived at Red Rocks with Sissy and James. He didn't feel like making the drive alone. As they pulled into the parking area, security escorted them to a reserved area. Driving into the security area was a job in itself, as the crowd walking into the amphitheater stopped upon recognizing Garland sitting in the backseat. Many of his fans took advantage of the situation and began to take pictures, each one setting off a sea of flashbulbs.

Garland slowly departed the backseat, feeling his way along the frame of the car. Each time a flashbulb went off, it made it difficult to see for a few seconds afterward. Kevin met the Summerses, escorting them into the dressing area behind the stage. As Garland joined

Adam and Brandon, their memories of the contest began to flood their minds. The memories of Summer's Solstice were sometimes good and sometimes painful.

Joe Moss greeted the boys and began to go over the program for the evening. There would be several city dignitaries in attendance. The mayor would make a proclamation designating the upcoming Saturday as Aurora's Fire Day in Denver. This special day included a key to the city as well. Aurora's Fire were the first entertainers to have a day proclaimed in their honor.

"After the dignitaries are done, I have a special announcement for the American Invasion tour," Joe said. He then insisted this would make them world superstars and would place them on the rock-and-roll stage with the most-popular artists of the day.

As Joe left for the stage, Harley's wheelchair made its way into the room. They were all glad to see him.

"Guess who will be your emcee this evening!" Harley said.

"Harley, you will be perfect for this evening," Brandon said as he shook Harley's hand and patted him on the shoulder.

"You know, Harley, in so many ways, 'Touch' is as much yours as mine," Garland said.

"You were right the other day. If you hadn't made the mistake with the record that night, it would have never been discovered," Adam said.

"Hey, I gave the listeners a choice that night," Harley said. "To this day, I still have that segment each week, with every new record released. Unfortunately, though, I haven't been able to find another 'Touch.' Maybe that shows what a great song it really is!"

"Harley, it's time to get the show started," Kevin said.

Harley rolled his chair out of the room, promising he would meet them onstage shortly.

They were all very glad that Harley was a part of their celebration.

As Garland began to close the door after Harley's exit, Suzanna stopped, making sure she had his attention. Garland closed the door and made his way to where she was standing.

"Suzanna, you look very nice this evening," Garland said.

Garland couldn't keep his eyes from her beauty. This was exactly what Suzanna had planned. She had the hook set and baited; now all she needed was the catch, and her catch was getting nibbles. Just when she thought she had Garland hooked, Sissy entered the hallway.

"Wow, Suzanna, are you doing a shoot here tonight? Are any of these cameras here for you this evening?" Sissy said. Sissy couldn't resist the temptation. She knew Suzanna was trying to lure her son.

"Hello, Sissy, it's nice to see you. I am here to celebrate with the rest of Colorado tonight. I think the show is about to start. I hope I will see you afterward at the private party. Perhaps we can enjoy a cocktail together," Suzanna said as she smiled and walked away.

Harley began the evening's ceremony by playing a video with Aurora's Fire's songs in the background. This was the cue for the band to join him onstage. After the video, Joe Moss was introduced.

"This evening, I am here to honor six young men who have touched our lives. One short year ago, I felt I had something very special with these guys. I had no idea of how special they would become," Joe said.

Joe paused; this was emotional for him. As he regained his composure, Joe began to inform the audience of the biggest event for any American artist in history.

"In one month, Britain will never be the same. We will do to England what the British Invasion did to us in the mid-sixties. The American Invasion will have four groups performing at four different venues for four different nights. They will all come together for one all-day concert at England's Wembley Stadium. This event will be attended by more than one hundred thousand people," Joe barked into the microphone.

This announcement brought the crowd to its feet. This was truly big news for a band from Aurora, Colorado.

The biggest compliment of the evening was Garland. Sand Dollar's first album had just gone platinum. Joe Moss presented the award to the band. As the lead singer took to the microphone to acknowledge the award, she paused and motioned for Garland to join her at the microphone.

"Garland Summers, this is just as much yours as it ours. You wrote several of the songs on the album, and you were the one who convinced Joe Moss to take a chance on a band from San Diego, California. We all love and thank you," she said.

Garland hugged her as she kissed his cheek. It meant a lot to Garland to be acknowledged in this way, a way that made him feel very humble.

Garland took his place at the microphone, and the remaining members of Aurora's Fire slipped behind the curtain. As Garland departed the front of the stage, the big curtain began to open. Already in their places were his bandmates, ready to perform. The curtain opening kept the crowd on its feet. Garland joined the others. No one had clued Garland about this event. He would rely on Rudy to start the song intro. Garland picked up his old Gibson. Rudy began the intro, an intro everyone in the crowd knew. Emotions began to overwhelm Garland as he began the first verse of "Touch." The crowd joined hands and began to sway as Garland sang. Garland knew "Touch" would never be loved any more than it was by the audience that night.

As the show wrapped up, Aurora's Fire exited the stage and returned to the dressing room.

Sissy, still trying to recover from the California trip, informed Garland that she and James wouldn't be attending the private party. She reluctantly kissed Garland, insisting that he be very careful tonight. Woman's intuition told her that something would happen if he wasn't careful.

Kevin assured Sissy everything would be all right and that he would bring Garland to the party and then home. This made Sissy feel much better; there was no one she trusted her son's life with more than Kevin. Sissy left the room and entered the hallway. Once again, she caught a glimpse of Suzanna; this time, she was talking to Garland. Kevin walked up to Garland and Suzanna.

"Garland, if you are ready, it's time to head over to the party," Kevin said.

Garland turned to leave with Kevin.

"I hope to see you at the party, Garland," Suzanna said.

Kevin patted Garland on the back, shaking his head as they left the amphitheater.

Garland arrived at the party, along with Kevin and Adam. As the three walked into the reception area, once again, there was a sea of flashbulbs. Garland was beginning to recover from the first round of flashes. This party was adult oriented, with alcoholic drinks the mainstay of the gala.

Garland wasn't known to be a man who often drank alcoholic spirits. As Garland began to walk around the room, a waiter approached him, offering a drink.

Not knowing his liquor combinations, Garland ordered a drink unfamiliar to the waiter. Not wanting to feel any more embarrassed than he already was, Garland ordered a bourbon and Coke. This was one drink he had heard of in the movies. The waiter proceeded to the bar and returned with Garland's drink. Garland, not wanting to feel out of place, took a very large drink. The strong bourbon content took his breath away as he swallowed. The second sip was more pleasant than the first.

Garland finished his drink and ordered a second drink. The waiter returned with his drink.

"Hey, Garland, take it easy with the firewater," a voice said.

The voice startled Garland. He had no idea someone was right behind him as he took a drink from the glass. There was only one person Garland knew who would refer to booze as firewater. As a hostess walked by, Brandon refilled his napkin with the appetizers from her serving tray. He was hooked on these southwest egg rolls.

"Garland, I have to confess something to you. I am not so sure about these concerts in England. I don't want to be away from Tobie and Skye. Going out on the road is becoming harder and harder for me," Brandon said.

"I know, Brandon. I am sure I would feel just as you do, if I were married and a father," Garland said.

Brandon placed his used napkin on a nearby tray and excused himself.

Garland was finishing his second drink when Suzanna caught a glimpse of him.

This is the perfect time to solve our problems, Suzanna thought as she sultrily approached Garland. Her plan to wow him this evening was now in play. She planned to erase Brenda from his mind, and the way she looked this evening, that memory would be tested.

Suzanna, drinking a cocktail, gave Garland a hug and a big kiss. Garland was shocked, but he also took time to enjoy Suzanna's warm welcome. Suzanna was very beautiful this evening, and her kisses matched her beauty. The two left the party through a door leading to a patio. The moon was very bright, making her long black hair shimmer like silk. The patio door opened, with a waiter offering them each a drink. This time, the type of drink didn't matter. The alcohol was beginning to fuel their desires.

Suzanna once again made another pass at Garland. It was time to really test his willpower.

"Does my hair look as good as the girl in the pictures at your mother's house?" she said.

Garland refused to answer her, once again finishing the last few sips of his drink.

Suzanna began to match Garland drink for drink; she was determined that enough alcohol would make Garland her slave. She was confident her plan was working.

Then, it happened! Garland was drunk. This was a first for the young musical prodigy. Suzanna wrapped her arm around Garland as they went back indoors. Garland began to stumble, and his speech was beginning to slur.

"Garland, the party is almost over. Are you ready for me to drive you home?" Adam said.

"Adam, Garland has asked me to take him home after the party," Suzanna said.

Adam, wanting to be satisfied this was Garland's wish, inquired as to whether this was indeed his decision. Garland assured Adam that he wanted to ride home with Suzanna.

"I will talk to you tomorrow," Adam said as he left the party.

Garland and Suzanna began to make their way to Suzanna's car. As Garland stumbled in his drunkenness, looking for the car, Suzanna led him toward her new red Lincoln Mark V.

Although Suzanna had enjoyed herself throughout the evening, she wasn't inebriated. She began to inquire about Garland and Brenda's relationship. Unfortunately, Garland wasn't cooperating, which interfered with Suzanna's plans.

"Brenda, when did you get a new car?" Garland asked Suzanna when they reached her car.

This really upset Suzanna. Already irritated that Garland did not seem to be taking her bait, his calling her by another woman's name—her rival, no less—just added fuel to the fire. This was especially infuriating because she wanted to erase Brenda from his memory.

Garland helped Suzanna into the driver's seat, once again calling her Brenda. This wasn't funny to Suzanna. Using the car to keep his balance, Garland walked around the car until he reached the passenger door. It was a good thing her new car was a two-door. Garland slid into the front seat, closing the door behind him.

"Brenda, let's go home, baby!" Garland said as he passed out.

Suzanna shook Garland awake, refusing to accept that her plan wasn't working. She then began to let Garland know what her intentions were. She slowly undressed herself, joining Garland in the passenger seat. She was determined to be with Garland one last time to erase Brenda from his heart. In his inebriated state, Garland gave in to Suzanna's desires once again. However, Suzanna's satisfied desire was soon to be interrupted when Garland whispered Brenda's name in her ear.

Being called by her rival's name infuriated Suzanna even more now than before. She burned rubber as she left the parking lot, almost hitting KARO's van. Suzanna, thinking of revenge, began to drive faster and faster. She sometimes made the tires squeal on her car as she turned corners. Suzanna turned the volume up on the radio; she loved the sound system in her new car. The radio was playing one of her favorite songs. Once again, she adjusted the volume and began to sing along with the lyrics. The song made her think of the days when she and Garland were together. It reminded her of the happiness of those days. The song began to end, giving way to "Touch." This was the last song she wanted to hear. She immediately turned the radio off. The night air was erotic. Suzanna rolled both windows down to enjoy the sensual breezes.

Several blocks from the party, Suzanna, her mind flowing with the breeze slammed on the brakes as the traffic light turned red. Several feet from the curb was a bench for public-transportation riders. A man and his girlfriend were waiting for the next bus when Suzanna's quick stop caught their attention.

"Look!" the man said to his girlfriend. "Do you know who is in that car?" ked his girlfriend.

She paused, at first not recognizing Garland's face.

"That is Garland Summers. He won four awards on the Grammys," the man said.

His girlfriend took a closer look. "Oh my God! You are right! It is him! I think he is asleep!"

Her loud voice woke Garland, and he sat up in the passenger seat.

"Baby, get your camera out!" the man shouted.

Not wanting to miss out on this moment, she pulled a camera from her purse and took Garland's picture. The flash exploded in Garland's inebriated consciousness.

Dazed, Garland turned toward the camera as the young man took another picture.

The man and his girlfriend thought it was magic to be waiting for a bus and have a celebrity almost fall into their laps.

The light suddenly changed, and Suzanna sped away. Once again, the tires squealed, leaving marks behind on the roadway.

Catching the first red light had its reward. With traffic lights, often synchronized, it made it easier for her to catch green lights for the next few blocks. Suzanna's Mark V began to gain speed with each green light. She never thought twice about slowing down. The higher speed made the erotic winds calming. She needed something to calm her. Her plan for Garland was a failure. Suzanna was unfamiliar with failure. This was a new territory for her, and it only angered her more.

The timing of the traffic lights became a game to her. She felt they were one thing that she had conquered this evening. Occasionally, she glanced at Garland, making sure he was unconscious.

Suzanna was approaching her thirteenth block without catching one red light.

This is awesome! she thought.

The city blocks were becoming longer, and the lights were farther apart now. Her speed now exceeded seventy miles per hour. This part of the street was unfamiliar to her. The street began to have curves. These made the drive more fun for her. It reminded her of the roller coaster Garland had made her ride at Elitch Gardens. She remembered how much it had scared her. Garland laughing at her fear then added to her anger now. Soon the curves became much sharper, adding to the thrill of the drive.

Just around the next curve was Officer Tuck Foster. This was Officer's Foster last night before retiring. Officer Foster stopped to retrieve a piece of lumber in the street. He knew this would be very dangerous to any driver during the daytime hours, and even more so at night. Suzanna was nearing eighty miles an hour now. As Officer Foster began to make his way from the street, two headlights appeared, headed his way. The car was closing in very fast. Officer Foster froze in his tracks, as if he knew this would be the end of his long career.

The darkness, coupled with Suzanna's high rate of speed, made it impossible for Suzanna to see. She swerved at the last minute, trying to miss whatever it was in the street. The timing worked against Officer Foster and Suzanna. She timed her lane change at the exact moment the officer stepped into the same lane. She slammed on her brakes, but it was too late. The front of her car lifted the officer and threw him up and over the back of the Lincoln. Suzanna became hysterical. This was a human she had run over. It would take quick thinking to get her out of this dilemma.

Struggling to calm herself, Suzanna finally brought her car to a stop. She turned to see the stricken officer lying in the street. First, she looked to see if there were any witnesses. Being such a late hour, there wasn't any traffic in the streets. Suzanna pulled her car onto the sidewalk. Garland remained unconscious. She knew he was very drunk. The accident had caused Garland's head to hit the dash.

What can I do to get out of this? she thought frantically.

She began to gather up her purse and other personal belongings. She had to make out like her car had been stolen. After taking her purse from the car, Suzanna ran into a dark alley and onto the next street over. Eventually, she came upon a pay phone and called the police.

"Hello, I want to report a stolen car," she said to the dispatcher.

"Ma'am, what type of car was stolen?" the dispatcher inquired.

"It's a 1970 red Lincoln Mark V," Suzanna answered. She hung the phone up after giving the police department the temporary tag number.

As part of her escape, Suzanna left the driver's door open and the motor running. The cooler night air began to awaken Garland. He sat up in the car. Garland ran his hand over his forehead, feeling the knot that had formed. He couldn't imagine how he had arrived in this car. As he began to exit the car, the hangover began to remind him who was in charge. Garland climbed into the driver's seat, closing the door. He began to drive slowly until he found a nearby park and pulled into the park's parking lot. Once again, his hangover took charge, and Garland passed out again—this time, behind the wheel, with the motor still running.

A police cruiser turned on Estes Parkway. Two officers were about to finish their shift. The cruiser began its way into the curve. As the officers entered a part of the street where the lights gave way to the darkness, parked on the shoulder was a police cruiser. The red and blue lights were flashing atop the cruiser. Their rays bounced off an object lying in the street close by. The cruiser stopped, and the officers jumped out of the car and into the street. The officers unfastened their flashlights, shining them into the street where the object lay. Both officers ran to get a closer look. As they approached the scene, their worst fear became a reality: it was a body. They quickly determined it was the body of another police officer.

Officer Travis ran back to the cruiser to request emergency assistance.

"We have an officer down!" he shouted into the police radio's microphone.

Officer Bowie remained with the fallen officer, making sure there wasn't another accident. This was a very dark part of the street.

Officer Travis once again requested emergency assistance. This time, his request was answered.

"We need an ambulance at Estes Parkway, near Coors Park," he said.

After the dispatcher acknowledged the location, Officer Travis returned to assist Officer Foster. Officer Tuck Foster was alive, but just barely.

Several nearby cruisers arrived, as did the ambulance. The paramedics loaded Officer Foster into the ambulance and departed for the nearest hospital. They, too, knew this was to be Foster's last day of duty. The two officers arriving first at the scene, Officers Travis and Bowie, returned to their cruiser and began to wrap up their shift. Their cruiser made its way to a median, and they turned around to return to headquarters.

The officers were making a U-turn, when their headlights revealed a car parked in the park's parking lot. This was not normal; the park had closed several hours earlier. They entered the parking lot to investigate the red Lincoln. As they approached the vehicle, they parked the cruiser behind the Lincoln to block any attempt by the driver to flee. Both officers exited the cruiser, taking normal precautions as they approached the car.

The officers separated, with each selecting a door for safety, uncertainty of the number of occupants inside the vehicle. Each officer directed his flashlight inside the red Lincoln, searching the back for any surprises. Slumped over, with his head resting on the steering wheel, was an unconscious man. After several attempts to get his attention, without any response, they opened the car doors. Officer Travis shook the man and leaned him against the seat's back, shining his flashlight on the man's face.

"Sir, are you all right?" Officer Travis asked.

He wasn't sure if the man was hurt. He broke open a capsule, holding it under the man's nostrils, bringing him to consciousness.

Officer Bowie returned to the cruiser and called in a trace on the vehicle's registration. The dispatcher indicated this was a vehicle stolen earlier in the evening. As he returned to the Lincoln, Officer Bowie walked around the car, discovering the front was damaged. He had a hunch this was the car involved in Tuck Foster's accident.

Officer Travis turned the car's engine off, helping the man from the seat and leaning him up against the side of car. The man's breath indicated he was intoxicated. Further examination with a flashlight into his eyes confirmed that he was. Officer Travis turned the man around, leaning him over the trunk while searching for identification. Finding a wallet in the left rear pocket, he retrieved it. Shining his flashlight into the wallet, he found the man's driver's license. He began to slide the license from the plastic holder to reveal the owner. The answer was so much of a shock that Officer Travis dropped his flashlight.

This can't be true. There is no way this man could be involved with an incident such as this, Officer Travis thought.

Several of the other arriving officers gathered to assist Officer Travis. One retrieved the fallen wallet and driver's license. Officer Travis insisted on being the one to place handcuffs on the prisoner. His behavior took them all by surprise.

Officer Travis kept the secret as long as he could. He escorted the prisoner to his cruiser, opening a rear door and placing the prisoner inside. Officer Bowie, realizing his partner was somehow in shock, entered the cruiser. He insisted on driving to the station. Officer Travis radioed headquarters to pick up the Lincoln and return the car to headquarters. The vehicle was now a crime scene.

"What did you see in his wallet that shook you up so bad?" Officer Bowie asked.

Officer Travis turned to his partner with tears in his eyes. "Tonight, we may have lost a brother on the force, and Colorado may have lost its biggest new star."

"What do you mean by that?" Officer Bowie asked.

Officer Travis, finding it difficult to speak, finally said, "Our prisoner is Garland Summers. This is one sad day for the Denver area. A day it will take us a long time to recover from."

Garland Summers was booked that evening. If Officer Foster died, Garland would be charged vehicular manslaughter.

||||||||

In North Carolina, an hour before daylight, Brenda was tossing and turning in her sleep. Something was wrong. She rushed into the bathroom, feeling sick to her stomach. This was becoming a common occurrence. She refused to admit the reality of the cause of her problems; she hoped it was just a passing phase. The reality was that the phase was an everyday happening. She was a month late now, and the time to face reality had come.

A pregnant unmarried girl wasn't accepted very well in society in the seventies. She would make an appointment in the morning to see a doctor in Raleigh, but she was sure what the results would be. She had mixed emotions about what she already knew. Garland would be a wonderful father, and if he still wanted to get married, nothing would make her happier.

||||||||

Garland was processed into the city jail. The jailer took Garland's mug shot. The local media, having access to police scanners, already began to pick up on the story. Calls were coming into KARO, wanting confirmation that this was the Grammy-winning Garland Summers. One of the scanners was in the newsroom at KARO. Timmy Towns, the all-night on-air personality, heard the news over the scanner. Not wanting to call the Summerses without any further details, he called Kevin instead.

Kevin's alarm rang simultaneously with the phone. He turned over and pushed the Snooze button, thinking he would catch a few more minutes of sleep. Kevin suddenly realized the phone was ringing as well. Maybe it would stop if he left it alone. Kevin slowly reached for the phone on his nightstand and answered it.

"Kevin, are you awake? I want you to be awake when I tell you this. I don't want you thinking it was a bad dream, because this is a bad dream that is real!" Timmy said.

"Timmy is there a problem at the station? You know you should be calling James, if there is one," Kevin said.

"Kevin, you need to get down here as fast as you can. There has been a terrible accident, and it involved Garland!" Timmy shouted.

The tone of Timmy's voice let Kevin know something very bad had happened. Kevin threw on some clothes and drove to KARO.

|||||||

Garland was beginning to sober up. He sat up on the cot in his cell. Garland began to look around, noticing the small quarters with bars all around him. He walked over to the sink, filled his cupped hands with cold water, and splashed his face. His head was splitting. Hangovers were new to Garland.

"Does anyone have an aspirin?" he asked.

The jailer approached Garland. "I am glad to see Sleeping Beauty is finally awake."

Turning to see to whom the jailer was speaking, Garland asked, "Are you talking to me?"

The jailer laughed at Garland's attempt to play innocent.

"Do you have any idea where you are?" the jailer said.

Garland shook his head. Once again, Garland's attempt to play innocent tried the jailer's patience.

"Boy, after what you did last night, you will beg to see the sun again," the jailer said.

Garland, in no mood for the jailer's attitude, folded his pillow and lay back on the cot. He would have to wait out the headache and hangover.

Word began to spread in the remaining cells about a cop being hit and the driver leaving the scene. Garland heard others talking but didn't have a clue he was the subject of their conversations. Nor did he have any idea why he was locked up in a cell.

||||||||

Kevin arrived at the radio station. Several news crews had assembled in the parking lot. It was now just a matter of time before the news would be released. This was a nightmare—one that, if true, would never go away. Kevin paced his office, trying to think of a way to break the news to James and Sissy. They were his best friends in the world, and there was no one he thought more highly of than Garland. Kevin did the only thing he could think of in the moment and immediately left for the Summerses' home. He knew they would need him at a time like this.

Kevin arrived at James and Sissy's house in record time. He pulled into the driveway, got out of the car, and ran onto the front porch. Kevin, rather than ringing the doorbell, began pounding the door. He wanted to make sure he would be heard. Sissy, the lighter sleeper of the two, was awakened and grabbed her housecoat. She turned on a nearby lamp and went to the door. She knew not to open the door at that hour. Sissy turned her porch light on and peeped through the privacy hole in the door. Kevin began to pound on the door once again; this time, he began to shout for James and Sissy.

Sissy, realizing something was very wrong, opened the front door and invited Kevin inside. By now, all the commotion had brought James into the living room.

"What on earth is going on, Kevin? Why are you acting like this?" James asked.

Kevin tried to catch his breath before he spoke. He knew he would need every breath to break the news to them.

Kevin walked over to Sissy and held both of her hands.

"This is the hardest thing I have ever had to tell anyone in my life. I am not sure how to say it or where to start," Kevin's said.

Kevin's behavior began to upset Sissy. As if by instinct, she sat down on the sofa.

Kevin continued, "Last night, after the party, Garland was involved in an accident. He is okay, but he is being held in jail. He is accused of a hit-and-run with a stolen car. The person who was hit is a Denver police officer."

Sissy, as if in a trance, began to deny the accusation against Garland. She refused to believe what Kevin was telling her.

"Garland is in his room, asleep," Sissy said. "I will show you. Let me go get him."

Sissy left the living room and proceeded to Garland's bedroom. The bed had not been slept in. She walked back into the living room and collapsed.

This was the beginning of the worst day of their lives.

26

THE CITY JAIL was suddenly overtaken by the reporters rushing in. There was a news conference going on at the hospital, with reporters from all three major networks. Garland was recovering from his hangover, wishing he could recollect the night before. Screams of disbelief began to fill the jail. Officers were rushing in to confirm what the news conference was reporting. The police chief stood behind a podium filled with many microphones.

"At 7:30 a.m. mountain time, Officer Tuck Foster was pronounced dead. He was a twenty-year veteran of the Denver police department. We have a suspect in custody in the city jail. Garland Summers is being charged with manslaughter with a stolen vehicle. The vehicle was reported as stolen by its owner earlier in the evening," the chief said.

Several of Officer Foster's colleagues entered the jail area where Garland was being detained.

"Will someone tell me what all the sadness is about?" Garland said.

Two officers had to be restrained from entering Garland's cell. They found it hard to believe, and took it as Garland being a smart-ass. Garland backed away from the bars, realizing the officers' anger was directed at him. Still unaware he was the suspect, Garland sat down on his cot.

||||||||

The news conference from the hospital was being fed nationally. This was a tragic event. Several blocks away, Tobie began to fix Brandon's breakfast and feed Skye. For some reason this morning, she turned on the television in the den. Brandon, already awake, was taking his morning shower. Tobie opened the refrigerator door, searching for eggs to cook for Brandon's breakfast. She found the eggs and closed the refrigerator door.

A news flash suddenly interrupted the regular program. The reporter began to report the fatal accident involving a Denver police officer. Tobie was cracking the eggs over a bowl to prepare Brandon's favorite, a southwestern omelet, when the reporter announced the suspect was Garland Summers. She picked up Skye, rushing to hear the news, making sure she had heard what she couldn't believe. As the news reporter began to profile Garland, Tobie dropped to her knees. This couldn't be the Garland she knew and loved.

Brandon entered the room to see Tobie kneeling on the floor, in tears. His first fear was that something was wrong with Skye, and he rushed to her side. Tobie turned to Brandon and began to cry more intensely. Brandon had never seen her this upset before. After closely examining Skye, Brandon helped Tobie to her feet. Her tears refused to let up.

"Baby, what is wrong? Why are you so upset?" he asked.

Tobie tried very hard to answer Brandon, but there wasn't any way she could. Brandon hugged Tobie, assuring there was nothing bad enough to make her this upset.

Holding his wife and daughter, Brandon began to see an image of Garland on the television. The announcer began to update the story. As the reporter continued, Tobie felt Brandon's heart beating like it was trying to jump out of his bare chest. Brandon clutched her like he never had before. This was the second time she had seen her husband cry, but never more intensely than that morning as he watched the news about his best friend.

||||||||

Brenda was driving into Raleigh for her doctor's appointment. This morning, her mind was on Garland, on how to tell him he would be a father. She started her journey this morning with the car's radio turned off. She drove into the parking lot of the doctor's office, wiping the tear marks from her face. She reported in to the receptionist, signing the appointment log and waiting for her turn. As she began to take a seat in waiting area, a nurse came to the door, informing Brenda she was next. The nurse led Brenda into an examining room where Brenda informed her of the reason of her visit.

"You are here for a pregnancy test," the nurse confirmed.

Brenda answered that yes, that was why she was there, as the nurse began to ask her questions about her feminine cycle.

"I am six weeks late," Brenda informed the nurse.

The nurse gave Brenda a container for a urine sample. Shortly after the nurse took Brenda's container, the doctor entered the examining room. He began to examine Brenda and, without any hesitation, congratulated her on her upcoming baby. It was true that Brenda was going to be a mother.

Brenda was getting dressed as the doctor informed her of when he would like to see her again. In seven and a half months, she would give Garland a child; after her final semester of school, they could be married. Brenda left the examining room, making her way to the business office to settle her bill. She stood at the desk for several minutes. Where was everyone? She wanted to pay and return home. Out in the waiting room, the television was breaking the news.

The receptionist saw Brenda waiting at her desk and rushed over to take care of the bill and schedule her next appointment. She was in tears.

"I am sorry for making you wait," she said as she searched for a Kleenex to wipe her eyes.

Brenda, not wanting to appear nosy, told her she hoped everything would be okay.

"Honey, the sorrow is not for me. My sorrow is for that young man who, just the other night, won all those awards," she said.

Brenda's heart skipped a beat; she hoped the woman was not

referring to Garland. Exiting through the door, Brenda stopped at the television. Her worst fears came true. Garland *was* the one they were talking about. She tried to make her way to the door, but her legs buckled as she fainted. The nurses rushed her back into a room, wiping her face with a wet cloth. Brenda came to and became hysterical. What was to have been the most exciting day of her life suddenly became the worst.

IIIIIIII

The news about Garland filled the national airwaves, both on television and radio. Nowhere was the news received harder than at Magic Sounds. Joe Moss's plans for the invasion of Britain was wiped out. His marquee act and its star were in danger of becoming a memory. Joe did the only thing he could think of: he contacted Mathew Stein. Mathew was the premier defense attorney in the state of Colorado. Joe knew Garland would need the best there was. Under Colorado law, if convicted, Garland Summers could receive the death penalty—a charge that the Summerses and their friends were not aware of.

Sissy answered the phone when Joe called.

"Sissy, this is Joe Moss. I want to help Garland in any way I can. I am a very good friend of the best defense attorney Colorado has to offer. His name is Mathew Stein, and he has agreed to accept Garland's case."

"Joe, thank you," Sissy said. "We have no idea where to begin. This is such a shock."

"Sissy, I want you to know that we all believe Garland is innocent. There has to be some kind of mistake," Joe said.

Sissy knew Joe was trying to help and appreciated his efforts.

Joe told Sissy that Mathew Stein was on his way to the jail to meet with Garland.

Once again, Sissy thanked Joe, and they said goodbye and ended the call.

IIIIIIII

Later that same day, the prosecutor began to gather evidence for the state's case against Garland. Suzanna's car was sent to forensics. Attached to the damaged Lincoln were clothing fibers that had to be examined. Crime-scene investigators compared the angles of the damage with the injuries on Officer Tuck Foster's body. It soon became conclusive that this was the vehicle involved in the accident. Although Garland was a very popular celebrity, killing a police officer was a very serious charge in Colorado, and there wasn't a more respected officer.

Garland was sitting on his cot when two guards approached his cell door and unlocked it. Without saying a word, one of the guards grabbed Garland and pushed him into the cell's doorway. The other guard then took over and shoved him into the open hallway.

"Come on, boy. We are going to take a little trip," one of the guards said.

Garland and the two guards began their walk down a long hallway. With each step, the guards harassed Garland about being a cop killer. Once, when Garland stopped to respond to the accusations, a baton pushed into his backside reminded him that this was not a social walk.

Finally, the three arrived at a room. One guard opened the door, pushing Garland inside. As Garland stumbled into the doorway, a well-dressed man sitting at a table sprang to his feet, protesting the treatment Garland received.

"I suggest you stop this treatment while you still have a job," the man said.

The guard shook his head as he looked into the man's eyes. He took offense at the man's interference but left the room without saying a word.

The man walked over to Garland and introduced himself. "Hello, Garland. I am a friend of Joe Moss. My name is Mathew Stein, and I will be your attorney."

Garland shook his attorney's hand. "Mathew, in the time I have been here, no one has told me why I am here. I have no idea what I have done. I think they think I have done something to a police officer."

Mathew informed Garland of the charges pending against him, and Garland broke down and cried like a baby.

"Mathew, I swear to God that I have not done this. This has to be a mistake," Garland said.

"Tomorrow, the prosecution will announce the state's case against you. This will not be an easy trial, Garland. The state could seek the death penalty," Mathew said.

Now realizing that Garland was unaware of not only why he was being held but also what was at stake, Mathew decided it was best to conclude the meeting.

"Garland, I will be back in the morning; I want to know everything you remember," Mathew said.

Mathew approached the door and motioned for a guard to return Garland to his cell.

Turning back to face Garland, he said, "Garland, let me know if any of the asshole guards do anything to you without cause."

Mathew only hoped that his earlier threat would make the guards stop the treatment he'd witnessed earlier.

IIIIIII

Brenda returned home from her doctor's appointment. As she walked into the house, her mother ran to her side.

"Baby, we are shocked. This cannot be the Garland Summers we all know and love," Valerie said.

Thinking their daughter was weak from the shock of the news, Valerie and Michael Fisher led their daughter into the den, helping her to a seat on the sofa. This was going to be a very high-profile trial, with a celebrity like Garland involved in the death of a police officer.

Brenda, at a loss for words, reached into her purse, searching for the results of her pregnancy test. After retrieving paper with the test results, she handed it to her mother. Valerie took the piece of paper and began to read it. Valerie's silence clued her husband that the paper was of some concern. Brenda slumped over on the couch and began to cry. She felt so alone. At this moment, she very much needed the man she loved.

"Brenda, I don't know what to say," Valerie said.

Michael Fisher began to read the results of the test.

Brenda knew her dad would be the most upset of all about her situation.

Michael walked over to the sofa where Brenda was lying. He reached out a helping hand to his daughter, saying, "Brenda, take my hand."

Brenda reluctantly took her father's hand, and he gently pulled her until she was sitting upright on the couch. Michael then took a seat next to his daughter. Brenda took a very deep breath. Her heart was racing almost as fast as the tears were falling from her eyes and down her cheeks.

"Sweetheart, I know this is something you never expected to happen," Michael said. "With the events of the day, this has to be very hard for you. I want you to know that I love you, and we will get through this. We will keep the news to ourselves for the time being."

Brenda needed her dad's love and support, and his words made her realize why she loved him as much as she did.

IIIIIII

Each passing day brought more evidence against Garland. With each news conference concerning the case, the crowd became larger and much angrier.

Suzanna called her agent about a photo shoot in Paris. She wanted to get away; she needed time to form her story. There couldn't be any mistakes or holes in her story. The prosecution was seeking the death penalty; her story had to be airtight.

Suzanna left the states the next day, informing her dad and the police that she didn't have any immediate plans on returning to Colorado. Being out of the country would make it difficult for her to be questioned by defense counsel prior to the trial. Since Suzanna was not a suspect, and the police had her car, there was no objection to her departure. She had no plans to return for the trial, and no one said she was required to.

||||||||

Mathew Stein met with Garland, trying to re-create the events of that tragic night. Each time, Garland drew a blank; he couldn't remember anything. The police and the prosecutor felt they had an ironclad case against Garland. Mathew questioned Garland daily, trying to find any clue that would help in Garland's defense. No matter how hard Mathew tried, Garland just couldn't remember the events of that night. He wasn't able to provide any help for his defense. The state's case was further enhanced by Garland's blood-alcohol level, which, at the time of booking, was twice that of the legal limit for intoxication.

"Mathew, I can't even tell you how I got into any car that night, much less one I searched out to steal," Garland said.

"The stolen car belongs to Suzanna Royal, whom you left the party with. You told me you remember that you left with Suzanna. What type of car Suzanna does she drive?" Mathew asked.

"I only remember her red Mustang. When we left the party, she had a new car, but I don't remember what kind of car it was," Garland said.

"Garland, the grand jury will meet to assess the charges against you. If the grand jury indicts you, under Colorado law, the prosecution could seek the death penalty. We have our work cut out for us," Mathew said.

Mathew realizing the stress on Garland, summoned a jailer.

"Tomorrow, we will know exactly what the state is seeking. Please try to remember what happened that night. Anything you can remember will help," Mathew said as he left Garland.

||||||||

The next day arrived, with a full courtroom. News media sat along the front steps awaiting the results of the grand jury's decision.

James and Sissy arrived early that morning. Mathew had arranged for them to see their son and escorted them into the room where Garland was being detained. A jailer opened the door, letting Sissy and James in. Garland looked as if he had not slept in days. Sissy couldn't remember seeing him in worse shape. Garland's condition made Sissy weep. She darted to her son's side to hold him. It was as if she were not able to hold her son tight enough that day. This was a feeling all new to her. Garland returned Sissy's hug, and then he and James hugged as well.

"Mother, Dad, I swear to you, I have not done what they are accusing me of. Has someone found Suzanna? She will clear this all up," Garland said.

Sissy hugged her son with an even greater amount of compassion. "Baby, Suzanna is the one accusing you of auto theft, and she has left the country. It may be days before she returns—if she ever does return."

A bailiff opened the door to escort Garland and Mathew into the courtroom. The grand jury had reached a decision, and it was time to reveal that decision.

As Garland, Mathew, Sissy, and James entered the courtroom, along the back row sat Kevin, Adam, Brandon, and the other members of Aurora's Fire.

Mathew and Garland took a seat at a table in front of the grand jury.

A grand jury spokesman began to inform the judge of the grand jury's decision regarding the state's case against Garland Summers for vehicular manslaughter with a stolen vehicle used in the death of Officer Tuck Foster.

The judge said, "Garland Summers, if you are convicted of the charges brought against you this day, you could receive a maximum sentence of the death penalty."

The announcement caused Sissy to faint.

This was like the worst nightmare imaginable, except it was a bad dream that she couldn't awaken from.

IIIIIII

The news from the courtroom began to spread like wildfire. The reporters began to disclose the story to their audiences and readers. Nowhere was the news received any harder than in North Carolina. The national news broke the story as the Fishers were about to eat lunch that afternoon.

Brenda watched Sissy and James as they left the courthouse steps. She had never seen Sissy like this before. This classy, wonderful delight of a woman was hurting very badly. Brenda wanted to reach out to Sissy and James. She loved them as much as if they were her own parents. There was only one thing she could do to help lighten the pain in their hearts.

IIIIIII

Later that evening, as the news began to form public opinions about the case, Sissy and James were watching a national report. Meanwhile, radio stations were forming a boycott of Aurora's Fire records, banishing them from the airwaves. Just weeks earlier, they had been on top of the music world. It seemed Garland had been found guilty even before the trial started.

The next day's news would add even more pain. Record stores began to pull Aurora's Fire from their stores, and fans began to drop their records off to be destroyed. This was a way to pay tribute to a fallen hero, Officer Tuck Foster.

The next morning, was Officer Foster's funeral. This funeral was the largest the Denver area had ever witnessed. There was a police escort from the church to the cemetery, and the streets were lined with citizens. The crowd was so large, the cemetery was closed to all but family members and close friends.

Several of the local television stations captured an aerial view and fed a national audience. Suzanna, in Paris, watched one of those broadcasts. She watched as Officer Foster's family left the cemetery. She had succeeded in escaping this terrible crime. The revenge she wanted on Garland was now changing the lives of many people—forever.

IIIIIIII

Later that same evening, Brenda sat alone in her bedroom. She opened her drawer and took out the paper bag that Garland had written a song on that day in the park in Raleigh. Somehow, the words contained in this song now had a much more profound meaning, touching her heart even more deeply. Alongside the song was the box containing the ring Garland had given her at the airport.

Everyone thought she had returned it to Garland that day at the airport. Maybe if she had said yes that day, Garland wouldn't have been at that party all alone. She would have been there with him, and this would not have happened.

Valerie Fisher entered Brenda's room to see her crying.

"Mother, I have to do something I think will mean a lot to Sissy. I feel she really needs this at this time," Brenda said as she began to massage her stomach.

Valerie knew what her daughter was intending to do and agreed it would be a good time.

Brenda picked up the phone from her nightstand and dialed the Summerses in Colorado.

"Sissy, hello," Brenda said when Sissy answered.

"Brenda, is that you? Baby, your voice is soothing for the soul," Sissy said.

Brenda could feel Sissy's pain.

"Sissy, I am speechless about all of this. I cannot believe what has happened. I know Garland is innocent," Brenda said.

"Brenda, you do know that my son loves you very much," Sissy said.

"Yes, Sissy I do, and I love him as well," Brenda said. She paused and then added, "Sissy, I have something to tell you, but I don't want Garland to know. In seven months, you are going to be a grandmother."

Sissy's sad tone of voice changed immediately as she said, "Brenda, are you sure?"

"Yes, I am positive. I didn't want to say anything with everything that is going on right now, but then I thought that maybe it would help you and James," Brenda said.

James walked into the room to see Sissy crying but smiling.

"Honey, you are going to be a pawpaw," Sissy told him.

Sissy and James were very excited and agreed to keep the secret, as Brenda requested. They also didn't want Garland to worry about Brenda's pregnancy during this terrible time. They agreed with Brenda that they would tell him when the news would be good news.

After saying goodbye to Brenda, Sissy hung up the phone. She couldn't remember the last time she or James had smiled.

27

BRENDA'S FINAL SEMESTER at Duke was now into the last weeks. Her radiance increased each day of her pregnancy. She was determined not to let her pregnancy keep her from her goal. Early one afternoon after class, Brenda arrived at home to find a very special letter in the mail. She began to open the envelope, hoping the contents inside contained the news she had worked so hard for during the past four years. She paused for a few seconds, trying to regain her composure, and then she continued opening the envelope.

Valerie Fisher entered the kitchen just as her daughter began to read the letter. Valerie approached the spot where Brenda stood.

Brenda smiled and handed the letter to her mother.

The letter was from the dean of the Duke law school. "Dear Miss Fisher," the letter stated. "We are pleased to inform you that you have been accepted into the Duke University School of Law for the upcoming fall semester."

This was wonderful news for the Fishers.

Brenda left the room and retired to her bedroom. She was excited about the good news but knew she would never be able to attend law school now. Motherhood had a higher priority, and raising a new baby wouldn't leave time for law school. Perhaps there would be another time for her to pursue her dream. She wanted to be the best mother for her baby. Someday, she would continue her education. She wanted to go to law school very badly, but she wanted her baby even more. She was now less than a month away from her due date.

Garland's trial would begin within the week, and the entire nation was interested in the outcome. After several weeks, a jury was finally selected for the trial. Many of the judicial experts were anticipating a long trial. A long trial meant the verdict might not come until after the baby was born. Brenda was keeping a scrapbook of court proceedings; she wanted to know everything she could. The legal process fascinated her; after all, law was her chosen future profession.

‖‖‖‖‖‖‖

Sissy and James were sitting down to their morning coffee when the doorbell rang. James left the kitchen and went through the living room to see who was at the front door.

Mathew Stein stood at the front door.

James opened the door, and the two men exchanged greetings.

"James, may I come in?" Mathew asked. "I would like to talk to you and Sissy."

James led Mathew into the kitchen.

Sissy greeted Mathew and fixed him a cup of coffee.

Mathew sat down and took the coffee from Sissy.

From Mathew's sad eyes and long face, Sissy could tell there was something troubling him.

"Mathew, is there something wrong?" Sissy asked.

Mathew took a sip of the hot coffee, hoping it would help him pronounce the words he dreaded saying out loud.

"Sissy, James, for the first time in my legal career, I have a case that I am afraid I cannot win. I find myself in unfamiliar territory. I am 100 percent certain that Garland is innocent, but I cannot find any evidence to support that," Mathew said.

Sissy began to fall apart again. James was beside her, trying to comfort her.

No one felt worse than Mathew did.

"Tomorrow, when Garland's trial begins, I want you to know that I will do everything I can to save him," Mathew said.

Sissy nodded, still sobbing and unable to speak.

James escorted Mathew from the room, led him to the door, and thanked him as the two men said their goodbyes.

IIIIIII

Suzanna was wrapping up her photo shoot in Paris. Her plan was a success. She wasn't a suspect in the accident. She had pulled it off. Being out of the country had kept her from any questioning by the defense attorneys, just as she'd hoped. She planned to stay in Paris after her shoot was over. She loved Paris and thought about moving there permanently. She would monitor the trial as much as she could, with the limited news from the states.

IIIIIII

The day finally arrived. It was the day Sissy Summers had been dreading for the last six months. Sissy and James entered the courtroom that morning, took their seats, and waited for the judge to enter. Today was the day Garland's trial would begin. Garland entered the courtroom, with Mathew Stein and his legal staff at his side.

On the other side of the courtroom sat the prosecution team, looking very confident about their case. The state's representative was a very young attorney named Adam Watkins. Even though Watkins's legal career was very brief so far, it was also very successful. Watkins had never lost a case for the state. He was confident the state's evidence would result in a conviction.

As the courtroom clock struck 9:00 a.m., Judge Daniel Sands entered the courtroom. The bailiff instructed everyone to rise as the judge took his seat. He began to announce the state's case against Garland Summers. He informed Garland that if he was convicted, the state could seek the death penalty.

Once again, the news made Sissy distraught. Under a doctor's guidance, Sissy had taken a mild sedative before arriving at the courthouse.

The trial was to be closed to the press, with no cameras, and only a court-appointed artist sketching courtroom scenes.

"Counselors, we will begin with your opening statements," Judge Sands said.

Adam Watkins approached the jury stand and began his opening statements.

"We intend to prove that, on the morning of October 25, 1971, Officer Tuck Foster was struck by a stolen vehicle and was abandoned by the driver," he said. "The stolen vehicle was later determined to be the vehicle involved in the accident. The automobile was found at a nearby park, with the defendant, Garland Summers, unconscious behind the steering wheel. Mr. Summers was later determined to be inebriated at the scene."

With each remark, the jury stared at Garland, occasionally turning to look at Officer Foster's family, who were present in the courtroom.

Adam Watkins thanked the jury for performing their civic duty during a high-profile trial.

"Mr. Stein, would you like to address the jury with your opening statement?" Judge Sands said.

Mathew approached the jury stand, with much less confidence than his courtroom adversary had displayed.

"Ladies and gentlemen of the jury, I also want to thank you for performing your civic duty during this trial," Mathew said.

Mathew walked up and down in front of the jury stand, looking into each juror's eyes, trying to read what the prosecution—and the media—had already implanted in their minds.

"In this country, a person is considered innocent until proven guilty," Mathew said. "The state has the burden to prove beyond a reasonable doubt that Garland Summers was the driver of the stolen vehicle that night. They must prove that there is no doubt that this crime was committed by the defendant. I intend to prove that there is doubt as to whether my client was the person who stole and was driving the car that killed Officer Foster. We owe it to Garland Summers and to Officer Foster to seek the truth and deliver justice based on that truth."

Mathew once again thanked the jury. He also thanked Officer Foster's family for his service to the community. He left the jury stand, hoping he had proved that there could be doubt in this case. Now he had to produce the evidence to support his theory.

During both attorneys' opening statements, Garland found it hard to keep from thinking about Brenda. She was his rock; she was the strength he needed that day.

IIIIIII

Brenda was entering the parking lot of her doctor's office. This was the last scheduled doctor's visit before her big day. Her thoughts and prayers were in Colorado that morning. She wished she could be there for Garland and Sissy. It was very difficult for her to not be with them.

The nurse brought Brenda into the examining room, and she waited for the doctor to arrive.

Dr. Sharp entered the examining room and greeted Brenda. He sensed there was something troubling her.

"Brenda, you look like you are very upset. Do you feel like something is wrong with your baby?" he asked.

Brenda began to cry.

"No, Doctor, I feel fine. I'm sure everything is wonderful with the baby. I just miss the father," she said as the tears began to fly more freely.

"Well, let's have a look," the doctor said as he began his examination.

He stood up when he had finished, giving Brenda a thumbs-up sign. "You will be a mother in less than two weeks. I hope the father is excited about the big day."

Dr. Sharp's last comment only made Brenda more upset. He patted her on the hand, assuring her that everything would be okay.

IIIIIII

Shortly after the attorneys made their opening statements to the jury, the judge adjourned court for the day. Witnesses would begin taking the stand the next morning.

Mathew Stein sat at the defense table, reviewing the prosecution's witness list. He perused their list carefully, pausing to make notes of questions he would use during his cross-examination. Just like his opening statement, each question he would pose was designed to create reasonable doubt.

A deputy of the court escorted Garland back to his cell that afternoon. They entered the customary elevator to make the six-story journey. As the elevator doors closed shut, Garland recognized a song playing on the speakers of the elevator. It was the same song he had heard the night of the accident. As the song continued to play, Garland's memory of the evening began to come back. This was the first time in more than six months that he remembered anything about that horrible night.

The elevator reached its destination, and the doors opened. The deputy took Garland by the arm and led him to his cell. Once they arrived at the cell, he signaled for the doors to be remotely opened. Garland stepped inside the cell, moving aside for the doors to be shut. The deputy began to leave when Garland spoke out.

"I must see my lawyer. Can you please see if you can reach Mathew Stein before he leaves the courtroom?" Garland asked.

The deputy promised Garland that he would try to catch Mathew before he vacated the premises.

Mathew gathered his notes and left the courtroom as the deputy entered the hallway.

"Mr. Stein, Garland Summers needs to see you immediately. He was determined for me to catch you before you left," the deputy said.

"Is he all right?" Mathew asked.

"He appeared to be physically all right, sir, but he was excited about something," the deputy said.

Mathew agreed to accompany the deputy to Garland's cell. The defense needed anything Mathew could muster. He was fighting an uphill battle.

Garland stood up from his cot at the sound of footsteps approaching his cell.

"Garland the deputy said you need to speak with me," Mathew said when he reached the door to the cell.

Garland told Mathew, "I have heard that sometimes, when a person has a loss of memory, an event will occur that will restore their memory. Tonight, that event happened in the elevator as I returned to my cell."

"Garland we need to talk. Let me arrange for one of the interrogation rooms," Mathew said as he left the cell block, promising Garland he would be right back.

Garland and Mathew entered the interrogation room together. Mathew took out a tape recorder. He didn't want to miss anything Garland had to say.

As he turned on the recorder and pressed the Record button, Mathew signaled Garland to begin speaking.

"There was this song playing on the elevator speaker. It was the same song that was playing on the car's radio that night. When I heard the song again, everything began to come back to me about what happened when I left the party," Garland said.

Perhaps there was a clue now that would clear up what really happened that night. Mathew told Garland to keep reviewing the events in his mind, and they would speak again in the morning before the trial resumed. He told Garland to try to recall as many details as he could. Mathew left his interview with Garland feeling that there was a glimmer of hope now. Although it was a small glimmer, at least now there *was* a glimmer.

Garland would spend the rest of the evening retrieving the little things he remembered before he passed out. He hoped that would be enough.

Slowly Garland's memory began to recollect the events of the party. Drinking was all new to him, and so he didn't have the slightest idea of how much tolerance he had to liquor. Not only was it the amount of alcohol he had consumed, but also the speed at which he had consumed it. He began to remember talking to Adam before he left the party. The subject of their conversation was still cloudy. As much as he tried, Garland couldn't remember leaving the party with Adam. He knew he must have left with Suzanna, but how that had transpired remained a mystery to him.

IIIIIII

Mathew arrived the next morning to gather information from Garland, now that he was beginning to remember some of the events at the party. The prosecution would begin the day with some expert witnesses detailing the crime scene and evidence leading to Garland's arrest. Mathew felt more comfortable starting the second day of the trial than he had felt the first day.

Mathew and Garland left the jail cell, making their way into the courtroom. Sissy was standing near the doorway to the courtroom. She wanted to speak with Garland before he entered the courtroom. Mathew and Garland stopped for a moment where Sissy was standing. Mathew knew both Garland and Sissy needed contact with each other.

Sissy hugged Garland, never knowing how much a hug from her son meant to her until this morning. It was one of those things people took for granted—never knowing how important a hug was until you couldn't have another one. The jailer insisted that they enter the courtroom. The judge had given strict orders for a punctual start of the day's proceedings. Garland kissed Sissy and told her he loved her as the two separated.

Mathew and Garland proceeded to the defense table, awaiting Judge Sands' arrival.

Adam Watkins began the second day of the trial by calling an expert forensic investigator to the witness stand. Watkins began to question his witness as to the speed at which the Lincoln was driven that night. The witness informed the court that the car had reached speeds exceeding seventy miles per hour and that the skid marks on the pavement indicated the speed of impact was well beyond sixty miles per hour when the car struck Officer Foster. The witness's testimony caused anger among many of the attendees in the courtroom that day. Watkins wanted to create a sense of the crime's brutality, and he was succeeding marvelously.

Mathew approached the witness stand for his cross-examination. He needed to create reasonable doubt; this would be Garland's only chance.

"Mr. Smith, I see you have a very impressive background in automobile casualty research. You seem to have a very good eye for details, and I compliment you on that talent," Mathew said.

Mr. Smith thanked Mathew for his astute observation of him.

"Garland, please stand up for the court and Mr. Smith," Mathew said.

Garland stood alongside the table, in plain view of Mr. Smith.

"Mr. Smith, how tall would you say the defendant is?" Mathew asked.

"I would say he is about six feet tall," Mr. Smith answered.

Mathew turned from the witness, looked at Garland, and thanked him for his cooperation.

"Very good, Mr. Smith. Garland is actually just under six feet, one inch tall," Mathew said.

"Mr. Smith, what was the position of the driver's seat in relation to the tilt steering wheel on the Lincoln?" Mathew asked.

"It was positioned fairly close to the steering wheel," Mr. Smith replied.

Mathew paused and rubbed his forehead for a moment.

"So you are saying that the seat was adjusted for someone much shorter than the defendant?" Mathew asked.

Mr. Smith paused and looked at Adam Watkins.

"I would say that it was adjusted for a driver much shorter than Mr. Summers," Mr. Smith said.

"Is it your expert opinion that someone of the defendant's height, in relation to the seat position, would have difficulty driving and controlling that vehicle?" Mathew asked.

Once again, Mr. Smith paused, looking toward Adam Watkins before answering Mathew.

"It would not be easy for a man of the defendant's height to drive in that position," Mr. Smith answered.

"Thank you, Mr. Smith," Mathew said as he returned to the defense table. He indicated to the court that he was through with his cross-examination of the witness.

Adam Watkins approached the witness.

"Mr. Smith, it has been determined that the defendant was intoxicated that night. Alcohol, being a relaxant, would enable someone of Mr. Summer's height to fit in that position, would it not?" Watkins asked.

"A person who is intoxicated has less body rigidity and would not feel the discomfort in that short distance between the seat and steering wheel," Mr. Smith said.

Watkins thanked Mr. Smith for his testimony, and Judge Sands dismissed him from the witness stand.

Mathew hoped the seat issue had created reasonable doubt in the minds of the jurors that day. Only time would tell if he had succeeded.

Mathew had given Sissy some hope. She had watched the jury's reaction to Mathew's cross-examination of the auto expert, and she thought it had given them something to think about.

She whispered into James's ear, "I think Mathew made some good points to the jury about the seat position. He told us the only hope we had was to create reasonable doubt, and I saw that doubt on some of the jurors' faces today."

James clasped Sissy's hand. After seeing Mathew in action, James also had hope now.

Judge Sands adjourned the court, informing one and all that the trial would resume on Monday morning.

Mathew wanted to take advantage of the weekend to gather more momentum for the defense he would present on Monday morning.

"Garland, I will meet you back at your cell. I want to see if you have any more details coming back to you about that night," Mathew said.

Mathew wanted to find a witness who had actually seen Garland—or the actual driver—driving that car out of the parking lot. Someone had to have seen them exit the lot. He really wanted that needle to be found; but, in order to find it, he would have to tear down the haystack. Mathew intended just to do that.

|||||||

Sissy and James arrived home that afternoon to find the phone ringing. Sissy rushed in to answer the phone, picking up after many rings.

"Hello," Sissy said.

The voice on the other end of the line said, "I was afraid I wouldn't be able to reach you, Sissy. How is the trial going?"

James entered the room in time to see the glow on Sissy's face, indicating the caller was someone his wife enjoyed talking to. James walked over to Sissy, whispering for her to tell him who the caller was. Sissy motioned for him to come closer, holding the receiver away from her ear. James smiled instantly when he heard the voice on the phone.

"Hello, Brenda, am I a pawpaw yet?" James said.

Sissy poked James in the ribs, showing her disbelief.

Brenda laughed at James's question. "No, Pawpaw, your grandson has not shown up yet."

"Sissy, is she holding out on us? Does she know for sure it's a boy?" James asked.

"James, I don't know if it's a boy or a girl, but I do know that the baby will be well loved," Brenda said.

There was a silence on both ends of the phone as the three took a moment to savor the thought of a new baby in the family.

James left the room, and Sissy and Brenda continued their conversation.

|||||||

The trial was into its second week. Mathew felt hopeless. The prosecution marched expert after expert to take the witness stand. Each witness seemed to provide more-convincing testimony than that of the previous witness. Mathew took notes searching for any chance to create reasonable doubt in the minds of the jurors. If only Garland could remember more about that evening; perhaps his recollection would create that one thing they needed so badly.

One day, after the trial had adjourned, Garland returned to his cell. He lay back on his cot, closing his eyes. For some reason, his mind focused on Suzanna. He remembered leaving the parking lot with Suzanna, who was driving her new car. The drive began at a slow pace. Even though he was intoxicated, he was able to enjoy the crisp autumn night. This was the first time Garland had any memory of Suzanna after the party. Several witnesses testified to seeing Garland and Suzanna arguing at the party. The prosecution took advantage of the arguments to enhance their case of auto theft.

Mathew made his nightly rounds to Garland's cell, discussing the highlights of the trial that trial. That evening, Mathew noticed Garland seemed a little different.

"Garland, we are beginning to look really bad. We desperately need a break in our favor," Mathew said.

Mathew looked at Garland as he lay motionless on his cot. Garland was in another world and didn't respond to his attorney's remarks.

"Damn it, Garland, you have to give me something to work with. This is your life on the line, and I cannot save it!" Mathew shouted.

Garland did not respond to Mathew.

"Garland, I am going to call it a day. I will stop by in the morning before we go to the trial," Mathew said.

Mathew summoned a guard and left the jail.

Several hours had passed when a new jailer approached Garland's cell. He was listening to KARO on a transistor radio. The volume was loud enough that Garland could hear the music.

"Garland, my name is Chase Flemming, and I am new to your block," the guard said.

Garland sat up on his cot.

"Chase, what is that song you are listening to?" Garland asked.

Chase paused to turn the volume down, and then he said, "It is a new release by a group called Sand Dollar."

Garland walked over to the door of the cell to listen to the song.

He soon recognized it as a song he had written during one of their tours. It was a song about his broken relationship with Suzanna.

"Chase, thanks for letting me listen to that song," Garland said.

"You are welcome, Garland. You are my daughter's favorite musical artist," Chase said.

"Tell your daughter I thank her for being a fan," Garland said.

He returned to his cot as Chase continued along the block.

The song on Chase's radio began to bring back Garland's memory of Suzanna on the night of the party. For some reason, Garland began to remember Adam walking with him and Suzanna from a room at the party. Maybe Adam had some input about the evening.

"Chase! Can you come here please? "Garland shouted down the hallway.

Chase, hearing the urgency in Garland's voice, realized something was troubling him. He walked back to Garland's cell.

"Is there something wrong?" Chase asked.

"Can you call my attorney, Mathew Stein? It is very important," Garland said.

Chase agreed and walked to use the phone in the guards' office.

Chase made several failed attempts to contact Mathew.

"Garland, I cannot reach Mr. Stein. I am working a twelve-hour shift, and I will try to reach him in the morning," Chase said.

Garland thanked Chase for his efforts.

Garland's message reached Mathew the next morning. Mathew arrived for his daily pretrial meeting with Garland.

"Mathew, I remember talking to my best friend, Adam English, and he agreed to give me a ride home that evening. I knew I wasn't in any condition to drive. He must have seen me talking to Suzanna that night," Garland said.

Mathew jotted down notes from their conversation and promised Garland he would speak to Adam. Adam attended the trial daily; Garland had been his best friend since their days back in Texas.

Mathew approached Adam. "Adam, I would like to talk to you about the night of the party. Can I have a moment of your time?"

Adam and Mathew left the courtroom and went to a nearby conference room.

"Adam, did you see Garland and Suzanna together?" Mathew asked.

At first, Adam was hesitant, and Mathew sensed Adam's loyalty to Garland.

"Adam, Garland needs your help. He insists that it was Suzanna he left with that night. Did you witness the two leaving together?" Mathew asked.

"Mr. Stein, I did see Garland and Suzanna talking together, and I did agree to take Garland home that evening. However, I did not see Garland leave with any one. I attempted to find him but without any success," Adam said.

Mathew thanked Adam for his honesty. This meant that Mathew had to continue his desperate search for a witness to aid Garland's defense.

Mathew approached the prosecution's table, whispering into Adam Watkins ear. He then gave Watkins a piece of paper. The two attorneys ended their conversation with a handshake and a nod of approval. Mathew returned to the defense table, awaiting Judge Sand's entrance. Judge Sands entered the courtroom, and the bailiff opened the day's proceedings. Mathew then stood, asking if he and the prosecutor could approach the bench. The judge agreed, and Mathew gave Judge Sands the paper he had presented to Adam Watkins earlier. The judge reviewed the paper, asking Adam Watkins a question. Watkins nodded his approval, and the two attorneys returned to their tables.

Mathew patted Garland on the shoulder and then made his announcement to the court, saying. "Your Honor, the defense would like to call Adam English to the stand."

Adam froze for a moment. He turned toward Kevin and then slowly rose from his seat and approached the witness stand. The bailiff swore Adam in.

Mathew wanted to begin his questioning of Adam with a personal testimonial to his and Garland's friendship. He thought this would help Adam adjust to the questioning.

"Adam, how long have you known the defendant?" Mathew asked.

Adam responded that their friendship went back to their days in Texas when they were in their early teens.

"How would you describe the defendant's relationship with Suzanna Royal?" Mathew asked.

"They were very close. In fact, they were inseparable," Adam answered.

"On the night of the party, did you witness the two together?" Mathew questioned.

"Yes, I saw them together," Adam said.

"Did the defendant ask you for a ride home that evening?" Mathew asked.

"Yes, and I agreed to take Garland home," Adam answered.

"Did you witness Suzanna Royal leaving with the defendant?" Mathew asked.

"No, sir. I did not see the two leave together that evening," Adam said.

Mathew thanked Adam for his time and returned to the defense table.

Adam Watkins approached the witness stand, rubbing his chin as he faced the witness.

"Adam, you testified that the defendant and Miss Royal were inseparable. Was that still the case on the evening of the party?" Watkins asked.

Adam looked toward Garland before shaking his head no.

"So would you say that something had occurred between the two of them that ended their relationship?" Watkins asked.

Mathew jumped up, objecting to the line of questioning.

"Your Honor, I am just trying to establish a motive for the defendant's desire to take Miss Royal's car," Watkins replied.

Judge Sands overruled Mathew's objection, letting the prosecution's question stand.

"Mr. English, you will need to answer the question," Judge Sands said.

"The relationship ended because Suzanna's pregnancy was terminated," Adam said.

"How was the pregnancy terminated?" Watkins asked.

"I am not sure," Adam answered.

"So Garland was upset at Miss Royal for losing the baby?" Watkins asked.

"Objection!" shouted Mathew.

This time, Judge Sands ruled in Mathew's favor, instructing the jury to disregard the prosecution's remark.

"No further questions, Your Honor," Watkins said.

The prosecutor returned to his seat, with a smile on his face. Although his question was thrown out, he knew the jurors wouldn't be able to erase it from their minds.

Adam returned to his seat beside Kevin.

That day, the prosecution failed to produce a witness that saw Garland driving Suzanna's car out of the parking lot. Although Mathew felt he once again had created that reasonable doubt in the minds of the jurors, he was very troubled by the prosecution's effort to establish a motive. The day's proceedings came to a close.

Adam approached Mathew, wanting him and Garland to both know that he hoped he had not damaged Garland's defense.

Garland was sitting on his cot, rubbing the small knot that remained on his forehead, when Mathew entered his cell. Mathew walked over to Garland's cot, sitting next to him. Garland, with his head hanging down, continued to rub his forehead.

"Are you all right?" Mathew asked.

At first, it seemed that Garland didn't even know Mathew was in the room.

Finally, Garland replied, "Yes. This knot is almost gone now."

"Is that the knot you said you could only remember vaguely?" Mathew asked.

Garland turned to Mathew, nodding that it was the same knot.

"I remember awakening, sitting up, and things going black again," Garland said. "Every time I look at my face in the mirror, I can feel a slap against my head, but I can never see what caused the knot."

Mathew remembered seeing the knot recorded in the arresting police officer's report. Maybe he could create more reasonable doubt with the knot. Mathew left Garland that afternoon, eager to pursue his newest idea.

Mathew opened the passenger door of Suzanna's car. He eased himself into the seat, as if to determine what had caused the knot. Mathew and Garland were the same height. Mathew began to lean forward, as if to re-create a passenger whose head was thrown onto the passenger dash. With his head resting on the dash, Mathew marked the place of impact on his forehead.

Mathew left the car and returned to his office to research the description and pictures of the knot on Garland's forehead. The knot on Garland's forehead was lower down than the impact point of Mathew's simulation. He knew he was on to something but wasn't sure as to just what it was. Mathew called the crime lab to set up a re-creation with a dummy with the same height parameters as Garland. There had to be something that made the knot form lower on Garland's face.

The next day, Mathew arrived at the lab to find his request had been completed. There was a dummy with same proportions as those of Garland. Mathew, with the dummy, drove Suzanna's car to a test area. He noted the posted speed limit of the street on which Officer Foster was killed. Mathew placed a small area of clay over the dummy's forehead to record the impact spot.

Mathew placed the car in gear and began to drive until he reached the posted speed limit of thirty-five miles per hour. Once he reached the posted speed, Mathew slammed on the brakes, throwing the dummy into the dash. The clay worked marvelously, leaving an indention at the impact point. Mathew compared the dummy's point of impact with that on his face and the picture of Garland's forehead. The dummy's impact was in a lower position than Mathew's but a higher one than Garland's. There was still something Mathew was overlooking.

Mathew took the measurements of the test and left the test site. He returned to the scene of the accident and began to read more of the CSI report. The accident report stated that the speed of the vehicle that struck Officer Foster was exceeding seventy miles per hour. The skid marks left on the asphalt confirmed it was a high speed.

Mathew returned to the test area. He removed the clay; smoothing it for another test run. Mathew once again approached thirty-five miles per hour. This time, he wanted to test the impact of a collision at seventy miles per hour. Once the Lincoln reached a speed of seventy miles per hour, Mathew slammed on the brakes, and the dummy once again crashed into the dash. This time, because of the speed, the dummy's head was thrown farther onto the dash, thus leaving an impact point lower down on the face.

Mathew recorded the point of impact and compared it to his own and Garland's. This time, the point was lower than Mathew's but identical to Garland's. Mathew now had his reasonable doubt. He needed the permission of both Judge Sands and Adam Watkins to admit his findings as evidence.

IIIIIII

As the next day's trial proceedings were about to begin, Mathew entered the courtroom with a much different attitude than he had displayed up to that point. He looked very confident, which the courtroom had not witnessed until that day.

Judge Sands entered the courtroom and opened the proceedings.

"Your Honor, I would like to submit as evidence a test I have conducted," Mathew said. "I have had the results authenticated by automotive experts the prosecution introduced to the court at the beginning of the trial. I am sure the prosecution will attest to their expert knowledge."

"Counselor, it is a little late to be submitting evidence in this case. I will let you admit this, but this is the last time for new evidence," Judge Sands said.

"Thank you, sir. This is crucial to my client's case," Mathew said.

Mathew began setting up four easels. The first easel contained four pictures.

"Ladies and gentlemen, this is a picture of my client on the night of the accident. Please note the location of the knot on his forehead," Mathew said.

Sissy turned to James, perplexed. *What is Mathew up to?* she wondered.

Mathew then removed a second picture from the easel. It was picture of a dummy with the impact mark on its face.

"Please note the impact point on the second picture. Note the impact point on the forehead. This is the impact point of a head being thrown onto a dash from a vehicle not moving," Mathew said.

Mathew placed the pictures side by side, giving everyone a chance to examine the difference between the impact points. He then placed the second picture on the easel on the far end.

Mathew returned to the first easel, removing a third picture.

"Notice the impact point on the forehead. This is the impact point at thirty-five miles per hour, the posted speed limit on the road where the accident occurred. The knot is higher on the forehead than the knot in the picture of the previous example," Mathew said.

Mathew then compared this picture to Garland's, stating, "The impact point is below that of my client's, at thirty-five miles per hour."

Mathew took the third example, placing it next to the end.

"The last picture is of a dummy, with the impact speed of sixty miles per hour, the same estimated speed of the vehicle that struck Officer Foster," Mathew said.

He removed the picture and placed it next to Garland's picture, stating, "Notice that the impact point of the two knots is identical."

"Exactly what is your point, Counselor?" Adam Watkins asked.

"That my client was in the passenger seat and was not the driver. This point of impact could not be received behind the wheel," Mathew barked.

Mathew returned to the defense table.

"Your Honor, the defense would like to call Mr. Smith back to the stand," Mathew said.

Mr. Smith returned to the witness stand. The bailiff reminded him that he was still under oath.

"Mr. Smith, is it your expert opinion that the marks shown on

Garland Summers's forehead could not have been received from behind the wheel but only when seated as a passenger?" Mathew said.

Mr. Smith looked at the four easels, studying the impact points on all four examples.

"I would have to concur that a driver's point of impact to the same area would be impossible," Mr. Smith said.

"Thank you, Mr. Smith. I have no further questions," Mathew Stein said.

Mathew turned to observe the jury. He saw that some were now having doubts. Mathew looked more confident after the day's events than he did before the proceedings started.

Judge Sands adjourned the court for the day. The momentum was swinging toward the defense for the first time during the trial. The prosecution still had the burden of proof beyond a reasonable doubt.

⫿⫿⫿⫿⫿

Sissy and James returned home that evening with a much more optimistic attitude about the trial. Sissy opened the door of her blue convertible to hear the Summerses' phone ringing. She rushed into the house to pick up the phone in the kitchen.

"Hello," she answered.

"Sissy, I have been worried about Garland's trial. Here on the East Coast, we receive only brief news reports," the voice said.

By this time, James had entered the house. Sissy whispered to James the identity of the caller.

James couldn't resist the temptation and took the phone from his wife. "How is my favorite girl, and how is my future grandson doing?"

Brenda was about to answer James when a sharp pain overcame her.

"Brenda, are you all right?" James said.

There was a loud noise as the phone dropped to the floor. As James clutched the phone, he could hear Brenda shouting, "Mother, I think it's time to go to the hospital!"

It only took one shout from Brenda for her mother to come to her aid.

"We need to gather up your things and head to Memorial Hospital." Valerie said.

Valerie picked up the phone's receiver from the floor as she helped her daughter to her feet.

Once Brenda was standing, she began to speak into the phone. "James, your grandson is having a fit to enter this world. You will soon be a pawpaw."

Brenda said goodbye to James and Sissy, and Valerie hung up the phone.

Michael Fisher helped his daughter into the family sedan. For months, the route to the hospital had been planned. For some reason, the route seemed to take much longer that day than it had during the many practice runs.

"Dad, is there any way you can speed up? Why are you driving so slowly? Do you want your grandchild to be born in the backseat of a car?" Brenda said.

Each remark became more comical than the ones before. It was her way of taking her mind off the pain. Finally, the car approached the emergency entrance.

Michael ran into the emergency entrance, leaving the car running and the driver's door open. Valerie exited the front passenger seat to accept the wheelchair her husband was delivering to the car.

"Honey, you park the wheelchair, and I will drive the car into the emergency room!" Michael said.

Valerie smiled at her husband's confusion.

"I think I will take the wheelchair inside, and you can park the car," she answered as she kissed her husband.

"Nurse, we are having a baby!" Brenda yelled.

The nurse wheeled Brenda into a nearby room and pulled the curtain, asking, "Honey, what is your doctor's name?"

Brenda took a deep breath, trying to remember her doctor's name. The contractions were much more frequent now. Once again, she tried to answer the nurse as another contraction came. Footsteps suddenly came around the corner. The footsteps were soon stopped by the nurse exiting the room. The nurse turned to pull the curtain when Brenda answered the nurse.

"My doctor is Dr. Sharp!" Brenda shouted.

The nurse turned to Brenda as the owner of the footsteps peeked into the room.

"Dr. Sharp, what took you so long?" Brenda said, her forehead and bangs wet with perspiration.

Dr. Sharp's timing was a shock, as much as it was welcomed. He stepped inside to exam his patient.

"Brenda, it is time for you to become a mother," he said.

Dr. Sharp ordered the nurses to take Brenda to the delivery room immediately.

"I will meet you in the delivery room," he said as he left with a sense of urgency about his pace.

Brenda entered the delivery room, thinking how cold it was. Dr. Sharp made sure he was there for anything she would require. The nurses transferred Brenda into the bed for her delivery. Dr. Sharp once again examined his patient.

"Brenda you are beginning to really dilate. You are doing very well. I want you to begin to take quick breaths. They will help you feel more comfortable," Dr. Sharp said.

Brenda looked at the clock on the nearby wall, thinking she had been there much longer than she actually had. The time was beginning to crawl. A very big contraction suddenly took her breath away. This was the worst one up to that point. She began to breathe much more rapidly.

"Okay, Brenda, you will need to take deep breaths and push," Dr. Sharp said.

Brenda followed his instructions and pushed again.

The baby's head began to make its way out of its mother.

"One more push, Brenda," Dr. Sharp said.

Brenda pushed once again, as instructed, and then, with one sudden movement, she felt doctor Sharp begin to remove her baby.

At first, there was no sound, and it startled the new mother.

"Is my baby all right?" she cried.

One of the nurses, realizing the fear of the new mother, began to comfort her. "She is beautiful; we just need to clean her up and take some vital statistics."

For what seemed like an hour, the nurse kept the baby away from Brenda's bed. As the nurse turned around to return to Brenda, there was a very loud cry. She walked over to Brenda and laid the baby on her stomach.

"Congratulations, honey, you have a very healthy baby girl. She is beautiful," the nurse said.

Brenda began to peek inside the pink blanket. This was the most beautiful sight she had ever seen. She took the baby to her face and kissed her hands.

"I love you Ashton Rene Summers. You are so beautiful," Brenda said.

Brenda began to cry. These were tears of both joy and sorrow.

Ashton entered the world that day, but no one had any idea of how special this little girl would become.

28

THE EVENING HOURS turned into the early morning hours, and Sissy was distraught. To feel closer to Garland and Brenda, Sissy sat in Garland's bedroom. In one corner of the room sat the old Gibson guitar. While sitting on the side of Garland's bed, Sissy retrieved the old friend and began to clutch it as if it were her son. She rested her head against the guitar's neck and began to hug it as she gently stroked the strings. Each stroke produced a soothing sound; she began to lose herself in the sound.

Thoughts of Garland as a baby began to fill Sissy's mind. That time now seemed priceless. The thought of soon being a grandmother began to give her comfort. With Brenda leaving for the hospital as they ended their last phone call, Sissy wondered how she was doing and hoped she was okay. A long, empty loneliness took over her thoughts.

James awoke to find his wife was not in their room. He began to search the house, seeking to find her and comfort her. He soon found Sissy lying on Garland's bed. His first thought was to wake her and escort her back to their room. As he approached his wife, James saw a look of peace on her face, an expression that had been absent ever since Garland's arrest.

James gently removed the old Gibson and replaced it with two pillows: one for her lovely head, and the other for her to hug for comfort. He proceeded to a nearby chair, retrieved a light blanket, unfolded it, and placed it across his wife's body. He paused to savor that, throughout all the years and the recent heartache, Sissy remained a very beautiful woman. James kissed Sissy's forehead and departed the room, turning off the lamp as he exited.

IIIIIIII

Mathew arrived at Garland's cell for their daily pretrial meeting. Garland sensed a difference in Mathew that morning.

"Mathew, you look as if you are worn out," Garland said.

Mathew entered the cell and, without saying word, sat next to his client. Several minutes passed before Mathew gathered the words he wanted to say.

"Garland, I told you from the start that I would give you everything I had to win this case. After weeks of ironclad evidence and every attempt to create reasonable doubt, I have nothing more to offer you. We tried our best, and soon it will be up to the jury," Mathew said.

Mathew's solemnness left Garland speechless.

As Mathew left the cell block, Chase was making his rounds.

"I think Garland could use a friend right about now, Chase," Mathew said as he entered the elevator.

Chase, following Mathew's suggestion, stopped at Garland's cell.

"Hey, Chase! How is your daughter?" Garland asked.

"She is doing great and is still your biggest fan!" Chase said.

Garland smiled, telling Chase to thank his daughter for her loyalty.

"You are a lucky man, Chase. I once thought I was going to be a father. I would have loved to relive my childhood with a child of my own," Garland said.

With his left hand, Chase retrieved his wallet. He opened the wallet to reveal a foldout of pictures. Every picture was of his wife and daughter.

"This is your daughter? "Garland asked.

"Yes, Garland, that is your biggest fan," Chase said with a smile and a wink.

Garland pressed against the bars of the cell and extended his hand through one of the spaces between the bars.

Chase firmly shook Garland's hand, wishing him good luck with the upcoming verdict.

|||||||

Sissy was sitting in front of her makeup vanity, getting ready for the day's trial proceedings.

James entered the bedroom and was already dressed.

"Honey, I don't think I will be able to go to court today. I am not feeling very well," Sissy said.

James patted her shoulder and kissed her neck, wishing her a speedy recovery.

"I will tell Garland you send him your love," James said.

The weeks of the trial were wearing Sissy down. She left her bedroom to take the sedative her physician had prescribed. Sissy was in the kitchen, about to take the pill and chase it with a glass of water, when the phone began to ring.

At first, Sissy decided not to answer it. But, after several rings, Sissy picked up the receiver.

"Hello," Sissy said very slowly.

"Hello, Sissy. Is Pawpaw there?" the voice said.

Sissy's attitude suddenly received the push it needed.

"Brenda, is that really you? I have been so worried, and I have felt so lost not being able to do anything. Hold on a second," Sissy said.

Sissy placed the receiver on the table and rushed to the garage to stop James before he left.

"James, you need to come back into the house!" Sissy screamed.

James immediately stopped and ran into the house. His first fear was for Garland.

Sissy returned to the phone and motioned for James to take the receiver.

"Hello, this is James," he said.

"Pawpaw, how are you doing? I have some bad news for you," Brenda said.

James's heart began to race, and his mouth found it hard to answer her.

"Brenda, are you okay?" he finally managed to say.

"Well, yes, I am, Pawpaw. The bad news is, you don't have a grandson; you have the most beautiful granddaughter who ever lived," she said.

James sat down and tried to answer Brenda once again, saying, "It's a girl?"

Brenda laughed. "Yes, Pawpaw, and I know you and Sissy will be so proud of her."

Brenda was sitting in her hospital room, talking to James and Sissy, when the nurse brought Ashton in for a visit. The nurse wheeled the bassinet over to her bed and handed Ashton to Brenda.

"Pawpaw, I want you to meet your granddaughter. Say hello to Ashton Rene Summers," Brenda said.

Sissy watched as James began to cry. His emotions overcame him that morning.

"Brenda, I think someone has stolen Pawpaw's heart this morning," Sissy said.

Brenda began to fill Sissy in on all the details about her new granddaughter. Sissy thanked Brenda for calling—and for the beautiful grandbaby.

After hanging up the phone, Sissy said, "James, if you can wait a few minutes, I think I will accompany you to court today after all."

Revitalized, Sissy walked briskly out of the kitchen to get dressed.

IIIIIIII

The news in the media was that the trial would soon be sent to the jury for deliberation, and the crowds were becoming larger. As Garland entered the courtroom, his attention focused on where Sissy and James were sitting. In the row immediately behind them were all his friends: Joe Moss, Kevin and Adam English, and Rudy and Sam Stamps. Garland was about to take his seat, wondering where Brandon was, when the rear door suddenly swung open.

Garland turned to see a man in a wheelchair, escorted by Brandon and Tobie. The wheelchair stopped at the aisle occupying the rest of Garland's friends. Brandon and Tobie slid into their seats on the aisle, leaving the wheelchair parked in the aisle. Garland tried to contain himself at this wonderful sight, but his emotions overwhelmed him when Harley raised his closed fist in support of his friend. It was hard to tell who was having the harder time fighting back tears, Garland or Harley.

Several of the jury members were also touched by the support of Garland's friends and family.

Judge Sands entered the courtroom. As he approached the bench, the sight of the jury and courtroom attendees directing their attention to Garland took Judge's Sands's opening words right out of his mouth. In all his years of courtroom experience as both an attorney and a judge, he had never witnessed such a sight.

After a moment, Judge Sands opened the proceedings to Adam Watkins and the prosecution.

Adam Watkins began by introducing the biggest surprise of the trial thus far.

"Your Honor, the prosecution would like to call Garland Summers to the witness stand," Watkins said.

The request took the court by surprise.

Garland took his seat in the witness stand, and the bailiff swore him in.

The courtroom suddenly became intense as everyone awaited the prosecution's first remarks and questions.

Watkins opened by asking, "Mr. Summers, are you acquainted with Suzanna Royal?"

"Yes, sir, I have known Suzanna since our days at Hinckley High School," Garland replied.

Watkins began turning the pages in his hand. "During the time you knew Miss Royal, what type of relationship did the two of you have?"

"We were involved and tried a long-distance relationship while she was in California," Garland replied.

"So the long-distance part didn't work out for the two of you?" Watkins asked.

"I tried to make it work," Garland said.

"What was the cause of the relationship coming to an end?" Watkins asked.

Mathew said, "Objection, Your Honor! Where is Mr. Watkins going with these questions?"

"Mr. Watkins, what is the purpose of this line of questioning?" Judge Sands asked.

"I am trying to establish a motive for the possible auto theft that led to Officer Foster's death, Your Honor," Watkins said.

Judge Sands granted permission for Watkins to continue his questioning, instructing Garland to answer the question directed to him.

"We both changed, and the relationship no longer worked for either of us," Garland said.

Mathew sat at the defense table, taking notes. He did not anticipate Garland taking the stand today. When the time came for his chance to cross-examine Garland, he wanted to once again try to create that reasonable doubt in the minds of the jurors.

"Mr. Summers, did you and Miss Royal talk at the party at the country club?" Watkins asked.

"Yes, sir, Suzanna and I engaged in a conversation," Garland said.

"One of the employees reported seeing you and Miss Royal having an argument," Watkins said.

Garland hesitated.

"Mr. Summers, did the two of you have an argument during the party?" Watkins asked.

"Yes, we did," Garland answered.

"Your Honor, I have no further questions for Mr. Summers at this time," Mr. Watkins said.

"Mr. Stein, do you have any questions for the witness?" Judge Sands said.

"Your Honor, I have no questions at this time, but I want to reserve the right to call Mr. Summers back to the stand at a later date," Mathew said.

"Mr. Stein, I do not see any reason to keep delaying these proceedings. If you want to question Mr. Summers, you will need to do it at this time," the judge ordered.

The judge's remark to Mathew made a stir in the courtroom. The jury and all the attendees were shocked.

Mathew approached the witness stand but turned his attention to the jury. He did not want the judge to think he was baiting the jury; that was something Judge Sands would not tolerate.

"Garland, when you left the party that evening, what method of transportation did you use?" Mathew asked.

"I was a passenger in a vehicle," Garland said.

"If you were a passenger, who was the driver of the vehicle?" Mathew asked.

"I was the passenger, and Suzanna Royal was the driver," Garland said.

"A witness reported seeing you and Miss Royal having an argument. Why would you leave with a person you were arguing with?" Mathew asked.

Mathew knew that this questioning was risky, but it was the only way he could create any doubt in the jurors' minds.

"She was upset because I wouldn't leave the party to meet up with her afterward," Garland said.

"Objection, Your Honor!" Watkins interjected. "Miss Royal is not here to substantiate the witness's claims."

"Overruled," Judge Sands said. "I will let the witness answer the question."

"Why would you leave with a person you were arguing with?" Mathew asked.

"I was going to leave with my friend, Adam English. I was intoxicated and couldn't drive. Suzanna insisted that I leave with her," Garland said.   "Please tell the court what happened next," Mathew said.

"At first, I thought that, because I was drunk, I couldn't find Suzanna's car," Garland said.

"Garland, what was the car you were searching for?" Mathew asked.

"When we were together, Suzanna drove a red Ford Mustang convertible," Garland said. He then repeated, "I thought the only reason I couldn't find her car was because I was drunk."

"You were not aware she owned a different car?" Mathew asked.

"No, sir, I was not," Garland answered.

"I guess it would be difficult to steal someone's car for revenge if you weren't aware of the type of car they owned," Mathew said.

Once again, Adam Watkins objected to Mathew's remark.

"Counselor, I will not allow that last remark. I am ordering the jury to disregard Mr. Stein's remark," Judge Sands said.

"Garland, how did you arrive at the car you were a passenger in?" Mathew asked.

"Suzanna took me to her new Lincoln. I would have been there all night, looking for her Mustang," Garland said.

Mathew and Garland made eye contact. The two were in sync with establishing that reasonable doubt.

"So, prior to leaving with Miss Royal, you thought she had driven her Mustang and were not aware that she had arrived by another method of transportation that evening. Is that correct?" Mathew asked.

"Yes, sir, that is correct. I was not aware that she arrived by another method of transportation," Garland replied.

Mathew thanked Garland for his time and said that he had no further questions.

Judge Sands asked the prosecution if they wanted to cross-examine the witness.

"I have no further questions, Your Honor," Adams Watkins responded.

Judge Sands looked through some papers.

"It is the court's opinion that this trial is ready for the jury. Tomorrow, the defense and prosecution will present their closing statements to the jury," Judge Sands declared.

IIIIIIII

Mathew worked on his closing statement well into the early hours of the morning. This was his last chance to create reasonable doubt in the minds of the jurors. The prosecution would present their case first. Mathew loved being the home team when it came to delivering his closing statements. This would open the door for some improvising, if need be. He always felt this was an advantage.

IIIIIIII

The morning hours flew by. This was the day that created fear in the hearts of the entire Summers family and all their friends.

As Mathew arrived at the Denver County Courthouse that morning, the media coverage was very large. The courthouse was completely surrounded by news-crew trucks. Of all the trials in Mathew's career, this one had the largest media presence.

He entered the courtroom to find Garland's parents and close friends gathered in the back of the courtroom trying to console one another. He took a moment to deposit his briefcase on the defense table and then returned to the rear of the courtroom. He could feel the tension as he approached the family.

Sissy's emotions had drained her spirit. This was a spirit no one had ever thought could be drained. Mathew patted Sissy on the back as she turned to face him. She fought to hold back her tears, but, the moment Mathew touched Sissy, she could no longer control her emotions.

"Sissy, you and James must not give up on me. I have saved the best for last," Mathew said.

Sissy squeezed his hand, trying to release of her fears.

"Mathew, you have done all you could have possibly done. Both Sissy and I are aware of that," James said.

Mathew was about to return to his seat at the table when the courtroom door opened, and Garland was escorted to his seat. The jurors also entered the courtroom, taking their seats in the jury box. Mathew excused himself from the Summers family and made his way to where Garland was already sitting.

The bailiff entered the courtroom, and those inside the courtroom found their seats. They all knew the time was here.

Judge Sands entered the room and took his seat. The judge declared the proceedings open and said the prosecution would present the first closing statement to the jury. He then instructed Adam Watkins to deliver his closing statement.

Watkins confidently approached the jury box and began by thanking them for having done their civic duty.

"You have all listened to the evidence against Garland Summers. We are here to deliver justice for the lost life of Officer Tuck Foster," Watkins said as he pointed to the Foster family members in attendance.

"The defendant was intoxicated and stole the car of a female whose relationship with the defendant ended with hostile feelings. His motive was revenge," Adam Watkins said.

Watkins paused for a moment as he walked back and forth in front of the jurors. Several times, he paused as he was about to speak, turning toward the Foster family.

"You have seen the evidence that the defendant was found in the driver's seat of a stolen vehicle owned by the female member of that failed relationship and that the stolen vehicle was the same vehicle that struck Officer Foster. The defendant then left the scene of the accident, without rendering aid to one of Denver's finest servants," he added.

As Watkins turned to face the courtroom, tears ran down his cheek.

"The state is asking you to remember that favorite son by finding the defendant guilty of the charges presented in this case. Officer Foster deserves that!" Watkins said.

Throughout the courtroom there were sounds of sniffles from the police officers and members of the Foster family.

"I know you will do the right thing," Watkins said as he turned and returned to his seat.

The courtroom was silent except for the sound of sniffles.

"Mr. Stein, you may present your closing statements when you are ready," Judge Sands said.

Mathew sat at the defense table, with his hands covering the right side of his forehead, when Judge Sands gave him the floor to make his statements. Mathew slowly stood up behind the table, pushing back his chair. He approached the jury stand, rubbing his forehead with his right hand, as if he were suffering from a headache.

"Ladies and gentlemen of the jury, my colleague is absolutely correct when he says we need to obtain justice for Officer Tuck Foster. He deserves nothing less than the truth," Mathew said.

Mathew raised his head and removed his right hand from his forehead. He looked into the eyes of each member of the jury, as a shocked look appeared on their faces.

Mathew continued, "The prosecution has proved that the defendant was indeed a passenger in the car. They have not proved that he was the driver of that car. It has been proved that the car's driver's seat was not adjusted for someone of the defendant's size to drive that car. There were no witnesses at a very crowded party and parking lot who saw the defendant drive the car off the parking lot, and we certainly have not been able to question the car's owner as to where she was when the car was taken."

Mathew continued looking into the eyes of the jury as he presented his statements. "I want each and every one of you to look at my face. Is there any doubt about who was driving that car that evening? The evidence we have provided shows that it was not Garland Summers."

Mathew backed away from the jury stand.

"You can see from my face that he was not the driver," Mathew said.

As Mathew turned to face the courtroom, there was a startling reaction from those in attendance. Mathew was wearing a piece of clay marking the impact point that was identical to the impact point on Garland's face from the accident.

Mathew thanked the jury and returned to his seat.

Judge Sands wrapped up the day's proceedings shortly afterward.

"Members of the jury, you have heard the case presented both by the prosecution and the defense in the case involving Officer Tuck Foster," the judge said. "You will be asked to determine if the defendant is guilty or not guilty. The law says you must do this without any reasonable doubt."

The judge then instructed the bailiff to lead the jury to a room for their deliberation.

No one was anticipating a fast verdict.

An officer escorted Garland back to his cell to await the jury's deliberation.

Mathew took this time to talk to Sissy and James.

"The jury will be asked to render a verdict. If it is a guilty verdict, they will then be asked to deliver within the limits of the law the punishment for the crime of which Garland has been found guilty," Mathew said.

Sissy sat next to James, with her head on his shoulder. She felt this was the only safe place for her. She was almost asleep when she felt two strong hands begin to rub her shoulders. Long deep rubs soon relieved the tension that had her shoulders so very tight. As the hands stopped their massaging actions, Sissy leaned her head back to discover who her wonderful masseur was.

"Hey, darling, we are here for you and James for as long as you need us," the masseur said.

James turned to see Brandon kiss Sissy on her forehead.

"Brandon, thanks for being here. You are like our second son," James said.

Brandon smiled and patted James on the head, and then he resumed massaging Sissy's shoulders.

Another familiar voice followed Brandon's, saying, "James, is there anything we can do to help you and Sissy?"

"Kevin, you are my best friend, and you have always been there for us all," James said.

Kevin took a seat in the row in front of James and Sissy. He, too, wanted to be there for his friends.

Mathew turned to witness a sight rarely seen in a courtroom. There was a friendship and bond between these people that he seldom observed.

The wait reached the two-hour mark.

"Mathew, you said it would be a long deliberation. What time frame did you anticipate?" Sissy asked.

"I have seen it take more than a day, Sissy," Mathew answered. "The longer they take, the better for us."

The rear courtroom door swung open as a messenger entered the courtroom. His journey took him to the row occupied by the Summerses.

"Sissy Summers, you have a phone call in the lobby," he said.

Sissy gathered up her purse and made her way to his side, following him out to the lobby.

"You can take your call at the phone sitting on the security guard's desk," he said.

Sissy picked up the headset sitting on the counter.

"Hello, this is Sissy," she said.

"Sissy, how are you holding up?" the voice said.

Sissy's eyes watered, and her face was a grin from ear to ear. "I am doing okay. You have no idea how much I have been worrying about you."

"Sissy, you need not worry about me. I am doing just fine. Ashton and I came home from the hospital today. I have been worrying about the trial. The news said the case was delivered to the jury," Brenda said.

"Yes, they have my baby's life in their hands," Sissy said as she broke down.

The nearby security guard, realizing Sissy was having a hard time, offered a box of tissues.

"I am so afraid Brenda. I had so much hope we had a chance. Mathew said the longer the jury is out, the better it will be for Garland," Sissy said.

"You know I am praying for you all. When this is over, I am bringing Ashton to meet her grandmother and pawpaw," Brenda said.

Sissy thanked Brenda for her concern.

"I can't wait to meet Ashton, Brenda. I know Garland would be so proud," Sissy said.

She ended the call and returned to the courtroom, hoping for some good news.

Several more hours passed, and there still was no verdict. Mathew left the courtroom. He took the time to try to find out if there was any news. He knew that if a verdict was not rendered soon, they all would be asked to leave the building.

"Sissy and James, they may sequester the jury all night," Kevin said.

A court official entered the courtroom from a door the jury used to exit the courtroom. He approached Judge Sands.

They all held their breath, thinking that this was the moment they had been waiting for.

"The jury has not reached a verdict. We are therefore asking you all to go home for the evening. You may return here tomorrow at 9:00 a.m.," he said.

The Summerses and their friends agreed that it would be best to wait out the decision at home.

Brandon and Tobie were the first ones to leave. They assured Sissy that they would meet them at the Summerses' house. Kevin and Adam left shortly afterward. Sissy and James were lucky to have very good friends.

On the way home, Sissy informed James that the phone call was from Brenda and that she and Ashton were now home. They now had a way to talk to Brenda when they needed her.

James pulled into the driveway; Brandon and Tobie arrived shortly afterward. Brandon walked around to the trunk of his car and opened it. Inside the trunk was food he had picked up.

"Brandon, you didn't have to do this," James said as he thanked him.

Brandon and James grabbed the boxes of food and took them into the house.

Kevin and Adam arrived, also with some food. They came prepared to sit out the wait with their friends, for as long as it took. In one of the boxes Adam was carrying there were several folders, which were a surprise for later.

Sissy welcomed Kevin and Adam into the kitchen, and they all sat down to try to enjoy a meal.

"Brandon, this barbecue is wonderful. Where in the world did you ever find it?" Sissy asked.

"Well, it's Tobie's uncle Charlie's specialty. He cooked it while he was babysitting Skye," Brandon said.

Everyone agreed it was the best barbecue any of them had tasted. They didn't realize they were this hungry until they sat down and began to eat. The food disappeared very fast.

After they all had filled their bellies and the kitchen was cleaned up, Kevin insisted that they all take a seat in the living room. He wanted to reveal the secret of the contents of the box Adam had brought. They all gathered in the living room, each taking a seat.

"Adam has something he would like to share with us all at this very difficult time," Kevin said.

Adam began to empty the box. Inside was a slide projector. Adam sat the projector on the coffee table and directed it toward a nearby wall.

"Dad, will you turn off the lamp?" Adam asked.

Kevin obliged his son.

Adam began to show the slides in the projector.

"The first one is of Garland and me back in Texas when we first started," Adam said.

The sight of Adam and Garland playing their instruments at the age of twelve was touching. The second picture was of Brandon during the stunt Kevin pulled on him as he auditioned his drum playing. This picture made them all laugh aloud.

Each picture had a special memory for everyone in the room. Some memories were happy ones, and some were sad. Each one showed how much Garland had touched all their lives.

Adam turned to Sissy as he continued the slide show. Sissy's smile made the whole night worthwhile. This was good therapy for each of them.

During the final slide, Adam stopped to observe the others. There wasn't a dry eye in the room. He savored the moment before he reached for the switch to turn the lights back on. This moment was priceless for him. These were not just friends in the room; they were family.

||||||||

Early the next morning, the silence was broken by the ringing of the Summerses' phone. Sissy answered the phone on the fourth ring.

"Sissy, this is Mathew Stein. I have received a phone call that the jury has reached a decision. They will read the verdict at 10:00 a.m.," Mathew said.

Sissy thanked Mathew for the call. She turned to see the bedroom clock, which showed 7:00 a.m.

James was lying on his side, taking a moment to collect his thoughts about the upcoming news from the courtroom. He overhead Sissy's conversation with Mathew.

Sissy got up, went to the bench at the foot of their bed, and put on her housecoat. She went out of the bedroom to start her the morning.

As she made her way down the hallway and into the kitchen, Sissy knocked on the other bedroom doors. Adam and Kevin occupied one room, while Brandon and Tobie resided in the other. They had slept over, not wanting to be away from James and Sissy when the news came down. Sissy arrived in the kitchen and began to make coffee and cook breakfast. She needed something to take her mind off the morning's upcoming events. Tobie was the first to arrive in the kitchen and immediately began to help Sissy with the breakfast preparation. The aroma of bacon cooking soon brought the others into the kitchen.

There was a subdued silence about the breakfast table as they sat down to eat the day's first meal.

Sissy sat in a chair, staring at her plate. She began to form a face, with the two fried eggs as the eyes, and a sausage patty as the nose. She then took a bite of her half piece of toast and placed it at the bottom of the plate, as if the face were wearing a frown. She stopped and stared at the plate as a tear began to run down her cheek. A fork suddenly entered the plate from the right side, turning the frowning piece of toast upside down and into a smile. She turned to see her coartist.

"Baby, everything will be all right," Brandon said, setting down the fork and wiping away Sissy's tears with his napkin. "You need to eat your breakfast, Sissy. You know that Garland would not want you to worry about him."

Sissy smiled and patted Brandon's hand. "You have always been my Rock of Gibraltar, Brandon. I really don't know what I would do without you. I thank you, and I love you like a son."

It was time to do the dishes and get dressed for the courtroom.

Within the hour the morning chores were finished, and the long lonely trip to the courthouse was about to begin.

"James, I want to take Garland's car today. We may not see him for long time, and it will make me feel close to him," Sissy said.

James agreed that this was be a wonderful idea. He went into the garage to back the car into the driveway.

IIIIIII

Garland was awakened that morning with the best breakfast throughout his time in jail.

Chase wanted to be the one who delivered the special meal.

"Good morning, Garland. I heard the news that the jury arrived at their decision, and I want to wish you good luck. I want you to know I think you are not guilty," Chase said as he unlocked the door and placed the breakfast tray at the foot of Garland's cot.

"Thank you, Chase. I will always remember the special kindness you have shown me while I have been here. Your daughter is fortunate to have a father such as you," Garland said.

Chase thanked Garland for the compliment.

"I would have loved to have been the kind of father you are. I, too, have a great dad," Garland said as he began to open the top of his breakfast tray.

Chase, not wanting to show his emotions, turned and left the cell, locking the door behind him.

Two police officers escorted Garland into the courtroom. As Garland made his way to his seat, his eyes met his mother's. Garland saturated his memory with Sissy that morning, not knowing when he would see her again.

Sissy grabbed her husband's hand, trying to hold back the pain she felt when she saw the anguish in her son's face that morning.

James glanced down at his right hand to see the skin change color as Sissy's grip became more intense. He gently placed his left hand on top of Sissy's hand and began to comfort her. As he continued the strokes of tenderness, he felt Sissy's grip beginning to ease, and the color started to return to his hand. Without saying a word, James Summers comforted his wife in a very special way.

Judge Sands entered the room for the final time in this trial. The courtroom became silent, with the silence occasionally interrupted by a hum of the ceiling fan's blade. The jury foreman gave the jury's decision to the bailiff. The bailiff retrieved the piece of paper and handed it to Judge Sands. He remained standing at the front of the judge's bench.

"Mr. Foreman, has the jury reached a verdict?" the judge asked.

The foreman promptly answered that the jury did indeed have a verdict.

"Please read that verdict for the court," Judge Sands instructed.

"For the charge of auto theft, we find the defendant guilty. For the charge of involuntary manslaughter of Officer Tuck Foster, we find the defendant guilty," the foreman barked out.

With the foreman's announcement, the courtroom was divided between cheers and cries of disbelief. Both sounds filled the courtroom.

Judge Sands began to hammer his gavel, trying to bring the courtroom back to order. His actions were not well received. He began hammering louder and louder.

"Quiet in the courtroom!" the judge shouted. "We need quiet!"

The judge's instructions were not followed.

"If there isn't order in this court, I will clear the courtroom!" he shouted into his microphone.

The crowd slowly began to calm down.

Garland remained standing as the judge began to announce his sentencing.

"Garland Summers, for auto theft, you are to serve ten years in the Colorado state correctional institution. For the charge of involuntary manslaughter of Officer Foster, you will serve thirty years in the state correctional institution," Judge Sands said.

This meant that Garland would serve a combined sentence of forty years.

Mathew was shocked. He believed he had created reasonable doubt in the minds of several of the jurors. He was sure of it, based on the jury's deliberation time.

The police officers escorted Garland from the courtroom quickly. Mathew also left the courtroom with Garland as they returned to his cell.

The news media immediately rushed from the courtroom, headed to their stations in the streets near the courthouse. The news would be released in a flash to the rest of the nation.

After assurances that Garland was safely returned to his cell, Mathew returned to the courtroom. He sought out James and Sissy, wanting to speak with them both. Both James and Sissy were entering the outside hallway when Mathew found them.

"James and Sissy, can I have a word with the two of you?" Mathew shouted down the hallway.

James and Sissy paused, waiting for Mathew to reach the spot where they stood.

Mathew escorted them to a nearby conference room. He wanted to have some privacy, especially with all the news media frenzy. This was not the time for a reporter to approach either of them with the news just received.

The three of them ducked into the small room, and Mathew locked the door.

"I want you both to know I am very sorry I failed Garland's defense, and I am already making plans for an appeal," Mathew said.

"Mathew, I have not been able to speak with Garland since the day he was arrested," Sissy said. "You have no idea how hard it is to take not knowing when I will next hear my son's voice."

Sissy could read the disappointment in Mathews face and eyes. She knew how much Mathew believed in her son's innocence and thanked Mathew for everything he had tried to accomplish.

29

AFTER WHAT SEEMED to be the longest night of Sissy's life, she began to awaken. The previous day was a day from hell. The events were such that a parent never dreams will ever happen to them. She rolled over to find James had abandoned his side of the bed. A quick glance revealed the time was late into the morning. She tried to remember the last time she had slept this late. She slowly crept out of bed and began to dress for the day. After several weeks of Garland's trial, Sissy began to wonder if she would ever enjoy happiness again. Something needed to happen in her life to restore a reason to go on.

She made her way into the kitchen, opening a nearby cabinet for a glass. This was one of those mornings when a good strong alcoholic drink would have been very welcome. She opted for a glass of cold orange juice, to be enjoyed without any spirits. She raised her glass and pressed it against her forehead, wanting to enjoy the coolness. She slowly lowered the glass down to her lips and began to enjoy the sweet nectar as she swallowed.

After a nice long drink, the phone began to ring. She slowly began to enjoy another long swallow from her glass as the phone continued to ring. This was one time the phone could wait until after her refreshment. After several relaxing moments, Sissy finished the orange juice and placed the dirty glass in the kitchen sink. As she turned to exit the kitchen, the phone began to ring again. Once again, she opted to let the phone go unanswered.

Sissy exited the front door and took a seat on a nearby chair on the porch. She wanted to escape into the late morning's sunshine. There was a light southerly breeze blowing through her hair that day, and the sound of songbirds filled her ears. This was an almost heavenly escape of the mind. An escape she needed so badly.

The tranquil morning was interrupted once again by a ringing phone. She hoped that whomever was calling would finally get the message that no one in the Summers house was in the mood to be disturbed. She began to slowly rock and suddenly started to hum in tune, as if to answer the songbirds. It was almost as if they were carrying on a conversation with Sissy, telling her everything was going to be okay.

A black sedan entered the driveway, stopping near the front porch. The driver's door began to open, and out stepped Mathew Stein.

"Sissy, I have been trying to reach you all morning. Garland will soon be sent to the state correctional institution. I have arranged a visitation for you and James before he is transported there. I know it has been way too long since you have been able to talk to each other," Mathew said.

Sissy turned to thank Mathew. It was almost like Sissy was in another world that morning. She showed no emotion toward Mathew. The numbness of being alone and without her son was beginning to set in.

Mathew took a seat next to Sissy. He was very worried about her. He wished there was something he could do to get her out of this state of mind.

A mail carrier's Jeep pulled up in front of the Summerses' house. The postman, noticing Sissy was sitting on the porch, decided to hand deliver the day's mail. As he approached the front porch, his hands revealed a very large envelope.

"Hi, Sissy, it's good to see you. I wanted to bring your mail to you," he said.

Sissy turned to accept the mail and thanked the postman for his kindness. She placed the envelope into her lap as she continued to rock her chair. The catatonic look on her face indicated to Mathew that Sissy's mental state was somewhere far, far away. Mathew left his seat and stepped down off the front porch. He paused as Sissy began to open the large envelope to reveal its contents. Slowly she tried to open the flap of the heavily taped envelope but was not successful.

"Sissy, would you like me to help you with that?" Mathew asked.

Sissy, without a word, gave Mathew the package. Mathew reached into his pocket and retrieved his pocketknife, cutting the tape away from the flap. Mathew returned the envelope to Sissy. She opened the envelope and began to remove its contents. Inside was a letter, along with another smaller envelope. As she read the letter, a smile began to form on her face. There suddenly came a sense of urgency. Mathew, noticing that sudden change, stopped to make sure Sissy was all right.

Sissy, like a small child on Christmas morning, ripped open the smaller envelope. It was apparent the letter had clued her as to what the contents of the smaller envelope were. Reaching inside the envelope, she slid out several pictures. The pictures were all turned upside down, not revealing their subjects. As she picked up the first photo, she began to read the writing on the back.

The picture indicated it was Ashton Rene Summers. Sissy immediately turned the picture over and began to smile even more. There was the cutest picture of a baby girl in a pink blanket. In the second picture, Ashton's eyes were wide open. This was the medicine Sissy badly needed. The final picture was one of Ashton as she left the hospital, wearing a new outfit. After just a few days, Ashton Rene Summers was healing the hearts that needed her.

Sissy slowly began to look at each picture a second time. She suddenly stopped.

"Mathew, when did you get here?" she asked.

Mathew paused for a moment, realizing Sissy was back.

"I just got here, my dear. I wanted to check in on you," he said.

Sissy thanked Mathew and began to show Ashton's pictures to him.

"Mathew, this is my new granddaughter. I want you to promise me that you will not say anything about her to Garland. I don't want him to suffer any more than he must. In time, he will be told of her existence," Sissy said.

Mathew agreed to respect Sissy's wishes. He, too, did not want Garland to be hurt more at this time in his life.

"Mathew, did you say I could see Garland in a week?" she asked.

"Yes, Sissy, you will be able to talk to him after he has been relocated," he answered.

"Mathew, I am going to take a trip. I will be back before he is relocated," she said.

"A trip? Where will you go?" Mathew asked.

"I am going to see Ashton and her mother," she said with a smile.

Mathew agreed it was a good idea and offered to help Sissy in any way he could.

|||||||

Brenda was lying awake in her bed, trying to muster the energy to attend to her daughter. She rolled and rolled in her bed, placing her pillow over her head and trying to muffle the sound of Ashton's cries. At last, she sprang to her feet, putting on her housecoat, and dashed off into the nursery. She was discovering very quickly that motherhood was a full-time job with a newborn. Brenda's discontent was soon erased with just one look from Ashton's beautiful blue eyes. They were the kind of eyes a person could drown in. As if Ashton's eyes weren't enough to erase away all your troubles, she had this big toothless smile that made your heart laugh. It was a feeling that made you feel good all over, just adoring and holding her.

"Hey, baby, do you want Mommy to change you?" she asked, as if she were waiting for an answer.

"After we change your diaper, baby, we will go to the kitchen, and Mommy will feed you. And after we eat, Mommy will give you a nice warm bath with some fresh powder to make you feel like a big girl," Brenda said with a big grin.

She picked Ashton up from her crib and met her mother in the hallway. Valerie stopped to kiss her grandbaby and daughter. Ashton had stolen Valerie Fisher's heart as well. The three continued their journey to the kitchen. They turned from the hallway just as the doorbell began to ring.

"Here, Mother, you take Ashton into the kitchen, and I will see who is as the front door," Brenda said.

The doorbell rang a second time, as if the visitor were running out of patience. Brenda looked through the peephole, trying to see who would be on their doorstep this early in the morning. The visitor's movements made it hard for Brenda to focus on who was at their door. The doorbell rang for the third time; this time, accompanied by a heavy knock on the door. Brenda began to unlock the deadbolt and door latch. As she cracked the door slowly, the visitor was looking away and was not aware the door was beginning to open.

"May I help you?" Brenda asked.

Her response startled the visitor. The visitor began to turn around.

Brenda was at a loss for words as the identity of her visitor was revealed.

"Oh my God! Sissy, I can't believe you are really here!" Brenda shouted.

Brenda jumped across the porch and threw her arms around Sissy, clasping her in a tight hug.

Sissy needed this warm welcome very badly. After just a few seconds, she realized her trip to North Carolina was the best thing for her at this time.

"Brenda, I hope I am not imposing on your family. I needed to be with someone I could lean on," Sissy said.

Neither Sissy nor Brenda wanted to let the other go. It was difficult to determine which one needed the other the most at that moment.

Brenda and Sissy were entering the house when Brenda suddenly stopped.

"Sissy, are those your bags we left on the porch?" Brenda asked.

"Yes, dear. I will need to call a cab to take me to a hotel," Sissy said.

Brenda turned and pointed her finger at Sissy. "You will do no such thing. You will stay here for as long as you want to."

Sissy smiled at the affection Brenda showered upon her at that moment.

Valerie called out from the kitchen, "Brenda, who was that at the door?"

Sissy and Brenda entered the kitchen, where Valerie and Michael stood.

"Oh my God!" Valerie said. "Sissy I have been so worried about you."

The two women embraced, then separated, holding hands and admiring each other.

"I hate to interrupt the reunion, ladies, but there is a little young lady who would like to meet her grandmother," Michael said.

As Michael spoke, Sissy stopped, turning toward the nearby countertop where an infant carrier sat. She slowly walked over to admire its contents, placing her hands on the sides of the carrier and then gently stroking the blanket.

"Sissy Summers, I want you to meet Miss Ashton Rene Summers," Brenda said.

Sissy was at a loss for words. With the swift but gentle movements of motherly instinct, she removed Ashton from the carrier. She held the infant in her arms with the softest and gentlest touch.

Ashton suddenly opened her eyes, gazing at the face of the person holding her. It was like a staring contest between the two.

"Would you like to give Ashton her breakfast?" Brenda asked.

Sissy nodded and took a seat at the nearby table. Brenda gave Sissy Ashton's bottle. Ashton began to nurse from the bottle, never taking her eyes off Sissy. Sissy's eyes were full of joy. This was a joy she needed in the worst way.

As Ashton continued to enjoy her bottle, Sissy began to hum softly. She then sang an angelic melody. The Fishers were taken by the angelic voice, but not as much as Ashton was. The ending of Sissy's melody was timed perfectly with the last drops of the bottle. Sissy placed the empty bottle on the countertop and began rocking baby Ashton in her arms as she began another chorus.

"Here you go, Momma; I don't mean to monopolize your daughter," Sissy said.

As Sissy gave Ashton to Brenda, Ashton began to cry.

"Looks like Ashton wants to monopolize you, Sissy," Brenda said, laughing.

"That was the same song I used to sing to Garland when we would have our early morning feedings back in New Mexico. For an instant, I was back in that time," Sissy said.

The four walked into the den to continue their reunion.

As she took a seat on the couch, Sissy continued to hold Ashton.

Brenda wanted the two to have as much time together as Sissy needed. It was a nice break for Brenda as well.

Picking up the picture album sitting on the coffee table, Valerie said, "Let me turn the pages while you enjoy Ashton, Sissy."

Inside were pictures of Ashton and Brenda at the hospital, followed by their welcome-home pictures.

"Brenda, you are going to have to fight the boys off this young lady. She is very special indeed," Sissy said with a smile.

Valerie continued turning the pages of the album. As she turned to the final page, there was one last picture. It was of Garland.

Sissy began to cry.

"Ashton, I know you are too young to understand, but that boy is your father. You look so much like him," Sissy said.

Valerie paused, looking at Garland's picture. "Sissy, you are absolutely right. She does look very much like Garland."

Sissy nodded as the tears ran down her cheeks. As she held Ashton closer, she was no longer able to control her emotions.

Ashton's deep-blue eyes soon absorbed Sissy into them. There was a special twinkle deep within them that sparkled. Sissy kissed Ashton's forehead and began to sing once again. Her soft melody mesmerized the tiny baby, as if Ashton were memorizing the moment and the words Sissy was singing.

Sissy paused for a moment, remembering that, twenty years ago, Garland had shown the same talent. Could it be that Ashton would be as talented as Garland? After enjoying that special thought but keeping it to herself, Sissy continued her serenade.

Both Brenda and Valerie smiled at Sissy's melody. One day, they, too, would discover what Sissy had already realized.

||||||||

Sissy's stay with the Fishers went by very quickly. It seemed like only yesterday that Sissy had arrived at the Fishers' front door. Sissy retired to her room that evening, wishing she could stay longer. She was about to go to bed when there was a knock on her door.

"Sissy, are you asleep?" Brenda asked.

"No, Brenda. Come on in," Sissy answered.

Brenda entered the room, holding a small box in one hand and a brown-paper lunch bag in the other. It was no secret what the box contained, but Sissy wondered what was in the bag.

Brenda sat on the bed, beside Sissy, opening the box to reveal the ring Garland had used to propose to her that day at the airport in California.

"Baby, this is very pretty. I know how proud you must be of it and how proud Garland was to give it to you," Sissy said.

Brenda began to cry. "If I had said yes that day, Garland would not be in the mess he is in right now."

"You can't blame yourself for that," Sissy said. "We both know he is not guilty, and we must keep trying to exonerate him."

Brenda nodded, wiping away her tears.

"What do you have in the brown-paper bag?" Sissy asked.

Brenda unfolded the bag to reveal the words written on it. She handed the bag to Sissy.

Sissy began to read the verses of the song. As she read the words, Sissy smiled in recognition.

"Did you write this, Brenda?" Sissy asked.

"No, Garland wrote it one day at a park in Raleigh. He wrote it for me," Brenda answered.

"I can tell it was written for someone very dear to the songwriter," Sissy said.

"I will keep this song, hoping that, someday, the songwriter will be able to finish the music in his heart to match these beautiful words," Brenda said.

"I think that is a wonderful idea, dear. It is important that you do that for us all," Sissy said.

Brenda smiled and kissed Sissy, wishing her a good night.

||||||||

The next morning arrived, with Sissy packing her bags. She wanted the Fishers to know how much she'd enjoyed her stay and thanked them for the pictures of Ashton that they had given her.

"I have to be back in time to see Garland. Before they transfer him to the state correctional institution, our attorney has arranged a visit for James and me to see Garland. I will finally get to talk to my son. I don't know when I will have that chance again," Sissy said.

They said their goodbyes.

Sissy added, "I have decided not to tell Garland about Ashton yet. I don't want him to suffer any more than he already has. When the time is right, I will tell him all about his precious daughter."

A cab arrived in the Fishers' driveway, and soon Sissy was gone, leaving all the Fishers with an awful empty feeling. Sometimes life just wasn't fair. So many people were suffering when they should have been rejoicing in a new birth.

||||||||

Mathew Stein arrived at the county detention facility early that morning. This was the last day Garland would be one of its inmates.

"Good morning, Garland," a voice said.

Garland looked up to see that ever-present smile.

"Good morning, Chase. How are you this morning?" Garland replied.

"I am very well. I am going to miss you. It has been a pleasure getting to know you, even under these circumstances," Chase said.

Chase opened the door as Mathew approached the cell.

"Garland, I have a surprise for you this morning. Before they move you to the state facility, there's someone I want you to see. I have arranged some time for you in a visitation room," Mathew said.

Chase escorted Garland down the hall and into a visitation room.

Who could it be? Garland wondered. He knew the person he hoped it would be.

Inside the room was a table with four chairs. Garland sat in one of the empty seats, waiting for his visitor.

Several minutes later, Mathew entered the room to check on Garland.

"Garland, your visitors are here. You will have one hour to visit with them. I know you need this very much, and I hope their visit is a comfort to you," Mathew said as he left the room.

The door opened before Garland could sit back down. The suddenness took Garland by surprise, but nowhere near the surprise felt by the people entering the room. His visitors were anxious too.

"Mom, Dad, you are a sight for sore eyes," Garland said as he rushed to hug them both.

Garland hugged Sissy very intensely. It was evident he didn't plan on letting her leave that day.

"I have missed you so much. During the trial, it was all I could do to sit there and listen to the lies and misleading statements by the prosecution," Sissy said.

James hugged both Garland and Sissy. This was a much-needed group hug.

Garland led them both over to the table. James took the closest seat to the door. Garland took the seat next to his father. Sissy began to walk around the table, to take the remaining unoccupied seat, when she was detoured by her son's strong hand. The hand escorted Sissy to its owner's lap.

"I want to devour you, Mother," Garland said as he guided Sissy into his waiting lap.

Sissy and James began to catch Garland up on the outside world.

"Have you talked to Brenda?" was the first question Garland asked.

Before Sissy had the chance to answer her son, out came another question. "Did she finish school?"

Sissy laughed at her son's sense of urgency. She had no doubt as to his feelings for Brenda.

"Garland, she is fine. And, yes, she graduated."

"Is she going to law school?" he asked.

Sissy hesitated, not wanting to tell him about Ashton, and then she said, "She is taking a break this semester before entering law school."

"I miss her so much. After I get moved, I want to write her, if they will let me," Garland said.

"I think she will like that very much, baby," Sissy said.

Garland wanted to know about the gang.

"What happened to the band?" he asked.

"The band is finishing the tour Joe arranged," James said.

"How are Brandon, Tobie, and Skye?" Garland asked.

"After the tour, Brandon is retiring from the music business. He is taking a job at the radio station with your dad. He and Tobie are expecting another child," Sissy said.

"Wow! Cochise didn't waste any time! I know he must be a wonderful father. Tell him I think he is the luckiest guy I know," Garland said.

Sissy could feel Garland's sincerity about Brandon's fatherhood. Although it hurt not to tell Garland about Ashton, she knew it would only be painful for him now—more pain than she wanted her son to endure.

"Mathew is working on an appeal to the district courts. He feels Suzanna should have been sequestered for the trial, but, because she was out of the country, there was nothing he could do," Garland said.

Sissy felt the anger her son held in his heart toward Suzanna.

"At first, I couldn't understand why she would do this to me, but then I stopped to think about it. It was her way out, setting me up for her mistake, which she didn't want to face," Garland said.

This was the first time Sissy and James heard firsthand from Garland what happened that evening.

Everyone knew that Suzanna put herself first; everything was always all about her. If she had to pay for having made a horrible mistake that early morning, she would find someone else to take the blame. The person who paid the price definitely wouldn't be Suzanna.

The hour rushed by faster than the Summerses were prepared for.

Mathew entered the room and began to explain that the prisoner transfer that was about to take place.

"I will let you know when Garland is settled in," Mathew told James and Sissy.

Chase entered the room to escort James and Sissy out. Turning to Garland, Chase said, "Garland, I will return afterward to do your transfer."

Sissy and James said goodbye to their son. Today's visitation was far too short, but it had been wonderful to finally have contact with Garland. They needed that as much as he did.

After Sissy and James left, Chase returned to escort Garland for the thirty-minute trip. The state correctional facility would be Garland's home for the remaining forty years of his sentence.

Garland and Chase arrived at the facility and began their long walk down the hall to cell block C. Each time they passed a prison cell, an inmate turned to stare at the two as they made their journey. Garland's cell was almost at the end of the hall. Chase stopped and signaled for the guard at the post to open Garland's cell door. As the door opened, Chase bent down and unlocked the shackles around Garland's ankles and then sprang to his feet to unlock the shackles around Garland's hands.

Garland entered the cell and turned to thank Chase for being his friend at the county facility.

"Chase, it has been nice meeting you and getting to know about your daughter. Please tell her that I thank her for not giving up on me," Garland said.

Chase nodded and then signaled for the door to be shut.

Garland took a seat on his bunk. His transfer was now completed.

30

IT WAS 1976, and the country would celebrate its bicentennial. Garland was entering the fifth year of his sentence. The year before, the United States Court of Appeals refused to review Garland's case, finding no evidence that would have altered the outcome of his trial.

One morning, a pleasant surprise came Garland's way. It was 6:30 a.m., time for breakfast. Garland was washing his face when a guard stopped at his door; this wasn't a normal occurrence. There was a sudden clearing of the throat. At first, Garland paid no attention. As he began to dry his face, there came another clearing of the throat, much louder and longer than the first one.

Garland placed the towel on the sink and turned to make his way to the door for breakfast.

"Aren't you going to say, 'Good morning'?" the guard.

Garland paused at the door, recognizing the face of his friend from the county facility.

"Chase, is that you?" he asked.

"Are you surprised to see me?" Chase said.

Garland controlled his emotions. He knew there would be an audience and did not wish to cause any trouble for Chase.

This was a very welcome surprise for Garland.

"I will escort you to the mess hall for breakfast this morning," Chase said.

"What are you doing here this morning?" Garland asked.

"Well, I have been transferred over here to the state facility. It was by luck that I was assigned this cell block. The first thing I did was look up the inmate population to find your cell number. I have been worried about you," Chase said.

Chase walked Garland to the mess hall and then departed.

Garland entered the mess hall and, after going through the serving line, took his usual seat and table.

After breakfast, Chase returned to escort Garland back to his cell.

"I will return shortly, Garland. Would you like some magazines to read?" Chase asked.

Garland nodded yes. Up to that point, Garland hadn't felt any desire to keep up with the happenings on the outside.

Chase returned with a cart loaded with magazines and books.

"Take your pick, Garland, which would you like?" Chase asked.

Not sure which ones to select, Garland left the decision up to Chase.

Chase selected a few magazines he thought would capture Garland's interest.

"I will pick them up at the end of my shift," Chase said as he departed

Garland took a seat on his bunk and began to thumb through the first selection: *Newsweek*. There was a feature on the new music phenomenon. Chase knew that any articles about the music scene would capture Garland's interest. Garland began to read about the new dance-craze music that the article referred to as "disco." Not only did the music create a new sound, but it appeared to have a fashion following as well. The new sound even launched several new dances.

What in the world is the "hustle"? he wondered. *What is this new sound everyone is in love with?*

The Bee Gees, a well-established group, were credited with creating much of the new sound. Garland was familiar with their sound. He never realized the sound he was familiar with was such a trendsetter. He began to wonder what kind of career Aurora's Fire would have had.

The second magazine Garland began to thumb through had articles focused on various people impacting the nation and the world.

He began to turn the pages briskly; there were no stories that grabbed his attention. Garland tossed the magazine to the side and began to look through the final magazine. This was a copy of *Rolling Stone,* a magazine in a newspaper print and format that covered the music industry. Once again, he read about the disco craze. There were so many new groups, and very few of the old groups he was familiar with appeared in any of the articles. It was evident the music world was changing very fast.

After scanning through *Rolling Stone* and recalling the old music he had grown up listening to, Garland felt wistful about the songs on the charts in those days. He wanted something different to read about. There, sitting on the other side of his bunk, was the magazine with the stories about people. When he tossed aside the magazine, it landed with a page folded and was now open to a story. After closely examining the picture in the article, Garland immediately reached to pick up the magazine. His sudden movement caused the magazine to close. He quickly tried to find the page with the picture that had caught his attention. Finally, the page appeared.

Garland paused, and his eyes began to tear. There in the article was a photo of a beautiful woman and the most precious little girl he had ever seen. It was as if God had made an angel and then improved upon the first angel with the second, smaller version. He began to read about this wonderful woman. Against all odds, she had made a career for herself as a very successful attorney. Garland began to read until his eyes were so engulfed with tears that he couldn't see. He paused to wipe his eyes and then continued to read the article.

"Brenda Fisher is the youngest assistant district attorney Wayne County, North Carolina, has ever known," the article stated. The impact she was making was changing a lot of lives in the Raleigh area.

After reading further into the article, Garland discovered who the little girl was. She was Brenda's daughter. He stroked the child's face. There was something special about this little girl, he felt.

The reality hit Garland all at once: this was the daughter of Brenda and her husband. He had lost the love of his life to another man. How fortunate this man was to have Brenda and such a precious daughter.

Once again, Garland felt the emptiness of never becoming a father. It was the same kind of feeling he had about Brandon and Skye.

"Congratulations, baby. I always knew you would be a wonderful mother someday," he said aloud.

Garland continued to look at the picture of the two until he could no longer resist the temptation. He tore the picture of Brenda and Ashton from the magazine and placed it inside his pillowcase. Garland closed the magazines, pushing them to the floor. He then lay down, placing his head on the pillow, wanting to feel close to Brenda. He was very tired and soon fell asleep.

As promised, Chase returned to pick up the magazines. Garland sat up, retrieving the periodicals from the floor. As he handed them to Chase, it was evident a page had been removed from one of them. Chase, not wanting any trouble for Garland, placed the magazine at the bottom of the stack. He would discard the magazine once back in the prison library.

IIIIIIII

Sissy went to the mailbox the next day. Inside there was another of those special envelopes from North Carolina. Just as always happened, the anticipation would not let her wait to open the envelope before reaching the front porch. She took a seat on her comfortable ladder-back rocking chair and began to thumb through the latest pictures of Ashton. The pictures were of Ashton's first day of kindergarten. Her beautiful long blonde hair was draped across her shoulders. Brenda really had a talent for dressing this young little lady. It seemed like only yesterday that Ashton had arrived in the world, and now she was beginning school.

As Sissy began to put away Ashton's latest pictures, she couldn't help but think about just how much Garland would enjoy this little angel. Each day, Ashton looked more and more like her daddy. It was almost five years since Sissy had visited the Fishers. Maybe it was time for another visit. There were so many childhood firsts that Sissy wished Garland could have enjoyed with his daughter. Each one made her sad as she thought about how father and daughter were both missing out on each other.

||||||||

Garland was sitting on his bunk when Chase made his morning rounds after breakfast.

"Garland, is there anything you would like to read today? I have some new magazines you have not had the chance to read," he said.

Garland turned toward Chase. "No, thanks, Chase. I am not in a reading mood this morning."

Chase turned the reading cart around and returned to the guard station.

Garland reached into his pillowcase and removed the picture of Brenda and Ashton.

His mind began to wander that morning, more so than usual. Looking at Ashton's picture was becoming a morning ritual with him. He began thinking of what it would be like to experience all those firsts that a father had the joy of experiencing. There was that first word spoken by a child, the first steps taken, the first Christmas, the first tooth—and on and on. Garland thought that all these firsts would be wonderful, but second to the most important of all: the first childhood hug and kiss. Those were the tops. There were no words that could describe that first.

Brenda's career made Garland feel very proud. She truly was the most remarkable woman Garland had ever known. Brenda had set a very high goal for herself, reached for and captured that goal, and done it all while being a mother. Once again, Garland thought about the very lucky man back in North Carolina who had such a wonderful wife and daughter. Perhaps, one day, he would be able to meet the man and tell him just how lucky he was. Garland placed the picture back inside his pillowcase.

Perhaps tomorrow's view of the photo would take him on an entirely different journey.

|||||||

It was a typical morning rush for the Fishers. Brenda was discovering how challenging a five-year-old could be, wondering where Ashton got all that energy. Brenda's morning was running late, and the last thing she needed was Ashton's burst of energy.

"Ashton Rene, where are you? It is time for you to go to school, and I am running late!" Brenda shouted.

Brenda had earlier discovered that silence was not always golden with Ashton. It usually meant she was into something. Brenda began a room-to-room search. Finally, she discovered a curious five-year-old in her own bedroom dresser drawer.

"Ashton, what are you doing in my drawer?" Brenda asked.

Brenda's sudden arrival startled the five-year-old. She turned to her mother and ran to her instantly. As she leaped into her mother's arms, Brenda noticed there was an item in her tiny hands.

"What do you have in your hand, baby?" she asked.

Ashton instantly tried to conceal her newfound secret. After some very effective sweet-talking, Ashton relinquished the item to her mother's welcoming hand.

As Brenda relieved the tiny hand of its contents, Ashton climbed down from her mother's arms. What was it that had captured her daughter's desire? Brenda unfolded the object to discover a picture of her and Garland. It was a picture she had forgotten, taken during Garland's trip to North Carolina. She began to smile, remembering that night when Garland arrived trying to show his support for Brenda's college. He was wearing a T-shirt from the wrong school. The moment brought a smile and much-needed laugh.

Both reactions puzzled little Ashton.

"Mommy, who is that man, and why are you laughing?" she asked.

Brenda shrugged her shoulders. With a tear in her eye, she said, "Baby, he is a very good friend I miss very much."

"Mommy, can we go see your friend?" Ashton asked.

Ashton's question seized Brenda's heart. She tried to answer her daughter, but the words were hard to form.

"Ashton, maybe one day you can meet him. I know he would love you as much as I do," she finally managed to say.

Brenda returned the picture to the dresser drawer from which it had come.

Ashton dashed from Brenda's bedroom and raced into the living room.

"Mommy, I am going to be late for school if you don't hurry up!" Ashton shouted.

The day was just beginning, and Ashton's energy had already worn her mother down. Brenda gathered up her keys, took Ashton by the hand, and rushed to the car. The trip to Ashton's school was a fifteen-minute drive, with traffic. That morning, it seemed as if every red light along the route was timed to catch Brenda and Ashton.

Ashton impatiently rocked in her seat. Brenda turned to see that it was all her daughter could do to stay seated. She turned on the car radio. As luck would have it, there was a commercial playing on their usual station. Ashton immediately began pushing the preset radio buttons until she arrived at a station playing a song.

Brenda's mind focused on a meeting she had with a client later in the day, thinking about the meeting and watching the road, she did not notice that music was playing in the car.

Ashton's attention was on the song playing on the radio. When Ashton turned up the volume, Brenda snapped out of her thoughts.

"Ashton, you will blow the speakers playing the radio that loud," she said as she lowered the volume.

Her first reaction was to reprimand her daughter, but just as she was about to speak, that precious little girl's head was turning from side to side. She was really into the song playing.

"Do you like that song, baby?" Brenda asked.

Ashton just nodded vigorously, indicating her approval of the song.

Brenda laughed and then paused: the song Ashton was enjoying on the radio was "Touch." Brenda couldn't resist relishing the moment of her daughter enjoying a song on the radio. This was a first for

Ashton. And *that* song, no less. A driver behind Brenda began to honk the horn. The light was now green.

After watching her daughter's fascination with "Touch," Brenda began to think. Maybe after her latest trial was over, she should take time away for a bit to enjoy her daughter. Ashton was changing more and more each day. Yes, a trip would be a great thing for both of them. She would surprise Ashton that evening after dinner. The drive after work to pick up Ashton would seem like an eternity. Brenda wanted to hurry home and begin to plan their trip. Events earlier in the day would now make it possible for the trip to begin.

After dinner, Brenda and Ashton were sitting in Ashton's bedroom. Brenda began to comb through Ashton's beautiful long blonde hair. Ashton leaned back onto one of pillows.

"Hey, baby, I have a surprise for you. How would you like to take a short trip with your mother?" she said.

Ashton, being only five, did not know what a trip was all about.

"Ashton, we will pack some of your clothes and things, and we will get on an airplane and fly to a place I think you will really enjoy. I think we are both ready for this trip," Brenda said.

Brenda then spent the rest of the evening preparing Ashton for the trip.

IIIIIII

Michael Fisher loaded the final piece of luggage for the trip. They were now all ready for their journey to begin. Brenda, although she described the trip, did not inform Ashton of their destination. Brenda and Ashton arrived at the airport well in advance of their flight. As always, Brenda wanted to be prepared for any unexpected surprises. Michael escorted Brenda and Ashton to their gate and began the anticipated wait for their plane to depart. Ashton took the opportunity to lay her head in her granddad's lap and take nap.

"I hope you enjoy the trip. I know it will be something special for the two of you," Michael said to Brenda.

Ashton's nap was shortened by the announcement that it was now time to board their flight.

"Ashton, hug your granddad and kiss him goodbye," Brenda said as she, too, kissed her dad and boarded the plane.

Shortly after they took their seats and fastened their seat belts, the pilot welcomed the passengers aboard.

"We will arrive at our destination in a little over two hours," the pilot said.

Ashton began to rock back and forth in her seat, anticipating the takeoff. Brenda laughed at her daughter's excitement. She reached into a bag and took out a camera to capture the moment. She had a knack of knowing the perfect time to collect these moments—moments that would be appreciated in the future. The plane began to make the journey down the tarmac and onto the runway. Ashton's deep-blue eyes were filled with excitement and were as blue as the sky she soon would be flying through.

The flight landed on time, and Brenda made ground arrangements to take them away from the airport. A nearby skycap loaded their luggage into a taxi. Brenda and Ashton sat in the backseat as the cab driver secured the trunk.

"Where can I drive you ladies?" the driver inquired.

Brenda removed a piece of paper from her purse, revealing their destination.

"We will be there in about an hour," the driver said.

The scenery from the airport was gorgeous. This was Brenda's first trip to this part of the country, and she was taken away by the scenery as much as her five-year-old was. Brenda took advantage of the hour-long drive to freshen up. As she began to apply her makeup, Ashton insisted that she was old enough to wear it as well. Brenda smiled as she dabbed her cheeks with a little rouge and a slight touch of lipstick.

"Mommy, can I see?" Ashton asked.

Brenda took a small mirror from her purse, holding it while the amazingly grown-up five-year-old primped.

"Ashton, what am I going to do with you in ten years?" Brenda said with a laugh and a smile.

"Ma'am, we will be arriving at your destination in approximately five minutes. I will assist you with your luggage," the cab driver said.

"Will you please remain in the cab?" Brenda asked. "We will proceed to a hotel afterward."

The driver, looking into the rearview mirror to make eye contact with Brenda, nodded yes. The driver then turned down the street and drove slowly, looking for the exact address on the paper Brenda had given him. Just after the street curved, the driver saw the house with the same number written on the paper. He pulled into the driveway and alongside the walkway leading to the front porch. After the cab stopped, the driver jumped from the driver's seat and rushed to open the back door for his passengers.

Brenda exited the cab and took little Ashton by the hand, leading her to the porch.

"Mommy, where are we?" Ashton asked.

Brenda smiled as her daughter climbed into the ladder-back rocking chair on the porch.

Brenda nervously pressed the doorbell. She wanted to surprise the owner. Once again, Brenda pressed the doorbell, impatiently waiting.

"Mommy, are you sure we are at the right house?" the five-year-old asked.

"Yes, baby, this is the right house; I don't think anyone is home, though," Brenda said as she tried the doorbell a third time. This time, she pressed the bell multiple times. There still was no answer. Had she done the wrong thing by showing up unannounced?

Brenda took Ashton's hand and began to lead her back to taxi. They arrived at the back door of the cab, and Brenda opened the door, helping Ashton inside. Just then, a blue Camaro convertible pulled into the driveway, slowing alongside the cab. Ashton waited inside the cab as her mother paused to speak to the driver of the Camaro.

The convertible stopped, and out jumped the driver, without turning off the motor.

"Oh my God! I cannot believe my eyes!" Sissy said as she ran around the car to hug Brenda. "This is a wonderful surprise. Is something wrong with Ashton?"

Brenda smiled at Sissy as a voice came from within the taxi.

"My name is Ashton," said the dainty voice.

Sissy immediately bent down to see where that sweet voice was coming from. Ashton began to scoot along the edge of the seat until she exited the car.

"Can I have a hug?" Sissy asked.

Ashton hesitated, uncomfortable with the request for a hug from someone she didn't know.

"I am sorry, baby; I didn't mean to scare you," Sissy said, stepping aside to let Ashton run to Brenda's side.

"Ashton, it's okay, baby. This lady will never do you any harm," Brenda said.

Ashton stared at Sissy, still unsure about the situation.

"Baby, this is your grandmother," Brenda said.

Ashton slowly walked over to Sissy and held out her hand. Sissy laughed and obliged the handshake. After all, it had been five years since she had seen her granddaughter, and Ashton couldn't possibly remember her.

"You should have called us Brenda. We could have met you at the airport," Sissy said.

"I wanted to surprise you," Brenda said. "I have a room reserved at a nearby hotel."

"Well, they will just have to give that room to someone else; you will not be using it," Sissy said. Turning to the cab driver, she added, "Driver, can you please open the trunk? We need to get their luggage out of the car."

The driver began to approach the rear of the taxi when an orange Camaro convertible entered the driveway and stopped behind Sissy's blue Camaro. James stepped out from the driver's side.

"Sissy, do you know your car's motor is still running?" James said as he jogged to the open car door, reaching in to shut off the engine and remove the keys.

James walked around Sissy's car and then stopped in his tracks.

"Am I dreaming? Brenda, is that really you?" James said as he ran to where Brenda stood and hugged her like he never wanted to let go.

Once again, Ashton was overwhelmed by the actions of a stranger.

"It is so good to see you, Brenda. How is my grandson?" James said with a wink.

"I am not a little boy; I am a little girl," a tiny voice said.

James looked down to see Ashton.

"Yes, you are, baby, and a very pretty little girl at that," James said as he lifted her up in his arms and kissed her cheek.

"Ashton, this is your other pawpaw," Brenda said.

Ashton paused to memorize James's face.

"James, I think you may have scared the little angel," Sissy said.

James was about to put Ashton down, but she clung to him, hugging him around the neck. This surprised everyone. Brenda and Sissy had expected Ashton to have the same reaction with James that she had with Sissy.

"Mommy, you mean I have two pawpaws?" Ashton asked.

Brenda laughed. "Yes, Ashton, you do indeed have two pawpaws."

James and the cab driver carried Brenda's and Ashton's things into the house.

"Let me show you where to take Brenda's and Ashton's things," Sissy said as she led the whole group to the bedroom that Brenda and Ashton would occupy.

As Sissy turned down the hallway, James instantly knew exactly what was on her mind.

"James, I think they will be comfortable in this bedroom," Sissy said.

James smiled in agreement as he opened the closet door, setting Brenda's and Ashton's things inside and then settling up with the cab driver—despite Brenda's protest—and seeing him out.

Brenda paused to soak in what her eyes were telling her heart.

Ashton, not wanting her mother to wander very far away from her in a strange house, clung to Brenda's leg. She turned to Sissy, with a very satisfying smile.

"Sissy, you seem to always know exactly what to do," Brenda said.

"It just seemed like the right thing to do. I know you miss him as much as I do," Sissy said as she excused herself, leaving Brenda and Ashton to unpack their things.

Garland's bedroom was indeed perfect.

IIIIIII

Brenda awakened from a much-needed nap. As she was lying on the bed, the Summerses' doorbell began to ring. Not wanting to be nosy, Brenda at first ignored the sound of the arriving visitor. There seemed to be three guests entering the house. Brenda continued lying on the bed as Ashton began to stir from her nap. Those big blue eyes opened, and, just as they had always done since the day she was born, captured her mother's heart.

"Mommy, where are we?" the tiny voice asked.

"Baby, we are at your grandma Sissy and pawpaw James's house," Brenda said.

Brenda knew the day would soon arrive when her daughter would begin to question who her father was. Brenda was not prepared for how to answer that question.

"Come on, baby, let's get up. I think we may have company," Brenda said.

With that, the two left the bedroom and went to the living room.

Sitting on the couch was a family of three: a man, a woman, and a little girl.

Sissy greeted Brenda and Ashton as they entered the living room.

"Ashton, can I have a hug?" Sissy asked.

Ashton very timidly moved away from Brenda and then ran to Sissy and climbed into her lap. Her sudden reaction brought a laugh from the couch's occupants.

"Brandon, is that you?" Brenda said.

"Yes, Brenda, it's me," Brandon answered as he stood up and greeted Brenda with a hug.

"Do you remember my wife, Tobie?" Brandon asked.

"Yes, I do. How are you Tobie?" Brenda asked as she turned from Brandon to greet Tobie.

"Well, other than being a little bit pregnant, I am wonderful," Tobie replied as she struggled to her feet.

"My mommy is expecting my little brother," a little voice behind Tobie proclaimed.

Brenda smiled at the little girl who was not at all shy.

"Brenda, this is our daughter, Skye," Brandon proudly announced.

"Skye, you have the prettiest black hair and the blackest eyes I have ever seen. You are a very pretty little girl. Where did you ever get those cute little dimples?" Brenda said.

"My daddy gave them to me," Skye said.

Brenda laughed and turned to Brandon. "Well, sweetie, you are absolutely right. He did indeed."

Ashton remained sitting in Sissy's lap, staring at Skye. Ashton had little interactions with other children until she began kindergarten.

Brenda, Brandon, and Tobie each took a seat, wanting to be more comfortable.

"Brandon, Tobie, Skye, this is my daughter, Ashton," Brenda said.

Ashton hid her face in Sissy's bosom, not knowing how to react to these strangers. Her shyness generated laughter from the adults in the room.

Each time a question was directed her way, Ashton would hide her face, not knowing what to say. On several occasions, Sissy encouraged Ashton to talk, without any results.

Each time Ashton hid her face, Skye became more interested in the other little person in the room. Finally, her curiosity got the best of her, and she climbed down from the couch she occupied with her parents. Skye's next move would surprise everyone: she rushed to Sissy's chair and began to take Ashton's hand.

Ashton turned to see who was taking her hand and trying to get her attention.

There was a sudden face-to-face meeting of the two little angels.

"My name is Skye. I am six years old. What is your name?"

Just when everyone anticipated that Ashton would once again hide her face, she climbed from Sissy's lap.

"My name is Ashton, and I am five years old."

Ashton and Skye took a seat in the floor, still holding hands, not wanting to be separated. It was difficult to determine which hand did not want to be without the other. The two little girls formed a bond that day—one that would be special for the rest of their lives.

Ashton was beginning to do what Brenda had hoped for on this trip. She was beginning to open up to people. Soon after taking a seat on the floor with Skye, Ashton's personality and confidence level blossomed. The initially timid, shy, and quiet little girl suddenly did not want to stop talking.

The adults continued their conversations, occasionally stopping to listen to the conversations of their little girls.

Something soon happened that would touch the hearts of them all. Ashton began to hum a song. At first, everyone thought she was just humming the song. But then, she began to sing verses of the song. The room suddenly grew quiet, with everyone's attention focused on the five-year-old. Although the words weren't in the correct order, it became apparent what she was trying to sing.

"Ashton, sweetie, where did you hear that song?" Sissy asked.

Ashton paused, turning toward Sissy to answer her question. "I have it in my head."

"Inside your head? Have you heard that song before?" Sissy asked.

Ashton nodded and then resumed singing. Her pleasant little voice was very good.

"Oh my God!" Brenda exclaimed as she now recognized the tune as well. "Sissy, we heard that song on the car radio on the way to school one morning. That is the only time she has ever heard it, and she sang along with the song as it played in the car."

Brandon also recognized the tune and was touched. "Do you guys know the song she is mimicking?"

Ashton stopped singing and ran back to Sissy's lap and arms. Sissy hugged and kissed her granddaughter.

"Yes, Brandon, we all know the tune she is singing," Sissy said.

The song Ashton was singing that day, after only hearing it once, was "Touch." Without any awareness of what she had done, Ashton Rene Summers showed that she was more special than anyone in that room could ever have guessed.

Brandon, Tobie, and Skye were about to leave that evening.

"Ashton you have been a pleasure to meet. I know your grandmother and mother are very proud of you. I have something I want to give you," Tobie said as she opened her purse to find her wallet.

Tobie opened the wallet, removed an item, and motioned to Ashton to take it as a gift.

Ashton, her eyes wide with pleasure, took the present from Tobie and then returned to Brenda's lap.

"Look, Mommy!" Ashton said.

Brenda obliged her daughter, seeing a picture of Skye. With a smile, Brenda left the room.

At first, Tobie thought her actions had upset Brenda. Her concern was soon relieved when Brenda appeared with an item and instructed Ashton to take it to Tobie.

Brenda had reciprocated the gift exchange by providing a picture of Ashton. Tobie smiled, complimenting Ashton on what a good picture it was.

Brandon's curiosity overtook him, and he insisted that Tobie share it with him.

Gazing at Ashton's picture, Brandon smiled and said, "Ashton, you are a living doll."

Brandon's initial response had been to say that Ashton looked just like her father, but he caught himself. He had no doubt that Garland was Ashton's father.

The great trips taken in life always end too soon, and this was the case with Brenda and Ashton's trip to Colorado.

"Brenda, are you sure you and Ashton can't stay longer? It seems like you have only been here for a few hours, not two whole days," Sissy said.

"I wish we could stay longer," Brenda said. "I have had such a wonderful time, and so has Ashton. I am so glad she got to meet you and James."

Ashton rushed to her grandmother's side, jumping up and into her open arms.

Sissy, holding back the tears, grabbed the little five-year-old and returned the hug. "I love you, little Ashton. I cannot wait until the next time I get to see you."

Sissy carried Ashton into Garland's bedroom.

"I have something I want for you to have," Sissy said.

Sissy opened a drawer and retrieved a brown paper bag.

"Ashton, when you get back home, have your mother play this record for you," Sissy said.

Ashton jumped down from Sissy's arms, running into the next room to show her mother her new treasure.

"Ashton, what is that special item you have in your hand?" Brenda asked.

"Grandma Sissy said for you to play this when we get back home," Ashton said.

Brenda took the gift from Ashton, removing it from the brown paper bag. The record Brenda removed from the brown paper bag that day was one of the original demos for "Touch."

Walking into Garland's room, Brenda smiled at Sissy, shaking her head. She knew how hard this was for Sissy to let go of, and parting with it showed how much she loved Ashton.

31

GARLAND CELEBRATED HIS thirtieth birthday in prison. Once again, the federal appellate court had turned down his appeal. It had become evident that he would serve his full sentence. The eighties were entering their second year. Prison limited his exposure to the outside world. The prison's periodicals were mostly about the national scene; there wasn't much news about the local area. Sometimes the magazines were several months old by the time they made their rounds to the inmates' cells.

Chase made his rounds one morning, bringing the periodicals currently in stock. *Newsweek* was dated from the second week of December 1980. A picture on the front cover grabbed Garland's attention. The week's entire publication was devoted to John Lennon.

"Chase, I will take that magazine with John Lennon's picture on the cover," Garland said.

Chase folded the magazine and passed it through the cell's bars. Below Lennon's picture was a caption with the years 1940–1980. Garland knew that such a caption could only mean one thing. As he opened the magazine, Garland was shocked by what he read.

Who could have done such a thing? he wondered.

What was the outside world coming to if someone took a person's life for no reason other than to gather their own fame, at the expense of the family, friends, and fans who loved the victim?

As a music lover and Beatles fan, Garland had found their breakup was hard to take. However, the murder of one of the members was even harder to take. As much as any other fan, Garland had always hoped that, someday, there would have been a reunion concert. It would have been an event that could never be topped. Now it could never happen.

IIIIIIII

Ashton Summers was now a ten-year-old beginning fifth grade. It was an early spring Saturday morning; Ashton was lying on the bed with her mother. Ashton turned to Brenda, with a deeply concerned look in her eyes. Brenda sensed there was something bothering her daughter.

"Baby, is there something troubling you?" Brenda asked.

Ashton hesitated, as if not quite sure where to begin. She sprang from Brenda's bed and retrieved a box from the closet.

Brenda instantly recognized the box in Ashton' hands as she returned, taking a seat on the bed.

Ashton opened the box, searching its contents. Finally, she removed an item from the box. Ashton placed the ring on her small finger.

"Mom, is this the ring my dad gave to you?" she asked.

Brenda removed the ring from Ashton's finger and placed it on her own left ring finger. She had forgotten how beautiful a ring it was.

"Yes, baby, this is the ring your father gave to me when he asked me to marry him," Brenda answered.

"Is my father dead? I never hear anyone talk about him," Ashton said.

Brenda paused, not sure of the correct response. She had always promised herself that she would not lie to Ashton when the time came for her to learn more about Garland. With tears in her eyes, Brenda turned to answer her daughter.

"Ashton, your father is alive, and I have no doubt that, if he knew about you, he would spoil you to no end. He was—he is—a very good man," Brenda said.

"He doesn't know about me?" Ashton asked.

Ashton's question broke her mother's heart.

"No, baby, he doesn't," Brenda confirmed.

"Is he ashamed of me?" Ashton asked.

This time, Ashton's question made Brenda clutch her daughter, breaking down.

"Will you tell me about him? Mom, I know you will think it is strange, but I can feel him," Ashton said.

"Ashton, please believe me when I say that your father would be with us if he could and that, someday, he may join us. I really believe that day will come, and, when it does, Ashton, you will see what a great man your dad is," Brenda said.

Brenda turned to the box and began to reminisce about the items inside it. There were the pictures of her and Garland, along with that lunch bag with the song lyrics Garland had written that day in the park in Raleigh.

"Mom, you kept these pictures of the man you said was a very good friend. Is he also in the photo of you as a little girl with the boy playing a guitar? Is he the boy in the photo?" Ashton asked.

Brenda smiled before answering Ashton.

"Baby, he is much more than that," Brenda said.

Ashton stared at the picture of Garland with his Gibson. "Mom, that guitar is the same guitar in Grandma Sissy's house. Is he a friend of Grandma Sissy's too?"

"No, baby, he is not Grandma Sissy's friend. He is her son," Brenda said.

Ashton smiled. She was beginning to figure things out about Sissy and Garland.

"Your special friend is my father, isn't he, Mom?"

Brenda hugged her daughter.

Brenda and Ashton spent the rest of the afternoon going through the box, with Brenda explaining the significance of each item in the box. Her daughter was growing up and was beginning to appreciate stories about Garland. She wanted to tell Ashton about Garland's career, but that would have to wait until she was old enough to understand the events that happened after his success as a recording artist.

"Mom, do you think we can buy a guitar for my birthday?" Ashton asked.

"Ashton, do you like music that much? Do you want to take lessons?" Brenda asked.

"I love music. It takes me away to a place I cannot describe, far, far away. I want to try out for the school choir. Can I?" Ashton said.

"Baby, you can try out for anything you want," Brenda said.

|||||||

The weekend rolled around. The choir tryouts were to be held on Saturday afternoon. The Fisher family was all in attendance that afternoon, giving their support to Ashton. There would be two occasions for Ashton to sing. One song would be a solo, accompanied by a piano player, to be sung before the choir director. The second song would be a group song. This song would show the singer's ability to harmonize with a group. Each participant would sing the same individual song. Ashton would perform her group song first. It was decided that the best singers performing the group song would then advance to perform the individual song.

Ashton was selected to perform her group song with another girl and two boys. The four took the stage and began their audition. The Fishers sat on the edges of their chairs as the song began. At first, the girls would perform a two-part harmony, followed by a two-part harmony from the boys. The song would end with a four-part harmony. As Ashton and her partner began their harmonies, there was one voice that was off key. After several choruses, it became clear which voice was off key. The girls stepped back, making space for the boys. The boy's harmonies were very good. It was now time for the group's four-part harmony. Once again, there seemed to be one voice out of key from the other three. As the song ended, the choir director instructed the four to remain on the stage for the results.

The choir director stepped forward to reveal her decision. She began with the two boys, informing them that they both would advance to the solo round.

She turned to confer with the piano player, and then she said, "We would like for you two girls to repeat your harmonies together."

Brenda turned to her mother. It was unusual to request a repeat audition during a tryout.

The girls began their number. Once again, there was a different key from one of the girls.

The choir director stood with her hand on her chin. This was something very different. It was something she had never witnessed before. The number came to a close.

"Please remain on the stage, girls. We have a dilemma," the choir director said, adding, "Ashton Summers, can you and your parents meet with us in private?"

Brenda's heart fell that day. She knew how much her daughter wanted this. The Fishers left their seats to meet with the choir director. They were appreciative that she wanted to break the news to Ashton in private.

"Ashton, how do you think you did today?" the choir director asked.

Ashton turned to her family before answering.

After a moment, she said, "I think I did well."

"This is the first time we have come across what has happened today. At first, we thought the difference was because of an off note you were hitting. That is why we wanted you to sing again. Ashton, you were hitting a much harder note. A note we have never heard from someone your age," the choir director said.

"Is that a good thing? Or, does that mean I didn't make the choir? "Ashton asked.

"Quite the opposite, Ashton; in fact, you do not have to do the solo song. You are a very talented young lady," the choir director said.

Ashton began to jump up and down. As the Fishers departed their meeting with the choir director, Ashton's excitement drew much attention from those sitting in the crowd. The Fishers left the auditions that day with something none of them had ever expected from a ten-year-old girl.

The Fishers arrived home that afternoon with a ten-year-old who thought she had just landed on the moon, only she didn't need a rocket to get there with.

|||||||

"Ashton, we are very proud of what you did today. You should be very proud of yourself," Brenda told her daughter.

"Do you think my daddy would be proud of me today?" Ashton asked.

Ashton's question took her mother by surprise.

"Baby, I don't *think* he would be proud; I *know* he would be. You know, I remember him when he was your age. You have his spirit, and now it looks like you have his talent too," Brenda said.

"Mom, do you know what I want to do?" Ashton asked.

"No, baby, what would you like to do?" Brenda asked.

"I want to call Grandma Sissy and tell her the good news. I want her to tell my daddy," Ashton said as she ran into the den, where a phone was sitting on a table.

Brenda followed her daughter, reaching into a drawer for a book with phone numbers. She turned to the page with Sissy's number, saying, "Here you go, baby. Call your grandmother and tell her the good news."

Ashton anxiously dialed Sissy's phone number. The phone began to ring. Ashton turned to Brenda, with a puzzled look on her face. This was not a good time for no one to be at home. She was bursting with good news and wanted to share it with her grandparents. Ashton paused, looking at the phone. She was about to hang up when she finally heard a voice on the other end.

"Hello," a male voice said.

"Pawpaw, this is Ashton."

"How is my grandson? Is everything okay?" James said jokingly.

Ashton continued talking to James. She didn't often have the opportunity to talk to him.

Sissy entered the room. She knew there was someone special on the line for James to be engaged in a phone conversation for this long.

James winked at Sissy as she took a nearby seat.

"Tell your mother I love her. I will let you talk to your grandmother," James said.

"Ashton, is everything all right?" Sissy asked.

"I have a big surprise for you, Grandma. I tried out for the school choir and made it as a soloist," Ashton proudly stated.

"That is wonderful, Ashton. I have always loved singing," Sissy said.

"We have a concert in three weeks, and I wish you could be here," Ashton said.

Sissy paused for a moment, thinking of a response. Finally, she realized she didn't have a better answer than saying that she would attend.

"My mom would like to say something to you, Grandma. I am so excited you will be here," Ashton said.

"Hello, Sissy," Brenda said. "I had no idea she would put you on the spot like that. She did the same thing to me the other day when she saw that picture of Garland at my tenth-birthday party in Charleston, with his Gibson. She immediately recognized it as the one you have in Garland's room."

"She was always a very bright little girl," Sissy said.

"Sissy, I couldn't lie to my daughter. She knows Garland is her dad, but she has no idea of his whereabouts. I am sorry, but it was something I had to do," Brenda said.

"Brenda, you did the right thing by not lying to her," Sissy said.

"Sissy, if you are able to make it to her first program, it would mean the world to her. I have to warn you, though: she will ask you a lot of questions about her dad," Brenda said.

"I will be there, Brenda. It has been five years since I have seen her. I still have the memory of her and Skye sitting on the floor together. I could always use some updated memories," Sissy said.

For the next three weeks, Ashton's choir practice was the center of conversation at the dinner table each night. Ashton's love for music seemed relentless, and it was clear she couldn't get enough of music.

During the last rehearsal before the show, the choir director made it a point to catch Brenda before she and Ashton left practice.

"Brenda, your daughter is advancing so fast. We have discussed what would be best for her musical future. There is an advanced choir that is normally for older students, but we feel that, with her talent, she will do very well as a member. I would like your permission to move her up after the program," the choir director said.

Brenda was very proud of her daughter and agreed that, if Ashton wanted to pursue the advanced choir, it would be all right with her.

The morning of the choir program arrived. Ashton ran into her mother's bedroom.

"Mom, is Grandma Sissy coming today? Have you heard from her?" Ashton asked as she jumped on the bed.

Brenda, barely awake, tried to provide her daughter with the answers she sought. She knew Ashton was very excited about this day and wanted all her loved ones around to share it with her.

"No, baby, I have not heard from her. The program doesn't start until 6:00 p.m. She hasn't called saying she wouldn't be here," Brenda answered.

Ashton let her head drop to the nearby pillow, landing next to her mother's head.

"You are growing up so fast, Ashton. It scares me that the time is getting away from us so fast," Brenda said.

Ashton calmed down and fell asleep in her mother's welcoming arms.

Shortly after lunch that afternoon, the welcome sight they anticipated finally arrived. A cab pulled into the driveway, delivering two passengers.

Ashton heard the car doors shutting and rushed to the front door.

"They are here! They are here!" she shouted as she darted out the front door to greet not only Sissy but James as well.

"Pawpaw, I didn't know you were coming too," Ashton said.

"Did you think I would miss the making of a superstar?" James said as he lifted Ashton into his arms.

The driver opened the trunk and began unloading its contents. He first removed two suitcases, followed by a makeup bag. He struggled for the last item. It was a very large bag, and it was all wrapped up to hide its identity.

Brenda and Valerie greeted the Summerses and helped with their luggage. James carried the present into the house and then into the guest room, escorted by Brenda.

Ashton was very excited to see her grandparents, waiting anxiously for James to emerge from the guest room. James returned to the den, where the other family members were sitting.

Ashton dashed from the den. She returned shortly, carrying a brown paper bag, and took a seat on the couch, as close as she could possibly get to Sissy.

"What is it in your bag, Ashton?" Sissy asked.

Ashton smiled and removed a box.

Brenda, sitting in a nearby chair, knew what was about to happen.

"This box is my mom's," Ashton said.

Ashton opened the box and began to show Sissy its contents, explaining the significance of each item. She stopped at the final item: the picture of Garland and his guitar at Brenda's tenth-birthday party.

"Grandma, my mom says this boy is my daddy," Ashton said.

Even with Brenda's warning, Ashton's remarks shocked Sissy.

"Can I please see the picture Ashton?" Sissy asked.

Ashton handed the picture to Sissy.

It had been a very long time since Sissy had seen that picture.

"Yes, baby, that is your daddy," Sissy said.

"Do you know where my daddy is? Can I see him?" Ashton asked.

Sissy paused, thinking of an answer for her granddaughter.

Finally, she said, "Baby, if there was any way your daddy could be with you, he would. Someday, perhaps he'll be able to."

"Does he love me?" Ashton asked.

This time, Sissy couldn't answer Ashton's question.

"Ashton, we have talked about your daddy. He does love you," Brenda answered.

Ashton began to sniffle, trying to hide her tears. It was hard to understand where her dad might be, and why it was such a big secret.

Sissy left the room at that moment.

"Ashton, you have upset your grandmother," Brenda said.

Hurting Sissy's feelings was the last thing Ashton wanted to do.

The few hours remaining before Ashton's program turned into a few minutes, and soon it was time to leave for the show.

Michael Fisher rounded up the VIPs, including the evening's star attraction.

Ashton returned to the den. She was wearing a lacy yellow dress. Her blonde hair was in two ponytails on either side of her head, tied with two small yellow ribbons that matched the lace on her dress.

"Ashton, you are a very beautiful little lady," Sissy said.

James stood, holding out his arm. Just when Brenda thought her daughter would know what her pawpaw was offering, Ashton took her escort's arm and departed for the car. Brenda and Sissy both shook their heads in disbelief, wondering who had taught that move to Ashton.

They arrived at the school's auditorium, to a capacity crowd. It was to be a full house this evening. Ashton and her family entered the auditorium. As her family was escorted to their seats, an usher greeted Ashton. He escorted her to the area where the choir was assembling.

Sissy sat in her chair; she was excited for Ashton and eager for the show to begin. Sissy began to thumb through the show's program. The songs were listed in the order in which they would be performed, but there was no listing of who would perform them. Ashton's family would just have to sit tight and enjoy the show, waiting for her big moment.

The first song of the evening was an all-boys song. The boys were all dressed in sport coats and ties. Midway into the song, one boy approached the front of the stage, took the microphone, and began to sing the lead for the chorus of the remaining boys. The song ended with all the boys coming together in harmony. It was a very good number to open the show. By this time, the auditorium was more than full, and people began to stand along the walls of the auditorium. Many times, the darkness of the auditorium was flooded with camera flashes.

After the crowd's applause, the lights on the stage drew into a small spotlight on the stage. A backdrop of lights creating a rainbow suddenly appeared on a background developed for the show. The song's introduction was an old favorite from one of Hollywood's favorite family movies. As the intro came to an end, a figure appeared on the stage, sitting on a stool.

The spotlight revealed a small girl sitting with a stuffed dog. Sissy reached for Brenda's hand as the little girl began to sing. Ashton began to sing with the zest of a much more-experienced performer. When Ashton began "Somewhere over the Rainbow," a chill came over both Brenda and Sissy. The notes were very pure and on key. Sissy turned to James to see the illuminated look in his eyes as Ashton made the audience her own. They looked at each other. It was just like Garland had done at the Red Rocks Amphitheatre.

Brenda knew that her little girl had a special talent, a talent that ran deep into her veins and through her heart, and it came from Garland. She had forgotten that special feeling Garland made them all feel whenever he took the stage; now this feeling was more alive than ever. It was a way for them all to feel Garland through Ashton—a way that she would grasp later in her life and never let go, giving her and whomever she touched with her voice a sense of disbelief from their ears but not their hearts. She was Garland Summers's daughter.

Ashton made "Somewhere over the Rainbow" sound as if she had been singing it for a very long time. She accomplished that in just three weeks of rehearsing. When Ashton stood up from her stool to bring home the final chorus, the crowd all got to its feet as well. Her song ended with a standing ovation and a sea of flashbulbs.

Ashton then did the only thing she would do that night that was typical of a ten-year-old: she ran off the stage and into the waiting arms of her mother. Shortly after being treated with the amazement of the audience and the compliment of a standing ovation, Ashton's retreat broke the crowd into a very warm chorus of "Aw!" This was an incredible night for both the singer and her audience.

The program ended in a very big success. People were congratulating the Fishers and Ashton. Many of them were strangers to the family.

The choir director took the time to return Ashton's little stuffed dog, which she had dropped on the stage after her song. The trip back to the Fishers' was very enjoyable. It was difficult to determine who was the proudest that night.

Ashton was sitting in the front seat when she began to hear a sound from the car's radio. The adults all recounted the events of the show and did not hear the sound coming from the radio. Ashton began to lean forward to hear if she was hearing what she thought she was hearing. She soon recognized it as a song that had captivated her five years earlier. Ashton's family was too excited to notice the ten-year-old. Ashton, wanting to hear the music, turned up the volume to the radio. The small hand increased the volume until it was very loud.

At first, the loudness grabbed their attention only because it was loud; but then, it happened. They all turned to watch Ashton. As much as Ashton had mesmerized them earlier that evening, the song on the radio now mesmerized Ashton. The car's passengers, who had been talking very loudly, suddenly became very quiet. They were touched once again by this ten-year-old. The song she was captivated by was "Touch." Everyone, without saying a word, thought that this was a fitting way to end a perfect evening.

The next morning arrived way too soon for them all. It was a reminder that the Summerses' trip would soon be over, and they would return to Colorado.

Sissy joined Brenda in the den that morning. Brenda's box containing the memorabilia was sitting on the table from the day before.

"Brenda, do you mind if I look at some of your things?" Sissy asked.

Brenda nodded her approval to Sissy.

There were so many memories in that box, and they refreshed Sissy. Some brought tears, and others brought smiles and even laughter.

"Sissy, how long has it been since you saw Garland?" Brenda asked.

"The new warden has changed things at the prison. Beginning next month, we can visit Garland once a month. Until now, we only had visits every six months," Sissy answered.

"Does he know about Ashton?" Brenda asked.

"No, Brenda. I didn't want to hurt him any more than he has already been hurt," Sissy said.

Their conversation was soon interrupted by Ashton snuggling in between Sissy and Brenda. She was now awake for the day.

"Sissy, look at Ashton. You know how proud of her we all are and how she made us all feel about her last night. Don't you think it's time for Garland to have some of that in his life?" Brenda asked.

Sissy turned to Ashton pulling her closer for a hug. Brenda did have a point. Ashton made everyone feel good. Maybe it was time for Garland to have those same feelings.

Sissy left the room.

Brenda, at first, thought she had overstepped her boundaries and hurt Sissy's feelings. Brenda's concerns would soon be allayed when Sissy entered the room, carrying a wrapped package.

"Here, baby, I want you to have this," Sissy said as she gave the present to Ashton.

As Ashton began to tear the paper away from the present, there were some occasional pinging sounds. It was not long before the paper was all torn away. Ashton began to hold Garland's old Gibson. Ashton turned over the old Gibson. Underneath there was a name written.

"Grandma, this is Garland's guitar. It says so on the back," Ashton said.

Ashton with the Gibson in her lap reached into Brenda's box. Not only was there a picture of Garland with the old Gibson at Brenda's tenth-birthday party, but there was also a picture of Garland and the Gibson on the jacket of a demo record.

"Grandma is that Garland in the picture? Is this record in the box the demo?" Ashton asked.

Although Ashton had seen the record many times, it never registered in her mind what the record was.

"Ashton, that is the same guitar on the record you are holding. The record inside that picture is the song you loved on the radio during the trip home from your show. That record is a song called 'Touch.' Ashton, the man in the picture and singing the song you love so much is your daddy," Sissy said as she hugged Ashton.

Ashton was very excited to have "Touch," but now it was even more special; it was her dad's song, and the old Gibson was his too.

Brenda shook her head, with tears in her eyes. She knew how much the Gibson meant to Sissy, and giving it to Ashton was a true act of love.

32

A BRIGHT-RED CHEVROLET pickup truck pulled into the prison personnel parking lot one morning. The driver's-side door swung open, and the large frame of the truck's driver and owner emerged. Thaddeus Charles Rucker then began his journey into the Colorado state correctional institution. Passing through the gate, Thad towered over the guard. He nodded to the guard, walking past him and into the prison yard. Thad crossed through the yard, entered the prison, and proceeded down the hallway and toward the administration offices. All eyes focused on Thad's six-foot-eight frame; this was a very intimidating sight.

"Good morning," Thad said to a young black lady sitting at the reception desk.

"Good morning, sir. May I assist you in your visit with us today?" she asked.

"My name is Thaddeus Charles Rucker. Please show me to the warden's office," Thad said.

The guard pointed to a nearby door and pressed a button that gave access to this wing of the prison.

Thad continued his walk, arriving at the warden's office. Outside the office was the desk of the warden's secretary.

"Yes, sir, may I be of assistance to you this morning?" the woman seated behind the desk said.

Thad looked at the well-dressed middle-aged lady. Sitting on the desk was a nameplate with the identity of his greeter.

"My name is Thaddeus Rucker, and I see that your name is Rosemary House."

Rosemary opened her top desk drawer, removing a set of keys.

"I think you will need these, sir," Rosemary said as she stretched out her hand, offering the keys to Thad. "I am your secretary, Mr. Rucker."

The keys disappeared inside the huge hand that received them, and then the deep voice said, "Rosemary, please give me a few minutes to get settled in and then come into my office."

"Certainly, Mr. Rucker," Rosemary said.

Thad entered his new office and placed his briefcase on the credenza behind the mahogany overhang desk. He walked over and opened the blinds. This window overlooked one of the prison yards that the inmates used daily for recreation. Thad returned to his desk and tried out his new desk and chair. The desk was fantastic, but something had to be done about the chair. His predecessor was a much smaller man. Good family man that he was, Thad opened his briefcase and removed a framed photo of his wife and two sons, placing it on the credenza. As he turned around from the credenza, Thad felt a sharp pain in his legs. There was no way this chair was going to work without some modifications.

Rosemary entered Thad's office. Thad was bent over, rubbing his knees with both hands.

"Mr. Rucker, are you all right?" Rosemary asked.

"Rosemary, I need you to contact maintenance to send someone up to look at this chair," Thad said.

"Yes, sir, Mr. Rucker. I will get right on that," Rosemary said.

Rosemary's reaction made it apparent that she, too, was quite intimidated by Thad. With his door partially open, he listened as Rosemary called maintenance, insisting that someone get to his office as soon as possible. Rosemary ended the phone call.

Several minutes later, Rosemary returned to Thad's office.

"Mr. Rucker, I didn't know how you liked your coffee, so I brought both cream and sugar," she said.

"Thank you, Rosemary. I do like my coffee black, though," Thad said.

Rosemary delivered the coffee to Thad and turned to exit the office.

"Rosemary, if it's okay with you, you can call me Thad. My dad was Mr. Rucker," he said.

At that moment, a special working relationship began between Thad and Rosemary. She realized that, even though Thad had an intimidating presence, he was a very nice man.

The next morning, as Thad arrived, Rosemary promptly delivered a cup of black coffee, along with a pleasant good morning.

"Good morning to you, Rosemary. I will need a list of all the inmates here and their profiles. It's time for me to get acquainted with my roommates," Thad said.

Rosemary soon returned with the information Thad requested in one hand and a fresh pot of coffee in the other.

Thad smiled. "Thank you, Rosemary, for the information and the coffee."

Thad began to read about each and every inmate at the facility. He wanted to know the sentences and the crimes they were sentenced for. As he read through the first group of inmate records, there were no postings for any visitations by family members, and the other visitations listed were infrequent. Family visitation was something Thad believed in very strongly; part of the rehabilitation of the inmate involved the family as well.

Some of these inmates could be saved. No one knew this better than Thad himself. His own father was proof of it. After serving his sentence, Thad's father graduated from college and made it possible for Thad to obtain not only his undergraduate degree but also two postgraduate degrees from the University of Colorado. Sometimes, after paying their debt to society, all people needed was a second chance.

"Rosemary, I intend to make some changes here, and I want to start today. Please accompany me to lunch," Thad said.

At first, Rosemary was not sure of his intentions. She knew Thad was a married man with a family.

"You and I will have lunch in the prison cafeteria today," Thad said.

Rosemary almost instantly exhaled when Thad clarified the venue. She had been holding her breath, not sure of how to respond to what had initially seemed to be a request for a luncheon date.

Rosemary and Thad entered the cafeteria that afternoon. As they made their way through the serving line, every eye in the cafeteria focused on them. The inmates couldn't believe what they saw. They had heard that there was to be a new warden, and this was their first exposure to him. Many of them had served several years in the facility and only had seen pictures of the previous wardens. They never expected to have the new warden eat in the cafeteria with them.

Thad and Rosemary took a seat at the end of one table where were four inmates were finishing their meal.

"What did you guys have for lunch today?" Thad asked.

None of the inmates responded.

"Just as I thought. The food was so good, it made you speechless," Thad said.

Once again, his remarks did not result in any responses. He knew it would take some time for them to feel the changes, but time was not something these men were short on.

Rosemary and Thad returned to their office.

"Rosemary, please have a few of the guards meet me in the recreation yard during the afternoon rec time," Thad requested.

Rosemary paused, trying to understand what Thad had in mind. It appeared to her that his first attempt at change had failed during lunch. Nevertheless, she carried out his instructions.

Thad viewed a list of the inmates who would be in the rec yard at the time he had set aside. During this rec time, several of the young black inmates played a pickup game of basketball. Thad made it a point to know the case of everyone who would be in the yard at the time, including the remaining time of each of their sentences.

The two guards were waiting at the rec-yard gate.

"Mr. Rucker, are you sure you want to go through with this?" one guard said, looking up at Thad.

Thad looked down at the guards and patted them both on the top of their heads. "Fellas, you know what they say, don't you?"

"And just what is that, sir?" one of the guards asked.

"Well, only that size *does* matter," Thad said with a laugh.

Thad entered the yard with the guards, assuring them everything would be fine.

Thad walked through the yard, greeting every inmate he came upon. Once again, there were no responses to his advances. He made his way over to the basketball court, where the daily game was in progress. Thad arrived at courtside to watch a few exchanges on the court.

"What is the score?" he asked.

Several players diverted their focus to Thad, and, at that point, the other team scored. This did not sit well with the team that was on defense at that moment.

Once again, there was no response to his question.

As Thad continued watching the game, a sudden break in play came when the ball was knocked out of bounds and rolled over to Thad's feet. Thad reached down and picked up the ball, hesitating to return it to the game.

"Fellas, you can have the ball back as soon as someone advises me as to what the score is in the game," Thad said.

At first, there was no answer. Then, just as Thad was about to turn and leave with the ball, an answer came to his question.

"It is a tie. Now give us back the goddamn ball," a voice said.

Thad walked over to the player who had answered the question.

"Did I hear you correctly? The game is tied?" Thad asked.

The young black man nodded yes.

"I think it's time that we break that tie. Don't you?" Thad said.

No one in the yard expected what was to happen next. Thad, standing near the basketball goal, wearing street shoes and a suit, took one giant step toward the basketball hoop and did a reverse one-handed dunk. The ball dropped to the ground, returning to Thad.

"Fellas, I think the game is no longer a tie," he said as he flipped the basketball back to a player.

Thad left the rec yard. This time, although no one answered him verbally, they did mentally. The times were indeed a changing in the Colorado state correctional facility.

Thad returned to his office.

"Rosemary, can you please bring me the next list to review?" Thad said.

Rosemary quickly delivered the next series to be examined by her boss.

"Thad, you are reviewing the inmates' records very closely," Rosemary observed.

"Yes, Rosemary. I want to save everyone I can. Maybe, someday, I can give them back their lives," he said.

Rosemary smiled, realizing her boss was more than just a nice man; he had a heart as big as outer frame.

Thad began to review the inmates of cell block C. Each page indicated the number of visitations for that inmate, the names of each of the visitors, and their relationship to that inmate. The rest of the file was dedicated to the charges against each of the inmates and the notes from each of their trials.

As Thad turned the page listing the inmates of the cell block, he found the records of Garland Summers. Thad paused for moment, wondering if this was the same Garland Summers whom he watched perform at the Red Rocks contest. As he continued reading Garland's file, Thad found his answer. How did a person who had everything in the world going for him ever get in a situation to be sent here? These were the mental notes Thad took that day.

"Rosemary, tomorrow, I want you to arrange for a guard on cell block C to come to my office. I want to take a tour of that block," Thad said as he left for the day.

|||||||

Sissy and James were enjoying some quiet time one evening, watching the local news. At the end of the newscast, there was a feature about the new warden at the state correctional facility. This story captured their interest, as it related to the issue closest to their hearts.

The reporter opened by stating, "Thad Rucker wants to bring about a change for the inmates of the Colorado state correctional institution."

An interview with Thad Rucker, the new warden, then followed. This interview held special meaning for the Summerses.

"I am changing the inmate visitations. Each of the inmates' families will be receiving the details of my new program," Thad Rucker said.

"I hope this is a good step for us all," James said as he turned to Sissy.

Sissy agreed. Any additional time they could have with Garland would be appreciated. The rumors that the new warden planned to change things seemed to be true.

||||||||

As Thad made his way into his office, a prison guard was waiting outside the door.

"Good morning, sir," the guard said. "My name is Chase Flemming, and I will be your escort into cell block C today."

"Chase, come into my office," Thad said, turning to Rosemary and adding, "Rosemary, please bring Chase a cup of coffee."

Once inside his office, Thad said, "Chase, please have a seat. I want to ask you about some of the population on cell block C."

"Yes, sir," Chase said as he sat down.

Rosemary almost instantly returned with the coffee.

"Thank you, ma'am," Chase said as Rosemary handed the coffee to him.

Chase then informed Thad about his tenure with the prison and the amount of time he had served on the "C," as it was called by those who worked and stayed there.

Thad opened the prisoner log, turning to the page bookmarked. He slid the book toward Chase.

"Chase, please look at the inmate on that page. Tell me everything you know about that inmate," Thad said.

Chase looked over the rim of his coffee cup, reading the inmate name at the top of the page.

"Yes, sir. I know him better than any of the other inmates on the C. Garland Summers was a talent this country had never known before," Chase said.

"I cannot find any incidences concerning his conduct while he has been serving his sentence," Thad said.

"No, sir, Garland has been a delight. Many of the inmates who have contacts on the outside believe he was never guilty of the charges against him. Some of those men were arrested by the officer whose death Garland was charged with," Chase said.

"Yes, Chase, I had the same impression of the young man's talent when I saw him perform several years ago. I have never seen a singer with such a passion for music. I have read the transcripts from the trial, and none of it adds up," Thad said.

Chase agreed.

"Today, I want to take a tour during your shift. I want to meet Garland Summers," Thad said.

Chase finished his coffee, and then he led Thad into the C. The two entered the C through a door near the guard station. The C was the home of inmates serving a very long incarceration. Only cell block D was home to the inmates that were there for harsher crimes, some even awaiting the death penalty.

Midway down the hall from the guard station, Chase and Thad arrived at Garland's cell. Their approach took Garland by surprise; he did not hear them coming. Garland sat on his bunk, with a folded piece of paper in his hands.

"Garland, what is that in your hand?" Chase asked.

Chase's remark startled Garland, causing him to drop the picture he was holding. It fell to the floor. As it landed, the other two men saw a picture of a woman and a little girl. Garland stooped down, retrieving the picture of Brenda and little Ashton, which he folded and placed in his shirt pocket.

"Garland, this is Mr. Rucker. He is the new warden," Chase said.

Garland stood and walked over to the bars of his cell.

"Garland, may I see the picture you have in your pocket?" Thad asked.

Garland reluctantly took the picture from his pocket. Once the warden had the picture in his possession, Garland knew that he would never see it again. This was the only thing he had with him to remember the love of his life. Thad took the picture from Garland, unfolding it on the other side of the cell's bars.

"Garland, why is this picture of importance to you?" Thad asked.

"She was someone I loved and asked to be my wife. As you can see in the picture, she has a daughter now. I have lost her to another man," Garland said.

Thad read the paragraph under Brenda's picture, seeing that she was a very successful attorney.

Garland turned from the bars, with his head hung low. He took a seat on his bunk.

"Garland, here is your picture back. I can see why you wanted to marry this lovely lady," Thad said.

Garland rose and crossed to the cell's bars, taking the picture from Thad.

"Tell me, Garland, does she write to you?" Thad asked.

"Write to me? No, sir, the prison will not let me receive letters from anyone other than the people on my visitors' list," Garland said, surprised that the warden had asked.

"Would you like for her to write to you?" Thad asked.

"Yes, sir, I would like that very much," Garland said.

"Chase, please bring Garland some stationery and an envelope. Garland, you can borrow my pen," Thad said.

Garland could barely contain his excitement as he accepted Thad's pen.

"Thank you, sir. You have no idea of how much this means to me. Maybe her husband will let her write me back, "Garland said.

Chase returned with the paper and envelope, passing them through the cell's bars to Garland.

"We can continue your tour, Mr. Rucker. You have only seen half of the C," Chase said.

"That will not be necessary, Chase. I found out what I wanted to know. We can continue our tour another day," Thad said.

Thad returned to the warden's office, and Chase resumed his duties.

"Rosemary, I need for you to take a memo, please," Thad said. "I want to add to the inmates' write-to lists. It is time to help those on the outside with their sense of loss. I want to let each inmate add to the list of people they would like to write to, outside their visitors' lists."

Rosemary smiled as she wrote down the information Thad dictated.

IIIIIII

Ever since James and Sissy's visit to North Carolina, Ashton had played "Touch" every day. One day, as Brenda passed by Ashton's bedroom door, she paused, hearing something very special. Ashton was playing "Touch" at a very low volume that day. The volume was loud enough for someone to hear the music. As Brenda began to listen, her precious little girl sent chills up and down her neck and back. Ashton began to sing "Touch." She knew every verse to the song. It was like an angel had arrived to sing.

Brenda began to partially open the shut door. She wanted to look at the angel serenading her heart and soul. The cracked-open door revealed something Brenda would cherish for the rest of her life. Ashton was sitting in a chair, clutching the old Gibson. Brenda could see the desire in her daughter's eyes that day; Ashton clearly wished that she could play the old Gibson. It was time to get Ashton set up for guitar lessons. "Touch" was ending on the record player. Brenda was about to shut the door when Ashton approached the record player and replayed "Touch"; it was if she were performing an encore performance.

Brenda rushed into the den. She began to dial the phone. She had to tell someone of the experience she'd just had.

"Hello, Sissy," she said when the phone was answered on the second ring.

"Brenda, how are you doing, darling?" Sissy said.

"Sissy, I have to tell someone, and you are the only one I know who would appreciate what I was just treated to as much as I did," Brenda said.

"Oh, what happened?" Sissy asked.

Brenda began by describing the sound of Ashton's voice.

"You will never guess what she was trying to do, Sissy. She was holding the guitar as if she were entertaining an audience. Sissy, she now knows every verse to 'Touch,' and when she sings that song, it is like an angel. It gave me chills," Brenda said.

"Brenda, when did she take lessons? I never knew she knew how to play," Sissy said.

"Sissy, that is the hardest part. I can see how much she wants to play, but she doesn't know how," Brenda said.

"Brenda, when is the next time the two of you can make it to Colorado?" Sissy asked.

"Sissy, Ashton will be out of school next week," Brenda said.

"Well, if you and Ashton can make it to Colorado, I think I know someone Ashton will love to meet. Kevin is the one who taught Garland, and I cannot think of a better person for the job. Kevin would be very touched, I am sure," Sissy said.

"We will be there next week, Sissy. I will surprise Ashton," Brenda said.

||||||||

Garland folded the piece of stationery and placed it into the envelope Chase had given him during the warden's visit.

"Chase, can you come here please?" Garland shouted.

Chase rushed to Garland's cell, thinking something was wrong.

"Is everything all right?" Chase asked.

"Fine," Garland said, adding, "Chase, can you please see that this letter gets mailed? I know every letter leaving has to be reviewed, so I did not seal the envelope."

Chase looked down at the envelope bearing a North Carolina address.

"Garland, do you have family in North Carolina?" Chase asked.

"No, Chase, it's a letter to the woman I loved and lost a long time ago. The one I told the warden about. I just wanted to tell her I am sorry," Garland said.

Chase, seeing the sense of loss filling Garland's face, promised he would mail the letter immediately.

The next morning, Garland was awakened by Chase's excitement.

"Garland, have you forgotten what today is?" Chase said.

"Well, yes, Chase. You know, the days do begin to run together when you have been here for as long as I have," Garland replied.

"Today is visitation day. I was reviewing the list of visitors, and I see that both your mother and father are coming today," Chase said.

"Chase, have you been smoking something? Visitation comes every six months, and they were here just last month," Garland replied.

Chase grinned and then laughed heartily. "No, Garland. You know that I do not smoke. This is Warden Rucker's new program."

Garland stood up, confused. There had been promises that were never fulfilled by the former warden, for whatever reason.

Later that afternoon, Chase escorted Garland into one of the visitation rooms. The rooms were divided by safety glass that separated the visitors from the inmates, and each room was equipped with a phone line so that the inmates could communicate with their visitors. Garland took his seat, awaiting his visitors. Sissy and James entered the room and sat on the opposite side of the glass from Garland. Garland placed his hand on the glass, the closest he could come to holding Sissy's hand.

"Mother, what is this new plan the warden has in place for inmate visits?" Garland asked.

"Baby, Warden Rucker has changed the visitation schedule to monthly visits," Sissy said.

Garland took a deep breath and sighed. He needed contact with his family. The more frequent the visits, the better, as far as he was concerned.

"He has also given us an extended write-to list. At first, I thought it was another promise to be broken, but, maybe, he really does want to make some changes," Garland said.

"Garland, did you add anyone to your write-to list?" Sissy asked.

Garland smiled as if his facial expression should be a sufficient answer for his mother. "Sissy Summers, you never cease to amaze me. You already know the answer to that question. As a matter of fact, after being informed of the new program, I had a letter in the mail within a few hours."

Sissy held her composure. She wanted so much to tell Garland that Brenda was coming for a visit. This was a very hard secret to keep.

A voice over the prison's public-address system announced that visitation hours were ending. Garland kissed the two fingertips on his right hand and pressed them against the glass, just opposite Sissy's hand. The visiting hours always seemed to go by very fast.

Sissy and James exited the visitation room, entering a hallway that would take them to the exit. A very large man was walking on the opposite side of the hallway that afternoon.

This is the largest man I have ever seen up close, Sissy thought as he approached her and James.

"Excuse me, folks, did the two of you exit visitation room number four?" the man asked.

James turned, confirming that room number four was the room they had been in.

"Yes, sir, we were visiting our son. We are very thankful for the warden's new visitation policy," Sissy said.

"I am glad you approve, ma'am. You know, sometimes it takes a person that has come from a situation to really understand that situation," Thad said. "My name is Thad Rucker, and I am the new warden."

"Mr. Rucker, we are James and Sissy Summers," James replied.

"You were visiting Garland Summers?" Thad asked.

"Yes, Mr. Rucker. Garland is our son," Sissy said.

"I have been reviewing Garland's records here during his stay. I was a very big fan of your son. He is a very talented man," Thad said.

"Thank you. Once again, I want to say that I am very appreciative for your involvement. Garland's very close friend is coming from North Carolina next week for a visit," Sissy said.

Thad paused, remembering the picture and story Garland held in his pocket about an attorney from North Carolina. The woman Garland said he loved and then lost because of his incarceration.

"Is that friend an attorney?" Thad asked.

In unison, James and Sissy said, "Yes."

"Garland doesn't know that she and her daughter are both coming for a visit," Sissy added.

"It was a pleasure meeting you both. If there is anything that I can help your family with, please give me a call. I must finish my rounds," Thad said and excused himself.

IIIIIIII

The morning arrived for Ashton and Brenda's trip to Colorado. All the bags were packed. Ashton rushed from the house, with a guitar case in her hand. She was very excited about seeing her grandparents and having the chance to start guitar lessons. Brenda, making sure everything was packed, returned to lock the front door. As she turned to make her way to the car, the postman handed her the daily mail. Brenda began to glance through several of the periodicals in the stack. Thinking these would help her occupy her on the plane, she tossed them into a travel bag.

They arrived at the Raleigh airport just in time for baggage check-in.

"Mom, do we have to put the guitar in check-in? Will my guitar be safe?" Ashton asked.

A nearby airline attendant sensed Ashton's concern for her guitar.

"Ma'am, you can do a carry-on and let one of the stewardesses secure your guitar inside the cabin of the aircraft," he told Brenda.

His suggestion calmed Ashton. Brenda and Ashton rushed to the departure gate and entered the plane.

"Miss, would you like me to take your guitar and place it in the pilot's closet?" the stewardess asked Ashton.

"Do you think it will be okay in there?" Ashton asked.

The stewardess smiled. "I think it will be just fine in there."

Ashton and Brenda took their seats, awaiting the takeoff.

Brenda placed her bag on the floor underneath the seat in front of her. Soon afterward, the plane began to lift into the sky. Ashton was sitting in the seat next to the window and began to plug her ears with her fingers as the plane reached its flight altitude. The stewardess came around, taking a beverage order now that the plane was at cruising speed and altitude. Brenda reached for the travel bag and removed the stack of mail delivered earlier that morning.

Brenda released the lock from the back of the seat in front of her, releasing the tray. She would be more comfortable using the tray as she started to read the mail. Today's stack was bigger than normal. She began to examine the headlines on the periodicals, searching for an article that would catch her interest. As she removed the second magazine, there was a letter facing downward. She opened the envelope, removing its contents. Brenda turned to Ashton to make sure her daughter was comfortable.

"Ma'am, I have your drink orders," the stewardess announced.

The stewardess passed Ashton her soda. Brenda placed the letter down on the tray, making sure Ashton had control of her drink.

The stewardess then passed Brenda her beverage. She placed the cup into the cup holder built into the tray. With one hand, Brenda began to unfold the letter to read it; with the other hand, she lifted the cup for a drink of refreshment. Her eyes glanced down at the writing as she continued to sip from the cup. Brenda began to read the contents of the letter. Her eyes were glancing from one side of the page to the other when, suddenly, her beverage began to spray from her mouth.

A nearby stewardess rushed to her side. "Ma'am, are you all right? Do you need any medical attention?"

The stewardess's actions startled Ashton, making her scream.

Brenda, being embarrassed by the situation, assured the steward-ess that everything was fine.

Brenda, not wanting a repeat performance, elected to try reading the letter without any liquid in her mouth this time. She couldn't be-lieve her eyes. To reassure herself, Brenda turned over the envelope to confirm what she was reading. The letter's return address was from Garland Summers in the Colorado state correctional institution. This was a letter that hit Brenda straight in the heart. Garland touched emotions within Brenda that she had not felt since the last time she was with him. It wasn't long before the tears began to flow.

"Mom, what is wrong with you? Why are you so sad?" Ashton asked.

Brenda turned to her daughter and kissed her. "I am not sad, baby, I am very, very happy. This letter is from you daddy."

As if by magic, Brenda's tears began to fill Ashton's eyes. The two held each other as they embraced the moment—a moment that was soon interrupted.

A box of tissues appeared in front of Brenda and Ashton.

"Ladies, I have brought you some tissues," the stewardess said.

Brenda thanked her.

"Ashton, I'll bet that stewardess thinks I am the worst passenger she has ever seen," Brenda said.

33

AS THE PLANE made its approach to Denver's Stapleton Airport, Ashton looked out a nearby window, for an awesome view of the Rocky Mountains. The snowcapped peaks glistened in the sunlight. Even to a youngster, this was a very majestic sight. This picturesque moment was shortened as the plane descended onto the airport's runway. Maybe it was becoming older that made Ashton see things in a different way. Soon she and Brenda would exit the plane into the welcoming arms of James and Sissy, inside the gate.

Ashton was holding on to Brenda's hand as the two entered the gate. The flight from Raleigh was witnessing a full waiting area. Ashton began to get excited, but she was not being able to find her grandparents. She just knew they would be the first sight she would enjoy as they entered through the doors into the gate area.

"Ashton! Ashton!" a voice cried.

The voice was not the expected voice they had come to love. This voice was coming from the area of the plane from which they had just departed. Brenda and Ashton stopped to see who was calling Ashton. As they turned around to locate the voice, another voice began to shout Ashton's name. Once again, the voice came from behind the two of them. This time, the shout was from a familiar voice.

"Mom, how are we hearing my name called from two different directions?" Ashton asked.

"Baby, I think we just *thought* it was coming from the plane. We now know it was coming from the crowd. That was Grandma Sissy's voice, Ashton," Brenda said.

Ashton smiled, wanting to find her grandmother. Brenda and Ashton turned toward the gate to find the owner of the familiar voice.

"Ashton! Ashton!" came the voice from the rear once again; but, this time, the voice was much closer than the time before.

Brenda and Ashton stopped in their tracks once again.

"Ashton, you have forgotten something," the voice said.

Ashton turned to see the stewardess approaching them, carrying the guitar that was safeguarded in the captain's closet during the flight.

"Oh my God, Ashton! I cannot believe we almost left your guitar!" Brenda said.

The stewardess smiled, remembering how particular Ashton had been when she boarded the plane. Ashton hugged the stewardess, thanking her, while Brenda carried the guitar. This time, when the two turned to make their final way into the gate area, there was that wonderful sight they had sought earlier.

"Grandma, I couldn't find you earlier," Ashton said.

"Earlier? Baby, what do you mean by 'earlier'?" Sissy asked.

Brenda, not wanting to worry Sissy, replied, "The walk from the plane was crowded, and Ashton's view was blocked by the crowd. She was worried she wouldn't be able to find you."

Sissy smiled as she hugged her granddaughter.

"You make me very happy," Sissy told Ashton.

James retrieved the guitar from Brenda.

"Sissy, I'll bet you never expected to see the old Gibson again so soon," James said.

"Pawpaw, enjoy it while you can. I am not leaving it behind," Ashton proclaimed.

Sissy and Brenda laughed. There was nothing as good as family to help mend the pain they were feeling.

The next morning, Brenda awakened. Not wanting to disturb her sleeping beauty, she quietly dressed, leaving the bedroom.

James and Sissy were sitting around the small breakfast table in the kitchen.

"Good morning, Brenda. Would you like some coffee or juice?" James asked.

"Coffee, please," Brenda said. "I'll get it."

"Brenda, have a seat. I will get you a cup of coffee," James said.

Brenda thanked James as she took a sip of the hot beverage.

"Sissy, yesterday morning before we left North Carolina, the postman delivered our mail. In the stack of mail was a letter from Garland. It meant so much to me that words cannot describe the feelings I had as I read the letter," Brenda said.

"Brenda, there is a new warden; he wants to make some changes. He is a very sincere man. Your letter is just one of his new programs implemented. You will also be able to write Garland," Sissy said.

Brenda fought back the tears. After ten long years, she would be able to express to Garland the love she never lost for him, not even with all that happened.

Brenda's and Sissy's conversation was interrupted that morning by the entrance of a not-quite-awake youngster. Ashton climbed into the chair with Sissy. Sissy relished the moment, not wanting it to end.

"Ashton, are you hungry, baby?" Sissy asked.

Ashton with her head resting on Sissy's shoulder began moving her head while resting it on her grandmother. From the movement of Ashton's head against her shoulder, Sissy soon determined the answer to her question.

"James, would you turn the oven on? Our granddaughter is hungry; it is time for me to get breakfast started," Sissy said as she hugged and kissed Ashton, leaving the seat entirely to her.

Shortly after the breakfast dishes were washed, dried, and put away, Sissy informed Ashton of a special trip she had arranged for Ashton's stay in Aurora.

"Ashton, we are going to take a trip to Pawpaw's work. There is someone I want you to meet," Sissy said.

Ashton dashed from the kitchen to get ready for their trip.

Sissy smiled at her granddaughter's enthusiasm.

This was going to be a fun trip, and Ashton's stay would be one she would never forget. After Ashton dressed, she dashed back into the kitchen, informing the entire house that she was now ready for her adventure.

Once again, Sissy laughed. "We will leave shortly. I will get dressed as well. Brenda, you need to do the same. This trip will be good for you as well."

As Brenda and Sissy were getting dressed, James went into the garage and started one of the cars. Without saying a word, James left the car in the driveway and came back into the house.

Brenda and Ashton were sitting on the living-room couch when Sissy entered the room.

"Grandma, I think Pawpaw has already left without us. I heard him take his car from the garage," Ashton said.

"Oh, he did, did he? Well, I have a car we can use. I think you will like it better than Pawpaw's car, baby," Sissy said.

Brenda and Ashton met Sissy at the front door. As they stepped out onto the front porch, sitting in the driveway was the most beautiful orange Camaro. Ashton began jumping up and down at the excitement of being a passenger in that car.

Ashton, the smallest of the three, climbed into the backseat of the convertible.

"Grandma, can we ride with the top down? I have never ridden in a car without a top on it," Ashton said.

Sissy laughed as she released the latches holding the top to the windshield and pressed the button, letting the top down.

"Hold on to your hats, ladies," Sissy said.

Sissy was going to enjoy the short trip to the KARO.

Ashton felt the breeze as it flowed through her long blonde hair. Brenda turned to enjoy that special moment. It was truly one of those moments that would be captured for a lifetime. The Camaro pulled into the radio station's parking lot. Sissy pulled into a parking spot next to where James stood. James opened the passenger door for Brenda and Ashton.

"Ashton, are you ready to see where Pawpaw works?" James asked.

Ashton climbed out of the car, ran to his side, and took his hand.

James escorted Ashton into the radio station's lobby and showed her the trophy case. This was Brenda's first trip to KARO as well.

"Pawpaw, there are so many trophies," Ashton said.

James began explaining the awards and their significance. As they reached the final award in the showcase, two other showcases across the room caught Ashton's eye.

"Pawpaw, are we going to look at the ones in those cases too?" Ashton asked.

James paused, looking at Sissy.

Brenda also noticed the showcase and turned to see how James would respond to Ashton.

"Ashton, I think that is a great idea," Sissy said.

Sissy escorted them to the other showcases. The first showcase contained a platinum record in recognition of record sales.

"Mom, that record has 'Touch' printed on it," Ashton said.

"Yes, baby, you are right. It does indeed have 'Touch' written on the record," Brenda said.

"Is this the same 'Touch' my daddy did?" Ashton asked.

Sissy wiped the tears from her eyes. "Yes, baby, that is your daddy's record."

Ashton walked up to the case and put her hand on the glass, as if to touch the platinum record.

"There are four things shaped like old-time record players. What are those?" Ashton asked.

"Those are the statuettes of the four Grammy Awards your daddy won that year," Sissy said.

"What is a Grammy?" Ashton asked.

"Grammys are the most prestigious award in the music industry, and your daddy won four in one night," Sissy proudly proclaimed.

The last showcase contained a set of drumsticks.

"Why are these drumsticks in there?" Ashton asked.

Sissy was about to answer Ashton when she was interrupted.

"Those were my drumsticks," a voice said.

Sissy knew the story of the drumsticks.

"Brandon, it has been too long since I last saw you," Sissy said as she rushed for a hug and kiss.

"This must be Ashton. Do you remember me?" Brandon asked.

Ashton shook her head no, but then she remembered.

"You are Skye's dad," she said.

Brandon laughed. "You have a very smart child, Brenda. I am sorry; I didn't mean to ignore you. I was just so caught up in your daughter. She looks so much like Garland."

Brenda smiled and accepted his sincere apology.

"Grandma, what is the story about the drumsticks?" Ashton asked.

"Ashton, I think the story of the drumsticks will mean more to you coming from me than Sissy," Brandon said. "A long time ago, we were in a music contest. On the night of the finals, my father, whom I had not seen since I was a small child, attended the contest. That night, he informed me that my mother was dying and wanted to see me before she died. The news affected my performance, and we lost the competition. There was a lot of pain for everyone that night, and things were said that were not meant."

Brandon's story was interrupted when Tobie and their son arrived at the radio station. After greeting them, he resumed telling Ashton his story.

"I left Colorado to be with my mother and sister until my mother died. Those drumsticks were the only thing I left behind. I was gone for a while. The other members of the band held on to them. It was their way of always having a part of me around them," Brandon said.

Tobie stood at Brandon's side.

"Tobie, it is good to see you and that handsome little boy again," Sissy said.

Sissy hugged Tobie and gave Brandon another hug too.

"Brandon, you have a wonderful family," Sissy said.

Sissy lifted the five-year-old and hugged him.

"What is your name?" Brenda asked the child. "You look like a little Brandon to me. I'll bet your name is Brandon Jr."

Brandon began to rub his hand along his son's long dark hair.

"Brenda, we call him Gar," Brandon said.

"I don't believe I have ever heard that name before," Brenda said.

Brandon smiled. "Brenda, Gar is short for Garland. His name is Garland; I named my son after my best friend."

Sissy held little Gar very tight. She didn't want anyone to see the tears in her eyes. Every time she thought of how Brandon and Tobie had named their son after Garland, it touched her heart deeply.

"Ashton, I want you to meet someone who has been your pawpaw's and my best friend for a long time. I have arranged for him to give you some guitar lessons while you are here," Sissy said.

Sissy began to gather Brenda and Ashton together when a warm arm hugged Sissy from behind.

"Sissy, is this my new pupil?" the voice behind her said.

"Ashton, this is Kevin English. He is our dearest friend," Sissy said.

"Your grandmother has told me a lot about you Ashton. She is a great judge of talent, and it will be my privilege to get you started as a musician," Kevin said.

"Grandma, is Mr. English the one who taught my daddy to play?" Ashton asked.

"Yes, baby, he taught your daddy too," Sissy said.

Ashton smiled at Kevin; it was a smile that took Kevin back many years.

"Ashton, I want to show you something that I think you will enjoy very much," Kevin said.

As the group walked through the halls of the radio station, a room appeared on the right. It was the studio broadcasting the current on-air show. Speakers mounted outside the room aired the show in progress.

"Let's continue our tour," Kevin said.

Soon the radio show was drowned out by another sound coming from a larger room.

"Where is that sound coming from, and what is that sound?" Ashton asked.

Several steps down the hall revealed their answer.

"This was our music room back in the old days," Kevin said.

Everyone's attention was directed inside the room. Their answer as to the source of the sound was then revealed.

Someone was playing on the drum set in the room. Brandon opened the door, letting everyone inside the room. A girl wearing a set of headphones was keeping time to a song inside the headset. At first, she paid little attention to her audience, but then, suddenly, as if she were performing a concert, she began to draw a sense of satisfaction. Brandon eventually caught her attention, giving her the cut sign. It was time for a break. She climbed down from the drummer's stool, rushing to meet Brandon.

"Brandon, is this Skye?" Brenda asked.

Before Brandon could answer Brenda, Skye rushed over to Ashton.

"I know who you are. You're the little girl who sang that song in Sissy's house when we sat on the floor that day," Skye said.

Although Skye was only a year older than Ashton, she was much more mature than Ashton physically. She was a very beautiful girl.

"Ashton and Skye, this room holds many memories. Music history began right here in this room," Kevin said.

Ashton began to explore the room. An item in one corner began to draw Ashton to it. A guitar stand contained an electric guitar with very vivid colors painted on its face.

"Mom, this is the prettiest guitar I have ever seen," Ashton said.

Sissy knew Brenda was not familiar with the guitar's history.

"Ashton, that is a Fender electric guitar. It was your father's too," Sissy said.

"The psychedelic design was from the sixties. Your dad loved playing it," Kevin said.

Ashton took the Fender from its stand. The Fender was much heavier than the old Gibson. She wanted to learn the electric guitar as well as the acoustic guitar. She wanted to be just like her daddy; she wanted to learn to play the instruments he had played.

Kevin continued the tour of the room. Not only was the history interesting to Ashton, but it meant a lot to Skye as well. She, too, wanted to follow in her dad's footsteps. Skye ran back to the drummer's stool and continued her practice session, driving everyone from the room.

"Ashton, tomorrow your grandma can bring you and the old Gibson to the station, and we will get started with your lessons," Kevin said.

Ashton was very thankful for the opportunity. "Thank you, Mr. English. I will try very hard to be a good pupil for you."

IIIIIIII

The next morning, Sissy said, "Brenda, you can rest in this morning. I will take Ashton to KARO to start her lessons with Kevin. I have a few errands I need to run."

Brenda, although she felt a little guilty, knew the rest would be welcome. It would also give Sissy and Ashton some time together alone. Brenda could only imagine the questions Ashton would have for Sissy.

Sissy and Ashton arrived at the station. Ashton wanted to carry the Gibson by herself, and she did.

Kevin met the two of them at the door.

"She is all yours for the day, Kevin," Sissy said with a wink. "You will not be able to keep her, though. She is mine."

Kevin grinned as he put his hand on Ashton's shoulder, telling her they would get started in a few minutes.

Sissy smiled and chuckled, saying goodbye to Ashton and then heading toward James's office.

"James, I need to make a phone call," Sissy said as she entered his office.

Sissy retrieved a card from her purse and began to dial the phone number on the card.

"Hello, this is Sissy Summers. May I please speak with Mr. Rucker?" Sissy said.

"One moment. Let me see if Mr. Rucker is available," Rosemary said.

Sissy waited, and soon a deep voice spoke on the other end of the line.

"Why, good morning, Mrs. Summers. Is there something I can help you with?" Thad said.

Sissy began to tell the warden about Brenda and Ashton being in town.

"Mrs. Summers, are they the ones in the magazine picture Garland has kept in his shirt pocket?" Thad asked.

"I am not sure, Mr. Rucker. I have never seen the picture you are referring to. They are from North Carolina. Garland is the father of Brenda's daughter, Ashton," Sissy said.

Thad recalled the details of the incident the day he met Garland. The woman and little girl in that picture were the same ones now visiting with the Summerses.

"Mr. Rucker, I know Garland's visiting day occurred earlier in the week. I was hoping you would grant another visit for Brenda and me to see Garland. My husband and I are willing to give up next month's visit in order to have this opportunity," Sissy said.

"Mrs. Summers, your family is one I especially want to help. I will grant you the favor, on one condition," Thad said.

"Anything, sir. Anything. Please just tell me what we need to do," Sissy said.

"Mrs. Summers, just make sure you and your husband are available to see your son next month, as usual," Thad said.

Sissy thanked Mr. Rucker.

"My secretary will phone you with the day and time for the visit," Thad said.

They said their goodbyes and ended the call.

"James, Mr. Rucker is a very good man. I told you that the day we met him," Sissy said as she filled James in on the details.

After kissing her husband goodbye, Sissy departed to run her errands for the day.

As Sissy left the radio station, Kevin and Ashton began Ashton's first lesson.

"Ashton, I want you to hold the old Gibson as if she were your best friend. You do right by her, and she will do right by you. You need to be a team," Kevin instructed.

Ashton nodded as she cradled the Gibson.

"We will start with you learning three chords today. These are the most-popular chords," Kevin said.

Ashton placed her fingers on the strings and frets of the guitar's neck.

After adjusting Ashton's fingers to make several chord changes, Kevin reached into his pocket, retrieving a guitar pick.

"Ashton, the pick will make your notes more precise, and the chord changes will be much easier on your fingers," Kevin said.

After an hour of practice, Kevin wanted to give his new pupil a well-deserved break.

"I will be back in fifteen minutes, Ashton. We will perform your first song on the guitar when we resume," Kevin said.

"My first song?" Ashton asked.

"Yes. It will be a simple three-chord song. You will be able to make the chord changes and hear the notes you are playing," Kevin said.

As Kevin exited, Skye entered the room, taking a seat next to Ashton.

"Ashton, everyone says you have a heavenly voice. I remember you singing that day, like I said. I would love to hear you sing again sometime," Skye said.

"You know, Skye, it would really be something if you and I continued where our dads left off, wouldn't it?" Ashton said.

Skye loved music, but she had never really thought about performing with a group. The idea appealed to her. She smiled at Ashton.

"Skye, if I give you my phone number and address, will you call me and write to me? Will you be my friend?" Ashton asked.

The thought touched Skye. She had very few friends. Skye's heritage was not an asset when it came to making friends in Colorado. She knew Ashton couldn't care less about her Native American background.

The two girls exchanged phone numbers and addresses. A very special bond was formed that day—one that would make music history.

Kevin returned, informing Skye that she could have her practice session in an hour. Much to Kevin's surprise, Skye hugged Ashton before leaving the room.

"Did you have a nice visit with Skye during your break, Ashton?" Kevin asked.

"Yes, Mr. English. Skye and I have decided that we want to be friends forever," Ashton said.

"That's wonderful, Ashton. Skye could really use a very genuine friend," Kevin said.

Kevin placed the old Gibson in his hand and began to show the chord changes for Ashton's first song. He counted off the notes as he played the song, making each chord change at the appropriate time.

Ashton watched very closely.

"Ashton, now it's your turn. Give it a try," Kevin said.

Ashton placed the guitar in her lap and began to pick the chords as Kevin instructed. After counting out the notes and making the chord changes, Ashton recognized the song she was now playing. "Row, Row Your Boat" was a song she'd frequently sung in kindergarten. She smiled at Kevin, and he grinned back.

|||||||

Brenda was preparing the evening meal when Ashton and Sissy arrived home from the station.

Ashton greeted Brenda with a hug and a very big smile. This had been a very busy and exciting day for the youngster.

"Ashton, what is this piece of paper you have?" Brenda asked.

"Mom, can you keep it for me? It has Skye's phone number and address. Do you mind if we call her sometimes and if I write to her?" Ashton asked.

"Baby, that would be wonderful. I think you may have found a very good friend," Brenda said.

"Yes, Mom. Skye and I have decided to become forever friends," Ashton said as she left the kitchen, heading for the guest room.

Ashton's quietness concerned Brenda. The table was set, and dinner would be served shortly. Brenda peeked into the bedroom, looking for her daughter. There was no sign of Ashton on the bed. She began to walk around the bed to see Ashton lying on the floor next to the bed. Ashton had fallen asleep with another piece of paper in her hand and several colored markers on the floor. Brenda placed the caps on the pens.

"Ashton, it is time to wash up for dinner," Brenda said, gently stroking her daughter's shoulder to rouse her from her nap.

Ashton began to sit up on the floor.

"Baby, what do you have in your hand now?" Brenda asked.

Ashton gave the paper to her mother. "Mom, it's a picture of the guitar we saw yesterday. I want to give it to my dad someday."

Brenda looked at the drawing, recognizing the designs they had seen on the electric guitar. This was the Fender with the psychedelic designs.

||||||||

Each day at the station brought a new adventure for Ashton. She was getting an education in music and also discovering how talented Garland's family and friends were. Ashton and Skye remained inside the music studio during the breaks Kevin gave Ashton. Sometimes the girls talked about the future each one wanted, and sometimes they tried to play together. Both girls were becoming more talented with each passing day.

One afternoon, Kevin returned from his break. As he approached the entrance to the music studio, he paused to listen in on the activity inside the room. Ashton was playing the Gibson as if she were playing a flat guitar. She used her right hand to play the chords, while she placed the fingers of her left hand on the strings up and down the frets of the guitar's neck. The speed at which Ashton began to change chords was miraculous for someone who had just begun to play two days earlier.

What song is she playing? Kevin wondered as he continued to observe his pupil.

The answer to his own question dawned on Kevin after he listened for another few seconds. Although it was a little off key, the song was recognizable to anyone who knew it. Ashton was attempting, after just two days of guitar lessons, to play "Touch." There was something special about this little girl.

Kevin was about to enter the room when a hand reached from behind him and began to close the door.

"Dad, let's listen a little longer," Kevin heard his son's voice say.

"Adam, I had no idea you were in town," Kevin said as he turned around and hugged his son. "Let me introduce you to someone, Adam. I think you will be shocked when you meet her."

Adam and Kevin walked into the room, and each took a nearby seat. Ashton wasn't aware they were in the room as she continued to play.

Ashton began to play the final chords of the song. There was still a very long way to go before she would have the entire song down. Her finale was interrupted by the two men sitting on the stools behind her.

"Ashton, please take a break. I want you to meet someone," Kevin said.

Ashton left her seat and walking to the stool Kevin occupied.

"Ashton, this is my son, Adam," Kevin said.

"I am glad to—" Adam began, and then his greeting stopped as he did a double take at the sight of the face of the girl whose guitar playing had mesmerized him earlier.

After a few seconds, Adam said, "I am pleased to meet you, Ashton."

Like Brandon, Adam was shocked by Ashton's resemblance to Garland.

"Ashton, forgive me. Seeing you took me back so many years. It is almost like I am seeing double," Adam said.

Ashton smiled and then laughed.

"Adam, since I have been here, I have heard several people making the same comment. I guess my daddy marked me very well," Ashton said.

Both Adam and Kevin laughed at Ashton's reply.

The laughter suddenly quieted when Adam and Kevin heard what Ashton said next: "I hope, one day, I will get a chance to meet my dad."

||||||||

The next morning, Sissy entered the guest room. She began to shake Brenda lightly, trying to rouse her from sleep. Brenda slowly began to open her eyes, raising her head from the comfortable pillow.

"Brenda, come into the kitchen. I have a surprise for you today," Sissy whispered.

Sissy helped Brenda with her housecoat as they left the room.

The two walked to the kitchen and sat down at the table.

"Brenda, after we drop Ashton off at the station, I want you to take a trip with me. I have planned something very special for you today," Sissy said.

Brenda wondered what this special occasion might be.

After they left Ashton with Kevin, Sissy pulled out of the KARO parking lot.

"Brenda, our trip this morning will take us about an hour. You can enjoy the scenery as we make our way," Sissy said.

Brenda agreed the scenery was magnificent. Denver was a very beautiful town.

"Sissy, I see what you like about this part of Colorado. For a big city, Denver is very clean and beautiful," Brenda said.

They approached their destination, entering a very large building complex.

"Sissy, is this the Colorado state correctional facility?" Brenda asked.

"Yes, Brenda, it is indeed," Sissy said.

At first, Brenda thought that the purpose of the trip was for Sissy to show Brenda where Garland was being kept. She realized that was not the case when Sissy pulled into the visitors' parking area.

"Sissy, why are we stopping?" Brenda asked.

Without saying word, Sissy parked the car in a visitor's space. When Sissy stopped the car's motor and opened the door, Brenda knew there was a specific reason for their trip, but she would have to wait to see what that reason. Brenda exited the car and linked her arm through Sissy's. The long walk down the spruce-lined sidewalk led to a door.

The sign on the door read, "All visitors must report to the guard station."

Sissy opened the door leading into the guard station.

Brenda froze at the thought of entering.

"Sissy, as much as I need and want to do this, I am not sure I can," Brenda said.

Sissy took Brenda by the hand. "Brenda, everything will be okay. I initially had the same thoughts you are having now."

Brenda squeezed Sissy's hand, and the two continued toward the guard station.

||||||||

Chase arrived at Garland's cell. "Garland, Warden Rucker wants me to take you to see him immediately."

Garland obliged Chase, as he always did, and prepared to walk to the warden's office. After passing through the guard station, Chase escorted Garland in the opposite direction from that of the warden's office.

"Chase, I thought you said we were going to the warden's office," Garland said.

Chase ignored Garland's comment and continued to lead him in the opposite direction.

"Chase, why are we going to the visitation rooms?" Garland asked.

"Garland, I have no idea. I am just following my orders, "Chase said.

Chase escorted Garland to the inmates' side of the visitation area.

Garland took his usual seat, awaiting the arrival of his visitor. He knew it was too soon for Sissy and James's monthly visit. Several minutes passed by, and there was no sign of a visitor. This was not the norm. Visitors always awaited the inmates' arrival, not the other way around.

The minutes crept by, seeming like hours. Garland began to hold the phone receiver in his hand, wishing there was someone on the other end. Perhaps if he would press his head against the glass, he could imagine a voice coming through the phone. With the phone receiver held up to his right ear, Garland did just that, resting his forehead against the glass, closing his eyes and trying to envision a visitor.

This started to work. Garland began to envision a visitor entering the room and taking a seat across from him on the opposite side of the glass. His face glowed with the idea, and a smile spread from ear to ear. Slowly the door on the visitors' side began to open. Sissy led the way into the room, arriving at the two visitor chairs. Garland wasn't aware the two seats were occupied. Sissy lifted her headset and began to whisper into the mouthpiece. Her words crept into Garland's vision, while his eyes were still closed, making him think that his dream was real.

"How have you been, baby?" Sissy whispered into the phone.

Garland's smile grew even larger. "Mother, it is good to be home."

"Garland, I wished you were home," Sissy replied.

Garland opened his eyes immediately. This was too real to be just a dream.

"Garland, I am not a dream. I am here today," Sissy said.

Garland's heart suddenly began to pound inside his chest. The beat was as fast as it was strong.

"Brenda, is that you?" Garland asked.

Brenda began to cry. She desperately tried to answer Garland, but the words wouldn't come out of her mouth. Brenda suddenly placed her hand against the glass, as if inviting Garland's hand to meet hers. Oh, how she wished their fingers could be intertwined—one hand and one heart.

Garland took a deep breath. His mother had spoken the truth: this wasn't a dream. His first response was to try to wipe the tears from each of her cheeks.

Brenda's tears intensified in response to his tenderness. Once again, she tried to respond to Garland, but the words wouldn't come. As her tears continued, she began to slap the window with her hand.

Garland began to trace Brenda's fingers with his own fingertips from the other side of the glass.

Once again, Garland's loving tenderness deeply touched Brenda.

"Brenda, you look as beautiful as you did the last time I saw you," Garland said.

Garland's hand rested against the glass, with his fingers spread apart, as if trying to join their two hands. As he began to once again trace Brenda's left hand, he suddenly paused. There was no sign of a wedding band on her left ring finger.

"Garland, I have missed you so much. You have no idea how much," Brenda said.

"Brenda, I have thought about you every day for the past ten years. Every time I look at your picture, I am reminded of what I have lost. Your husband is a very lucky man to have both you and a precious daughter, "Garland said.

"Garland, what makes you think that I am married and that I have a daughter?" Brenda asked.

"I have seen her," Garland replied.

Garland placed the phone receiver on the ledge at the bottom of the glass. With his free hand, Garland began to retrieve a folded piece of paper from inside the pocket of his shirt. Garland's shaking hands made it difficult to unfold the badly worn creases. Eventually, the picture was completely unfolded. Garland placed the picture against the window for Brenda to see. The creases of the folding were so worn that holes had formed, fading the once-pristine picture.

"Garland, that picture was taken five years ago. You have had this picture that long?" Brenda asked.

"Yes, and there isn't a day that goes by that I do not look at it several times a day, wishing I was the man you married. He is the luckiest man on earth to have you and your daughter. I have almost worn out this picture by all the times I've looked at it," Garland said.

Brenda then placed the phone receiver down on the ledge on her side.

Garland paused, thinking something he said had upset Brenda. That was the last thing he ever wanted to do.

Brenda rose from her seat and left the room.

"Mother, please tell her I am sorry and ask her to come back inside," Garland said.

Sissy stood and went to the door, returning to her seat in a few moments.

"It's okay, baby. Just wait," Sissy told Garland.

Brenda's and Sissy's purses were checked at the guard station. Those items were not allowed into the visitation room.

Brenda reentered the visitors' side of the room and returned to her seat. She was holding a piece of paper wrapped in tissue paper. Brenda sat down and began to unwrap the item.

"Garland, I have something I want you to see," she said.

Brenda removed a picture from the tissue and placed it against the glass.

Garland instantly went into a trance, savoring the wonderful sight.

"Brenda, is this your daughter? She is growing into a beautiful young girl," Garland said.

"Yes, Garland, this is my daughter, Ashton. She is so much like her father. She has his talent and passion, a passion that I have only seen once in my life. I want you to have this picture," Brenda said.

Garland placed his hand against the glass, trying to touch Ashton's cheeks in the photo.

The emotion overcame Sissy at that moment.

"Mother, why are you crying?" Garland asked.

It seemed there was a voice-stealing spirit in the room that day. Just as Brenda had experienced earlier, Sissy couldn't find the words to say.

"Garland, I think I know why your mother is crying. Those are not tears of sorrow; they are tears of joy," Brenda said.

"Brenda, you said your daughter is like her father and has his passion. What kind of passion does she have?" Garland asked.

"She has his passion for music, and she cannot wait to meet him one day to enjoy the passion share," Brenda said.

"Meet him one day? What do you mean?" Garland asked.

"Garland, Ashton is your daughter," Brenda said.

Brenda's answer was more than Sissy could endure. Her tears flowed in a river.

"Ashton is so much like you, Garland," Brenda said. "She found the copy of 'Touch' that you sent me when it was released, and she took to music from that day. Garland, she knows every word to that song. Even though she has never met you, she loves you very much."

For the first time in more than ten years, Garland wanted to perform again. This was the best day of his life.

"Brenda, you are the love of my life. You always have been. Sometimes it takes a person a lifetime to realize that, but I already know it. With the warden's new program, I will write to Ashton. I want to be a part of her life. I know I cannot offer her anything, but please tell her I love her," Garland said.

Finally able to speak, Sissy said, "Baby, you have given Ashton much more than you know. She is so talented, and that talent emerged the day she found out about you."

A red light above the visitation-room door signaled that the visitation period was over.

"Ladies, you will need to say your goodbyes. When I return, it will be time to leave," Chase said.

Sissy and Brenda touched the glass with their hands.

"I love you both. I now have three special girls in my life," Garland said.

Chase reentered the room.

"Will you please see to it that Garland receives this picture?" Brenda asked Chase.

"May I look at the picture?" Chase asked.

Sissy knew Chase from her and James's previous visitations. He was a good man and a friend to Garland.

"Yes, Chase, you may see it. It is a current picture of Garland's daughter," Sissy said.

"This is the little girl in the magazine picture Garland has cherished for five years. His dream came true today," Chase said.

"What dream is that, Chase?" Brenda asked.

"He is a daddy. That is the special feeling he has wanted ever since the day I met him ten years ago," Chase said.

34

THE FISHERS' PHONE began to ring early one morning. Ashton, nearest to the phone in the den, answered its beckoning ring.

"Happy birthday to you, happy birthday, dear Ashton," Sissy sang when her granddaughter answered.

Ashton's smile indicated she was delighted.

"Thanks, Grandma, for the song and the birthday present," Ashton said.

Ashton was still smiling when Brenda entered the room to see who had called.

"I wanted to wish my sixteen-year-old a happy birthday," Sissy said.

"I am taking my driver's test this morning before I go to school," Ashton said.

"You know, Ashton, it seems like only yesterday that you were born," Sissy said.

"Grandma, I want to thank you and Pawpaw for the airline tickets. I cannot wait to use them," Ashton said.

"You're welcome, baby," Sissy said, adding, "I want to ask a favor of your mother. Is she nearby?"

Ashton turned to summon her mother to the phone.

Brenda's nearby ear was the recipient of a loud "Mom! Grandma Sissy is on the phone for you!"

"Hello, Sissy. How are you?" Brenda said.

"Hey, baby, I am doing fine. I want to ask you for a favor, Brenda. I would love for Ashton to come to Colorado and spend the summer with us, but only if she wants to," Sissy said.

Brenda paused, turning to her daughter.

"Do you think you and James could put up with her all summer long, Sissy?" Brenda asked.

Ashton's mouth opened wide in shock. Brenda didn't have to relay the question to her daughter.

"Grandma, I want that very much!" Ashton said loudly, as if she were trying to talk to Sissy in Colorado without a long-distance line on the phone.

"I think you heard how excited she is about the idea," Brenda said, laughing.

Brenda ended the call with Sissy just in time. Her anxious sixteen-year-old was dressed and ready for her big test.

"Mom, can I drive to the office to get my license?" Ashton asked.

Brenda answered her daughter by giving her the keys to the car, Brenda's new Tornado.

"You need to be extra careful driving my new car, baby. You haven't driven it much. Maybe we should take Pawpaw's car for you to drive to take your test," Brenda said.

"You want me to take my driver's test in a station wagon?" Ashton said.

Brenda laughed. She couldn't resist the look she received from Ashton. Brenda's dad didn't look like he felt any better about Ashton taking his car to the test than Ashton did.

Brenda's black Tornado pulled into the crowded parking lot of the Department of Motor Vehicles.

"Ashton, after you have taken your written exam—and if you pass that exam—we can proceed to your actual driving test," Brenda said.

"Mom, there is no *if* about me passing my written test," Ashton replied. "The driving part, however, may be a different story."

With much nervousness, Ashton began the written test. The first five questions covered topics she knew quite well. Ashton paused for a moment, looking up from the test to locate her mother, who sat in the room opposite the test area. The two rooms were divided by a glass partition. At the exact same moment, Brenda took a break from the magazine she had brought along to read to pass the time while waiting for Ashton. Their eyes met, and Ashton smiled at Brenda, giving her the thumbs-up sign. This test was going to be a snap.

Ashton turned in her finished written exam and waited for her grade. The test was fed into a machine. In a matter of seconds, the machine would score the answers to the exam's multiple-choice questions. The clerk guided the test into the machine. Seconds later, the test exited the other end of the machine, complete with Ashton's test results.

"Congratulations, young lady. Your score is a perfect 100," the clerk said as he returned Ashton's test to her.

Brenda stood at the doorway, anxiously awaiting the results. Ashton approached her mother, wearing a very large frown on her face. Brenda took a deep breath. She had prepared herself for Ashton's possible disappointment.

"Baby, we can come back tomorrow for another try," Brenda said as she hugged her daughter.

As she returned her mother's hug, Ashton slowly slipped the test into her mother's empty hand.

Once again, Brenda took a deep breath, trying to gather the courage to look at the test results. Brenda turned the test over to reveal the grade. Her eyes focused at the top of the page.

"Ashton! I am going to ring your neck, young lady. You scared the hell out of me," Brenda said.

"I got you, Brenda Fisher," Ashton said with a big laugh, loving the trick she had pulled off.

"Well, let's see how well you do driving Pawpaw's station wagon," Brenda retorted.

"Mom, that wasn't funny the first time you said it," Ashton said.

To Brenda, the thought of Ashton driving a station wagon for her test was very funny.

The more Ashton tried to stop her mom's laughter, the more Brenda laughed.

"Okay, Mom, you got me back. Can we please head over to the driving part of the test?" Ashton begged.

Brenda, still trying to stop her laughter, nodded yes to her daughter's request, and they headed toward the driving part of the exam.

Much to Brenda's surprise, Ashton passed the driving part of her exam with flying colors.

"Mother, may I be your chauffeur this morning?" Ashton asked as she led her mother to the passenger side of the car, opening the door.

"To school, Ashton, to school," Brenda instructed her sixteen-year-old chauffeur.

"Yes, ma'am, it will be my pleasure, but we are taking the scenic route," Ashton replied.

She wanted to arrive in time for lunch, showing off her newfound status as a driver to anyone in the school's courtyard.

||||||||

Garland glanced at a nearby clock in the prison cafeteria. He knew from some of Ashton's letters that today was the biggest day of her sixteen years. Colorado time was two hours behind that of the East Coast, and he had no doubt his little girl was going for the biggest achievement of her young life. Obtaining a driver's license was a milestone in the life of both parent and child. Once again, he had been robbed of one of life's special pleasures. How many more times would pain and suffering remind him of his loss? At times like this, Garland drew strength from the picture of his little girl, which he always kept in his shirt pocket.

||||||||

The days leading up to Ashton's summer trip to Colorado went by as quick as a breath on a cold glass of water. Ashton was so excited that her bags were packed days before the big day arrived. This would be her first trip away from home on her own, a trip that had her both excited and unsure.

As Ashton entered the plane that morning, a familiar face greeted her.

"Well, hello, Ashton. It is good to see you again," the voice the face belonged to said.

Ashton smiled and replied, "It is good to see you again too. I can't believe you remember me."

The stewardess's smile comforted Ashton.

"I see you have your familiar friend with you for this trip. I will be glad to secure your guitar in the customary place," the stewardess said.

"Thank you very much. This time, I promise you will not have to hunt me down inside the terminal to retrieve her," Ashton said with a laugh.

Ashton took her seat and fastened her seat belt. As she began to get comfortable, another stewardess came by to take the customary refreshment order and offer several periodicals. Ashton gladly accepted a stack of current magazines to read. Reading would help pass the time. Ashton began to thumb through her selections until she came across one particular cover that touched her. It was a picture of Aurora's Fire. Inside was a feature covering the story of the group since the downfall of its superstar. This was a chance for Ashton to discover just how big a star Garland and Aurora's Fire had once been.

Turning pages until she got to the featured article, she saw several pictures of the group from 1971, followed by updated pictures. Ashton began to compare the then and now photos of each band member. She began to laugh aloud as she read the caption below one of the seventies pictures. She could feel just how special Brandon was. It was obvious who had kept the group loose. She turned to the current picture of Brandon. As handsome as Brandon was as a young man, he was even handsomer now. The years had been kind to him.

Ashton wasn't familiar with some of the band members; she only knew the members who had been in Summer's Solstice. The years hadn't been nearly as kind to Adam, Beau, and Harley as they had been to Brandon. Ashton paused after turning the page. As she began to read the article, her emotions overwhelmed her. A picture of Garland appeared. This was the first picture she had seen of her dad during this time, and there was look on his face that indicated just how special these times had been to him. She knew how happy his music had made him; this was something she, too, possessed.

Below Garland's picture was a picture of a red Lincoln. A feeling of pain and anger began to fill her heart as she read about the car. Deep inside, she felt there was something about what happened to her father that just wasn't right; he didn't deserve what had happened to him. At that moment, Ashton decided that the purpose of this trip was to meet Garland. She dedicated herself to fulfilling that purpose. It was time to fill the emptiness in her heart from not having a dad. The distinct feeling that something needed to be done about her father's case persisted. After all, Ashton was not just the daughter of a very talented musician; she was also the daughter of a very smart and talented lawyer.

||||||||

Some things in this world just cannot be explained. This was one of those occasions. Just as Ashton was reading the article while flying in the skies over Tennessee, Garland was reading the same article in his cell in Colorado. It was good to learn about what the guys were doing these days and where they were.

"Garland, here is your mail," Chase said as he looked in on his friend.

"Send it to me airmail," Garland said.

"You bet, Garland," Chase said as he flipped the letter toward Garland.

With the instincts of an infielder, Garland snatched the letter in its flight.

Garland glanced at the opened envelope and began to remove the contents. Inside was a letter from Ashton. The letter informed Garland that his sixteen-year-old daughter was coming to spend the summer with Sissy and James.

The letter read, "Dad, I am coming to spend the summer with

Grandma and Pawpaw. I am bringing your old Gibson too. The last time I was in Colorado, Kevin gave me lessons."

Garland smiled at the thought of Kevin teaching his daughter and using the same guitar that Garland had loved so much. He had no idea of the talent his daughter possessed, a talent instilled within her from Garland himself, and now a passion for music from that same source.

||||||||

The literature Ashton devoured made the trip go by very fast. Although the article wasn't that long, the mental images she composed as she read it captivated her. It was almost as if she had lived those moments with Garland; the mental images were intense and seemed real.

The stewardess came by, informing the passengers that the captain was about to make the final approach into Denver.

Ashton placed her tray in the upright position. She returned the magazines into the pocket on the seat in front of her, minus one—that one magazine she snuck into her purse. Ashton placed her purse in her lap as she looked out the window. The same view that had mesmerized Ashton the first time she saw it did so just as much this time.

The plane stopped at its gate, and the stewardess instructed the passengers that it was okay to depart the plane. As Ashton approached the exit, the stewardess stood in a hallway entering the cockpit of the plane.

"Ashton, here is your guitar. It was very good to see you, and it, again," she said with a smile.

Ashton hugged the stewardess, thanking her for her caring.

Ashton entered the gate area, looking for a familiar face.

"Ashton, here we are!" a voice called.

Ashton paused to locate the voice's owner. Standing there was someone Ashton thought she was imagining.

"Skye, is that you? Excuse me. My eyes are playing tricks on me," Ashton said.

"Playing tricks on you? Are you all right?" Skye said.

"Oh yes. I just read an article about Aurora's Fire. There was a picture of your dad when he was younger. I can't believe how much you look like him," Ashton said.

"Ashton, that is nice of you to say. I take that as a compliment. I know my dad was handsome back then," Skye said with a smile and a big hug for her friend.

"We are going to have a wonderful summer together. We have so much to talk about," Skye said.

"I have dreamed about this trip ever since my grandma invited me," Ashton said.

As Skye and Ashton began to separate from their hug, a young and very beautiful girl approached them, seeming to enjoy the affection the two had for each other.

"Ashton, I want you to meet a friend of mine. This is Brooklyn. Her uncle is a friend of your dad's," Skye said.

"Skye has told me so much about you, Ashton. My uncle is very fond of your dad," Brooklyn said.

"Thanks, Brooklyn. If you are a friend of Skye's, I know you are truly a wonderful person. She is a very good judge of people," Ashton said.

The three girls continued their chat as they made their way out of the terminal.

It was during the drive to Sissy and James's house that day that another friendship began. Brooklyn and Ashton found that they shared a common interest. Brooklyn, too, loved Garland's music, and she knew more about it than anyone Ashton had encountered.

"My sister was a very big fan of your dad. She has all of his records and many pictures of him and the band," Brooklyn said.

Ashton glowed with each of Brooklyn's stories. "Ashton, Brooklyn not only loves music, but she is also a musician. Maybe we can all meet during the summer at the old studio at KARO," Skye said.

"That would be awesome, Skye. Maybe we can get Kevin to listen in and give us some advice," Ashton said.

The excitement made the trip seem like just a jaunt.

Skye pulled into the Summerses' driveway. Something was different that day.

"I don't understand," Skye said.

"What do you mean, Skye?" Ashton asked.

"Sissy has always come out on the porch every time I have driven up. This is not normal," she said.

Skye's concern upset Ashton. She ran quickly onto the porch and into the house.

"Grandma? Grandma? Where are you?" Ashton shouted as she ran from room to room.

Each time Ashton called for Sissy, there was no answer.

By this time, Skye and Brooklyn had entered the house. They joined the search.

Ashton, exhausted from her emotions, fell onto the couch.

Both Skye and Brooklyn rushed to her aid.

"I can't find her anywhere," Ashton said as she broke down.

Her tears made it difficult for Skye and Brooklyn to understand her. Skye rushed into the kitchen to get Ashton a glass of water.

These emotions were new to Ashton.

As Skye was departing the kitchen, carrying the glass of water, the phone began to ring. The ring startled her. Without hesitating, Skye answered the phone. Maybe it would be a clue as to Sissy's whereabouts.

"Hello. Who is this?" the voice on the other end said.

"This is Skye. Who is it you are trying to reach?"

"Skye, this is Brenda Fisher. I'm calling to check in with my daughter to make sure she made it safely to Sissy and James's house."

"Brenda, I picked Ashton up at the airport and drove her here," Skye replied.

Ashton, hearing Skye's end of the conversation, entered the kitchen, requesting the phone from Skye.

"Mother!" Ashton cried.

From the tone of her daughter's voice, Brenda sensed that something was wrong.

"Ashton, are you all right? Is there something wrong?" Brenda asked.

"Grandma Sissy is not here. We have searched the house, and she isn't here," Ashton said.

Ashton's fear began to scare Brenda as well.

The frantic afternoon ended as James pulled into the driveway. He was immediately swarmed by three very concerned girls.

"Pawpaw, where is Grandma Sissy? She isn't anywhere to be found!" Ashton screamed.

"Baby, everything is all right. Your grandmother is visiting your father today. A national news channel is doing a story about Garland, and they wanted to interview Sissy as well," James said.

That afternoon, Ashton found comfort not only in James's answer but in his strong arms as well.

"The news channel will air the program in the fall, to kick off their new season. I think you will be very proud of your daddy when you get to see the show, baby," James said.

The first day of Ashton's summer-long visit began with much excitement and anticipation. For the first time in her life, she got a taste of being in the public eye of fame.

Sissy arrived shortly afterward, with hugs all around, and filled her husband and visitors in on the big event.

"Ashton, tomorrow, Kevin is expecting you at KARO. He has some new ideas as well as some surprises that I think you will enjoy," Sissy said.

Ashton smiled at the thought of furthering her musical interests with Kevin. She enjoyed both his enthusiasm and his knowledge very much.

||||||||

Ashton arrived at KARO much earlier than the time Kevin had scheduled. She pulled the orange Camaro into the parking lot, just minutes ahead of Kevin.

"Hey, girl! You are getting more beautiful every time I see you," Kevin said with a hug and a kiss.

"Kevin, I have missed our sessions very much. I never knew how much music meant to me until I was away from Aurora," Ashton said.

Kevin smiled and led Ashton into the radio station.

"Ashton, you can go to the music studio, and I will join you there after I check my messages," Kevin said.

Ashton made her way toward the studio.

As she turned to pick up her guitar, her grasp was interrupted by a hand picking up the guitar's case.

"Here, let me help you with that," a voice said.

Ashton turned to discover whose voice and hand she had come upon this morning. She tried to reply to the voice but was taken by the handsomest young man she had ever seen.

"Are you Ashton?" he asked.

Ashton nodded. It was the only response she could manage.

A gentle smile and laugh took her breath away.

"My name is Cory Baker. I am an intern at the station this summer. I attend the university in Boulder."

"It is very nice to meet you, Cory," Ashton said, finally finding her voice.

As Cory opened the studio's door, Skye and Brooklyn made their way into the studio as well. Both girls paused to see the glow on Ashton's face and the sparkle in her eyes.

"Hey, Cory. I see you have met Ashton," Skye said with a laugh.

Ashton turned toward Skye to give her approval of the view she was experiencing.

Cory excused himself as the girls began to pick up their instruments.

"Ashton, I am looking forward to practicing with you. Skye has told me so much about the times you guys played together," Brooklyn said.

Skye began to perform a few drumrolls and the introduction to the song she and Ashton had last practiced, hoping it would create a magical moment. Brooklyn, recognizing the beat, began to play a few chords on the keyboard. Then, just as suddenly as Skye began, she paused. Ashton was not in tune with the moment. Skye and Brooklyn turned to each other and smiled, shaking their heads in disbelief.

"Ashton, when you come down off of your cloud, we would like you to join us," Skye said.

"I thought you girls wanted to practice," Kevin said as he entered the studio.

"We would love to, but Ashton is in la-la land," Brooklyn said.

Kevin walked over to Ashton.

"Ashton, what kind of music do they have in la-la land?" Kevin said with a very large smile.

His remarks brought a loud roar of laughter from the two other girls.

Without any further hesitation, Ashton began to play the song that followed Skye's intro.

Kevin took a seat in the room. He wanted to see where these girls were with their talent. Soon Skye's beat and Brooklyn's notes were accompanied by an incredible sound. Kevin, sitting on the stool, with his right hand on his chin, was blown away. This was truly a magical moment.

Ashton began to sing an angelic melody, suddenly overwhelming Kevin. As the girls' first number came to a close, Kevin excused himself from the room, saying, "I have to make very important phone call, girls. I will be right back."

Kevin's departure surprised the girls. They wondered if they had performed badly.

Skye and Brooklyn began to tease Ashton about her lost moment in la-la land.

"I think I was in heaven a moment ago, and I saw an angel," Ashton said.

Both Skye and Brooklyn laughed aloud.

"Let's see. I'll bet this angel's name was Cory? Right?" Skye teased.

Ashton blushed at Skye's remarks. She couldn't hide the feeling she was enjoying, and she didn't want to.

Kevin soon reentered the room.

"Girls, I have someone coming over I want you to meet. If you can create the same moment for him that you did for me a while ago, this could be a very special day. I want you to replay 'Touch' from the beginning," Kevin said.

The girls began to play as Kevin returned to his perch on the stool. As the girls began "Touch," Kevin leaned over the console and turned the recorder on. This time, the magical moment wasn't going to be lost. Midway through the song, Kevin made another discovery: Brooklyn and Ashton's two-part harmony sent chills up his spine.

Kevin sprang from his seat to interrupt the song.

"Girls, stop!" he shouted.

Once again, the girls stopped, thinking something wasn't going very well.

Kevin began to walk through the song, explaining what he wanted from them.

"Brooklyn, I want you to sing along with Ashton on the chorus lines," Kevin directed.

Brooklyn, shocked by Kevin's request, smiled and nodded.

"Okay, let's do it again now," Kevin said.

He once again turned the recorder on as the girls began their song. And then, once again, he interrupted the song.

"Skye, I want you to pick up the tempo a little as Ashton and Brooklyn sing the chorus lines," Kevin said.

Skye wiped her hands on a towel and promptly agreed.

Kevin began to count off the start for the girls. On his signal, the girls began to play. The song was even better. Kevin couldn't believe his ears. These girls, in just three takes, were perfect with their sound. This time, Kevin captured the entire number on the recorder. This was something very, very special.

"Girls, I want you come over here and listen to something," Kevin said.

The girls had no idea that Kevin had captured their performance on tape.

Kevin began the playback. The girls took a break. As the song began, a man stopped in the doorway. It was soon obvious that he, too, was awestruck by the girl's sound. As the song ended, he entered the room, applauding their number. The girls hadn't even seen him come into the studio.

Kevin turned to shake his hand.

"Thanks, Joe, for coming on such a short notice. You know I wouldn't have insisted on you doing that if this were not something I think you need to hear," Kevin said.

"Kevin, I felt the excitement in your voice. I have only heard that excitement once before in your voice, and you know what the result of that excitement was," Joe said.

"Ashton, Skye, and Brooklyn, I want you to meet Joe Moss; he is the president of Magic Sounds. Joe, Ashton is Garland Summers's daughter," Kevin said.

Joe did something no one expected that day. He walked over to where Ashton sat, took her hand, and kissed it.

"Ashton, this is a very special day," Joe said.

The moment overwhelmed Joe emotionally.

"Please forgive me, girls. This is very big surprise for me. Ashton, I had no idea Garland had a daughter. You have his special gift. Your father was the best artist I have ever heard. The pleasure of meeting you is all mine," Joe said with a tear in his eye.

Ashton smiled, deeply touched to meet the man responsible for launching her dad's musical career.

"Joe, I want you to hear something. This time, I want you to hear all I am about to play for you," Kevin said.

Joe stopped in his tracks as Kevin started the recorder. The look on Joe's face showed that he couldn't hide his excitement. As the girl's song came to an end, Joe once again applauded.

"This is absolutely wonderful!" he shouted.

"Joe, are you thinking what I am thinking?" Kevin asked.

"Yes, Kevin, I am." Joe replied.

Kevin hugged Joe around the neck. Neither of them could control their emotions during this very special moment.

The three girls didn't have a clue as to what Joe and Kevin were referring to.

"Girls, we need to come up with a name for your act. I want to record your music," Joe said.

Skye and Brooklyn quickly ran to hug each other as they began to jump up and down at the news.

Ashton, meanwhile, was reacting very differently.

"Ashton, are you all right?" Kevin asked.

Ashton began to cry, shaking her head.

"No, Kevin, I am not all right," she said.

"What's wrong?" Joe asked.

"I want to make music very much, and I owe so much to my dad. But I have never been able to meet him. I have gone my entire life without ever being able to look into the eyes of my own dad," Ashton said.

Ashton's pain was felt by everyone in the room that day.

"Ashton, we are going to change that. We will see to it that you do get to meet Garland. You and he both have been deprived of that, and it cannot be ignored any longer," Kevin said.

Ashton smiled at the idea of finally seeing her dad in person. Just as Garland had done with her picture, she had worn out the pictures of him.

35

ASHTON ARRIVED AT her grandparents' home that evening feeling as if her feet would never touch the ground. The look on her face soon indicated to her grandparents this had been a wonderful day.

"Hey, baby, by the look on your face, I can tell you must have really enjoyed your session with Kevin today at the radio station," Sissy said.

James smiled knowingly but let Ashton relay the day's events to Sissy.

Ashton turned to Sissy, treating her grandmother to a wonderful sight for any grandparent to behold: a beloved grandchild's beaming smile.

"Grandma, Kevin arranged for a man to hear us perform today. I think you might know him. His name is Joe Moss, and he knows my dad!" Ashton exclaimed.

"Yes, Ashton, Joe is a very good man. Your dad thought the world of Joe," Sissy said.

Ashton continued, "Kevin recorded us playing a song today. We were playing 'Touch' when Joe walked into the studio. At first, we all thought we had disappointed Kevin and Mr. Moss. But then, Mr. Moss, with much excitement, told us we needed to come up with a name for our group because he wants to record our music."

Ashton immediately ran to Sissy and hugged her with much emotion.

"Ashton, you know I have always been very proud of you. This makes me even prouder of you than I ever thought I could be," Sissy said.

"Grandma, I met someone else today who is very special," Ashton said.

Ashton's comment brought a loud chuckle from James. "Let me guess who that might be, Ashton. I'll bet his name is Cory."

With an even louder laugh, James enjoyed the rosy blush in his granddaughter's cheeks from the embarrassment she felt.

"Cory is a very nice boy, Ashton. Everyone really thinks highly of him," James confirmed.

"He is much more than that, Pawpaw. He is the cutest boy I have ever met. There are no boys like him back in North Carolina," Ashton said with a smile.

"Ashton, I have another surprise for you, baby. Remember how, when you arrived, I was visiting your dad? They are doing a television special about his story, and they want to meet you as well," Sissy said.

At first, Ashton wasn't sure that she would be able to meet them.

"They want you to come to the prison for the interview," Sissy said.

Ashton looked down at the floor. She paused, taking a deep breath. After several moments, Ashton began to cry.

"Ashton, are you okay, baby?" James asked.

Ashton failed to answer her grandfather.

Sissy, realizing her granddaughter was struggling with the idea, gave Ashton a warm hug. Ashton returned the hug, relishing in the comfort and security of her grandmother's presence.

"Baby, if you don't want to do this, you don't have to," Sissy said.

Ashton continued to struggle with the idea.

Finally, with tears filling her eyes, Ashton raised her head from Sissy's shoulder, asking, "Grandma, does this mean that, after sixteen years, I will be able to meet my dad?"

"That will be up to the prison officials, baby," Sissy said. "They will have the final say as to whether you will be able to meet Garland. I know the producers of the special want the two of you to meet."

Once again, Ashton paused, trying to find the right words. "Grandma, you have seen my dad. Does he want to see me?"

Sissy stroked the cheeks of her granddaughter, wiping away her tears.

"Baby, from the moment your father found out about you, there has not been anything in this world that he wanted more," Sissy said as she wiped away her own tears.

IIIIIIII

At sunrise the next morning, the television crew arrived at the penitentiary. This was going to be a very exciting day at the prison. As the show's producer reached the entrance, the automatic doors swung open, welcoming him. Shortly after he entered the building, a very large man blocked the entrance.

"I want to welcome you to the Colorado state correctional institution. My name is Thad Rucker, and I am the warden," Thad said.

"Hey, Thad, thanks for the welcome. My name is Peter House, and I am the producer for this project."

Thad assured the crew that they would have anything they needed during their stay.

"Hey, fellas, if you like, I can make arrangements for you to spend the night," Thad said.

A pause came in response, followed by loud laughter. Although Thad's good intentions were sincere, they were received with certain trepidation.

"Follow me, Peter. We have a room reserved for your crew to set up their equipment," Thad said.

Thad and Peter entered the room, which was a normal visitation room equipped with a glass partition and phones.

Although Peter had envisioned a different setup, he looked around and then nodded his head.

"This is perfect. This will really create a sense of reality as to what goes on inside a prison," Peter said.

At Peter's signal, several men carrying video and audio equipment entered the room and began to set up.

||||||||

Chase made his way down the hall, headed for Garland's cell.

"Garland, today will be a very special day for you. Warden Rucker wants me to take you to a visitation room," Chase said.

It was all Chase could do to restrain himself from breaking the news of what was about to happen.

"What are you so happy about today?" Garland asked.

When Chase didn't answer, Garland asked again. This went on several times. Each time Garland repeated his question, Chase just laughed, each time a little louder than the time before. Not once did Chase answer his friend.

As they arrived at the visitation room, Chase turned to open the door for Garland. This time, the smile had been replaced with tears.

"Garland, this is a day you have waited a long time for. I am so glad it is finally happening today," Chase said.

Garland paused, wondering why Chase had so quickly gone from laughter to tears.

As Garland entered the room, Peter House greeted him.

"Garland, my name is Peter House, and I am with ABC Television. We are here to do a special about Aurora's Fire."

The bright lights and cameras took Garland by surprise.

"This special will air during our fall premiere week," Peter said. "Later in the interview, we will be joined by others guests. I guarantee that one guest will touch you like you have never been touched in your life."

Peter's comment intrigued Garland. He must have meant one of the band members. But which one would it be? Adam? Brandon? His mind raced. It would be wonderful to see either one of them after all these years.

As Garland took a seat, he noticed a slide projector pointed in the direction of a nearby wall.

"Garland, I hope you will enjoy what you are about to see. I know I have enjoyed it very much," Peter said.

Peter motioned for a guard to dim the lights and then instructed one of the crew members to begin the show. Each time the crew member pressed a handheld remote, the slide carousel would turn, revealing a new vision on the wall.

"Garland, I want to capture your feelings as to what you are experiencing as you see the pictures. Feel free to say whatever you are feeling," Peter said.

At first, Garland sat in silence, as if removed from his own emotions.

Peter began to think that maybe this wasn't a good idea after all.

Then, it hit!

"Will you please go back to the prior slide?" Garland asked.

The crew member reversed the slide and smiled at Peter. The slide was a picture of Garland and his old Gibson guitar that James had purchased in Roswell, New Mexico.

"I haven't seen her in many years," Garland said.

Several slides followed before Garland reacted again. This time, Garland began to laugh.

"That one is from the day when Adam and I invited Brandon over to Adam's house to play the drums for Adam's dad, Kevin, who was our music coach. Brandon was very cocky, but it didn't take long for Kevin to take the cockiness out of Brandon. Eventually, though, Brandon came through with his talent," Garland said.

Thinking about the memory, Garland again laughed out loud.

From that frame on, all throughout the day, Garland re-created the event depicted in every remaining slide he viewed, bringing his memories to life. Peter then realized his idea wasn't a failure but a very big success. The small recorder on the table captured every single one of Garland's comments.

Once again, Garland requested for a frame to be shown again.

"Garland, do you remember this frame?" Peter asked.

"Yes. That is the night Summer's Solstice lost the contest at Red

Rocks; this is the last picture that was taken of the group. Summer's Solstice never performed again," Garland said.

"Guard, can you please catch the lights?" Peter said.

The guard turned the overhead lights back on. A knock began on the other side of the door, and the guard turned to open it. A wheelchair entered to the room, escorted by three other men.

"Thank you for coming today," Peter said to the group. "My name is Peter House."

Garland turned to see to whom Peter was introducing himself.

Garland wasn't prepared for what he saw: standing in the room that day was the rest of the original Summer's Solstice.

"Garland, when Peter informed us of what he was planning, a team of wild horses could not keep us from being here with you today," Harley said.

The five men hugged each other.

The room began to fill with the flashes from the cameras. This was more than written words would be able to describe.

Peter stood in silence as he witnessed a friendship between five men like he had never experienced before.

"Fellas, we are very glad you are here today for this occasion. This has already been a special treat for me. When America sees this special, I know that it will be a night they will never forget," Peter said.

One by one, the other members of Summer's Solstice sat on the floor around Harley's wheelchair. Garland returned to his seat.

The others each told stories not only of Garland but of how much the other members of the group had meant to each of them. Some stories made the entire room erupt with laughter, while others made the room so quiet that a pin could have been heard hitting the tile floor, if it weren't for the sniffles of emotion.

Garland stood from his seat and began to share a personal moment. "There was a dark event in the life of the Summers family. It was the kind of night you think you'll only hear about on the late news. It was a night when my mother faced the possibility of losing her own life, had it not been for someone else putting aside his own safety to ensure hers. At first, when we heard of her savior, we thought that her head injury or the medication she had received had made her delirious. This savior she described was someone who had vanished from all our lives for quite some time, and there just wasn't any way that this man could be our devoted hero. But he was. Brandon, you saved my mother's life that night in that dark parking lot, and I have never been able to let you or anyone else know just what you have meant to me. Today, I want to say, 'Thank you,'" Garland said.

Brandon stood up from the floor and walked to where Garland now stood.

"Garland, that night, I was not only defending your mother, but a lady I consider to be my mother as much as you do," Brandon said.

The two men stood toe-to-toe, clasping each other in a bear hug.

"How are Tobie and Skye?" Garland asked.

"Tobie's great. Skye has grown up so fast," Brandon said.

"Brandon, I know you must be a great dad. I often had visions of you with a son, though," Garland said.

Brandon smiled and began to remove his wallet from his left rear pocket. He opened the wallet and removed a family picture.

Garland began to gaze at the picture, as if he were trying to memorize it.

"Hey, is that your son, Cochise?" Garland asked.

"Yes, Garland, that is our son," Brandon said.

"Wow, I never knew you had a son. He is the spitting image of his old man too! What is his name?" Garland said.

"We call him Gar," Brandon said.

"Gar? That is a unique name, Brandon," Garland said.

"Well, yes, it is, and so is the person he bears the name of. His real name is Garland," Brandon said with a proud grin.

The moment left Garland speechless and deeply touched.

Peter, not wanting to lose any of this special time, began to ask the other members about their present-day lives.

Harley told stories of the radio station, including the night when he made "Touch" the biggest-selling record of all time.

Adam talked about his dad and doing some studio work for a local record label.

"Beau, you haven't said much. How are things with Chad and Suzanna?" Garland asked.

Garland's question about Suzanna shocked everyone.

"She is in Paris, Garland. I hope you don't hold any of it against me—I mean, what she did," Beau said. "My dad was just diagnosed with cancer."

Garland hugged Beau, assuring him that everything was all right between the two of them and telling him he hoped Chad would be okay.

"Have any of you guys kept in touch with Joe Moss?" Garland asked.

"Well, Garland, Joe is still pursuing new acts. You know, you guys are a very hard act to follow," Peter said.

"I heard that Joe really wanted to be here today, but there was this other engagement, one he has waited a very long time for, and so he couldn't make it," Brandon said.

"Garland, we did invite Joe. And Brandon is correct: at this moment, Joe is signing up a new star whom he feels will be the biggest and most talented star he has ever signed. He said she is the greatest vocalist and musician he has ever had the privilege of hearing," Peter said.

"That's great. Joe deserves another break after what happened to him because of me," Garland said.

At that moment, there was a knock on the door. The guard at the door opened it a crack and then delivered a note to Peter. Peter unfolded the message. He whispered into the guard's ear, nodding his approval as the guard left the room. The interruption gathered everyone's attention. Soon afterward, there was another knock was on the door. Peter nodded for the guard to escort the visitor into the room.

The door slowly began to open. Standing on the threshold was an image all the guys recognized. There was no need for any introduction as to who this man was. Joe Moss entered the room and immediately proceeded to where Garland stood in shock. Joe firmly placed his hands on Garland's shoulders, as if never wanting to remove them.

"I have waited a long time for this," Garland said.

Joe smiled. "Yes, Garland, you have. Far more than you even know."

Garland was confused as to what Joe was referring to.

"Joe, Brandon said you have found a very talented act," Garland said.

"Yes, I have, Garland. I think they are the most talented I have ever seen, given their limited experience," Joe said.

"When I heard of your prior engagement, Joe, I never expected to see you here today," Garland said.

"Garland, I didn't cancel my other engagement today. Seeing you today was much too important to me. So I have decided to do something very special both for her and you," Joe said.

"Joe, I am glad you are here, but you should take care of a chance that comes around once in a lifetime. There may never be another opportunity," Garland said.

"Oh, I thought about that," Joe said with a laugh. "But, you see, being here today in this room with you is an even bigger event in her life than any record contract I could give her."

"Guards, will you please bring our next guest in," Peter said.

The room filled with excitement as to the act that Joe was so taken with. Two very beautiful young women entered the room. Garland immediately recognized Skye from Brandon's family photo and began to congratulate him. The two girls entered and stood behind Joe and Garland. No one could understand why the door remained open. It seemed the best had been saved for last as another young girl entered the room.

"Garland, I want you to meet my new star," Joe said.

Garland began to tremble, trying to gain control of his emotions.

"Garland, this is Ashton Summers," Joe said.

Ashton rushed to Garland. This was the moment, sixteen years in the making. Garland placed his hands alongside Ashton's cheeks, wiping away her tears.

"Ashton, you are the most beautiful sight I have ever seen in my life. You look so much like your mother," Garland said.

"No, I am just like my dad," Ashton said.

"Garland, as much as I hate to admit it to you, your daughter is the best I have ever heard," Joe said.

"Mr. Moss, there will never be anyone better than my dad," Ashton said as she devoured the arms she had longed to have hold her for her entire life.

In all his years in television, Peter House had never dreamed he would have a story like the one he would soon bring to the entire nation.

The special reunion would soon be enjoyed by the many fans Aurora's Fire had touched. Thirty minutes had passed that afternoon when Peter informed the guys the session was coming to an end. This was a goodbye none of them wanted. After all, it could very well be another seventeen years before such an opportunity arrived for a similar occasion. One by one, each said their goodbyes to Garland, each deeply touched by a meeting that was long, long overdue. As Joe made his way to the door, he turned to Peter, winking as he closed the door behind him.

"Ashton and Garland, I have arranged for some private time for the two of you," Peter said as he left the room.

Ashton, still overwhelmed by it all, struggled to contain her emotions.

Garland sensed the emotions of his daughter and escorted her to a seat next to his.

"Ashton, you make me so very, very proud. I have worn out the pictures you sent to me. I never thought this day would actually arrive," Garland said.

Ashton began to feel the warmth of the man whom so many articles had depicted as evil.

"Dad, I have wanted to see and feel you for such a long time. Grandma and Pawpaw miss you so much," Ashton said. "I can feel it in my heart that there is no way you could have ever done the things they have you in here for."

"No, baby, your heart leads you right. I was so blind that night. I lost something that night that it took me many years to get back," Garland said.

Garland could tell by the look on Ashton's face that she was lost as to what he was talking about.

"Your mother and I, after many years apart, were back together, and Suzanna knew it. I don't think it was her intention that early morning to kill an innocent person. What she wanted was to teach me a lesson, and, boy, did she ever teach me one hell of a lesson. I have been deprived of the woman I love and our daughter," Garland said.

Ashton nodded in understanding.

"Enough said about me, baby. Tell me all about this great news that has Joe so excited," Garland said.

Ashton left her seat and sat on Garland's lap. "I have wanted to sit on my daddy's lap ever since I was a little girl, and I am going to enjoy this moment."

While sitting on Garland's lap, Ashton placed her head on his shoulder and began to hum a chorus. Soon the hum became words. Ashton removed her head from Garland's shoulder and began to sing, looking directly into his eyes. Midway through Ashton's serenade, something happened! Garland joined her song. Garland paused to absorb this moment. His little girl was singing his song, and she did it so well!

Peter and his crew returned to the room.

"Ashton and Garland, I would give anything in this world if I did not have to wrap up this reunion. It really kills me to end it, but the prison has already given us more time than we asked for," Peter said.

Chase entered the room to escort Garland back to his cell. Chase also wished that this moment could last forever.

Garland and Ashton said their final goodbyes, and Garland left the room.

"Ashton, I would like to interview you tomorrow. I hope you will give me that honor," Peter said.

Ashton smiled and agreed.

"Okay, guys, I think it's time to pack things up and get ready for tomorrow," Peter said.

It just so happened that the cameras used to record the interviews were the last items to be packed. One of the cameramen began to disassemble his camera, when he noticed the green light was on.

"Peter, I can't believe I did this," the cameraman said.

"What is it that you did?" Peter asked.

"I left the camera on when we left room. The camera was on the entire time we were out of the room," the man said.

Peter rushed over to the camera.

"Are you thinking what I am thinking?" Peter asked.

The two men smiled and anxiously rewound the recording. Their ears and eyes were treated to a heavenly event. Caught on that camera was sight and sound of Ashton and Garland singing "Touch." The cameraman turned off the camera and looked at Peter. The two men's eyes couldn't hide what their hearts knew. That afternoon, they had captured more than anyone could have dreamed possible.

36

THE WEEKS AFTER Garland and Ashton's meeting flew by. During Ashton's last two weeks in Colorado, Brooklyn, Skye, and Ashton were introduced to another aspiring young musician. One afternoon during a jam session at KARO, a man wearing a prison guard's uniform pulled into the station's parking lot. As the man entered the station's hallway, the view from the studio revealed he was not alone.

"Oh my gosh! He is the prison guard who escorted my dad that day to meet us!" Ashton screamed.

The first thing entering Ashton's mind was that something bad had happened to her dad. She rushed into the hall to meet the two visitors.

"Is my dad all right? I recognized you from that day at the prison," Ashton said.

"Yes, Ashton everything is just fine. My name is Chase Flemming, and I have known your dad for many years. I consider him a dear friend."

Ashton breathed a sigh of relief.

"We have talked about you from the day he found out you existed. We have shared many important events in our lives with each other," Chase said.

Standing next to Chase was a slender and very tall girl.

"When your dad found out about your band and career, he remembered I had a niece who worshipped the ground your dad walked on," Chase said. "This is my niece, Shanda. She loves music just like you girls do."

Ashton was joined by Brooklyn and Skye.

"What kind of music do you like, Shanda?" Skye asked.

"I enjoy all kinds of music, and I can play five different instruments," Shanda replied.

"Five? Wow, that is a lot!" Skye said.

"Who are some of the artists you enjoy?" Ashton asked.

Shanda began to name many of the stars from the sixties.

"Wow, you like the oldies, huh?" Ashton said.

"Yep, and I love everything Aurora's Fire did. I'll bet I know some songs you don't know," Shanda said.

Shanda looked through the studio window to see the instruments on hand. She went past the other girls and took a seat on a stool in the studio.

Brooklyn looked at Skye, shrugging her shoulders.

"It seems she would like to audition for us," Brooklyn said.

Shanda discovered Garland's old Gibson resting on a guitar stand next to her and immediately retrieved the instrument.

"Hey, be careful with her! She is very delicate and special," Ashton warned.

Shanda grinned, tossing her long red hair to one side to make room for the guitar strap.

The three other girls sat on the remaining stools as Shanda began to play several chords. As she continued to play, the song wasn't familiar to any of the others. Shanda began to sing lyrics to a song as unfamiliar as the musical chords she was playing. Although Ashton, Skye, and Brooklyn didn't know the tune, it did not take them long to realize that Shanda was a talented musician and singer.

As Shanda began to perform the final notes of this wonderful unknown song, Kevin, undetected, entered the room to listen as well.

"That was a beautiful song, Shanda, but none of us ever heard that tune before. Did you write that song?" Ashton asked.

Shanda laughed at Ashton's remarks and then said, "Don't any of you recognize that song?"

Kevin folded his arms and smiled.

Skye, noticing the Kevin had entered the studio, asked, "Kevin, what has you so content?"

"Girls, this young lady has just trumped all of you," Kevin replied.

"What do you mean?" Skye asked.

Kevin laughed loudly and then paused, creating even more curiosity.

"The song Shanda has just performed is entitled 'Forever.' It was released as the A side to a song that became a very big hit. 'Forever' was supposed to have been the hit side. You have just heard the flip side to 'Touch.' Ashton, 'Forever' is another Aurora's Fire song," Kevin said.

"Shanda, I think we have just found a missing link to our group," Kevin said.

Ashton took a seat next to Shanda.

"You really are a big fan of Aurora's Fire and my father's music, aren't you?" Ashton said.

"Ashton, there isn't any music I have ever enjoyed more than the music your dad gave us," Shanda said.

"Shanda, I don't think there will be any problems with the girls or Joe Moss if you want to join our group," Kevin said.

Ashton now had the final piece to her new band.

Kevin's call to Joe was received with much enthusiasm.

"Kevin, did I understand you to say that Shanda plays five instruments?" Joe asked.

"Yes, Joe, and if she plays the others as well as she played Garland's old Gibson, you will have a lot of versatility," Kevin said.

Kevin smiled as he began to hold the phone's receiver farther away from his ear. Joe's excitement not only filled Kevin's ear but the entire room as well.

"Shanda, Mr. Moss would like to have a word with you," Kevin said.

Shanda walked to Kevin's desk and placed the phone next to her ear, which was covered by her long red hair.

Several times, Shanda said, "Yes, sir," and then she placed the receiver back on the phone. With her head hung down, Shanda began to walk back to her seat on a nearby stool. Just as she was about to sit, she turned to the others and began to instantly jump up and down.

"I am in! I am in!" Shanda shouted.

Shanda's excitement was well received by the other three girls.

"Now that we have all of our missing pieces together, girls, we need to come up with a name for our little group here," Kevin said. "Tomorrow, we will begin to lay down the tracks to a few songs. When you arrive, we will discuss a name."

"I'd like to make a suggestion for our group's name," Skye said.

"Let's hear your idea, Skye," Kevin said.

"Well, if it weren't for Ashton, I don't think any of us would have this great opportunity. It's all right by me if we are referred to as 'Ashton,'" Skye said.

Skye's suggestion humbled Ashton.

"Skye, you and the other girls are part of this group too. I don't want to slight any of you by using just my name," Ashton said.

"Ashton, Skye is right. We should use your name," Brooklyn said.

"What about 'Summer's Sound'? I think it is the perfect name; it blends the old with the new," Shanda said.

"I agree, Shanda. That is the perfect name," Skye said.

"Ashton, I think they are right," Brooklyn said.

"All right. It's unanimous: our name will be Summer's Sound," Ashton said with a very big smile.

"Kevin, tell Mr. Moss to get the printers ready," Skye said.

IIIIIIII

Ashton's summer in Colorado would only last a few more weeks, and every day would be very busy. The next day, Ashton arrived at KARO to pick up the old Gibson. As she entered the station, a familiar voice greeted her.

"Hello, Ashton. Let me be the first to congratulate you," Cory said.

Ashton began to blush; she was very inexperienced when it came to the opposite sex.

"Thank you very much, Cory," she said.

"Ashton, I am pleased that you remembered my name. After all, we haven't spent much time together and really haven't had a chance to talk much," Cory said.

Once again, Ashton was taken away by Cory's flirtation.

"Kevin tells me that Mr. Moss wants to record you and the other girls," Cory said.

"Yes, Cory, and we must have it wrapped all up in less than two weeks," Ashton said.

"Two weeks?" Cory said.

"Yes, that is when I have to go back to North Carolina to finish up my senior year of high school," Ashton said.

"Ashton, I am both glad and sad. I am happy for your chance to follow in your dad's footsteps, and I am sad because I wanted to get to know you better," Cory said.

Ashton smiled, blushing once again.

Kevin, overhearing Cory and Ashton's conversation, popped his head out of his office.

"Cory, I think it would be a very nice gesture if you accompanied Miss Summers to the Magic Sounds Studio," Kevin said.

This time, it was Cory's turn to blush. Cory picked up the Gibson and escorted Ashton to one of the station's vans.

As the van pulled away from the radio station that morning, Cory turned the van's radio on. There was nothing like music to break the ice and create a mood for conversation. It was hard to tell who was more nervous.

"I really would like to spend some time with you before you return to North Carolina, Ashton," Cory said.

Ashton began to blush once more. No boy had ever shown Ashton this kind of attention, especially not one who was this cute.

"Cory, I would love to spend time with you before I leave," Ashton said.

The ride to Magic Sounds that morning seemed to go by as fast as the breath on a cold glass of water disappears. Ashton felt like she could listen to Cory forever. She found herself opening up more and more.

"Cory, do you think Kevin would mind if you waited to take me home after I am done with Mr. Moss today?" Ashton asked.

Cory smiled, thinking Ashton's request was indeed the request he wanted to hear.

"I don't think Kevin would mind if I stayed around until you were done," Cory said.

As Cory pulled the van into the parking lot, Skye and Brooklyn were sitting on a bench.

"Skye, are you thinking what I am thinking?" Brooklyn asked.

Skye giggled. "Oh yeah, without a doubt."

"Hey, Cory, will you be attending our session this morning?" Skye asked.

"Well, as a matter of fact, I will be," Cory answered.

As Cory and Ashton approached the bench occupied by Skye and Brooklyn, there was an amazed look on both girls' faces. The glass reflection revealed the smile on Ashton's face as Cory placed her hand within his hand.

The four entered the front lobby together.

"I hope Shanda will get here soon. I am anxious to hear what Mr. Moss has planned for us," Skye said.

As they approached Joe's office, his secretary welcomed them inside. Sitting at a conference table in Joe's office were Joe and Shanda. It was apparent that Shanda was as serious about this day as the others were.

"Ladies, the music business is changing very fast these days. There are more avenues to promote our artists than ever before," Joe said.

The girls smiled at Joe's excitement.

"I'm sure you all have seen music videos. They have become almost as important as the record itself these days," Joe said.

"I love them. I can watch them all day long on MTV," Shanda said.

Joe turned and smiled at Shanda.

"Well, you girls will be our first attempt at doing a video," Joe said.

"We are going to do all of this in just two weeks, Mr. Moss?" Ashton asked.

"We will take our time these two weeks and try to come up with an intro song and the video. We want to do it right," Joe said.

After a long day of decision making, Ashton was ready to get away for some private time with her new chauffeur.

"Ashton, you look as if you could use something to eat. I know a place I think you will enjoy," Cory said.

The drive took them into an area in downtown Denver.

"I think a radio station's van might have some pull in this place," Cory said, laughing.

Cory pulled into the crowded parking lot and drove up to the valet stand. Just as if a celebrity were in the van, several valets rushed the van at once, each wanting to be of service.

"Sir, are you here for someone special this evening? They never tell us when any VIPs are in the restaurant," he said.

Cory smiled at Ashton, as if to ask for her permission before saying what he was about to say. As fast as the thought entered Cory's mind, Ashton read what was going on inside his head and smiled in agreement.

"Well, yes, as a matter of fact I am," Cory said.

The valet waited with much anticipation for Cory to expand his answer.

"I have with me the lead singer of Summer's Sound," Cory said.

The valet immediately rushed to Ashton's side of the van, opening her door.

"This is my first week working here. I never dreamed I would be parking the van of a star," he said.

"Would you please see to it that Miss Summers's transportation is well taken care of?" Cory asked.

"Yes, sir. You have my word," the valet said.

Ashton laughed at the young man's naïveté.

"You know, Cory, you should be ashamed of yourself," Ashton said with big smile.

"Well, it's true, Ashton. You are the lead singer, and you will soon be a new star," Cory said.

As they climbed the steps into the restaurant, Ashton was in awe. There were so many people waiting to get a seat inside.

"Wow, Cory! Is there really someone famous here for all these people to see?" Ashton asked.

Cory approached the hostess, whispering into her ear. The hostess turned to Ashton and smiled. Cory turned and winked at Ashton.

"I think I have a table that will be perfect. Follow me, please," the hostess said.

Without any hesitation, Ashton took Cory's hand.

"Will this table be all right, sir?" the hostess asked.

"Yes, it is perfect," Cory replied.

Cory immediately pulled out Ashton's chair for her.

"What in the world did you do to get us seated this quick?" Ashton asked.

As Ashton took her seat, Cory whispered in her ear, "I handed her a twenty-dollar bill."

Cory smiled as he pushed Ashton's chair in, and then he bent and kissed the back of her right hand.

Soon afterward, a waitress greeted them. "Welcome to the Hard Rock Café. My name is Samantha, and I will be your waitress this evening."

Cory informed Samantha that they would require a few minutes to make their selections.

As Ashton read through the menu, she noticed that each item was named either for a song or an artist. The walls were covered with album covers and enlarged concert tickets, complete with show dates and seat sections.

"Cory, I have heard of the Hard Rock Café, but I never dreamed I would ever visit one. I just love the music they play," Ashton said.

Samantha returned to take their order.

"Thank you, Cory. It is very special to be here and to be here with you," Ashton said.

"Believe it or not, Ashton, this is also my first time coming here; they haven't been open very long," Cory said.

Ashton's first date was one she would always remember.

"Ashton, I have no doubt that, one day, I will dine here, and I will be treated to one of your many hits to come," Cory said.

Ashton smiled. Cory knew exactly how to make a young woman feel heavenly.

"Cory, you will make it very hard for me to leave here in a few weeks. This summer has been better than I ever anticipated. Please take your time driving us back to Aurora," Ashton said.

Cory placed Ashton's hands inside his own and began to gently trace her fingers with his. The gentleness of his touch sent goose bumps up Ashton's arms.

Ashton took a deep breath, closing her eyes. She did not want to open her eyes and find that this entire evening had been a dream. As Ashton began to gently tilt her head to one side, she was taken in by the most pleasant surprise of the evening. Cory, no longer controlling his urges, leaned toward Ashton. Once again, Ashton took what seemed to be a deep breath, slowly exhaling. Ashton thought there wasn't anything to make the evening any more perfect, but her thought was soon proved wrong. Cory began to gently kiss Ashton's lips. It was as if she felt the warmth of Cory's heart as he continued to press his very soft lips against hers.

Ashton's tender first kiss would most definitely be filed deep in her memory. There were no words to describe what she was feeling.

"Excuse me, sir. I will leave your check on the table. Please feel free to take your time," Samantha said.

Cory and Ashton interrupted their kiss, which seemed to Ashton to have lasted forever.

"I am sorry, Ashton. I really couldn't help myself," Cory said.

"Cory, the only thing you have to apologize for is stopping," Ashton said.

Cory's smile at Ashton's comment was abruptly interrupted. Ashton leaned toward Cory. This time, the kiss would end when she wanted it to, not from a waitress's interruption.

37

SUMMER'S SOUND ARRIVED at the Magic Sounds Studio. Recording their first record was becoming much harder than the ambitious young musicians had anticipated. Just when the girls thought they had nailed their last take, Joe Moss immediately instructed them to do another take. Each take diminished their enthusiasm.

"Girls, we are so, so close to getting this thing right," Joe barked through the studio control room's microphone.

Each time Joe barked his insistence for another take, it led to angry and tired looks from his young stars.

"I am about to give up. I have no idea what he wants of us," Ashton said.

After several hours of take after take, Joe dismissed the girls. He sensed that no matter how hard he drove them, today was not going to be the day that he would receive the sounds on tape that he had in his head. Perfection, and nothing less than perfection, was the only thing that he would accept.

"Girls, let's call it a day. When you get serious about your music, maybe we can get this right!" Joe shouted.

The girls were seeing a different side of Joe, one they never knew existed.

Ashton arrived at James and Sissy's, feeling like she would never satisfy Joe Moss.

As she entered the house, it was very evident to Sissy that something was very, very wrong.

"Grandma, I am not very hungry tonight. I want to take a nice hot bath and go to bed," Ashton said.

She immediately retrieved her pajamas and began to run a bath of hot water and nice soothing bubbles. As she eased into the tub, the soothing bubbles began to coat her soft young skin. Ashton slid down into the tub, leaning against the sloped back until only her face was visible. She could not remember the last time a hot bubble bath felt this relaxing.

Ashton could hear Joe Moss's voice in her head, echoing over and over. What was Joe was trying to get from them? After all the takes they'd done that afternoon, how could none be good enough? She thought they had sounded very good. She closed her eyes, trying to relax again, struggling to get Joe's voice out of her head.

Ashton was almost asleep in the tub when a loud knock came from the other side of the bathroom door.

"Ashton, are you okay, baby?" Sissy said.

At first, Ashton thought she was hearing her grandmother's voice in a dream. But then, there was another knock on the door.

"Ashton, can I come in?" Sissy asked.

"Grandma, I am okay. I am getting out of the tub," Ashton answered as she reached for the nearby towel and began to dry herself off.

Ashton opened the door, startled by the sight of her grandmother sitting on a nearby bench in the hallway. As Ashton approached the bench, Sissy slid over to one side and insisted that her granddaughter take a seat. Ashton obliged her grandmother, sitting beside her.

"Ashton, what has you so troubled?" Sissy said as she held Ashton's hand.

Ashton tried very hard to fight back her tears but didn't succeed.

"Grandma, I don't know if I am cut out for this," she said.

Sissy, sensing the pain in her granddaughter, held her hand tighter.

"Ashton, you have to trust Joe; he will make all of you better," Sissy said. "You are not a quitter. You have a very special talent, and he will bring that talent out better than anyone else."

Ashton smiled at Sissy as she left her seat. "I feel a lot better now. It is very nice to have someone to talk to. Thanks for listening, Grandma. I love you very much."

"Get a good night's rest Ashton," Sissy said. "Remember, tomorrow will be another day."

The four girls arrived at the Magic Sounds Studio the next morning, dreading the task of the day. As Joe walked into the recording studio, coldness overtook him. One by one, Joe looked at each of the four girls' faces. How could he erase the fear he saw in their faces?

"Does anyone here want to call it quits?" he asked.

Each of the girls turned to another, searching for someone to speak up. There was no volunteer to answer Joe's question. Joe began to walk about the room. One by one, he escorted each girl to her instrument.

"Girls, take a minute. I want each of you to hold your instrument. It is the one real thing that will never fail you. It will always be there for you," Joe said.

The girls did what Joe told them to do.

"All right. I want all of you to close your eyes and go to a place that makes you feel very safe," he said.

Ashton began to smile as she held the old Gibson. One by one, the faces of the other girls soon wore smiles.

"I want you all to keep your eyes closed," Joe instructed.

Joe began to play the recording of the prior day. The music began to fill the young musicians' ears. He observed the girls as they absorbed the music. Then, as quick as a flash, Joe stopped the recording.

"Remember to keep your eyes closed," he reiterated.

Joe flipped the switch on the control panel and began to play another song. As the song continued to play, he once again observed the reaction of the four girls. Each of the four girls made a terrible face in response to the sounds they heard. The longer the music played, the more intense the looks became, and they placed their hands over their ears.

Some of the facial expressions made Joe laugh. He hoped the news he was about to break to them would make a difference in their confidence. Joe turned the music off. This time, there was a look of relief on the girls' faces.

"You can all open your eyes now," Joe said. "Do I have a volunteer to tell me her thoughts about what she heard?"

This time, the response he sought came immediately.

"Where on earth did you ever come up with that stuff?" Skye asked.

"Please tell us this was a joke," Shanda added with a very loud laugh.

"Who were those guys on that tape?" Ashton asked.

Joe began to laugh again, amused by the girls' reactions. He removed the tape from the console.

"I am going to pass this around, and I want each of you to read the name on the label," Joe said as he handed the tape to Brooklyn.

Brooklyn paused in awe as she passed the tape to Skye.

The look on girl's face was identical when she read the label on the tape. Each of the girls knew the song. It was a very big hit.

"So you see, girls, you can do this. Two of you already have it in your blood," Joe said.

A different look suddenly appeared on the girls' faces: one of determination. Now more than ever, they wanted to succeed. It was comforting to them that even Aurora's Fire had struggled at first.

During the next few days, the girls spent many hours at the Magic Sounds Studio. Although they made great progress in the recording studio, Joe still wasn't wowed with the finished product. There was just something missing that he just couldn't put his finger on, something necessary for them to get the right mixture. Soon Ashton would have to return to North Carolina. Maybe it was time to give the girls a day away from the pressure.

On Saturday morning, Ashton was finishing her breakfast and getting ready to go to the studio.

The phone rang, and Ashton answered.

"Ashton, this is Joe Moss. I think it would be a good idea if you and the girls took today and Sunday off. We can get back to work on Monday."

"Mr. Moss, are you sure about that? I will be leaving for North Carolina on Wednesday," Ashton said.

"Yes, I'm sure," Joe said. "I wanted to have the record and the video wrapped up before you left, but we have come along way. We may only need to finish things when you come back. It is important for you to finish your school. You are almost finished; we can wait one more semester to wrap it up."

Ashton ended her conversation with Joe Moss, shrugging her shoulders.

Turning toward Sissy, she asked, "Grandma, what is the phone number to the radio station?"

Sissy told Ashton the phone number and then laughed, saying, "Ashton, it's a little early to call the station to make a request for a song to be played."

"Ha-ha! Aren't you funny, Grandma?" Ashton replied.

Ashton immediately dialed the station's number. As the phone began to ring on the other end of the line, Ashton impatiently paced back and forth in Sissy's kitchen. The phone rang for what seemed to be an eternity.

"Thank you for calling KARO radio," the voice said.

Ashton collapsed into one of the kitchen table's chairs, relieved to have finally gotten through to the station.

"Cory, is that you?" she asked.

"Hey, Ashton. I thought you would be at the studio wrapping things up," Cory said.

"Well, Mr. Moss thought it best for us to take a break for the next two days," Ashton explained.

"Oh, he did, did he? So now you have two days with nothing to do on your hands, huh?" Cory teased.

"Cory, I have just four days remaining before I have to go back home," Ashton said.

Cory paused for a moment, thinking of how things would be in his life once Ashton returned home.

"I get off at noon, Ashton. I will pick you up then, and we will spend the day together," Cory said.

Cory's invitation excited Ashton. Her face lit up at the thought of seeing him.

That afternoon, as Cory drove to the Summerses' house, he kept thinking of a special treat for Ashton. As he approached the freeway's exit ramp, he spotted a nearby billboard advertising Elitch Gardens. This would be a great way to introduce Ashton to her dad's early beginnings, and it would also be a fun way for her to unwind.

Ashton watched anxiously through the living-room curtains for the arrival of the KARO van. Soon the entire household would know of its arrival. Ashton rushed out onto the front porch, leaving the door to be closed by Sissy.

Sissy shook her head in disbelief at her granddaughter's excitement. It wouldn't be long before Sissy would miss being in the midst of a teenager's emotional ups and downs.

Cory pulled into the driveway, stopping instantly. He sprang from the driver's seat, running to open the passenger-side door.

Ashton glowed and felt like her feet weren't even touching the ground. There was a bug going around Aurora, and Ashton was definitely affected by that little bug.

"I have a surprise for you today, Ashton. One I think you will really connect with, and it will also be a lot of fun," Cory said.

Ashton smiled. She could no longer resist the temptation, and she kissed her suitor.

"Cory, I am sure that I will love whatever you have planned for us today. I just want to spend time with you," Ashton said.

"You know, there is one thing I do not like about this van," Ashton said.

"Oh, and what is that?" Cory asked.

"I cannot sit next to you during the drive," Ashton said with a frown.

Cory pulled the van into a nearby parking lot. Sitting in the rear of the van was a crate that looked like it would be a perfect fit. Sure enough, the crate managed to fit snuggly in between the two front seats.

Ashton smiled at Cory's ingenuity and promptly took a seat next to Cory. She was now ready for the drive.

Ashton opened up to Cory, sharing the difficulty the girls were having trying to capture on tape what Joe Moss had in his head.

Although Cory wasn't familiar with the recording process, he knew Ashton needed to vent to someone, and he wanted to be her confidant. As Cory listened to Ashton's troubles, the van began its final approach to Elitch's parking lot.

"Wow, I totally forgot that this is the last week for summer hours at the park," Cory said.

Ashton looked through the windshield, taking in the scenery.

"Ashton, what do you know about Elitch Gardens?" Cory asked.

"I think it's an amusement park," she replied.

"Yes, it is, and it is much more than that. This is the park where Joe Moss discovered Aurora's Fire," Cory said.

Ashton was touched that Cory wanted to help her learn more about her dad. Cory was indeed a rare find these days, and a find that she wanted very much.

"I think we shall start with the roller coaster. It is a killer of a ride and will give you a really big rush," Cory said with loud laugh.

The two made their way over to the roller coaster. Ashton caught a glimpse of a sign pointing the way to an outdoor amphitheater. As they approached the entrance to the amphitheater, a sudden chill came over Ashton.

"Ashton, is everything all right?" Cory asked.

Ashton began to nod her head affirmatively. This was the first time Ashton had been to a place that her dad enjoyed very much. Ashton turned to Cory and hugged him very, very close. Her sniffles showed just how much the sight had touched her heart.

"You know, there is something I want to show you, Ashton," Cory said.

Cory led his date into the amphitheater. Outside the main entrance was a showcase of the acts that had performed during the years. Ashton arrived at one particular picture inside the main showcase.

"Oh my God, Cory! That is Brandon! He really was a very

handsome guy. Skye would be so proud of her daddy if she saw this," Ashton said with a smile.

"Ashton, I want you look at the picture above Brandon. Do you recognize who that is?" Cory said.

Ashton reached to touch the glass-covered picture with one hand while trying to hide her quivering lip with the other.

Cory stepped behind Ashton and wrapped his arms around her.

"That is my dad, with the old Gibson!" she screamed.

"Yes, baby, that is Garland," Cory said as he squeezed Ashton tightly.

"You know, Cory, I didn't think our dinner at the Hard Rock Café could be topped, but this really has touched me in a way I have never been touched before," Ashton said.

"Take all the time you want here, Ashton. When you are ready, we can head on over to the rides in the park," Cory said.

"Cory, thank you for this moment. We can leave for the rides now. But, first, there is one more thing I want to do," Ashton said.

"Whatever you like, baby," Cory said.

Ashton removed Cory's arms and turned around to face him. Without any hesitation, Ashton wrapped her arms around Cory and kissed him passionately. Ashton's desire soon caused a traffic jam around the showcase.

"Excuse us, but I am in love with this guy, and you will have to wait to see the pictures until I am finished showing him," Ashton said.

Ashton and Cory spent the rest of the park hours enjoying the roller coaster and other thrilling rides. The park's public address system announced that the park would be closing soon.

"Where has the time gone?" Ashton asked.

They began to make their way to the park entrance. Cory took Ashton's hand, leading her into a gift shop.

Immediately upon entering the shop, Cory spotted an Elitch T-shirt.

The clerk informed the two shoppers that the store was about to close.

"This will not take long. I want two of those T-shirts: one large and one medium," Cory said.

The clerk retrieved the T-shirts and placed them in a shopping bag as Cory paid him.

"Ashton, every time you wear this T-shirt, I want you to think about our time here together, just as I will whenever I wear mine," Cory said.

The day and night at Elitch provided just what the doctor—and Joe Moss—had ordered. Ashton spent Sunday getting some rest. She wanted to spend some quality time with Sissy. Grandmother and granddaughter spent hours enjoying each other's company. Sissy enjoyed hearing Ashton's recap of Elitch.

"You know, Ashton, I remember those days as if they happened yesterday. It was a very good time in all of our lives," Sissy said.

"Hey, Grandma. Cory and I have matching T-shirts to wear. It's our way of being together when we are apart," Ashton said.

"I can tell you like Cory very much. He is a very well-liked young man and will do well in life. He wants to be a lawyer, just like your mom," Sissy said.

Ashton smiled at Sissy's comment.

"I think I will get some rest now, Grandma. Tomorrow, we have to meet with Joe Moss again," Ashton said.

||||||||

Monday morning arrived, and Ashton was determined she could deliver whatever Joe Moss wanted of her.

"Ashton, why don't you drive Garland's convertible to the studio?" Sissy said.

Ashton smiled. She loved Garland's car.

"I love your new T-shirt, Ashton," Sissy said.

"Well, it makes me feel very good, and I want to feel the best I can this morning," Ashton said.

Ashton kissed Sissy goodbye and left to take care of business.

Ashton was the first to arrive at the studio. Shortly afterward, the other girls arrived. All of them were early that morning.

Ashton began telling the others about her date with Cory. When she finished, she added, "Skye, your dad was one fine hunk."

"Hey, how do you know?" Skye asked.

"Skye there is a showcase containing pictures of 'Aurora's Fire' inside the amphitheater at Elitch. There is one of Brandon," Ashton said.

Ashton could tell by Skye's reaction that she wasn't familiar with the picture.

"You really need to see it, Skye. I was as proud of your dad as I was of mine," Ashton said.

Skye smiled and thanked Ashton for the compliment and the information.

Joe entered the studio and said, "I see the rest did everyone some good."

The girls all agreed that they might have been too intense during the previous week.

Joe began to convey his idea about the sound he wanted to achieve. He once again began to replay prior week's tape.

"If you ladies are ready, Skye, give us the count, and we can begin," Joe said.

Skye began the count on her drums, and the rest of the girls picked up their cues to join in.

Joe stood up immediately and interrupted them.

"Ladies, we don't want to replay live what you have just heard on tape. Let's try it again, from the top," he said.

Skye once again began her count.

One by one, each girl picked up her cue to join in.

Once again, Joe stood up, shaking his head.

"Ashton, why are you two counts behind the beat?!" Joe shouted.

Ashton began to shake in fear at Joe's ire.

"I am sorry, Mr. Moss. I thought my tempo was in check." Ashton said.

Joe's anger toward Ashton shocked the other girls.

"Okay, once again, from the top," Joe said.

This time Joe, didn't interrupt the song. The girls finished the take, feeling that they had delivered.

"Way to go Ashton, Brooklyn, and Skye. We nailed it!" Shanda shouted.

Joe walked over to where Shanda was sitting behind her keyboard.

"Nailed it?! Whatever gave you that idea, young lady?!" Joe shouted.

Hour after hour passed, and it seemed Monday's session was no different from Friday's. Each time the girls built up momentum, Joe stopped the recorder.

"Girls, let's break for lunch. Maybe this afternoon will be better," Joe said as he rushed out of the studio.

Once again, the girls felt like total failures.

"You guys can do me a favor. Tell Joe I will not return this afternoon," Ashton said as she ran into the parking lot, crying.

The confidence Ashton displayed earlier that morning had been destroyed by Joe Moss. She was beginning to hate that man. She kept playing over and over in her mind what Sissy had told her about Joe. This couldn't be the same Joe Moss Sissy had known. Ashton needed a friend; she needed someone who could understand what she was experiencing. As she sat in her dad's Camaro, it came to her. It was almost as if she were being summoned. Ashton left the studio's parking lot. She knew what she must try to do. Without any approval, Ashton drove to the state prison. There was something she must try.

It was almost 4:00 p.m., Monday afternoon, when Ashton entered Thad Rucker's office.

"Excuse me, miss. Do you have an appointment?" Rosemary asked.

"I must see Mr. Rucker, please. It's very important," Ashton cried.

"You are Ashton Summers, aren't you?" Rosemary inquired.

"Yes, ma'am, I am. Can I please see Mr. Rucker?" Ashton said.

Rosemary informed Ashton that she would see if he was available. While Ashton waited, Rosemary entered Thad's office. Shortly afterward, the office door swung open, and Thad Rucker stood in the doorway, inviting Ashton inside.

Ashton began to explain the reason behind her visit. She finished by saying, "I have no one else to turn to on this matter, Mr. Rucker. There is only one person who can help me."

"Aren't you going back to North Carolina soon?" Thad asked.

"Yes, sir, I leave for home Wednesday," Ashton replied.

The tears in Ashton's eyes touched Thad's heart that day. If Ashton were his daughter, he would want someone to help her.

"Rosemary! Can you come in here please?" Thad said through his intercom.

Rosemary entered Thad's office as he was writing on a piece of paper. Thad folded the note and handed it to her, instructing, "Rosemary, please deliver this for me."

"Yes, sir," Rosemary replied.

Thad and Ashton continued their conversation as Rosemary left the room.

Rosemary entered the hallway and proceeded to the guard's desk. She stopped at the desk and began to open the note. It read, "Please have Garland Summers escorted to my office immediately." Rosemary smiled as she delivered the note to a guard. It was occasions such as this that made her proud to work for a man such as Thad. She returned to inform Thad that his request was being followed.

Thad felt Ashton's loss.

Ashton's tears began to slow as she once again explained the situation. "This is very hard, Mr. Rucker. I had no idea of the demands this would require. I just wish I had someone I could talk to."

"You are a very talented young lady, Ashton. I want to help you as much as I can," Thad said.

Thad took a seat on the corner of his desk and offered Ashton a tissue.

Ashton accepted the tissue and began to dab her pretty blue eyes.

There was a knock on the door.

"You may enter," Thad said.

As the door began to open, Ashton was still wiping her tear-filled eyes.

"Warden, you wished to see me. Is something wrong?" said the man who entered.

"There is a young lady who needs your help, Garland. I wouldn't entrust her to anyone else in this world," Thad said.

Ashton sprung to her feet. Her ears must have deceived her. As she turned, she realized there was no deception.

"Daddy! Oh, how I need you!" Ashton cried as she ran to Garland's open arms.

"Ashton, is something wrong? Is everyone in the family all right?" Garland asked as he kissed his daughter's cheek.

"Yes, Daddy, we are all just fine," Ashton said through her tears.

"Garland, have a seat," Thad said. "Your daughter needs your help."

"Warden, there isn't anything I wouldn't do to help my little girl," Garland said, all choked up.

Garland, too, was having a hard time speaking through the emotions. He moved a nearby chair next to Ashton and wrapped his arm around her.

Ashton began to explain the group's troubles. "We just can't please Mr. Moss, Daddy. We've tried for days, without any success."

Garland took his hand and began to wipe away the tears from Ashton's cheeks.

"Ashton, from the day I found out you were mine, I have waited for a moment like this, baby," Garland said.

Ashton gave Garland step-by-step details of their failures.

"Joe is a tough one, baby, but he knows what it takes. He will do anything for you; I promise you that. He is the real deal and a rare friend," Garland said.

"But how do I connect with what he wants from us?" she asked.

Ashton began to sing the song with the tempo she thought was right.

"Ashton, tomorrow, I want you to go back into the studio and change the meter to your song. Have Skye change the beat counts to what I am about to show you. Do you think you will be able to remember what we will do here today?" Garland asked.

"Show me, Daddy," Ashton said.

"I want you to count your beat meter to me as I show you what I think will work, "Garland said.

Garland began to count the new tempo, and then he made Ashton repeat it over and over until she remembered it.

"Ashton, remember that you have Sissy's and my blood in you. You are a thoroughbred," Garland said as he kissed his daughter's forehead.

"Do you really think it is as simple as changing the tempo and beat count, Daddy?" Ashton asked.

Garland smiled. "Yes, baby, I really do. I'll bet you get it the first time you try it. I am that sure of you," Garland said.

"Daddy, why is it I feel so wonderful every time I am around you?" Ashton said as she once again began to cry.

"Ashton, I want you to promise me that you will not tell anyone about what has happened here today," Thad said.

"Yes, sir, as hard as it will be not to be brag about my dad, I will respect your wish," Ashton said.

She was smiling now; the tears were all gone.

|||||||

Ashton left for the studio very early on Tuesday morning. Once again, she was the first one to arrive. Ashton sat on her familiar stool and held the old Gibson. With each strumming of the strings, she smiled, thinking about how great it was to be Garland Summers's daughter.

Skye, Brooklyn, and Shanda were shocked to see Ashton at the studio that morning. Each gave her a hug, telling her how glad they were to see her.

"What happened to you yesterday afternoon?" Shanda asked.

Ashton smiled, saying, "I had the best afternoon of my life yesterday."

"Oh, so you left us for Cory again?" Skye teased.

Ashton smiled again. She now had two wonderful men in her life.

Joe Moss entered the studio to discover a very pleasant surprise.

"Well, Miss Ashton, I do owe you an apology. I was out of line yesterday," Joe said.

"Thank you, Mr. Moss. After today, no one will owe anyone an apology. I am going to nail this on the first take today," Ashton said.

Joe shook his head. "Nothing like self-confidence, I suppose."

"Let me have a word with the girls first, Mr. Moss, before we get started," Ashton said.

Ashton began to explain to Skye the change of the tempo and count. Each time, the two girls counting them out together. Finally, all four girls started counting.

"Mr. Moss, you will only need one take this morning," Ashton said.

"Okay, girls, let's do it then," Joe said.

The girls all took their seats at their instruments. Ashton smiled at the other girls, giving Skye the cue. Skye counted out the new count, and the girls hit their marks. Joe began to make the adjustments as the girls played. The chord changes were all on key and on time. Joe looked up over the top of his glasses, thinking that this couldn't be happening. As the song was about to end, Ashton began to conduct the others as to when they would end their notes, all in unison. The moment Ashton dropped her arm, the timing was perfect. This time, there was no mistakes. The girls, filled with joy, all sprang to their feet, hugging each other. Just when they expected their celebration to be halted, it was joined by one more celebrant: Joe Moss.

"I cannot believe what I just heard. Now that wowed me!" Joe shouted.

"We have the music tracks, and now we can step into the booths and do the vocal tracks," Joe said.

The girls took their seats in the booth and began the vocals that would be mixed in. This was the fun they had anticipated.

"Congratulations, girls. We now have a record we can promote," Joe said.

The girls began to pack up their things.

"Ashton, what happened to you yesterday?" Joe asked.

"Mr. Moss, I forgot who I am. That is one mistake I will never make again," Ashton said with a proud smile.

"Come on, girls, we need to celebrate this evening. I want everyone to spend the night at my house tonight. This is our last night with Ashton for a long time," Shanda said.

|||||||

The girls arrived at Shanda's parents' house that evening.

"I am very proud of you girls. Congratulations!" Shanda's mom, Lisa Flemming, said.

"Mom, I have invited the girls to spend the night. Tomorrow, Ashton will be going back to North Carolina," Shanda said.

"Well, then, we need to make this a very special evening," Lisa said.

Shanda led the girls into the den. The den was a very large room and would be the perfect accommodations for the night's celebration.

"I am going to order pizza; that way, I can visit with you girls, not having any kitchen duty," Lisa said with a laugh.

"Shanda, you have a great mom," Brooklyn said.

"Well, she sometimes can be overbearing. But, today, I think she has a reason to be," Shanda said.

Shanda threw some pillows into the middle of the room, saying, "Let's get comfortable."

Shanda opened a nearby desk drawer. She removed an old photo album for the girls to enjoy. There were family photos of the Flemmings; Shanda was in most of the photos. There were pictures of Santa and Shanda, family vacations, and one with very cute boy.

"Shanda, who is the hunk in the picture?" Ashton asked.

Shanda blushed. "He was my first crush."

A while later, Shanda's mother entered the room, carrying the pizza boxes.

"Oh, look at Chucky. He was Shanda's kindergarten boyfriend," Lisa told her daughter's friends.

The girls laughed as they began to view other pictures.

Lisa retrieved the album before she opened one of the pizza boxes, saying, "I think we'd best not mix the pictures with the pizza."

Each of the girls looked at Shanda, feeling that this was one of the overbearing moments that Shanda had alluded to earlier. Lisa walked over to the desk drawer and put the album back inside.

"Hey, girls, look what I found inside the drawer," Lisa said as she displayed a camera and glanced down at its indicator. "I don't believe this. There is film in this camera. I don't think this camera has been used in seventeen or eighteen years."

"Hey, Mom, why don't you take a picture of us with the camera? We can take the film to the drugstore and have the one-hour developing," Shanda said.

Lisa took several pictures. Some were of all four girls, and some were in pairs, each time creating a different pair of girls.

"When you take the film in to be developed, tell them you want double prints, Shanda; that way, your friends can each take some home," Lisa said.

"Ashton, can we all go in your Camaro? It really is an awesome car," Shanda said.

Ashton smiled and nodded that it would be all right.

The girls wolfed down their pizza and then raced to the drugstore. Shanda jumped from the convertible and rushed inside to drop off the film.

"I hope this film turns out okay. We just found it in a really old camera of my dad's." Shanda said.

"I will give special care of your film," the clerk said.

Shanda thanked him, asked for double prints, and returned to the parking lot.

"What are we going to do for the next hour? I don't want to go home and have to come right back," Shanda said.

Ashton drove out of the parking lot, entering the intersection of two streets.

"Shanda, I have no idea where we are," Ashton said.

"Turn right onto Estes Parkway; we are not far from the Red Rocks Amphitheatre," Shanda said.

Ashton followed the orders of her navigator, following the signs to Red Rocks. Estes Parkway was a scenic road with long blocks in between intersections.

It was at one of these few intersections that a very eerie feeling came over Ashton. She proceeded through the stoplight, approaching a very large park on the right. As the car passed the park, the feeling became more intense.

"Ashton, is something wrong?" Skye asked.

"Did any of you feel that?" Ashton asked.

"No, Ashton, none of us felt anything," Skye said.

There was real fear on Ashton's face that evening.

Ashton drove through the next intersection, pulling over and stopping in the far-right lane. She took a deep breath and proceeded to make a U-turn. As the Camaro swung around, completing its U-turn, a self-made memorial appeared.

"Does anyone know the significance of the marker?" Ashton asked.

Shanda was the only one who knew anything about this part of the city, but she didn't have a clue as to the significance of the maker.

Ashton straightened the nose of the Camaro when the feeling came over her once again. This was a feeling she had never witnessed before; whatever it was, she did not want to have it again.

"By the time we get back to the drugstore, I think the film will be ready," Shanda said.

Shanda once again jumped from the convertible and rushed into the drugstore.

"Are my pictures ready?" Shanda asked.

"Yes, they are. You were right; there were some very old pictures on the film. I did as you requested and made double prints; however, there is one shot that I could make only one copy of," the clerk said.

Shanda thanked the clerk for his dedication.

The girls arrived at the Flemmings' home, with their mission completed. Their arrival was announced with all the excitement of four teenage girls.

"Mom, you will not believe this," Shanda declared.

"What is it I will not believe, Shanda?" her mother asked.

"There were some very old pictures on the film," Shanda said.

"Yes, I said that when I looked at the camera," Lisa said.

"But, I mean, *really* old, Mom," Shanda persisted.

"Okay, Shanda, I get it," Lisa said in a warning tone.

Shanda turned and winked at her friends.

The girls all formed a circle and began to distribute the pictures.

"Since we have double prints, I think Ashton can take a full set back to North Carolina to help her remember us all," Shanda said.

Ashton smiled at Shanda's offer and said, "I would like that very much."

Ashton placed the photo packet among her things; she didn't want to forget it.

"Mom, do you recognize any of these pictures?" Shanda asked.

Her mother smiled and laughed aloud. "Yes, of course. Shanda, those *old* pictures were taken before you born. Those are pictures of your father and me before we married."

The pictures of Shanda's parents in their youth gathered the girls' attention for the remainder of the evening.

The next morning arrived, with none of the girls asleep.

"I will always remember this night. I have found three very special friends," Ashton said.

"Well, you did keep us up all night long, Ashton," Brooklyn said.

The girls were too tired to laugh.

"Ashton, you are going to be so tired today," Shanda said.

"Hey, it's all right. I have a three-hour flight home," Ashton said.

Ashton packed her belongings, making sure not to leave her picture packet behind. The girls all hugged Ashton as she left. Soon the tired eyes were all filled with tears.

Sissy and James escorted Ashton to the airport early that afternoon.

"Grandma I want to leave the old Gibson. I am graduating in December, and I want to get back as soon as I can. We have a lot of work to do on our record," Ashton said.

"Honey, we will always be glad to have you anytime we can. Maybe your mom can come back the next time," Sissy said.

Ashton hugged both James and Sissy and made her way to the gate. As she began to enter the plane, a very pleasant voice once again greeted her.

"Hello, Ashton. I see you are traveling alone on this flight," the stewardess said.

Ashton smiled with tears in her eyes. "More than you will ever know."

38

SOMEWHERE OVER ARKANSAS, Ashton removed the photo packet. It was almost time to eat. She had just enough time to remember her summer by looking at the pictures of her friends. She removed the twenty-four photos and began to view them. Each one brought both smiles and tears. Each girl held a special place in her heart and in a unique way from the others. The clerk at the drugstore had done a very good job with the old pictures of Shanda's mom and dad. The pictures indicated the years had been very good to Shanda's mom.

As Ashton viewed each picture, she put it back into the packet, not wanting any damage to occur. She was looking at the final picture when the stewardess arrived with the food cart.

"Ashton, I have your meal," the stewardess said with a smile.

Without viewing the final picture, Ashton returned it into the packet.

"Thank you. I am starved," Ashton said.

Ashton's flight soon landed into Raleigh. Although Ashton talked to Brenda during the very busy past three months, she had missed her mother very much. Ashton entered the arrival gate.

"Thanks for flying with us, Ashton, please hurry back!" the stewardess said as she shook Ashton's hand.

"Oh, I will! I have to come back after the holidays," Ashton said.

As Ashton entered the arrival waiting area, it was very evident to Brenda that her daughter was very tired.

"Are you all right, Ashton?" Brenda asked.

"Yes, Mom. I am operating on no sleep from last night," Ashton said.

"We will get you home, and you can get some rest," Brenda said.

After they retrieved Ashton's luggage, they walked through the airport and outside to Brenda's car. Ashton climbed into the car and almost immediately fell asleep.

For two days, Ashton rested from her busy summer. Monday would bring about the first day of school. Finally, after some much-deserved rest, Ashton unpacked her things. She removed the photo packet and placed it in a drawer containing many keepsake items. Brenda entered the hallway, hearing Ashton's closet doors closing.

"Are you awake, baby?" Brenda asked.

"Yes, Mom, I am awake," Ashton replied.

Brenda entered her daughter's bedroom. "I have never seen you this exhausted before, Ashton. I was really worried about you."

"Mom, this summer was so wonderful," Ashton said.

Ashton spent the next several hours describing the highlights of the summer to Brenda and her grandparents.

"Baby, we are so proud of your new record deal. You, too, should be very proud of what you have done," Valerie said.

"Thank you, Grandma. Although the record deal is something I hope will change my life, I had two more events that changed it too. Maybe even more so," Ashton said.

"Two more? And even more so? Does one involve a boy?" Michael asked with a wink.

"Well, Pawpaw, it actually involves two men," Ashton said.

"So it's men now instead of boys, huh?" Michael said with a laugh.

Ashton blushed at his remarks. "Well, yeah, Pawpaw. Two men."

Brenda and Valerie exchanged a glance.

"I met this wonderful, caring, and, of course, gorgeous guy at the radio station. I know you all would really like him as much as I do," Ashton said.

"What is his name?" Brenda asked.

Ashton paused, as if just the mention of his name took her breath away. "His name is Cory. Mom, I know you will like this too. He is studying to be a lawyer."

Ashton's comment made Brenda smile, and then she said, "Wow, gorgeous and ambitious!"

"He treats me like I am really something special," Ashton said.

Ashton's description of Cory left the entire family wanting to know more about him.

"I said there were *two* men. Cory is awesome, but the other man has changed my life." Ashton said, then she paused, gathering her emotions, before she added, "I never knew how much he would change my life, or how much I needed him."

It was becoming more difficult for Ashton to talk. She stopped altogether for a few moments.

Ashton continued, "He is even kinder and more wonderful than any words I can come up with. Now I don't have just a picture to hold and caress. I can hear his voice, I can feel his touch, and I know he loves me very much. I am so proud to be his daughter."

With that, Ashton lost control of her emotions and left the room.

Brenda immediately left the room; she was concerned about her daughter. As she entered Ashton's bedroom, Ashton sat on the edge of her bed, clutching a pillow as she rocked back and forth.

"Ashton, you saw in Garland what I have always seen in him. His goodness is what makes the tragedy so horrible," Brenda said.

"Mom, I actually got to see him twice," Ashton said.

"Twice?" Brenda said.

"Yes," Ashton said. "The first time was for the TV interview Grandma Sissy told you about. I promised the warden I would not tell anyone about the second time, but I have to tell you, Mom."

"This will be our little secret," Brenda assured Ashton.

"After almost a week in the studio, we all were about to give up because we couldn't give Joe Moss the sound he wanted. It was just terrible, and I walked away. I had made up my mind I wasn't going back," Ashton said.

"Ashton, it must have been really bad for you to want to quit," Brenda said.

"It was, Mother," Ashton said, and then she continued the story. "Grandma Sissy let me drive Daddy's Camaro. When I left the studio that day, I went to the prison to see Mr. Rucker. He arranged for me to see Daddy. He walked into Mr. Rucker's office and saw that I was crying and began to wipe away my tears as if he had wiped them away since I was a little girl. I knew at that moment he loved me very much."

It was hard to determine whose eyes were filled with more tears.

"Daddy listened to my count and changed the tempo. The next day, I returned to the studio; we got the sound Joe wanted with the first take. I could have not done that without Daddy, Mom. But now that I know his talent is in me, I can do whatever I want. I am Garland Summers's daughter, and there is nothing that can change that. I am special," Ashton said.

"Yes, you are Ashton; you are very special," Brenda said.

Ashton spent the last few days of her summer vacation recuperating. The next few months of school were going to be very lonely. She now had a new and exciting life back in Colorado.

Monday morning arrived much quicker than Ashton was prepared for. This was the start of her final semester of high school. The fall term of the school year always brought a sense of excitement and new beginnings for the Fishers, and this year would not be any different; in fact, the sense would be stronger now than in any past year.

"Ashton, since this is your final semester, why don't you drive yourself to school?" Brenda said.

Ashton smiled. As much as she enjoyed Brenda's company during the drive to school, driving herself to school was a step toward her independence. It felt very good.

Ashton entered the school corridor leading to her first class. As she glanced down at the schedule of classes, first on the schedule was an honor's English class. Ashton entered the classroom and found a seat. After years of not being very popular, Ashton found there were no familiar faces in the classroom.

Two girls sitting across from her, dressed in their cheerleader uniforms, were deep in conversation. It wasn't difficult to hear the subject of their conversation. There was much enthusiasm about this year's new fall television schedule, and the premiere of a news magazine show was scheduled for that night. ABC, the network carrying the show, had promoted the premiere very well during the summer months.

Soon the school bell began to ring, interrupting the two girls' conversation. Both girls turned to face the front, catching a glimpse of Ashton as they did so. Ashton felt there was a look in their eyes indicating that they felt they were much better than she was. The teacher entered the room just as the cheerleader sitting in the rear seat, Lisa, whispered into the ear of Marti, the girl in the front seat. Both girls laughed aloud as they once again glanced in Ashton's direction.

"Good morning, class. Welcome to Honors English. My name is Ms. Childress," the teacher said as she wrote her name on a nearby blackboard.

Ms. Childress took a seat and began taking attendance, saying, "As I call your name, please answer."

After she finished the roll call, Ms. Childress said, "For the next fifteen minutes, I want each of you to write an essay describing the highlight of your summer."

Ashton opened her notebook, removed a pen from her purse, and immediately began the assignment. As Lisa and Marti paused, each trying to gather her thoughts, Ashton was off like a rocket. It was as if her pen couldn't keep up with her brain.

"Okay, class, time is up," Ms. Childress said. "I want you to hand your essay to the person sitting directly across from you."

Ashton removed the four pages she had composed in the fifteen-minute time frame and exchanged essays with Lisa, the cheerleader sitting across the aisle from her. The look on Lisa's face was one of utter shock; she had barely written down anything, and she was receiving a four-page essay in return.

Ms. Childress walked down every aisle, observing each student's reaction as the class began to read the essays. Ms. Childress's approach to Ashton's aisle was halted by several loud laughs. It was obvious one of her students had written something very comical. She turned to discover that the laughter was coming from Lisa, the cheerleader reading Ashton's essay. As she approached Lisa's seat, Ms. Childress stopped alongside her seat.

"I take it you have discovered something very amusing," Ms. Childress said.

"Yes, ma'am. This is very funny," Lisa replied.

Lisa's remarks embarrassed and hurt Ashton. She failed to find anything humorous about her summer adventure, and it was painful to see that her description of her summer experiences would make anyone laugh.

"Well, since you have discovered such a wonderful essay, you can read it aloud for us all to enjoy," Ms. Childress said.

Lisa immediately sprang to her feet to begin her oration of Ashton's essay.

"'What I Did during the Summer,' by Ashton Summers," Lisa read. She then began to read Ashton's essay aloud. Several times, laughter from the entire class interrupted her; each time, the laughter was led by Lisa's own laughter.

Lisa paused and began to deliver what she thought would create the loudest laugh of all in response to the essay. "My record company wanted to capitalize on the idea of signing my deal with me meeting my dad in prison. There were film crews filming this event for a TV special."

Lisa returned to her seat, trying to hold back the tears from her laughter.

"Ashton, you have written a very good essay. Congratulations on your eventful summer," Ms. Childress said.

As Ms. Childress returned to her seat at the front of the room, she was trying to hide that she, too, was amused by Ashton's essay.

The bell rang, and not a minute too soon for Ashton. She felt she had been humiliated by the entire class that day. The news of Ashton's essay began to spread throughout the school. After all, there was nothing like being in a class with two cheerleaders to make that to happen.

Ashton walked to her final class of the day. She was thankful she had signed up for music one more time. Entering the music hall that day, Ashton felt this was one room where she would be protected;

after all, most of the students in this class she knew very well. Ashton took a seat near the rear of the room, as she preferred not having any attention during this class period. Soon the room began to fill with students. They immediately turned their attention to the rear of the room, where Ashton was sitting. Ashton, once again, began to try to hide her face and emotions. Was this ever going to stop?

Several of her closest friends rushed to the rear. Ashton gathered her emotions. She was not prepared for this.

"Ashton, we have all heard what happened in your English class. What happened to you in there was uncalled for," one girl said.

"We all believe that, one day, you will have the last laugh. You will really be something special, and those cheerleaders will have nothing but the memory of having been cheerleaders," another friend said.

Ashton smiled and thanked her friends; she needed some friends now.

As the class began, the teacher paused for a moment, then asked, "Ashton, would you mind sharing what you did on your summer vacation?"

Ashton paused, removing her essay from a folder, and then began to read the essay in the way it was meant to be read. All eyes were glued on Ashton as she stood and read her essay. When she finished reading the essay, the room was filled with not laughter but tears. This time, the audience hearing the essay believed in Ashton, and believers always make a difference.

Ashton arrived home that afternoon exhausted from the emotions of the day. This was the first day of her last year of school, and it was nothing like she had expected or wanted.

"How was your day at school?" Valerie asked.

"Grandma, I almost walked out of that school this morning," Ashton said.

"What happened?" Valerie asked.

Ashton retrieved the essay she had written for her English class and gave it to Valerie to read. As Valerie read the essay, Ashton began to relate what had occurred during that class.

"They did that to you just for writing the truth?" Valerie asked.

Ashton nodded yes, trying to hold back the shame, pain, and tears.

"Well, something is going happen tonight that I think will change everything that happened today," Valerie said with a very big smile as she gave Ashton a very big hug.

Brenda arrived home from work and was filled in by Valerie about Ashton's day at school.

"Ashton, I want you to see something on TV tonight," Brenda said.

"Mother, I don't think I want to watch any television this evening," Ashton said.

"Believe me, baby, you will want to see this!" Brenda said.

"Do you have any homework?" Valerie asked.

"No, we never do on the first day of school," Ashton said.

"Well, then go upstairs and get comfortable. We are all going to enjoy this," Brenda said.

Ashton followed her mother's advice and did as she requested.

Eight o'clock arrived, with Ashton entering the Fishers' den.

"You are just in time for a new show premiering this evening," Michael said.

Ashton threw two pillows onto the floor in front of the TV. The news magazine show made its premiere with a story about a talented father and daughter.

The story began with Garland's special musical talent and career, and then described how it was all erased by an unfortunate incident. As the story proceeded, it began to trace Garland's life in prison. It then showed the reunion of Aurora's Fire in the prison the day of the interview, explaining that it was a reunion seventeen years in the making.

"That reunion was awesome, Mom. I wish you could have seen the love those guys have for each other," Ashton said.

Then, the story began to describe the emergence of a budding musical star with a lot of raw talent. There were slides of Ashton on the TV.

Brenda felt there was no one any prouder of her daughter that night than she was, but she was very wrong.

Back in Colorado, Thad Rucker had made arrangements for the

entire prison population to view this show. In one of those rooms there was indeed someone just as proud of Ashton as Brenda was. Garland stood near the television set in the room where he was viewing the show. Each time Ashton's face appeared on the screen, Garland would caress Ashton's cheek on the screen with the back of his hand.

The narrator began telling the story of Ashton's musical talent, explaining that the same record company that had recorded Garland and Aurora's Fire would sign her to a record deal as well. Caught on film were not only the signing of Ashton's recording contract but also her long-awaited meeting with her dad.

"Oh my God! Ashton, that is your dad!" Brenda cried.

Something very special was about to happen. It was an event unknown to anyone other than the producers. The producers included the moment when Peter House and the cameraman left the room and a camera was left on inadvertently. Brenda, sensing what was about to happen, rushed to take a seat next to her daughter on the floor. At that moment, Ashton and Garland began to sing together, without anyone—including the two of them—knowing it was being taped. It was the highlight of the show.

"Mom, do you recognize the song we are singing?" Ashton said.

Brenda, with tears rolling down her cheeks, was about to answer.

But Valerie beat her to it, interjecting, "That is 'Touch'!"

Valerie, too, was overwhelmed by her emotions.

"Although our story is over, the saga has just begun," the narrator said as the show ended.

Ashton and Brenda each helped the other up from the floor.

"I told you, baby, I think things are about to change for you," Brenda said.

Ashton and Brenda's hugs were interrupted by the nearby telephone. Ashton, closest to the phone, answered it.

"Ashton, you were awesome on the show. How was your first day of school?" the voice on the other end of the line said.

Ashton began to blush. "Well, thanks for the compliment about the show; my first day of school was terrible."

As Ashton continued her conversation, her blush deepened.

"I don't think that is Sissy on the phone," Michael said, laughing.

Ashton turned to her grandfather, shaking her head to signify that he was definitely correct with his assumption.

"Thanks for calling, Cory. I miss you very much," Ashton said as she hung up the phone.

"I think school will be much different tomorrow," Ashton said as she kissed everyone good night.

Ashton arrived at school the next morning. Once again, as she made her way through the hallways to her English class, there were stares and whispers among the students. She began to take her time making her way to her classroom. As Ashton entered the classroom, the bell began to ring as she made her way to her seat. Once again, Lisa and Marti were engaged in conversation as she sat down.

Ms. Childress, already at her desk, began take attendance. After the roll call, Ms. Childress walked around to the front of her desk and took a seat.

"Yesterday, I gave an assignment to write about a special event that happened to you during the summer. Unfortunately, we made the mistake of not believing the content of one of those essays, and we were wrong. Ashton, I want to apologize to you for what happened here yesterday, and I can promise you that it will never happen again in my class," Ms. Childress said.

Ashton smiled. Ms. Childress did what Ashton had hoped she would.

"Ashton, we all would be grateful if you would tell us more about your summer. When you said that you met your dad, it didn't connect with me that you were Garland Summers's daughter. Your dad was very talented. I, too, do not think he is guilty of the charges against him," Ms. Childress said.

Ashton thanked Ms. Childress.

"Ms. Childress, I am not any different than I was yesterday," Ashton said, and then she related the rest of her summer adventure.

As Ashton finished her story, one student asked if the class could ask questions.

"Do you mind answering questions, Ashton?" Ms. Childress asked.

Smiling at the two cheerleaders sitting next to her, Ashton said, "No, ma'am, I don't mind at all. I would be glad to answer questions."

For the remaining classroom period, Ashton answered questions from the other students. Not one question came from Lisa or Marti. The cheerleaders were too ashamed to ask her anything.

39

ASHTON'S FINAL SEMESTER was moving right along. Summer's Sound's first release was now in the top twenty of both the *Billboard* and *Cashbox* music charts. There was still the need for a music video; Joe Moss didn't want to release "Touch" as Summer's Sound's first song. Each night after doing her homework, Ashton retreated to her bedroom. She thought there was something special on the tape of her and Garland.

"Touch" had always been her favorite song, not only from her dad but from any artist. After all, it was hard to argue against a song that was such a huge hit; in fact, to date, it was still the biggest-selling song ever recorded. She began to change the melody and adjust the harmonies to "Touch"; each take was captured on the portable cassette recorder given to her by her mother. There had to be a way of playing the vocals over a music track. If only she had a more sophisticated recorder!

Ashton, feeling defeated, left her bedroom one evening to join the rest of her family in the den.

"Well, have you finally decided to come out of hibernation?" Michael inquired.

Ashton smiled. "Sorry, Pawpaw, it's just that I have this idea in my head, and I cannot produce it with the cassette recorder I have in my bedroom."

"Is something wrong with the recorder?" Michael asked.

"Well, no, it's just that I cannot mix any vocals with the music I have in my head," Ashton said.

"Hmm. Well, Ashton, you lost me with all that mixing talk, but I have a recorder you can borrow. Maybe you can record a separate tape of your music," Michael said.

"That's a great idea, Pawpaw. You have no idea of how much that would help me." Ashton said.

Michael smiled at Ashton's excitement and proceeded to retrieve the recorder.

Ashton rushed back into her bedroom. At least now she had a way to record the music for the vocals. As she pondered the musical arrangement, Ashton popped a cassette of "Touch" into her recorder. She pressed the Play button on the recorder, lying across her bed. About halfway through "Touch," Ashton jumped up. She grabbed the recorder and rushed down the stairs with an empty cassette.

"Hey, Ashton, your room isn't on fire, is it?" Brenda asked.

"No, Mother. I have an idea," Ashton said as she ran into the living room, taking a seat behind her grandmother's piano.

Ashton began to hum the lyrics and instantly picked out the notes on the piano.

"Brenda, it looks like those piano lesson Ashton took might come in handy," Michael said.

"Dad, that would be great, but I don't recognize the notes she is attempting to play," Brenda said.

"You two should be ashamed of yourselves. I cannot believe you do not recognize that song," Valerie said.

Brenda listened more closely, smiling as she recognized the song.

"Oh my, after all these years, this is the first time I have ever heard 'Touch' performed on a piano," Brenda said.

To Brenda, as good a song as "Touch" was, it was even more spectacular on the piano.

Brenda listened as Ashton performed different renditions of the arrangement. Then, it happened! Ashton played an up-tempo version, suddenly slowing the tempo down for the chorus of "Touch." After the chorus, Ashton returned to the up-tempo, each time slowing the tempo for the chorus. Ashton closed the arrangement to a warm, welcoming applause from her mother.

"Ashton! That was awesome!" Brenda said.

Ashton greeted her mother with a big grin, showing her appreciation of the compliment. Ashton also liked the up-tempo with the slower chorus, and the piano was the perfect instrument to accomplish that.

During the next few weeks, Ashton spent many hours working on the piano arrangement. Late one Saturday night, Ashton recorded the final take for her instrumental track. As she began to replay the finished taped version, Ashton pressed the Record button on the other cassette recorder. Although it was a raw version, it was time to mix the vocals with the music track.

Each time, Ashton erased the previous recording. She found herself becoming like Joe Moss and laughed at the thought. Ashton had an idea. There was enough room on the tape to make several takes. So, after each take, Ashton rewound the musical track, recording another vocal track. Soon she would have four takes completed. Although she was very satisfied with the results, there was something missing.

Thanksgiving arrived, leaving just a month before the end of the semester and graduation. Summer's Sound's first record had dropped from the top-forty charts. There was much anticipation from radio stations to release a follow-up song. No one wanted Summer's Sound to be a one-hit wonder. The Fishers were enjoying their Thanksgiving meal when the phone rang. Ashton answered the beckoning rings.

"Happy Thanksgiving," the voice on the other end said.

"Happy Thanksgiving to you, Grandma," Ashton replied.

"Ashton, I have a surprise for you, honey," Sissy said.

"Grandma, I always love your surprises," Ashton said.

"Ashton, may I please talk to your mom?" Sissy asked.

"Mother, Grandma wants to talk to you," Ashton said as she passed the phone to Brenda.

"Hello, Sissy, it has been too long since we last talked," Brenda said.

"Yes, baby, it has. Brenda, James and I would like to attend Ashton's graduation and spend the Christmas holidays with you and her," Sissy said.

Brenda's face glowed at the thought. "Sissy we would love that."

"I have a present I think Ashton will really love and never forget," Sissy said.

Brenda thanked Sissy for the call and hung up the phone.

"What was that all about?" Ashton asked.

"Well, Ashton, it appears we will have company for the Christmas holidays and your graduation," Brenda said.

"Sissy and James are coming for the holidays?" Valerie asked.

"Yes, Mother, they are," Brenda answered.

Ashton scooted her chair over to the nearby hutch, opening a drawer and retrieving a calendar. She opened the calendar and began to count the number of days remaining until the end of the semester and the start of the holidays. The last remaining days of school would be special now.

IIIIIII

Thanksgiving went by, and school resumed for the semester's final month. Ashton was determined that no one would ruin those last few days for her. As she walked into her final class on that first day back from the holiday, Lisa and Marti stood outside the music room. As she approached the two girls, they giggled and walked off, turning around occasionally to laugh at her again. Ashton wished she could shut them up—just once.

Ashton arrived home that evening, retreating to her bedroom. Tonight's dinner would require longer preparation. After changing into something more comfortable, Ashton relaxed on her bed, listening to her tapes. As the tapes began to play, Ashton began to remember the summer. The memories created tears and laughs. Thoughts ran through her mind about Skye, Brooklyn, and Shanda. It seemed like forever since she had seen them. Then, it dawned on her that she had the pictures Shanda's mom had taken of the four of them.

Ashton sprang to her feet opening a nearby drawer and searching for the envelope containing the pictures. Finally, underneath some clothing, there was the photo packet. Ashton removed the envelope and fell onto her bed. She began to look through the photos of Skye, Brooklyn, and Shanda. They seemed so real! At times, she could even hear the tones of their voices. Even the old pictures of the Flemmings made her laugh.

Ashton retrieved the last picture from the envelope. The picture was turned upside down. Ashton reversed the picture. She started to look at the picture just as her mother opened the bedroom door, informing her that it was time for dinner.

"I am starved, Mother," Ashton said, as she began to return the picture to the envelope.

The days following Thanksgiving were flying by much faster than Ashton had ever anticipated. It seemed as if Thanksgiving had only been yesterday when semester exams began. The semester exams were the final events of the semester.

Lisa and Marti occupied their usual seats as Ashton entered her English classroom for the final time. Ashton placed her notebook on her desk. She was making her way to her seat when Lisa suddenly grabbed her notebook from the desk.

"Oh my!" Lisa said as she unfolded the piece of paper.

As she read its contents, she began to laugh aloud.

"Hey, don't be stingy! I want to see what's so funny!" Marti exclaimed.

"Do you really believe you can write a song?" Lisa said with a very loud laugh.

As the teacher entered the room, her attention was once again immediately directed to the two cheerleaders and their antics. Ms. Childress captured the evidence of the commotion, silently making her way to the girls' seats.

"Where in the world did you ever come up with some of these lines?" Lisa said.

She was about to make another comment when the piece of paper was intercepted by Ms. Childress. Ms. Childress opened the paper and began to read the contents. Once again, the piece of paper created a very loud laugh, this time from Ms. Childress.

"Lisa and Marti, do you think the lyrics of the biggest-selling record of all time are funny?" Ms. Childress asked.

Lisa and Marti paused. Once again, their desire to make Ashton look like a fool backfired. It was their lack of knowledge that brought about a large laugh, this time from the entire classroom. Ms. Childress returned Ashton's paper.

The school bell rang that afternoon, ending the school day. Ashton paused for a moment to relish the moment; this was the last time she would listen to the bell as a student. All the prior school years seem to fill her memory for a moment, erased only by the thought of graduation and finally returning to the new life she was so ready for. Midterm graduation ceremonies were scheduled the next evening in the school auditorium. Ashton's emotions were like a roller coaster that afternoon on her final drive home. This was the last day of school, but it was also just hours away from being reunited with her grandparents.

As Ashton entered the house, Brenda was ending a phone call.

"Mother, who was that?" Ashton asked.

"How was your last day of school?" Brenda asked.

"It was okay, but who was that on the phone? Was it Sissy giving you her flight information?" Ashton asked.

"Ashton, I was talking to Sissy, but there isn't going to be any flight information," Brenda answered.

Brenda immediately observed the disappointment in her daughter's face.

"Please don't tell me they cannot come tomorrow night for my graduation," Ashton said.

"I didn't say they weren't coming; I just meant they will not be flying here," Brenda said.

"Then, how will they arrive?" Ashton asked.

"Well, your grandmother informed me that in order to deliver your surprise, it would be necessary for them to rent a van," Brenda said.

Ashton's face immediately lit up; almost as much as the family Christmas tree in the nearby room.

Brenda could see the wheels turning inside her daughter's young mind as she attempted to solve the mystery of her surprise.

"You do know that it will keep me up all night long trying to figure out what in the world my surprise is," Ashton said as she left the room.

Ashton retreated to her bedroom to find comfort in the one thing that had always been there for her: music. She retrieved the recorder from a nearby drawer and began to listen to the mixed playbacks. Just as music had always done, it soothed her nervousness, and she soon fell asleep.

|||||||

It was finally graduation day! There were so many things to do. Which was good, since all the activities helped the time pass quickly.

Every hour, Ashton inquired as to where Sissy and James were. "Mother, have you heard any news concerning their whereabouts?"

Brenda laughed each time, giving the same answer as she did the hour before.

The morning hours soon gave way to the afternoon, and Brenda returned from shopping.

"Have you heard anything from your grandmother?" Brenda asked.

"Why are you asking me that question? I thought you were the one keeping track of them," Ashton replied.

Brenda paused for a moment, keeping her thoughts to herself. She didn't want to worry her young graduate, but she had concerns.

"Ashton, I think it's time to start getting dressed for your big evening," Brenda suggested.

Ashton slowly nodded; she, too, knew this was a good idea. Ashton returned to her bedroom and began to prepare herself.

The afternoon was fading, and there still was no word from Sissy.

"Mother, how much longer can we wait? When do we need to leave?" Ashton asked.

"Ashton, we really need to leave now. You really look very good in your cap and gown. I want to get some pictures of you wearing them once we get to the school," Brenda said.

The Fishers all climbed into the family station wagon, making their journey to the high-school auditorium.

It was a short drive to the school, but the tension of James and Sissy's unknown whereabouts made it seem much longer. Michael Fisher let the ladies out at the door. He then drove down several rows of parking spaces. Eventually, he found an empty space next to a big white van and carefully maneuvered the station wagon into the tight spot. He briskly walked from the parking lot to the auditorium, not wanting to miss out on any of the activities.

"Dad, we are over here!" Brenda shouted to as she waved her arms, wanting to make sure they would be all be reunited before the ceremonies began.

As Ashton entered the auditorium, Lisa and Marti continued their usual bullying. It had never occurred to Ashton that Lisa and Marti would also be graduating at midterm. The girls marched into the auditorium, single file, taking their assigned seats. The Fishers took seats in the front row seat, not wanting to miss any of the evening's program. As Ashton turned to take her seat, she focused in on the area where her family sat, giving each a very big smile and thumbs-up sign. She wasn't about to let anyone spoil this night! Her only concern was the whereabouts of James and Sissy; she hoped they were all right.

The principal welcomed the families and the graduates. "Tonight, we have the largest midterm graduating class in our school's history. It is a compliment to these students that they achieved their educational goals ahead of their scheduled graduation, and a tribute to how much they are ready to become a more productive part of society."

Her opening statement was greeted with a very loud applause from the audience.

The first graduate approached the stage and received his diploma. The commencement was now under way. Ashton left her seat, waiting in the line at the foot of the stage. As she approached the first step of the stage, her heart began beating more rapidly; almost as if in a musical time, her heartbeat kept time with each step. She now stood on the last step of the stage, awaiting the announcement of her name.

"Ashton Rene Summers," the principal called.

As Ashton shook the principal's hand and received her diploma, there were two areas showing their enthusiasm. She turned to the first area, where her family sat, but who and where were the others? The entire row sitting behind the Fishers all were standing! At first glance, there appeared to be a group of seven people standing, not wanting to end their applause.

Ashton left the stage and returned to her seat, trying to catch another glimpse of the row behind her family. This time, the row's applause was drowned out as the next graduate's family began to show their support. Marti relished the thought that Ashton's contingent of fans was overtaken by her own. Lisa immediately followed Marti in the procession and was equally supported. Lisa, the final graduate of the evening, returned to her seat, and all the graduates remained standing.

"Ladies and gentlemen, I present to you the midterm graduating class of Goldsboro High School," the principal said.

The announcement brought the entire audience to its feet, showing respect and support for the graduates. The graduation march began to play as the students made their way into a nearby room, soon joined by their families and friends.

The class entered the school cafeteria. Soon family and friends began to also fill the room for the celebration.

As Ashton entered the cafeteria, once again, Lisa and Marti were standing nearby, with their friends and family around them. Brenda was the first of the Fishers to enter the room, and she rushed over immediately to hug Ashton.

"Ashton, we are so very proud of you," Brenda said.

Ashton returned her mother's hug as Michael and Valerie entered the room.

"Brenda, I want to get a picture of you and Ashton. Both of you, smile!" Michael said.

Ashton and Brenda obliged him for several shots.

Michael and Valerie each hugged Ashton.

"Mother, when I received my diploma, there was another area of people applauding. Have you heard anything from Sissy?" Ashton asked.

"No, baby, but we heard the applause too," Brenda said.

Marti and Lisa both had a very large crowd of family and friends around them. Marti glanced at Ashton and began to make a face, as if to rub it in that they had a larger group joining them. Ashton instinctively turned her head away, not wanting to give Marti the satisfaction she sought. As Ashton turned away, the most awesome sight entered the room. Ashton dashed to the door.

"You have no idea how worried I was, Grandma!" Ashton said with tears in her eyes.

"Honey, you know your pawpaw and I wouldn't miss this for the world," Sissy said.

Ashton continued to hug Sissy, showing her just how much she loved her grandma.

The Fishers came over to join James and Sissy.

Sissy and James caught Marti's attention. She once again made the face, indicating she wasn't impressed with the two new arrivals.

"Honey, there are some others who wanted to share this night with you," Sissy said.

"Others, Grandma?" Ashton said.

Sissy began to answer Ashton as Joe Moss entered the room.

"Mr. Moss, thank you for coming," Ashton said.

Joe reached into his pocket and retrieved an envelope. "Ashton, I promised your dad that I would see that you get this, and I figured there was no better way than to deliver it to you in person."

Ashton opened the envelope, revealing a handwritten letter by Garland. This letter was a total surprise to Sissy and James as well. Ashton began to read Garland's letter.

When she finished, she said, "Mr. Moss, other than my dad being here today, this is the best graduation present I could receive."

Sissy smiled. She was very proud of her son this evening.

Ashton began to fold the letter, returning it to its envelope, when a loud outburst erupted.

Three girls rushed into the room, shouting in unison, "Happy graduation!"

"Oh my God! Skye, Brooklyn, and Shanda, I cannot believe you are here! This means so much to me! You have no idea!" Ashton screamed.

Ashton's antics created a stir in the room. This time, both Lisa and Marti's faces showed a different look upon them. Ashton smiled at the changed looks upon their faces. This evening was getting better with each moment.

Both Marti and Lisa suddenly focused on the next person entering the room. The two cheerleaders seemed to be in awe.

"Oh my God! Do you see what I see?" Marti screamed.

"Oh yes, I do! Who is that hunk? And just look—he is all alone too," Lisa chimed in.

As he entered the room, both Marti and Lisa immediately tried to make eye contact with him, but it was evident he was focused on finding someone.

He soon smiled and retrieved a small package from his coat pocket. It appeared he had found the person he sought. Skye, Brooklyn, and Shanda all smiled and created an opening.

"Happy graduation, Ashton," he said.

Ashton immediately ran into his open arms.

"Cory, I have missed you so much. You have no idea how much," Ashton said.

"Oh yes, I do, baby!" Cory said.

"Ashton, I have something I want to give you," Cory said as he dropped down on one knee and began to open the box.

With tears in her eyes and her lips trembling, Ashton placed her hand over her mouth, trying to calm her emotions.

"Ashton, from the moment I first met you, I have not been able to get you out of my heart. Will you marry me?" Cory asked.

As the tears ran down the sides of her face and onto her neck, Ashton vigorously nodded, saying, "Yes, Cory!"

Cory placed the ring on her left ring finger. He then sprang to his feet and sealed the deal with a kiss.

Loud applause followed, from the entire room, as everyone had witnessed the entire event.

Ashton turned to see the looks on Marti and Lisa's faces. Both Marti and Lisa had left the room. It seemed the person who smiled last had the best reason to smile.

40

FEELING AS IF she had died and gone to heaven, Ashton Summers arrived at the Fisher home with the rest of her family. She couldn't help but smile as she glanced out into the driveway, viewing the huge van. She mentally began to place herself inside the van for the return trip to Colorado as soon as the Christmas holiday was over.

Ashton's entourage retreated to the family's den. Ashton prepared seating for three on the sofa. On one side sat Cory, holding Ashton's left hand; on the right side sat Sissy, holding's Ashton's other hand. Ashton held her grandmother's hand with just as much intensity as she held Cory's hand. The happiness in Ashton's heart was truly an awesome feeling.

"Grandma, the only thing that would make this moment more special would be for my dad to be sitting with the three of us," Ashton said.

Ashton's comment brought a very large smile to Sissy's face.

"Yes, honey, I know. He would be so proud of you tonight. Cory, I have no doubt that there is anyone he would rather see his little girl spend the rest of her life with than you. Always remember that, and know just how special it is to spend the rest of your life with that one very special person. There are too many people in this world who never get to experience that," Sissy said as her smile began to disappear.

Brenda sat across the room with her head hanging down. She

knew exactly the feelings Sissy was referring to. Brenda suddenly broke the mood, searching for a much happier atmosphere.

"Ashton, why don't you let everyone hear your project?" Brenda said.

Ashton smiled; she knew exactly which project her mother was referring to. Ashton rushed from her seat and returned quickly with Michael's cassette recorder.

"Mr. Moss, I think you are going to really love what you are about to hear. I think you may actually get 'wowed,'" Brenda said.

Ashton placed the cassette player on a stool in the center of the room; she wanted everyone to have the same hearing advantage. She pushed the Play button and raised the volume. There was a short piano introduction. The intro was perfect for what was about to follow. It wasn't long before Ashton's voice gave away the cassette's very special secret. As the song began to play, each person connected to another person in the room that night; no one wanted to miss the emotion that consumed the room. Although raw, there was something very special about the way the piano complemented the up-tempo of the song that switched each time, slowly giving way to the chorus. As the tape came to its close, Ashton pressed the Stop button on the player.

There was a silence that controlled the room. That control was suddenly released.

"Ashton Summers, I salute you! You have wowed me with a masterpiece of which I would have never thought I would have the pleasure of hearing in my lifetime," Joe Moss said.

Ashton sprang to her feet and rushed to where Joe was sitting, throwing her arms around him and hugging him.

"Do you really like it, Mr. Moss?" she asked.

As he did only on rare occasions, Joe became choked up; this was unfamiliar territory for him.

"You know, the entire time you were playing that, Ashton, I kept thinking of how much we could improve your song in the studio," Joe said. "But then, I realized it was the rawness and the affection of what we just heard that made it perfect. Ashton, there isn't any studio on earth that would make it better. It is already perfect."

"Well, there is one thing I want to add to the song, Mr. Moss," Ashton said.

"And what is that, Ashton?" Joe countered.

"I want to mix in harmonies with Skye, Brooklyn, and Shanda. That is the only thing I feel is missing, and the harmonies would really make it special. You see, Mr. Moss, the song is already perfect, and my daddy made it that way," Ashton said.

"Yes, he did indeed do that, Ashton," Joe said, adding, "Brenda, you really do have a very, very special daughter."

Ashton returned to the cassette recorder, removing the tape. She returned to where Joe was sitting and placed the tape in his hand. "Mr. Moss, now it's your turn to take care of my daddy's song."

Joe paused for a moment, trying to come up with something to say.

Finally, he said, "You know, we are going to make music history with this."

"History, Mr. Moss?" Ashton inquired.

"Yes, history, Ashton. You see, there has never been a father and daughter who have recorded the same song with each version making it to number one on the charts. But this one will!" Joe shouted.

Joe's excitement made the entire room laugh.

As Joe Moss's excitement began to die down, Michael Fisher departed his seat to exit the room. As he began his walk across the room, Michael paused, trying to regain his balance.

"Daddy, are you all right?" Brenda said as she sprang from her seat.

Brenda escorted her father to a vacant seat on the couch, next to where she was sitting.

Michael slowly made himself comfortable.

"I am sorry if I scared anyone," Michael said apologetically.

"Honey, you did give a scare for a moment," Valerie admitted.

Michael Fisher placed his hand upon Ashton's nearby hand. It was obvious he was very upset about something.

"Ashton, I want to share something with you, honey. This is a night that, by all rights, I shouldn't have been able to enjoy."

Michael's comments frightened Ashton.

"Pawpaw, what are you trying to tell me?" Ashton asked.

Michael took a deep breath before he continued.

"This is a story that neither you nor the Summerses are aware of. Ashton, a few years before you were born, I was involved in a very serious car accident, as you know," Michael said as he began to hold Ashton's hand more tightly. "The accident required several complicated surgeries. The medical bills were enormous. Although the surgeries helped me make fantastic progress in my recovery, there remained one more surgery that I needed very much. Because of the amount of the medical expenses, the operation would have to be postponed. If the surgery was to be postponed, it would have jeopardized my life."

Michael paused as he searched for the words to continue.

"Daddy, you should go to your room and rest," Brenda urged.

"No, Brenda, I will not do that!" Michael retorted, and then he continued his story. "A local newspaper and television station covered the story of the accident and my situation with the medical expenses. Ashton, within a few days, there was a benefit concert by a young, talented, and, most of all, compassionate young musician to raise money to help us with the hospital bills."

Ashton turned toward her mother, seeing the tears in her eyes.

"Mother, what is wrong?" she asked.

Brenda, now trying to gain control of her emotions, clutched her daughter. "Ashton, the person responsible for that concert was your father."

"So you see, Ashton, if it weren't for Garland, I never would have survived to be here this night, "Michael said.

After a night filled with emotion, Joe Moss arrived at the Fisher home the next morning. He was on his way to the airport to return to Colorado.

"Ashton, after the holidays, when the four of you return to Colorado, we will set up a session in the studio to wrap up your project. You should be very proud of what you have created," Joe said.

Ashton thanked Joe, assuring him that she was more than ready for this special opportunity.

||||||||

Christmas Day was almost upon them. Although the holidays brought a very special and warm family feeling, Brenda knew that, shortly afterward, Ashton would be leaving. As Christmas Day arrived, it was becoming more apparent to Brenda that Ashton was ready to begin a new life in Colorado, with the Summerses and a new husband. Oh, how much she envied her daughter! Brenda, too, would have loved to begin a new life in Colorado with the love of her life. She only prayed that no one would take that away from Ashton; she was way too familiar with the feeling of having something that precious ripped right out of your heart.

The family moved into the den, enjoying a special fire in the fireplace for Christmas morning. Ashton entered the room that morning, admiring the Christmas tree as the glow from the fireplace made the needles sparkle. She took a seat on the floor to enjoy the warmth of the fire. Her deep thoughts were interrupted by two hands upon her shoulders gently stroking her long blonde hair.

"Ashton, let me show you how to really sit on the floor," the voice behind her said.

Ashton didn't know which pleasure consumed her the most: the fire or the comforting hands upon her shoulders. Soon the hands were removed from her shoulders as the body behind her flopped down upon the floor.

"Hey, don't hog the fire!" Skye said. "Let me show you a better way to sit. First, you bend your knees, and then you place one foot under one leg as you place the opposite foot on top of the leg of the foot that was underneath the first leg."

"Oh, you mean to sit Indian style?" Ashton asked.

"Now you are getting it!" Skye said with a laugh.

Ashton laughed too.

"Ashton, there is nothing like the flames of a fire dancing to take your mind far away. I could tell when I saw you that your mind was indeed far, far, away," Skye said.

"You are right, Skye. Although I have heard many times about my grandfather's car accident, until last night, I never knew my dad was the one responsible for helping the family," Ashton said.

"Ashton, my dad tells me that almost everything good that has ever happened to him involved your dad. They really were almost like brothers," Skye said.

"From the first time I saw him, I could tell that my dad was very special," Ashton said.

"Yes, honey, your dad was—and is—wonderful. Skye, scoot over a bit, and I will join you ladies," Brenda said as she joined the two girls on the floor to enjoy the fire.

Soon the stories about Garland began to flow. This was the first time Brenda had ever really talked about Garland; until now, the memories had always been too painful. Some stories made them laugh, and others made them cry.

"Garland was the love of my life," Brenda said. "He still is. No other man could ever take his place."

Ashton loved to hear about Garland from both Brenda and Skye.

"Mom, you really did love my dad very much, didn't you?" Ashton said.

Brenda hugged her daughter. "Yes, baby, I did and still do. I love him more than life itself."

"Mother, I will not open a present this Christmas that will mean as much to me as what this moment does," Ashton said.

Soon the three ladies were joined by friends and family entering the room.

Shortly after the breakfast dishes were put away, the phone began to ring.

Who in the world would be calling on a Christmas morning? they all wondered.

"Merry Christmas!" Brenda said as she picked up the phone.

"Brenda, I hope you are all having a wonderful Christmas. This is Kevin English."

"Yes, Kevin this Christmas has been very good," Brenda replied.

"Brenda, we received some bad news last evening. Can I speak to James or Sissy please?" Kevin said.

Brenda's heart began to race at the thought of what the bad news might be, especially so bad that Kevin would call James and Sissy on Christmas morning. She prayed it wasn't about Garland.

"James, Kevin would like to speak to you," Brenda said.

James retrieved the phone from Brenda.

"Merry Christmas, Kevin," James said.

"Merry Christmas to you, James. Last night, Beau Royal called me. Chad now has advanced pancreatic cancer. The doctors have told him there is nothing they can do," Kevin said.

James's voice began to crack as he continued to talk to Kevin, thanking him for the call. James informed the room of the solemn news about Chad. Everyone who knew Chad thought very highly of him.

"Brenda, I am sorry, but we are going to have to return to Colorado tomorrow," James said.

Ashton returned to her bedroom. She had a lot of packing to do. She knew it could be a very long time before she would return to North Carolina. Cory soon joined her in packing. As the two began to pack Ashton's luggage, Cory occasionally turned to look at things in her bedroom. He wanted to know all he could about his future wife. Ashton removed the envelope from the top nightstand drawer. As she placed the envelope upon her bed, the contents fell from the open end onto the bed.

"Ashton, let me put them back inside while you continue to pack," Cory said.

"Those are the pictures we took last summer at Shanda's house," Ashton said.

"Wow, from what I see in those pictures, you girls had a great time!" Cory said.

Ashton laughed. "Oh yeah, it really was that, and Shanda's mom is just like one of the girls."

Cory smiled, hoping Ashton would feel at home with his parents.

Cory returned the final picture into the envelope, sealing the opened end.

"You can put the envelope back into the nightstand drawer. I don't want to take a chance of anything happening to those pictures. One day, I want to look back and remember how special those moments were," Ashton said.

Cory followed Ashton's wishes and returned the envelope to the drawer.

41

A SOFT WHITE blanket of snow welcomed the group back home to Colorado. Although there were occasional snowfalls in North Carolina, they rarely deposited the amount already accumulated in Aurora.

"Grandma, the snow is very beautiful," Ashton said.

Sissy smiled at her granddaughter's excitement.

"Honey, you will learn to tire of the snow. Although it is very beautiful when it first falls, it doesn't take long for that beauty to wear thin," Sissy said with a laugh.

The year 1990 was just around the corner. Very busy times lay ahead, with the release of a new record and a wedding as well. It was indeed going to be a very, very special year.

||||||||

Shortly after the New Year began, the girls arrived at the Magic Sounds Studio. The girls entered to the recording room, awaiting Joe Moss's arrival. Ashton arrived first. As she entered the studio that morning, she noticed a picture on the wall in the lobby. This was a very special picture, but she hadn't noticed it during any of her prior visits to the studio.

Each of the girls took a seat in the studio, and the adrenaline was very evident this morning. None of the girls noticed Joe Moss's presence already in the room.

Joe took this moment to relish the girls' excitement. He remembered the excitement of another talented group. This indeed would be a very special time for everyone involved.

"Hey, Summer's Sound, are you ready to get started?" Joe said.

His voice startled the girls. They would all have to wonder as to how much of their conversation had been overheard by Joe.

Joe began to play an updated and improved copy of Ashton's cassette tape. As the music began, the girls were all taken by the moment. The studio's equipment created a much better sound than the acoustics in the Fishers' house in North Carolina.

Ashton began to direct the chorus version for the girls. One great advantage of the studio's equipment: tracks could be added to and overlaid on the original.

"Mr. Moss, as proud as I am of the tape you have, I would like to record a new one right here in the studio," Ashton said.

Ashton immediately took a seat behind the studio's piano and began to play a slightly different introduction. The changes made the song flow much more fluidly than the raw original.

"Ashton, let's get the other girls to accompany you with their instruments," Joe said.

Skye's drumming added perkiness to the beat. Brooklyn began to strum chords on Ashton's old Gibson. Shanda, primarily their keyboard player, immediately knew that a keyboard couldn't enhance this song; she simply savored the sounds she was treated to.

Skye and Brooklyn followed Ashton's piano lead and began to arrive at the song's closing notes. The girls finished their first take and immediately turned their eyes to the control room, hoping for an approval from Joe. Minutes went by as the girls waited for some indication from Joe. Headphones adorned Joe's head; he wanted to hear the direct sound, using different mixes of the trebles and midranges. The girls began to become impatient.

"Damn it, Joe, are you ever going to make up your mind?" Shanda said, forgetting that her microphone was still open into the control room, where every word was received by Joe.

Joe shocked the girls with his next move. He proceeded to the control-room door, turning off the light. He left the room without saying word to the girls inside the studio.

"Wow, I cannot believe what I have just seen. He has left the room without saying anything to us!" Skye shouted.

The studio door suddenly swung open.

"Ashton, may I please see you for a moment?" Joe said.

Ashton shrugged her shoulders as she left the room. She followed Joe into another soundproof room.

"Ashton, I want you to hear what we have just done," Joe said.

Ashton took a seat as Joe began to replay the new remix. The sound was pure; there were no imperfections from echoes or feedbacks.

Joe reached for the Power button and turned the power off.

"Ashton, congratulations! Your song is now ready for your chorus lines to be added," Joe said.

Ashton hugged Joe and rushed into the studio where the other girls waited.

Ashton entered the room to a barrage of comments and questions.

"I cannot hear what you are saying. You are all talking over each other, and I cannot understand what you are saying!" Ashton shouted.

Ashton's shout brought immediate silence from the other girls. Ashton turned to the other girls, savoring the moment; she knew this was a moment none of them would ever forget.

Ashton was about to reveal her excitement when the room suddenly began to be filled with the playback Joe had recently replayed for her. Once again, no one noticed Joe slipping back into the control room. The girls immediately paused to hear the music. As if they had all be instructed to, they immediately glanced into the control room. They now had their answer. Joe Moss was smiling from ear to ear and giving them the thumbs-up sign.

"Congratulations, ladies! You wowed me with the very first take," he bellowed.

The girls cheered, hugging each other and laughing.

592 \ DAVID WILLIS

"If you girls are ready, we can begin the vocal tracks," Joe said.

The girls all agreed, with much enthusiasm.

"Ashton, I want the other girls to join me in the control room while we do your vocals. After we do your vocals, the girls can rejoin you, and we will start the harmonies," Joe said.

Skye, Brooklyn, and Shanda joined Joe in the control room.

"Ashton, when I cue you, I want you to start," Joe said.

As Joe gave Ashton her first cue, Ashton paused.

"One moment, please, Mr. Moss," Ashton said as she left the room.

Skye began to rush for the door but was immediately blocked by Joe. He had a very good idea of what was happening to his young star.

"Let's give her a moment. She will be just fine." Joe insisted.

After several minutes, Ashton returned to the room, holding to what appeared to be a piece of paper.

"I am sorry, Joe. I am ready when you are," Ashton declared.

"Are you sure?" Joe asked.

"Oh yeah. I am now," Ashton said as she gave the thumbs-up sign and placed the headphones over her ears to hear the musical tracks.

Joe immediately gave Ashton her cue and began the recorders.

Ashton began the vocals to "Touch," with a passion none of her friends had ever witnessed. Her voice seemed to reach a level in a league of its own. Each previous verse was overshadowed by the next verse. Then, it happened. Ashton reached a high note, signaling the harmonies that would be mixed in. This was angelic. Each time the note was achieved, Ashton clutched the piece of paper in her hand, as if she were singing directly to the paper. As the song began to reach the closing verses, the girls rushed from the control room to await Ashton. They wanted to share this special moment with their friend. Ashton's voice began to fade as the lyrics came to a close.

The girls all rushed in, each kissing and hugging Ashton; this was one very compassionate group hug.

Joe Moss entered the studio, once again undetected. "Ashton, every time I think I have heard the ultimate, you amaze me all over again. You create something more spectacular each and every time."

As the girls began to release their hugs, Ashton stepped back, with tears flowing from Joe's remarks.

Still clutching the piece of paper to her breast, Ashton began to move her hands. As her hands opened, the subject of the piece of paper was revealed.

Joe smiled as he took the paper from Ashton's hand, showing the other side to the other girls.

"Mr. Moss, today, when I was singing, I wasn't singing alone," Ashton said as she broke down.

The piece of paper Ashton was holding that day was a picture of Garland the night he received the Grammy for "Touch." It was a picture Ashton had never seen of her dad until that morning when she entered the studio.

"Girls, grab your headphones and step into the next booth. I want to pipe in the musical track overplayed with Ashton's voice. You will hear the mixed version, and we can record the harmonies in the chorus lines," Joe said.

With a perky briskness of excitement in their steps, the girls entered the designated sound booth. Ashton and Skye stood behind one mic, with Brooklyn and Shanda occupying the other. A bright-red recording sign soon illuminated the room as the tracks began to play.

The girls would follow Ashton's lead for the harmonies. Ashton would signal by a count of fingers as to how many refrains would be required. The booth began to fill with the two prior mixes awaiting the final harmonies. As the first chorus approached, Joe was nervous. He knew that the mixing of harmonies rarely took less than a half dozen takes. Each time the harmonies began, the girls' timing fell in perfectly. Time after time, the harmonies were right on the mark. It was now time to do the fadeaway for the final notes of "Touch." This would end the record and would be controlled by the engineers in the recording room.

"Girls, please remain in the booth. We want to hear the playback of the harmony mixes," Joe said.

The girls waited nervously as Joe and the engineers began the mixed playback. It soon became apparent, from the gestures of the three men, that they weren't in agreement about something. The two engineers were in agreement and appeared to be trying to convince Joe Moss.

"Ladies, let's try it one more time. This time, instead of singing the chorus line twice, I want to do each one three times," Joe said.

Once again, the girls took their places behind the microphones as the recording light became illuminated. Once again, the girls were impeccable with their timing and harmony as they added the third refrain.

The girls remained inside the booth as the engineers and Joe Moss once again began the playback in the control room. The recording light soon was turned off as the three men met. The three began talking, once again with multiple gestures.

Joe and the engineers returned to the control panel. The minutes seemed liked hours as they appeared to be replaying the recorded mix. This time, the three of them remained sitting far apart.

What could possibly be wrong? The girls whispered among themselves in the sound booth; time was really beginning to creep along now.

"It sure would be nice to know what is going on up there," Skye said.

"Oh, well, girls. We might as well get ready for another take," Shanda said.

The girls removed their headphones and sat on the stools in the room.

Soon there was a glimmer of hope from the control room. Joe Moss began to laugh about something. Following his lead were the laughs of the two sound engineers. The two men shook Joe's hand and departed the room. Joe flipped on the microphone piped into the recording booth.

"Are you girls going to stay in there all day?" he said with a chuckle.

The girls sprang to their feet and dashed into the control room. They wanted to share in whatever was making Joe happy.

"Ladies, have a seat. I want you to hear the final results," Joe said as he began the playback.

The playback for "Touch" was much more than any of the girls could have imagined. They couldn't believe their ears. Goose bumps overcame the girls and Joe Moss. This was something very, very special.

"Mr. Moss, when the second take took so long for the three of you to come to a decision, we just knew something still wasn't right," Ashton said.

"No, Ashton. It was perfect. During the time delay you witnessed, we created a master and dubbed four more copies," Joe said.

"Four copies and a master? What is a master?" Skye asked.

"The master will be forever locked up inside the studio's vault. The master will be used to create any further copies to be mass produced, and I have a very good feeling it will be used several times," Joe said with a laugh and a smile.

The girls grinned.

"Tomorrow, we will begin a photo shoot for 'Touch.' I have a film crew that I have notified to be here as well. As special as 'Touch' is, it will need a special video as well. Congratulations, once again, ladies! Your lives have all just been changed," Joe said with a wink and smile.

Joe opened the doors as the girls began to depart.

"Ashton, I want to talk to you about something before you leave," Joe said.

Ashton remained and took a seat, and Joe began to share his idea about the video.

As Ashton visualized his concept, it brought tears to her eyes. She told Joe that his idea was awesome.

The other girls remained in the hallway, awaiting Ashton. When Ashton came out, all four girls exited the studio. There was Cory, sitting outside on a bench.

This day keeps getting better by the moment, Ashton thought.

"Well, I see you will not need a ride, Ashton," Brooklyn said as the other girls laughed aloud.

Joe rushed to where the young people stood.

"Cory, you are just the person I wanted to see," Joe said as he handed Cory a package. "Deliver this package to KARO, and give it to Kevin. Inside is a note giving him instructions and my suggestion. He'll understand."

"Yes, sir," Cory said. "I will deliver the package before taking Ashton home."

Cory and Ashton left the studio, making their journey to KARO.

"Ashton, have you decided on a date for our wedding?" Cory asked.

"Cory, I would love to get married in June," Ashton said.

"Well, that gives us six months to prepare for the big day," Cory said.

"Oh my, oh my," Ashton said.

"What is it, Ashton?" Cory asked.

"I just remembered that June is the month when my grandparents, Sissy and James, were married," Ashton said.

The KARO van arrived at the station.

"I will only be a minute, baby," Cory said. "Let me deliver Joe Moss's package to Kevin, and then we'll talk about our wedding date."

Cory dashed from the van, running into the station and down the hall leading to Kevin's office. As he entered Kevin's office, Cory was out of breath.

"Hey, Cory, where is the fire?" Kevin asked.

"There is no fire, Kevin," Cory said with a smile. "Joe Moss told me to deliver this to you immediately. He said you'd understand."

Kevin unwrapped the package and removed a tape reel.

The note attached to the tape read, "Please have Harley play this tonight on his show. This is an exclusive. You will have it exclusively until it is released next week."

Kevin glanced down at the label affixed to the reel. The label read, "'Touch,' by Summer's Sound, featuring Ashton Summers." Kevin relished the moment. He, too, knew this was unique.

Cory and Ashton arrived at the Summerses' house.

"Ashton, I thought you left here this morning with Shanda," Sissy said.

"Yes, Grandma, I did, but Cory was at the studio when we finished. Mr. Moss wanted a package delivered to Kevin at the radio station. Although I like Shanda, I do enjoy Cory's company a little bit more," Ashton said as she hugged Cory.

Cory grinned at his fiancée's compliment.

"Grandma, we have set a date for the wedding," Ashton said.

"That's wonderful, baby," Sissy said.

Ashton turned to Cory, seeking his approval of their earlier conversation. She nodded, and Cory nodded to signal his approval.

"All right. What is all this nodding about?" Sissy said.

"Grandma, I want to be a June bride, and I know June is the month you and Pawpaw were married. We want our wedding day to be on the same day you were married," Ashton said.

The emotion overwhelmed Sissy as she tried to speak. Sissy hugged Cory with one arm and Ashton with the other.

"Ashton, I would be touched for you to be married on the same day your pawpaw and I were married," Sissy said.

James entered the kitchen from the garage just in time to witness the moment.

"Is there something wrong?" he asked.

Sissy smiled and reached for his hand. "James, Ashton and Cory have set their wedding date. They are to be married on June 26," Sissy said.

James paused for a moment before he realized that was also his and Sissy's wedding day.

"We need to go out to dinner this evening and celebrate the big day," James said.

Sissy and Ashton departed the room to get ready.

"Cory, you and Ashton have just made Sissy a very happy woman. This will be the only wedding she will ever be a part of, other than our own, of course," James said.

Cory paused for a moment; this was not something that had occurred to either Ashton or him. What James had revealed made the upcoming wedding day even more special.

When Ashton and Sissy returned, Cory said, "Now that you ladies are ready, I know of a special place."

"Okay, Cory, you can drive and take the lead. It's all in your hands," James said.

Cory drove into Denver. It wasn't long before they arrived at a familiar place. He pulled into the valet parking, leaving the car for the valet.

"Cory! This is where you took me on our first date!" Ashton shouted.

Cory smiled. "Yes, baby, and I couldn't think of a better place to share this night with your family."

The Hard Rock Café held a special place in Ashton's heart. This was a perfect.

"Ashton, how did things go at the studio today?" Sissy asked once they were seated.

"Grandma, you should have seen Joe Moss. He was like a little boy on Christmas morning. We recorded what he referred to as 'a master and four other copies,'" Ashton said.

"In just one day you wowed old Joe?" James asked.

They all laughed at the thought of Joe being wowed.

"Joe wants us back at the studio tomorrow to take publicity photos and to set up a video. He didn't say what he had in mind for the video, only that it would be something very special for a very special song," Ashton said, keeping the details Joe had shared to herself so that the others would have a wonderful surprise.

"I see the Hard Rock now plays our signal. I wonder how Kevin managed to get that pulled off," James said.

The waitress arrived taking the special night's dinner selections. Although the selections weren't very extravagant, the finest restaurant in Denver couldn't compete with the atmosphere for this night.

"James, isn't that Harley on the radio?" Sissy asked.

James paused for a moment. "Yes, it sure is Harley. I guess he must be doing his old time slot this evening."

The waitress promptly delivered the meals. The four were enjoying their meals when something happened that none of them expected.

"Tonight, ladies and gentlemen, KARO has something very special to announce. This is a very special event. Nothing like this has hit our airwaves in more than twenty years, when an error was made on my very own show," Harley said.

"I wonder what Harley has come up with now," Sissy said.

James shrugged his shoulders.

"KARO radio will be the only frequency on the radio dial where you will be able to listen to the debut of what we have for you this evening. It is a rare privilege for me to play the debut of this song," Harley said.

Harley's announcement created total quiet inside the restaurant. Everyone eagerly waited to hear whatever it was that Harley deemed to be so special.

"Denver, I give you the world premiere of 'Touch,' by Summer's Sound, featuring Ashton Summers!" Harley proclaimed.

Ashton froze. Joe Moss was truly amazing. He had done this right under her nose, without Ashton having any idea of what was going on.

People in the Hard Rock, as if frozen in time, all stopped their activities. It was as if no one wanted to miss out on this happening.

Sissy couldn't remove her eyes from her granddaughter. She was very, very proud of her.

Cory held Ashton's hand; he was very proud of his future bride.

The magical spell continued in the restaurant as the girl's harmonies began. After twenty long years, it was very nice to have "Touch" back, and it was back like no other song ever experienced—before or since.

Back at KARO, as "Touch" finished playing, Harley immediately began answering the phones. Each phone call was broadcast live over the radio inside the restaurant. Harley's radio show now became a talk show for fans to voice their amazement. Harley would air phone calls, nonstop, for the next forty-five minutes.

"Hello, Denver, this is something I have never experienced and will never experience again. With that, I give you 'Touch' once again," Harley said as he replayed the song.

Musical history was about to be rewritten.

42

THE EXCITEMENT THE next morning at Magic Sounds was electrifying. None of the girls could believe the reaction they received the previous night on the radio.

As Joe entered the studio that morning, he could barely contain himself from joining the girls in their celebratory mood.

"Mr. Moss, you never cease to amaze us with your surprises!" Skye shouted as he made his way into his office.

"I am glad you liked the debut, girls, but, today, we must get started on the video. I want the video to coincide with the record release. We have just two weeks to shoot, edit, and mix the video," Joe said.

As the girls entered the studio that morning, the room was almost entirely filled with video cameras.

"Girls, I want you to meet someone who is an icon in our business when it comes to shooting music videos. There is no one any better in his field," Joe said as he introduced Kenny Marshal.

Kenny immediately took control, positioning the girls behind their instruments.

"We will begin by shooting a re-creation of the recording of 'Touch,'" Kenny said.

As the girls took their spots, two cameramen took their places alongside them in the recording room.

"Girls, we will do a lip-sync to the tape. Your microphones will not be turned on. We are trying to capture the energy of the recording session," Kenny said.

"I will cue you when to start," Kenny said as he left the room and went to the control room to take his position as director.

The girls began to play their instruments when Kenny delivered the signal.

As the first take came to an end, Joe Moss left the control room, saying, "Girls, that was great!"

"I want to shoot it again," Kenny said and immediately delivered the start cue for the second take.

As the second take came to an end, Kenny rearranged the cameramen's positions.

"Ladies, I will cue you for our third take," Kenny said.

The girls began to wonder what it would take to wow Kenny. They ended the third take, awaiting the cue for a fourth take.

Kenny stood up from his stool, signaling with a hand motion under his chin.

"What is he trying to tell us?" Skye asked.

Skye's question brought about loud laughter from the two cameramen inside the room.

"That means it's a wrap," one of the men said.

The girls placed their instruments on their stands and left the room.

Joe Moss was standing outside.

"Girls, you were great! Skye, Brooklyn, and Shanda, you girls can go home and get some rest. Ashton, I need to see you in my office," Joe said.

Ashton hugged her friends as they left the studio, and then she accompanied Joe to his office.

"Ashton, have a seat," Joe said as they entered his office.

Ashton obliged Joe, wondering what this was all about. Her curiosity was soon answered as five men walked into Joe's office. A sixth man followed in a wheelchair. Each of the men moved toward the chair Ashton occupied.

"Ashton, I think you know the remaining members of Aurora's Fire," Joe said.

Ashton greeted each of the men with a hug and a kiss.

"Ashton, as I briefly explained to you already, we are going to do something never done in a music video before. We are going to blend some current footage of Summer's Sound with Aurora's Fire footage from yesterday and today," Joe said.

Ashton was touched to see that all the band members were there.

"All we need is Garland, Joe," Brandon said.

Brandon's remark made Ashton pause.

Joe smiled at Ashton as he responded to Brandon, saying, "That is the best part. We can split the video screen with footage of Garland and Ashton."

"Guys, let's head on into the recording room. Kenny wants to shoot a few takes of you," Joe said.

As Aurora's Fire entered the recording room, the cameramen escorted them to their positions. Rudy, Sam, Brandon, Beau, Adam, and Harley had not performed together for almost twenty years.

"Guys, I will cue you when to start," Kenny said.

Brandon sat behind his daughter's drums. The music began to wash away the years as it was piped into the sound booth.

Ashton took a seat inside the control room, alongside Joe and Kenny. It wasn't long before she recognized a familiar sound.

"Okay, guys, let's do it again," Kenny said.

Kenny's remarks brought about a smile from Ashton. It was comforting to know that even the best needed more than one take. Soon they were on the fifth take.

"Kenny, what are they doing wrong?" Ashton asked.

Kenny smiled at Ashton before answering her. "Nothing, Ashton, I am just relishing the moment. This is a wonderful sight for these eyes."

Ashton now returned the smile; she, too, enjoyed the moment.

"All right, guys, we have what we need," Kenny said.

Aurora's Fire removed their instruments and departed the room. Each of them thanked Joe and Kenny for this opportunity.

"You know, Kenny, if you had wanted a hundred more takes, we would have gladly done them. This was special to us as well," Brandon said.

Ashton hugged each of the men as they left the Magic Sounds Studio.

"Mr. Moss, are we done for today?" Ashton asked.

Joe escorted Ashton to her car.

"I have less than two weeks to mix and edit these takes. We have already committed to a debut. The video will premiere the same day as the single will be released. Ashton, if I am right about this, we are about to do something bigger than the music industry has ever witnessed before. What we have is that good," Joe said.

The days leading up to the premiere of the video and single for "Touch" flew by. Every day, "Touch" was the number-one requested song at KARO. Other stations were requesting the rights to play the tape as well. The popularity of "Touch" was spreading faster than wildfire, and the record hadn't even been released. KARO limited the number of stations receiving permission to air "Touch." In each of those markets the results were identical to the results in Denver.

‖‖‖‖‖‖

The day before "Touch" was to be released, Chase Flemming was making his daily mail rounds.

"Hey, Garland, you have a letter today," Chase said.

Garland rose up from his bunk to accept the letter from Chase.

"Thanks, Chase," Garland said.

As Chase delivered the letter to Garland, a quick glance indicated the letter was from Ashton.

"I hope nothing is wrong, Garland," Chase said.

"I haven't heard anything about her musical career," Garland said.

Although Chase had been kept abreast of the situation by Shanda, he wanted Ashton to be the one to inform her dad.

Garland began to read Ashton's letter.

Dear Dad,

How have you been? My life has been going so fast lately. Grandma, Pawpaw, and Mom are doing great. You know too well how demanding the music business can be. I have finished school and have moved to Colorado to finish a follow-up record. We have just wrapped up the final mixes. I can see why you love Colorado.

Daddy, I have mixed emotions about sharing some news. I met this boy, Cory, and we are engaged. We are going to be married on June 26, Grandma and Pawpaw's anniversary. I know you would really like Cory. He is a very kind; in so many ways he reminds me of what I know about you. Even though that big day is very special to me, I have a very big hole inside me. I wish you could be there with me that day. It would have been the most important thing in my life to have you walk me down the aisle and give me away to the man I love.

Garland dropped Ashton's letter without reading its final lines. It was a painful reminder of his failure to Ashton.

"I hope everything is all right," Chase said, searching for a way to comfort his friend.

"I have failed my little girl once again, Chase. She is getting married, and I cannot be there to walk her down the aisle and present her to the man she loves," Garland said as he lay down in his bunk, turning to face the wall.

||||||||

Joe began to dial the Summerses' home. He wanted to remind them that the video for "Touch" would premiere on MTV that evening at 8:00 p.m.

Sissy answered the phone and assured Joe that the Summers household would be glued to the television that night.

"Sissy, I hope you like what we have developed with the video," Joe said.

Sissy thanked Joe for the phone call and promised she would remind Ashton about the premiere of the video—as if Ashton could have possibly forgotten.

IIIIIII

Chase was finishing up his shift that afternoon when he came up with an idea. He immediately rushed to Thad Rucker's office to catch him before he left for the day.

"Rosemary, has Mr. Rucker left for the day?" Chase asked.

Rosemary buzzed Thad's intercom button."

"Yes, Rosemary, I am still here. I was about to lock up my desk and retrieve my coat," Thad answered.

"Mr. Rucker, Chase Flemming would like to see you," Rosemary said.

"Send him in, Rosemary," Thad replied.

Chase entered the room and immediately proceeded to Thad's desk.

"Mr. Rucker, I would like to ask you for a favor. Today, Garland Summers received a letter from his daughter. Whatever was inside the letter really upset Garland very badly," Chase said.

"Do you have any idea what might have disturbed him?" Thad asked.

"From what Garland shared with me after he read the letter, Ashton is to be married in about four months, and Garland won't be able to walk her down the aisle," Chase said.

"Chase, as much as I would like to help Garland, there is nothing I can do," Thad said.

A moment of silence overtook both men.

"Maybe there is something we can do to lift Garland's spirits, Mr. Rucker," Chase said.

"And what would that be?" Thad asked.

"Well, sir, tonight is the premiere of Ashton's music video, and tomorrow is the release of her new record. If we can arrange for Garland to view the premiere, it would mean so much," Chase said.

"I think we can do that much for Garland. In fact, I will sign off for him to watch the video in the prison library," Thad said.

Chase smiled. "Mr. Rucker, thank you very, very much. If it is all right with you, I want to stay and view the premiere with Garland."

Thad smiled at Chase's excitement.

"Mr. Flemming, I think Garland Summers is fortunate to have a friend such as you," Thad said as he retrieved his coat and shook Chase's hand before leaving his office.

Chase left Thad's office and proceeded immediately to the prison library. The television in the library was connected to cable, but Chase wasn't sure if MTV was a channel included in the prison's cable package. Chase began to locate the channel lineup on the cable company's listings. Slowly he began to scan down the guide until he came across the MTV listing. Chase immediately turned the television's power on. Reaching with his free hand, Chase began to scan through the channels on the cable converter box, stopping at the channel that the guide indicated was MTV. The look on Chase's face indicated he had found his treasure. In the bottom right corner, the MTV logo appeared; in the lower left corner of the screen was a message. The message revealed the countdown to the world premiere of "Touch." Chase stood for a moment, as if in a deep trance, while the countdown soon erased five minutes from the countdown.

Chase glanced at a clock on a nearby wall, realizing the inmates were in the dining hall. He ran down the two flights of stairs leading to the dining hall. As he entered the dining hall, Chase proceeded to the area where Garland usually dined. Garland was sitting in a chair, with his back to the dining hall's entrance. Chase approached Garland. Garland was about to take a bite from a dinner roll when he felt two hands begin to grasp his shoulders. At first, the hands took Garland by surprise, but there was comfort contained in those hands as they stroked his shoulders. This was the touch of a friend.

Garland glanced upward over his right shoulder to find the hand's owner.

"Chase, what are you still doing here this late? Your shift ended an hour ago," Garland said.

Chase smiled as he began to whisper into Garland's ear.

"Have you finished your meal, Garland?" Chase asked.

"Well, yes, I am, Chase. Why do you ask?" Garland replied.

"Well, today, I know you received news in Ashton's letter that upset you, and I think I have something that will help you. I have something I want to show you," Chase said as the two men made their way to the dining hall's door.

Chase and Garland journeyed up the two flights of stairs to the prison library. Chase unlocked the library door.

"Chase, after reading Ashton's letter, I am not in the mood for any additional reading this evening," Garland said.

Chase smiled at Garland as he patted him on the shoulder. Chase then removed another key from his pocket and unlocked the video room.

"Have a seat Garland," Chase insisted.

Garland obliged his friend as Chase glanced at the nearby clock. He wanted his timing to be perfect for this occasion.

"Why do you keep watching the clock, Chase?" Garland asked.

Chase shook his head in amazement. He then proceeded to the television, turning the power on.

"Garland, have you ever watched MTV?" Chase asked.

"Although I know about the channel from articles I have read, I have never watched MTV before now," Garland said.

"Well, Garland, after tonight, you will remember MTV forever!" Chase said.

"Chase, the bottom left-hand corner indicates we are a minute away from a world premiere. What is it they are premiering?" Garland asked.

Chase smiled and then laughed.

Chase's laugh was interrupted as the screen reached zero on the countdown. An MTV VJ began the introduction of what the world was about to witness.

"Without further ado, America, I now give you the world premiere music video of 'Touch,' by Summer's Sound, featuring Ashton Summers," the VJ said.

The "Touch" video began with Ashton's piano intro, combined with some old footage of Aurora's Fire performing. As Ashton's voice began, Garland felt like he was listening to an angel. The video continued with more footage of Aurora's Fire, occasionally mixing in Ashton, Skye, Brooklyn, and Shanda. Then, as if done magically, the screen combined Aurora's Fire and Summer's Sound singing "Touch" simultaneously. The harmonies of the girls were perfectly in time with the harmonies of Aurora's Fire. The emotion contained in Ashton's voice, combined with the old footage of the band, overwhelmed Garland.

After three and a half minutes, "Touch" began to wind down. As the chorus lines for the fadeaway began, the video switched once again to old footage of Aurora's Fire, fading into present-day footage of Brandon, Adam, Beau, Harley, Rudy, and Sam. Garland approached the television and began to stroke the faces of his little girl and his friends as they appeared. As the video ended, the VJ struggled to find the words he was looking for. It was apparent to the world that on this night, Garland's little girl touched everyone watching the video.

"Chase, this afternoon, I wanted my life to end. I had nothing to live for. But, tonight, I feel like I am the luckiest man alive. I do have a very special daughter," Garland said as he broke down.

Chase, good friend that he was, hugged Garland.

"Someday, Garland, I know you will be reunited with your little girl. You have to believe in that," Chase said as he began to wipe the tears from his own eyes.

|||||||

The next day, the results of the "Touch" release and video premiere began to come in. Joe Moss spent the entire morning on the phone. Record stores nationwide were reporting lines outside stores, with people waiting for their chance to buy "Touch." Joe couldn't wait to call Ashton with the good news.

"Hello, Sissy, this is Joe. Can I please speak to Ashton?" Joe said as Sissy answered the phone.

Sissy called out to Ashton, who rushed to the phone.

"Hello, Mr. Moss," she replied.

"Ashton, the results from MTV are in. You have the most-watched video premiere in their history. Congratulations!" Joe shouted.

"Thanks, Mr. Moss," Ashton said as she hung up the phone and slowly began to return to her room.

Sissy, sensing something was terribly wrong with Ashton, followed her into her bedroom.

"Ashton, you should be very proud of what you have done," Sissy said.

Ashton buried her head in one of her pillows.

Sissy sat beside her distraught granddaughter. She had never seen Ashton this upset before.

As she began to regain some of her composure, Ashton turned toward Sissy and tried to answer her.

"Grandma, Mr. Moss made a wonderful video. It was too powerful," Ashton said.

"Too powerful!" Sissy replied.

"Yes, until I watched the video, Grandma, the words to "Touch" were just that: words. But they are so much more than just words. 'Touch' is about the feeling you get from the people who are important in your life. Although life has taken my dad from me, his touch is deep inside my heart and soul, and I will never lose that," Ashton said.

"Ashton, you now feel what I have felt for more than twenty years," Sissy said.

Ashton smiled at Sissy. They were connected much more deeply now than just as grandmother and granddaughter. They were *touched*.

In the first week of its release, the single of "Touch" climbed into the number-one spot on the charts faster than any song in history. MTV was overwhelmed. The video demolished all others in viewership and requests. There was a phenomenon in the country, and it was catching.

Garland kept up with the progress of "Touch" by reading the weekly magazines supplied by the prison as well as by listening to the news Chase fed him, based on what Shanda relayed to him. Chase, too, had family bragging rights and was very proud of Shanda.

For the first time in a very long time, things were looking up for the Summers family. Perhaps there was a light at the end of the tunnel.

43

"TOUCH" SOARED TO the top of the charts faster than any song in history. After eight weeks, "Touch" remained in the number-one spot on the charts. Ashton and the girls were overwhelmed by the record's success and the demands of their fans. Joe was organizing a short tour; he wanted to maximize every opportunity that the success of "Touch" created for the girls.

Just two months remained before Ashton and Cory's big day. Ashton did her best to juggle the demands of wedding planning and the success of "Touch." This was a busy and exciting time for the Summerses.

One morning, as James was preparing to leave for work, the phone rang.

"Good morning, James. This is Kevin."

"Good morning, Kevin. I was just about to leave for work when the phone rang," James responded.

"James, Beau Royal called me this morning. Chad was admitted to the hospital this morning. His cancer has spread faster than the doctors expected," Kevin said.

"How is Beau holding up?" James asked.

"About as well as one could expect, given the situation," Kevin answered.

As Sissy walked through the kitchen for a refill of coffee, she heard James's end of the conversation.

James thanked Kevin for the call, told Sissy the bad news, and headed off to work.

|||||||

After making the call to Kevin, Beau looked at a nearby clock in Chad's living room, noting that it was now 8:00 a.m. mountain time. Beau began to count on his fingers, trying to determine the present time in Paris, France. He eventually calculated that it would be 4:00 p.m. there. Beau opened a drawer in a nearby desk, searching for Chad's personal address book. On the final page, he found the phone number he sought, written in black ink.

Beau nervously began to dial the number; he had not spoken to Suzanna in many years. He wondered what he should say to his sister. The phone began to ring. International calling was all new to him. After several rings without an answer, the phone was directed to an answering machine. The message on the answering matching was in French. Neither speaking nor understanding French, Beau waited for the voice on the message to finish.

After the beep, Beau left a message, stating, "Suzanna, this your brother, Beau. Will you please call me at dad's house as soon as you can? This is an emergency."

Maybe Suzanna had not yet arrived home from work that afternoon. Chad had not heard from Suzanna in several years. Although Chad and Beau had tried to establish a long-distance relationship with Suzanna, she rejected all their many attempts. It became apparent that she no longer needed or wanted contact with her family.

Beau waited a few minutes, hoping Suzanna would call back, to no avail. He then left Chad's home and returned to be with his dad at the hospital. He would have to tell Chad that his attempt to reach Suzanna failed.

|||||||

"Ashton, Shanda called this morning," Sissy informed her granddaughter. "She wants Skye, Brooklyn, and you to come over to spend the night. She wants the four of you to have some girl time together, just like the old days."

"I could use one of those nights, Grandma," Ashton said. "Mrs. Flemming is a lot of fun to be around."

Ashton packed a few things and headed over to the Flemmings' house.

Lisa Flemming warmly welcomed Ashton and the other three girls that evening, giving each a hug.

"Girls, I am so proud of all of you! Ashton, Skye, and Brooklyn, I consider you my three other daughters," Lisa said.

The girls spent the early hours that evening sharing stories of their newfound popularity; this was something none of them had experienced.

As Lisa Flemming passed the doorway to the den, Ashton said, "Mrs. Flemming, are you going to join us this evening? We all really enjoyed your company the last time we had a sleepover."

Lisa smiled. "As soon as I finish up some things in the kitchen, I would love to join you girls."

As if they were sitting around a campfire, the girls formed a circle on the den floor.

"Shanda, remember when we found your mom and dad's camera the last time we were here? Can we look at those pictures again?" Ashton asked.

"Hey, great idea, Ashton! Can we, Shanda? That would be cool," Skye added.

Shanda leaped from her seat to retrieve the pictures. She opened the familiar desk drawer, searching for the envelope containing the pictures. The envelope was missing.

"Mom, do you know where the envelope containing those old pictures is? The girls would like to look at them again," Shanda shouted from the den.

Shanda's question was soon answered when she found a photo album at the rear of the drawer.

"Never mind, Mom! I have found what I was looking for," Shanda said.

Shanda placed the album inside the girl's circle, for all to enjoy. In the front of the album were the pictures taken at the last sleepover.

"You know, it seems like so much has happened since these pictures was taken," Shanda said.

The girls all agreed, amazed by all the changes in their young lives during the past few months.

Shanda continued turning the pages of the album; new pages appeared that hadn't been there the last time.

"Wow, look at these articles written all about us," Skye said.

Lisa Flemming kept every article about the girls' career that she could find. As the girls continued looking through the newly created scrapbook, realizing how much they had actually achieved in such a short time.

Shanda turned to the remaining pages of the album.

"Hey, Shanda, there are the old pictures of your mom and dad," Brooklyn said.

The girls began to laugh at the retro styles of Shanda's parents. The laughter became so loud that Lisa Flemming could no longer resist the fun. She came into the den and joined the girls. Lisa, as if she were twenty years younger, sat on the floor.

As Shanda pointed to each picture, her mom gave a brief description of what had occurred at the time the photo was taken.

The girls enjoyed sharing Lisa's memories.

Some pictures brought tears, and some brought very loud laughs; each photo held very precious memories for the Flemmings.

"Hey, Mom, I guess this last picture was a blank, huh?" Shanda joked as she pointed to a picture without any images.

Lisa laughed at her daughter's comment and then said, "No, silly! The picture is turned upside down."

Lisa retrieved the picture and turned it right side up to reveal its image. As she looked at the picture, a solemn silence overcame Lisa.

Looking at Lisa's face, the girls immediately sensed that something was wrong.

"Mom, what is this picture?" Shanda asked.

Lisa stared at the picture for a moment or two, not answering Shanda.

Finally, she said, "I have not looked at this picture since the night you had the film developed, Shanda. But I remember the night when it was taken."

While Lisa continued to stare at the picture, Shanda asked, "What is so important about this picture, Mom?"

"Shanda, your dad and I were coming home from a concert that night—actually, it was very early in the morning. We were standing at a bus stop, and this car squealed to a stop at the traffic light," Lisa said.

Shanda retrieved the picture from Lisa, saying, "Mom, this is just a picture of a man sitting in the passenger seat of a car."

"Oh no, Shanda; it's much, much more than that," Lisa said.

"Why is that, Mom? Do you know this man?" Shanda asked.

Lisa paused before answering, "I don't know him personally, Shanda. The man in the car is Garland Summers."

"Look, Ashton! Your dad is in this picture," Shanda said, passing the photo to Ashton.

Ashton took the picture from Shanda, looked at it, and went pale. To everyone's surprise, Ashton then sprang to her feet, clutching the picture in her hand. It was obvious something about the photo disturbed Ashton.

"Mrs. Flemming, can I please use your phone?" Ashton asked.

"Sure, Ashton," Lisa said. "Is something wrong?"

"Are these the same pictures that I have the extra prints of?" Ashton said as she dashed to the phone and began to dial a number.

"Yes, they are," Shanda confirmed.

"Mom, I need your help!" Ashton said as Brenda answered the phone.

"Ashton, what's wrong?" Brenda asked.

"This is very important, Mom! I need you to look in the top right-hand dresser drawer in my bedroom. There is an envelope containing some old pictures," Ashton said.

"Let me go upstairs, baby," Brenda said. "I will look in the drawer and then pick up the extension in your bedroom. Hold on."

Brenda raced up the stairs and into Ashton's room, arriving at the drawer. Removing several items from the drawer, she found the envelope, emptying the pictures onto Ashton's bed.

"Ashton, I have the pictures out on your bed," Brenda said as she picked up the extension.

"I need you to look for one particular picture, Mom," Ashton said.

Brenda began describing the pictures to Ashton, asking, "What is it you are looking for?"

"Have you looked at all the pictures, Mom?" Ashton asked.

"Yes, baby, I have," Brenda answered.

"There was one I so wanted you to see. I thought I had the same picture there," Ashton said as her heart began to fall.

As Brenda began to return the pictures to the envelope, she discovered that one picture had remained inside the envelope when she emptied the others onto the bed.

"Wait, Ashton! There was one picture that remained inside the envelope when I emptied the others," Brenda said.

"Can you look at it and tell me what you see, Mom?" Ashton asked.

Brenda removed the picture from the envelope. "Ashton, it's a picture of a man inside a car. It looks like he must have been awakened when this picture was taken. Maybe by the flash going off," Brenda said.

"Mom, I want you to look very closely at the man in the picture!" Ashton said with a tone of urgency.

As Brenda closely reexamined the photo, it appeared that the same chill Ashton felt in Colorado had made its way to North Carolina.

"Oh my God! Oh my God!" Brenda shouted.

Brenda's cries brought her parents to Ashton's room. They rushed inside, thinking something bad happened.

"Mom, are you still there? I need for you to tell me who that man is," Ashton shouted into the phone.

"Ashton, that man is your dad." Brenda answered.

Ashton began to cry with joy.

"Do you know what this means, Mother?" Ashton said.

Brenda paused, searching for the answer her daughter sought.

"Mother, I think that is the car Daddy was accused of stealing, and the photo proves he wasn't the driver that night. There appears to be a woman driving the car," Ashton said.

Brenda further examined the photo, following Ashton's observation.

"Yes, Ashton, you're right! There appears to be a female driver," Brenda said.

"Do you realize what this means, Mother?" Ashton asked once again.

"Yes, baby, I do. This confirms what we have known all along. Your dad is innocent, and now I have the evidence to prove it!" Brenda shouted.

Brenda's last statement resounded through the Flemmings' den.

Ashton hung the phone up and began to hug the girls and Shanda's mom.

"This is the best thing that has ever happened to me!" Ashton shouted with joy.

It was time to get started on the vindication of Garland Summers.

||||||||

As the grandfather clock in Chad's den struck midnight, Beau once again began to dial Paris. If he couldn't reach Suzanna during the afternoon, then, just maybe, he could reach her in the morning. The dial tone soon gave way to a phone ringing. After several rings, Beau was about to accept that, once again, he was unsuccessful in trying to reach his sister.

"Bonjour," a voice said.

"Suzanna, is that you?" Beau asked.

"Who is this calling?" the voice asked.

"Well, if you are the person I believe you to be, I am your brother," Beau said.

Beau's statement yielded silence on the other end of the line.

"Suzanna, I left a message on your answering service," Beau said. "I am not calling you for me. I am calling for dad. He has cancer and doesn't have very much time left. I am fulfilling one of his last wishes."

Once again, Beau's remarks were unanswered.

"At least I have the comfort of knowing I tried to fulfill that wish for him by calling you. It is now up to you as to whether that wish comes true," Beau said.

This time, Beau's words were not ignored.

"Beau, how much time do they think he has?" Suzanna asked.

"They are trying to control his pain, but they aren't sure how much longer he can last. He is very sick. For some reason, he wants to see you. I hope you will fulfill that wish and come to see him while he can still know you are there," Beau said.

"Beau, I can't promise I can do that," Suzanna said.

"That is something you will have to live with, you self-centered bitch," Beau said as he slammed down the phone, disgusted with his sister.

Beau could not understand how a person raised in the same way that he had been raised—in the same house, no less—had grown up to become something so different. It was hard to determine which hurt him the most: watching his father dying or witnessing the way Suzanna reacted to the news about their father.

44

BRENDA FISHER ARRIVED in Denver early one May morning. In order to prove Garland's innocence, she would need to stay in Colorado. Sissy and James were eager to help Brenda in any way possible, and she would stay with them in Aurora. Shortly after arriving at the Summerses' house, Brenda phoned Mathew Stein, Garland's defense attorney.

"Mr. Stein, this is Brenda Fisher. I have something I would like to discuss with you. It is evidence in Garland Summers's case," Brenda said.

After looking at his schedule for the week, Mathew told Brenda that he was available any time the next afternoon.

"I promise you, Mr. Stein, this is something we all have been waiting for during the past nineteen years," Brenda said.

Mathew gave Brenda directions to his office, and they ended the call.

Brenda would reside in the Summerses' guest bedroom.

"Sissy, I really do appreciate your hospitality in letting me stay here. I can get so much more accomplished by staying in Colorado," Brenda said.

"Brenda, you are family," Sissy said, and then she asked, "Do you really believe you have the key to getting my son vindicated?"

"Sissy, I don't *believe* I have the key; I absolutely *know* that I do," Brenda said confidently.

Sissy smiled. For the first time in years, she believed there was hope.

"Sissy, although I am very confident, I want you to promise me you will not mention any of this to Garland. I don't want him to have another letdown if, for some reason, this doesn't work," Brenda said.

Sissy agreed. She, too, thought it was in Garland's best interest not to bring up the new developments.

"I have a meeting with Mathew Stein tomorrow afternoon. He will have to file the necessary documents, as I am not licensed in Colorado," Brenda said.

Ashton and Cory arrived shortly afterward.

"Mom, you have made me very happy by coming here," Ashton said.

"Baby, I have a lot at stake with your dad's release too," Brenda said.

Sissy smiled at Brenda's reply. After all these years, it was obvious to Sissy that Brenda still loved Garland very much.

"Cory, I may need some help from an aspiring young law student," Brenda said.

"You got it, Brenda. Just tell me what I can do to help," Cory said as he held Ashton's hand very tightly.

|||||||

Beau arrived early the next morning at the University of Colorado's Cancer Center.

"Good morning, Dad. How are you feeling this morning?" Beau asked.

Chad was sitting up in bed, enjoying his breakfast and watching an early morning news show.

"Well, as bad as my condition is, I am in better shape than what is going on in the world," Chad replied, adding, I have been watching the local news, and it is all bad news. Do they ever cover any good news?"

Beau laughed at Chad's remarks, hoping that, perhaps, this would be one of his father's better days.

"Son, have you had a chance to talk to your sister?" Chad asked.

Not wanting to Chad to be hurt by Suzanna's attitude, Beau said that he had failed to contact her. He assured his father that he would continue to try to reach Suzanna.

IIIIIIII

Soon it was afternoon, and Brenda arrived at Mathew Stein's office at the appointed time.

"Good afternoon, Ms. Fisher. What do you have for me concerning Garland Summers?" Mathew asked.

Brenda and Mathew sat at a conference table in Mathew's office, and Brenda began to display the photo taken by the Flemmings.

"Do you recognize the man in this photo?" Brenda asked.

"Yes, I absolutely do! Where did you get this?" Mathew asked.

Brenda then displayed a photo enlargement that clearly showed Garland in the passenger seat and a female driver behind the wheel.

"I think this is the unturned stone we needed years ago," Brenda said, adding, "Mr. Stein, I have an assistant researching this car. If I am correct in my assumption, the Colorado Department of Motor Vehicles will have records to indicate that Suzanna Royal purchased this car on the same day as the accident."

"If we can prove that, then it would prove the photo could not have been taken before the night of the accident," Mathew said.

Brenda smiled and gladly accepted Mathew's enthusiastic pat on the back.

Mathew Stein's secretary buzzed him on the intercom, saying, "Excuse me, Mr. Stein. Ms. Fisher's assistant is here with some important information."

"Please send him in," Mathew said.

As if his feet were on fire, Cory raced into the room.

"Brenda, the state's records prove just what you thought: Suzanna Royal purchased the red Lincoln the day that the accident occurred, "Cory said with a very big smile.

"Brenda, I believe we now have the evidence to vindicate Garland," Mathew said.

"I will remain in Colorado, Mathew, to help with trying to get a new trial," Brenda said.

"Brenda, I am not seeking a new trial. I am going straight to the top with this," Mathew said.

"Straight to the top? You will seek a gubernatorial pardon for Garland?" Brenda asked.

"Yes. It will eliminate any mishaps, not to mention any appeals the prosecution may pursue. I believe it will be a closed case," Mathew said.

"If only we could get Suzanna back to Colorado. I would love to have a chance at that bitch!" Brenda said.

"I think you will have your chance, Brenda," Cory said. "Unfortunately, Chad is dying."

|||||||

Ashton and Sissy went to the church Ashton where the wedding ceremony was to take place. It was a small mountain church with a picturesque view.

"You know, Grandma, as perfect as this church is, it comes in at a far second," Ashton said.

"What do you mean, 'a far second'?" Sissy asked.

"Reverend Sawyer, would it be possible to have my wedding in the garden behind the church?" Ashton asked.

The reverend turned to admire the view Ashton had fallen in love with.

"Ashton, I think your idea would be perfect. There is no man-made backdrop to compare with this," Reverend Sawyer said.

"Grandma, this will be heavenly," Ashton said.

Ashton's remarks brought a laugh from Reverend Sawyer.

"Grandma, I want to meet with a dressmaker for the girls' dresses," Ashton said.

"The girls? How will you decide which one will be your maid of honor?" Sissy asked.

Ashton smiled as she suddenly hugged Sissy, whispering in her ear, "It was easy, Grandma. I didn't choose one of them. I chose you. I want you to be my matron of honor."

Sissy clutched Ashton tightly. There were no words to describe how deeply Ashton had touched her that day.

Ashton's wedding plans were almost complete now. She had her church, her bridesmaids, and her matron of honor.

"Grandma, I have a terrible dilemma. I don't want to hurt Pawpaw's feelings," Ashton said.

"Ashton, what in the world would ever make you think you would hurt your pawpaw's feelings?" Sissy asked.

"I need someone to walk me down the aisle. You know how much I love Pawpaw. It's just that Pawpaw Fisher has been the closest thing I ever had to a father," Ashton said.

"Ashton, I think Pawpaw Fisher would be a wonderful choice. Pawpaw James would be the first one to agree," Sissy said.

"I'm so relieved, Grandma! I think we can now leave to go to the dressmaker," Ashton said as they departed the church.

||||||||

"Son, I am getting very tired. I am going to catch a nap," Chad said.

"Dad, I will check in on you this afternoon," Beau said as he departed his father's hospital room.

As Beau began to depart the wing of the hospital, a nurse called out to him, trying to get his attention.

"Beau! Beau Royal! You have a phone call at the nurse's station," the nurse shouted.

"Hello," Beau said as he retrieved the phone's receiver from the nurse.

"Beau, how is dad doing?" Suzanna asked.

"Today is one of his good days, Suzanna. I am afraid these good days are becoming rare," Beau said.

"What you said to me the other day really hit close to home. I am making the arrangements to visit him. I should be there by this weekend," she said.

"I am glad, Suzanna. All we can do now is pray for a few more of those good days," Beau said.

"In case something happens and I am not able to arrange this, do not say anything to him about me coming," Suzanna said.

Beau agreed that it would hurt Chad deeply to have his hopes built up, only to have them pulled away from him.

IIIIIII

Day by day, Mathew Stein and Brenda prepared a case for Garland's pardon. They wanted to be sure there wasn't any shadow of doubt about the new evidence.

"Brenda, do you think we can get a statement from the Flemmings about this photo we want to enter into evidence? We now have the burden of proof of innocence. Their testimonial validating the date the picture was taken and the state's record for the vehicle sale should be sufficient evidence," Mathew said.

"I am sure that will not be an issue with the Flemmings," Brenda said.

"During the trial, a witness testified to seeing Garland and Suzanna together," Mathew said.

"If only we had ironclad proof that Suzanna is the person driving in the photo. The photo proves Garland was in no condition to drive," Brenda said.

"Well, we will just have to go with what we can prove, Brenda. I, too, would love more evidence connecting Suzanna as the driver," Mathew said.

IIIIIII

Saturday morning arrived in Denver, with Beau making his daily trip to the hospital to visit Chad. Beau's timing that morning was perfect.

As he entered Chad's room, his dad's doctor was inside with several nurses.

"Good morning, Doc. I hoped to catch you this morning," Beau said.

The doctor continued reviewing Chad's charts with the two nurses.

As hard as he tried, Beau couldn't hear their discussion.

Chad's doctor looked at one of the nurses as he closed Chad's charts.

Once again, Beau couldn't detect the instructions the doctor was relaying to the nurse.

Chad's doctor turned and approached Beau. "Beau, I have ordered the chemo treatments to stop. There is nothing more we can do. We will try to keep him as comfortable as possible."

"How much longer does my dad have?" Beau asked.

The doctor paused before answering.

"Beau, I don't think Chad will last through the weekend. I am very sorry," the doctor said as he patted Beau on the shoulder.

Once again, Beau's heart hurt for his dad. It would have really been nice if Suzanna had made the effort to see Chad.

Needing a break for a moment, Beau took advantage of Chad's nap. This would be a good time to make phone calls and grab a bite to eat. Maybe Chad would be awake when he returned. He wanted to be sure to say a proper goodbye to his dad. Beau departed the room and headed for the hospital cafeteria.

On his way back from the cafeteria, Beau noticed several pay phones in the corridor. Each phone call Beau made became harder. It wasn't easy to tell friends that his dad was about to pass away.

"Hello, Sissy," Beau said into the phone.

"Beau, we have been praying for you and Chad. How is he?" Sissy asked.

The pause and silence quickly indicated to Sissy that things were not good.

"The doctor just told me that Dad will not make it through the weekend," Beau said.

Trying to hold back her emotions, Sissy said, "Beau, James and I will be there as fast as we can."

Sissy's heart hurt for Beau; she didn't want him to endure all of this alone.

Beau thanked Sissy for her concern and began his journey back to Chad's room. Each step Beau took was harder than the one before. Beau paused, trying to muster the courage to enter Chad's room. Taking a deep breath, Beau was about to enter Chad's room when a voice came from down the hallway.

"Beau, please wait up!" the voice called.

Beau turned to see Sissy and James racing through the corridor. They stopped beside him, and each clasped in a big hug.

"Thank you for coming. It really means a lot to me to have to you here. You know that Dad has always thought the world of you both," Beau said.

As they slowly entered the room, they saw that Chad was sitting up in his bed. A woman in a red dress with her back to them as they entered was sitting beside the bed, talking to Chad. Sissy and James were reluctant to enter the room; they did so only at Beau's insistence. As they approached the bed, none of them could believe what they saw.

Chad was talking. The three stopped within several feet of the back of the woman's chair. The curtain around the bed was partially closed, and Chad couldn't see them. As the woman began to speak, Sissy clutched Beau's arm. Even if James and Beau didn't have a clue as to who the woman was, Sissy had no doubt about her identity.

Chad took a sip of water, cleared his throat, and said, "Suzanna, why have you stayed away so long? Why did you ever leave your brother and me? Why did you never respond to our attempts to contact you?"

Suzanna held the glass of water for Chad as he took another sip through the straw. Wanting closure and figuring she didn't have anything to lose, Suzanna decided to come clean about that night and tell Chad the truth.

Without any hesitation, Suzanna replied, "Sometimes a girl has to do what a girl has to do to save herself."

Chad looked into his daughter's eyes, trying to understand what she was trying to tell him.

"What does that mean?" Chad asked.

"I had my own life to think about that night, and going to Paris was the only way I could protect my career. France doesn't have any extradition laws," she said with a grin.

Once again trying to understand, Chad asked, "Why would you need that?"

Suzanna snickered at Chad's ignorance. She was about to answer Chad when Beau interrupted her.

"I will tell you what it means, Dad. It means that she lied about that night. Your little girl framed Garland," Beau said as he grabbed Suzanna's arm.

Suzanna tried to pry herself from Beau's grip, only to find Sissy standing on the opposite side.

"How long have you been standing there?" Suzanna asked.

"Long enough to know that you were the guilty one that night. You wouldn't be concerned about extradition laws unless you had a reason to be!" Beau shouted.

Suzanna denied the accusations, wrenched her arm free, and dashed from the room.

During the commotion, Chad slipped away into a coma. Sissy and James stayed at his side, awaiting a nurse, while Beau pursued Suzanna. Amazingly, she managed to slip away—again.

An empty-handed Beau returned to the room.

"Beau, I'm so sorry. Chad has slipped into a coma. There is nothing you can do for him now," Sissy said.

"Sissy, I am so sorry for what Suzanna did to Garland. I will help you in any way I can," Beau said.

Sissy hugged Beau, thanking him.

"Sissy, I know my dad would want me to," Beau said as he broke down, worn down by Chad's illness.

Chad Royal never came out the coma and died shortly after midnight. He was now at peace.

IIIIIIII

Sissy wasted no time informing Mathew Stein of the day's events, explaining that Suzanna was back in town.

"Thank you, Sissy. This is just what we need. I just wish we had another witness besides you and James. We don't need any accusation conflict of interest thrown at us," Mathew said.

"Mathew, we have a witness. Beau was in the room as well, and he doesn't have a conflict of interest. It is not easy to testify against your own sister," Sissy said.

Not wanting to waste time, Mathew convinced a judge that it was imperative to prevent Suzanna Royal from leaving the country. The judge gave Mathew the proper paperwork he would need to obtain a warrant for her arrest.

Mathew called the Summerses' home. When Sissy answered, he said, "Sissy, it is just a matter of time before we will have the rat in our trap."

IIIIIIII

Suzanna arrived at Stapleton International Airport early Sunday morning. Her flight was to leave for Paris, with a stopover in New York. As she began the walk to her flight's gate, she noticed there were a lot of security and police officers inside the airport. A nearby clock on the wall indicated her flight was about thirty minutes away from departure.

Suzanna turned her ticket in at the airline's ticket booth, receiving a boarding pass and taking a seat in the gate area. A stewardess announced boarding for the flight to Paris with a stopover in New York City. Suzanna proceeded to board the plane. As she departed the tunnel, entering the plane, another stewardess escorted Suzanna to her designated seat and checked her carry-on luggage in the overhead compartment above her seat.

The plane soon filled up. There weren't any empty seats on the flight. For long flights, Suzanna always preferred aisle seats; they were much more convenient for restroom trips. She found a magazine in the pocket at the back of the seat in front of her and began to flip through it. As she finished the magazine and reached for another, Suzanna began to think that there was something wrong. They had been on the ground too long.

A stewardess began the routine instructions for seat belts. Suzanna, bored with the presentation, resumed flipping through the second magazine.

The delay continued.

Suzanna stopped a different stewardess as she came down the aisle.

"Are we going to spend the night on this plane, or are we going to New York?" Suzanna said.

The stewardess, noting Suzanna's seat number and row, promised, "We will be departing shortly."

The stewardess walked toward the front of the plane, arriving at one of the microphones.

"Ladies and gentlemen, we apologize for the delay. We will be departing shortly," the stewardess said as she hung up the microphone.

The captain's voice then came over plane's speakers, saying, "We do apologize for the delay."

Suzanna returned the magazine to the pocket at the back of the seat in front of her. Just then, two Denver police officers entered the front of the plane and began to make their way down the aisle. They stopped at the aisle seat in the row in front of Suzanna. As Suzanna turned toward the seat across the aisle from where she sat, a glimpse of two more police officers caught her peripheral view.

The four officers wanted to be sure that they arrived at the correct seat and row.

"May we please see your passport?" one officer said.

Suzanna turned, wanting to be sure that he was speaking to her. She then nodded as she retrieved her passport from her purse.

The officer opened the passport, which revealed Suzanna's name.

"I am sorry, Ms. Royal, but you will have to come with us," the officer said.

With that, Suzanna began to cause a ruckus.

"What is the meaning of this? I want to talk to someone in charge!" Suzanna demanded.

"Ms. Royal, you can do exactly that by coming with us. We will gladly oblige your request," the officer replied.

The officers escorted Suzanna off the plane and back into the gate area.

A stewardess followed with Suzanna's carry-on bag.

"What is the meaning of this ridiculous action?" Suzanna shouted at the officer.

"Ms. Royal, you have the right to remain silent, anything you may say can be used against you in a court of law, and you have the right to attorney," the officer said.

Suzanna laughed, asking, "Are you reading me my *Miranda* rights?"

"Yes, ma'am we are," the officer said.

Suzanna was speechless as the officer continued to recite the *Miranda* rights.

The officer escorted Suzanna from the airport and immediately took her to the city jail. After nineteen long years, Suzanna was arrested for the death of Officer Tuck Foster.

45

DURING THE REMAINING few days before the wedding, Brenda and Mathew anxiously awaited the news from the governor's office. Their case was sufficiently reviewed and presented to the governor himself for viewing.

Also during one of those few remaining days, Ashton began to reflect on her life. Could it really be that everything was falling into place so perfectly?

Brenda took some time each day leading up to her daughter's wedding, wanting to help with the preparations. This was her only child, and she would only get married once.

While they were working on the preparations, Sissy said, "You know, Ashton, for good luck, it's customary for the bride to have four important items in her possession at the time of her wedding. The custom is for her to have something old, something new, something borrowed, and something blue."

"Grandma, when it comes to Cory, I am already lucky," Ashton said.

Sissy smiled at the love in her granddaughter's heart.

"Your pawpaw and I have talked it over, and I must admit that the chat didn't take long. We were in perfect agreement on this," Sissy said.

Sissy's remarks intrigued Ashton.

"In fact, I believe we can see to it that you have all four of the good luck charms by giving you just one item," Sissy said.

Ashton's perplexed expression soon gave way to one of utter disbelief.

"Grandma, are you saying what I believe you to be saying? I can only think of one item you have that is blue," Ashton replied.

Ashton unexpectedly dashed off to her bedroom, in tears.

Brenda, returning from Mathew Stein's office, witnessed Ashton's rapid takeoff.

"Sissy, what on earth is wrong with my daughter?" she asked.

"I'm afraid you will have to ask her that question. I have no idea," Sissy said.

Brenda and Sissy followed Ashton into her bedroom.

"Ashton, what on earth is the matter with you?" Brenda asked.

Ashton lay on the bed, with her face pressed into the pillow. She slowly turned over, trying to answer her mother's question, but she couldn't find the words. Eventually, Ashton regained enough composure to answer Brenda.

"Mother, Grandma was telling me about the four good luck charms I needed for my wedding day," Ashton said.

"Oh yes. I cannot speak from experience, but I do remember hearing about those items," Brenda said.

Both Brenda and Ashton turned to see a smiling Sissy.

"Mother, Grandma is giving me her blue Camaro convertible," Ashton said as she once again began to cry.

Brenda, feeling as much disbelief as Ashton, hugged Sissy.

"You are the most special woman in the world, Sissy. I love you very much," Brenda said as the three women began to control their emotions.

IIIIIII

The morning of Monday, June 25, 1990, Ashton awoke before dawn. She propped up her two pillows to enjoy the sight of daybreak, which she watched through a nearby window.

With just as much excitement as her daughter, Brenda also savored the moment. It seemed like only yesterday that Ashton was a little girl in pigtails, running around the Fisher house and carrying a stuffed dog. One memory of Ashton's childhood would give way to another.

Brenda tiptoed out of the guest room and over to Ashton's room. Finding her daughter awake, Brenda quietly entered the room.

Ashton, as if instinctively knowing her mom was observing her actions, began to admire her beautiful engagement ring.

"Mother, don't you think my wedding ring will look awesome alongside my engagement ring?" Ashton asked.

Ashton's question startled Brenda. She was in her deep reminiscent thoughts.

Brenda stepped over to join Ashton, taking a seat on her bedside.

"Baby, I have never seen your wedding ring," Brenda said.

Ashton laughed. "I forgot, Mom. Cory has been guarding it with his life."

Brenda took Ashton's hand in hers and began to slide the ring from Ashton's finger. She slowly began to slip the gorgeous carat-and-a-half ring onto her own left ring finger.

Once again, Brenda had the look of being in another world.

Ashton, not wanting to diminish her mom's moment, smiled as she lay her head in Brenda's lap.

"Mother, are you all right?" Ashton asked.

Brenda's radiant smile was soon replaced with tears as she began to slide the ring from her finger.

"Ashton, I am very proud of you," Brenda said as she slid the ring back onto Ashton's finger.

"Mom, what is the reason for your tears?" Ashton asked.

Brenda took a deep breath as she tried to answer her daughter. "Baby, I was just trying to imagine what a wedding ring would have looked like on my finger."

Ashton felt the emptiness in her mother's heart.

"Mom, I wish my ring looked as good on my finger as it does on yours," Ashton said.

"Ladies, we do have a lot to do today," Sissy said from the bedroom doorway. "This is our last day to prepare. After all, Ashton, this time tomorrow, you will be an old married woman."

Ashton, wanting to enjoy the beauty of the small mountain church, had chosen a sunrise wedding. The sunrise in the mountains was magnificent beyond words.

Brenda collected herself, controlled her emotions, and began to prepare for a meeting with Mathew Stein. Somewhere deep within her was a glimmer of hope that there would be an answer from the governor's office. Freeing Garland would be the best wedding present she could give her daughter.

||||||||

Brenda joined Mathew at his conference table. They began to review, step-by-step, the information they had prepared for the governor's office.

"My sources from the governor's office indicate that Governor Roomer has received the new evidence," Mathew said. "Brenda, I have never had a case reach the governor for a pardon, but I do have a very good feeling about this. I think the evidence in our favor is overwhelming, especially since we have a witness to Suzanna's confession, along with the state's records on the purchase of the Lincoln."

The early afternoon hours gave way to early evening hours. Mathew's sources at the capitol informed him that the governor was still in his office; perhaps something would be announced shortly. Mathew and Brenda only hoped it would the news they needed so very badly.

Brenda, noticing the clock on the wall, began to pack up her things.

"Mathew, it's almost 10:00 p.m. I have a very early appointment tomorrow morning; one that has been in the making for eighteen years," Brenda said as she shook Mathew's hand, thanking him for all his efforts.

"Brenda, I will see you at the wedding tomorrow morning," Mathew said.

Brenda left for the Summerses' house, accepting that they had failed in their quest.

|||||||

Governor Roomer sat in his office, along with some of the state's best prosecutors. Issuing a governor's pardon for someone who was arrested in the death of a popular police officer would not be received favorably.

"We all know what the repercussions will be if I issue a pardon," the governor said.

Among the prosecutors in the governor's office was Adam Watkins, the prosecuting attorney during Garland's trial.

"Yes, sir, but what about justice? Justice overdue for nineteen years," Watkins said.

"What are you suggesting, Adam?" the governor asked.

"Sir, I have sent the information over to Judge Daniel Sands. He presided over the trial. I want his opinion. I am expecting a phone call from him any minute now," Watkins said.

The governor nodded.

"I believe we have punished an innocent man," Watkins added.

The governor held Adam Watkins in very high regard and valued his opinion. In fact, the governor himself had already reached the same conclusion Watkins had.

The governor's assistant rushed into the room, saying, "Mr. Watkins, Judge Sands is on the phone."

Adam excused himself and went to the phone on a nearby table.

"Hello, Judge Sands," Watkins said. "Thank you for getting back to me so quickly."

"Adam, I have reviewed the evidence, along with the confession," Judge Sands said. "As a judge, it is my opinion that, with that same evidence and confession during the trial, Garland Summers would have been acquitted."

"Your Honor, do you mind if I put you on speakerphone? I want the governor and the other prosecutors to hear your opinion," Watkins said.

The judge gave Adam his permission.

"Good evening, Judge," the governor said.

"You are keeping late hours on this one, Roy," the judge said.

"Yes, Daniel we are, but justice has no time clock," the governor said.

"Judge, this is Adam. Will you please reiterate your opinion so that everyone can hear it directly?" Watkins asked.

"Certainly, Adam. As a judge, it is my opinion that, with that same evidence and confession during the trial, Garland Summers would have been acquitted," Judge Sands said.

Once again, Adam thanked the judge for the prompt return of the call, especially at such a late hour, and they ended the call.

"Well, Governor, you now have two opinions: one from the prosecutor and one from the presiding judge. Pardoning Garland Summers is the right thing to do, in terms of both ethics and the law," Watkins said.

"Adam, you and Judge Sands only reaffirmed the decision I had already reached. I will issue a pardon for Garland Summers and authorize his release tomorrow," the governor said.

"Sir, his daughter's wedding is to take place tomorrow morning, in a sunrise ceremony. This would be a fantastic wedding present," Watkins said.

The governor smiled as he opened his Rolodex, searching for a number. Finding it, he picked up the receiver and then dialed the number.

"Hello," the voice on the other end of the line said.

"Thad, this is Governor Roy Roomer. I am sorry to call you at this late hour. I am issuing a gubernatorial pardon for Garland Summers, authorizing his release tomorrow. I understand his daughter's wedding is tomorrow at sunrise."

"Sir, we all have waited for this a very long time. I am getting dressed now. I will go directly to my office to start his release," Thad said. "Thank you, Governor."

Thad arrived at the penitentiary shortly after midnight. He began all the necessary paperwork to exonerate Garland Summers. The documents he filed would erase the conviction; it would be as if Garland's conviction had never occurred. All state and federal records had to be updated. Thad filled out a requisition for some civilian clothes to be brought to his office. There had to be something around that would be suitable for a man to wear to his daughter's wedding.

Thad now needed someone who could drive Garland to the wedding. There was only one person suitable; a man perfect to carry out this special delivery. Thad called the supervisor on duty for Garland's block.

"What time does Chase Flemming arrive for his shift?" Thad asked.

The supervisor checked his records. "Sir, Chase is off today. He is attending a wedding."

"Do you have his home phone number? It is very important that I get in touch with him," Thad said.

The supervisor retrieved Chase's number for Thad.

"Hello," a very sleepy voiced answered.

"Chase, this is Thad Rucker. You know I wouldn't call you at home at this hour if it wasn't something very important and urgent. I need you to get down here as fast as you can," Thad said.

"Mr. Rucker, I have a wedding to attend this morning," Chase said.

"I know, and that is why I need you, and only you, for this delivery. It will not take long. After you are finished here, you can leave for the wedding immediately," Thad said.

"I will be there in less than an hour," Chase said as he hung up the phone.

||||||||

Garland Summers was just awakening when a guard began to open his cell door.

"Garland, I am to take you to Warden Rucker's office immediately," the guard said.

Garland and the guard quickly walked to Thad's office.

"Sir, here is Mr. Summers," the guard said.

"I want you to bring all of Mr. Summer's things to my office," Thad ordered the guard.

The guard went back to Garland's cell.

"What is going on, sir? Am I being transferred to another block?" Garland asked.

"Let's just say you are being transferred, all right; it's just not to another block," Thad said with a smile.

Garland looked puzzled.

"I want you to read this letter from Governor Roomer," Thad said as he passed the letter to Garland.

Garland read the governor's letter and then asked, "Mr. Rucker, is this for real?"

"Yes, Garland. In fact, those clothes hanging up over there are for you," Thad said.

Garland turned to view the clothes hanging on a nearby coat hanger.

"Aren't these a little fancy for someone being released from prison?" Garland asked.

"Well, yes, they are Garland. But not everyone leaves prison and goes directly to attend a wedding," Thad said.

Garland broke into a grin and immediately hugged Thad. After all these years, Garland would soon be a free man.

As Garland stepped into a corner and began to dress, there was a knock on Thad's office door.

"Come in," Thad said.

"I'm here for your delivery, sir," Chase Flemming said.

Thad smiled as he shook Chase's hand and thanked him for coming on such a short notice.

"I have a special wedding present I want you to take to the wedding for me," Thad said.

Thad's request confused Chase. "I suppose that's the delivery you mentioned on the phone, sir. It's just that it's so early in the morning. I am sure Ashton would appreciate any gift you have for her, even after her wedding."

"I apologize for the early hour, Chase, but this gift needs to be there before the wedding is over," Thad replied with a laugh.

Chase was still unsure as to why Thad was so insistent that he make the delivery, but he awaited further instructions. He then caught a glimpse from the corner of one of his eyes. There was a man standing in the corner of the office.

"Good morning, Chase," the man said.

Garland's voice startled Chase, causing him to drop the set of keys he was juggling in his hand.

"Garland, where did you get those threads?" Chase asked.

"Chase, *this* is the package I need you to deliver to the wedding," Thad said.

Chase smiled at Thad. "Warden, I think it's wonderful you are letting Garland out to attend Ashton's wedding."

Once again, Thad laughed. This time, Garland joined in.

"Chase, I have been pardoned," Garland said.

The good news left Chase speechless.

"You two need to get going if you are to arrive at the church on time for the wedding," Thad said.

With that, Chase and Garland rushed from Thad's office.

46

AS JUNE 26 arrived, there wasn't a tired eye in the Summerses' home. The pure adrenaline was more than enough to let everyone make it through the night without any sleep. If it had been six months later or earlier, it could have easily been the morning after Christmas, with a group of kids all enjoying their new toys from Santa. As the kitchen clock struck 4:00 a.m., it was apparent that no one was going to bed this day.

"Ashton, let me help you with your hair," Sissy said.

Ashton met Sissy at the kitchen sink, while her grandmother prepared a warm rinse. Ashton bent over the sink, awaiting the warm mist of water from the sink's spray nozzle. The warm water soon saturated her long blonde hair and was quickly joined by a cool, creamy sensation delivered by shampoo. The herbal scent from the shampoo soon filled the nostrils of both the shampooer and her client.

Sissy's fingers began to gently massage Ashton's scalp. Each stroke was pure heaven as the fingers softly rubbed the suds from the shampoo into Ashton's long hair. The suds began to disappear as the spray of warm water rinsed the shampoo clean. Sissy's fingers then guided any traces of shampoo from Ashton's hair.

"Oh my, Grandma! You do know how to spoil a girl," Ashton said as she raised her head, receiving a warm towel wrap.

"Ashton, take a seat at the kitchen table while I blow-dry your hair," Sissy instructed.

The warm air from the blow-dryer slowly began to dry Ashton's long hair. Her blonde hair appeared to be glowing. Sissy said that she had never seen Ashton's hair look as radiant as it did that morning.

"Ashton, after you have put your wedding dress on, we will use a curling iron for the finishing touches to your hair," Sissy said.

James and the Fishers entered the kitchen for their morning coffee. Each of them stopped to enjoy the sight of Ashton's radiance.

"Is anyone hungry for breakfast?" Sissy asked.

"Sissy, the time is getting away from us this morning. It is already past 5:00 a.m.," James said.

"James, I'm sure it won't matter. I think we're all too excited to have any appetite for breakfast this morning," Valerie said.

"Grandma, will you and Mother help me with my dress?" Ashton asked.

Without another word, the three women departed the kitchen and headed for Ashton's bedroom.

"Ashton, we all need to leave the house at six," Sissy said.

Ashton slipped carefully into her wedding dress. The dress clung to Ashton's figure, assuring a perfect fit.

"Ashton, as beautiful as your dress is, on this morning, its beauty is a far second in this room," Sissy said.

Brenda and Sissy left Ashton's room and went to put their own dresses on.

Sissy soon returned to Ashton's room, dressed for the wedding.

"Are you ready for the finishing touches to your hair?" Sissy asked.

Ashton took a seat on a chair in front of the dresser's mirror as Sissy began to treat her beautiful long hair.

"Ashton, I have an idea for your hair. Your dad always loved a woman's hair in a waterfall, and I think you have the perfect hair for that style," Sissy said.

Ashton smiled and nodded her approval.

Brenda, too, returned to Ashton's bedroom.

"Ashton, you look awesome! Your grandmother's touch to your hair is breathtaking. I wish your dad could see you; he always loved my hair in a waterfall," Brenda said.

Brenda placed her hand on Ashton's shoulder, and Ashton placed her hand on top of Brenda's hand.

Valerie entered Ashton's bedroom, holding a small tiara made of miniature red roses. Valerie placed the tiara on Ashton's head, aligning it with the part in hair forming the waterfall.

"Every princess needs a crown, darling," Valerie said as she kissed the top of Ashton's head.

"Ladies, I think it is time for us to leave for the church," James said.

Sissy looked at her watch, agreeing with James.

"If we leave now, we will get to the church about an hour before the wedding is scheduled to begin," Sissy said.

The caravan pulled out of the Summerses' driveway, greeted by a very beautiful June morning. The weather was better than any of them could have hoped for.

IIIIIII

Cory was the first to arrive at the church that morning. Ashton was completely; Cory was just the opposite. Time after time, he would retrieve the small box from his tuxedo pocket, assuring himself that the ring was still inside.

"Good morning, Cory," Reverend Sawyer said. "Would you like to join me for a hot cup of coffee? You do know that caffeine can calm you down just as easily as it charges you up, don't you? You look like a man who could really use a good hot cup of joe."

Cory accompanied the reverend to a nearby coffee bar in the church.

IIIIIII

Chase knew that, the later he and Garland arrived, the larger the press coverage of the wedding would be. As Chase and Garland entered the church's parking lot, there was already a rather large crowd of paparazzi and journalists preparing their equipment for Ashton's arrival. Chase laughed to himself, imagining the crowd size if they only knew who was also attending the wedding. Chase turned down a small alley that lead to the rear of the church; this would enable him and Garland to enter the church undetected by the crowd at the front of the church.

"Chase, I don't want to take away from Ashton's big day. I would like to stay back here until the wedding starts," Garland said.

Chase agreed and led Garland to small area just off the garden area. Garland paused to admire the sun as it began to slowly creep over a mountain peak. Taking a seat on a nearby bench, Garland's admiration of the mountains was quickly interrupted as another sight appeared—a sight absent from view for nineteen years. Garland's dash to the object quickly grabbed Chase's attention.

It soon became obvious that the object of Garland's attention was Ashton's getaway car.

"Chase, I haven't seen this beauty for nineteen years, and she is just as gorgeous as the day I bought her," Garland said.

"This was your car?" Chase asked.

"No, Chase, this was a birthday present I bought for my mother with one of my first royalty checks," Garland said.

"She really is beautiful, Garland," Chase said.

Garland opened the driver's door and took a seat behind the wheel.

"Garland, I want to check on the activity out front," Chase said.

The bridal party was arriving, followed by a mad dash from the paparazzi. The swarm of photo opportunists made it difficult for the Summerses and Fishers to exit their vehicles.

Ashton, Brenda, and Sissy began to struggle making their way. Each step proved more difficult than the step before. The overzealous crowd caused the ladies to retreat to their car.

"How are we ever going to get out of this car? The crowd is becoming larger and more controlling," Ashton said.

Sissy, Ashton, and Brenda, holding on to each other, were about to give up on escaping for the church.

"Look! There seems to be a parting of these idiots," Ashton said.

With that, Sissy's door swung open.

"Ladies, are you ready to make your way into the church? Sissy, let me give you a hand," their rescuer said.

As Sissy emerged from the rear of the car, she looked at their rescuer.

"Brandon, you are always my bodyguard," Sissy said. "Ladies, our path will not be blocked any longer. We couldn't be in any safer hands."

"Adam, please escort Sissy into the church," Brandon said as he delivered Sissy to Adam.

"Hey, baby girl, it's your turn now," Brandon said as he helped Ashton from her seat, delivering her to Rudy.

"Brenda, let's get you to your little girl's wedding," Brandon said as he personally led Brenda into the church.

The church was filling up quickly.

"Brandon, you have always been there for me whenever I needed you," Sissy said.

"Ashton, we need to head on over to the bridal room. It is bad luck for the groom to see you before you are officially married," Brenda said.

"I hope Cory doesn't have any trouble getting here on time," Ashton said.

"You can relax, Ashton. Cory is already here. In fact, Reverend Sawyer informed me that Cory has been here for more than two hours," Brandon said with a laugh.

James, Valerie, and Michael soon joined Ashton, Brenda, and Sissy in the bridal room.

Brenda and Sissy then began to apply Ashton's final touches.

Reverend Sawyer cracked open the door, asking, "Is everyone almost ready?"

Ashton took a deep breath and assured the reverend that everything was under control.

The reverend's departure was quickly replaced with the entrance of Skye, Brooklyn, and Shanda, Ashton's bridesmaids.

"Ladies, you look awesome!" Michael said with a smile.

"Will you ladies please excuse me for a minute? I want to get a breath of fresh air," Sissy said as she departed the room.

Sissy stopped at a nearby folding door, observing that the garden area's seating was almost full. Only the front two rows on the bride's side, reserved for her family, remained unoccupied. As Sissy began to close the door, she noticed a very disturbing sight that she could not ignore. Sitting all alone in the back row was a man in a dark-blue suit. Sissy immediately approached the man, taking a seat next to him.

"Beau, I want to tell you again how sorry I am about Chad. You know we all loved him dearly," Sissy said, giving him a hug.

"Thank you, Sissy," Beau said. "I had mixed feelings about coming to Ashton's wedding today. I am so ashamed of what my sister has done to your family, and I wasn't sure if I would be allowed to attend."

"You listen to me, Beau Royal! No one here has any ill feelings toward you or Chad for what Suzanna did or for what she is," Sissy said very firmly.

"Now that my dad is gone, Aurora's Fire is the only family I have left," Beau said.

Without saying a word, Sissy reached for Beau's hand and led him to a row behind the bride's family seats. Sissy hugged Beau once again.

"You see, Beau, we are the ones who need to thank you. What you did was very hard to do. Thanks to you, I believe that, someday, my son will be with me again," Sissy said.

Beau entered the row and took a seat.

Sissy's attempt to turn around and go back to the bridal room was soon blocked as Adam, Brandon, Rudy, and Sam all made their way to where Beau was sitting, each stopping to hug and greet him. Aurora's Fire was all present for this wonderful occasion. As Brandon whispered in Beau's ear, Beau stood and turned to wave to Harley, seated in his wheelchair at the end of the row where the band members were sitting.

Sissy walked toward the bridal room, stopping to knock on a door across the aisle.

"Come in," Cory called from inside the room.

Sissy entered the room and said, "Cory, you look very handsome. This occasion brings back memories of forty years ago."

Cory greeted Sissy with a big hug. "Happy anniversary, Grandma!

I hope you don't mind me calling you Grandma. My grandmothers are both gone now."

Sissy kissed Cory on the cheek. "I would be honored for you to call me that."

Reverend Sawyer gave the final reminder; it was time to get the wedding started. Ashton's bridesmaids were the first to depart the room, leaving Brenda, Ashton, Valerie, and Michael in the room. Next, Valerie departed the room.

Brenda, sitting on a chair in the corner, opened her small purse, searching for Ashton's special present. She began to retrieve the special gift, nestled at the bottom of the bag and tucked away very safely in a piece of material. Brenda opened the material, revealing its treasure: the engagement ring Garland had given her many years before. She had kept the ring tucked away all this time; it was a painful reminder of the biggest mistake of her life—not saying that she would marry the only man she had ever loved.

"Mother, I am glad you brought the ring with you. Will you wear it today—for me?" Ashton said.

Brenda was touched deeply. "I can't, baby. I just can't."

Brenda began to cry.

"Brenda, we are about to start; your escort is here to take you to your seat in the garden," Reverend Sawyer said.

Brenda hugged and kissed her dad and Ashton, clutching the wrapped ring in her hand. If she couldn't wear the ring, she could at least hold it in its protective cloth.

"Ashton, it means so much to me to be the one to give you away on this special day. I always dreamed of one day doing this for your mom," Michael said.

"I know, Pawpaw; she wanted that very much too," Ashton said, trying to fight off the tears.

Michael kissed Ashton's cheek and then opened the door as "Here Comes the Bride" began to play.

Garland approached the garden area to take a seat just out of the view of those attending the wedding. Suddenly, as if an old lost friend were trying to contact Garland, a young girl sitting just beyond his reach began playing "Here Comes the Bride." There was something very special about the song. It wasn't just the song; it was the instrument playing the song was accompanied. Garland couldn't shake the feeling that an old lost friend had summoned him. It was true: Shanda Flemming was playing "Here Comes the Bride" on his old Gibson. After all these years, it was as if the old Gibson herself showing off to the one who had held her so many times. Garland and the old Gibson were reunited for the greatest, happiest day of his life.

||||||||

As Ashton and Michael entered the aisle leading to the pulpit area, the congregation began to stand, showing their appreciation for the beautiful bride. Ashton took her first step into the aisle. As she approached the first row of spectators, Ashton was greeted by a very warm smile, the smile that, on one particular morning back in North Carolina, had rescued Ashton from the verbal abuse of two cheerleaders. Ms. Childress patted Ashton on the shoulder as she passed by. Ashton smiled, noticing how beautiful Ms. Childress was when not wearing her schoolteacher attire.

Row after row contained people whom Ashton admired, and now it was their turn to show their admiration for the young star on her wedding day. A cool mountain breeze began to softly feather the layers of Ashton's blonde hair. Shanda and the old Gibson were about to finish as Ashton approached the final rows. Ashton made a slight detour around the wheelchair marking the row Aurora's Fire occupied. She loved all these men dearly and paused to greet them all.

Valerie Fisher, Joe Moss, Kevin English, and James Summers occupied seats on the front row, the farthest from the aisle. The aisle seat was reserved for one very nervous and proud mother.

Ashton stopped to greet her mother with the final hug of her unmarried life.

"Thanks for always being there for me," Ashton whispered into Brenda's ear.

Needing something to comfort her as Ashton broke away from

the hug and continued to join Reverend Sawyer, Brenda began to grip the ring inside the cloth in her hand.

Shanda placed the old Gibson in a stand and joined Sissy and the bridesmaids.

The mountains provided a backdrop a thousand words could never do justice to.

Ashton and Michael stood in front of Reverend Sawyer. Cory, with a tear in his eye, smiled at the beauty of his bride.

"Who gives this woman in marriage?" Reverend Sawyer asked.

Michael Fisher, choked with emotion, struggled to answer the question.

"I do," Michael said as Cory now stood alongside Ashton.

Reverend Sawyer began the ceremony.

Michael entered the family row, taking a seat between Valerie and Brenda.

Sissy smiled at her radiant granddaughter, remembering how happy she herself had been as a bride on this same day forty years ago.

Brenda smiled at Sissy, trying to calm her nervousness. Once again, Brenda began to clutch the piece of cloth in her hands.

Michael, trying to calm Brenda, wrapped his arm around her, thinking how happy Brenda would have been if she'd had her own wedding day.

As Ashton and Cory began to deliver the vows each had written for this day, Garland's eyes received a treat. Every person who mattered in his life was gathered there today. There was his pride and joy, Ashton, experiencing the one thing he had wanted in life: marrying his true love. As much as he tried to fight the emotion, tears began to fill his eyes. Sitting as a family were all the members of Aurora's Fire, along with their own families—plus Harley., After all these years, a very strong bond existed between them that nothing could destroy.

Cory and Ashton finished their vows to each other. Reverend Sawyer began to declare the symbolism of the wedding rings and instructed the two to exchange rings.

The ring exchange opened the floodgate of Brenda's emotions. As happy as she was for Ashton, emptiness overwhelmed her heart.

Without her true love, even clutching her own engagement ring did not comfort the emptiness or the loss.

Ashton placed Cory's ring on his finger, completing the ring exchange.

"Cory, you may now kiss your bride," Reverend Sawyer commanded.

Cory, without any hesitation, took Ashton in his arms.

The river that flowed through the mountains in the background of the church's garden seemed to have found its way into Garland's eyes. Although Garland knew this day would be hard, this was much more than he had anticipated.

As Cory and Ashton kissed, Garland's eyes were treated to a view that made his heart race. There was Brenda, sitting in the row with her parents. She seemed to be clutching a piece of cloth in her hand. She was more beautiful today than ever. He recalled the day back in Charleston during his tenth-birthday party: Brenda Fisher had captured his heart then, and it was still hers. Garland's treat was suddenly interrupted. Ashton and Cory stood hand in hand, blocking Garland's view of Brenda.

As Garland tried to move to regain his view of Brenda, he caught a glimpse of someone returning for the old Gibson. Sitting on each side of an easel of flowers were pictures of Ashton as a little girl. On one side of Ashton's picture was a picture of Brenda. It was a picture taken the year Ashton was born. On the other side was a picture of Garland, taken shortly before the accident.

Focusing his attention on the pictures near the easel, Garland missed the person taking a seat and holding his old Gibson.

Sissy soon began to play "Touch" on the old Gibson. This was her special gift to Ashton. Sissy began singing Garland's version of "Touch."

Ashton took comfort in Cory's arms; she had never heard Sissy's angelic voice perform this song. This was perfect.

Sissy began the second verse of "Touch," with even more passion than the first verse. Once again, the old Gibson began reaching out to

Garland. He stood, with his eyes closed, enjoying his mother's voice. Sissy completed the second verse of "Touch" and began the chorus.

As she started the chorus, two very passionate hands caressed her shoulders. There wasn't a reason for Sissy to be startled by this touch. A voice suddenly joined Sissy's, creating a perfect harmony. Sissy's voice began to crack for the first time in her life while singing. As if on cue with Sissy's voice cracking, Garland took over "Touch."

With the change of voices, Ashton and Cory turned to the seat occupied by Sissy, now holding, but not playing the Gibson. As Garland continued with "Touch," Sissy stood and immediately clutched Garland as he belted out one of the notes that only Garland Summers could deliver. Garland's note gave his daughter goose bumps. This was the first time Ashton had ever heard her dad sing and play the Gibson at the same time.

Every eye in the church, all of them filled with tears, now focused on the spot where Garland stood. Everyone knew immediately the voice they were hearing.

Garland, realizing the entire crowd was now focused on him, immediately ended "Touch."

Sissy with her eyes full of tears and both arms wrapped around her son's neck, turned to her granddaughter.

Garland, holding his mother's hand, led her to where Ashton and Cory stood. Ashton, too, hugged Garland's neck, and then she began to kiss him.

"Daddy, you have made this a perfect day. I am glad they let you out for my wedding. What time do you have to be back?" Ashton asked.

Chase Flemming entered the area. "Ashton, your dad isn't going back. He has been pardoned by the governor, and all charges have been erased."

"Daddy, is that really true?" Ashton asked.

"Yes, Ashton, after all these years, you finally have a dad," Garland said.

"This makes this day complete and the happiest day of my life. All my dreams have come true," Ashton said.

Garland turned and made his way to the front row, stopping where Brenda stood, now in tears.

"Ashton, this wonderful day isn't quite complete yet," Garland said over his shoulder.

"Brenda, I have always dreamed of what I would do if this day ever came about," Garland said.

Brenda, still clutching the piece of cloth, kissed Garland. After a long kiss, Brenda placed her head on Garland's chest, thinking what a wonderful feeling that was.

"Brenda Fisher, I was thinking that, if I had a ring, since we already have a preacher here, I know what would make this day complete," Garland said.

Brenda smiled as she opened the piece of cloth she had been holding throughout the wedding.

"Garland, this is the ring you bought me when you asked me to marry you," Brenda said.

Garland smiled. "Brenda Fisher, since we have all of our family and friends here, will you be my wife?"

Brenda jumped into Garland's arms, wrapping both her arms around his neck. "Yes, Garland, I will! I am not going to make the same mistake twice."

Garland took Brenda's hand and led her to the front of the church.

"Ladies and gentlemen, we are going to have another wedding. If any of you would like to stay, I am sure Garland and Brenda would love to have you here," Reverend Sawyer said.

There wasn't one person who left the church that morning.

Garland and Brenda, after almost twenty years of separation, were finally reunited.

"All those years, love was held together by a touch. Not the record-breaking song—first by a father and then by his daughter—but the touch of two hearts, sharing love and refusing to let go," Joe Moss said.

The wheels in Joe's head began to turn, envisioning all the possibilities there would be with a combined tour of Aurora's Fire and Summer's Sound.

Those observing the look on Joe's face all smiled, knowing how his mind worked.

"Boy, are the paparazzi going to be surprised. They were here covering Ashton's wedding, only to have an even bigger story land right in their laps," Joe said with a laugh.

CPSIA information can be obtained
at www.ICGtesting.com
Printed in the USA
BVHW030952211119
564442BV00006B/29/P